SHOW BOAT • SO BIG • CIMARRON

Three Living Novels of American Life

SHOW BOAT
SO BIG
CIMARRON

Three Living Novels
of American Life
by

EDNA FERBER

Garden City, New York
DOUBLEDAY & COMPANY, INC.

SO BIG

SHOW BOAT

CIMARRON

SHOW BOAT

To

WINTHROP AMES

Who First Said Show Boat

to Me

INTRODUCTION

"Show Boat" is neither history nor biography, but fiction. This statement is made in the hope that it will forestall such protest as may be registered by demon statisticians against certain liberties taken with characters, places, and events. In the Chicago portion of the book, for example, a character occasionally appears some three or four years after the actual date of his death. Now and then a restaurant or gambling resort is described as running full blast at a time when it had vanished at the frown of civic virtue. This, then, was done, not through negligence in research, but because, in the attempt to give a picture of the time, it was necessary slightly to condense a period of fifteen or twenty years.

E. F.

I

Bizarre as was the name she bore, Kim Ravenal always said she was thankful it had been no worse. She knew whereof she spoke, for it was literally by a breath that she had escaped being called Mississippi.

"Imagine Mississippi Ravenal!" she often said, in later years. "They'd have cut it to Missy, I suppose, or even Sippy, if you can bear to think of anything so horrible. And then I'd have had to change my name or give up the stage altogether. Because who'd go to see—seriously, I mean —an actress named Sippy? It sounds half-witted, for some reason. Kim's bad enough, God knows."

And as Kim Ravenal you doubtless are familiar with her. It is no secret that the absurd monosyllable which comprises her given name is made up of the first letters of three states—Kentucky, Illinois, and Missouri—in all of which she was, incredibly enough, born—if she can be said to have been born in any state at all. Her mother insists that she wasn't. If you were an habitué of old South Clark Street in Chicago's naughty '90s you may even remember her mother, Magnolia Ravenal, as Nola Ravenal, soubrette—though Nola Ravenal never achieved the doubtful distinction of cigarette pictures. In a day when the stage measured feminine pulchritude in terms of hips, thighs, and calves, she was considered much too thin for beauty, let alone for tights.

It had been this Magnolia Ravenal's respiratory lack that had saved the new-born girl from being cursed through life with a name boasting more quadruple vowels and consonants than any other in the language. She had meant to call the child Mississippi after the tawny untamed river on which she had spent so much of her girlhood, and which had stirred and fascinated her always. Her accouchement had been an ordeal even more terrifying than is ordinarily the case, for Kim Ravenal had actually been born on the raging turgid bosom of the Mississippi River itself, when that rampageous stream was flooding its banks and inundating towns for miles around, at five o'clock of a storm-racked April morning in 1889. It was at a point just below Cairo, Illinois; that region known as Little Egypt, where the yellow waters of the Mississippi and the olive-green waters of the Ohio so disdainfully meet and refuse, with bull-necked pride, to mingle.

From her cabin window on the second deck of the Cotton Blossom Floating Palace Theatre, Magnolia Ravenal could have seen the misty shores of three states—if any earthly shores had interested her at the moment. Just here was Illinois, to whose crumbling clay banks the show boat was so perilously pinioned. Beyond, almost hidden by the rain veil, was Missouri; and there, Kentucky. But Magnolia Ravenal lay with her eyes shut because the effort of lifting her lids was beyond her. Seeing her, you would have said that if any shores filled her vision at the moment they were heavenly ones, and those dangerously near. So white, so limp, so spent was she that her face on the pillow was startlingly like one of the waxen blossoms whose name she bore. Her slimness made almost no outline beneath the bedclothes. The coverlet was drawn up to her chin. There was only the white flower on the pillow, its petals closed.

Outside, the redundant rain added its unwelcome measure to the swollen and angry stream. In the ghostly gray dawn the grotesque wreckage of flood-time floated and whirled and jiggled by, seeming to bob a mad obeisance as it passed the show boat which, in its turn, made stately bows from its moorings. There drifted past, in fantastic parade, great trees, uprooted and clutching at the water with stiff dead arms; logs, catapulted with terrific force; animal carcasses dreadful in their passivity; chicken coops; rafts; a piano, its ivory mouth fixed in a death grin; a two-room cabin, upright, and moving in a minuet of stately and ponderous swoops and advances and chassés; fence rails; an armchair whose white crocheted antimacassar stared in prim disapproval at the wild antics of its fellow voyagers; a live sheep, bleating as it came, but soon still; a bed with its covers, by some freak of suction, still snugly tucked in as when its erstwhile occupant had fled from it in fright—all these, and more, contributed to the weird terror of the morning. The Mississippi itself was a tawny tiger, roused, furious, bloodthirsty, lashing out with its great tail, tearing with its cruel claws, and burying its fangs deep in the shore to swallow at a gulp land, houses, trees, cattle—humans, even; and roaring, snarling, howling hideously as it did so.

Inside Magnolia Ravenal's cabin all was snug and warm and bright. A wood fire snapped and crackled cosily in the little pot-bellied iron stove. Over it bent a veritable Sairey Gamp stirring something hot and savoury in a saucepan. She stirred noisily, and talked as she stirred, and glanced from time to time at the mute white figure in the bed. Her own bulky figure was made more ponderous by layer on layer of ill-assorted garments of the kind donned from time to time as night wears on by one who, having been aroused hastily and in emergency, has arrived scantily clad. A gray flannel nightgown probably formed the basis of this costume, for its grizzled cuffs could just be seen emerging from the man's coat whose sleeves she wore turned back from the wrists for comfort and convenience. This coat was of box cut, double-breasted, blue with brass buttons and gold braid, of the sort that river captains wear. It gave her a racy and nautical look absurdly at variance with her bulk and occupation. Peeping beneath and above and around this, the baffled eye could just glimpse oddments and elegancies such as a red flannel dressing gown; a flower-besprigged challis sacque whose frill of doubtful lace made the captain's coat even more incongruous; a brown cashmere skirt, very bustled and bunchy; a pair of scuffed tan kid bedroom slippers (men's) of the sort known as romeos. This lady's back hair was twisted into a knob strictly utilitarian; her front hair bristled with the wired ends of kid curlers assumed, doubtless, the evening before the hasty summons. Her face and head were long and horse-like, at variance with her bulk. This, you sensed immediately, was a person possessed of enormous energy, determination, and the gift of making exquisitely uncomfortable any one who happened to be within hearing radius. She was the sort who rattles anything that can be rattled; slams anything that can be slammed; bumps anything that can be bumped. Her name, by some miracle of fitness, was Parthenia Ann Hawks; wife of Andy Hawks, captain and owner of the Cotton Blossom Floating Palace Theatre; and mother of this Magnolia Ravenal who, having just been delivered of a daughter, lay supine in her bed.

Now, as Mrs. Hawks stirred the mess over which she was bending, her spoon regularly scraped the bottom of the pan with a rasping sound that would have tortured any nerves but her own iron-encased set. She removed the spoon, freeing it of clinging drops by rapping it smartly and metallically against the rim of the basin. Magnolia Ravenal's eyelids fluttered ever so slightly.

"Now then!" spake Parthy Ann Hawks, briskly, in that commanding tone against which even the most spiritless instinctively rebelled, "Now then, young lady, want it or not, you'll eat some of this broth, good and hot and stren'th'ning, and maybe you won't look so much like a wet dish rag." Pan in one hand, spoon in the other, she advanced toward the bed with a tread that jarred the furniture and set the dainty dimity window curtains to fluttering. She brought up against the side of the bed with a bump. A shadow of pain flitted across the white face on the pillow. The eyes still were closed. As the smell of the hot liquid reached her nostrils, the lips of the girl on the bed curled in distaste. "Here, I'll just spoon it right up to you out of the pan, so's it'll be good and hot. Open your mouth! Open your eyes! I say open—— Well, for land's sakes, how do you expect a body to do anything for you if you——"

With a motion shocking in its swift unexpectedness Magnolia Ravenal's hand emerged from beneath the coverlet, dashed aside the spoon with its steaming contents, and sent it clattering to the floor. Then her hand stole beneath the coverlet again and with a little relaxed sigh of satisfaction she lay passive as before. She had not opened her eyes. She was smiling ever so slightly.

"That's right! Act like a wildcat just because I try to get you to sup up a little soup that Jo's been hours cooking, and two pounds of good mutton in it if there's an ounce, besides vegetables and barley, and your pa practically risked his life getting the meat down at Cairo and the water going up by the foot every hour. No, you're not satisfied to get us caught here in the flood, and how we'll ever get out alive or dead, God knows, and me and everybody on the boat up all night long with your goings on so you'd think nobody'd ever had a baby before. Time I had you there wasn't a whimper out of me. Not a whimper. I'd have died, first. I never saw anything as indelicate as the way you carried on, and your own husband in the room." Here Magnolia conveyed with a flutter of the lids that this had not been an immaculate conception. "Well, if you could see yourself now. A drowned rat isn't the word. Now you take this broth, my fine lady, or we'll see who's——" She paused in this dramatic threat to blow a cooling breath on a generous spoonful of the steaming liquid, to sup it up with audible appreciation, and to take another. She smacked her lips. "Now then, no more of your monkey-shines, Maggie Hawks!"

No one but her mother had ever called Magnolia Ravenal Maggie Hawks. It was unthinkable that a name so harsh and unlovely could be applied to this fragile person. Having picked up the rejected spoon and wiped it on the lace ruffle of the challis sacque, that terrible termagant grasped it firmly against surprise in her right hand and, saucepan in left, now advanced a second time toward the bed. You saw the flower on the pillow frosted by an icy mask of utter unyieldingness; you caught a word that sounded like shenanigans from the woman bending over the bed, when the cabin door opened and two twittering females entered attired in garments strangely akin to the haphazard costume worn by Mrs. Hawks. The foremost of these moved in a manner so bustling as to be unmistakably official. She was at once ponderous, playful, and menacing —this last attribute due, perhaps, to the rather splendid dark moustache which stamped her upper lip. In her arms she carried a swaddled bundle under one flannel flap of which the second female kept peering and uttering strange clucking sounds and words that resembled izzer and yesseris.

"Fine a gal's I ever see!" exclaimed the bustling one. She approached the bed with the bundle. "Mis' Means says the same and so"—she glanced contemptuously over her shoulder at a pale and haggard young man, bearded but boyish, who followed close behind them—"does the doctor."

She paused before the word doctor so that the title, when finally it was uttered, carried with it a poisonous derision. This mysterious sally earned a little snigger from Mis' Means and a baleful snort from Mrs. Hawks. Flushed with success, the lady with the swaddled bundle (unmistakably a midwife and, like all her craft, royally accustomed to homage and applause) waxed more malicious. "Fact is, he says only a minute ago, he never brought a finer baby that he can remember."

At this the sniggers and snorts became unmistakable guffaws. The wan young man became a flushed young man. He fumbled awkwardly with the professionally massive watch chain that so unnecessarily guarded his cheap nickel blob of a watch. He glanced at the flower-like face on the pillow. Its aloofness, its remoteness from the three frowzy females that hovered about it, seemed to lend him a momentary dignity and courage. He thrust his hands behind the tails of his Prince Albert coat and strode toward the bed. A wave of the hand, a slight shove with the shoulder, dismissed the three as nuisances. "One moment, my good woman. . . . If you please, Mrs. Hawks. . . . Kindly don't jiggle . . ."

The midwife stepped aside with the bundle. Mrs. Hawks fell back a step, the ineffectual spoon and saucepan in her hands. Mis' Means ceased to cluck and to lean on the bed's footboard. From a capacious inner coat pocket he produced a stethoscope, applied it, listened, straightened. From the waistcoat pocket came the timepiece, telltale of his youth and impecuniosity. He extracted his patient's limp wrist from beneath the coverlet and held it in his own strong spatulate fingers— the fingers of the son of a farmer.

"H'm! Fine!" he exclaimed. "Splendid!"

An unmistakable sniff from the midwife. The boy's florid manner dropped from him. He cringed a little. The sensitive hand he still held in his great grasp seemed to feel this change in him, though Magnolia Ravenal had not opened her eyes even at the entrance of the three. Her wrist slid itself out of his hold and down until her fingers met his and pressed them lightly, reassuringly. The youth looked down, startled. Magnolia Ravenal, white-lipped, was smiling her wide gay gorgeous smile that melted the very vitals of you. It was a smile at once poignant and brilliant. It showed her gums a little, and softened the planes of her high cheek-bones, and subdued the angles of the too-prominent jaw. A comradely smile, an understanding and warming one. Strange that this woman on the bed, so lately torn and racked with the agonies of childbirth, should be the one to encourage the man whose clumsy ministrations had so nearly cost her her life. That she could smile at all was sheer triumph of the spirit over the flesh. And that she could smile in sympathy for and encouragement of this bungling inexpert young medico was incredible. But that was Magnolia Ravenal. Properly directed and managed, her smile, in later years, could have won her a fortune. But direction and management were as futile when applied to her as to the great untamed Mississippi that even now was flouting man-built barriers; laughing at levees that said so far and no farther; jeering at jetties that said do thus and so; for that matter, roaring this very moment in derision of Magnolia Ravenal herself, and her puny pangs and her mortal plans; and her father Captain Andy Hawks, and her mother Parthenia Ann Hawks, and her husband Gaylord Ravenal, and the whole troupe of the show boat, and the Cotton Blossom Floating Palace Theatre itself, now bobbing about like a cork on the yellow flood that tugged and sucked and tore at its moorings.

Two tantrums of nature had been responsible for the present precarious position of the show boat and its occupants. The Mississippi had furnished one; Magnolia Ravenal the other. Or perhaps it might be fairer to fix the blame, not on nature, but on human stupidity that had failed to take into account its vagaries.

Certainly Captain Andy Hawks should have known better, after thirty-five years of experience on keelboats, steamboats, packets, and show boats up and down the great Mississippi and her tributaries (the Indians might call this stream the Father of Waters but your riverman respectfully used the feminine pronoun). The brand-new show boat had done it. Built in the St. Louis shipyards, the new *Cotton Blossom* was to have been ready for him by February. But February had come and gone, and March as well. He had meant to be in New Orleans by this time, with his fine new show boat and his troupe and his band of musicians in their fresh glittering red-and-gold uniforms, and the marvellous steam calliope that could be heard for miles up and down the bayous and plantations. Starting at St. Louis, he had planned a swift trip downstream, playing just enough towns on the way to make expenses. Then, beginning with Bayou Teche and pushed by the sturdy steamer *Mollie Able*, they would proceed grandly upstream, calliope screaming, flags flying, band tooting, to play every little town and landing and plantation from New Orleans to Baton Rouge, from Baton Rouge to Vicksburg; to Memphis, to Cairo, to St. Louis, up and up to Minnesota itself; then over to the coal towns on the Monongahela River and the Kanawha, and down again to New Orleans, following the crops as they ripened—the corn belt, the cotton belt, the sugar cane; north when the wheat yellowed, following with the sun the ripening of the peas, the tomatoes, the crabs, the peaches, the apples; and as the farmer garnered his golden crops so would shrewd Captain Andy Hawks gather his harvest of gold.

It was April before the new *Cotton Blossom* was finished and ready to take to the rivers. Late though it was, when Captain Andy Hawks beheld her, glittering from texas to keel in white paint with green trimmings, and with Cotton Blossom Floating Palace Theatre done in letters two feet high on her upper deck, he was vain enough, or foolhardy enough, or both, to resolve to stand by his original plan. A little nervous fussy man, Andy Hawks, with a horrible habit of clawing and scratching from side to side, when aroused or when deep in thought, at the little mutton-chop whiskers that sprang out like twin brushes just below his leather-visored white canvas cap, always a trifle too large for his head, so that it settled down over his ears. A capering figure, in light linen pants very wrinkled and baggy, and a blue coat, double-breasted; with a darting manner, bright brown eyes, and a trick of talking very fast as he clawed the mutton-chop whiskers first this side, then that, with one brown hairy little hand. There was about him something grotesque, something simian. He beheld the new *Cotton Blossom* as a bridegroom gazes upon a bride, and frenziedly clawing his whiskers he made his unwise decision.

"She won't high-water this year till June." He was speaking of that tawny tigress, the Mississippi; and certainly no one knew her moods better than he. "Not much snow last winter, north; and no rain to speak of, yet. Yessir, we'll just blow down to New Orleans ahead of French's *Sensation*"—his bitterest rival in the show-boat business—"and start to work the bayous. Show him a clean pair of heels up and down the river."

So they had started. And because the tigress lay smooth and unruffled now, with only the currents playing gently below the surface like muscles beneath the golden yellow skin, they fancied she would remain complaisant until they had had their way. That was the first mistake.

The second was as unreasoning. Magnolia Ravenal's child was going to be a boy. Ma Hawks and the wise married women of the troupe knew the signs. She felt thus-and-so. She had such-and-such sensations. She was carrying the child high. Boys always were slower in being born than girls. Besides, this was a first child, and the first child always is late. They got together, in mysterious female conclave, and counted on the fingers of their two hands—August, September, October, November,

December—why, the end of April, the soonest. They'd be safe in New
Orleans by then, with the best of doctors for Magnolia, and she on land
while one of the other women in the company played her parts until
she was strong again—a matter of two or three weeks at most.

No sooner had they started than the rains began. No early April
showers, these, but torrents that blotted out the river banks on either
side and sent the clay tumbling in great cave-ins, down to the water,
jaundicing it afresh where already it seethed an ochreous mass. Day after
day, night after night, the rains came down, melting the Northern ice
and snow, filtering through the land of the Mississippi basin and finding
its way, whether trickle, rivulet, creek, stream, or river, to the great
hungry mother, Mississippi. And she grew swollen, and tossed and flung
her huge limbs about and shrieked in labour even as Magnolia Ravenal
was so soon to do.

Eager for entertainment as the dwellers were along the little Illinois
and Missouri towns, after a long winter of dull routine on farm and in
store and schoolhouse, they came sparsely to the show boat. Posters
had told them of her coming, and the news filtered to the back-country.
Town and village thrilled to the sound of the steam calliope as the
Cotton Blossom Floating Palace Theatre, propelled by the square-cut
clucking old steamer, *Mollie Able*, swept grandly down the river to the
landing. But the back-country roads were impassable bogs by now, and
growing worse with every hour of rain. Wagon wheels sank to the hubs
in mud. There were crude signs, stuck on poles, reading, "No bottom
here." The dodgers posted on walls and fences in the towns were rain-
soaked and bleary. And as for the Cotton Blossom Floating Palace
Theatre Ten Piece Band (which numbered six)—how could it risk ruin
of its smart new red coats, gold-braided and gold-buttoned, by marching
up the water-logged streets of these little towns whose occupants only
stared wistfully out through storm-blurred windows? It was dreary even
at night, when the show boat glowed invitingly with the blaze of a
hundred oil lamps that lighted the auditorium seating six hundred (One
Thousand Seats! A Luxurious Floating Theatre within an Unrivalled
Floating Palace!). Usually the flaming oil-flares on their tall poles stuck
in the steep clay banks that led down to the show boat at the water's
edge made a path of fiery splendour. Now they hissed and spluttered
dismally, almost extinguished by the deluge. Even when the bill was St.
Elmo or East Lynne, those tried and trusty winners, the announcement
of which always packed the show boat's auditorium to the very last seat
in the balcony reserved for Negroes, there was now only a damp handful
of shuffle-footed men and giggling girls and a few children in the cheaper
rear seats. The Mississippi Valley dwellers, wise with the terrible wis-

dom born of much suffering under the dominance of this voracious
and untamed monster, so ruthless when roused, were preparing against
catastrophe should these days of rain continue.

Captain Andy Hawks clawed his mutton-chop whiskers, this side and
that, and scanned the skies, and searched the yellowing swollen stream
with his bright brown eyes. "We'll make for Cairo," he said. "Full steam
ahead. I don't like the looks of her—the big yella snake."

But full steam ahead was impossible for long in a snag-infested river,
as Andy Hawks well knew; and in a river whose treacherous channel
shifted almost daily in normal times, and hourly in flood-time. Cautiously they made for Cairo. Cape Girardeau, Gray's Point, Commerce
—then, suddenly, near evening, the false sun shone for a brief hour. At
once everyone took heart. The rains, they assured each other, were over.
The spring freshet would subside twice as quickly as it had risen. Fit-
tingly enough, the play billed for that evening was Tempest and Sunshine, always a favourite. Magnolia Ravenal cheerfully laced herself into
the cruel steel-stiffened high-busted corset of the period, and donned
the golden curls and the prim ruffles of the part. A goodish crowd
scrambled and slipped and slid down the rain-soaked clay bank, torch-
illumined, to the show boat, their boots leaving a trail of mud and
water up and down the aisles of the theatre and between the seats. It
was a restless audience, and hard to hold. There had been an angry
sunset, and threatening clouds to the northwest. The crowd shuffled its
feet, coughed, stirred constantly. There was in the air something electric,
menacing, heavy. Suddenly, during the last act, the north wind sprang
up with a whistling sound, and the little choppy hard waves could
be heard slapping against the boat's flat sides. She began to rock, too,
and pitch, flat though she was and securely moored to the river bank.
Lightning, a fusillade of thunder, and then the rain again, heavy, like
drops of molten lead, and driven by the north wind. The crowd scrambled up the perilous clay banks, slipping, falling, cursing, laughing,
frightened. To this day it is told that the river rose seven feet in twenty-
four hours. Captain Andy Hawks, still clawing his whiskers, still bent
on making for Cairo, cast off and ordered the gangplank in as the last
scurrying villager clawed his way up the slimy incline whose heights
the river was scaling inch by inch.

"The Ohio's the place," he insisted, his voice high and squeaky with
excitement. "High water at Cincinnati, St. Louis, Evansville, or even
Paducah don't have to mean high water on the Ohio. It's the old yella
serpent making all this kick-up. But the Ohio's the river gives Cairo the
real trouble. Yessir! And she don't flood till June. We'll make for the
Ohio and stay on her till this comes to a stand, anyway."

Then followed the bedlam of putting off. Yells, hoarse shouts, bells ringing, wheels churning the water to foam. Lively now! Cramp her down! Snatch her! SNATCH her!

Faintly, above the storm, you heard the cracked falsetto of little Captain Andy Hawks, a pilot for years, squeaking to himself in his nervousness the orders that river etiquette forbade his actually giving that ruler, that ultimate sovereign, the pilot, old Mark Hooper, whose real name was no more Mark than Twain's had been: relic of his leadsmen days, with the cry of, "Mark three! Mark three! Half twain! Quarter twain! M-A-R-K twain!" gruffly shouted along the hurricane deck.

It was told, on the rivers, that little Andy Hawks had been known, under excitement, to walk off the deck into the river and to bob afloat there until rescued, still spluttering and shrieking orders in a profane falsetto.

Down the river they went, floating easily over bars that in normal times stood six feet out of the water; clattering through chutes; shaving the shores. Thunder, lightning, rain, chaos outside. Within, the orderly routine of bedtime on the show boat. Mis' Means, the female half of the character team, heating over a tiny spirit flame a spoonful of goose grease which she would later rub on her husband's meagre cough-racked chest; Maudie Rainger, of the general business team, sipping her bedtime cup of coffee; Bert Forbush, utility man, in shirt sleeves, check pants, and carpet slippers, playing a sleep-inducing game of canfield—all this on the stage, bare now of scenery and turned into a haphazard and impromptu lounging room for the members of this floating theatrical company. Mrs. Hawks, in her fine new cabin on the second deck, off the gallery, was putting her sparse hair in crimpers as she would do if this were the night before Judgment Day. Flood, storm, danger—all part of river show-boat life. Ordinarily, it is true, they did not proceed down river until daybreak. After the performance, the show boat and its steamer would stay snug and still alongside the wharf of this little town or that. By midnight, company and crew would have fallen asleep to the sound of the water slap-slapping gently against the boat's sides.

To-night there probably would be little sleep for some of the company, what with the storm, the motion, the unwonted stir, and the noise that came from the sturdy *Mollie Able*, bracing her cautious bulk against the flood's swift urging; and certainly none for Captain Andy Hawks, for pilot Mark Hooper and the crew of the *Mollie Able*. But that, too, was all part of the life.

Midnight had found Gaylord Ravenal, in nightshirt and dressing gown, a handsome and distraught figure, pounding on the door of his mother-in-law's cabin. From the cabin he had just left came harrowing sounds—whimpers, and little groans, and great moans, like an animal in agony. Magnolia Ravenal was not one of your silent sufferers. She was too dramatic for that. Manœuvred magically by the expert Hooper, they managed to make a perilous landing just above Cairo. The region was scoured for a doctor, without success, for accident had followed on flood. Captain Andy had tracked down a stout and reluctant midwife who consented only after an enormous bribe to make the perilous trip to the levee, clambering ponderously down the slippery bank with many groanings and forebodings, and being sustained, both in bulk and spirit, by the agile and vivacious little captain much as a tiny fussy river tug guides a gigantic and unwieldy ocean liner. He was almost frantically distraught, for between Andy Hawks and his daughter Magnolia Ravenal was that strong bond of affection and mutual understanding that always exists between the henpecked husband and the harassed offspring of a shrew such as Parthy Ann Hawks.

When, an hour later, Gaylord Ravenal, rain-soaked and mud-spattered, arrived with a white-faced young doctor's assistant whose first obstetrical call this was, he found the fat midwife already in charge and inclined to elbow about any young medical upstart who might presume to dictate to a female of her experience.

It was a sordid and ravaging confinement which, at its climax, teetered for one dreadful moment between tragedy and broad comedy. For at the crisis, just before dawn, the fat midwife, busy with ministrations, had said to the perspiring young doctor, "D'you think it's time to snuff her?"

Bewildered, and not daring to show his ignorance, he had replied, judicially, "Uh—not just yet. No, not just yet."

Again the woman had said, ten minutes later, "Time to snuff her, I'd say."

"Well, perhaps it is." He watched her, fearfully, wondering what she might mean; cursing his own lack of knowledge. To his horror and amazement, before he could stop her, she had stuffed a great pinch of strong snuff up either nostril of Magnolia Ravenal's delicate nose. And thus Kim Ravenal was born into the world on the gust of a series of convulsive a-CHOOs!

"God almighty, woman!" cried the young medico, in a frenzy. "You've killed her."

"Run along, do!" retorted the fat midwife, testily, for she was tired by now, and hungry, and wanted her coffee badly. "H'm! It's a gal. And they had their minds all made up to a boy. Never knew it to fail." She turned to Magnolia's mother, a ponderous and unwieldy figure at the foot of the bed. "Well, now, Mis'—Hawks, ain't it?—that's right—

Hawks. Well, now, Mis' Hawks, we'll get this young lady washed up and then I'd thank you for a pot of coffee and some breakfast. I'm partial to a meat breakfast."

All this had been a full hour ago. Magnolia Ravenal still lay inert, unheeding. She had not even looked at her child. Her mother now uttered bitter complaint to the others in the room.

"Won't touch a drop of this good nourishing broth. Knocked the spoon right out of my hand, would you believe it! for all she lays there looking so gone. Well! I'm going to open her mouth and pour it down."

The young doctor raised a protesting palm. "No, no, I wouldn't do that." He bent over the white face on the pillow. "Just a spoonful," he coaxed, softly. "Just a swallow?"

She did not vouchsafe him another smile. He glanced at the irate woman with the saucepan; at the two attendant vestals. "Isn't there somebody——?"

The men of the company and the crew were out, he well knew, with pike poles in hand, working to keep the drifting objects clear of the boats. Gaylord Ravenal would be with them. He had been in and out a score of times through the night, his handsome young face (too handsome, the awkward young doctor had privately decided) twisted with horror and pity and self-reproach. He had noticed, too, that the girl's cries had abated not a whit when the husband was there. But when he took her writhing fingers, and put one hand on her wet forehead, and said, in a voice that broke with agony, "Oh, Nola! Nola! Don't. I didn't know it was like . . . Not like this. . . . Magnolia . . ."—she had said, through clenched teeth and white lips, surprisingly enough, with a knowledge handed down to her through centuries of women writhing in childbirth, "It's all right, Gay. . . . Always . . . like this . . . damn it. . . . Don't you worry. . . . It's . . . all . . ." and the harassed young doctor had then seen for the first time the wonder of Magnolia Ravenal's poignant smile.

So now when he said, shyly, "Isn't there somebody else——" he was thinking that if the young and handsome husband could be spared for but a moment from his pike pole it would be better to chance a drifting log sent crashing against the side of the boat by the flood than that this white still figure on the bed should be allowed to grow one whit whiter or more still.

"Somebody else's fiddlesticks!" exploded Mrs. Hawks, inelegantly. They were all terribly rude to him, poor lad, except the one who might have felt justified in being so. "If her own mother can't——" She had reheated the broth on the little iron stove, and now made a third advance, armed with spoon and saucepan. The midwife had put the swaddled bundle on the pillow so that it lay just beside Magnolia Ravenal's arm. It was she who now interrupted Mrs. Hawks, and abetted her.

"How in time d'you expect to nurse," she demanded, "if you don't eat!"

Magnolia Ravenal didn't know and, seemingly, didn't care.

A crisis was imminent. It was the moment for drama. And it was furnished, obligingly enough, by the opening of the door to admit the two whom Magnolia Ravenal loved in all the world. There came first the handsome, haggard Gaylord Ravenal, actually managing, in some incredible way, to appear elegant, well-dressed, dapper, at a time, under circumstances, and in a costume which would have rendered most men unsightly, if not repulsive. But his gifts were many, and not the least of them was the trick of appearing sartorially and tonsorially flawless when dishevelment and a stubble were inevitable in any other male. Close behind him trotted Andy Hawks, just as he had been twenty-four hours before—wrinkled linen pants, double-breasted blue coat, oversize visored cap, mutton-chop whiskers and all. Together he and Ma Hawks, in her blue brass-buttoned coat that was a twin of his, managed to give the gathering quite a military aspect. Certainly Mrs. Hawks' manner was martial enough at the moment. She raised her voice now in complaint.

"Won't touch her broth. Ain't half as sick as she lets on or she wouldn't be so stubborn. Wouldn't have the strength to be, 's what I say."

Gaylord Ravenal took from her the saucepan and the spoon. The saucepan he returned to the stove. He espied a cup on the washstand; with a glance at Captain Andy he pointed silently to this. Andy Hawks emptied its contents into the slop jar, rinsed it carefully, and half filled it with the steaming hot broth. The two men approached the bedside. There was about both a clumsy and touching but magically effective tenderness. Gay Ravenal slipped his left arm under the girl's head with its hair all spread so dank and wild on the pillow. Captain Andy Hawks leaned forward, cup in hand, holding it close to her mouth. With his right hand, delicately, Gay Ravenal brought the first hot revivifying spoonful to her mouth and let it trickle slowly, drop by drop, through her lips. He spoke to her as he did this, but softly, softly, so that the others could not hear the words. Only the cadence of his voice, and that was a caress. Another spoonful, and another, and another. He lowered her again to the pillow, his arm still under her head. A faint tinge of palest pink showed under the waxen skin. She opened her eyes; looked up at him. She adored him. Her pain-dulled eyes even then said so. Her lips moved. He bent closer. She was smiling almost mischievously.

"Fooled them."

"What's she say?" rasped Mrs. Hawks, fearfully, for she loved the girl. Over his shoulder he repeated the two words she had whispered.

"Oh," said Parthy Ann Hawks, and laughed. "She means fooled 'em because it's a girl instead of a boy."

But at that Magnolia Ravenal shook her head ever so slightly, and looked up at him again and held up one slim forefinger and turned her eyes toward the corners with a listening look. And in obedience he held up his hand then, a warning for silence, though he was as mystified as they. And in the stillness of the room you heard the roar and howl and crash of the great river whose flood had caught them and shaken them and brought Magnolia Ravenal to bed ahead of her time. And now he knew what she meant. She wasn't thinking of the child that lay against her arms. Her lips moved again. He bent closer. And what she said was:

"The River."

II

SURELY no little girl had ever had a more fantastic little girlhood than this Magnolia Ravenal who had been Magnolia Hawks. By the time she was eight she had fallen into and been fished out of practically every river in the Mississippi Basin from the Gulf of Mexico to Minnesota. The ordinary routine of her life, in childhood, had been made up of doing those things that usually are strictly forbidden the average child. She swam muddy streams; stayed up until midnight; read the lurid yellow-backed novels found in the cabins of the women of the company; went to school but rarely; caught catfish; drank river water out of the river itself; roamed the streets of strange towns alone; learned to strut and shuffle and buck-and-wing from the Negroes whose black faces dotted the boards of the Southern wharves as thickly as grace notes sprinkle a bar of lively music. And all this despite constant watchfulness, nagging, and admonition from her spinster-like mother; for Parthy Ann Hawks, matron though she was, still was one of those women who, confined as favourite wife in the harem of a lascivious Turk, would have remained a spinster at heart and in manner. And though she lived on her husband's show boat season after season, and tried to rule it from pilot house to cook's galley, she was always an incongruous figure in the gay, careless vagabond life of this band of floating players. The very fact of her presence on the boat was a paradox. Life, for Parthy Ann Hawks, was meant to be made up of crisp white dimity curtains at kitchen windows; of biweekly bread bakings; of Sunday morning service and Wednesday night prayer meeting; of small gossip rolled evilly under the tongue. The male biped, to her, was a two-footed animal who tracked up a clean kitchen floor just after it was scoured and smoked a pipe in defiance of decency. Yet here she was—and had been for ten years—leading an existence which would have made that of the Stratford strollers seem orderly and prim by comparison.

She had been a Massachusetts school teacher, living with a henpecked fisherman father, and keeping house expertly for him with one hand while she taught school with the other. The villagers held her up as an example of all the feminine virtues, but the young males of the village were to be seen walking home from church with this or that plump twitterer who might be a notoriously bad cook but who had an undeniable way of tying a blue sash about a tempting waist. Parthenia Ann, prayer book clasped in mitted hands, walked sedately home with her father. The vivacious little Andy Hawks, drifting up into Massachusetts one summer, on a visit to fishermen kin, had encountered the father, and, through him, the daughter. He had eaten her light flaky biscuit, her golden-brown fries; her ruddy jell; her succulent pickles; her juicy pies. He had stood in her kitchen doorway, shyly yet boldly watching her as she moved briskly from table to stove, from stove to pantry. The sleeves of her crisp print dress were rolled to the elbow, and if those elbows were not dimpled they were undeniably expert in batter-beating, dough-kneading, pan-scouring. Her sallow cheeks were usually a little flushed with the heat of the kitchen and the energy of her movements, and, perhaps, with the consciousness of the unaccustomed masculine eye so warmly turned upon her. She looked her bustling best, and to little impulsive warm-hearted Andy she represented all he had ever known and dreamed, in his roving life, of order, womanliness, comfort. She was some years older than he. The intolerance with which women of Parthenia Ann's type regard all men was heightened by this fact to something resembling contempt. Even before their marriage, she bossed him about much as she did her old father, but while she nagged she also fed them toothsome viands, and the balm of bland, well-cooked food counteracted the acid of her words. Then, too, Nature, the old witch-wanton, had set the yeast to working in the flabby dough of Parthy Ann's organism. Andy told

her that his real name was André and that he was descended, through
his mother, from a long line of Basque fisher folk who had lived in the
vicinity of St. Jean-de-Luz, Basses-Pyrénées. It probably was true, and
certainly accounted for his swarthy skin, his bright brown eyes, his im-
pulsiveness, his vivacious manner. The first time he kissed this tall,
raw-boned New England woman he was startled at the robustness with
which she met and returned the caress. They were married and went
to Illinois to live in the little town of Thebes, on the Mississippi. In the
village from which she had married it was said that, after she left, her old
father, naturally neat and trained through years of nagging to superneat-
ness, indulged in an orgy of disorder that lasted days. As other men turn
to strong drink in time of exuberance or relief from strain, so the tidy
old septuagenarian strewed the kitchen with dirty dishes and scummy
pots and pans; slept for a week in an unmade bed; padded in stocking
feet; chewed tobacco and spat where he pleased; smoked the lace curtains
brown; was even reported by a spying neighbour to have been seen seated
at the reedy old cottage organ whose palsied pipes had always quavered
to hymn tunes, picking out with one gnarled forefinger the chorus of a
bawdy song. He lived one free, blissful year and died of his own cooking.

As pilot, river captain, and finally, as they thrived, owner and captain
of a steamer accommodating both passengers and freight, Captain Andy
was seldom in a position to be guilty of tracking the white-scoured
kitchen floor or discolouring with pipe smoke the stiff folds of the window curtains. The prim little Illinois cottage saw him but rarely during
the season when river navigation was at its height. For many months
in the year Parthy Ann Hawks was free to lead the spinsterish existence
for which nature had so evidently planned her. Her window panes glittered, her linen was immaculate, her floors unsullied. When Captain
Andy came home there was constant friction between them. Sometimes
her gay, capering little husband used to look at this woman as at a
stranger. Perhaps his nervous habit of clawing at his mutton-chop whiskers had started as a gesture of puzzlement or despair.

The child Magnolia was not born until seven years after their marriage. That Parthy Ann Hawks could produce actual offspring was a
miracle to give one renewed faith in certain disputed incidents recorded
in the New Testament. The child was all Andy—manner, temperament,
colouring. Between father and daughter there sprang up such a bond of
love and understanding as to make their relation a perfect thing, and so
sturdy as successfully to defy even the destructive forces bent upon it
by Mrs. Hawks. Now the little captain came home whenever it was
physically possible, sacrificing time, sleep, money—everything but the
safety of his boat and its passengers—for a glimpse of the child's piquant

face, her gay vivacious manner, her smile that wrung you even then.

It was years before Captain Andy could persuade his wife to take a river trip with him on his steamer down to New Orleans and back again, bringing the child. It was, of course, only a ruse for having the girl with him. River captains' wives were not popular on the steamers their husbands commanded. And Parthy Ann, from that first trip, proved a terror. It was due only to tireless threats, pleadings, blandishments, and actual bribes on the part of Andy that his crew did not mutiny daily. Half an hour after embarking on that first trip, Parthy Ann poked her head into the cook's galley and told him the place was a disgrace. The cook was a woolly-headed black with a rolling protuberant eye and the quick temper of his calling.

Furthermore, though a capable craftsman, and in good standing on the river boats, he had come aboard drunk, according to time-honoured custom; not drunk to the point of being quarrelsome or incompetent; but entertaining delusions of grandeur, varied by ominous spells of sullen silence. In another twelve hours, and for the remainder of the trip, he would be sober and himself. Captain Andy knew this, understood him, was satisfied with him.

Now one of his minions was seated on an upturned pail just outside the door, peeling a great boiler full of potatoes with almost magic celerity and very little economy.

Parthy Ann's gimlet eye noted the plump peelings as they fell in long spirals under the sharp blade. She lost no time.

"Well, I declare! Of all the shameful waste I ever clapped my eyes on, that's the worst."

The black at the stove turned to face her, startled and uncomprehending. Visitors were not welcome in the cook's galley. He surveyed without enthusiasm the lean figure with the long finger pointing accusingly at a quite innocent pan of potato parings.

"Wha' that you say, missy?"

"Don't you missy me!" snapped Parthy Ann Hawks. "And what I said was that I never saw such criminal waste as those potato parings. An inch thick if they're a speck, and no decent cook would allow it."

A simple, ignorant soul, the black man, and a somewhat savage; as mighty in his small domain as Captain Andy in his larger one. All about him now were his helpers, black men like himself, with rolling eyes and great lips all too ready to gash into grins if this hard-visaged female intruder were to worst him.

"Yo-all passenger on this boat, missy?"

Parthy Ann surveyed disdainfully the galley's interior, cluttered with the disorder attendant on the preparation of the noonday meal.

"Passenger! H'mph! No, I'm not. And passenger or no passenger, a filthier hole I never saw in my born days. I'll let you know that I shall make it my business to report this state of things to the Captain. Good food going to waste——"

A red light seemed to leap then from the big Negro's eyeballs. His lips parted in a kind of savage and mirthless grin, so that you saw his great square gleaming teeth and the blue gums above them. Quick as a panther he reached down with one great black paw into the pan of parings, straightened, and threw the mass, wet and slimy as it was, full at her. The spirals clung and curled about her—on her shoulders, around her neck, in the folds of her gown, on her head, Medusa-like.

"They's something for you take to the Captain to show him, missy."

He turned sombrely back to his stove. The other blacks were little less grave than he. They sensed something sinister in the fury with which this garbage-hung figure ran screaming to the upper deck. The scene above decks must have been a harrowing one.

They put him off at Memphis and shipped another cook there, and the big Negro, thoroughly sobered now, went quite meekly down the gangplank and up the levee, his carpet bag in hand. In fact, it was said that, when he had learned it was the Captain's wife whom he had treated thus, he had turned a sort of ashen gray and had tried to jump overboard and swim ashore. The gay little Captain Andy was a prime favourite with his crew. Shamefaced though the Negro was, there appeared something akin to pity in the look he turned on Captain Andy as he was put ashore. If that was true, then the look on the little captain's face as he regarded the miscreant was certainly born of an inward and badly concealed admiration. It was said, too, but never verified, that something round and gold and gleaming was seen to pass from the Captain's hairy little brown hand to the big black paw.

For the remainder of the trip Mrs. Hawks constituted herself a sort of nightmarish housekeeper, prowling from corridor to cabins, from dining saloon to pantry. She made life wretched for the pert yellow wenches who performed the cabin chamber-work. She pounced upon them when they gathered in little whispering groups, gossiping. Thin-lipped and baleful of eye, she withered the very words they were about to utter to a waiter or deck-hand, so that the flowers of coquetry became ashes on their tongues. She regarded the female passengers with suspicion and the males with contempt. This was the latter '70s, and gambling was as much a part of river-boat life as eating and drinking. Professional gamblers often infested the boats. It was no uncommon sight to see a poker game that had started in the saloon in the early evening still in progress when sunrise reddened the river. It was the day of the flowing moustache, the broad-brimmed hat, the open-faced collar, and the diamond stud. It constituted masculine America's last feeble flicker of the picturesque before he sank for ever into the drab ashes of uniformity. A Southern gentleman, particularly, clad thus, took on a dashing and dangerous aspect. The rakish angle of the hat with its curling brim, the flowing ends of the string tie, the movement of the slender virile fingers as they stroked the moustache, all were things to thrill the feminine beholder. Even that frigid female, Parthenia Ann Hawks, must have known a little flutter of the senses as she beheld these romantic and—according to her standards—dissolute passengers seated, silent, wary, pale, about the gaming table. But in her stern code, that which thrilled was wicked. She belonged to the tribe of the Knitting Women; of the Salem Witch Burners; of all fanatics who count nature as an enemy to be suppressed; and in whose veins the wine of life runs vinegar. If the deep seepage of Parthy Ann's mind could have been brought to the surface, it would have analyzed chemically thus: "I find these men beautiful, stirring, desirable. But that is an abomination. I must not admit to myself that I am affected thus. Therefore I think and I say that they are disgusting, ridiculous, contemptible."

Her attitude was somewhat complicated by the fact that, as wife of the steamer's captain, she was treated with a courtly deference on the part of these very gentlemen whom she affected to despise; and with a gracious cordiality by their ladies. The Southern men, especially, gave an actual effect of plumes on their wide-brimmed soft hats as they bowed and addressed her in their soft drawling vernacular.

"Well, ma'am, and how are you enjoying your trip on your good husband's magnificent boat?" It sounded much richer and more flattering as they actually said it. ". . . Yo' trip on yo' good husband's ma-a-a-ygnif'cent . . ." They gave one the feeling that they were really garbed in satin, sword, red heels, lace ruffles.

Parthenia Ann, whose stays always seemed, somehow, to support her form more stiffly than did those of any other female, would regard her inquirers with a cold and fishy eye.

"The boat's well enough, I suppose. But what with the carousing by night and the waste by day, a Christian soul can hardly look on at it without feeling that some dreadful punishment will overtake us all before we arrive at the end of our journey." From her tone you would almost have gathered that she hoped it.

He of the broad-brimmed hat, and his bustled, basqued alpaca lady, would perhaps exchange a glance not altogether amused. Collisions, explosions, snag-founderings were all too common in the river traffic of the day to risk this deliberate calling down of wrath.

Moving away, the soft-tongued Southern voices would be found to be as effective in vituperation as in flattery. "Pole cat!" he of the phantom plumes would say, aside, to his lady.

Fortunately, Parthy Ann's dour misgivings did not materialize. The trip downstream proved a delightful one, and as tranquil as might be with Mrs. Hawks on board. Captain Andy's steamer, though by no means as large as some of the so-called floating palaces that plied the Mississippi, was known for the excellence of its table, the comfort of its appointments, and the affability of its crew. So now the passengers endured the irritation of Mrs. Hawks' presence under the balm of appetizing food and good-natured service. The crew suffered her nagging for the sake of the little captain, whom they liked and respected; and for his wages, which were generous.

Though Parthenia Ann Hawks regarded the great river—if, indeed, she noticed it at all—merely as a moist highway down which one travelled with ease to New Orleans; untouched by its mystery, unmoved by its majesty, unsubdued by its sinister power, she must still, in spite of herself, have come, however faintly and remotely, under the spell of its enchantment. For this trip proved, for her, to be the first of many, and led, finally, to her spending seven months out of the twelve, not only on the Mississippi, but on the Ohio, the Missouri, the Kanawha, the Big Sandy. Indeed, her liking for the river life, together with her zeal for reforming it, became so marked that in time river travellers began to show a preference for steamers other than Captain Andy's, excellently though they fared thereon.

Perhaps the attitude of the lady passengers toward the little captain and the manner of the little captain as he addressed the lady passengers did much to feed the flame of Parthy Ann's belligerence. Until the coming of Andy Hawks she had found favour in no man's eyes. Cut in the very pattern of spinsterhood, she must actually have had moments of surprise and even incredulity at finding herself a wife and mother. The art of coquetry was unknown to her; because the soft blandishments of love had early been denied her she now repudiated them as sinful; did her hair in a knob; eschewed flounces; assumed a severe demeanour; and would have been the last to understand that any one of these repressions was a confession. All about her—and Captain Andy—on the steamship were captivating females, full of winning wiles; wives of Southern planters; cream-skinned Creoles from New Orleans, indolent, heavy-lidded, bewitching; or women folk of prosperous Illinois or Iowa merchants, lawyers, or manufacturers making a pleasure jaunt of the Southern business trip with husband or father.

And, "Oh, Captain Hawks!" they said; and, "Oh, Captain Andy! Do come here like a nice man and tell us what it means when that little bell rings so fast? . . . And why do they call it the hurricane deck? . . . Oh, Captain Hawks, is that a serpent tattooed on the back of your hand! I declare it is! Look, Emmaline! Emmaline, look! This naughty Captain Andy has a serpent . . ."

Captain Andy's social deportment toward women was made up of that most devastating of combinations, a deferential manner together with an audacious tongue. A tapering white finger, daringly tracing a rosy nail over the blue coils of the tattooed serpent, would find itself gently imprisoned beneath the hard little brown paw that was Andy's free hand.

"After this," the little captain would say, thoughtfully, "it won't be long before that particular tattoo will be entirely worn away. Yes, ma'am! No more serpent."

"But why?"

"Erosion, ma'am."

"E—but I don't understand. I'm so stupid. I——"

Meltingly, the wicked little monkey, "I'll be so often kissing the spot your lovely finger has traced, ma'am."

"Oh-h-h-h!" A smart tap of rebuke with her palm-leaf fan. "You *are* a saucy thing. Emmaline, did you hear what this wicked captain said!"

Much of the freedom that Magnolia enjoyed on this first trip she owed to her mother's quivering preoccupation with these vivacious ladies.

If the enchantment of the river had been insidious enough to lure even Mrs. Hawks, certainly the child Magnolia fell completely under its magic spell. From that first trip on the Mississippi she was captive in its coils. Twenty times daily, during that leisurely journey from St. Louis to New Orleans, Mrs. Hawks dragged her child, squirming and protesting, from the pilot house perched atop the steamer or from the engine room in its bowels. Refurbished, the grime removed from face and hands, dressed in a clean pinafore, she was thumped on one of the red plush fauteuils of the gaudy saloon. Magnolia's hair was almost black and without a vestige of natural curl. This last was a great cross to Mrs. Hawks, who spent hours wetting and twining the long dank strands about her forefinger with a fine-toothed comb in an unconvincing attempt to make a swan out of her duckling. The rebellious little figure stood clamped between her mother's relentless knees. Captured thus, and made fresh, her restless feet in their clean white stockings and little strapped black slippers sticking straight out before her, her starched skirts stiffly spread, she was told to conduct herself as a young lady of her years and high position should.

"Listen to the conversation of the ladies and gentlemen about you,"

Mrs. Hawks counselled her, severely, "instead of to the low talk of those greasy engineers and pilots you're always running off to. I declare I don't know what your father is thinking of, to allow it. . . . Or read your book. . . . Then where is it? Where is the book I bought you especially to read on this trip? You haven't opened it, I'll be bound. . . . Go get it and come back directly."

A prissy tale about a female Rollo so prim that Magnolia was sure she turned her toes out even in her sleep. When she returned with a book (if she returned at all) it was likely to be of a quite different sort —a blood-curdling tale of the old days of river-banditry—a story, perhaps, of the rapacious and brutal Murrel and his following of ten hundred cut-throats sworn to do his evil will; and compared to whom Jesse James was a philanthropist. The book would have been loaned her by one of the crew. She adored these bloody tales and devoured them with the avidity that she always showed for any theme that smacked of the river. It was snatched away soon enough when it came under her mother's watchful eye.

Magnolia loathed the red plush and gilt saloon except at night, when its gilding and mirrors took on a false glitter and richness from the kerosene lamps that filled wall brackets and chandeliers. Then it was that the lady passengers, their daytime alpacas and serges replaced by silks, sat genteelly conversing, reading, or embroidering. Then, if ever, the gentlemen twirled their mustachios most fiercely so that the diamond on the third finger of the right hand sparkled entrancingly. Magnolia derived a sensory satisfaction from the scene. The rich red of the carpet fed her, and the yellow glow of the lamps. In her best cashmere dress of brown with the polonaise cut up the front and around the bottom in deep turrets she sat alertly watching the elaborate posturings of the silken ladies and the broadcloth gentlemen.

Sometimes one of the ladies sang to the hoarse accompaniment of the ship's piano, whose tones always sounded as though the Mississippi River mist had lodged permanently in its chords. The Southern ladies rendered tinkling and sentimental ballads. The Midwestern wives were wont to deliver themselves of songs of a somewhat sterner stuff. There was one song in particular, sung by a plain and falsetto lady hailing from Iowa, that aroused in Magnolia a savage (though quite reasoning) loathing. It was entitled Waste Not, Want Not; Or: You Never Miss The Water Till The Well Runs Dry. Not being a psychologist, Magnolia did not know why, during the rendition of the first verse and the chorus, she always longed to tear her best dress into ribbons and throw a barrel of flour and a dozen hams into the river. The song ran:

When a child I lived at Lincoln,
With my parents at the farm,
The lessons that my mother taught,
To me were quite a charm.
She would often take me on her knee,
When tired of childish play,
And as she press'd me to her breast,
I've heard my mother say:

CHORUS: *Waste not, want not, is a maxim I would teach——*

Escape to the decks or the pilot house was impossible of accomplishment by night. She extracted what savour she could from the situation. This, at least, was better than being sent off to bed. All her disorderly life Magnolia went to bed only when all else failed. Then, too, once in her tiny cabin she could pose and swoop before the inadequate mirror in pitiless imitation of the arch alpacas and silks of the red plush saloon; tapping an imaginary masculine shoulder with a phantom fan; laughing in an elegant falsetto; grimacing animatedly as she squeaked, "Deah, yes!" and "Deah, no!" moistening a forelock of her straight black hair with a generous dressing of saliva wherewith to paste flat to her forehead the modish spit-curl that graced the feminine adult coiffure.

But during the day she and her father often contrived to elude the maternal duenna. With her hand in that of the little captain, she roamed the boat from stem to stern, from bunkers to pilot house. Down in the engine room she delightedly heard the sweating engineer denounce the pilot, decks above him, as a goddam Pittsburgh brass pounder because that monarch, to achieve a difficult landing, had to ring more bells than the engineer below thought necessary to an expert. But best of all Magnolia loved the bright, gay, glass-enclosed pilot house high above the rest of the boat and reached by the ultimate flight of steep narrow stairs. From this vantage point you saw the turbulent flood of the Mississippi, a vast yellow expanse, spread before you and all around you; for ever rushing ahead of you, no matter how fast you travelled; sometimes whirling about in its own tracks to turn and taunt you with your unwieldy ponderosity; then leaping on again. Sometimes the waters widened like a sea so that one could not discern the dim shadow of the farther shore; again they narrowed, snake-like, crawling so craftily that the side-wheeler boomed through the chutes with the willows brushing the decks. You never knew what lay ahead of you—that is, Magnolia never knew. That was part of the fascination of it. The river curved and twisted and turned and doubled. Mystery always lay just around the corner of the next bend. But her father knew. And Mr. Pepper, the chief pilot, always knew. You couldn't believe that it was possible for any human brain to remember the things that Captain Andy and Mr. Pepper knew about that treacherous, shifting, baffling river. Magnolia delighted to test them. She played a game with Mr. Pepper and with her father, thus:

"What's next?"

"Kinney's woodpile."

"Now what?"

"Ealer's Bend."

"What'll be there, when we come round that corner?"

"Patrie's Plantation."

"What's around that bend?"

"An old cottonwood with one limb hanging down, struck by lightning."

"What's coming now?"

"A stump sticking out of the water at Higgin's Point."

They always were right. It was magic. It was incredible. They knew, too, the depth of the water. They could point out a spot and say, "That used to be an island—Buckle's Island."

"But it's water! It couldn't be an island. It's water. We're—why, we're riding on it now."

Mr. Pepper would persist, unmoved. "Used to be an island." Or, pointing again, "Two years ago I took her right down through there where that point lays."

"But it's dry land. You're just fooling, aren't you, Mr. Pepper? Because you couldn't take a boat on dry land. It's got things growing on it! Little trees, even. So how could you?"

"Water there two years ago—good eleven foot."

Small wonder Magnolia was early impressed with this writhing monster that, with a single lash of its tail, could wipe a solid island from the face of the earth, or with a convulsion of its huge tawny body spew up a tract of land where only water had been.

Mr. Pepper had respect for his river. "Yessir, the Mississippi and this here Nile, over in Egypt, they're a couple of old demons. I ain't seen the Nile River, myself. Don't expect to. This old river's enough for one man to meet up with in his life. Like marrying. Get to learn one woman's ways real good, you know about all there is to women and you got about all you can do one lifetime."

Not at all the salty old graybeard pilot of fiction, this Mr. Pepper. A youth of twenty-four, nerveless, taciturn, gentle, profane, charming. His clear brown eyes, gazing unblinkingly out upon the river, had tiny golden flecks in them, as though something of the river itself had taken possession of him, and become part of him. Born fifty years later, he would have been the steel stuff of which aviation aces are made.

Sometimes, in deep water, Mr. Pepper actually permitted Magnolia to turn the great pilot wheel that measured twice as high as she. He stood beside her, of course; or her father, if he chanced to be present, stood behind her. It was thrilling, too, when her father took the wheel in an exciting place—where the water was very shoal, perhaps; or where the steamer found a stiff current pushing behind her, and the tricky dusk coming on. At first it puzzled Magnolia that her father, omnipotent in all other parts of the *Creole Belle*, should defer to this stripling; should actually be obliged, on his own steamer, to ask permission of the pilot to take the wheel. They were both beautifully formal and polite about it.

"What say to my taking her a little spell, Mr. Pepper?"

"Not at all, Captain Hawks. Not at all, sir," Mr. Pepper would reply, cordially if ambiguously. His gesture as he stepped aside and relinquished the wheel was that of one craftsman who recognizes and respects the ability of another. Andy Hawks had been a crack Mississippi River pilot in his day. And then to watch Captain Andy skinning the wheel—climbing it round and round, hands and feet, and looking for all the world like a talented little monkey.

Magnolia even learned to distinguish the bells by tone. There was the Go Ahead, soprano-voiced. Mr. Pepper called it the Jingle. He explained to Magnolia:

"When I give the engineer the Jingle, why, he knows I mean for him to give her all she's got." Strangely enough, the child, accustomed to the sex of boats and with an uncannily quick comprehension of river jargon, understood him, nodded her head so briskly that the hand-made curls jerked up and down like bell-ropes. "Sometimes it's called the Soprano. Then the Centre Bell—the Stopping Bell—that's middle tone. About alto. This here, that's the Astern Bell—the backup bell. That's bass. The Boom-Boom, you call it. Here's how you can remember them: The Jingle, the Alto, and the Boom-Boom."

A charming medium through which to know the river, Mr. Pepper. An enchanting place from which to view the river, that pilot house. Magnolia loved its shining orderliness, disorderly little creature that she was. The wilderness of water and woodland outside made its glass-enclosed cosiness seem the snugger. Oilcloth on the floor. You opened the drawer of the little table and there lay Mr. Pepper's pistol, glittering and sinister; and Mr. Pepper's Pilot Rules. Magnolia lingered over the title printed on the brick-coloured paper binding:

PILOT RULES

FOR THE

RIVERS WHOSE WATERS FLOW INTO THE GULF OF MEXICO AND THEIR TRIBUTARIES

AND FOR

THE RED RIVER OF THE NORTH

The Red River of the North! There was something in the words that thrilled her; sent little delicious prickles up and down her spine.

There was a bright brass cuspidor. The expertness with which Mr. Pepper and, for that matter, Captain Hawks himself, aimed for the centre of this glittering receptacle and sustained a one-hundred-per-cent. record was as fascinating as any other feature of this delightful place. Visitors were rarely allowed up there. Passengers might peer wistfully through the glass enclosure from the steps below, but there they were confronted by a stern and forbidding sign which read: No Visitors Allowed. Magnolia felt very superior and slightly contemptuous as she looked down from her vantage point upon these unfortunates below. Sometimes, during mid-watch, a very black texas-tender in a very white starched apron would appear with coffee and cakes or ices for Mr. Pepper. Magnolia would have an ice, too, shaving it very fine to make it last; licking the spoon luxuriously with little lightning flicks of her tongue and letting the frozen sweet slide, a slow delicious trickle, down her grateful throat.

"Have another cake, Miss Magnolia," Mr. Pepper would urge her. "A pink one, I'd recommend, this time."

"I don't hardly think my mother——"

Mr. Pepper, himself, surprisingly enough, the father of twins, was sure her mother would have no objection; would, if present, probably encourage the suggestion. Magnolia bit quickly into the pink cake. A wild sense of freedom flooded her. She felt like the river, rushing headlong on her way.

To be snatched from this ecstatic state was agony. The shadow of the austere and disapproving maternal figure loomed always just around the corner. At any moment it might become reality. The knowledge that this was so made Magnolia's first taste of Mississippi River life all the more delicious.

III

GRIM force though she was, it would be absurd to fix upon Parthy Ann Hawks as the sole engine whose relentless functioning cut down the profits of Captain Andy's steamboat enterprise. That other metal monster, the railroad, with its swift-turning wheels and its growing network of lines, was weaving the doom of river traffic. The Prince Albert coats and the alpaca basques were choosing a speedier, if less romantic, way to travel from Natchez to Memphis, or from Cairo to Vicksburg. Illinois, Minnesota, and Iowa businessmen were favouring a less hazardous means of transporting their merchandise. Farmers were freighting their crops by land instead of water. The river steamboat was fast becoming an anachronism. The jig, Captain Andy saw, was up. Yet the river was inextricably interwoven with his life—was his life, actually. He knew no other background, was happy in no other surroundings, had learned no other trade. These streams, large and small of the North, the Midwest, the South, with their harsh yet musical Indian names—Kaskaskia, Cahokia, Yazoo, Monongahela, Kanawha—he knew in every season: their currents, depths, landings, banks, perils. The French strain in him on the distaff side did not save him from pronouncing the foreign names of Southern rivers as murderously as did the other rivermen. La Fourche was the Foosh. Bayou Teche was Bayo Tash. As for names such as Plaquemine, Paincourteville, and Thibodaux—they emerged mutilated beyond recognition, with entire syllables lopped off, and flat vowels protruding everywhere. Anything else would have been considered affected.

Captain Andy thought only in terms of waterways. Despite the prim little house in Thebes, home, to Andy, was a boat. Towns and cities were to him mere sources of supplies and passengers, set along the river banks for the convenience of steamboats. He knew every plank in every river-landing from St. Paul to Baton Rouge. As the sky is revealed, a printed page, to the astronomer, so Andy Hawks knew and interpreted every reef, sand bar, current, and eddy in the rivers that drained the great Mississippi Basin. And of these he knew best of all the Mississippi herself. He loved her, feared her, respected her. Now her courtiers and lovers were deserting her, one by one, for an iron-throated, great-footed, brazen-voiced hussy. Andy, among the few, remained true.

To leave the river—to engage, perforce, in some landlubberly pursuit was to him unthinkable. On the rivers he was a man of consequence. As a captain and pilot of knowledge and experience his opinion was deferred to. Once permanently ashore, penduluming prosaically between the precise little household and some dull town job, he would degenerate and wither until inevitably he who now was Captain Andy Hawks, owner and master of the steamboat *Creole Belle*, would be known merely as the husband of Parthy Ann Hawks, that Mistress of the Lace Curtains, Priestess of the Parlour Carpet, and Keeper of the Kitchen Floor. All this he did not definitely put into words; but he sensed it.

He cast about in his alert mind, and made his plans craftily, and put them warily, for he knew the force of Parthenia's opposition.

"I see here where old Ollie Pegram's fixing to sell his show boat." He was seated in the kitchen, smoking his pipe and reading the local newspaper. "*Cotton Blossom*, she's called."

Parthy Ann was not one to simulate interest where she felt none. Bustling between stove and pantry she only half heard him. "Well, what of it?"

Captain Andy rattled the sheet he was holding, turned a page leisurely, meanwhile idly swinging one leg, as he sat with knees crossed. Each movement was calculated to give the effect of casualness.

"Made a fortune in the show-boat business, Ollie has. Ain't a town on the river doesn't wait for the *Cotton Blossom*. Yessir. Anybody buys that outfit is walking into money."

"Scallywags." Thus, succinctly, Parthenia thought to dismiss the subject while voicing her opinion of water thespians.

"Scallywags nothing! Some of the finest men on the river in the show-boat business. Look at Pegram! Look at Finnegan! Look at Hosey Watts!"

It was Mrs. Hawks' habit to express contempt by reference to a ten-foot pole, this being an imaginary implement of disdain and a weapon of defence which was her Excalibur. She now announced that not only would she decline to look at the above-named gentlemen, but that she could not be induced to touch any of them with a ten-foot pole. She concluded with the repetitious "Scallywags!" and evidently considered the subject closed.

Two days later, the first pang of suspicion darted through her when Andy renewed the topic with an assumption of nonchalance that failed to deceive her this time. It was plain to this astute woman that he had been thinking concentratedly about show boats since their last brief conversation. It was at supper. Andy should have enjoyed his home-cooked meals more than he actually did. They always were hot, punctual, palatable. Parthenia had kept her cooking hand. Yet he often ate abstractedly and unappreciatively. Perhaps he missed the ceremony, the animation, the sociability that marked the meal hours in the dining saloon of the *Creole Belle*. The Latin in him, and the unconsciously theatrical in him, loved the mental picture of himself in his blue coat with brass buttons and gold braid, seated at the head of the long table while the alpacas twittered, "Do you think so, Captain Hawks?" and the Prince Alberts deferred to him with, "What's your opinion, sir?" and the soft-spoken black stewards in crackling white jackets bent over him with steaming platters and tureens.

Parthenia did not hold with conversation at meal time. Andy and Magnolia usually carried on such talk as occurred at table. Strangely enough, there was in his tone toward the child none of the usual patronizing attitude of the adult. No what-did-you-learn-at-school; no have-you-been-a-good-girl-to-day. They conversed like two somewhat rowdy grown-ups, constantly chafed by the reprovals of the prim Parthenia. It was a habit of Andy seldom to remain seated in his chair throughout a meal. Perhaps this was due to the fact that he frequently was called away from table while in command of his steamer. At home his jumpiness was a source of great irritation to Mrs. Hawks. Her contributions to the conversation varied little.

"Pity's sake, Hawks, sit still! That's the third time you've been up and down, and supper not five minutes on the table. . . . Eat your potato, Magnolia, or not a bite of cup cake do you get. . . . That's a fine story to be telling a child, I must say, Andy Hawks. . . . Can't you talk of anything but a lot of good-for-nothing drunken river roustabouts! . . . Drink your milk, Maggie. . . . Oh, stop fidgeting, Hawks! . . . Don't cut away all the fat like that, Magnolia. No wonder you're so skinny I'm ashamed of you and the neighbours think you don't get enough to eat."

Like a swarm of maddening mosquitoes, these admonitions buzzed through and above and around the conversation of the man and the child.

To-night Andy's talk dwelt on a dramatic incident that had been told him that day by the pilot of the show boat *New Sensation*, lately burned to the water's edge. He went on vivaciously, his bright brown eyes sparkling with interest and animation. Now and then, he jumped up from the table the better to illustrate a situation. Magnolia was following his every word and gesture with spellbound attention. She never had been permitted to see a show-boat performance. When one of these gay water travellers came prancing down the river, band playing, calliope tooting, flags flying, towboat puffing, bringing up with a final flare and flourish at the landing, there to tie up for two or three days, or even, sometimes, for a week, Magnolia was admonished not to go near it. Other children of the town might swarm over it by day, enchanted by its mystery, enthralled by its red-coated musicians when the band marched up the main street; might even, at night, witness the performance of a play and actually stay for the song-and-dance numbers which comprised the "concert" held after the play, and for which an additional charge of fifteen cents was made.

Magnolia hungered for a glimpse of these forbidden delights. The little white house at Thebes commanded a view up the river toward Cape Girardeau. At night from her bedroom window she could see the lights shining golden yellow through the boat's many windows, was fired with excitement at sight of the kerosene flares stuck in the river bank to light the way of the lucky, could actually hear the beat and blare of the band. Again and again, in her very early childhood, the spring nights when the show boats were headed downstream and the autumn nights when they were returning up river were stamped indelibly on her mind as she knelt in her nightgown at the little window of the dark room that faced the river with its dazzling and forbidden spectacle. Her bare feet would be as icy as her cheeks were hot. Her ears were straining to catch the jaunty strains of the music, and her eyes tried to discern the faces that passed under the weird glow of the torch flares. Usually she did not hear the approaching tread of discovery until the metallic, "Magnolia Hawks, get into your bed this very minute!" smote cruelly on her entranced ears. Sometimes she glimpsed men and women of the show-boat troupe on Front Street or Third Street, idling or shopping. Occasionally you saw them driving in a rig hired from Deffler's Livery Stable. They were known to the townspeople as Show Folks, and the term carried with it the sting of opprobrium. You could mark them by something different in their dress, in their faces, in the way they walked. The women were not always young. Magnolia noticed that often they were actually older than her mother (Parthy was then about thirty-nine). Yet they looked lively and somehow youthful, though their faces bore wrinkles. There was about them a certain care-free gaiety, a jauntiness. They looked, Magnolia decided, as if they had just come from some interesting place and were going to another even more interesting. This was rather shrewd of her. She had sensed that the dulness of village and farm life, the look that routine, drudgery, and boredom stamp indelibly on the countenance of the farm woman or the village housewife, were absent in these animated and often odd faces. Once

she had encountered a little group of three—two women and a man—
strolling along the narrow plank sidewalk near the Hawks' house. They
were eating fruit out of a bag, sociably, and spitting out the seeds, and
laughing and chatting and dawdling. One of the women was young and
very pretty, and her dress, Magnolia thought, was the loveliest she had
ever seen. Its skirt of navy blue was kilted in the back, and there were
puffs up each side edged with passementerie. On her head, at a saucy
angle, was a chip bonnet of blue, trimmed with beaded lace, and ribbon,
and adorable pink roses. The other woman was much older. There were
queer deep lines in her face—not wrinkles, though Magnolia could not
know this, but the scars left when the gashes of experience have healed.
Her eyes were deep, and dark, and dead. She was carelessly dressed,
and the box-pleated tail of her flounced black gown trailed in the street,
so that it was filmed with a gray coating of dust. The veil wound round
her bonnet hung down her back, imparting a Spanish and mysterious
look. The man, too, though young and tall and not bad-looking, wore
an unkempt look. His garments were ill assorted. His collar boasted no
cravat. But all three had a charming air of insouciance as they strolled
up the tree-shaded village street, laughing and chatting and munching
and spitting out cherry stones with a little childish ballooning of the
cheeks. Magnolia hung on the Hawks' fence gate and stared. The older
woman caught her eye and smiled, and immediately Magnolia decided
that she liked her better than she did the pretty, young one, so after a
moment's grave inspection she smiled in return her sudden, brilliant
wide smile.

"Look at that child," said the older woman. "All of a sudden she's
beautiful."

The other two surveyed her idly. Magnolia's smile had vanished now.
They saw a scrawny sallow little girl, big-eyed, whose jaw conformation
was too plainly marked, whose forehead was too high and broad, and
whose black hair deceived no one into believing that its dank curls were
other than tortured.

"You're crazy, Julie," remarked the pretty girl, without heat; and
looked away, uninterested.

But between Magnolia and the older woman a filament of live liking
had leaped. "Hello, little girl," said the older woman.

Magnolia continued to stare, gravely; said nothing.

"Won't you say hello to me?" the woman persisted; and smiled again.
And again Magnolia returned her smile. "There!" the woman exclaimed,
in triumph. "What did I tell you!"

"Cat's got her tongue," the sloppy young man remarked as his contribution to the conversation.

"Oh, come on," said the pretty girl; and popped another cherry into her mouth.

But the woman persisted. She addressed Magnolia gravely. "When you grow up, don't smile too often; but smile whenever you want anything very much, or like any one, or want them to like you. But I guess maybe you'll learn that without my telling you. . . . Listen, won't you say hello to me? H'm?"

Magnolia melted. "I'm not allowed," she explained.

"Not——? Why not? Pity's sake!"

"Because you're show-boat folks. My mama won't let me talk to show-boat folks."

"Damned little brat," said the pretty girl, and spat out a cherry stone. The man laughed.

With a lightning gesture the older woman took off her hat, stuffed it under the man's arm, twisted her abundant hair into a knob off her face, pulled down her mouth and made a narrow line of her lips, brought her elbows sharply to her side, her hands clasped, her shoulders suddenly pinched.

"Your mama looks like this," she said.

"Why, how did you know!" cried Magnolia, amazed. The three burst into sudden loud laughter. And at that Parthy Hawks appeared at the door, bristling, protective.

"Maggie Hawks, come into the house this minute!"

The laughter of the three then was redoubled. The quiet little village street rang with it as they continued their leisurely care-free ramble up the sun-dappled leafy path.

Now her father, at supper, had a tale to tell of these forbidden fascinators. The story had been told him that afternoon by Hard Harry Swager, river pilot, just in at the landing after a thrilling experience.

"Seems they were playing at China Grove, on the Chappelia. Yessir. Well, this girl—La Verne, her name was, or something—anyway, she was on the stage singing, he says. It was the concert, after the show. She comes off and the next thing you know there's a little blaze in the flies. Next minute she was afire and no saving her." To one less initiated it might have been difficult to differentiate in his use of the pronoun, third person, feminine. Sometimes he referred to the girl, sometimes to the boat. "Thirty years old if she's a day and burns like greased paper. Went up in ten minutes. Hard Harry goes running to the pilot house to get his clothes. Time he reaches the boiler deck, fire has cut off the gangway. He tries to lower himself twelve feet from the boiler deck to the main, and falls and breaks his leg. By that time they were cutting the towboat away from the *Sensation* to save her. Did save her, too, finally. But the *Sensation* don't last long's it takes to tell it. Well, there he was, and what did they have to do but send four miles inland for a doctor, and when he comes, the skunk, guess what?"

"What!" cries Magnolia not merely to be obliging in this dramatic crisis, but because she is frantic to know. Captain Andy is on his feet by this time, fork in hand.

"When the doc comes he takes a look around, and there they all are in any kind of clothes they could grab or had on. So he says he won't set the leg unless he's paid in advance, twenty-five dollars. 'Oh, you won't, won't you!' says Hard Harry, laying there with his broken leg. And draws. 'You'll set it or I'll shoot yours off so you won't ever walk again, you son of a bitch!' "

"Captain Andy Hawks!"

He has acted it out. The fork is his gun. Magnolia is breathless. Now both gaze, stricken, at Mrs. Hawks. Their horror is not occasioned by the word spoken but by the interruption.

"Go on!" shouts Magnolia; and bounces up and down in her chair. "Go *on!*"

But the first fine histrionic flavour has been poisoned by that interruption. Andy takes his seat at table. He resumes the eating of his pork steak and potatoes, but listlessly. Perhaps he is a little ashamed of the extent to which he has been carried away by his own recital. "Slipped out," he mumbled.

"Well, I should say as much!" Parthy retorted, ambiguously. "What kind of language can a body expect, you hanging around show-boat riff-raff."

Magnolia would not be cheated of her dénouement. "But did he? Did he shoot it off, or did he fix it, or what? What did he do?"

"He set it, all right. They gave him his twenty-five and told him to get the h—— to get out of there, and he got. But they had to get the boat out—the towboat they'd saved—and no pilot but Hard Harry. So next day they put him on the hurricane deck, under a tarpaulin because the rain was pouring the way it does down there worse than any place in the world, just about. And with two men steering, he brings the boat to Baton Rouge seventy-five miles through bayou and Mississippi. Yessir."

Magnolia breathed again.

"And who's this," demanded Mrs. Hawks, "was telling you all this fol-de-rol, did you say?"

"Swager himself. Harry. Hard Harry Swager, they call him." (You could see the ten-foot pole leap of itself into Mrs. Hawks' hand as her fingers drummed the tablecloth.) "I was talking to him to-day. Here of

late he's been with the *New Sensation.* He piloted the *Cotton Blossom*
for years till Pegram decided to quit. Well, sir! He says five hundred
people a night on the show boat was nothing, and eight hundred on
Saturday nights in towns with a good back-country. Let me tell you right
here and now that runs into money. Say a quarter of 'em's fifty centers,
a half thirty-five, and the rest twenty-five. The niggers all twenty-five up
in the gallery, course. Naught . . . five times five's . . . five and carry
the two . . . five times two's ten carry the one . . . five . . ."

Parthy was no fool. She sensed that here threatened a situation demanding measures even more than ordinarily firm.

"I may not know much"—another form of locution often favoured by
her. The tone in which it was spoken utterly belied the words; the
tone told you that not only did she know much, but all. "I may not
know much, but this I do know. You've got something better to do
with your time than loafing down at the landing like a river rat with
that scamp Swager. Hard Harry! He comes honestly enough by that
name, I'll be bound, if he never came honestly by anything else in his
life. And before the child, too. Show boats! And language!"

"What's wrong with show boats?"

"Everything, and more, too. A lot of loose-living worthless scallywags,
men *and* women. Scum, that's what. Trollops!" Parthy could use a
good old Anglo-Saxon word herself, on occasion.

Captain Andy made frantic foray among the whiskers. He clawed like
a furious little monkey—always the sign of mental disturbance in him.
"No more scum than your own husband, Mrs. Hawks, ma'am. I used
to be with a show-boat troupe myself."

"Pilot, yes."

"Pilot be damned." He was up now and capering like a Quilp. "Actor,
Mrs. Hawks, and pretty good I was, too, time I was seventeen or eighteen. You ought to've seen me in the after-piece. Red Hot Coffee it was
called. I played the nigger. Doubled in brass, too. I pounded the bass
drum in the band, and it was bigger than me."

Magnolia was enchanted. She sprang up, flew round to him. "Were
you really? An actor? You never told me. Mama, did you know? Did you
know Papa was an actor on a show boat?"

Parthy Ann rose in her wrath. Always taller than her husband, she
seemed now to tower above him. He defied her, a terrier facing a mastiff.

"What kind of talk is this, Andy Hawks! If you're making up tales
to tease me before the child I'm surprised at you, that though nothing
you could do would ever surprise me again."

"It's the truth. The *Sunny South,* she was called. Captain Jake Bofinger, owner. Married ten times, old Jake was. A pretty rough lot we were in those days, let me tell you. I remember time we——"

"Not another word, Captain Hawks. And let me tell you it's a good thing for you that you kept it from me all these years. I'd never have married you if I'd known. A show-boat actor!"

"Oh, yes, you would, Parthy. And glad of the chance."

Words. Bickering. Recriminations. Finally, "I'll thank you not to mention show boats again in front of the child. You with your La Vernes and your Hard Harrys and your concerts and broken legs and fires and ten wives and language and what not! I don't want to be dirtied by it, nor the child. . . . Run out and play, Magnolia. . . . And let this be the last of show-boat talk in this house."

Andy breathed deep, clung with both hands to his whiskers, and took the plunge. "It's far from being the last of it, Parthy. I've bought the *Cotton Blossom* from Pegram."

IV

Many quarrels had marked their married life, but this one assumed serious proportions. It was a truly sinister note in the pageant of mis-mating that passed constantly before Magnolia's uncomprehending eyes in childhood. Parthenia had opposed him often, and certainly always when a new venture or plan held something of the element of uncon-ventionality. But now the Puritan in her ran rampant. He would dis-grace her before the community. He was ruining the life of his child. She would return to her native New England. He would not see Mag-nolia again. He had explained to her—rather, it had come out piecemeal —that his new project would necessitate his absence from home for months at a time. He would be away, surely, from April until November. If Parthy and the child would live with him on the show boat part of that time—summers—easy life—lots to see—learn the country——

The storm broke, raged, beat about his head, battered his diminutive frame. He clutched his whiskers and hung on for dear life. In the end he won.

All that Parthy ever had in her life of colour, of romance, of change, he brought her. But for him she would still be ploughing through the

drifts or mud of the New England road on her way to and from the
frigid little schoolhouse. But for him she would still be living her barren
spinster life with her salty old father in the grim coast town whence she
had come. She was to trail through the vine-hung bayous of Louisiana;
float down the generous rivers of the Carolinas, of Tennessee, of Mississippi, with the silver-green weeping willows misting the water's edge.
She was to hear the mellow plaintive voices of Negroes singing on the
levees and in cabin doorways as the boat swept by. She would taste
exotic fruits; see stirring sights; meet the fantastic figures that passed
up and down the rivers like shadows drifting in and out of a weird
dream. Yet always she was to resent loveliness; fight the influence of
each new experience; combat the lure of each new face. Tight-lipped,
belligerent, she met beauty and adventure and defied them to work a
change in her.

For three days, then, following Andy's stupendous announcement,
Parthenia threatened to leave him, though certainly, in an age that
looked upon the marriage tie as well-nigh indissoluble by any agent
other than death, she could not have meant it, straight-laced as she was.
For another three days she refused to speak to him, conveying her com-
munications to him through a third person who was, perforce, Magnolia.
"Tell your father thus-and-so." This in his very presence. "Ask your
father this-and-that."

Experience had taught Magnolia not to be bewildered by these tactics;
she was even amused, as at a game. But finally the game wearied her; or
perhaps, child though she was, an instinctive sympathy between her
and her father made her aware of the pain twisting the face of the man.
Suddenly she stamped her foot, issued her edict. "I won't tell him another single word for you. It's silly. I thought it was kind of fun, but
it isn't. It's silly for a great big grown-up person like you that's a
million years old."

Andy was absent from home all day long, and often late into the
night. The *Cotton Blossom* was being overhauled from keel to pilot
house. She was lying just below the landing; painters and carpenters
were making her ship-shape. Andy trotted up and down the town and
the river bank, talking, gesticulating, capering excitedly. There were
numberless supplies to be ordered; a troupe to be assembled. He was
never without a slip of paper on which he figured constantly. His pockets
and the lining of his cap bristled with these paper scraps.

One week following their quarrel Parthy Ann began to evidence
interest in these negotiations. She demanded details. How much had
he paid for that old mass of kindling wood? (meaning, of course, the
Cotton Blossom). How many would its theatre seat? What did the

troupe number? What was their route? How many deck-hands? One cook or two? Interspersed with these questions were grumblings and dire predictions anent money thrown away; poverty in old age; the advisability of a keeper being appointed for people whose minds had palpably given way. Still, her curiosity was obviously intense.

"Tell you what," suggested Andy with what he fancied to be infinite craft. "Get your hat on come on down and take a look at her."

"Never," said Parthenia; and untied her kitchen apron.

"Well, then, let Magnolia go down and see her. She likes boats, don't you, Nola? Same's her pa."

"H'm! Likely I'd let her go," sniffed Parthy.

Andy tried another tack. "Don't you want to come and see where your papa's going to live all the months and months he'll be away from you and ma?"

At which Magnolia, with splendid dramatic sense, began to cry wildly and inconsolably. Parthy remained grim. Yet she must have been immediately disturbed, for Magnolia wept so seldom as to be considered a queer child on this count, among many others.

"Hush your noise," commanded Parthy.

Great sobs racked Magnolia. Andy crudely followed up his advantage. "I guess you'll forget how your papa looks time he gets back."

Magnolia, perfectly aware of the implausibility of any such prediction, now hurled herself at her father, wrapped her arms about him, and howled, jerking back her head, beating a tattoo with her heels, interspersing the howls with piteous supplications not to be left behind. She wanted to see the show boat; and, with the delightful memory of the *Creole Belle* trip fresh in her mind, she wanted to travel on the *Cotton Blossom* as she had never wanted anything in her life. Her eyes were staring and distended; her fingers clutched; her body writhed; her moans were heart-breaking. She gave a magnificent performance.

Andy tried to comfort her. The howls increased. Parthy tried stern measures. Hysteria. The two united then, and alarm brought pleadings, and pleadings promises, and finally the three sat intertwined, Andy's arm about Magnolia and Parthenia; Parthenia's arm embracing Andy and Magnolia; Magnolia clinging to both.

"Come get your hair combed. Mama'll change your dress. Now stop that crying." Magnolia had been shaken by a final series of racking sobs, real enough now that the mechanics had been started. Her lower lip quivered at intervals as the wet comb chased the strands of straight black hair around Mrs. Hawks' expert forefinger. When finally she appeared in starched muslin petticoats and second-best plaid serge, there followed behind her Parthy Ann herself bonneted and cloaked for the street. The thing was done. The wife of a showman. The Puritan in her shivered, but her curiosity was triumphant even over this. They marched down Oak Street to the river landing, the child skipping and capering in her excitement. There was, too, something of elation in Andy's walk. If it had not been for the grim figure at his side and the restraining hand on his arm, it is not unlikely that the two—father and child—would have skipped and capered together down to the water's edge. Mrs. Hawks' tread and mien were those of a matronly Christian martyr on her way to the lions. As they went the parents talked of unimportant things to which Magnolia properly paid no heed, having had her way. . . . Gone most of the time. . . . It wouldn't hurt her any, I tell you. . . . Learn more in a week than she would in a year out of books. . . . But they *ain't*, I tell you. Decent folks as you'd ever want to see. Married couples, most of 'em. . . . What do you think I'm running? A bawdy-boat? . . . Oh, language be damned! . . . Now, Parthy, you've got this far, don't start all over again. . . . There she is! Ain't she pretty! Look, Magnolia! That's where you're going to live. . . . Oh, all right, all right! I was just talking . . .

The *Cotton Blossom* lay moored to great stobs. Long, and wide and plump and comfortable she looked, like a rambling house that had taken perversely to the nautical life and now lay at ease on the river's broad breast. She had had two coats of white paint with green trimmings; and not the least of these green trimmings comprised letters, a foot high, that smote Parthy's anguished eye, causing her to groan, and Magnolia's delighted gaze, causing her to squeal. There it was in all the finality of painter's print:

CAPT. ANDY HAWKS' COTTON BLOSSOM FLOATING PALACE THEATRE

Parthy gathered her dolman more tightly about her, as though smitten by a chill. The clay banks of the levee were strewn with cinders and ashes for a foothold. The steep sides of a river bank down which they would scramble and up which they would clamber were to be the home path for these three in the years to come.

An awninged upper deck, like a cosy veranda, gave the great flat boat a curiously homelike look. On the main deck, too, the gangplank ended in a forward deck which was like a comfortable front porch. Pillars, adorned with scroll-work, supported this. And there, its mouth open in a half-oval of welcome, was the ticket window through which could be seen the little box office with its desk and chair and its wall rack for tickets. There actually were tickets stuck in this, purple and red and blue. Parthy shut her eyes as at a leprous sight. A wide doorway led into the entrance hall. There again double doors opened to reveal a stairway.

"Balcony stairs," Andy explained, "and upper boxes. Seat hundred and fifty to two hundred, easy. Niggers mostly, upstairs, of course." Parthy shuddered. An aisle to the right, an aisle to the left of this stairway, and there was the auditorium of the theatre itself, with its rows of seats and its orchestra pit; its stage, its boxes, its painted curtain raised part way so that you saw only the lower half of the Venetian water scene it depicted; the legs of gondoliers in wooden attitudes; faded blue lagoon; palace steps. Magnolia knew a pang of disappointment. True, the boxes bore shiny brass railings and boasted red plush upholstered seats.

"But I thought it would be all light and glittery and like a fairy tale," she protested.

"At night," Andy assured her. He had her warm wriggling little fingers in his. "At night. That's when it's like a fairy tale. When the lamps are lighted; and all the people; and the band playing."

"Where's the kitchen?" demanded Mrs. Hawks.

Andy leaped nimbly down into the orchestra pit, stooped, opened a little door under the stage, and beckoned. Ponderously Parthy followed. Magnolia scampered after. Dining room and cook's galley were under the stage. Great cross-beams hung so low that even Andy was forced to stoop a little to avoid battering his head against them. Magnolia could touch them quite easily with her finger-tips. In time it came to seem quite natural to see the company and crew of the *Cotton Blossom* entering the dining room at meal time humbly bent as though in a preliminary attitude of grace before meat.

There were two long tables, each accommodating perhaps ten; and at the head of the room a smaller table for six.

"This is our table," Andy announced, boldly, as he indicated the third. Parthy snorted; but it seemed to the sensitive Andy that in this snort there was just a shade less resentment than there might have been. Between dining room and kitchen an opening, the size of a window frame, had been cut in the wall, and the base of this was a broad shelf for convenience in conveying hot dishes from stove to table. As the three passed from dining room to kitchen, Andy tossed over his shoulder further information for the possible approval of the bristling Parthy. "Jo and Queenie—she cooks and he waits and washes up and one thing another—they promised to be back April first, sure. Been with the *Cotton Blossom*, those two have, ten years and more. Painters been cluttering up here, and what not. And will you look at the way the

kitchen looks, spite of 'em. Slick's a whistle. Look at that stove!" Crafty
Andy.

Parthenia Ann Hawks looked at the stove. And what a stove it was!
Broad-bosomed, ample, vast, like a huge fertile black mammal whose
breast would suckle numberless eager sprawling bubbling pots and
pans. It shone richly. Gazing upon this generous expanse you felt that
from its source could emerge nothing that was not savoury, nourishing,
satisfying. Above it, and around the walls, on hooks, hung rows of
pans and kettles of every size and shape, all neatly suspended by their
pigtails. Here was the wherewithal for boundless cooking. You pictured
whole hams, sizzling; fowls neatly trussed in rows; platoons of brown
loaves; hampers of green vegetables; vast plateaus of pies. Crockery,
thick, white, coarse, was piled, plate on plate, platter on platter, behind
the neat doors of the pantry. A supplementary and redundant kerosene
stove stood obligingly in the corner.

"Little hot snack at night, after the show," Andy explained. "Coffee
or an egg, maybe, and no lighting the big wood burner."

There crept slowly, slowly over Parthy's face a look of speculation,
and this in turn was replaced by an expression that was, paradoxically,
at once eager and dreamy. As though aware of this she tried with words
to belie her look. "All this cooking for a crowd. Take a mint of money,
that's what it will."

"Make a mint," Andy retorted, blithely. A black cat, sleek, lithe, at
ease, paced slowly across the floor, stood a moment surveying the two
with wary yellow eyes, then sidled toward Parthy and rubbed his arched
back against her skirts. "Mouser," said Andy.

"Scat!" cried Parthy; but her tone was half-hearted, and she did not
move away. In her eyes gleamed the unholy light of the housewife who
beholds for the first time the domain of her dreams. Jo and Queenie to
boss. Wholesale marketing. Do this. Do that. Perhaps Andy, in his zeal,
had even overdone the thing a little. Suddenly, "Where's that child!
Where's—— Oh, my goodness, Hawks!" Visions of Magnolia having
fallen into the river. She was, later, always to have visions of Magnolia
having fallen into rivers so that Magnolia sometimes fell into them out
of sheer perversity as other children, cautioned to remain in the yard,
wilfully run away from home.

Andy darted out of the kitchen, through the little rabbit-hutch door.
Mrs. Hawks gathered up her voluminous skirts and flew after; scrambled
across the orchestra pit, turned at the sound of a voice, Magnolia's, and
yet not Magnolia's, coming from that portion of the stage exposed below
the half-raised curtain. In tones at once throaty, mincing, and falsely
elegant—that arrogant voice which is childhood's unconscious imitation

of pretence in its elders—Magnolia was reciting nothing in particular, and bringing great gusto to the rendition. The words were palpably made up as she went along—"Oh, do you rully think so! . . . My little girl is very naughty . . . we are rich, oh dear me yes, ice cream every day for breakfast, dinner, and supper. . . ." She wore her mother's dolman which that lady had unclasped and left hanging over one of the brass railings of a box. From somewhere she had rummaged a bonnet whose jet aigrette quivered with the earnestness of its wearer's artistic effort. The dolman trailed in the dust of the floor. Magnolia's right hand was held in a graceful position, the little finger elegantly crooked.

"Maggie Hawks, will you come down out of there this instant!" Parthy whirled on Andy. "There! That's what it comes to, minute she sets foot on this sink of iniquity. Play acting!"

Andy clawed his whiskers, chuckling. He stepped to the proscenium and held out his arms for the child and she stood looking down at him, flushed, smiling, radiant. "You're about as good as your pa was, Nola. And that's no compliment." He swung her to the floor, a whirl of dolman, short starched skirt and bonnet askew. Then, as Parthy snatched the dolman from her and glared at the bonnet, he saw that he must create again a favourable impression—contrive a new diversion—or his recent gain was lost. A born showman, Andy.

"Where'd you get that bonnet, Magnolia?"

"In there." She pointed to one of a row of doors facing them at the rear of the stage. "In one of those little bedrooms—cabins—what are they, Papa?"

"Dressing rooms, Nola, and bedrooms, too. Want to see them, Parthy?" He opened a little door leading from the right-hand box to the stage, crossed the stage followed by the reluctant Parthenia, threw open one of the doors at the back. There was revealed a tiny cabin holding a single bed, a diminutive dresser, and washstand. Handy rows of shelves were fastened to the wall above the bed. Dimity curtains hung at the window. The window itself framed a view of river and shore. A crudely coloured calendar hung on the wall, and some photographs and newspaper clippings, time-yellowed. There was about the little chamber a cosiness, a snugness, and, paradoxically enough, a sense of space. That was the open window, doubtless, with its vista of water and sky giving the effect of freedom.

"Dressing rooms during the performance," Andy explained, "and bedrooms the rest of the time. That's the way we work it."

Mrs. Hawks, with a single glance, encompassed the tiny room and rejected it. "Expect me to live in a cubby-hole like that!" It was, unconsciously, her first admission.

Magnolia, behind her mother's skirts, was peering, wide-eyed, into the room. "Why, I *love* it! Why, I'd love to live in it. Why, look, there's a little bed, and a dresser, and a——"

Andy interrupted hastily. "Course I don't expect you to live in a cubby-hole, Parthy. No, nor the child, neither. Just you step along with me. Now don't say anything; and stop your grumbling till you see. Put that bonnet back, Nola, where you got it. That's wardrobe. Which room 'd you get it out of?"

Across the stage, then, up the aisle to the stairway that led to the balcony, Andy leading, Mrs. Hawks following funereally, Magnolia playing a zigzag game between the rows of seats yet managing mysteriously to arrive at the foot of the stairs just as they did. The balcony reached, Magnolia had to be rescued from the death that in Mrs. Hawks' opinion inevitably would result from her leaning over the railing to gaze enthralled on the auditorium and stage below. "Hawks, will you look at that child! I declare, if I ever get her off this boat alive I'll never set foot on it again."

But her tone somehow lacked conviction. And when she beheld those two upper bedrooms forward, leading off the balcony—those two square roomy bedrooms, as large, actually, as her bedroom in the cottage, she was lost. The kitchen had scored. But the bedrooms won. They were connected by a little washroom. Each had two windows. Each held bed, dresser, rocker, stove. Bedraggled dimity curtains hung at the windows. Matting covered the floors. Parthy did an astonishing—though characteristic—thing. She walked to the dresser, passed a practised forefinger over its surface, examined the finger critically, and uttered that universal tongue-and-tooth sound indicating disapproval. "An inch thick," she then said. "A sight of cleaning this boat will take, I can tell you. Not a curtain in the place but'll have to come down and washed and starched and ironed."

Instinct or a superhuman wisdom cautioned Andy to say nothing. From the next room came a shout of joy. "Is this my room? It's got a chair that rocks and a stove with a res'vore and I can see my whole self in the looking glass, it's so big. Is this my room? Is it? Mama!"

Parthy passed into the next room. "We'll see. We'll see. We'll see." Andy followed after, almost a-tiptoe; afraid to break the spell with a sudden sound.

"But is it? I want to know. Papa, make her tell me. Look! The window here is a little door. It's a door and I can go right out on the upstairs porch. And there's the whole river."

"I should say as much, and a fine way to fall and drown without anybody being the wiser."

But the child was beside herself with excitement and suspense. She could endure it no longer; flew to her stern parent and actually shook that adamantine figure in its dolman and bonnet. "Is it? Is it? Is it?"

"We'll see." A look, then, of almost comic despair flashed between father and child—a curiously adult look for one of Magnolia's years. It said: "What a woman this is! Can we stand it? I can only if you can."

Andy tried suggestion. "Could paint this furniture any colour Nola says——"

"Blue," put in Magnolia, promptly.

"—and new curtains, maybe, with ribbons to match——" He had, among other unexpected traits, a keen eye for colour and line; a love for fabrics.

Parthy said nothing. Her lips were compressed. The look that passed between Andy and Magnolia now was pure despair, with no humour to relieve it. So they went disconsolately out of the door; crossed the balcony, clumped down the stairs, like mutes at a funeral. At the foot of the stairs they heard voices from without—women's voices, high and clear—and laughter. The sounds came from the little porch-like deck forward. Parthy swooped through the door; had scarcely time to gaze upon two sprightly females in gay plumage before both fell upon her lawful husband Captain Andy Hawks and embraced him. And the young pretty one kissed him on his left-hand mutton-chop whisker. And the older plain one kissed him on the right-hand mutton-chop whisker. And, "Oh, dear Captain Hawks!" they cried. "Aren't you surprised to see us! And happy! Do say you're happy. We drove over from Cairo specially to see you and the *Cotton Blossom*. Doc's with us."

Andy flung an obliging arm about the waist of each and gave each armful a little squeeze. "Happy ain't the word." And indeed it scarcely seemed to cover the situation; for there stood Parthy viewing the three entwined, and as she stood she seemed to grow visibly taller, broader, more ominous, like a menacing cloud. Andy's expression was a protean thing in which bravado and apprehension battled.

Magnolia had recognized them at once as the pretty young woman in the rose-trimmed hat and the dark woman who had told her not to smile too often that day when, in company with the sloppy young man, they had passed the Hawks' house, laughing and chatting and spitting cherry stones idly and comfortably into the dust of the village street. So she now took a step forward from behind her mother's voluminous skirts and made a little tentative gesture with one hand toward the older woman. And that lively female at once said, "Why, bless me! Look, Elly! It's the little girl!"

Elly looked. "What little girl?"

"The little girl with the smile." And at that, quite without premeditation, and to her own surprise, Magnolia ran to her and put her hand in hers and looked up into her strange ravaged face and smiled. "There!" exclaimed the woman, exactly as she had done that first time.

"Maggie Hawks!" came the voice.

And, "Oh, my God!" exclaimed the one called Elly, "it's the——" sensed something dangerous in the air, laughed, and stopped short.

Andy extricated himself from his physical entanglements and attempted to do likewise with the social snarl that now held them all. "Meet my wife Mrs. Hawks. Parthy, this is Julie Dozier, female half of our general business team and one of the finest actresses on the river besides being as nice a little lady as you'd meet in a month of Sundays. . . . This here little beauty is Elly Chipley—Lenore La Verne on the bills. Our ingénue lead and a favourite from Duluth to New Orleans. . . . Where's Doc?"

At which, with true dramatic instinct, Doc appeared scrambling down the cinder path toward the boat; leaped across the gangplank, poised on one toe, spread his arms and carolled, "Tra-da!" A hard-visaged man of about fifty-five, yet with kindness, too, written there; the deep-furrowed, sad-eyed ageless face of the circus shillaber and showman.

"Girls say you drove over. Must be flush with your spondulicks, Doc. . . . Parthy, meet Doc. He's got another name, I guess, but nobody's ever used it. Doc's enough for anybody on the river. Doc goes ahead of the show and bills us and does the dirty work, don't you, Doc?"

"That's about the size of it," agreed Doc, and sped sadly and accurately a comet of brown juice from his lips over the boat's side into the river. "Pleased to make your acquaintance."

Andy indicated Magnolia. "Here's my girl Magnolia you've heard me talk about."

"Well, well! Lookit them eyes! They oughtn't to go bad in the show business, little later." A sound from Parthy who until now had stood a graven image, a portent. Doc turned to her, soft-spoken, courteous. "Fixin' to take a little ride with us for good luck I hope, ma'am, our first trip out with Cap here?"

Mrs. Hawks glanced then at the arresting face of Julie Dozier, female half of our general business team and one of the finest actresses on the river. Mrs. Hawks looked at Elly Chipley (Lenore La Verne on the bills) the little beauty, and favourite from Duluth to New Orleans. She breathed deep.

"Yes. I am." And with those three monosyllables Parthenia Ann Hawks renounced the ties of land, of conventionality; forsook the staid orderliness of the little white-painted cottage at Thebes; shut her ears to the scandalized gossip of her sedate neighbours; yielded grimly to the urge of the river and became at last its unwilling mistress.

V

WHEN April came, and the dogwood flashed its spectral white in the woods, the show boat started. It was the most leisurely and dreamlike of journeys. In all the hurried harried country that still was intent on repairing the ravages of a Civil War, they alone seemed to be leading an enchanted existence, suspended on another plane. Miles—hundreds—thousands of miles of willow-fringed streams flowing aquamarine in the sunlight, olive-green in the shade. Wild honeysuckle clambering over black tree trunks. Mules. Negroes. Bare unpainted cabins the colour of the sandy soil itself. Sleepy little villages blinking drowsily down upon a river which was some almost forgotten offspring spawned years before by the Mississippi. The nearest railroad perhaps twenty-five miles distant.

They floated down the rivers. They floated down the rivers. Sometimes they were broad majestic streams rolling turbulently to the sea, and draining a continent. Sometimes they were shallow narrow streams little more than creeks, through which the *Cotton Blossom* picked her way as cautiously as a timid girl picking her way among stepping stones. Behind them, pushing them maternally along like a fat puffing duck with her silly little gosling, was the steamboat *Mollie Able*.

To the people dwelling in the towns, plantations, and hamlets along the many tributaries of the Mississippi and Ohio, the show boat was no longer a novelty. It had been a familiar and welcome sight since 1817 when the first crude barge of that type had drifted down the Cumberland River. But familiarity with these craft had failed to dispel their glamour. To the farmers and villagers of the Midwest; and to the small planters—black and white—of the South, the show boat meant music, romance, gaiety. It visited towns whose leafy crypts had never echoed the shrill hoot of an engine whistle. It penetrated settlements whose backwoods dwellers had never witnessed a theatrical performance in all their lives—simple child-like credulous people to whom the make-believe villainies, heroics, loves, adventures of the drama were so real as sometimes to cause the *Cotton Blossom* troupe actual embarrassment. Often quality folk came to the show boat. The perfume and silks and broadcloth of the Big House took frequent possession of the lower boxes and the front seats.

That first summer was, to Magnolia, a dream of pure delight. Nothing could mar it except that haunting spectre of autumn when she would have to return to Thebes and to the ordinary routine of a little girl in a second-best pinafore that was donned for school in the morning and thriftily replaced by a less important pinafore on her return from school in the late afternoon. But throughout those summer months Magnolia was a fairy princess. She was Cinderella at the ball. She shut her mind to the horrid certainty that the clock would inevitably strike twelve.

Year by year, as the spell of the river grew stronger and the easy indolence of the life took firmer hold, Mrs. Hawks and the child spent longer and longer periods on the show boat; less and less time in the humdrum security of the cottage ashore. Usually the boat started in April. But sometimes, when the season was mild, it was March. Mrs. Hawks would announce with a good deal of firmness that Magnolia must finish the school term, which ended in June. Later she and the child would join the boat wherever it happened to be showing at the time.

"Couple of months missed won't hurt her," Captain Andy would argue, loath as always to be separated from his daughter. "May's the grandest month on the rivers—and April. Everything coming out fresh. Outdoors all day. Do her good."

"I may not know much, but this I do know, Andy Hawks: No child of mine is going to grow up an ignoramus just because her father has nothing better to do than go galumphing around the country with a lot of riff-raff."

But in the end, when the show boat started its leisurely journey, there was Mrs. Hawks hanging fresh dimity curtains; bickering with Queenie; preventing, by her acid presence, the possibility of a too-saccharine existence for the members of the *Cotton Blossom* troupe. In her old capacity as school teacher, Parthy undertook the task of carrying on Magnolia's education during these truant spring months. It was an acrimonious and painful business ending, almost invariably, in temper, tears, disobedience, upbraidings. Unconsciously Andy Hawks had done much for the youth of New England when he ended Parthy's public teaching career.

"Nine times seven, I said. . . . No, it isn't! Just because fifty-six was the right answer last time it isn't right every time. That was seven times eight and I'll thank you to look at the book and not out of the window. I declare, Maggie Hawks, sometimes I think you're downright simple."

Magnolia's under lip would come out. Her brow was lowering. She somehow always looked her plainest and sallowest during these sessions with her mother. "I don't care what nine times seven is. Elly doesn't know, either. I asked her and she said she never had nine of anything, much less nine times seven of anything; and Elly's the most beautiful person in the world, except Julie sometimes—and me when I smile. And my name isn't Maggie Hawks, either."

"I'd like to know what it is if it isn't. And if you talk to me like that again, young lady, I'll smack you just as sure as I'm sitting here."

"It's Magnolia—Magnolia—uh—something beautiful—I don't know what. But not Hawks. Magnolia—uh——" a gesture with her right hand meant to convey some idea of the exquisiteness of her real name.

Mrs. Hawks clapped a maternal hand to her daughter's somewhat bulging brow, decided that she was feverish, needed a physic, and promptly administered one.

As for geography, if Magnolia did not learn it, she lived it. She came to know her country by travelling up and down its waterways. She learned its people by meeting them, of all sorts and conditions. She learned folkways; river lore; Negro songs; bird calls; pilot rules; profanity; the art of stage make-up; all the parts in the *Cotton Blossom* troupe's repertoire including East Lynne, Lady Audley's Secret, Tempest and Sunshine, Spanish Gipsy, Madcap Margery, and Uncle Tom's Cabin.

There probably was much that was sordid about the life. But to the imaginative and volatile little girl of ten or thereabouts it was a combination playhouse, make-believe theatre, and picnic jaunt. Hers were days of enchantment—or would have been were it not for the practical Parthy who, iron woman that she was, saw to it that the child was properly fed, well clothed, and sufficiently refreshed by sleep. But Parthy's interests now were too manifold and diverse to permit of her accustomed concentration on Magnolia. She had an entire boatload of people to boss—two boatloads, in fact, for she did not hesitate to investigate and criticize the manners and morals of the crew that manned the towboat *Mollie Able*. A man was never safe from her as he sat smoking his after-dinner pipe and spitting contemplatively into the river. It came about that Magnolia's life was infinitely more free afloat than it had ever been on land.

Up and down the rivers the story went that the *Cotton Blossom* was the sternest-disciplined, best-managed, and most generously provisioned boat in the business. And it was notorious that a sign back-stage and in each dressing room read: "No lady of the company allowed on deck in a wrapper." It also was known that drunkenness on the *Cotton Blossom* was punished by instant dismissal; that Mrs. Captain Andy Hawks was a holy terror; that the platters of fried chicken on Sunday were inexhaustible. All of this was true.

Magnolia's existence became a weird mixture of lawlessness and order; of humdrum and fantasy. She slipped into the life as though she had been born to it. Parthy alone kept her from being utterly spoiled by the members of the troupe.

Mrs. Hawks' stern tread never adjusted itself to the leisurely rhythm of the show boat's tempo. This was obvious even to Magnolia. The very first week of their initial trip she had heard her mother say briskly to Julie, "What time is it?" Mrs. Hawks was marching from one end of the boat to the other, intent on some fell domestic errand of her own. Julie, seated in a low chair on deck, sewing and gazing out upon the yellow turbulence of the Mississippi, had replied in her deep indolent voice, without glancing up, "What does it matter?"

The four words epitomized the divinely care-free existence of the *Cotton Blossom* show-boat troupe.

Sometimes they played a new town every night. Sometimes, in regions that were populous and that boasted a good back-country, they remained a week. In such towns, as the boat returned year after year until it became a recognized institution, there grew up between the show-boat troupe and the townspeople a sort of friendly intimacy. They were warmly greeted on their arrival; sped regretfully on their departure. They almost never travelled at night. Usually they went to bed with the sound of the water slap-slapping gently against the boat's flat sides, and proceeded down river at daybreak. This meant that constant warfare raged between the steamboat crew of the *Mollie Able* and the show-boat troupe of the *Cotton Blossom*. The steamer crew, its work done, retired early, for it must be up and about at daybreak. It breakfasted at four-thirty or five. The actors never were abed before midnight or one o'clock and rose for a nine o'clock breakfast. They complained that the steamer crew, with its bells, whistles, hoarse shouts, hammerings, puffings, and general to-do attendant upon casting off and getting under way, robbed them of their morning sleep. The crew grumbled and cursed as it tried to get a night's rest in spite of the noise of the band, the departing audience, the midnight sociability of the players who, still at high tension after their night's work, could not yet retire meekly to bed.

"Lot of damn scenery chewers," growled the crew, turning in sleep.

"Filthy roustabouts," retorted the troupers, disturbed at dawn. "Yell because they can't talk like human beings."

They rarely mingled, except such members of the crew as played in the band; and never exchanged civilities. This state of affairs lent spice to an existence that might otherwise have proved too placid for comfort. The bickering acted as a safety valve.

It all was, perhaps, the worst possible environment for a skinny, high-strung, and sensitive little girl who was one-quarter French. But Magnolia thrived on it. She had the solid and lumpy Puritanism of Parthy's presence to counteract the leaven of her volatile father. This saved her from being utterly consumed.

The life was at once indolent and busy. Captain Andy, scurrying hither and thither, into the town, up the river bank, rushing down the aisle at rehearsal to squeak a false direction to the hard-working company, driving off into the country to return in triumph laden with farm produce, was fond of saying, "We're just like one big happy family."

Captain Andy knew and liked good food (the Frenchman in him). They ate the best that the countryside afforded—not a great deal of meat in the height of summer when they were, perhaps, playing the hot humid Southern river towns, but plenty of vegetables and fruit—great melons bought from the patch with the sun still hot on their rounded bulging sides, and then chilled to dripping deliciousness before eating; luscious yams; country butter and cream. They all drank the water dipped out of the river on which they happened to be floating. They quaffed great dippersful of the Mississippi, the Ohio, and even the turbid Missouri, and seemed none the worse for it. At the stern was the settling barrel. Here the river water, dipped up in buckets, was left to settle before drinking. At the bottom of this receptacle, after it was three-quarters empty, one might find a rich layer of Mississippi silt intermingled with plummy odds and ends of every description including, sometimes, a sizable catfish.

In everything but actual rehearsing and playing, Magnolia lived the life of the company. The boat was their home. They ate, slept, worked, played on it. The company must be prompt at meal time, at rehearsals, and at the evening performances. There all responsibility ended for them.

Breakfast was at nine; and under Parthy's stern régime this meant nine. They were a motley lot as they assembled. In that bizarre setting the homely, everyday garb of the men and women took on a grotesque aspect. It was as though they were dressed for a part. As they appeared in the dining room, singly, in couples, or in groups, with a cheerful or a dour greeting, depending on the morning mood of each, an onlooker could think only of the home life of the Vincent Crummleses. Having seen Elly the night before as Miss Lenore La Verne in the golden curls, short skirts, and wide-eyed innocence of Bessie, the backwoodsman's daughter, who turned out, in the last act, to be none other than the

Lady Clarice Trelawney, carelessly mislaid at birth, her appearance at breakfast was likely to have something of the shock of disillusionment. The baby stare of her great blue eyes was due to near-sightedness to correct which she wore silver-rimmed spectacles when not under the public gaze. Her breakfast jacket, though frilly, was not of the freshest, and her kid curlers were not entirely hidden by a silk-and-lace cap. Elly was, despite these grotesqueries, undeniably and triumphantly pretty, and thus arrayed gave the effect of a little girl mischievously tricked out in her grandmother's wardrobe. Her husband, known as Schultzy in private and Harold Westbrook on the bills, acted as director of the company. He was what is known in actor's parlance as a raver, and his method of acting was designated in the show-boat world as spitting scenery. A somewhat furtive young man in very tight pants and high collar always a trifle too large. He was a cuff-shooter, and those cuffs were secured and embellished with great square shiny chunks of quartz-like stuff which he frequently breathed upon heavily and then rubbed with his handkerchief. Schultzy played juvenile leads opposite his wife's ingénue rôles; had a real flair for the theatre.

Sometimes they were in mid-river when the breakfast bell sounded; sometimes tied to a landing. The view might be plantation, woods, or small town—it was all one to the *Cotton Blossom* company, intent on coffee and bacon. Long before white-aproned Jo, breakfast bell in hand, emerged head first from the little doorway beneath the stage back of the orchestra pit, like an amiable black python from its lair, Mrs. Hawks was on the scene, squinting critically into cream jugs, attacking flies as though they were dragons, infuriating Queenie with the remark that the biscuits seemed soggy this morning. Five minutes after the bell was brandished, Jo had placed the breakfast on the table, hot: oatmeal, steaming pots of coffee, platters of fried eggs with ham or bacon, stacks of toast, biscuits fresh from the oven. If you were prompt you got a hot breakfast; tardy, you took it cold.

Parthy, whose breakfast cap, designed to hide her curl papers, always gave the effect, somehow, of a martial helmet, invariably was first at the small table that stood at the head of the room farthest from the little doorway. So she must have sat at her schoolhouse desk during those New England winters, awaiting the tardy morning arrival of reluctant and chilblained urchins. Magnolia was one of those children whom breakfast does not interest. Left to her own devices, she would have ignored the meal altogether. She usually entered late, her black hair still wet from the comb, her eyes wide with her eagerness to impart the day's first bit of nautical news.

"Doc says there's a family going down river on a bumboat, and they've got a teensy baby no bigger than a——"

"Drink your milk."

"—doll and he says it must have been born on the boat and he bets it's not more than a week old. Oh, I hope they'll tie up somewhere near——"

"Eat your toast with your egg."

"Do I have to eat my egg?"

"Yes."

If Magnolia was late, Andy was always later. He ate quickly and abstractedly. As he swallowed his coffee you could almost see his agile mind darting here and there, so that you wondered how his electric little body resisted following it as a lesser force follows a greater—up into the pilot house, down in the engine room, into the town, leaping ahead to the next landing; dickering with storekeepers for supplies. He was always the first to finish and was off at a quick trot, clawing the mutton-chop whiskers as he went.

Early or late, Julie and Steve came in together, Steve's great height ludicrously bent to avoid the low rafters of the dining room. Julie and Steve were the character team—Julie usually cast as adventuress, older sister, foil for Elly, the ingénue. Julie was a natural and intuitive actress, probably the best in the company. Sometimes she watched Elly's unintelligent work, heard her slovenly speech and her silly inflections, and a little contemptuous look would come into her face.

Steve played villains and could never have kept the job, even in that uncritical group, had it not been for Julie. He was very big and very fair, and almost entirely lacking in dramatic sense. A quiet gentle giant, he always seemed almost grotesquely miscast, his blondeur and his trusting faithful blue eyes belying the sable hirsuteness of villainy. Julie coached him patiently, tirelessly. The result was fairly satisfactory. But a nuance, an inflection, was beyond him.

"Who has a better right!" his line would be, perhaps. Schultzy, directing at rehearsal, would endeavour fruitlessly to convey to him its correct reading. After rehearsal, Julie could be heard going over the line again and again.

"Who has a better *right!*" Steve would thunder, dramatically.

"No, dear. The accent is on 'better.' Like this: 'Who has a *better* right!'"

Steve's blue eyes would be very earnest, his face red with effort. "Oh, I see. Come down hard on 'better,' huh? 'Who has a better *right!*'"

It was useless.

The two were very much in love. The others in the company sometimes teased them about this, but not often. Julie and Steve did not respond to this badinage gracefully. There existed between the two a relation that made the outsider almost uncomfortable. When they looked at each other, there vibrated between them a current that sent a little shiver through the beholder. Julie's eyes were deep-set and really black, and there was about them a curious indefinable quality. Magnolia liked to look into their soft and mournful depths. Her own eyes were dark, but not like Julie's. Perhaps it was the whites of Julie's eyes that were different.

Magnolia had once seen them kiss. She had come upon them quietly and unexpectedly, on deck, in the dusk. Certainly she had never witnessed a like passage of love between her parents; and even her recent familiarity with stage romance had not prepared her for it. It was long before the day of the motion picture fadeout. Olga Nethersole's famous osculation was yet to shock a Puritan America. Steve had held Julie a long long minute, wordlessly. Her slimness had seemed to melt into him. Julie's eyes were closed. She was quite limp as he tipped her upright. She stood thus a moment, swaying, her eyes still shut. When she opened them they were clouded, misty, as were his. The two then beheld a staring and fascinated little girl quite palpably unable to move from the spot. Julie had laughed a little low laugh. She had not flushed, exactly. Her sallow colouring had taken on a tone at once deeper and clearer and brighter, like amber underlaid with gold. Her eyes had widened until they were enormous in her thin dark glowing face. It was as though a lamp had been lighted somewhere behind them.

"What makes you look like that?" Magnolia had demanded, being a forthright young person.

"Like what?" Julie had asked.

"Like you do. All—all shiny."

"Love," Julie had answered, quite simply. Magnolia had not in the least understood; but she remembered. And years later she did understand.

Besides Elly, the ingénue, Schultzy, juvenile lead, Julie and Steve, character team, there were Mr. and Mrs. Means, general business team, Frank, the heavy, and Ralph, general utility man. Elly and Schultzy sat at table with the Hawkses, the mark of favour customary to their lofty theatrical eminence. The others of the company, together with Doc, and three of the band members, sat at the long table in the centre of the room. Mrs. Means played haughty dowagers, old Kentucky crones, widows, mothers, and middle-aged females. Mr. Means did bankers, Scrooges, old hunters and trappers, comics, and the like.

At the table nearest the door and the kitchen sat the captain and crew of the *Mollie Able*. There were no morning newspapers to read between sips of coffee; no mail to open. They were all men and women of experience. They had knocked about the world. In their faces was a lived look, together with an expression that had in it a curiously child-like quality. Captain Andy was not far wrong in his boast that they were like one big family—a close and jealous family needing no outside stimulus for its amusement. They were extraordinarily able to amuse themselves. Their talk was racy, piquant, pungent. The women were, for the most part, made of sterner stuff than the men—that is, among the actors. That the men had chosen this drifting, care-free, protected life, and were satisfied with it, proved that. Certainly Julie was a force stronger than Steve; Elly made a slave of Schultzy; Mrs. Means was a sternly maternal wife to her weak-chested and drily humorous little husband.

Usually they lingered over their coffee. Jo, padding in from the kitchen, would bring on a hot potful.

Julie had a marmoset which she had come by in New Orleans, where it had been brought from equatorial waters by some swarthy earringed sailor. This she frequently carried to the table with her, tucked under her arm, its tiny dark head with the tragic mask of a face peering out from beneath her elbow. To Mrs. Hawks' intense disgust, Julie fed the tiny creature out of her own dish. In her cabin its bed was an old seal-skin muff from whose depths its mournful dark eyes looked appealingly out from a face that was like nothing so much as that of an old old baby.

"I declare," Parthy would protest, almost daily, "it fairly turns a body's stomach to see her eating out of the same dish with that dirty little rat."

"Why, Mama! it isn't a rat any such thing! It's a monkey and you know it. Julie says maybe Schultzy can get one for me in New Orleans if I promise to be very very careful of it."

"I'd like to see her try," grimly putting an end to that dream.

The women took care of their own cabins. The detail of this occupied them until mid-morning. Often there was a rehearsal at ten that lasted an hour or more. Schultzy announced it at breakfast.

As they swept up a river, or floated down, their approach to the town was announced by the shrill iron-throated calliope, pride of Captain Andy's heart. Its blatant voice heralded the coming of the show boat long before the boat itself could be seen from the river bank. It had solid brass keys and could plainly be heard for five miles. George, who played the calliope, was also the pianist. He was known, like all calliope players, as the Whistler. Magnolia delighted in watching him at the instrument. He wore a slicker and a slicker hat and heavy gloves to protect his hands, for the steam of the whistles turned to hot raindrops and showered his hands and his head and shoulders as he played. As they neared the landing, the band, perched atop the show boat, forward, alternated with the calliope. From the town, hurrying down the streets, through the woods, dotting the levee and the landing, came eager figures, black and white. Almost invariably some magic-footed Negro, overcome by the music, could be seen on the wharf executing the complicated and rhythmic steps of a double shuffle, his rags flapping grotesquely about him, his mouth a gash of white. By nine o'clock in the morning every human being within a radius of five miles knew that the Cotton Blossom Floating Palace Theatre had docked at the waterfront.

By half-past eleven the band, augmented by two or three men of the company who doubled in brass, must be ready for the morning concert on the main street corner. Often, queerly enough, the town at which they made their landing was no longer there. The Mississippi, in prankish mood, had dumped millions of tons of silt in front of the street that faced the river. Year by year, perhaps, this had gone on, until now that which had been a river town was an inland town, with a mile of woodland and sandy road between its main street and the waterfront. The old serpent now stretched its sluggish yellow coils in another channel.

By eleven o'clock the band would have donned its scarlet coats with the magnificent gold braid and brass buttons. The nether part of these costumes always irritated Magnolia. Her colour-loving eye turned away from them, offended. For while the upper costume was splendidly martial, the lower part was composed merely of such everyday pants as the band members might be wearing at the time of the concert hour, and were a rude shock to the ravished eye as it travelled from the gay flame and gold of the jacket and the dashing impudence of the cap. Especially in the drum major did this offend her. He was called the baton spinner and wore, instead of the scarlet cap of the other band members, an imposing (though a slightly mangy) fur shako, very black and shaggy and fierce-looking, and with a strap under the chin. Pete, the bass drummer, worked in the engine room. Usually, at the last minute, he washed up hastily, grabbed his drum, buttoned on his coat, and was dazzlingly transformed from a sooty crow into a scarlet tanager.

Up the levee they scrambled—two cornets, a clarinet, a tuba, an alto (called a peck horn. Magnolia loved its ump-a ump-a ta-ta-ta-ta, ump-a ump-a ta-ta-ta-ta), a snare drummer who was always called a "sticks," and the bass drum, known as the bull.

When the landing was a waterfront town, the band concert was a pleasant enough interval in the day's light duties. But when a mile or more of dusty road lay between the show boat and the main street it became a real chore. Carrying their heavy instruments, their scarlet coats open, their caps in their hands, they would trudge, tired, hot, and sweating, the long dusty road that led through the woods. When the road became a clearing and they emerged abruptly into the town, they would button their coats, mop their hot faces, adjust cap or shako, stiffen their drooping shoulders. Their gait would change from one of plodding weariness to a sprightly strut. Their pepper-and-salt, or brown, or black trousered legs would move with rhythmic precision in time to the music. From tired, sticky, wilted plodders, they would be transformed into heroic and romantic figures. Up came the chest of the baton spinner. His left hand rested elegantly on his hip, his head and shoulders were held stiffly, arrogantly; his right hand twirled the glittering baton until it dazzled the eyes like a second noonday sun. Hotel waitresses, their hearts beating high, scurried to the windows: children rushed pell-mell from the school yard into the street; clerks in their black sateen aprons and straw sleevelets stood in the shop doorways; housewives left their pots a-boil as they lingered a wistful moment on the front porch, shading their eyes with a work-seamed hand; loafers spilled out of the saloons and stood agape and blinking. And as the music blared and soared, the lethargic little town was transformed for an hour into a gay and lively scene. Even the old white fly-bitten nags in the streets stepped with a jerky liveliness in their spring-halted gait, and a gleam came into their lack-lustre eyes as they pricked up their ears to the sound. Seeking out the busiest corner of the dull little main street, the band would take their stand, bleating and blaring, the sun playing magnificently on the polished brass of their instruments.

Although he never started with them, at this point Captain Andy always turned up, having overtaken them in some mysterious way. Perhaps he swung from tree to tree through the woods. There he was in his blue coat, his wrinkled baggy linen pants, his white canvas cap with the leather visor; fussy, nervous, animated, bright-eyed, clawing the mutton-chop whiskers from side to side. Under his arm he carried a sheaf of playbills announcing the programmes and extolling the talents of the players. After the band had played two lively numbers, he would make his speech, couched in the absurd grandiloquence of the showman. He talked well. He made his audience laugh, bizarre yet strangely appealing little figure that he was. "Most magnificent company of players ever assembled on the rivers . . . unrivalled scenery and costumes . . . Miss Lenore La Verne . . . dazzling array of talent . . . fresh from triumphs in the East . . . concert after the show . . . singing and dancing . . . bring the children . . . come one, come all. . . . *Cotton Blossom* troupe just one big happy family. . . ."

The band would strike up again. Captain Andy would whisk through the crowd with uncanny swiftness distributing his playbills, greeting an acquaintance met on previous trips, chucking a child under the chin, extolling the brilliance and gaiety of the performance scheduled for that evening. At the end of a half hour the band would turn and march playing down the street. In the dispersing crowd could be discerned Andy's agile little figure darting, stooping, swooping as he thriftily collected again the playbills that, once perused, had been dropped in the dust by careless spectators.

Dinner was at four, a hearty meal. Before dinner, and after, the *Cotton Blossom* troupe was free to spend its time as it would. The women read or sewed. There were always new costumes to be contrived, or old ones to mend and refurbish. The black-hearted adventuress of that morning's rehearsal sat neatly darning a pair of her husband's socks. There was always the nearby town to visit; a spool of thread to be purchased, a stamp, a sack of peppermint drops, a bit of muslin, a toothbrush. The indolence of the life was such that they rarely took any premeditated exercise. Sometimes they strolled in the woods at springtime when the first tender yellow-green hazed the forest vistas. They fished, though the catch was usually catfish. On hot days the more adventuresome of them swam. The river was their front yard, grown as accustomed as a stretch of lawn. They were extraordinarily able to amuse themselves. Hardly one that did not play piano, violin, flute, banjo, mandolin.

By six o'clock a stir—a little electric unrest—an undercurrent of excitement could be sensed aboard the show boat. They came sauntering back from the woods, the town, the levee. They drifted down the aisles and in and out of their dressing rooms. Years of trouping failed to still in them the quickened pulse that always came with the approach of the evening's performance.

Down in the orchestra pit the band was tuning up. They would play atop the show boat on the forward deck before the show, alternating with the calliope, as in the morning. The daytime lethargy had vanished. On the stage the men of the company were setting the scene. Hoarse shouts. Lift 'er up there! No—down a little. H'ist her up. Back! Closer! Dressing-room doors opened and shut. Calls from one room to another. Twilight came on. Doc began to light the auditorium kerosene lamps whose metal reflectors sent back their yellow glow. Outside the kerosene searchlight, cunningly rigged on top of the *Mollie Able's* pilot house, threw its broad beam up the river bank to the levee.

Of all the hours in the day this was the one most beloved of Magnolia's heart. She enjoyed the stir, the colour, the music, the people. Anything might happen on board the Cotton Blossom Floating Palace Theatre between the night hours of seven and eleven. And then it was that she was banished to bed. There was a nightly struggle in which, during the first months of their life on the rivers, Mrs. Hawks almost always won. Infrequently, by hook or crook, Magnolia managed to evade the stern parental eye.

"Let me just stay up for the first act—where Elly shoots him."

"Not a minute."

"Let me stay till the curtain goes up, then."

"You march yourself off to bed, young lady, or no trip to the pirate's cave to-morrow with Doc, and so I tell you."

Doc's knowledge of the gruesome history of river banditry and piracy provided Magnolia with many a goose-skinned hour of delicious terror. Together they went excursioning ashore in search of the blood-curdling all the way from Little Egypt to the bayous of Louisiana.

Lying there in her bed, then, wide-eyed, tense, Magnolia would strain her ears to catch the words of the play's dialogue as it came faintly up to her through the locked door that opened on the balcony; the almost incredibly naïve lines of a hackneyed play that still held its audience because of its full measure of fundamental human emotions. Hate, love, revenge, despair, hope, joy, terror.

"I will bring you to your knees yet, my proud beauty!"

"Never. I would rather die than accept help from your blood-stained hand."

Once Parthy, warned by some maternal instinct, stole softly to Magnolia's room to find the prisoner flown. She had managed to undo the special lock with which Mrs. Hawks had thought to make impossible her little daughter's access to the upper veranda deck just off her room. Magnolia had crept around the perilously narrow ledge enclosed by a low railing just below the upper deck and was there found, a shawl over her nightgown, knitted bed-slippers on her feet, peering in at the upper windows together with adventuresome and indigent urchins of the town who had managed somehow to scramble to this uncertain foothold.

After fitting punishment, the ban was gradually removed; or perhaps Mrs. Hawks realized the futility of trying to bring up a show-boat child according to Massachusetts small-town standards. With natural human perversity, thereafter, Magnolia frequently betook herself quietly to bed of her own accord the while the band blared below, guns were fired, love lost, villains foiled, beauty endangered, and blood spilled. Curiously enough, she never tired of watching these simple blood-and-thunder dramas. Automatically she learned every part in every play in the *Cotton Blossom's* repertoire, so that by the time she was thirteen she could have leaped on the stage at a moment's notice to play anything from Simon Legree to Lena Rivers.

But best of all she liked to watch the audience assembling. Unconsciously the child's mind beheld the moving living drama of a nation's peasantry. It was such an audience as could be got together in no other kind of theatre in all the world. Farmers, labourers, Negroes; housewives, children, yokels, lovers; roustabouts, dock wallopers, backwoodsmen, rivermen, gamblers. The coal-mining regions furnished the roughest audiences. The actors rather dreaded the coal towns of West Virginia or Pennsylvania. They knew that when they played the Monongahela River or the Kanawha there were likely to be more brawls and bloodshed off the stage than on.

By half-past six the levee and landing were already dotted with the curious, the loafers, the impecunious, the barefoot urchins who had gathered to snatch such crumbs as could be gathered without pay. They fed richly on the colour, the crowds, the music, the glimpses they caught of another world through the show boat's glowing windows.

Up the river bank from the boat landing to the top of the bluff flared kerosene torches suspended on long spikes stuck in the ground. Magnolia knew they were only kerosene torches, but their orange and scarlet flames never failed to excite her. There was something barbaric and splendid about them against the dusk of the sky and woods beyond, the sinister mystery of the river below. Something savage and elemental stirred in her at sight of them; a momentary reversion to tribal days, though she could not know that. She did know that she liked the fantastic dancing shadows cast by their vivid tongues on the figures that now teetered and slid and scrambled down the steep clay bank to the boat landing. They made a weird spectacle of the commonplace. The whites of the Negroes' eyes gleamed whiter. The lights turned their cheeks to copper and bronze and polished ebony. The swarthy coal miners and their shawled and sallow wives, the farmers of the corn and wheat lands, the backwoods poor whites, the cotton pickers of Tennessee, Louisiana, Mississippi, the small-town merchants, the shambling loafers, the lovers two by two were magically transformed into witches, giants, princesses, crones, gnomes, Nubians, genii.

At the little ticket window sat Doc, the astute, or Captain Andy. Later Mrs. Hawks was found to possess a grim genius for handling ticket-seeking crowds and the intricacies of ticket rack and small coins. Those dimes, quarters, and half dollars poured so willingly into the half-oval of the ticket window's open mouth found their way there, often enough, through a trail of pain and sweat and blood. It was all one to Parthy. Black faces. White faces. Hands gnarled. Hands calloused. Men in jeans. Women in calico. Babies. Children. Gimme a ticket. I only got fifteen. How much for her here? Many of them had never seen a theatre or a play. It was a strangely quiet crowd, usually. Little of laughter, of shouting. They came to the show boat timid, wide-eyed, wondering, like children. Two men of the steamboat crew or two of the musicians acted as ushers. After the first act was over they had often to assure these simple folk that the play was not yet ended. "This is just a recess. You come back to your seat in a couple of minutes. No, it isn't over. There's lots more to the show."

After the play there was the concert. Doc, Andy, and the ushers passed up and down between the acts selling tickets for this. They required an additional fifteen cents. Every member of the *Cotton Blossom* troupe must be able to sing, dance, play some musical instrument, or give a monologue—in some way contribute to the half hour of entertainment following the regular performance.

Now the band struck up. The kerosene lamps on the walls were turned low. The scuffling, shuffling, coughing audience became quiet, quiet. There was in that stillness something of fright. Seamed faces. Furrowed faces. Drab. Bitter. Sodden. Childlike. Weary. Sometimes, startlingly clear-cut in that half light, could be glimpsed a profile of some gaunt Southern labourer, or backwoodsman; and it was the profile of a portrait seen in some gallery or in the illustration of a book of history. A nose high-bred, aquiline; a sensitive, haughty mouth; eyes deep-set, arrogant. Spanish, French, English? The blood of a Stuart, a Plantagenet? Some royal rogue or adventurer of many many years ago whose seed, perhaps, this was.

The curtain rose. The music ceased jerkily, in mid-bar. They became little children listening to a fairy tale. A glorious world of unreality opened before their eyes. Things happened. They knew that in life things did not happen thus. But here they saw, believed, and were happy. Innocence wore golden curls. Wickedness wore black. Love triumphed, right conquered, virtue was rewarded, evil punished.

They forgot the cotton fields, the wheatfields, the cornfields. They forgot the coal mines, the potato patch, the stable, the barn, the shed. They forgot the labour under the pitiless blaze of the noonday sun; the bitter marrow-numbing chill of winter; the blistered skin; the frozen road; wind, snow, rain, flood. The women forgot for an hour their washtubs, their kitchen stoves, childbirth pains, drudgery, worry, disappointment. Here were blood, lust, love, passion. Here were warmth, enchantment, laughter, music. It was Anodyne. It was Lethe. It was Escape. It was the Theatre.

VI

It was the theatre, perhaps, as the theatre was meant to be. A place in which one saw one's dreams come true. A place in which one could live a vicarious life of splendour and achievement; winning in love, foiling the evildoer; a place in which one could weep unashamed, laugh aloud, give way to emotions long pent-up. When the show was over, and they had clambered up the steep bank, and the music of the band had ceased, and there was left only the dying glow of the kerosene flares, you saw them stumble a little and blink, dazedly, like one rudely awakened to reality from a lovely dream.

By eleven the torches had been gathered in. The show-boat lights were dimmed. Troupers as they were, no member of the *Cotton Blossom* company could go meekly off to sleep once the work day was over. They still were at high tension. So they discussed for the thousandth time the performance that they had given a thousand times. They dissected the audience.

"Well, they were sitting on their hands to-night, all right. Seemed they never would warm up."

"I got a big laugh on that new business with the pillow. Did you notice?"

"Notice! Yeh, the next time you introduce any new business you got a right to leave me know beforehand. I went right up. If Schultzy hadn't thrown me my line where'd I been!"

"I never thought of it till that minute, so help me! I just noticed the pillow on the sofa and that minute it came to me it'd be a good piece of business to grab it up like it was a baby in my arms. I didn't expect any such laugh as I got on it. I didn't go to throw you off."

From Schultzy, in the rôle of director: "Next time you get one of those inspirations you try it out at rehearsal first."

"God, they was a million babies to-night. Cap, I guess you must of threw a little something extra into your spiel about come and bring the children. They sure took you seriously and brought 'em, all right. I'd just soon play for a orphan asylum and be done with it."

Julie was cooking a pot of coffee over a little spirit lamp. They used the stage as a common gathering place. Bare of scenery now, in readiness for next night's set, it was their living room. Stark and shadowy as it was, there was about it an air of cosiness, of domesticity. Mrs. Means, ponderous in dressing gown and slippers, was heating some oily mess for use in the nightly ministrations on her frail little husband's delicate chest. Usually Andy, Parthy, Elly, and Schultzy, as the *haute monde*, together with the occasional addition of the *Mollie Able's* captain and pilot, supped together at a table below-stage in the dining room, where Jo and Queenie had set out a cold collation—cheese, ham, bread, a pie left from dinner. Parthy cooked the coffee on the kerosene stove. On stage the women of the company hung their costumes carefully away in the tiny cubicles provided for such purpose just outside the dressing-room doors. The men smoked a sedative pipe. The lights of the little town on the river bank had long been extinguished. Even the saloons on the waterfront showed only an occasional glow. Sometimes George at the piano tried out a new song for Elly or Schultzy or Ralph, in preparation for to-morrow night's concert. The tinkle of the piano, the sound of the singer's voice drifted across the river. Up in the little town in a drab cottage near the waterfront a restless soul would turn in his sleep and start up at the sound and listen between waking and sleeping; wondering about these strange people singing on their boat at midnight; envying them their fantastic vagabond life.

A peaceful enough existence in its routine, yet a curiously crowded and colourful one for a child. She saw town after town whose waterfront street was a solid block of saloons, one next the other, open day and night. Her childhood impressions were formed of stories, happenings, accidents, events born of the rivers. Towns and cities and people came to be associated in her mind with this or that bizarre bit of river life. The junction of the Ohio and Big Sandy rivers always was remembered by Magnolia as the place where the Black Diamond Saloon was opened on the day the *Cotton Blossom* played Catlettsburg. Catlettsburg, typical waterfront town of the times, was like a knot that drew together the two rivers. Ohio, West Virginia, and Kentucky met just there. And at the junction of the rivers there was opened with high and appropriate ceremonies the Black Diamond Saloon, owned by those picturesque two, Big Wayne Damron and Little Wayne Damron. From the deck of the *Cotton Blossom* Magnolia saw the crowd waiting for the opening of the Black Diamond doors—free drinks, free lunch, river town hospitality. And then Big Wayne opened the doors, and the crowd surged back while their giant host, holding the key aloft in his hand, walked down to the river bank, held the key high for a moment, then hurled it far into the yellow waters of the Big Sandy. The Black Diamond Saloon was open for business.

The shifting colourful life of the rivers unfolded before her ambient eyes. She saw and learned and remembered. Rough sights, brutal sights; sights of beauty and colour; deeds of bravery; dirty deeds. Through the wheat lands, the corn country, the fruit belt, the cotton, the timber region. The river life flowed and changed like the river itself. Shanty boats. Bumboats. Side-wheelers. Stern-wheelers. Fussy packets, self-important. Races ending often in death and disaster. Coal barges. A fleet of rafts, log-laden. The timber rafts, drifting down to Louisville, were steered with great sweeps. As they swept down the Ohio, the timbermen sang their chantey, their great shoulders and strong muscular torsos bending, straightening to the rhythm of the rowing song. Magnolia had learned the words from Doc, and when she espied the oarsmen from the deck of the *Cotton Blossom* she joined in the song and rocked with their motion out of sheer dramatic love of it:

> "*The river is up,*
> *The channel is deep,*
> *The wind blows steady and strong.*
> *Oh, Dinah's got the hoe cake on,*
> *So row your boat along.*
> *Down the river,*
> *Down the river,*
> *Down the O-hi-o.*
> *Down the river,*
> *Down the river,*
> *Down the O-*
>   *hi-*
>   *O!*"

Three tremendous pulls accompanied those last three long-drawn syllables. Magnolia found it most invigorating. Doc had told her, too, that the Ohio had got its name from the time when the Indians, standing on one shore and wishing to cross to the other, would cup their hands and send out the call to the opposite bank, loud and high and clear, "*O-HE-O!*"

"Do you think it's true?" Magnolia would say; for Mrs. Hawks had got into the way of calling Doc's stories stuff-and-nonsense. All those tales, it would seem, to which Magnolia most thrilled, turned out, according to Parthy, to be stuff-and-nonsense. So then, "Do you think it's true?" she would demand, fearfully.

"Think it! Why, pshaw! I know it's true. Sure as shootin'."

It was noteworthy and characteristic of Magnolia that she liked best

the rampant rivers. The Illinois, which had possessed such fascination for
Tonti, for Joliet, for Marquette—for countless *coureurs du bois* who had
frequented this trail to the southwest—left her cold. Its clear water, its
gentle current, its fretless channel, its green hillsides, its tidy bordering
grain fields, bored her. From Doc and from her father she learned a
haphazard and picturesque chronicle of its history, and that of like rivers
—a tale of voyageurs and trappers, of flatboat and keelboat men, of
rafters in the great logging days, of shanty boaters, water gipsies, steamboats. She listened, and remembered, but was unmoved. When the
Cotton Blossom floated down the tranquil bosom of the Illinois Magnolia read a book. She drank its limpid waters and missed the mud-tang
to be found in a draught of the Mississippi.

"If I was going to be a river," she announced, "I wouldn't want to
be the Illinois, or like those. I'd want to be the Mississippi."

"How's that?" asked Captain Andy.

"Because the Illinois, it's always the same. But the Mississippi is always different. It's like a person that you never know what they're going
to do next, and that makes them interesting."

Doc was oftenest her cicerone and playmate ashore. His knowledge
of the countryside, the rivers, the dwellers along the shore and in the
back country, was almost godlike in its omniscience. At his tongue's end
were tales of buccaneers, of pirates, of adventurers. He told her of the
bloodthirsty and rapacious Murrel who, not content with robbing and
killing his victims, ripped them open, disembowelled them, and threw
them into the river.

"Oh, my!" Magnolia would exclaim, inadequately; and peer with
some distaste into the water rushing past the boat's flat sides. "How did
he look? Like Steve when he plays Legree?"

"Not by a jugful, he didn't. Dressed up like a parson, and used to
travel from town to town, giving sermons. He had a slick tongue, and
while the congregation inside was all stirred up getting their souls saved,
Murrel's gang outside would steal their horses."

Stories of slaves stolen, sold, restolen, resold, and murdered. Murrel's
attempted capture of New Orleans by rousing the blacks to insurrection
against the whites. Tales of Crenshaw, the vulture; of Mason, terror of
the Natchez road. On excursions ashore, Doc showed her pirates' caves,
abandoned graveyards, ancient robber retreats along the river banks or
in the woods. They visited Sam Grity's soap kettle, a great iron pot half
hidden in a rocky unused field, in which Grity used to cache his stolen
plunder. She never again saw an old soap kettle sitting plumply in some
Southern kitchen doorway, its sides covered with a handsome black velvet coat of soot, that she did not shiver deliciously. Strong fare for a

child at an age when other little girls were reading the Dotty Dimple Series and Little Prudy books.

Doc enjoyed these sanguinary chronicles in the telling as much as Magnolia in the listening. His lined and leathery face would take on the changing expressions suitable to the tenor of the tale. Cunning, cruelty, greed, chased each other across his mobile countenance. Doc had been a show-boat actor himself at some time back in his kaleidoscopic career. So together he and Magnolia and his ancient barrel-bellied black-and-white terrier Catchem roamed the woods and towns and hills and fields and churchyards from Cairo to the Gulf.

Sometimes, in the spring, she went with Julie, the indolent. Elly almost never walked and often did not leave the *Cotton Blossom* for days together. Elly was extremely neat and fastidious about her person. She was for ever heating kettles and pans of water for bathing, for washing stockings and handkerchiefs. She had a knack with the needle and could devise a quite plausible third-act ball gown out of a length of satin, some limp tulle, and a yard or two of tinsel. She never read. Her industry irked Julie as Julie's indolence irritated her.

Elly was something of a shrew (Schultzy had learned to his sorrow that your blue-eyed blondes are not always doves). "Pity's sake, Julie, how you can sit there doing nothing, staring out at that everlasting river's more than I can see. I should think you'd go plumb crazy."

"What would you have me do?"

"Do! Mend the hole in your stocking, for one thing."

"I should say as much," Mrs. Hawks would agree, if she chanced to be present. She had no love for Elly; but her own passion for industry and order could not but cause her to approve a like trait in another.

Julie would glance down disinterestedly at her long slim foot in its shabby shoe. "Is there a hole in my stocking?"

"You know perfectly well there is, Julie Dozier. You must have seen it the size of a half dollar when you put it on this morning. It was there yesterday, same's to-day."

Julie smiled charmingly. "I know. I declare to goodness I hoped it wouldn't be. When I woke up this morning I thought maybe the good fairies would have darned it up neat's a pin while I slept." Julie's voice was as indolent as Julie herself. She spoke with a Southern drawl. Her I was Ah, Ah declah to goodness—or approximately that.

Magnolia would smile in appreciation of Julie's gentle raillery. She adored Julie. She thought Elly, with her fair skin and china-blue eyes, as beautiful as a princess in a fairy tale, as was natural in a child of her sallow colouring and straight black hair. But the two were antipathetic. Elly, in ill-tempered moments, had been known to speak of Magnolia as "that brat," though her vanity was fed by the child's admiration of her beauty. But she never allowed her to dress up in her discarded stage finery, as Julie often did. Elly openly considered herself a gifted actress whose talent and beauty were, thanks to her shiftless husband, pearls cast before the river-town swinery. Pretty though she was, she found small favour in the eyes of men of the company and crew. Strangely enough, it was Julie who drew them, quite without intent on her part. There was something about her life-scarred face, her mournful eyes, her languor, her effortlessness, her very carelessness of dress that seemed to fascinate and hold them. Steve's jealousy of her was notorious. It was common boat talk, too, that Pete, the engineer of the *Mollie Able*, who played the bull drum in the band, was openly enamoured of her and had tried to steal her from Steve. He followed Julie into town if she so much as stepped ashore. He was found lurking in corners of the *Cotton Blossom* decks; loitering about the stage where he had no business to be. He even sent her presents of imitation jewellery and gaudy handkerchiefs and work boxes, which she promptly presented to Queenie, first urging that mass of ebon royalty to bedeck herself with her new gifts when dishing up the dinner. In that close community the news of the disposal of these favours soon reached Pete's sooty ears. There had even been a brawl between Steve and Pete—one of those sudden tempestuous battles, animal-like in its fierceness and brutality. An oath in the darkness; voices low, ominous; the thud of feet; the impact of bone against flesh; deep sob-like breathing; a high weird cry of pain, terror, rage. Pete was overboard and floundering in the swift current of the Mississippi. Powerful swimmer though he was, they had some trouble in fishing him out. It was well that the *Cotton Blossom* and the *Mollie Able* were lying at anchor. Bruised and dripping, Pete had repaired to the engine room to dry, and to nurse his wounds, swearing in terms ridiculously like those frequently heard in the second act of a *Cotton Blossom* play that he would get his revenge on the two of them. He had never, since then, openly molested Julie, but his threats, mutterings, and innuendoes continued. Steve had forbidden his wife to leave the show boat unaccompanied. So it was that when spring came round, and the dogwood gleaming white among the black trunks of the pines and firs was like a bride and her shining attendants in a great cathedral, Julie would tie one of her floppy careless hats under her chin and, together with Magnolia, range the forests for wild flowers. They would wander inland until they found trees other than the willows, the live oaks, and the elms that lined the river banks. They would come upon wild honeysuckle, opalescent pink. In autumn they went nutting, returning with sackfuls of hickory and hazel nuts—anything but the black walnut which any show-boat dweller knows will cause a storm if brought aboard. Sometimes they experienced the shock of gay surprise that follows the sudden sight of gentian, a flash of that rarest of flower colours, blue; almost poignant in its beauty. It always made Magnolia catch her breath a little.

Julie's flounces trailing in the dust, the two would start out sedately enough, though to the accompaniment of a chorus of admonition and criticism.

From Mrs. Hawks: "Now keep your hat pulled down over your eyes so's you won't get all sunburned, Magnolia. Black enough as 'tis. Don't run and get all overheated. Don't eat any berries or anything you find in the woods, now. . . . Back by four o'clock the latest . . . poison ivy . . . snakes . . . lost . . . gipsies. . . ."

From Elly, trimming her rosy nails in the cool shade of the front deck: "Julie, your placket's gaping. And tuck your hair in. No, there, on the side."

So they made their way up the bank, across the little town, and into the woods. Once out of sight of the boat the two turned and looked back. Then, without a word, each would snatch her hat from her head; and they would look at each other, and Julie would smile her wide slow smile, and Magnolia's dark plain pointed little face would flash into sudden beauty. From some part of her person where it doubtless was needed Julie would extract a pin and with it fasten up the tail of her skirt. Having thus hoisted the red flag of rebellion, they would plunge into the woods to emerge hot, sticky, bramble-torn, stained, flower-laden, and late. They met Parthy's upbraidings and Steve's reproaches with cheerful unconcern.

Often Magnolia went to town with her father, or drove with him or Doc into the back country. Andy did much of the marketing for the boat's food, frequently hampered, supplemented, or interfered with by Parthy's less openhanded methods. He loved good food, considered it important to happiness, liked to order it and talk about it; was himself an excellent cook, like most boatmen, and had been known to spend a pleasant half hour reading the cook book. The butchers, grocers, and general store keepers of the river towns knew Andy, understood his fussy ways, liked him. He bought shrewdly but generously, without haggling; and often presented a store acquaintance of long standing with a pair of tickets for the night's performance. When he and Magnolia had time to range the countryside in a livery rig, Andy would select the smartest and most glittering buggy and the liveliest nag to be had. Being a poor driver and jerky, with no knowledge of a horse's nerves and mouth, the ride was likely to be exhilarating to the point of danger. The animal always was returned to the stable in a lather, the vehicle spattered with mud-flecks to the hood. Certainly, it was due to Andy more than Parthy that the *Cotton Blossom* was reputed the best-fed show boat on the rivers. He was always bringing home in triumph a great juicy ham, a side of beef. He liked to forage the season's first and best: a bushel of downy peaches, fresh-picked; watermelons; little honey-sweet seckel pears; a dozen plump broilers; new corn; a great yellow cheese ripe for cutting.

He would plump his purchases down on the kitchen table while Queenie surveyed his booty, hands on ample hips. She never resented his suggestions, though Parthy's offended her. Capering, Andy would poke a forefinger into a pullet's fat sides. "Rub 'em over with a little garlic, Queenie, to flavour 'em up. Plenty of butter and strips of bacon. Cover 'em over till they're tender and then give 'em a quick brown the last twenty minutes."

Queenie, knowing all this, still did not resent his direction. "That shif'less no-'count Jo knew 'bout cookin' like you do, Cap'n Andy, Ah'd git to rest mah feet now an' again, Ah sure would."

Magnolia liked to loiter in the big, low-raftered kitchen. It was a place of pleasant smells and sights and sounds. It was here that she learned Negro spirituals from Jo and cooking from Queenie, both of which accomplishments stood her in good stead in later years. Queenie had, for example, a way of stuffing a ham for baking. It was a fascinating process to behold, and one that took hours. Spices—bay, thyme, onion, clove, mustard, allspice, pepper—chopped and mixed and stirred together. A sharp-pointed knife plunged deep into the juicy ham. The incision stuffed with the spicy mixture. Another plunge with the knife. Another filling. Again and again and again until the great ham had grown to twice its size. Then a heavy clean white cloth, needle and coarse thread. Sewed up tight and plump in its jacket the ham was immersed in a pot of water and boiled. Out when tender, the jacket removed; into the oven with it. Basting and basting from Queenie's long-handled spoon. The long sharp knife again for cutting, and then the slices, juicy and scented, with the stuffing of spices making a mosaic pattern against the pink of the meat. Many years later Kim Ravenal, the actress, would serve at the famous little Sunday night suppers that she and her husband Kenneth Cameron were so fond of giving a dish that she called ham *à la* Queenie.

"How does your cook do it!" her friends would say—Ethel Barrymore or Kit Cornell or Frank Crowninshield or Charley Towne or Woollcott. "I'll bet it isn't real at all. It's painted on the platter."

"It is not! It's a practical ham, stuffed with all kinds of devilment. The recipe is my mother's. She got it from an old Southern cook named Queenie."

"Listen, Kim. You're among friends. Your dear public is not present. You don't have to pretend any old Southern aristocracy Virginia belle mammy stuff with *us*."

"Pretend, you great oaf! I was born on a show boat on the Mississippi, and proud of it. Everybody knows that."

Mrs. Hawks, bustling into the show-boat kitchen with her unerring gift for scenting an atmosphere of mellow enjoyment, and dissipating it, would find Magnolia perched on a chair, both elbows on the table, her palms propping her chin as she regarded with round-eyed fascination Queenie's magic manipulations. Or perhaps Jo, the charming and shiftless, would be singing for her one of the Negro plantation songs, wistful with longing and pain; the folk songs of a wronged race, later to come into a blaze of popularity as spirituals.

For some nautical reason, a broad beam, about six inches high and correspondingly wide, stretched across the kitchen floor from side to side, dividing the room. Through long use Jo and Queenie had become accustomed to stepping over this obstruction, Queenie ponderously, Jo with an effortless swing of his lank legs. On this Magnolia used to sit, her arms hugging her knees, her great eyes in the little sallow pointed face fixed attentively on Jo. The kitchen was very clean and shining and stuffy. Jo's legs were crossed, one foot in its great low shapeless shoe hooked in the chair rung, his banjo cradled in his lap. The once white parchment face of the instrument was now almost as black as Jo's, what with much strumming by work-stained fingers.

"Which one, Miss Magnolia?"

"I Got Shoes," Magnolia would answer, promptly.

Jo would throw back his head, his sombre eyes half shut:

I got a shoes, you got a shoes. All of God's chil-dren got a shoes;
When I get to Heav-en goin' to put on my shoes, Goin' to walk all
    over God's
Heav'n Heav'n, Heav'n, Ev-'ry bod-y talk-in' 'bout heav'n ain't go-in
    there;
Heav'n, Heav-en, Goin' to shout all over God's Heav'n

The longing of a footsore, ragged, driven race expressed in the tragically childlike terms of shoes, white robes, wings, and the wise and simple insight into hypocrisy: "Ev'rybody talkin' 'bout Heav'n ain't goin' there. . . ."

"Now which one?" His fingers still picking the strings, ready at a word to slip into the opening chords of the next song.

"Go Down, Moses."

She liked this one—at once the most majestic and supplicating of all the Negro folk songs—because it always made her cry a little. Sometimes Queenie, busy at the stove or the kitchen table, joined in with her high rich camp-meeting voice. Jo's voice was a reedy tenor, but soft and husky with the indescribable Negro vocal quality. Magnolia soon knew the tune and the words of every song in Jo's repertoire. Unconsciously, being an excellent mimic, she sang as Jo and Queenie sang, her head thrown slightly back, her eyes rolling or half closed, one foot beating rhythmic time to the music's cadence. Her voice was true, though mediocre; but she got into this the hoarsely sweet Negro overtone—purple velvet muffling a flute.

Between Jo and Queenie flourished a fighting affection, deep, true, and lasting. There was some doubt as to the actual legal existence of their marriage, but the union was sound and normal enough. At each season's close they left the show boat the richer by three hundred dollars, clean new calico for Queenie, and proper jeans for Jo. Shoes on their feet. Hats on their heads. Bundles in their arms. Each spring they returned penniless, in rags, and slightly liquored. They had had a magnificent time. They did not drink again while the *Cotton Blossom* kitchen was their home. But the next winter the programme repeated itself. Captain Andy liked and trusted them. They were as faithful to him as their childlike vagaries would permit.

So, filled with the healthy ecstasy of song, the Negro man and woman and the white child would sit in deep contentment in the show-boat kitchen. The sound of a door slammed. Quick heavy footsteps. Three sets of nerves went taut. Parthy.

"Maggie Hawks, have you practised to-day?"

"Some."

"How much?"

"Oh, half an hour—more."

"When?"

" 'Smorning."

"I didn't hear you."

The sulky lower lip out. The high forehead wrinkled by a frown. Song flown. Peace gone.

"I did so. Jo, didn't you hear me practising?"

"Ah suah did, Miss Magnolia."

"You march right out of here, young lady, and practise another half hour. Do you think your father's made of money, that I can throw fifty-cent pieces away on George for nothing? Now you do your exercises fifteen minutes and the Maiden's Prayer fifteen. . . . Idea!"

Magnolia marched. Out of earshot Parthy expressed her opinion of nigger songs. "I declare I don't know where you get your low ways from! White people aren't good enough for you, I suppose, that you've got to run with blacks in the kitchen. Now you sit yourself down on that stool."

Magnolia was actually having music lessons. George, the Whistler and piano player, was her teacher, receiving fifty cents an hour for weekly instruction. Driven by her stern parent, she practised an hour daily on the tinny old piano in the orchestra pit, a rebellious, skinny, pathetic little figure strumming painstakingly away in the great emptiness of the show-boat auditorium. She must needs choose her time for practice when a rehearsal of the night's play was not in progress on the stage or when the band was not struggling with the music of a new song and dance number. Incredibly enough, she actually learned something of the mechanics of music, if not of its technique. She had an excellent rhythm sense, and this was aided by none other than Jo, whose feeling for time and beat and measure and pitch was flawless. Queenie lumped his song gift in with his general shiftlessness. Born fifty years later he might have known brief fame in some midnight revue or Club Alabam' on Broadway. Certainly Magnolia unwittingly learned more of real music from black Jo and many another Negro wharf minstrel than she did from hours of the heavy-handed and unlyrical George.

That Mrs. Hawks could introduce into the indolent tenor of show-boat life anything so methodical and humdrum as five-finger exercises done an hour daily was triumphant proof of her indomitable driving force. Life had miscast her in the rôle of wife and mother. She was born to be a Madam Chairman. Committees, Votes, Movements, Drives, Platforms, Gavels, Reports all showed in her stars. Cheated of these, she had to be content with such outlet of her enormous energies as the *Cotton Blossom* afforded. Parthy had never heard the word Feminist, and wouldn't have recognized it if she had. One spoke at that time not of Women's Rights but of Women's Wrongs. On these Parthenia often waxed tartly eloquent. Her housekeeping fervour was the natural result of her lack of a more impersonal safety valve. The *Cotton Blossom* shone like a Methodist Sunday household. Only Julie and Windy, the *Mollie Able* pilot, defied her. She actually indulged in those most domestic of rites, canning and preserving, on board the boat. Donning an all-enveloping gingham apron, she would set frenziedly to work on two bushels of peaches or seckel pears; baskets of tomatoes; pecks of apples. Pickled pears, peach marmalade, grape jell in jars and pots and glasses filled shelves and cupboards. Queenie found a great deal of satisfaction in the fact that occasionally, owing to some culinary accident or to the unusual motion of the flat-bottomed *Cotton Blossom* in the rough waters of an open bay, one of these jars was found smashed on the floor, its

rich purple or amber contents mingling with splinters of glass. No one
—not even Parthy—ever dared connect Queenie with these quite explicable mishaps.

Parthy was an expert needlewoman. She often assisted Julie or Elly
or Mis' Means with their costumes. To see her stern implacable face
bent over a heap of frivolous stuffs while her industrious fingers swiftly
sent the needle flashing through unvarying seams was to receive the
shock that comes of beholding the incongruous. The enormity of it
penetrated even her blunt sensibilities.

"If anybody'd ever told me that I'd live to see the day when I'd be
sewing on costumes for show folks!"

"Run along, Parthy. You like it," Andy would say.

But she never would admit that. "Like it or lump it, what can I do!
Married you for better or worse, didn't I!" Her tone leaving no doubt as
to the path down which that act had led her. Actually she was having a
rich, care-free, and varied life such as she had never dreamed of and of
which she secretly was enamoured.

Dwellers in this or that river town loitering down at the landing to
see what manner of sin and loose living went on in and about this show
boat with its painted women and play-acting men would be startled to
hear sounds and sniff smells which were identical with those which
might be issuing that very moment from their own smug and godly
dwellings ashore. From out the open doors of the Cotton Blossom
Floating Palace Theatre came the unmistakable and humdrum sounds
of scales and five-finger exercises done painfully and unwillingly by
rebellious childish hands. Ta-ta-ta—TA—ta-ta-ta. From below decks
there floated up the mouth-watering savour of tomato ketchup, of boiling vinegar and spices, or the perfumed aroma of luscious fruits seething
in sugary kettles.

"Smells for all the world like somebody was doing up sweet pickles."
One village matron to another.

"Well, I suppose they got to eat like other folks."

Ta-ta-ta—TA—ta-ta-ta.

It was inevitable, however, that the ease and indolence of the life, as
well as the daily contact with odd and unconventional characters must
leave some imprint on even so adamantine an exterior as Parthy's. Little
by little her school-teacherly diction dropped from her. Slowly her
vowels began to slur, her aren'ts became ain'ts, her crisp New England
utterance took on something of the slovenly Southern drawl, her consonants were missing from the end of a word here and there. True, she
still bustled and nagged, managed and scolded, drove and reproached.
She still had the power to make Andy jump with nervousness. Whether

consciously or unconsciously, the influence of this virago was more definitely felt than that of any other one of the *Cotton Blossom's* company and crew. Of these only Julie Dozier, and Windy, the pilot (so called because he almost never talked) actually triumphed over Mrs. Hawks. Julie's was a negative victory. She never voluntarily spoke to Parthy and had the power to aggravate that lady to the point of frenzy by remaining limp, supine, and idle when Parthy thought she should be most active; by raising her right eyebrow quizzically in response to a more than usually energetic tirade; by the habitual disorder of the tiny room which she shared with Steve; by the flagrant carelessness and untidiness of her own gaunt graceful person.

"I declare, Hawks, what you keep that slatternly yellow cat around this boat for beats me."

"Best actress in the whole caboodle, that's why." Something fine in little Captain Andy had seen and recognized the flame that might have glorified Julie had it not instead consumed her. "That girl had the right backing she'd make her mark, and not in any show boat, either. I've been to New York. I've seen 'em down at Wallack's and Daly's and around."

"A slut, that's what she is. I had my way she'd leave this boat bag and baggage."

"Well, this is one time you won't have your way, Mrs. Hawks, ma'am." She had not yet killed the spirit in Andy.

"Mark my words, you'll live to regret it. The way she looks out of those black eyes of hers! Gives me the creeps."

"What would you have the girl look out of," retorted Andy, not very brilliantly. "Her ears?"

Julie could not but know of this antagonism toward her. Some perverse streak in her otherwise rich and gentle make-up caused her to find a sinister pleasure in arousing it.

Windy's victory was more definitely dramatic, though his defensive method against Parthy's attacks resembled in sardonic quiet and poise Julie's own. Windy was accounted one of the most expert pilots on the Mississippi. He knew every coil and sinew and stripe of the yellow serpent. River men used his name as a synonym for magic with the pilot's wheel. Starless night or misty day; shoal water or deep, it was all one to Windy. Though Andy's senior by more than fifteen years, the two had been friends for twenty. Captain Andy had enormous respect for his steersmanship; was impressed by his taciturnity (being himself so talkative and vivacious); enjoyed talking with him in the bright quiet security of the pilot house. He was absolute czar of the *Mollie Able* and the *Cotton Blossom*, as befitted his high accomplishments. No one ever dreamed of opposing him except Parthy. He was slovenly of person, careless of habit. These shortcomings Parthy undertook to correct early in her show-boat career. She met with defeat so prompt, so complete, so crushing as to cause her for ever after to leave him unmolested.

Windy had muddy boots. They were, it seemed, congenitally so. He would go ashore in mid-afternoon of a hot August day when farmers for miles around had been praying for rain these weeks past and return in a downpour with half the muck and clay of the countryside clinging to his number eleven black square-toed elastic-side boots. A tall, emaciated drooping old man, Windy; with long gnarled muscular hands whose enlarged knuckles and leathery palms were the result of almost half a century at the wheel. His pants were always grease-stained; his black string tie and gray shirt spattered with tobacco juice; his brown jersey frayed and ragged. Across his front he wore a fine anchor watch chain, or "log" chain, as it was called. And gleaming behind the long flowing tobacco-splotched gray beard that reached almost to his waist could be glimpsed a milkily pink pearl stud like a star behind a dirty cloud-bank. The jewel had been come by, doubtless, in payment of some waterfront saloon gambling debt. Surely its exquisite curves had once glowed upon fine and perfumed linen.

It was against this taciturn and omnipotent conquerer of the rivers that Parthy raised the flag of battle.

"Traipsin' up and down this boat and the *Mollie Able*, spitting his filthy tobacco and leaving mud tracks like an elephant that's been in a bog. If I've had those steps leading up to the pilot house scrubbed once, I've had 'em scrubbed ten times this week, and now look at them! I won't have it, and so I tell you. Why can't he go up the side of the boat the way a pilot is supposed to do! What's that side ladder for, I'd like to know! He's supposed to go up it; not the steps."

"Now, Parthy, you can't run a boat the way you would a kitchen back in Thebes. Windy's no hired man. He's the best pilot on the rivers, and I'm lucky to have him. A hundred jobs better than this ready to jump at him if he so much as crooks a finger. He's pulled this tub through good many tight places where any other pilot'd landed us high and dry on a sand bar. And don't you forget it."

"He's a dirty old man. And I won't have it. Muddying up my clean . . ."

Parthy was not one of your scolds who takes her grievances out in mere words. With her, to threaten was to act. That very morning, just before the *Cotton Blossom* was making a late departure from Greenville, where they had played the night before, to Sunnisie Side Landing, twelve miles below, this formidable woman, armed with hammer and nails, took advantage of Windy's temporary absence below decks to nail down the hatch above the steps leading to the pilot house. She was the kind of woman who can drive a nail straight. She drove ten of them, long and firm and deep. A pity that no one saw her. It was a sight worth seeing, this accomplished and indomitable virago in curl papers, driving nails with a sure and steady stroke.

Below stairs Windy, coming aboard from an early morning look around, knocked the ashes out of his pipe, sank his great yellow fangs into a generous wedge of Honest Scrap, and prepared to climb the stairs to the *Cotton Blossom* pilot house, there to manipulate wheel and cord that would convey his orders to Pete in the engine room.

Up the stairs, leaving a mud spoor behind. One hand raised to lift the hatch; wondering, meanwhile, to find it closed. A mighty heave; a pounding with the great fist; another heave, then, with the powerful old shoulder.

"Nailed," said Windy aloud to himself, mildly. Then, still mildly, "The old hell cat." He spat, then, on the hatchway steps and clumped leisurely down again. He leaned over the boat rail, looking benignly down at the crowd of idlers gathered at the wharf to watch the show boat cast off. Then he crossed the deck again to where a capacious and carpet-seated easy chair held out its inviting arms. Into this he sank with a grunt of relaxation. From his pocket he took the pipe so recently relinquished, filled it, tamped it, lighted it. From another pocket he took a month-old copy of the New Orleans *Times-Democrat*, turned to the column marked Shipping News, and settled down, apparently, for a long quiet day with literature.

Up came the anchor. In came the hawser. Chains clanked. The sound of the gangplank drawn up. The hoarse shouts from land and water that always attend the departure of a river boat. "Throw her over there! Lift 'er! Heh, Pete! Gimme hand here! Little to the left. Other side! Hold on! Easy!"

The faces of the crowd ashore turned expectantly toward the boat. Everything shipshape. Pete in the engine room. Captain Andy scampering for the texas. Silence. No bells. No steam. No hoarse shouts of command. God A'mighty, where's Windy? Windy! Windy!

Windy lowers his shielding newspaper and mildly regards the capering captain and bewildered crew and startled company. He is wearing his silver-rimmed reading spectacles slightly askew on his biblical-looking hooked nose. Andy rushes up to him, all the Basque in him bubbling. "God's sake, Windy, what's . . . why don't you take her! We're going."

Windy chewed rhythmically for a moment, spat a long brown jet of juice, wiped his hairy mouth with the back of one gnarled hand. "We ain't going, Cap'n Hawks, because she can't go till I give her the go-ahead. And I ain't give her the go-ahead. I'm the pilot of this here boat."

"But why? What the . . . Wh——"

"The hatch is nailed down above the steps leading to the pilot house, Cap'n Andy. Till that hatchway's open, I don't climb up to no pilot house. And till I climb up to the pilot house, she don't get no go-ahead. And till I give her the go-ahead, she don't go, not if we stay here along-side this landing till the *Cotton Blossom* rots."

He looked around benignly and resumed his reading of the New Orleans *Times-Democrat*.

Profanity, frowned upon under Parthy's régime, now welled up in Andy and burst from him in spangled geysers. Words seethed to the surface and exploded like fireworks. Twenty-five years of river life had equipped him with a vocabulary rich, varied, purple. He neglected neither the heavens above nor the earth beneath. Revolt and rage shook his wiry little frame. Years of henpecking, years of natural gaiety sup-pressed, years of mincing when he wished to stride, years of silence when he wished to sing, now were wiped away by the stream of undiluted rage that burst from Captain Andy Hawks. It was a torrent, a flood, a Mississippi of profanity in which hells and damns were mere drops in the mighty roaring mass.

"Out with your crowbars there. Pry up that hatch! I'm captain of this boat, by God, and anybody, man or woman, who nails down that hatch again without my orders gets put off this boat wherever we are, and so I say."

Did Parthenia Ann Hawks shrink and cower and pale under the blinding glare of this pyrotechnic profanity? Not that indomitable woman. The picture of outraged virtue in curl papers, she stood her ground like a Roman matron. She had even, when the flood broke, sent Magnolia indoors with a gesture meant to convey protection from the pollution of this verbal stream.

"Well, Captain Hawks, a fine example you have set for your company and crew I must say."

"*You* must say! You——! Let me tell you, Mrs. Hawks, ma'am, the less you say the better. And I repeat, anybody touches that hatchway again——"

"Touch it!" echoed Parthy in icy disdain. "I wouldn't touch it, nor the pilot house, nor the pilot either, if you'll excuse my saying so, with a ten-foot pole."

And swept away with as much dignity as a *Cotton Blossom* early morning costume would permit. Her head bloody but unbowed.

VII

JULIE was gone. Steve was gone. Tragedy had stalked into Magnolia's life; had cast its sable mantle over the *Cotton Blossom*. Pete had kept his promise and revenge had been his. But the taste of triumph had not, after all, been sweet in his mouth. There was little of the peace of satisfaction in his sooty face stuck out of the engine-room door. The arm that beat the bull drum in the band was now a listless member, so that a hollow mournful thump issued from that which should have given forth a rousing boom.

The day the *Cotton Blossom* was due to play Lemoyne, Mississippi, Julie Dozier took sick. In show-boat troupes, as well as in every other theatrical company in the world, it is an unwritten law that an actor must never be too sick to play. He may be sick. Before the performance he may be too sick to stand; immediately after the performance he may collapse. He may, if necessary, die on the stage and the curtain will then be lowered. But no real trouper while conscious will ever confess himself too sick to go on when the overture ends and the lights go down.

Julie knew this. She had played show boats for years, up and down the rivers of the Middle West and the South. She had a large and loyal following. Lemoyne was a good town, situated on the river, prosperous, sizable.

Julie lay on her bed in her darkened room, refusing all offers of aid. She did not want food. She did not want cold compresses on her head. She did not want hot compresses on her head. She wanted to be left alone—with Steve. Together the two stayed in the darkened room, and when some member of the company came to the door with offers of aid or comfort, there came into their faces a look that was strangely like one of fear, followed immediately by a look of relief.

Queenie sent Jo to the door with soup, her panacea for all ailments, whether of the flesh or the spirit. Julie made a show of eating it, but when Jo had clumped across the stage and down to his kitchen Julie motioned to Steve. He threw the contents of the bowl out of the window into the yellow waters of the Mississippi.

Doc appeared at Julie's door for the tenth time though it was only mid-morning. "Think you can play all right, to-night, though, don't you, Julie?"

In the semi-darkness of her shaded room Julie's eyes glowed suddenly wide and luminous. She sat up in bed, pushing her hair back from her forehead with a gesture so wild as to startle the old trouper.

"No!" she cried, in a sort of terror. "No! I can't play to-night. Don't ask me."

Blank astonishment made Doc's face almost ludicrous. For an actress to announce ten hours before the time set for the curtain's rising that she would not be able to go on that evening—an actress who had not suffered decapitation or an amputation—was a thing unheard of in Doc's experience.

"God A'mighty, Julie! If you're sick as all that, you'd better see a doctor. Steve, what say?"

The great blond giant seated at the side of Julie's bed did not look round at his questioner. His eyes were on Julie's face. "Julie's funny that way. She's set against doctors. Won't have one, that's all. Don't coax her. It'll only make her worse."

Inured as he was to the vagaries of woman, this apparently was too much for Doc. Schultzy appeared in the doorway; peered into the dimness of the little room.

"Funny thing. I guess you must have an admirer in this town, Jule. Somebody's stole your picture, frame and all, out of the layout in the lobby there. First I thought it might be that crazy Pete, used to be so stuck on you. . . . Now, now, Steve! Keep your shirt on! Keep your shirt on! . . . I asked him, straight, but he was surprised all right. He ain't good enough actor to fool me. He didn't do it. Must be some town rube all right, Julie, got stuck on your shape or something. I put up another one." He stood a moment, thoughtfully. Elly came up behind him, hatted and gloved.

"I'm going up to town, Julie. Can I fetch you something? An orange, maybe? Or something from the drug store?"

Julie's head on the pillow moved a negative. "She says no, thanks," Steve answered for her, shortly. It was as though both laboured under a strain. The three in the doorway sensed it. Elly shrugged her shoulders, though whether from pique or indifference it was hard to say. Doc still stood puzzled, bewildered. Schultzy half turned away. "S'long's you're all right by to-night," he said cheerfully.

"Says she won't be," Doc put in, lowering his voice.

"Won't be!" repeated Schultzy, almost shrilly. "Why, she ain't *sick*, is she! I mean, sick!"

Schultzy sent his voice shrilling from Julie's little bedroom doorway across the bare stage, up the aisles of the empty auditorium, so that it penetrated the box office at the far end of the boat, where Andy, at the ticket window, was just about to be relieved by Parthy.

"Heh, Cap! Cap! Come here. Julie's sick. Julie's too sick to go on. Says she's too sick to . . ."

"Here," said Andy, summarily, to Parthy; and left her in charge of business. Down the aisle with the light quick step that was almost a scamper; up the stage at a bound. "Best advance sale we've had since we started out. We never played this town before. License was too high. But here it is, not eleven o'clock, and half the house gone already." He peered into the darkened room.

From its soft fur nest in the old sealskin muff the marmoset poked its tragic mask and whimpered like a sick baby. This morning there was a strange resemblance between the pinched and pathetic face on the pillow and that of the little sombre-eyed monkey.

By now there was quite a little crowd about Julie's door. Mis' Means had joined them and could be heard murmuring about mustard plasters and a good hot something or other. Andy entered the little room with the freedom of an old friend. He looked sharply down at the face on the pillow. The keen eyes plunged deep into the tortured eyes that stared piteously up at him. Something he saw there caused him to reach out with one brown paw, none too immaculate, and pat that other slim brown hand clutching the coverlet so tensely. "Why, Jule, what's—— Say, s'pose you folks clear out and let me and Jule and Steve here talk things over quiet. Nobody ain't going to get well with this mob scene you're putting on. Scat!" Andy could distinguish between mental and physical anguish.

They shifted—Doc, Elly, Schultzy, Mis' Means, Catchem the torpid. Another moment and they would have moved reluctantly away. But Parthy, torn between her duty at the ticket window and her feminine curiosity as to the cause of the commotion at Julie's door became, suddenly, all woman. Besides—demon statistician that she was—she suddenly had remembered a curious coincidence in connection with this sudden illness of Julie's. She slammed down the ticket window, banged the box-office door, sailed down the aisle. As she approached Doc was saying for the dozenth time:

"Person's too sick to play, they're sick enough to have a doctor's what I say. Playing Xenia to-morrow. Good a stand's we got. Prolly won't be able to open there, neither, if you're sick's all that."

"I'll be able to play to-morrow!" cried Julie, in a high strained voice. "I'll be able to play to-morrow. To-morrow I'll be all right."

"How do you know?" demanded Doc.

Steve turned on him in sudden desperation. "She'll be all right, I tell you. She'll be all right as soon as she gets out of this town."

"That's a funny thing," exclaimed Parthy. She swept through the little crowd at the door, seeming to mow them down with the energy of her progress. "That's a funny thing."

"What?" demanded Steve, his tone belligerent. "What's funny?"

Captain Andy raised a placating palm. "Now, Parthy, now, Parthy. Sh-sh!"

"Don't shush *me*, Hawks. I know what I'm talking about. It came over me just this minute. Julie took sick at this very town of Lemoyne time we came down river last year. Soon as you and Doc decided we wouldn't open here because the license was too high she got well all of a sudden, just like that!" She snapped a thumb and forefinger.

Silence, thick, uncomfortable, heavy with foreboding, settled down upon the little group in the doorway.

"Nothing so funny about that," said Captain Andy, stoutly; and threw a sharp glance at the face on the pillow. "This hot sticky climate down here after the cold up north is liable to get anybody to feeling queer. None too chipper myself, far's that goes. Affects some people that way." He scratched frenziedly at the mutton-chop whiskers, this side and that.

"Well, I may not know *much*——" began Parthy.

Down the aisle skimmed Magnolia, shouting as she came, her child's voice high and sharp with excitement. "Mom! Mom! Look. What do you think! Julie's picture's been stolen again right out of the front of the lobby. Julie, they've taken your picture again. Somebody took one and Schultzy put another in and now it's been stolen too."

She was delighted with her news; radiant with it. Her face fell a little at the sight of the figure on the bed, the serious group about the doorway that received her news with much gravity. She flew to the bed then, all contrition. "Oh, Julie darling, I'm so sorry you're sick." Julie turned her face away from the child, toward the wall.

Captain Andy, simulating fury, capered a threatening step toward the doorway crowd now increased by the deprecating figure of Mr. Means and Ralph's tall shambling bulk. "Will you folks clear out of here or will I have to use force! A body'd think a girl didn't have the right to feel sick. Doc, you get down and 'tend to that ticket window, or Parthy. If we can't show to-night we got to leave 'em know. Ralph, you write out a sign and get it pasted up at the post office. . . . Sure you won't be feeling better by night time, are you, Julie?" He looked doubtfully down at the girl on the bed.

With a sudden lithe movement Julie flung herself into Steve's arms, clung to him, weeping. "No!" she cried, her voice high, hysterical. "No! No! No! Leave me alone, can't you! Leave me alone!"

"Sure," Andy motioned, then, fiercely to the company. "Sure we'll leave you alone, Julie."

But Tragedy, having stalked her victim surely, relentlessly, all the morning, now was about to close in upon her. She had sent emissary after emissary down the show-boat aisle, and each had helped to deepen the look of terror in Julie's eyes. Now sounded the slow shambling heavy tread of Windy the pilot, bearded, sombre, ominous as the figure of fate itself. The little group turned toward him automatically, almost absurdly, like a badly directed mob scene in one of their own improbable plays.

He clumped up the little flight of steps that led from the lower left-hand box to the stage. Clump, clump, clump. Irresistibly Parthy's eyes peered sharply in pursuit of the muddy tracks that followed each step. She snorted indignantly. Across the stage, his beard waggling up and down as his jaws worked slowly, rhythmically, on a wedge of Honest Scrap. As he approached Julie's doorway he took off his cap and rubbed his pate with his palm, sure sign of great mental perturbation in this monumental old leviathan. The yellow skin of his knobby bald dome-like head shone gold in the rays of the late morning sun that came in through the high windows at the side of the stage.

He stood a moment, chewing, and peering mildly into the dimness of the bedroom, Sphinx-like, it seemed that he never would speak. He stood, champing. The *Cotton Blossom* troupe waited. They had not played melodrama for years without being able to sense it when they saw it. He spoke. "Seems that skunk Pete's up to something." They waited. The long tobacco-stained beard moved up and down, up and down. "Skinned out half an hour back streaking toward town like possessed. He yanked that picture of Julie out of the hall there. Seen him. I see good deal goes on around here."

Steve sprang to his feet with a great ripping river oath. "I'll kill him this time, the ——"

"Seen you take that first picture out, Steve." The deep red that had darkened Steve's face and swelled the veins on his great neck receded now, leaving his china-blue eyes staring out of a white and stricken face.

"I never did! I never did!"

Julie sat up, clutching her wrapper at the throat. She laughed shrilly. "What would he want to steal my picture for! His own wife's picture. Likely!"

"So nobody in this town'd see it, Julie," said Windy, mildly. "Listen. Fifty years piloting on the rivers, you got to have pretty good eyesight.

Mine's as good to-day as it was time I was twenty. I just stepped down from the texas to warn you I see Pete coming along the levee with Ike Keener. Ike's the sheriff. He'll be in here now any minute."

"Let him," Andy said, stoutly. "Our license is paid. Sheriff's as welcome around this boat as anybody. Let him."

But no one heard him; no one heeded him. A strange and terrible thing was happening. Julie had sprung from her bed. In her white nightgown and her wrapper, her long black hair all tumbled and wild about her face, a stricken and hunted thing, she clung to Steve, and he to her. There came a pounding at the door that led into the show-boat auditorium from the fore deck. Steve's eyes seemed suddenly to sink far back in his head. His cheek-bones showed gaunt and sharp as Julie's own. His jaw was set so that a livid ridge stood out on either side like bars of white-hot steel. He loosened Julie's hold almost roughly. From his pocket he whipped a great clasp-knife and opened its flashing blade. Julie did not scream, but the other women did, shriek on shriek. Captain Andy sprang for him, a mouse attacking a mastodon. Steve shook him off with a fling of his powerful shoulders.

"I'm not going to hurt her, you fool. Leave me be. I know what I'm doing." The pounding came again, louder and more insistent. "Somebody go down and let him in—but keep him there a minute."

No one stirred. The pounding ceased. The doors opened. The boots of Ike Keener, the sheriff, clattered down the aisle of the *Cotton Blossom*.

"Stop those women screeching," Steve shouted. Then, to Julie, "It won't hurt much, darling." With incredible swiftness he seized Julie's hand in his left one and ran the keen glittering blade of his knife firmly across the tip of her forefinger. A scarlet line followed it. He bent his blond head, pressed his lips to the wound, sucked it greedily. With a little moan Julie fell back on the bed. Steve snapped the blade into its socket, thrust the knife into his pocket. The boots of Sheriff Ike Keener were clattering across the stage now. The white faces clustered in the doorway—the stricken, bewildered, horrified faces—turned from the two within the room to the one approaching it. They made way for this one silently. Even Parthy was dumb. Magnolia clung to her, wide-eyed, uncomprehending, sensing tragedy though she had never before encountered it.

The lapel of his coat flung back, Ike Keener confronted the little cowed group on the stage. A star shone on his left breast. The scene was like a rehearsal of a *Cotton Blossom* thriller.

"Who's captain of this here boat?"

Andy, his fingers clutching his whiskers, stepped forward. "I am.

What's wanted with him? Hawks is my name—Captain Andy Hawks, twenty years on the rivers."

He looked the sheriff of melodrama, did Ike Keener—boots, black moustaches, wide-brimmed black hat, flowing tie, high boots, and all. Steve himself, made up for the part, couldn't have done it better. "Well, Cap, kind of unpleasant, but I understand there's a miscegenation case on board."

"What?" whispered Magnolia. "What's that? What does he mean, Mom?"

"Hush!" hissed Parthy, and jerked the child's arm.

"How's that?" asked Andy, but he knew.

"Miscegenation. Case of a Negro woman married to a white man. Criminal offense in this state, as you well know."

"No such thing," shouted Andy. "No such thing on board this boat."

Sheriff Ike Keener produced a piece of paper. "Name of the white man is Steve Baker. Name of the negress"—he squinted again at the slip of paper—"name of the negress is Julie Dozier." He looked around at the group. "Which one's them?"

"Oh, my God!" screamed Elly. "Oh, my God! Oh, my God!"

"Shut up," said Schultzy, roughly.

Steve stepped to the window and threw up the shade, letting the morning light into the crowded disorderly little cubicle. On the bed lay Julie, her eyes enormous in her sallow pinched face.

"I'm Steve Baker. This is my wife."

Sheriff Ike Keener tucked the paper in his pocket. "You two better dress and come along with me."

Julie stood up. She looked an old woman. The marmoset whimpered and whined in his fur nest. She put out a hand, automatically, and plucked it from the muff and held it in the warm hollow of her breast. Her great black eyes stared at the sheriff like the wide-open unseeing eyes of a sleep walker.

Steve Baker grinned—rather, his lips drew back from his teeth in a horrid semblance of mirth. He threw a jovial arm about Julie's shrinking shoulder. For once she had no need to coach him in his part. He looked Ike Keener in the eye. "You wouldn't call a man a white man that's got Negro blood in him, would you?"

"No, I wouldn't; not in Mississippi. One drop of nigger blood makes you a nigger in these parts."

"Well, I got more than a drop of—nigger blood in me, and that's a fact. You can't make miscegenation out of that."

"You ready to swear to that in a court of law?"

"I'll swear to it any place. I'll swear it now." Steve took a step forward, one hand outstretched. "I'll do more than that. Look at all these folks here. There ain't one of them but can swear I got Negro blood in me this minute. That's how white I am."

Sheriff Ike Keener swept the crowd with his eye. Perhaps what he saw in their faces failed to convince him. "Well, I seen fairer men than you was niggers. Still, you better tell that——"

Mild, benevolent, patriarchal, the figure of old Windy stepped out from among the rest. "Guess you've known me, Ike, better part of twenty-five years. I was keelboatin' time you was runnin' around, a barefoot on the landin'. Now I'm tellin' you—me, Windy McKlain—that that white man there's got nigger blood in him. I'll take my oath to that."

Having thus delivered himself of what was, perhaps, the second longest speech in his career, he clumped off again, across the stage, down the stairs, up the aisle, looking, even in that bizarre environment, like something out of Genesis.

Sheriff Ike Keener was frankly puzzled. "If it was anybody else but Windy—but I got this straight from—from somebody ought to know."

"From who?" shouted Andy, all indignation. "From a sooty-faced scab of a bull-drumming engineer named Pete. And why? Because he's been stuck on Julie here I don't know how long, and she wouldn't have anything to do with him."

"Is that right?"

"Yes, it is," Steve put in, quickly. "He was after my wife. Anybody in the company'll bear me out. He wouldn't leave her alone, though she hated the sight of him, and Cap here give him a talking—didn't you, Cap? So finally, when he wouldn't quit, then there was nothing for it but lick him, and I licked him good, and soused him in the river to get his dirty face clean. He crawls out swearing he'll get me for it. Now you know."

Keener now addressed himself to Julie for the first time. "He says— this Pete—that you was born here in Lemoyne, and that your pop was white and your mammy black. That right?"

Julie moistened her lips with the tip of her tongue. "Yes," she said. "That's—right."

A sudden commotion in the group that had been so still. Elly's voice, shrill with hysteria. "I will! I'll tell right out. The wench! The lying black——"

Suddenly stifled, as though a hand had been clapped none too gently across her mouth. Incoherent blubberings; a scuffle. Schultzy had picked Elly up like a sack of meal, one hand still firmly held over her mouth; had carried her into her room and slammed the door.

"What's she say?" inquired Keener.

Again Andy stepped into the breach. "That's our ingénue lead. She's kind of high strung. You see, she's been friends with this—with Julie Dozier, here—without knowing about her—about her blood, and like that. Kind of give her a shock, I guess. Natural."

It was plain that Sheriff Ike Keener was on the point of departure, puzzled though convinced. He took off his broad-brimmed hat, scratched his head, replaced the hat at an angle that spelled bewilderment. His eye, as he turned away, fell on the majestic figure of Parthenia Ann Hawks, and on Magnolia cowering, wide-eyed, in the folds of her mother's ample skirts.

"You look like a respectable woman, ma'am."

Imposing enough at all times, Parthy now grew visibly taller. Cold sparks flew from her eyes. "I am."

"That your little girl?"

Andy did the honours. "My wife, Sheriff. My little girl, Magnolia. What do you say to the Sheriff, Magnolia?"

Thus urged, Magnolia spoke that which had been seething within her. "You're bad!" she shouted, her face twisted with the effort to control her tears. "You're a bad mean man, that's what! You called Julie names and made her look all funny. You're a——"

The maternal hand stifled her.

"If I was you, ma'am, I would bring up no child on a boat like this. No, nor stay on it, neither. Fine place to rear a child!"

Whereupon, surprisingly enough, Parthy turned defensive. "My child's as well brought up as your own, and probably better, and so I tell you. And I'll thank you to keep your advice to yourself, Mr. Sheriff."

"Parthy! Parthy!" from the alarmed Andy.

But Sheriff Ike Keener was a man of parts. "Well, women folks are all alike. I'll be going. I kind of smell a nigger in the woodpile here in more ways than one. But I'll take your word for it." He looked Captain Andy sternly in the eye. "Only let me tell you this, Captain Hawks. You better not try to give your show in this town to-night. We got some public-spirited folks here in Lemoyne and this fix you're in has kind of leaked around. You go to work and try to give your show with this mixed blood you got here and first thing you know you'll be riding out of town on something don't sit so easy as a boat."

His broad-brimmed hat at an angle of authority, his coat tails flirting as he strode, he marched up the aisle then and out.

The little huddling group seemed visibly to collapse. It was as though an unseen hand had removed a sustaining iron support from the spine of each. Magnolia would have flown to Julie, but Parthy jerked her back. Whispering then; glance of disdain.

"Well, Julie, m'girl," began Andy Hawks, kindly. Julie turned to him. "We're going," she said, quietly.

The door of Elly's room burst open. Elly, a rumpled, distraught, unlovely figure, appeared in Julie's doorway, Schultzy trying in vain to placate her.

"You get out of here!" She turned in a frenzy to Andy. "She gets out of here with that white trash she calls her husband or I go, and so I warn you. She's black! She's black! God, I was a fool not to see it all the time. Look at her, the nasty yellow——" A stream of abuse, vile, obscene, born of the dregs of river talk heard through the years, now welled to Elly's lips, distorting them horribly.

"Come away from here," Parthy said, through set lips, to Magnolia. And bore the child, protesting, up the aisle and into the security of her own room forward.

"I want to stay with Julie! I want to stay with Julie!" wailed Magnolia, overwrought, as the inexorable hand dragged her up the stairs.

In her tiny disordered room Julie was binding up her wild hair with a swift twist. She barely glanced at Elly. "Shut that woman up," she said, quietly. "Tell her I'm going." She began to open boxes and drawers.

Steve approached Andy, low-voiced. "Cap, take us down as far as Xenia, will you, for God's sake! Don't make us get off here."

"Down as far as Xenia you go," shouted Captain Andy at the top of his voice, "and anybody in this company don't like it they're free to git, bag and baggage, now. We'll pull out of here now. Xenia by afternoon at four, latest. And you two want to stay the night on board you're welcome. I'm master of this boat, by God!"

They left, these two, when the *Cotton Blossom* docked at Xenia in the late afternoon. Andy shook hands with them, gravely; and Windy clumped down from the pilot house to perform the same solemn ceremony. You sensed unseen peering eyes at every door and window of the *Cotton Blossom* and the *Mollie Able.*

"How you fixed for money?" Andy demanded, bluntly.

"We're fixed all right," Julie replied, quietly. Of the two of them she was the more composed. "We've been saving. You took too good care of us on the *Cotton Blossom*. No call to spend our money." The glance from her dark shadow-encircled eyes was one of utter gratefulness. She took up the lighter pieces of luggage. Steve was weighed down with the others—bulging boxes and carpet bags and bundles—their clothing and their show-boat wardrobe and their pitifully few trinkets and personal belongings. A pin cushion, very lumpy, that Magnolia had made for her at Christmas a year ago. Photographs of the *Cotton Blossom*. A book of pressed wild flowers. Old newspaper clippings.

Julie lingered. Steve crossed the gangplank, turned, beckoned with his head. Julie lingered. An unspoken question in her eyes.

Andy flushed and scratched the mutton-chop whiskers this side and that. "Well, you know how she is, Julie. She don't mean no harm. But she didn't let on to Magnolia just what time you were going. Told her to-morrow, likely. Women folks are funny, that way. She don't mean no harm."

"That's all right," said Julie; picked up the valises, was at Steve's side. Together the two toiled painfully up the steep river bank, Steve turning to aid her as best he could. They reached the top of the levee. They stood a moment, breathless; then turned and trudged down the dusty Southern country road, the setting sun in their faces. Julie's slight figure was bent under the weight of the burden she carried. You saw Steve's fine blond head turned toward her, tender, concerned, encouraging.

Suddenly from the upper deck that fronted Magnolia's room and Parthy's came the sound of screams, a scuffle, a smart slap, feet clattering pell-mell down the narrow wooden balcony stairs. A wild little figure in a torn white frock, its face scratched and tear-stained, its great eyes ablaze in the white face, flew past Andy, across the gangplank, up the levee, down the road. Behind her, belated and panting, came Parthy. Her hand on her heart, her bosom heaving, she leaned against the inadequate support offered by Andy's right arm, threatening momentarily to topple him, by her own dead weight, into the river.

"To think that I should live to see the day when—my own child—she slapped me—her mother! I saw them out of the window, so I told her to straighten her bureau drawers—a sight! All of a sudden she heard that woman's voice, low as it was, and she to the window. When she saw her going she makes for the door. I caught her on the steps, but she was like a wildcat, and raised her hand against me—her own mother—and tore away, with me holding this in my hand." She held out a fragment of torn white stuff. "Raised her hand against her own——"

Andy grinned. "Good for her."

"What say, Andy Hawks!"

But Andy refused to answer. His gaze followed the flying little figure silhouetted against the evening sky at the top of the high river bank. The slim sagging figure of the woman and the broad-shouldered figure of the man trudged down the road ahead. The child's voice could be heard high and clear, with a note of hysteria in it. "Julie! Julie! Wait for me! I want to say good-bye! Julie!"

The slender woman in the black dress turned and made as though to start back and then, with a kind of crazy fear in her pace, began to run away from the pursuing little figure—away from something that she had not the courage to face. And when she saw this Magnolia ran on yet a little while, faltering, and then she stopped and buried her head in her hands and sobbed. The woman glanced over her shoulder, fearfully. And at what she saw she dropped her bags and bundles in the road and started back toward her, running fleetly in spite of her long ruffled awkward skirts; and she held out her arms long before they were able to reach her. And when finally they came together, the woman dropped on her knees in the dust of the road and gathered the weeping child to her and held her close, so that as you saw them sharply outlined against the sunset the black of the woman's dress and the white of the child's frock were as one.

VIII

MAGNOLIA, at fifteen, was a gangling gawky child whose eyes were too big for her face and whose legs were too long for her skirts. She looked, in fact, all legs, eyes, and elbows. It was a constant race between her knees and her skirt hems. Parthy was for ever lengthening frocks. Frequently Magnolia, looking down at herself, was surprised, like Alice in Wonderland after she had eaten the magic currant cake, to discover how far away from her head her feet were. Being possessed of a natural creamy pallor which her mother mistook for lack of red corpuscles, she was dosed into chronic biliousness on cod liver oil, cream, eggs, and butter, all of which she loathed. Then suddenly, at sixteen, legs, elbows, and eyes assumed their natural proportions. Overnight, seemingly, she emerged from adolescence a rather amazing looking young creature with a high broad forehead, a wide mobile mouth, great dark liquid eyes, and a most lovely speaking voice which nobody noticed. Her dress was transformed, with Cinderella-like celerity, from the pinafore to the bustle variety. She was not a beauty. She was, in fact, considered rather plain by the unnoticing. Being hipless and almost boyishly flat of bust in a day when the female form was a thing not only of curves but of loops, she was driven by her mother into wearing all sorts of pads and ruffled corset covers and contrivances which somehow failed to conceal the slimness of the frame beneath. She was, even at sixteen, what might be termed distinguished-looking. Merely by standing tall, pale, dark-haired, next to Elly, that plump and pretty ingénue was transformed into a dumpy and rather dough-faced blonde in whose countenance selfishness and dissatisfaction were beginning to etch telltale lines.

She had been now almost seven years on the show boat. These seven years had spread a tapestry of life and colour before her eyes. Broad rivers flowing to the sea. Little towns perched high on the river banks or cowering flat and fearful, at the mercy of the waters that often crept like hungry and devouring monsters, stealthily over the levee and into the valley below. Singing Negroes. Fighting whites. Spawning Negroes. A life fantastic, bizarre, peaceful, rowdy, prim, eventful, calm. On the rivers anything might happen and everything did. She saw convict chain gangs working on the roads. Grisly nightmarish figures of striped horror, manacled leg to leg. At night you heard them singing plantation songs in the fitful glare of their camp fires in the woods; simple songs full of hope. Didn't My Lord Deliver Daniel? they sang. Swing Low Sweet Chariot, Comin' for to Carry Me Home. In the Louisiana bayou country she saw the Negroes perform that weird religious rite known as a ring shout, semi-savage, hysterical, mesmerizing.

Iowa, Illinois, and Missouri small-town housewives came to be Magnolia's friends, and even Parthy's. The coming of the show boat was the one flash of blazing colour in the drab routine of their existence. To them Schultzy was the John Drew of the rivers, Elly the Lillian Russell. You saw them scudding down the placid tree-shaded streets in their morning ginghams and calicoes, their bits of silver clasped in their work-seamed hands, or knotted into the corner of a handkerchief. Fifty cents for two seats at to-night's show.

"How are you, Mis' Hawks? . . . And the little girl? . . . My! Look at the way she's shot up in a year's time! Well, you can't call her little girl any more. . . . I brought you a glass of my home-made damson preserve. I take cup of sugar to cup of juice. Real rich, but it is good if I do say so. . . . I told Will I was coming to the show every night you were here, and he could like it or lump it. I been saving out of the housekeeping money."

They brought vast chocolate cakes; batches of cookies; jugs of home-brewed grape wine; loaves of fresh bread; jars of strained honey; stiff tight bunches of garden flowers. Offerings on the shrine of Art.

Periodically Parthy threatened to give up this roving life and take Magnolia with her. She held this as a weapon over Andy's head when he crossed her will, or displeased her. Immediately boarding schools, convents, and seminaries yawned for Magnolia.

Perhaps Parthy was right. "What kind of a life is this for a child!"

she demanded. And later, "A fine kind of a way for a young lady to be living—slopping up and down these rivers, seeing nothing but loafers and gamblers and niggers and worse. What about her Future?" Future, as she pronounced it, was spelled with a capital F and was a thin disguise for the word husband.

"Future'll take care of itself," Andy assured her, blithely.

"If that isn't just like a man!"

It was inevitable that Magnolia should, sooner or later, find herself through force of circumstance treading the boards as an actress in the Cotton Blossom Floating Palace Theatre company. Not only that, she found herself playing ingénue leads. She had been thrown in as a stop-gap following Elly's defection, and had become, quite without previous planning, a permanent member of the troupe. Strangely enough, she developed an enormous following, though she lacked that saccharine quality which river towns had come to expect in their show-boat ingénues. True, her long legs were a little lanky beneath the short skirts of the woodman's pure daughter, but what she lacked in one extremity she made up in another. They got full measure when they looked at her eyes, and her voice made the small-town housewives weep. Yet when their husbands nudged them, saying, "What you sniffling about?" they could only reply, "I don't know." And no more did they.

Elly was twenty-eight when she deserted Schultzy for a gambler from Mobile. For three years she had been restless, fault-finding, dissatisfied. Each autumn she would announce to Captain Andy her intention to forsake the rivers and bestow her talents ashore. During the winter she would try to get an engagement through the Chicago booking offices contrary to the custom of show-boat actors whose habit it was to hibernate in the winter on the savings of a long and economical summer. But the Chicago field was sparse and uncertain. She never had the courage or the imagination to go as far as New York. April would find her back on the *Cotton Blossom*. Between her and Schultzy the bickerings and the quarrels became more and more frequent. She openly defied Schultzy as he directed rehearsals. She refused to follow his suggestions though he had a real sense of direction. Everything she knew he had taught her. She invariably misread a line and had to be coached in it, word by word; inflection; business; everything.

Yet now, when Schultzy said, "No! Listen. You been kidnapped and smuggled on board this rich fella's yacht, see. And he thinks he's got you in his power. He goes to grab you. You're here, see. Then you point toward the door back of him, see, like you saw something there scared the life out of you. He turns around and you grab the gun off the table, see, and cover him, and there's your big speech. So and so and *so* and

so and *so* and so and *so* and so——" the *ad lib.* directions that have
held since the day of Shakespeare.

Elly would deliberately defy him. Others in the company—new members—began to take their cue from her.

She complained about her wardrobe; refused to interest herself in it,
though she had been an indefatigable needlewoman. Now, instead of
sewing, you saw her looking moodily out across the river, her hands
idle, her brows black. An unintelligent and unresourceful woman turned
moody and thoughtful must come to mischief, for within herself she
finds no solace.

At Mobile, then, she was gone. It was, they all knew, the black-
moustached gambler who had been following the show boat down the
river since they played Paducah, Kentucky. Elly had had dozens of ad-
mirers in her show-boat career; had received much attention from Southern gallants, gamblers, loafers, adventurers—all the romantic beaux of
the river towns of the '80s. Her attitude toward them had been puritani-
cal to the point of sniffiness, though she had enjoyed their homage and
always displayed any amorous missives or gifts that came her way.

True to the melodramatic tradition of her environment, she left a
note for Schultzy, written in a flourishing Spencerian hand that made
up, in part, for the spelling. She was gone. He need not try to follow
her or find her or bring her back. She was going to star at the head of
her own company and play Camille and even Juliet. He had promised
her. She was good and sick and tired of this everlasting flopping up
and down the rivers. She wouldn't go back to it, no matter what. Her
successor could have her wardrobe. They had bookings through Iowa,
Illinois, Missouri, and Kansas. She might even get to New York.
(Incredibly enough, she did actually play Juliet through the Mid-west,
to audiences of the bewildered yokelry.) She was sorry to leave Cap in
the lurch like this. And she would close, and begged to remain his loving
Wife (this inked out but still decipherable)—begged to remain, his
truly, Elly Chipley. Just below this signature the added one of Lenore
La Verne, done in tremendous sable downstrokes and shaded curlecues,
especially about the L's.

It was a crushing blow for Schultzy, who loved her. Stricken, he
thought only of her happiness. "She can't get along without me," he
groaned. Then, in a stunned way, "Juliet!" There was nothing of bitterness or rancour in his tone; only a dumb despairing wonder. "Juliet!
And she couldn't play Little Eva without making her out a slut." He
pondered this a moment. "She's got it into her head she's Bernhardt, or
something. . . . Well, she'll come back."

"Do you mean to say you'd take her back!" Parthy demanded.

"Why, sure," Schultzy replied, simply. "She never packed a trunk in her life, or anything. I done all those things for her. Some ways she's a child. I guess that's how she kept me so tight. She needed me all the time. . . . Well, she'll come back."

Captain Andy sent to Chicago for an ingénue lead. It was then, pending her arrival, that Magnolia stepped into the breach—the step being made, incidentally, over what was practically Parthy's dead body. For at Magnolia's calm announcement that she knew every line of the part and all the business, her mother stormed, had hysterics, and finally took to her bed (until nearly time for the rise of the curtain). The bill that night was The Parson's Bride. Show-boat companies to this day still tell the story of what happened during that performance on the *Cotton Blossom*.

They had two rehearsals, one in the morning, another that lasted throughout the afternoon. Of the company, Magnolia was the calmest. Captain Andy seemed to swing, by invisible pulleys, from the orchestra pit below to Parthy's chamber above. One moment he would be sprawled in the kerosene footlights, his eyes deep in wrinkles of delight, his little brown paws scratching the mutton-chop whiskers in a frenzy of excitement.

"That's right. That's the stuff! Elly never give it half the—— 'Scuse me, Schultzy—I didn't go for to hurt your feelings, but by golly, Nollie! I wouldn't of believed you had it in you, not if your own mother told——" Then, self-reminded, he would cast a fearful glance over his shoulder, that shoulder would droop, he would extricate himself from the welter of footlights and music racks and prompt books in which he squatted, and scamper up the aisle. The dim outline of a female head in curl papers certainly could not have been seen peering over the top of the balcony rail as he fancied, for when he had clattered up the balcony stairs and had gently turned the knob of the bedroom door, there lay the curl-papered head on the pillow of the big bed, and from it issued hollow groans, and plastered over one cheek of it was a large moist white cloth soaked in some pungent and nostril-pricking stuff. The eyes were closed. The whole figure was shaken by shivers. Mortal agony, you would have said (had you not known Parthy), had this stricken and monumental creature in its horrid clutches.

In a whisper—"Parthy!"

A groan, hollow, heartrending, mortuary.

He entered, shut the door softly, tiptoed over to the bed, laid a comforting brown paw on the shivering shoulder. The shoulder became convulsive, the shivers swelled to heaves. "Now, now, Parthy! What you taking on so for? God A'mighty, person'd think she'd done something to shame you instead of make you mighty proud. If you'd see her! Why, say, she's a born actress."

The groans now became a wail. The eyes unclosed. The figure raised itself to a sitting posture. The sopping rag rolled limply off. Parthy rocked herself to and fro. "My own daughter! An actress! That I should have lived to see this day! . . . Rather have . . . in her grave . . . why I ever allowed her to set foot on this filthy scow . . ."

"Now, Parthy, you're just working yourself up. Matter of fact, that time Mis' Means turned her ankle and we thought she couldn't step on it, you was all for going on in her part, and I bet if Sophy Means hadn't tied up her foot and gone on like a soldier she is, we'd of had you acting that night. You was rarin' to. I watched you."

"Me! Acting on the stage! Not that I couldn't play better than any Sophy Means, and that's no compliment. A poor stick if I couldn't." But her defence lacked conviction. Andy had surprised a secret ambition in this iron-armoured bosom.

"Now, come on! Cheer up! Ought to be proud your own daughter stepping in and saving us money like this. We'd of closed. Had to. God knows when that new baggage'll get here, if she gets here at all. What do you think of that Chipley! Way I've treated that girl, if she'd been my own daughter—well! . . . How'd you like a nice little sip of whisky, Parthy? Then you come on down give Nollie a hand with her costumes. Chipley's stuff comes up on her like ballet skirts.—Now, now, now! I didn't say she—— Oh, my God!"

Parthy had gone off again into hysterics. "My own daughter! My little girl!"

The time for severe measures had come. Andy had not dealt with actresses for years without learning something of the weapons with which to fight hysteria.

"All right. I'll give you something to screech for. The boys paraded this noon with a banner six feet long and red letters a foot high announcing the Appearance Extraordinaire of Magnolia the Mysterious Comedy Tragedienne in The Parson's Bride. I made a special spiel on the corner. We got the biggest advance sale we had this season. Yessir! Doc's downstairs raking it in with both hands and you had the least bit of gumption in you, instead of laying here whining and carrying on, you'd——"

"What's the advance?" spake up Parthy, the box-office expert.

"Three hundred; and not anywheres near four o'clock."

With one movement Parthy had flung aside the bedclothes and stepped out of bed revealing, rather inexplicably, a complete lower costume including shoes.

Andy was off, down the stairs, up the aisle, into the orchestra pit just in time to hear Magnolia say, "Schultzy, *please!* Don't throw me the line like that, I know it. I didn't stop because I was stuck."

"What'd you stop for, then, and look like you'd seen spooks!"

"I stopped a-purpose. She sees her husband that she hates and that she thought was dead for years come sneaking in, and she wouldn't start right in to talk. She'd just stand there, kind of frozen and stiff, staring at him."

"All right, if you know so much about directing go ahead and di——"

She ran to him, threw her arms about him, hugged him, all contrition. "Oh, Schultzy, don't be mad. I didn't go to boss. I just wanted to act it like I felt. And I'm awfully sorry about Elly and everything. I'll do as you say, only I just can't help thinking, Schultzy dear, that she'd stand there, staring kind of silly, almost."

"You're right. I guess my mind ain't on my work. I ought to know how right you are. I got that letter Elly left for me, I just stood there gawping with my mouth open, and never said a word for I don't know how long—— Oh, my God!"

"There, there, Schultzy."

By a tremendous effort (the mechanics of which were not entirely concealed) Schultzy, the man, gave way to Harold Westbrook, the artist.

"You're right, Magnolia. That'll get 'em. You standing there like that, stunned and pale."

"How'll I get pale, Schultzy?"

"You'll feel pale inside and the audience'll think you are." (The whole art of acting unconsciously expressed by Schultzy.) "Then Frank here has his sneery speech—*so* and so and *so* and so and *so* and so—and thought you'd marry the parson, huh? And then you open up with your big scene—*so* and so and *so* and so and *so* and so——"

Outwardly calm, Magnolia took only a cup of coffee at dinner, and Parthy, for once, did not press her to eat. That mournful matron, though still occasionally shaken by a convulsive shudder, managed her usual heartening repast and actually spent the time from four to seven lengthening Elly's frocks for Magnolia and taking them in to fit the girl's slight frame.

Schultzy made her up, and rather overdid it so that, as the deserted wife and school teacher and, later, as the Parson's prospective bride, she looked a pass between a healthy Camille and Cleopatra just before she applied the asp. In fact, in their effort to bridge the gap left by Elly's sudden flight, the entire company overdid everything and thus brought about the cataclysmic moment which is theatrical show-boat history.

Magnolia, so sure of her lines during rehearsal, forgot them a score of times during the performance and, had it not been for Schultzy, who threw them to her unerringly and swiftly, would have made a dismal failure of this, her first stage appearance. They were playing Vidallia, always a good show-boat town. The house was filled from the balcony boxes to the last row downstairs near the door, from which point very little could be seen and practically nothing heard. Something of the undercurrent of excitement which pervaded the *Cotton Blossom* troupe seemed to seep through the audience; or perhaps even an audience so unsophisticated as this could not but sense the unusual in this performance. Every one of the troupe—Schultzy, Mis' Means, Mr. Means, Frank, Ralph, the Soapers (Character Team that had succeeded Julie and Steve)—all were trembling for Magnolia. And because they were fearful for her they threw themselves frantically into their parts. Magnolia, taking her cue (literally as well as figuratively) from them, did likewise. As ingénue lead, her part was that of a young school mistress earning her livelihood in a little town. Deserted some years before by her worthless husband, she learns now of his death. The town parson has long been in love with her, and she with him. Now they can marry. The wedding gown is finished. The guests are invited.

This is her last day as school teacher. She is alone in the empty schoolroom. Farewell, dear pupils. Farewell, dear schoolroom, blackboard, erasers, water-bucket, desk, etc. She picks up her key. But what is this evil face in the doorway! Who is this drunken, leering tramp, grisly in rags, repulsive—— My God! You! My husband!

(Never was villain so black and diabolical as Frank. Never was heroine so lovely and frail and trembling and helpless and white—as per Schultzy's directions. As for Schultzy himself, the heroic parson, very heavily made up and pure yet brave withal, it was a poor stick of a maiden who wouldn't have contrived to get into some sort of distressing circumstance just for the joy of being got out of it by this godly yet godlike young cleric.)

Frank, then: "I reckon you thought I was dead. Well, I'm about the livest corpse you ever saw." A diabolical laugh. "Too damn bad you won't be able to wear that new wedding dress."

Pleadings, agony, despair.

Now his true villainy comes out. A thousand dollars, then, and quick, or you don't walk down the aisle to the music of no wedding march.

"I haven't got it."

"No! Where's the money you been saving all these years?"

"I haven't a thousand dollars. I swear it."

"So!" Seizes her. Drags her across the room. Screams. His hand stifles them.

Unfortunately, in their very desire to help Magnolia, they all exaggerated their villainy, their heroism, their business. Being a trifle uncertain of her lines, Magnolia, too, sought to cover her deficiencies by stressing her emotional scenes. When terror was required her face was distorted with it. Her screams of fright were real screams of mortal fear. Her writhings would have wrung pity from a fiend. Frank bared his teeth, chortled like a maniac. He wound his fingers in her long black hair and rather justified her outcry. In contrast, Schultzy's nobility and purity stood out as crudely and unmistakably as white against black. Nuances were not for show-boat audiences.

So then, screams, protestations, snarls, ha-ha's, pleadings, agony, cruelty, anguish.

Something—intuition—or perhaps a sound from the left upper box made Frank, the villain, glance up. There, leaning over the box rail, his face a mask of hatred, his eyes glinting, sat a huge hairy backwoodsman. And in his hand glittered the barrel of a businesslike gun. He was taking careful aim. Drama had come late into the life of this literal mind. He had, in the course of a quick-shooting rough-and-tumble career, often seen the brutal male mishandling beauty in distress. His code was simple. One second more and he would act on it.

Frank's hand released his struggling victim. Gentleness and love overspread his features, dispelling their villainy. To Magnolia's staring and open-mouthed amazement he made a gesture of abnegation. "Well, Marge, I ain't got nothin' more to say if you and the parson want to get married." After which astounding utterance he slunk rapidly off, leaving the field to what was perhaps the most abject huddle of heroism that ever graced a show-boat stage.

The curtain came down. The audience, intuitively glancing toward the upper box, ducked, screamed, or swore. The band struck up. The backwoodsman, a little bewildered but still truculent, subsided somewhat. A trifle mystified, but labouring under the impression that this was, perhaps, the ordinary routine of the theatre, the audience heard Schultzy, in front of the curtain, explaining that the villain was taken suddenly ill; that the concert would now be given free of charge; that each and every man, woman, and child was invited to retain his seat. The backwoodsman, rather sheepish now, took a huge bite of Honest Scrap and looked about him belligerently. Out came Mr. Means to do his comic Chinaman. Order reigned on one side of the footlights at least, though behind the heaving Venetian lagoon was a company saved from collapse only by a quite human uncertainty as to whether tears or laughter would best express their state of mind.

The new ingénue lead, scheduled to meet the *Cotton Blossom* at Natchez, failed to appear. Magnolia, following her trial by firearms, had played the absent Elly's parts for a week. There seemed to be no good reason why she should not continue to do so at least until Captain Andy could engage an ingénue who would join the troupe at New Orleans.

A year passed. Magnolia was a fixture in the company. Now, as she, in company with Parthy or Mis' Means or Mrs. Soaper, appeared on the front street of this or that little river town, she was stared at and commented on. Round-eyed little girls, swinging on the front gate, gazed at her much as she had gazed, not so many years before, at Elly and Julie as they had sauntered down the shady path of her own street in Thebes.

She loved the life. She worked hard. She cherished the admiration and applause. She took her work seriously. Certainly she did not consider herself an apostle of art. She had no illusions about herself as an actress. But she did thrive on the warm electric current that flowed from those river audiences made up of miners, farmers, Negroes, housewives, harvesters, backwoodsmen, villagers, over the footlights, to her. A naïve people, they accepted their theatre without question, like children. That which they saw they believed. They hissed the villain, applauded the heroine, wept over the plight of the wronged. The plays were as naïve as the audience. In them, onrushing engines were cheated of their victims; mill wheels were stopped in the nick of time; heroes, bound hand and foot and left to be crushed under iron wheels, were rescued by the switchman's ubiquitous daughter. Sheriffs popped up unexpectedly in hidden caves. The sound of horses' hoofs could always be heard when virtue was about to be ravished. They were the minstrels of the rivers, these players, telling in terms of blood, love, and adventure the crude saga of a new country.

Frank, the heavy, promptly fell in love with Magnolia. Parthy, quick to mark the sheep's eyes he cast in the direction of the ingénue lead, watched him with a tigress glare, and though he lived on the *Cotton Blossom*, as did Magnolia; saw her all day, daily; probably was seldom more than a hundred feet removed from her, he never spoke to her alone and certainly never was able to touch her except in the very public glare of the footlights with some hundreds of pairs of eyes turned on the two by the *Cotton Blossom* audiences. He lounged disconsolately after her, a large and somewhat splay-footed fellow whose head was too small for his shoulders, giving him the look of an inverted exclamation point.

His unrequited and unexpressed passion for Magnolia would have bothered that young lady and her parents very little were it not for the

fact that his emotions began to influence his art. In his scenes on the
stage with her he became more and more uncertain of his lines. Not
only that, his attitude and tone as villain of the piece took on a tender
note most mystifying to the audience, accustomed to seeing villainy
black, with no half tones. When he should have been hurling Magnolia
into the mill stream or tying her brutally to the track, or lashing her with
a horsewhip or snarling at her like a wolf, he became a cooing dove.
His blows were caresses. His baleful glare became a simper of adoration.

"Do you intend to speak to that sheep, or shall I?" demanded Parthy
of her husband.

"I'll do it," Andy assured her, hurriedly. "Leave him be till we get to
New Orleans. Then, if anything busts, why, I can always get some kind
of a fill-in there."

They had been playing the Louisiana parishes—little Catholic settlements between New Orleans and Baton Rouge, their inhabitants a mixture of French and Creole. Frank had wandered disconsolately through
the miniature cathedral which each little parish boasted and, returning,
had spoken darkly of abandoning the stage for the Church.

New Orleans meant mail for the *Cotton Blossom* troupe. With that
mail came trouble. Schultzy, white but determined, approached Captain
Andy, letter in hand.

"I got to go, Cap. She needs me."

"Go!" squeaked Andy. His squeak was equivalent to a bellow in a
man of ordinary stature. "Go where? What d'you mean, she?" But he
knew.

Out popped Parthy, scenting trouble.

Schultzy held out a letter written on cheap paper, lined, and smelling
faintly of antiseptic. "She's in the hospital at Little Rock. Says she's had
an operation. He's left her, the skunk. She ain't got a cent."

"I'll take my oath on that," Parthy put in, pungently.

"You can't go and leave me flat now, Schultzy."

"I got to go, I tell you. Frank can play leads till you get somebody,
or till I get back. Old Means can play utility at a pinch, and Doc can
do general business."

"Frank," announced Parthy, with terrible distinctness, "will play no
leads in this company, and so I tell you, Hawks."

"Who says he's going to! A fine-looking lead he'd make, with that
pin-head of his, and those elephant's hoofs. . . . Now looka here,
Schultzy. You been a trouper long enough to know you can't leave a
show in the ditch like this. No real show-boat actor'd do it, and you
know it."

"Sure I know it. I wouldn't do it for myself, no matter what. But it's her. I wrote her a letter, time she left. I got her bookings. I said if the time comes you need me, leave me know, and I'll come. And she needs me, and she left me know, and I'm coming."

"How about us!" demanded Parthy. "Leaving us in the lurch like that, first Elly and now you after all these years. A fine pair, the two of you."

"Now, Parthy!"

"Oh, I've no patience with you, Hawks. Always letting people get the best of you."

"But I told you," Schultzy began again, almost tearfully, "it's for her, not me. She's sick. You can pick up somebody here in New Orleans. I bet there's a dozen better actors than me laying around the docks this minute. I got to talking to a fellow while ago, down on the wharf. The place was all jammed up with freight, and I was waiting to get by so's I could come aboard. I said I was an actor on the *Cotton Blossom*, and he said he'd acted and that was a life he'd like."

"Yes," snapped Parthy. "I suppose he would. What does he think this is! A bumboat! Plenty of wharf rats in New Orleans'd like nothing better——"

Schultzy pointed to where a slim figure leaned indolently against a huge packing case—one of hundreds of idlers dotting the great New Orleans plank landing.

Andy adjusted the pair of ancient binoculars through which he recently had been scanning the wharf and the city beyond the levee. He surveyed the graceful lounging figure.

"I'd go ashore and talk to him, I was you," advised Schultzy.

Andy put down the glasses and stared at Schultzy in amazement. "Him! Why, I couldn't go up and talk to him about acting on no show boat. He's a gentleman."

"Here," said Parthy, abruptly, her curiosity piqued. She in turn trained the glasses on the object of the discussion. Her survey was brief but ample. "He may be a gentleman. But nobody feels a gentleman with a crack in his shoe, and he's got one. I can't say I like the looks of him, specially. But with Schultzy playing us this dirty trick—well, that's what it amounts to, and there's no sense trying to prettify it—we can't be choosers. I'd just step down talk to him if I was you, Hawks."

IX

THIS, then, turned out to be Magnolia's first glimpse of Gaylord Ravenal
—an idle elegant figure in garments whose modish cut and fine material
served, at a distance, to conceal their shabbiness. Leaning moodily
against a tall packing case dumped on the wharf by some freighter, he
gazed about him and tapped indolently the tip of his shining (and
cracked) boot with an exquisite little ivory-topped malacca cane. There
was about him an air of distinction, an atmosphere of richness. On
closer proximity you saw that the broadcloth was shiny, the fine linen
of the shirt front and cuffs the least bit frayed, the slim boots undeniably split, the hat (a delicate gray and set a little on one side) soiled as
a pale gray hat must never be. From the *Cotton Blossom* deck you saw
him as the son, perhaps, of some rich Louisiana planter, idling a moment at the water's edge. Waiting, doubtless, for one of the big river
packets—the floating palaces of the Mississippi—to bear him luxuriously
away up the river to his plantation landing.

The truth was that Gaylord Ravenal was what the river gamblers called
broke. Stony, he would have told you. No one had a better right to use
the term than he. Of his two possessions, save the sorry clothes he had
on, one was the little malacca cane. And though he might part with cuff
links, shirt studs and, if necessary, shirt itself, he would always cling to
that little malacca cane, emblem of good fortune, his mascot. It had
turned on him temporarily. Yet his was the gambler's superstitious nature. To-morrow the cane would bring him luck.

Not only was Gaylord Ravenal broke; he had just politely notified
the Chief of Police of New Orleans that he was in town. The call was not
entirely one of social obligation. It had a certain statutory side as well.

In the first place, Chief of Police Vallon, in a sudden political spasm
of virtue, endeavouring to clear New Orleans of professional gamblers,
had given them all twenty-four hours' shrift. In the second place, this
particular visitor would have come under the head of New Orleans un-
desirables on his own private account, even though his profession had
been that of philanthropist. Gaylord Ravenal had one year-old notch to
his gun.

It had not been murder in cold blood or in rage, but a shot fired in self-defence just the fraction of a second before the other man could turn the trick. The evidence proved this, and Ravenal's final vindication followed. But New Orleans gathered her civic skirts about her and pointed a finger of dismissal toward the door. Hereafter, should he enter, his first visit must be to the Chief of Police; and twenty-four hours—no more—must be the limit of his stay in the city whose pompano and crayfish and Creoles and roses and Ramos gin fizzes he loved.

The evening before, he had stepped off the river packet *Lady Lee*, now to be seen lying alongside the New Orleans landing together with a hundred other craft. His twenty-four hours would expire this evening.

Certainly he had not meant to find himself in New Orleans. He had come aboard the *Lady Lee* at St. Louis, his finances low, his hopes high, his erstwhile elegant garments in their present precarious state. He had planned, following the game of stud poker in which he immediately immersed himself, to come ashore at Memphis or, at the latest, Natchez, with his finances raised to the high level of his hopes. Unfortunately his was an honest and over-eager game. His sole possession, beside the little slim malacca cane (itself of small tangible value) was a singularly clear blue-white diamond ring which he never wore. It was a relic of luckier days before his broadcloth had become shiny, his linen frayed, his boots split. He had clung to it, as he had to the cane, through almost incredible hazards. His feeling about it was neither sentimental nor superstitious. The tenuous streak of canniness in him told him that, possessed of a clear white diamond, one can hold up one's head and one's hopes, no matter what the state of coat, linen, boots, and hat. It had never belonged, fiction-fashion, to his sainted (if any) mother, nor was it an old Ravenal heirloom. It was a relic of winnings in luckier days and represented, he knew, potential hundreds. In the trip that lasted, unexpectedly, from St. Louis to New Orleans, he had won and lost that ring six times. When the *Lady Lee* had nosed her way into the Memphis landing, and again at Natchez, it had been out of his possession. He had stayed on board, perforce. Half an hour before coming into New Orleans he had had it again, and had kept it. The game of stud poker had lasted days, and he rose from it the richer by exactly nothing at all.

He had glanced out of the *Lady Lee's* saloon window, his eyes bloodshot from sleeplessness, his nerves jangling, his hands twitching, his face drawn; but that face shaven, those hands immaculate. Gaylord Ravenal, in luck or out, had the habits and instincts of a gentleman.

"Good God!" he exclaimed now, "this looks like—it is New Orleans!" It was N'Yawlins as he said it.

"What did you think it was?" growled one of the players, who had temporarily owned the diamond several times during the journey down river. "What did you think it was? Shanghai?"

"I wish it was," said Gaylord Ravenal. Somewhat dazedly he walked down the *Lady Lee's* gangplank and retorted testily to a beady-eyed giant-footed gentleman who immediately spoke to him in a low and not unfriendly tone, "Give me time, can't you! I haven't been twenty-four hours stepping from the gangplank to this wharf, have I? Well, then!"

"No offence, Gay," said the gentleman, his eyes still searching the other passengers as they filed across the narrow gangplank. "Just thought I'd remind you, case of trouble. You know how Vallon is."

Vallon had said, briefly, later, "That's all right, Gay. But by this time to-morrow evening——" He had eyed Ravenal's raiment with a comprehending eye. "Cigar?" The weed he proffered was slim, pale, and frayed as the man who stood before him. Gaylord Ravenal's jangling nerves ached for the solace of tobacco; but he viewed this palpably second-hand gift with a glance of disdain that was a triumph of the spirit over the flesh. Certainly no man handicapped by his present sartorial and social deficiencies was justified in raising a quizzical right eyebrow in the manner employed by Ravenal.

"What did you call it?" said he now.

Vallon looked at it. He was not a quick-witted gentleman. "Cigar."

"Optimist." And strolled out of the chief's office, swinging the little malacca cane.

So then, you now saw him leaning moodily against a wooden case on the New Orleans plank wharf, distinguished, shabby, dapper, handsome, broke, and twenty-four.

It was with some amusement that he had watched the crew of the *Mollie Able* bring the flat unwieldy bulk of the *Cotton Blossom* into the wharfside in the midst of the confusion of packets, barges, steamboats, tugs, flats, tramp boats, shanty boats. He had spoken briefly and casually to Schultzy while that bearer of evil tidings, letter in hand, waited impatiently on the dock as the *Cotton Blossom* was shifted to a landing position farther upstream. He had seen these floating theatres of the Mississippi and the Ohio many times, but he had never before engaged one of their actors in conversation.

"Juvenile lead!" he had exclaimed, unable to hide something of incredulity in his voice. Schultzy, an anxious eye on the *Mollie Able's* tedious manoeuvres, had just made clear to Ravenal his own position in the *Cotton Blossom* troupe. Ravenal, surveying the furrowed brow, the unshaven cheeks, the careless dress, the lack-lustre eye, had involuntarily allowed to creep into his tone something of the astonishment he felt.

Schultzy made a little deprecating gesture with his hands, his shoulders. "I guess I don't look like no juvenile lead, and that's a fact. But I'm all shot to pieces. Took a drink the size of this"—indicating perhaps five fingers—"up yonder on Canal Street; straight whisky. No drinking allowed on the show boat. Well, sir, never felt it no more'n it had been water. I just got news my wife's sick in the hospital."

Ravenal made a little perfunctory sound of sympathy. "In New Orleans?"

"Little Rock, Arkansas. I'm going. It's a dirty trick, but I'm going."

"How do you mean, dirty trick?" Ravenal was mildly interested in this confiding stranger.

"Leave the show flat like that. I don't know what they'll do. I——" He saw that the *Cotton Blossom* was now snugly at ease in her new position, and that her gangplank had again been lowered. He turned away abruptly, without a good-bye, went perhaps ten paces, came back five and called to Ravenal. "You ever acted?"

"Acted!"

"On the stage. Acted. Been an actor."

Ravenal threw back his handsome head and laughed as he would have thought, ten minutes ago, he never could laugh again. "Me! An actor! N—" then, suddenly sober, thoughtful even—"Why, yes. Yes." And eyeing Schultzy through half-shut lids he tapped the tip of his shiny shabby boot with the smart little malacca cane. Schultzy was off again toward the *Cotton Blossom*.

If Ravenal was aware of the scrutiny to which he was subjected through the binoculars, he gave no sign as he lounged elegantly on the wharf watching the busy waterside scene with an air of indulgent amusement that would have made the onlooker receive with incredulity the information that the law was even then snapping at his heels.

Captain Andy Hawks scampered off the *Cotton Blossom* and approached this figure, employing none of the finesse that the situation called for.

"I understand you've acted on the stage."

Gaylord Ravenal elevated the right eyebrow and looked down his aristocratic nose at the capering little captain. "I am Gaylord Ravenal, of the Tennessee Ravenals. I failed to catch your name."

"Andy Hawks, captain and owner of the Cotton Blossom Floating Palace Theatre." He jerked a thumb over his shoulder at the show boat.

"Ah, yes," said Ravenal, with polite unenthusiasm. He allowed his patrician glance to rest idly a moment on the *Cotton Blossom*, lying squat and dumpy alongside the landing.

Captain Andy found himself suddenly regretting that he had not had her painted and overhauled. He clutched his whiskers in embarrassment, and, under stress of that same emotion, blurted the wrong thing. "I guess Parthy was mistaken." The Ravenal eyebrow became interrogatory. Andy floundered on. "She said that no man with a crack in the shoe——" he stopped, then, appalled.

Gaylord Ravenal looked down at the footgear under discussion. He looked up at the grim and ponderous female figure on the forward deck of the show boat. Parthy was wearing one of her most uncompromising bonnets and a gown noticeably bunchy even in that day of unsymmetrical feminine fashions. Black was not becoming to Mrs. Hawks' sallow colouring. Lumpy black was fatal. If anything could have made this figure less attractive than it actually was, Ravenal's glance would seem to have done so. "That—ah—lady?"

"My wife," said Andy. Then, mindful of the maxim of the sheep and the lamb, he went the whole way. "We've lost our juvenile lead. Fifteen a week and found. Chance to see the world. No responsibility. Schultzy said you said . . . I said . . . Parthy said . . ." Hopelessly entangled, he stopped.

"Am I to understand that I am being offered the position of—ah—juvenile lead on the—" the devastating glance upward—"Cotton Blossom Floating Palace——"

"That's the size of it," interrupted Andy, briskly. After all, even this young man's tone and manner could not quite dispel that crack in the boot. Andy knew that no one wears a split shoe from choice.

"No responsibility," he repeated. "A chance to see life."

"I've seen it," in the tone of one who did not care for what he has beheld. His eyes were on a line with the *Cotton Blossom's* deck. His gaze suddenly became concentrated. A tall slim figure in white had just appeared on the upper deck, forward—the bit of deck that looked for all the world like a nautical veranda. It led off Magnolia's bedroom. The slim white figure was Magnolia. Preparatory to going ashore she was taking a look at this romantic city which she always had loved, and which she, in company with Andy or Doc, had roamed a dozen times since her first early childhood trip on the *Creole Belle*.

Her dress was bunchy, too, as the mode demanded. But where it was not bunchy it was very tight. And its bunchiness thus only served to emphasize the slimness of the snug areas. Her black hair was drawn smoothly away from the temples and into a waterfall at the back. Her long fine head and throat rose exquisitely above the little pleated frill that finished the neckline of her gown. She carried her absurd beribboned and beflowered high-crowned hat in her hand. A graceful, pliant, slim young figure in white, surveying the pandemonium that was the New

Orleans levee. Columns of black rose from a hundred steamer stacks. Freight barrels and boxes went hurtling through the air, or were shoved or carried across the plank wharf to the accompaniment of shouting and sweating and swearing. Negroes everywhere. Band boxes, carpet bags, babies, drays, carriages, wheelbarrows, carts. Beyond the levee rose the old salt warehouses. Beyond these lay Canal Street. Magnolia was going into town with her father and her mother. Andy had promised her supper at Antoine's and an evening at the old French theatre. She knew scarcely ten words of French. Andy, if he had known it in his childhood, had quite forgotten it now. Parthy looked upon it as the language of sin and the yellow-back paper novels. But all three found enjoyment in the grace and colour and brilliance of the performance and the audience —both of a sort to be found nowhere else in the whole country. Andy's enjoyment was tinged and heightened by a vague nostalgia; Magnolia's was that of one artist for the work of another; Parthy's was the enjoyment of suspicion. She always hoped the play's high scenes were going to be more risqué than they actually were.

From her vantage point Magnolia stood glancing alertly about her, enjoying the babel that was the New Orleans plank wharves. She now espied and recognized the familiarly capering little figure below with its right hand scratching the mutton-chop whiskers this side and that. She was impatient to be starting for their jaunt ashore. She waved at him with the hand that held the hat. The upraised arm served to enhance the delicate curve of the pliant young figure in its sheath of white.

Andy, catching sight of her, waved in return.

"Is that," inquired Gaylord Ravenal, "a member of your company?"

Andy's face softened and glowed. "That? That's my daughter Magnolia."

"Magnolia. Magnol—— Does she—is she a——"

"I should smile she is! She's our ingénue lead, Magnolia is. Plays opposite the juvenile lead. But if you've been a trouper you know that, I guess." A sudden suspicion darted through him. "Say, young man— what's your name?—oh, yes, Ravenal. Well, Ravenal, you a quick study? That's what I got to know, first off. Because we leave New Orleans to-night to play the bayous. Bayou Teche to-morrow night in Tempest and Sunshine. . . . You a quick study?"

"Lightning," said Gaylord Ravenal.

Five minutes later, bowing over her hand, he did not know whether to curse the crack in his shoe for shaming him before her, or to bless it for having been the cause of his being where he was.

That he and Magnolia should become lovers was as inevitable as the cosmic course. Certainly some force greater than human must have been at work on it, for it overcame even Parthy's opposition. Everything conspired to bring the two together, including their being kept forcibly apart. Himself a picturesque, mysterious, and romantic figure, Gaylord Ravenal, immediately after joining the *Cotton Blossom* troupe, became the centre of a series of dramatic episodes any one of which would have made him glamorous in Magnolia's eyes, even though he had not already assumed for her the glory of a Galahad.

She had never before met a man of Ravenal's stamp. In this dingy motley company he moved aloof, remote, yet irresistibly attracting all of them—except Parthy. She, too, must have felt drawn to this charming and magnetic man, but she fought the attraction with all the strength of her powerful and vindictive nature. Sensing that here lay his bitterest opposition, Ravenal deliberately set about exercising his charm to win Parthy to friendliness. For the first time in his life he received rebuff so bristling, so unmistakable, as to cause him temporarily to doubt his own gifts.

Women had always adored Gaylord Ravenal. He was not a villain. He was, in fact, rather gentle, and more than a little weak. His method, coupled with strong personal attractiveness, was simple in the extreme. He made love to all women and demanded nothing of them. Swept off their feet, they waited, trembling deliciously, for the final attack. At its failure to materialize they looked up, wondering, to see his handsome face made more handsome by a certain wistful sadness. At that their hearts melted within them. That which they had meant to defend they now offered. For the rest, his was a paradoxical nature. A courtliness of manner, contradicted by a bluff boyishness. A certain shy boldness. He was not an especially intelligent man. He had no need to be. His up-turned glance at a dining-room waitress bent over him was in no way different from that which he directed straight at Parthy now; or at the daughter of a prosperous Southern lawyer, or at that daughter's vaguely uneasy mama. It wasn't deliberate evil in him or lack of fastidiousness. He was helpless to do otherwise.

Certainly he had never meant to remain a member of this motley troupe, drifting up and down the rivers. He had not, for that matter, meant to fall in love with Magnolia, much less marry her. Propinquity and opposition, either of which usually is sufficient to fan the flame, together caused the final conflagration. For weeks after he came on board, he literally never spoke to Magnolia alone. Parthy attended to that. He saw her not only daily but almost hourly. He considered himself lucky to be deft enough to say, "Lovely day, isn't it, Miss Magn——" before Mrs. Hawks swept her offspring out of earshot. Parthy was wise enough to see that this handsome, graceful, insidious young stranger would appear desirable and romantic in the eyes of women a hundredfold more sophisticated than the childlike and un-awakened Magnolia. She took refuge in the knowledge that this danger-ous male was the most impermanent of additions to the *Cotton Blossom* troupe. His connection with them would end on Schultzy's return.

Gaylord Ravenal was, in the meantime, a vastly amused and prodi-giously busy young man. To learn the juvenile leads in the plays that made up the *Cotton Blossom* troupe's repertoire was no light matter. Not only must he memorize lines, business, and cues of the regular bills—Uncle Tom's Cabin, East Lynne, Tempest and Sunshine, Lady Audley's Secret, The Parson's Bride, The Gambler, and others—but he must be ready to go on in the concert afterpiece, whatever it might be—sometimes A Dollar for a Kiss, sometimes Red Hot Coffee. The company rehearsed day and night; during the day they rehearsed that night's play; after the performance they rehearsed next night's bill. With some astonishment the *Cotton Blossom* troupe realized, at the end of two weeks, that Gaylord Ravenal was acting as director. It had come about naturally and inevitably. Ravenal had a definite theatre sense—a feeling for tempo, rhythm, line, grouping, inflection, characterization —any, or all, of these. The atmosphere had freshness for him; he was interested; he wished to impress Andy and Parthy and Magnolia; he considered the whole business a gay adventure; and an amusing inter-lude. For a month they played the bayous and plantations of Louisiana, leaving behind them a whole countryside whose planters, villagers, Negroes had been startled out of their Southern lethargy. These had known show boats and show-boat performances all their lives. They had been visited by this or that raffish, dingy, slap-dash, or decent and painstaking troupe. The *Cotton Blossom* company had the reputation for being the last-named variety, and always were patronized accord-ingly. The plays seldom varied. The performance was, usually, less than mediocre. They were, then, quite unprepared for the entertainment given them by the two handsome, passionate, and dramatic young people who now were cast as ingénue and juvenile lead of the Cotton Blossom Floating Palace Theatre company. Here was Gaylord Ravenal, fresh, young, personable, aristocratic, romantic of aspect. Here was Magnolia, slim, girlish, ardent, electric, lovely. Their make-believe ad-ventures as they lived them on the stage became real; their dangers and misfortunes set the natives to trembling; their love-making was a fra-grant and exquisite thing. News of this troupe seeped through from plantation to plantation, from bayou to bayou, from settlement to settle-ment, in some mysterious underground way. The *Cotton Blossom* did a record-breaking business in a region that had never been markedly profitable. Andy was jubilant, Parthy apprehensive, Magnolia starry-eyed, tremulous, glowing. Her lips seemed to take on a riper curve. Her skin was, somehow, softly radiant as though lighted by an inner glow, as Julie's amber colouring, in the years gone by, had seemed to deepen into golden brilliance. Her eyes were enormous, luminous. The gangling, hobbledehoy, sallow girl of seventeen was a woman of eighteen, lovely, and in love.

Back again in New Orleans there was a letter from Schultzy, a pathetic scrawl; illiterate; loyal. Elly was out of the hospital, but weak and helpless. He had a job, temporarily, whose nature he did not indicate. ("Porter in a Little Rock saloon, I'll be bound," ventured Parthy, shrewdly, "rubbing up the brass and the cuspidors.") He had met a man who ran a rag-front carnival company. He could use them for one attraction called The Old Plantation; or, The South Before the War. They were booked through the Middle West. In a few weeks, if Elly was stronger . . .

He said nothing about money. He said nothing of their possible return to the *Cotton Blossom*. That, Andy knew, was because of Elly. Unknown to Parthy, he sent Schultzy two hundred dollars. Schultzy never returned to the rivers. It was, after all, oddly enough, Elly who, many many years later, completed the circle which brought her again to the show boat.

Together, Andy, Parthy, and Doc went into consultation. They must keep Ravenal. But Ravenal obviously was not of the stuff of show-boat actors. He had made it plain, when first he came aboard, that he was the most impermanent of troupers; that his connection with the *Cotton Blossom* would continue, at the latest, only until Schultzy's return. He meant to leave them, not at New Orleans, as they had at first feared, but at Natchez, on the up trip.

"Don't tell him Schultzy ain't coming back," Doc offered, brilliantly.

"Have to know it some time," was Andy's obvious reply.

"Person'd think," said Parthy, "he was the only juvenile lead left in the world. Matter of fact, I can't see where he's such great shakes of an actor. Rolls those eyes of his a good deal, and talks deep-voiced, but he's got hands white's a woman's and fusses with his nails. I'll wager if you ask around in New Orleans you'll find something queer, for all he talks so high about being a Ravenal of Tennessee and his folks governors in the old days, and slabs about 'em in the church, and what not. Shifty, that's what he is. Mark my words."

"Best juvenile lead ever played the rivers. And I never heard that having clean finger nails hurt an actor any."

"Oh, it isn't just clean finger nails," snapped Parthy. "It's everything."

"Wouldn't hold that against him, either," roared Doc. The two men then infuriated the humourless Mrs. Hawks by indulging in a great deal of guffawing and knee-slapping.

"That's right, Hawks. Laugh at your own wife. And you, too, Doc."

"You ain't my wife," retorted Doc, with the privilege of sixty-odd. And roared again.

The gossamer thread that leashed Parthy's temper dissolved now. "I can't bear the sight of him. Palavering and soft-soaping. Thinks he can get round a woman my age. Well, I'm worth a dozen of him when it comes to smart." She leaned closer to Andy, her face actually drawn with fear and a sort of jealousy. "He looks at Magnolia, I tell you."

"A fool if he didn't."

"Andy Hawks, you mean to tell me you'd sit there and see your own daughter married to a worthless tramp of a wharf rat, or worse, that hadn't a shirt to his back when you picked him up!"

"Oh, God A'mighty, woman, can't a man look at a girl without having to marry her!"

"*Having* to marry her, Captain Hawks! *Having*—— Well, what can a body expect when her own husband talks like that, and before strangers, too. Having——!"

Doc rubbed his leathery chin a trifle ruefully. "Stretching a point, Mrs. Hawks, ma'am, calling me a stranger, ain't you?"

"All right. Keep him with the show, you two. Who warned you about that yellow-skinned Julie! And what happened! If sheriffs is what you want, I'll wager you could get them fast enough if you spoke his name in certain parts of this country. Wait till we get back to New Orleans. I intend to do some asking around, and so does Frank."

"What's Frank got to do with it?"

But at this final exhibition of male obtuseness Parthy flounced out of the conference.

On their return from the bayous the *Cotton Blossom* lay idle a day at the New Orleans landing. Early on the morning of their arrival Gaylord Ravenal went ashore. On his stepping off the gangplank he spoke briefly to that same gimlet-eyed gentleman who was still loitering on the wharf. To the observer, the greeting between them seemed amiable enough.

"Back again, Gay!" he of the keen gaze had exclaimed. "Seems like you can't keep away from the scene of the——"

"Oh, go to hell," said Ravenal.

He returned to the *Cotton Blossom* at three o'clock. At his appearance the idler who had accosted him (and who was still mysteriously lolling at the waterside) shut his eyes and then opened them quickly as though to dispel a vision.

"Cripes, Ravenal! Robbed a bank?"

From the tips of his shining shoes to the top of his pale gray hat, Ravenal was sartorial perfection, nothing less. The boots were hand-made, slim, aristocratic. The cloth of his clothes was patently out of England, and tailored for no casual purchaser, but for Ravenal's figure alone. The trousers tapered elegantly to the instep. The collar was moulded expertly so that it hugged the neck. The linen was of the finest and whitest, and cunning needlecraft had gone into the embroidering of the austere monogram that almost escaped showing in one corner of the handkerchief that peeped above his left breast pocket. The malacca stick seemed to take on a new lustre and richness now that it found itself once more in fitting company. With the earnings of his first two weeks on the *Cotton Blossom* enclosed as evidence of good faith, and future payment assured, Gaylord Ravenal had sent by mail from the Louisiana bayous to Plumbridge, the only English tailor in New Orleans, the order which had resulted in his present splendour.

He now paused a moment to relieve himself of that which had long annoyed him in the beady-eyed one. "Listen to me, Flat Foot. The *Cotton Blossom* dropped anchor at seven o'clock this morning at the New Orleans dock. I came ashore at nine. It is now three. I am free to stay on shore or not, as I like, until nine to-morrow morning. Until then, if I hear any more of your offensive conversation, I shall have to punish you."

Flat Foot, thus objurgated, stared at Ravenal with an expression in which amazement and admiration fought for supremacy. "By God, Ravenal, with any luck at all, that gall of yours ought to get you a million some day."

"I wouldn't be bothered with any sum so vulgar." From an inside pocket he drew a perfecto, long, dark, sappy. "Have a smoke." He drew out another. "And give this to Vallon when you go back to report. Tell him I wanted him to know the flavour of a decent cigar for once in his life."

As he crossed the gangplank he encountered Mrs. Hawks and Frank, the lumbering heavy, evidently shore-bound together. He stepped aside with a courtliness that the Ravenals of Tennessee could not have ex-celled in the days of swords, satins, and periwigs.

Mrs. Hawks was, after all, a woman; and no woman could look un-moved upon the figure of cool elegance that now stood before her. "Sakes alive!" she said, inadequately. Frank, whose costumes, ashore or afloat, always were négligée to the point of causing the beholder some actual nervousness, attempted to sneer without the aid of make-up and made a failure of it.

Ravenal now addressed Mrs. Hawks. "You are not staying long ashore, I hope?"

"And why not?" inquired Mrs. Hawks, with her usual delicacy.

"I had hoped that perhaps you and Captain Hawks and Miss Magnolia might do me the honour of dining with me ashore and going to the theatre afterward. I know a little restaurant where——"

"Likely," retorted Parthy, by way of polite refusal; and moved majestically down the gangplank, followed by the gratified heavy.

Ravenal continued thoughtfully on his way. Captain Andy was in the box office just off the little forward deck that served as an entrance to the show boat. With him was Magnolia—Magnolia minus her mother's protecting wings. After all, even Parthy had not the power to be in more than one place at a time. At this moment she was deep in conversation with Flat Foot on the wharf.

Magnolia was evidently dressed for a festive occasion. The skirt of her light écru silk dress was a polonaise draped over a cream-white surah silk, and the front of the tight bodice-basque was of the same cream-white stuff. Her round hat of Milan straw, with its modishly high crown, had an artful brim that shaded her fine eyes, and this brim was faced with deep rose velvet, and a bow of deep rose flared high against the crown. The black of her hair was all the blacker for this vivid colour. An écru parasol and long suède gloves completed the costume. She might have stepped out of *Harper's Bazaar*—in fact, she had. The dress was a faithful copy of a costume which she had considered particularly fetching as she pored over the pages of that book of fashion.

Andy was busy at his desk. Ranged in rows on that desk were canvas sacks, plump, squat; canvas sacks limp, lop-sided; canvas sacks which, when lifted and set down again, gave forth a pleasant clinking sound. Piled high in front of these were neat packets of greenbacks, ones and ones and ones, in bundles of fifty, each bound with a tidy belt of white paper pinned about its middle. Forming a kind of Chinese wall around these were stacked half dollars, quarters, dimes, and nickels, with now and then a campanile of silver dollars. In the midst of this Andy resembled an amiable and highly solvent gnome stepped out of a Grimm's fairy tale. The bayou trip had been a record-breaking one in point of profit.

". . . And fifty's six hundred and fifty," Andy was crooning happily, as he jotted figures down on a sheet of yellow lined paper, ". . . and fifty's seven hundred, and twenty-five's seven hundred twenty-five and twenty-five's . . ."

"Oh, Papa!" Magnolia exclaimed impatiently, and turned toward the little window through which one saw New Orleans lying so invitingly in the protecting arms of the levee. "It's almost four, and you haven't even changed your clothes, and you keep counting that old money, and Mama's gone on some horrid business with that sneaky Frank. I know it's horrid because she looked so pleased. And you promised me. We won't see New Orleans again for a whole year. You said you'd get a carriage and two horses and we'd drive out to Lake Pontchartrain, and have dinner, and drive back, and go to the theatre, and now it's almost four and you haven't even changed your clothes and you keep counting that old money, and Mama's——" After all, in certain ways, Magnolia the ingénue lead had not changed much from that child who had promptly had hysterics to gain her own ends that day in Thebes many years before.

"Minute," Andy muttered, absently. "Can't leave this money laying around like buttons, can I? Germania National's letting me in the side door as a special favour after hours, as 'tis, just so's I can deposit. . . . And fifty's eight-fifty, and fifty's nine . . ."

"I don't *care!*" cried Magnolia, and stamped her foot. "It's downright mean of you, Papa. You promised. And I'm all dressed. And you haven't even changed your——"

"Oh, God A'mighty, Nollie, you ain't going to turn out an unreasonable woman like your ma, are you! Here I sit, slaving away——"

"Oh! How beautiful you look!" exclaimed Magnolia now, to Andy's bewilderment. He looked up at her. Her gaze was directed over his head at someone standing in the doorway. Andy creaked hastily around in the ancient swivel chair. Ravenal, of course, in the doorway. Andy pursed his lips in the sky-rocket whistle, starting high and ending low, expressive of surprise and admiration.

"How beautiful you look!" said Magnolia again; and clasped her hands like a child.

"And you, Miss Magnolia," said Ravenal; and advanced into the cubby hole that was the office, and took one of Magnolia's surprised hands delicately in his, and bent over it, and kissed it. Magnolia was an excellent enough actress, and sufficiently the daughter of the gallant and Gallic Andy, to acknowledge this salute with a little gracious inclination of the head, and no apparent surprise whatever. Andy himself showed nothing of astonishment at the sight of this suave and elegant figure bent over his daughter's hand. He looked rather pleased than otherwise. But suddenly then the look on his face changed to one of alarm. He jumped to his feet. He scratched the mutton-chop whiskers, sure evidence of perturbation.

"Look here, Ravenal! That ain't a sign you're leaving, is it? Those clothes, and now kissing Nollie's hand. God A'mighty, Ravenal, you ain't leaving us!"

Ravenal flicked an imaginary bit of dust from the cuff of his flawless sleeve. "These are my ordinary clothes, Captain Hawks, sir. I mean to say, I usually am attired as you now see me. When first we met I was in temporary difficulties. The sort of thing that can happen to any gentleman."

"Certainly can," Andy agreed, heartily and hastily. "Sure can. Well, you gave me a turn. I thought you come in to give me notice. And while we're on it, you're foolish to quit at Natchez like you said, Ravenal. I don't know what you been doing, but you're cut out for a show-boat actor, and that's the truth. Stick with us and I'll raise you to twenty—" as Ravenal shook his head—"twenty-five—" again the shake of the head—"thirty! And, God A'mighty, they ain't a juvenile lead on the rivers ever got anywheres near that."

Ravenal held up one white shapely hand. "Let's not talk money now, Captain. Though if you would care to advance me a fifty, I . . . Thanks . . . I was going to say I came in to ask if you and Mrs. Hawks and Miss Magnolia here would do me the honour to dine with me ashore this evening, and go to the theatre. I know a little French restaurant——"

"Papa!" She swooped down upon little Andy then, enveloping him in her ruffles, in her surah silk, her rose velvet, her perfume. Her arms were about his neck. Her fresh young cheek pressed the top of his grizzled head. Her eyes were enormous—and they looked into Ravenal's eyes. "Papa!"

But years of contact with the prim Parthy had taught him caution. "Your ma——" he began, feebly.

Magnolia deserted him, flew to Ravenal, clutched his arm. Her lovely eyes held tears. Involuntarily his free hand covered her hand that clung so appealingly to his sleeve. "He promised me. And now, because he's got all that money to count because Doc was delayed at Baton Rouge and didn't meet us here like he expected he would this afternoon and Mama's gone ashore and we were to drive to Lake Pontchartrain and have dinner and he hasn't even changed his clothes and it's almost four o'clock—probably is four by now—and he keeps counting that old money——"

"Magnolia!" shouted Andy in a French frenzy, clutching the whiskers as though to raise himself by them from the floor.

Magnolia must have been enjoying the situation. Here were two men, both of whom adored her, and she them. She therefore set about testing their love. Her expression became tragic—but not so tragic as to mar her delightful appearance. To the one who loved her most deeply and un-selfishly she said:

"You don't care anything about me or my happiness. It's all this old boat, and business, and money. Haven't I worked, night after night, year in, year out! And now, when I have a chance to enjoy myself—it isn't as if you hadn't promised me——"

"We're going, I tell you, Nollie. But your ma isn't even here. And how did I know Doc was going to be stuck at Baton Rouge! We got plenty of time to have dinner ashore and go to the theatre, but we'll have to give up the drive to Pontchartrain——"

A heartbroken wail from Magnolia. Her great dark eyes turned in appeal to Ravenal. "It's the drive I like better than anything in the world. And horses. I'm crazy about horses, and I don't get a chance to drive—oh, well—" at an objection from Andy—"sometimes; but what kind of horses do they have in those little towns! And here you can get a splendid pair, all shiny, and their nostrils working, and a victoria and lovely long tails and a clanky harness and fawn cushions and the lake and soft-shell crabs——" She was becoming incoherent, but remained as lovely as ever, and grew more appealing by the moment.

Ravenal resisted a mad urge to take her in his arms. He addressed himself earnestly to the agonized Andy. "If you will trust me, Captain Hawks, I have a plan which I have just thought of. I know New Orleans very well and I am—uh—very well known in New Orleans. Miss Magnolia has set her heart on this little holiday. I know where I can get a splendid turnout. Chestnuts—very high steppers, but quite safe." An unadult squeal of delight from Magnolia. "If we start immediately, we can enjoy quite a drive—Miss Magnolia and I. If you like, we can take Mrs. Means with us, or Mrs. Soaper——"

"No," from the brazen beauty.

"—and return in time to meet you and Mrs. Hawks at, say, Antoine's for dinner."

"Oh, Papa!" cried Magnolia now. "Oh, Papa!"

"Your ma——" began Andy again, feebly. The stacks and piles still lay uncounted on the desk. This thing must be settled somehow. He scuttled to the window, scanned the wharf, the streets that led up from it. "I don't know where she's got to." He turned from the window to survey the pair, helplessly. Something about them—the very fitness of their standing there together, so young, so beautiful, so eager, so alive, so vibrant—melted the romantic heart within him. Magnolia in her holiday garb; Ravenal in his tailored perfection. "Oh, well, I don't see how it'll hurt any. Your ma and I will meet you at Antoine's at, say, half-past six——"

They were off. It was as if they had been lifted bodily and blown together out of the little office, across the gangplank to the landing. Flat
Foot stared after them almost benignly.

Andy returned to his desk. Resumed his contented crooning. Four
o'clock struck. Half-past four. His pencil beat a rat-a-tat-tat as he
jotted down the splendid figures. A gold mine, this Ravenal. A fine
figger of a boy. Cheap at thirty. Rat-a-tat-tat. And fifty's one thousand.
And twenty-five's one thousand twenty-five. And fifty's—and fifty's
—twelve twenty-five—gosh a'mighty!——

A shriek. A bouncing across the gangplank and into the cubby hole
just as Andy was rounding, happily, into thirteen hundred. A hand
clutching his shoulder frantically, whirling him bodily out of the creaking
swivel chair. Parthy, hat awry, bosom palpitating, eyes starting, mouth
working.

"On Canal Street!" she wheezed. It was as though the shriek she had
intended were choked in her throat by the very force of the feeling
behind it, so that it emerged a strangled thing. "Canal Street! The two of
them . . . with my own eyes . . . driving . . . in a . . . in a——"

She sank into a chair. There seemed to be no pretense about this.
Andy, for once, was alarmed. The tall shambling figure of Frank, the
heavy, passed the little ticket window, blocked the low doorway. He
stared, open-mouthed, at the almost recumbent Parthy. He was breathing heavily and looked aggrieved.

"She ran away from me," he said. "Sees 'em in the crowd, driving, and
tries to run after the carriage on Canal, with everybody thinking she's
gone loony. Then she runs down here to the landing, me after her.
Woman her age. What d'yah take me for, anyway!"

But Parthy did not hear him. He did not exist. Her face was ashen.
"He's a murderer!" she now gasped.

Andy's patience, never too long-suffering, snapped under the strain
of the afternoon's happenings. "What's wrong with you, woman! Have
you gone clean crazy! Who's a murderer! Frank? Who's he murdered?
For two cents I'd murder the both of you, come howling in here when a
man's trying to run his business *like* a business and not like a yowling
insane asylum——"

Parthy stood up, shaking. Her voice was high and quavering. "Listen
to me, you fool. I talked to the man on the docks—the one he was
talking to—and he wouldn't tell me anything and he said I could ask
the chief of police if I wanted to know about anybody, and I went to
the chief of police, and a perfect gentleman if there ever was one, and
he's killed a man."

"The chief of police! Killed a man! What man!"

"No!" shrieked Parthy. "Ravenal! Ravenal's killed a man."

"God A'mighty, when!" He started as though to rescue Magnolia.

"A year ago. A year ago, in this very town."

The shock of relief was too much for Andy. He was furious. "They didn't hang him for it, did they?"

"Hang who?" asked Parthy, feebly.

"Who! Ravenal! They didn't hang him?"

"Why, no, they let him go. He said he shot him in self——"

"He killed a man and they let him go. What does that prove? He'd a right to. All right. What of it!"

"What of it! Your own daughter is out driving in an open carriage this minute with a murderer, that's what, Andy Hawks. I saw them with my own eyes. There I was, out trying to protect her from contamination by finding out . . . and I saw her the minute my back was turned . . . your doings . . . your own daughter driving in the open streets in an open carriage with a murderer——"

"Oh, open murderer be damned!" squeaked Andy in his falsetto of utter rage. "I killed a man when I was nineteen, Mrs. Hawks, ma'am, and I've been twenty-five years and more as respected a man as there is on the rivers, and that's the truth if you want to talk about mur——"

But Parthenia Ann Hawks, for the first time in her vigorous life, had fainted.

X

GAYLORD RAVENAL had not meant to fall in love. Certainly he had not dreamed of marrying. He was not, he would have told you, a marrying man. Yet Natchez had come and gone, and here he was, still playing juvenile leads on the *Cotton Blossom*; still planning, days ahead, for an opportunity to outwit Mrs. Hawks and see Magnolia alone. He was thoroughly and devastatingly in love. Alternately he pranced and cringed. To-day he would leave this dingy scow. What was he, Gaylord Ravenal, doing aboard a show boat, play-acting for a miserable thirty dollars a week! He who had won (and lost) a thousand a night at poker or faro. To-morrow he was resolved to give up gambling for ever; to make himself worthy of this lovely creature; to make himself indispensable to Andy; to find the weak chink in Parthy's armour.

He had met all sorts of women in his twenty-four years. He had loved some of them, and many of them had loved him. He had never met a woman like Magnolia. She was a paradoxical product of the life she had led. The contact with the curious and unconventional characters that made up the *Cotton Blossom* troupe; the sights and sounds of river life, sordid, romantic, homely, Rabelaisian, tragic, humorous; the tolerant and meaty wisdom imbibed from her sprightly little father; the spirit of *laissez faire* that pervaded the whole atmosphere about her, had given her a flavour, a mellowness, a camaraderie found usually only in women twice her age and a hundredfold more experienced. Weaving in and out of this was an engaging primness directly traceable to Parthy. She had, too, a certain dignity that was, perhaps, the result of years of being deferred to as the daughter of a river captain. Sometimes she looked at Ravenal with the wide-eyed gaze of a child. At such times he wished that he might leap into the Mississippi (though muddy) and wash himself clean of his sins as did the pilgrims in the River Jordan.

On that day following Parthy's excursion ashore at New Orleans there had been between her and Captain Andy a struggle, brief and bitter, from which Andy had emerged battered but victorious.

"That murdering gambler goes or I go," Parthy had announced, rashly. It was one of those pronunciamentos that can only bring embarrassment to one who utters it.

"He stays." Andy was iron for once.

He stayed. So did Parthy, of course.

You saw the two—Parthy and Ravenal—eyeing each other, backs to the wall, waiting for a chance to lunge and thrust.

Cotton Blossom business was booming. News of the show boat's ingénue and juvenile lead filtered up and down the rivers. During the more romantic scenes of this or that play Parthy invariably stationed herself in the wings and glowered and made muttering sounds to which the two on stage—Magnolia starry-eyed as the heroine, Ravenal ardent and passionate as the lover—were oblivious. It was their only opportunity to express to each other what they actually felt. It probably was, too, the most public and convincing love-making that ever graced the stage of this or any other theatre.

Ravenal made himself useful in many ways. He took in hand, for example, the *Cotton Blossom's* battered scenery. It was customary on all show boats to use both sides of a set. One canvas side would represent, perhaps, a drawing room. Its reverse would show the greens and browns of leaves and tree trunks in a forest scene. Both economy and lack of stage space were responsible for this. Painted by a clumsy and unimaginative hand, each leaf daubed as a leaf, each inch of wainscoting drawn to scale, the effect of any *Cotton Blossom* set, when viewed from the other side of the footlights, was unconvincing even to rural and inexperienced eyes. Ravenal set to work with paint and brush and evolved two sets of double scenery which brought forth shrieks of ridicule and protest from the company grouped about the stage.

"It isn't supposed to look like a forest," Ravenal explained, slapping on the green paint with a lavish hand. "It's supposed to give the effect of a forest. The audience isn't going to sit on the stage, is it? Well, then! Here—this is to be a gate. Well, there's no use trying to paint a flat thing with slats that nobody will ever believe looks like a gate. I'll just do this . . . and this . . ."

"It does!" cried Magnolia from the middle of the house where she had stationed herself, head held critically on one side. "It does make you think there's a gate there, without its actually being . . . Look, Papa! . . . And the trees. All those lumpy green spots we used to have somehow never looked like leaves."

All unconsciously Ravenal was using in that day, and in that crude milieu, a method which was to make a certain Bobby Jones famous in the New York theatre of a quarter of a century later.

"Where did you learn to——" some one of the troupe would marvel; Magnolia, perhaps, or Mis' Means, or Ralph.

"Paris," Ravenal would reply, briefly. Yet he had never spoken of Paris.

He often referred thus casually to a mysterious past.

"Paris fiddlesticks!" rapped out Parthy, promptly. "No more Paris than he's a Ravenal of Tennessee, or whatever rascally highfalutin story he's made up for himself."

Whereupon, when they were playing Tennessee, weeks later, he strolled one day with Magnolia and Andy into the old vine-covered church of the village, its churchyard fragrant and mysterious with magnolia and ilex; its doorstep worn, its pillars sagging. And there, in a glass case, together with a tattered leather-bound Bible a century and a half old, you saw a time-yellowed document. The black of the ink strokes had, perhaps, taken on a tinge of gray, but the handwriting, clear and legible, met the eye.

WILL OF JEAN BAPTISTA RAVENAL.

I, Jean Baptista Ravenal, of this Province, being through the mercy of Almighty God of sound mind and memory do make, appoint, declare and ordain this and this only to be my last Will and Testament. It is my will that my sons have their estates delivered to them as they severally arrive at the age of twenty and one years, the eldest being Samuel, the second Jean, the third Gaylord.

I will that my slaves be kept to work on my lands that my estate be managed to the best advantage so as my sons may have as liberal

an education as the profits thereof will afford. Let them be taught to
read and write and be introduced into the practical part of Arithmetic,
not too hastily hurrying them to Latin and Grammar. To my sons,
when they arrive at age I recommend the pursuit and study of some
profession or business (I would wish one to ye Law, the other to
Merchandise).

"The other?" cried Magnolia softly then, looking up very bright-eyed
and flushed from the case over which she had been bending. "But the
third? Gaylord? It doesn't say——"

"The black sheep. My great-grandfather. There always was a Gaylord.
And he always was the black sheep. My grandfather, Gaylord Ravenal
and my father Gaylord Ravenal, and——" he bowed.

"Black too, are you?" said Andy then, drily.

"As pitch."

Magnolia bent again to the book, her brow thoughtful, her lips forming the words and uttering them softly as she deciphered the quaint
script.

> I give and bequeath unto my son Samuel the lands called Ashwood,
> which are situated, lying and being on the South Side of the Cumber-
> land River, together with my other land on the North side of said
> River. . . .
> I give and bequeath unto my son Jean, to him and his heirs and
> assigns for ever a tract of land containing seven hundred and forty
> acres lying on Stumpy Sound . . . also another tract containing one
> thousand acres . . .
> I give and bequeath to my son Samuel four hundred and fifty acres
> lying above William Lowrie's plantation on the main branch of Old
> Town Creek . . .

Magnolia stood erect. Indignation blazed in her fine eyes. "But, Gaylord!" she said.

"Yes!" Certainly she had never before called him that.

"I mean this Gaylord. I mean the one who came after Samuel and
Jean. Why isn't—why didn't——"

"Naughty boy," said Ravenal, with his charming smile.

She actually yearned toward him then. He could not have said anything more calculated to bind his enchantment for her. They swayed
toward each other over the top of the little glass-encased relic. Andy
coughed hastily. They swayed gently apart. They were as though mesmerized.

"Folks out here in the churchyard?" inquired Andy, briskly, to break
the spell. "Ravenal kin?"

"Acres of 'em," Gaylord assured him, cheerfully. "Son of . . . and daughter of . . . and beloved father of. . . . For that matter, there's one just beside you."

Andy side-stepped hastily, with a little exclamation. He cast a somewhat fearful glance at the spot toward which Ravenal so carelessly pointed. A neat gray stone slab set in the wall. Andy peered at the lettering it bore; stooped a little. "Here—you read it, Nollie. You've got young eyes."

Her fresh young cheek so near the cold gray slab, she read in her lovely flexible voice:

Here lies the body of M^{rs}. Suzanne Ravenal, wife of Jean Baptista Ravenal Esqr., one of his Majesty's Council and Surveyor General of the Lands of this Province, who departed this life Octr 19^t 1765. Aged 37 Years. After labouring ten of them under the severest Bodily afflictions brought on by Change of Climate, and tho' she went to her native land received no relief but returned and bore them with uncommon Resolution and Resignation to the last.

Magnolia rose, slowly, from the petals of her flounced skirt spread about her as she had stooped to read. "Poor darling!" Her eyes were soft with pity. Again the two seemed to sway a little toward each other, as though blown by a gust of passion. And this time little Captain Andy turned his back and clattered down the aisle. When they emerged again into the sunshine they found him, a pixie figure, leaning pensively against the great black trunk of a live oak. He was smoking a pipe somewhat apologetically, as though he hoped the recumbent Ravenals would not find it objectionable.

"I guess," he remarked, as Magnolia and Ravenal came up to him, "I'll have to bring your ma over. She's partial to history, her having been a schoolma'am, and all."

Like the stage sets he so cleverly devised for the show boat, Gaylord Ravenal had a gift for painting about himself the scenery of romance. These settings, too, did not bear the test of too close scrutiny. But in a favourable light, and viewed from a distance, they were charmingly effective and convincing.

His sense of the dramatic did not confine itself to the stage. He was the juvenile lead, on or off. Audiences adored him. Mid-western village housewives, good mothers and helpmates for years, were, for days after seeing him as the heroic figure of some gore-and-glory drama, mysteriously silent and irritably waspish by turn. Disfavour was writ large on their faces as they viewed their good commonplace dull husbands across the midday table set with steaming vegetables and meat.

"Why'n't you shave once in a while middle of the week," they would snap, "'stead of coming to the table looking like a gorilla?"

Mild surprise on the part of the husband. "I shaved Sat'dy, like always."

"Lookit your hands!"

"Hands? . . . Say, Bella, what in time's got into you, anyway?"

"Nothing." A relapse into moody silence on the part of Bella.

Mrs. Hawks fought a good fight, but what chance had her maternal jealousy against youth and love and romance? For a week she would pour poison into Magnolia's unwilling ear. Only making a fool of you . . . probably walk off and leave the show any day . . . common gambler . . . look at his eyes . . . murderer and you know it . . . rather see you in your grave. . . .

Then, in one brief moment, Ravenal, by some act of courage or grace or sheer deviltry, would show Parthy that all her pains were for nothing.

That night, for example, when they were playing Kentucky Sue. Ravenal's part was what is known as a blue-shirt lead—the rough brave woodsman, with the uncouth speech and the heart of gold. Magnolia, naturally, was Sue. They were playing Gains Landing, always a tough town, often good for a fight. It was a capacity audience and surprisingly well-behaved and attentive. Midway in the play's progress a drawling drunken voice from the middle of the house began a taunting and ridiculous chant whose burden was, "Is 'at so!" After each thrilling speech; punctuating each flowery period, "Is 'at so!" came the maddening and disrupting refrain. You had to step carefully at Gains Landing. The Cotton Blossom troupe knew that. One word at the wrong moment, and knives flashed, guns popped. Still, this could not go on.

"Don't mind him," Magnolia whispered fearfully to Ravenal. "He's drunk. He'll stop. Don't pay any attention."

The scene was theirs. They were approaching the big moment in the play when the brave Kentuckian renounces his love that Kentucky Sue may be happy with her villainous bridegroom-to-be (Frank, of course). Show-boat audiences up and down the rivers had known that play for years; had committed the speech word for word, through long familiarity. "Sue," it ran, "ef he loves yuh and you love him, go with him. Ef he h'ain't good to yuh, come back where there's honest hearts under homespun shirts. Back to Kaintucky and home!"

Thus the speech ran. But as they approached it the blurred and mocking voice from the middle of the house kept up its drawling skepticism. "Is 'at so! Is 'at so!"

"Damned drunken lout!" said Ravenal under his breath, looking unutterable love meanwhile at the languishing Kentucky Sue.

"Oh, dear!" said Magnolia, feeling Ravenal's muscles tightening under the blue shirt sleeves; seeing the telltale white ridge of mounting anger under the grease paint of his jaw line. "Do be careful."

Ravenal stepped out of his part. He came down to the footlights. The house, restless and irritable, suddenly became quiet. He looked out over the faces of the audience. "See here, pardner, there's others here want to hear this, even if you don't."

The voice subsided. There was a little desultory applause from the audience and some cries of, "That's right! Make him shut up." They refused to manhandle one of their own, but they ached to see someone else do it.

The play went on. The voice was silent. The time approached for the big speech of renunciation. It was here. "Sue, ef he loves yuh and you love him, go with him. Ef he——"

"Is 'at so!" drawled the amused voice, with an element of surprise in it now. "Is 'at so!"

Ravenal cast Kentucky Sue from him. "Well, if you will have it," he threatened, grimly. He sprang over the footlights, down to the piano top, to the keyboard, to the piano stool, all in four swift strides, was up the aisle, had plucked the limp and sprawling figure out of his seat by the collar, clutched him then firmly by this collar hold and the seat of his pants, and was up the aisle again to the doorway, out of the door, across the gangplank, and into the darkness. He was down the aisle then in a moment, spatting his hands briskly as he came; was up on the piano stool, on to the piano keyboard, on the piano top, over the footlights, back in position. There he paused a moment, breathing fast. Nothing had been said. There had actually been no sound other than his footsteps and the discordant jangle of protest that the piano keyboard had emitted when he had stepped on its fingers. Now a little startled expression came into Ravenal's face.

"Let's see," he said, aloud. "Where was I——"

And as one man the audience chanted, happily, "Sue, ef he loves yuh and you love him——"

What weapon has a Parthenia against a man like that? And what chance a Frank?

Drama leaped to him. There was, less than a week later, the incident of the minister. He happened to be a rather dirty little minister in a forlorn little Kentucky river town. He ran a second-hand store on the side, was new to the region, and all unaware of the popularity and good-will enjoyed by the members of the *Cotton Blossom* troupe. To him an actor was a burning brand. Doc had placarded the little town with dodgers and handbills. There was one, especially effective even in that day of crude photography, showing Magnolia in the angelic part of the ingénue lead in Tempest and Sunshine. These might be seen displayed in the windows of such ramshackle stores as the town's river front street boasted. Gaylord Ravenal, strolling disdainfully up into the sordid village that was little more than a welter of mud and flies and mules and Negroes, stopped aghast as his eye chanced to fall upon the words scrawled beneath a picture of Magnolia amidst the dusty disorderly mélange of the ministerial second-hand window. There was the likeness of the woman he loved looking, starry-eyed, out upon the passer-by. And beneath it, in the black fanatic penmanship of the itinerant parson:

A LOST SOUL

In his fine English clothes, swinging the slim malacca cane, Gaylord Ravenal, very narrow-eyed, entered the fusty shop and called to its owner to come forward. From the cobwebby gloom of the rear reaches emerged the merchant parson, a tall, shambling large-knuckled figure of the anaconda variety. You thought of Uriah Heep and of Ichabod Crane, experiencing meanwhile a sensation of distaste.

Ravenal, very elegant, very cool, very quiet, pointed with the tip of his cane. "Take that picture out of the window. Tear it up. Apologize."

"I won't do anything of the kind," retorted the holy man. "You're a this-and-that, and a such-and-such, and a so-and-so, and she's another, and the whole boatload of you ought to be sunk in the river you contaminate."

"Take off your coat," said Ravenal, divesting himself neatly of his own faultless garment as he spoke.

A yellow flame of fear leaped into the man's eyes. He edged toward the door. With a quick step Ravenal blocked his way. "Take it off before I rip it off. Or fight with your coat on."

"You touch a man of God and I'll put the law on you. The sheriff's office is just next door. I'll have you——"

Ravenal whirled him round, seized the collar of his grimy coat, peeled it dexterously off, revealing what was, perhaps, as maculate a shirt as ever defiled the human form. The Ravenal lip curled in disgust.

"If cleanliness is next to godliness," he remarked, swiftly turning back his own snowy cuffs meanwhile, "you'll be shovelling coal in hell." And swung. The minister was taller and heavier than this slight and dandified figure. But Ravenal had an adrenal advantage, being stimulated by the fury of his anger. The godly one lay, a soiled heap, among his soiled wares. The usual demands of the victor.

"Take that thing out of the window! . . . Apologize to me! . . . Apologize publicly for defaming a lady!"

The man crept groaning to the window, plucked the picture, with its offensive caption, from amongst the miscellany there, handed it to Ravenal in response to a gesture from him. "Now then, I think you're pretty badly bruised, but I doubt that anything's broken. I'm going next door to the sheriff. You will write a public apology in letters corresponding to these and place it in your filthy window. I'll be back."

He resumed his coat, picked up the malacca cane, blithely sought out the sheriff, displayed the sign, heard that gallant Kentuckian's most Southern expression of regard for Captain Andy Hawks, his wife and gifted daughter, together with a promise to see to it that the written apology remained in the varmint's window throughout the day and until the departure of the *Cotton Blossom*. Ravenal then went his elegant and unruffled way up the sunny sleepy street.

By noon the story was known throughout the village, up and down the river for a distance of ten miles each way, and into the back country, all in some mysterious word-of-mouth way peculiar to isolated districts. Ravenal, returning to the boat, was met by news of his own exploit. Business, which had been booming for this month or more, grew to phenomenal proportions. Ravenal became a sort of legendary figure on the rivers. Magnolia went to her mother. "I am never allowed to talk to him. I won't stand it. You treat him like a criminal."

"What else is he?"

"He's the——" A long emotional speech, ringing with words such as hero, gentleman, wonderful, honourable, nobility, glorious—a speech such as Schultzy, in his show-boat days as director, would have designated as a so-and-so-and-so-and-so-and-so-and-so.

Ravenal went to Captain Andy. I am treated as an outcast. I'm a Ravenal. Nothing but the most honourable conduct. A leper. Never permitted to speak to your daughter. Humiliation. Prefer to discontinue connection which can only be distasteful to the Captain and Mrs. Hawks, in view of your conduct. Leaving the *Cotton Blossom* at Cairo.

In a panic Captain Andy scampered to his lady and declared for a more lenient chaperonage.

"Willing to sacrifice your own daughter, are you, for the sake of a picking up a few more dollars here and there with this miserable upstart!"

"Sacrificing her, is it, to tell her she can speak civilly to as handsome a young feller and good-mannered as I ever set eyes on, or you either!"

"Young squirt, that's what he is."

"I was a girl like Nollie I'd run off with him, by God, and that's the truth. She had any spirit left in her after you've devilled her these eighteen years past, she'd do it."

"That's right! Put ideas into her head! How do you know who he is?"

"He's a Rav——"

"He says he is."

"Didn't he show me the church——"

"Oh, Hawks, you're a zany. I could show you gravestones. I could say my name was Bonaparte and show you Napoleon's tomb, but that wouldn't make him my grandfather, would it!"

After all, there was wisdom in what she said. She may even have been right, as she so often was in her shrewish intuition. Certainly they never learned more of this scion of the Ravenal family than the meagre information gleaned from the chronicles of the village church and graveyard.

Grudgingly, protestingly, she allowed the two to converse genteelly between the hours of five and six, after dinner. But no oriental princess was ever more heavily chaperoned than was Magnolia during these prim meetings. For a month, then, they met on the port side of the upper deck, forward. Their chairs were spaced well apart. On the starboard side, twenty-five feet away, sat Parthy in her chair, grim, watchful; radiating opposition.

Magnolia, feeling the gimlet eye boring her spine, would sit bolt upright, her long nervous fingers tightly interwoven, her ankles neatly crossed, the pleats and flounces of her skirts spread sedately enough yet seeming to vibrate with an electric force that gave them the effect of standing upright, a-quiver, like a kitten's fur when she is agitated.

He sat, one arm negligently over the back of his chair, facing the girl. His knees were crossed. He seemed at ease, relaxed. Yet a slim foot in its well-made boot swung gently to and fro. And when Parthy made one of her sudden moves, as was her jerky habit, or when she coughed raspingly by way of emphasizing her presence, he could be felt, rather than seen, to tighten in all his nerves and muscles, and the idly swinging foot took a clonic leap.

The words they spoke with their lips and the words they spoke with their eyes were absurdly at variance.

"Have you really been in Paris, Mr. Ravenal! How I should love to see it!" (How handsome you are, sitting there like that. I really don't care anything about Paris. I only care about you.)

"No doubt you will, some day, Miss Magnolia." (You darling! How I should like to take you there. How I should like to take you in my arms.)

"Oh, I've never even seen Chicago. Only these river towns." (I love the way your hair grows away from your temples in that clean line. I want to put my finger on it, and stroke it. My dear.)

"A sordid kind of city. Crude. Though it has some pleasant aspects. New York——" (What do I care if that old tabby is sitting there! What's to prevent me from getting up and kissing you a long long while on your lovely pomegranate mouth.)

Lowering, inflexible, sat Parthy. "She'll soon enough tire of that sort of popinjay talk," she told herself. She saw the bland and almost vacuous expression on the countenance of the young man, and being ignorant of the fact that he was famous from St. Louis to Chicago for his perfect poker face, was equally ignorant of the tides that were seething and roaring within him now.

They were prisoners on this boat; together, yet miles apart. Guarded, watched. They had their scenes together on the stage. These were only aggravations. The rather high planes of Magnolia's cheek-bones began to show a trifle too flat. Ravenal, as he walked along the grass-grown dusty streets of this or that little river town, switched viciously at weed and flower stalks with the slim malacca cane.

They hit upon a pathetic little scheme whereby they might occasionally, if lucky, steal the ecstasy of a good-night kiss. After the performance he would stroll carelessly out to the stern where stood the settling barrel. Ostensibly he was taking a bedtime drink of water. Magnolia was, if possible, to meet him there for a brief and perilous moment. It was rarely accomplished. The signal to him was the slamming of the screen door. But often the screen door slammed as he stood there, a tense quivering figure in the velvet dark of the Southern night, and it was Frank, or Mrs. Soaper, or Mis' Means, or puny Mr. Means, coughing his bronchial wheeze. Crack! went the screen door. Disappointment. Often he sloshed down whole gallons of river water before she came—if she came at all.

He had managed to save almost a hundred dollars. He was restless, irritable. Except for a mild pinochle game now and then with the men of the company, he had not touched a card in weeks. If he could get into a real game, somehow; manage a sweepstakes. Chicago. St. Louis, even. These little rotten river towns. No chance here. If he could with luck get together enough to take her away with him. Away from the old hell-cat, and this tub, and these damned eternal rivers. God, but he was sick of them!

They were playing the Ohio River—Paducah, Kentucky. He found himself seated at mid-afternoon round a table in the back room of a waterfront saloon. What time is it? Five. Plenty of time. Just for that raise you five. A few hundred dollars would do it. Six o'clock. Seven. Seven-thirty. Eight. Half-past—Who said half past! Ralph in the doorway. Can't be! Been looking everywhere for you. This's a fine way . . .

Come on outa here you. . . . Christ! . . . Ten dollars in his pocket. The curtain up at eight. Out, the shouts of the men echoing in his ears. Down to the landing. A frantic company, Andy clawing at his whiskers. Magnolia in tears, Parthy grim but triumphant, Frank made up to go on in Ravenal's part.

He dashed before the curtain, raised his shaking hand to quiet the cat-calling angry audience.

"Ladies and gentlemen, I ask your patience. There has been an unfortunate but unavoidable delay. The curtain will rise in exactly five minutes. In the name of the management I wish to offer you all apologies. We hope, by our performance, to make up for the inconvenience you have suffered. I thank you." A wave of his hand.

The band.

Parthy in the wings. "Well, Captain Hawks, I guess this settles it. Maybe you'll listen to your wife, after this. In a saloon—that's where he was—gambling. If Ralph hadn't found him—a pretty kettle of fish. Years building up a reputation on the rivers and then along comes a soft-soaping murdering gambler . . ."

Ravenal had got into his costume with the celerity of a fireman, and together he and Magnolia were giving a performance that was notable for its tempo and a certain vibratory quality. The drama that unrolled itself before the Paducah gaze was as nothing compared to the one that was being secretly enacted.

Between the lines of her part she whispered between immovable lips: "Oh, Gay, why did you do it?"

A wait, perhaps, of ten minutes before the business of the play brought him back within whispering distance of her.

"Money" (very difficult to whisper without moving the lips. It really emerged, "Uh-ney," but she understood). "For you. Marry you. Take you away."

All this while the lines of the play went on. When they stood close together it was fairly easy.

Magnolia (in the play): What! Have all your friends deserted you! (Mama'll make Andy send you away.)

Ravenal: No, but friendship is too cold a passion to stir my heart now. (Will you come with me?)

Magnolia: Oh, give me a friend in preference to a sweetheart. (But how can I?)

Ravenal: My dear Miss Brown—Miss Lucy——(Marry me).

Magnolia: Oh, please don't call me Miss Brown. (When?)

Ravenal: Lucy! (Where do we play to-morrow? Marry me there.)

Magnolia: Defender of the fatherless! (Metropolis. I'm frightened.)
Ravenal: Will you be a poor man's bride? (Darling!)

For fear of arousing suspicion, she did not dare put on her best dress
in which to be married. One's best dress does not escape the eye of a
Parthy at ten o'clock in the morning, when the landing is Metropolis.
With a sigh Magnolia donned her second best—the reseda sateen,
basqued, its overskirt caught up coquettishly at the side. She determined
on her Milan hat trimmed with the grosgrain ribbon and pink roses.
After all, Parthy or no Parthy, if one has a hat with pink roses, the time
to wear it is at one's wedding, or never.

Ravenal vanished beyond the river bank immediately after breakfast
next day; a meal which he had eaten in haste and in silence. He did not,
the general opinion ran, look as crushed as his misdemeanour warranted.
He had, after all, been guilty of the crime of crimes in the theatre, be it
a Texas tent show or an all-star production on Broadway; he had held
up the performance. For once the *Cotton Blossom* troupe felt that Mrs.
Hawks' bristling attitude was justified. All through the breakfast hour
the stern ribbon bow on her breakfast cap had quivered like a seismo-
graphic needle registering the degree of her inward upheaval.

"I think," said Magnolia, drinking her coffee in very small sips, and
eating nothing, "I'll just go to town and match the ribbon on my grosgrain striped silk——"

"You'll do nothing of the kind, miss, and so I tell you."

"But, Mama, why? You'd think I was a child instead of a——"

"You are, and no more. I can't go with you. So you'll stop at home."

"But Mis' Means is going with me. I promised her I'd go. She wants
to get some ointment for Mr. Means' chest. And a yard of elastic. And
half a dozen oranges. . . . Papa, don't you think it's unreasonable to
make me suffer just because everybody's in a bad temper this morning?
I'm sure I haven't done anything. I'm sure I——"

Captain Andy clawed his whiskers in a frenzy. "Don't come to me
with your yards of elastic and your oranges. God A'mighty!" He rushed
off, a distraught little figure, as well he might be after a wretched night
during which Mrs. Hawks had out-caudled Mrs. Caudle. When finally he
had dropped off to sleep to the sound of the monotonously nagging
voice, it was to dream of murderous gamblers abducting Magnolia who
always turned out to be Parthy.

In her second best sateen and the Milan with the pink roses Magnolia
went off to town at a pace that rather inconvenienced the short-breathed
Mis' Means.

"What's your hurry!" wheezed that lady, puffing up the steep cinder
path to the levee.

"We're late."

"Late! Late for what? Nothing to do all day till four, far's I know."

"Oh, I just meant—uh—I mean we started kind of late——" her voice trailed off, lamely.

Fifteen minutes later Mis' Means stood in indecision before a counter crawling with unwound bolts of elastic that twined all about her like garter snakes. The little general store smelled of old apples and broom straw and kerosene and bacon and potatoes and burlap and mice. Sixteen minutes later she turned to ask Magnolia's advice. White elastic half an inch wide? Black elastic three quarters of an inch wide? Magnolia had vanished from her side. Mis' Means peered through the dimness of the fusty little shop. Magnolia! White elastic in one hand, black in the other, Mis' Means scurried to the door. Magnolia had gone.

Magnolia had gone to be married in her second best dress and her hat with the pink roses. She flew down the street. Mis' Means certainly could have achieved no such gait; much less could she have bettered it to the extent of overtaking Magnolia. Magnolia made such speed that when her waiting bridegroom, leaning against the white picket fence in front of the minister's house next the church, espied her and came swiftly to meet her, she was so breathless a bride that he could make nothing out of her panted—"Elastic . . . Mis' Means . . . ran away . . ."

She leaned against the picket fence to catch her breath, a lovely flushed figure, and not a little frightened. And though it was early April with Easter just gone, there was a dogwood in bridal bloom in the minister's front yard, and a magnolia as well. And along the inside of the picket fence tulips and jonquils lifted their radiant heads. She looked at Gaylord Ravenal then and smiled her wide and gorgeous smile. "Let's go," she said, "and be married. I've caught my breath."

"All right," said Ravenal. Then he took from his pocket the diamond ring that was much too large for her. "Let's be engaged first, while we go up the path." And slipped it on her finger.

"Why, Gay! It's a diamond! Look what the sun does to it! Gay!"

"That's nothing compared to what the sun does to you," he said; and leaned toward her.

"Right at noon, in the minister's front yard!"

"I know. But I've had only those few moments in the dark by the settling barrel—it's been terrible."

The minister's wife opened the door. She looked at the two.

"I saw you from the parlour window. We were wondering—I thought maybe you'd like to be married in the church. The Easter decorations are still up. It looks lovely, all palms and lilies and smilax, too, from down South, sent up. The altar's banked with it. Mr. Seldon's gone there."

"Oh, I'd love to be married in church. Oh, Gay, I'd love to be married in church."

The minister's wife smoothed the front of her dress with one hand, and the back of her hair with the other, and, having made these preparations for the rôle of bridal attendant, conducted them to the little flower-banked church next door.

Magnolia never did remember very clearly the brief ceremony that followed. There were Easter lilies—whole rows of them—and palms and smilax, as the minister's wife had said. And the sun shone, picture-book fashion, through the crude yellows and blues and scarlets of the windows. And there was the Reverend Something-or-other Seldon, saying solemn words. But these things, strangely enough, seemed unimportant. Two little pig-tailed girls, passing by from school, had seen them enter the church and had tiptoed in, scenting a wedding. Now they were up in the choir loft, tittering hysterically. Magnolia could hear them above the Reverend Seldon's intonings. In sickness and in health—tee-hee-hee —for richer, for poorer—tee-hee-hee—for better, for worse—tee-hee-hee.

They were kneeling. Ravenal was wearing his elegantly sharp-pointed shoes. As he knelt his heels began to describe an arc—small at first, then wider and wider as he trembled more and more, until, at the end, they were all but striking the floor from side to side. Outwardly Magnolia was the bride of tradition, calm and pale.

. . . pronounce you man and wife.

Ravenal had a ten-dollar bill—that last ten-dollar bill—all neatly folded in his waistcoat pocket. This he now transferred to the Reverend Seldon's somewhat surprised palm.

"And," the minister's wife was saying, "while it isn't much—we're church mice, you see—you're welcome to it, and we'd be happy to have you take your wedding dinner with us. Veal loaf, I'm afraid, and butter beets——"

So Magnolia Ravenal was married in church, as proper as could be. And had her wedding dinner with the minister vis-à-vis. And when she came out of the church, the two little giggling girls, rather bold and rather frightened, but romantically stirred, pelted her with flowers. Pelted may be rather an exaggeration, because one threw a jonquil at her, and one a tulip, and both missed her. But it helped, enormously. They went to the minister's house and ate veal loaf and buttered beets and bread pudding, or ambrosia or whatever it was. And so they lived h—— and so they lived . . . ever after.

XI

EVEN after she had seen the Atlantic in a January hurricane, Kim Ravenal always insisted that the one body of water capable of striking terror to her was the Mississippi River. Surely she should have known. She had literally been born on that turbid torrent. All through her childhood her mother, Magnolia Ravenal, had told her tales of its vagaries, its cruelties, its moods; of the towns along its banks; of the people in those towns; of the boats that moved upon it and the fantastic figures that went up and down in those boats. Her grandfather, Captain Andy Hawks, had lost his life in the treacherous swift current of its channel; her grandmother, Parthenia Ann Hawks was, at eighty, a living legend of the Mississippi; the Flying Dutchman of the rivers, except that the boat touched many ports. One heard strange tales about Hawks' widow. She had gone on with the business after his tragic death. She was the richest show-boat owner on the rivers. She ran the boat like a female seminary. If an actor uttered so much as a damn, he was instantly dismissed from the troupe. Couples in the company had to show a marriage certificate. Every bill— even such innocuous old-timers as East Lynne and The Gambler's Daughter and Tempest and Sunshine—were subject to a purifying process before the stern-visaged female owner of the new *Cotton Blossom* would sanction their performance on her show boat.

Kim herself remembered many things about the Mississippi, though after her early childhood she did not see it for many years; and her mother rarely spoke of it. She even shook her head when Kim would ask her for the hundredth time to tell her the story of how she escaped being named Mississippi.

"Tell about the time the river got so high, and all kinds of things floated on it—animals and furniture and houses, even—and you were so scared, and I was born, and you wanted to call me Mississippi, but you were too sleepy or something to say it. And the place was near Kentucky and Illinois and Missouri, all at once, so they made up a name from the letters K and I and M, just till you could think of a real name. And you never did. And it stayed Kim. . . . People laugh when I tell them my name's Kim. Other girls are named Ellen and Mary and Elizabeth. . . .

Tell me about that time on the Mississippi. And the Cotton Blossom Floating Palace Theatre."

"But you know all about it. You've just told me."

"I like to hear you tell it."

"Your father doesn't like to have me talk so much about the rivers and the show boat."

"Why not?"

"He wasn't very happy on them. I wasn't, either, after Grandpa Hawks——"

Kim knew that, too. She had heard her father say, "God's sake, Nola, don't fill the kid's head full of that stuff about the rivers and the show boat. The way you tell it, it sounds romantic and idle and picturesque."

"Well, wasn't——?"

"No. It was rotten and sordid and dull. Flies on the food and filthy water to drink and yokels to play to. And that old harridan——"

"Gay!"

He would come over to her, kiss her tenderly, contritely. "Sorry, darling."

Kim knew that her mother had a strange deep feeling about the rivers. The ugly wide muddy ruthless rushing rivers of the Middle West.

Kim Ravenal's earliest river memories were bizarre and startling flashes. One of these was of her mother seated in a straight-backed chair on the upper deck of the *Cotton Blossom*, sewing spangles all over a high-busted corset. It was a white webbed corset with a pinched-in waist and high full bosom and flaring hips. This humdrum garment Magnolia Ravenal was covering with shining silver spangles, one overlapping the other so that the whole made a glittering basque. She took quick sure stitches that jerked the fantastic garment in her lap, and when she did this the sun caught the brilliant heap aslant and turned it into a glaze of gold and orange and ice-blue and silver.

Kim was enchanted. Her mother was a fairy princess. It was nothing to her that the spangle-covered basque, modestly eked out with tulle and worn with astonishingly long skirts for a bareback rider, was to serve as Magnolia's costume in The Circus Clown's Daughter.

Kim's grandmother had scolded a good deal about that costume. But then, she had scolded a good deal about everything. It was years before Kim realized that all grandmothers were not like that. At three she thought that scolding and grandmothers went together, like sulphur and molasses. The same was true of fun and grandfathers, only they went together like ice cream and cake. You called your grandmother grandma. You called your grandfather Andy, or, if you felt very roguish, Cap'n. When you called him that, he cackled and squealed, which was his way of laughing, and he clawed his delightful whiskers this side and that. Kim would laugh then, too, and look at him knowingly from under her long lashes. She had large eyes, deep-set like her mother's and her mother's wide mobile mouth. For the rest, she was much like her father—a Ravenal, he said. His fastidious ways (highfalutin, her grandmother called them); his slim hands and feet; his somewhat drawling speech, indirect though strangely melting glance, calculatedly impulsive and winning manner.

Another childhood memory was that of a confused and terrible morning. Asleep in her small bed in the room with her father and mother, she had been wakened by a bump, followed by a lurch, a scream, shouts, bells, clamour. Wrapped in her comforter, hastily snatched up from her bed by her mother, she was carried to the deck in her mother's arms. Gray dawn. A misty morning with fog hanging an impenetrable curtain over the river, the shore. The child was sleepy, bewildered. It was all one to her—the confusion, the shouting, the fog, the bells. Close in her mother's arms, she did not in the least understand what had happened when the confusion became pandemonium; the shouts rose to screams. Her grandfather's high squeaky voice that had been heard above the din —"La'berd lead there! Sta'berd lead! Snatch her! *SNATCH HER!*" was heard no more. Something more had happened. Someone was in the water, hidden by the fog, whirled in the swift treacherous current. Kim was thrown on her bed like a bundle of rags, all rolled in her blanket. She was left there, alone. She had cried a little, from fright and bewilderment, but had soon fallen asleep again. When she woke up her mother was bending over her, so wild-eyed, so frightening with her black hair streaming about her face and her face swollen and mottled with weeping, that Kim began to cry again in sheer terror. Her mother had snatched her to her. Curiously enough the words Magnolia Ravenal now whispered in a ghastly kind of agony were the very words she had whispered after the agony of Kim's birth—though the child could not know that.

"The river!" Magnolia said, over and over. Gaylord Ravenal came to her, flung an arm about her shoulder, but she shook him off wildly. "The river! The river!"

Kim never saw her grandfather again. Because of the look it brought to her mother's face, she soon learned not to say, "Where's Andy?" or— the roguish question that had always made him appear, squealing with delight: "Where's Cap'n?"

Baby though she was, the years—three or four—just preceding her grandfather's tragic death were indelibly stamped on the infant's mind.

He had adored her; made much of her. Andy, dead, was actually a more vital figure than many another alive.

It had been a startling but nevertheless actual fact that Parthenia Ann Hawks had not wanted her daughter Magnolia to have a child. Parthy's strange psychology had entered into this, of course—a pathological twist. Of this she was quite unaware.

"How're you going to play ingénue lead, I'd like to know, if you—when you—while you——" She simply could not utter the word "pregnant" or say, "while you are carrying your child," or even the simpering evasion of her type and class—"in the family way."

Magnolia laughed a little at that. "I'll play as long as I can. Toward the end I'll play ruffly parts. Then some night, probably between the second and third acts—though they may have to hold the curtain for five minutes or so—I'll excuse myself——"

Mrs. Hawks declared that she had never heard anything so indelicate in her life. "Besides, a show boat's no place to bring up a child."

"You brought me up on one."

"Yes," said Mrs. Hawks, grimly. Her tone added, "And now look at you!"

Even before Kim's birth the antagonism between Parthy and her son-in-law deepened to actual hatred. She treated him like a criminal; regarded Magnolia's quite normal condition as a reproach to him.

"Look here, Magnolia, I can't stand this, you know. I'm so sick of this old mud-scow and everything that goes with it."

"Gay! Everything!"

"You know what I mean. Let's get out of it. I'm no actor. I don't belong here. If I hadn't happened to see you when you stepped out on deck that day at New Orleans——"

"Are you sorry?"

"Darling! It's the only luck I've ever had that lasted."

She looked thoughtfully down at the clear colourful brilliance of the diamond on her third finger. Always too large for her, it now hung so loosely on her thin hand that she had been obliged to wind it with a great pad of thread to keep it from dropping off, though hers were the large-knuckled fingers of the generous and resourceful nature. It was to see much of life, that ring.

She longed to say to him, "Where do you belong, Gay? Who are you? Don't tell me you're a Ravenal. That isn't a profession, is it? You can't live on that."

But she knew it was useless. There was a strange deep streak of the secretive in him; baffling, mystifying. Questioned, he would say nothing.

It was not a moody silence, or a resentful one. He simply would not speak. She had learned not to ask.

"We can't go away now, Gay dear. I can't go. You don't want to go without me, do you? You wouldn't leave me! Maybe next winter, after the boat's put up, we can go to St. Louis, or even New Orleans—that would be nice, wouldn't it? The winter in New Orleans."

One of his silences.

He never had any money—that is, he never had it for long. It vanished. He would have one hundred dollars. He would go ashore at some sizable town and return with five hundred—a thousand. "Got into a little game with some of the boys," he would explain, cheerfully. And give her three hundred of it, four hundred, five. "Buy yourself a dress, Nola. Something rich, with a hat to match. You're too pretty to wear those home-made things you're always messing with."

Some woman wisdom in her told her to put by a portion of these sums. She got into the habit of tucking away ten dollars, twenty, fifty. At times she reproached herself for this; called it disloyal, sneaking, underhand. When she heard him say, as he frequently did, "I'm strapped. If I had fifty dollars I could turn a trick that would make five hundred out of it. You haven't got fifty, have you, Nola? No, of course not."

She wanted then to give him every cent of her tiny hoard. It was the tenuous strain of her mother in her, doubtless—the pale thread of the Parthy in her make-up—that caused her to listen to an inner voice. "Don't do it," whispered the voice, nudging her, "keep it. You'll need it badly by and by."

It did not take many months for her to discover that her husband was a gambler by profession—one of those smooth and plausible gentry with whom years of river life had made her familiar. It was, after all, not so much a discovery as a forced admission. She knew, but refused to admit that she knew. Certainly no one could have been long in ignorance with Mrs. Hawks in possession of the facts.

Ten days after Magnolia's marriage to Ravenal (and what a ten days those had been! Parthy alone crowded into them a lifetime of reproach), Mrs. Hawks came to her husband, triumph in her mien, portent in her voice:

"Well, Hawks, I hope you're satisfied now." This was another of Parthy's favourite locutions. The implication was that the unfortunate whom she addressed had howled heaven-high his demands for hideous misfortune and would not be content until horror had piled upon horror. "I hope you're satisfied now, Hawks. Your son-in-law is a gambler, and no more. A common barroom gambler, without a cent to his trousers longer'n it takes to transfer his money from his pocket to the table. That's what your only daughter has married. Understand, I'm not saying he gambles, and that's all. I say he's a gambler by calling. That's the way he made his living before he came aboard this boat. I wish he had died before he ever set foot on the *Cotton Blossom* gangplank, and so I tell you, Hawks. A smooth-tongued, oily, good-for-nothing; no better than the scum Elly ran off with."

"Now, Parthy, what's done's done. Why'n't you try to make the best of things once in a while, instead of the worst? Magnolia's happy with him."

"She ain't lived her life out with him yet. Mark my words. He's got a roving eye for a petticoat."

"Funny thing, Parthy. Your father was a man, and so's your husband, and your son-in-law's another. Yet seems you never did get the hang of a man's ways."

Andy liked Ravenal. There was about the fellow a grace, an ease, a certain elegance that appealed to the æsthetic in the little Gallic captain. When the two men talked together sometimes, after dinner, it was amiably, in low tones, with an air of leisure and relaxation. Two gentlemen enjoying each other's company. There existed between the two a sound respect and liking.

Certainly Ravenal's vogue on the rivers was tremendous. Andy paid him as juvenile lead a salary that was unheard of in show-boat records. But he accounted him worth it. Shortly after Kim's birth, Andy spoke of giving Ravenal a share in the *Cotton Blossom*. But this Mrs. Hawks fought with such actual ferocity that Andy temporarily at least relinquished the idea.

Magnolia had learned to dread the idle winter months. During this annual period of the *Cotton Blossom's* hibernation the Hawks family had, before Magnolia's marriage, gone back to the house near the river at Thebes. Sometimes Andy had urged Parthy to spend these winter months in the South, evading the harsh Illinois climate for a part of the time at least in New Orleans, or one of the towns of southern Mississippi where one might have roses instead of holly for Christmas. He sometimes envied black Jo and Queenie their period of absence from the boat. In spite of the disreputable state in which they annually returned to the *Cotton Blossom* in the early spring, they always looked as if they had spent the intervening months seated in the dappled shade, under a vine, with the drone of insects in the air, and the heavy scent of white-petalled blossoms; eating fruit that dripped juice between their fingers; sleeping, slack-jawed and heavily content, through the heat of the Southern mid-afternoon; supping greasily and plentifully on fried catfish and corn bread; watching the moon come up to the accompaniment of Jo's coaxing banjo.

"We ought to lazy around more, winters," Andy said to his energetic wife. She was, perhaps, setting the Thebes house to rights after their long absence; thwacking pillows, pounding carpets, sloshing pails, scouring tables, hanging fresh curtains, flapping drapes, banging bureau drawers. A towel wrapped about her head, turban-wise, her skirts well pinned up, she would throw a frenzy of energy into her already exaggerated housewifeliness until Andy, stepping fearfully out of the way of mop and broom and pail, would seek waterfront cronies for solace.

"Lazy! I've enough of lazying on that boat of yours month in month out all summer long. No South for me, thank you. Eight months of flies and niggers and dirty mud-tracking loafers is enough for me, Captain Hawks. I'm thankful to get back for a few weeks where I can live like a decent white woman." Thwack! Thump! Bang!

After one trial lasting but a few days, the Thebes house was found by Magnolia to be impossible for Gaylord Ravenal. That first winter after their marriage they spent in various towns and cities. Memphis for a short time; a rather hurried departure; St. Louis; Chicago. That brief glimpse of Chicago terrified her, but she would not admit it. After all, she told herself, as the astounding roar and din and jangle and clatter of State Street and Wabash Avenue beat at her ears, this city was only an urban Mississippi. The cobblestones were the river bed. The high grim buildings the river banks. The men, women, horses, trucks, drays, carriages, street cars that surged through those streets; creating new channels where some obstacle blocked their progress; felling whole sections of stone and brick and wood and sweeping over that section, obliterating all trace of its former existence; lifting other huge blocks and sweeping them bodily downstream to deposit them in a new spot; making a boulevard out of what had been a mud swamp—all this, Magnolia thought, was only the Mississippi in another form and environment; ruthless, relentless, Gargantuan, terrible. One might think to know its currents and channels ever so well, but once caught unprepared in the maelstrom, one would be sucked down and devoured as Captain Andy Hawks had been in that other turbid hungry flood.

"You'll get used to it," Ravenal told his bride, a trifle patronizingly, as one who had this monster tamed and fawning. "Don't be frightened. It's mostly noise."

"I'm not frightened, really. It's just the kind of noise that I'm not used to. The rivers, you know, all these years—so quiet. At night and in the morning."

That winter she lived the life of a gambler's wife. Streak o' lean, streak o' fat. Turtle soup and terrapin at the Palmer House to-day. Ham and eggs in some obscure eating house to-morrow. They rose at noon. They never retired until the morning hours. Gay seemed to know a great many people, but to his wife he presented few of these.

"Business acquaintance," he would say. "You wouldn't care for him."

Hers had been a fantastic enough life on the show boat. But always there had been about it an orderliness, a routine, due, perhaps, to the presence of the martinet, Parthenia Ann Hawks. Indolent as the days appeared on the rivers, they still bore a methodical aspect. Breakfast at nine. Rehearsal. Parade. Dinner at four. Make-up. Curtain. Wardrobe to mend or refurbish; parts to study; new songs to learn for the concert. But this new existence seemed to have no plot or plan. Ravenal was a being for the most part unlike the lover and husband of *Cotton Blossom* days. Expansive and secretive by turn; now high-spirited, now depressed; frequently absent-minded. His manner toward her was always tender, courteous, thoughtful. He loved her as deeply as he was capable of loving. She knew that. She had to tell herself all this one evening when she sat in their hotel room, dressed and waiting for him to take her to dinner and to the theatre. They were going to McVicker's Theatre, the handsome new auditorium that had risen out of the ashes of the old (to quote the owner's florid announcement). Ravenal was startled to learn how little Magnolia knew of the great names of the stage. He had told her something of the history of McVicker's, in an expansive burst of pride in Chicago. He seemed to have a definite feeling about this great uncouth giant of a city.

"When you go to McVicker's," Ravenal said, "you are in the theatre where Booth has played, and Sothern, and Lotta, and Kean, and Mrs. Siddons."

"Who," asked Magnolia, "are they?"

He was so much in love that he found this ignorance of her own calling actually delightful. He laughed, of course, but kissed her when she pouted a little, and explained to her what these names meant, investing them with all the glamour and romance that the theatre—the theatre of sophistication, that is—had for him; for he had the gambler's love of the play. It must have been something of that which had held him so long to the *Cotton Blossom*. Perhaps, after all, his infatuation for Magnolia alone could not have done it.

And now she was going to McVicker's. And she had on her dress with the open-throated basque, which she considered rather daring, though now that she was a married woman it was all right. She was dressed long before the time when she might expect him back. She had put out fresh linen for him. He was most fastidious about his dress. Accustomed to the sloppy deshabille of the show boat's male troupers, this sartorial niceness in Ravenal had impressed her from the first.

She regarded herself in the mirror now. She knew she was not beautiful. She affected, in fact, to despise her looks; bemoaned her high forehead and prominent cheek-bones, her large-knuckled fingers, her slenderness, her wide mouth. Yet she did not quite believe these things she said about herself; loved to hear Ravenal say she was beautiful. As she looked at her reflection now in the long gilt-framed mirror of the heavy sombre walnut bedroom, she found herself secretly agreeing with him. This was the first year of her marriage. She was pregnant. It was December. The child was expected in April. There was nothing distorted about her figure or her face. As is infrequently the case, her condition had given her an almost uncanny radiance of aspect. Her usually pallid skin showed a delicious glow of rosy colouring; her eyes were enormous and strangely luminous; tiny blue veins were faintly, exquisitely etched against the cream tint of her temples; her rather angular slimness was replaced by a delicate roundness; she bore herself well, her shoulders back, her head high. A happy woman, beloved, and in love.

Six o'clock. A little late, but he would be here at any moment now. Half-past six. She was opening the door every five minutes to peer up the red-carpeted corridor. Seven. Impatience had given way to fear, fear to terror, terror to certain agony. He was dead. He had been killed. She knew by now that he frequented the well-known resorts of the city, that he played cards in them. "Just for pastime," he told her. "Game of cards to while away the afternoon. What's the harm in that? Now, Nola! Don't look like your mother. Please!"

She knew about them. Red plush and gilt, mahogany and mirrors. Food and drink. River-front saloons and river-front life had long ago taught her not to be squeamish. She was not a foolish woman, nor an intolerant. She was, in fact, in many ways wise beyond her years. But this was 1888. The papers had been full of the shooting of Simeon Peake, the gambler, in Jeff Hankins' place over on Clark Street. The bullet had been meant for someone else—a well-known newspaper publisher, in fact. But a woman, hysterical, crazed, revengeful, had fired it. It had gone astray. Ravenal had known Simeon Peake. The shooting had been a shock to him. It had, indeed, thrown him so much off his guard that he had talked to Magnolia about it for relief. Peake had had a young daughter Selina. She was left practically penniless.

Now the memory of this affair came rushing back to her. She was frantic. Half-past seven. It was too late, now, for the dinner they had planned for the gala evening—dinner at the Wellington Hotel, down in the white marble café. The Wellington was just across the street from

McVicker's. It would make everything simple and easy; no rush, no hurrying over that last delightful sweet sip of coffee.

Eight o'clock. He had been killed. She no longer merely opened the door to peer into the corridor. She left the room door open and paced from room to hall, from hall to room, wildly; down the corridor. Finally, in desperation, down to the hotel lobby into which she had never stepped in the evening without her husband. There were two clerks at the office desk. One was an ancient man, flabby and wattled, as much a part of the hotel as the stones that paved the lobby. He had soft wisps of sparse white hair that seemed to float just above his head instead of being attached to it; and little tufts of beard, like bits of cotton stuck on his cheeks. He looked like an old baby. The other was a glittering young man; his hair glittered, his eyes, his teeth, his nails, his shirt-front, his cuffs. Both these men knew Ravenal; had greeted him on their arrival; had bowed impressively to her. The young man had looked flattering things; the old man had pursed his soft withered lips.

Magnolia glanced from one to the other. There were people at the clerks' desk, leaning against the marble slab. She waited, nervous, uncertain. She would speak to the old man. She did not want, somehow, to appeal to the glittering one. But he saw her, smiled, left the man to whom he was talking, came toward her. Quickly she touched the sleeve of the old man—leaned forward over the marble to do it—jerked his sleeve, really, so that he glanced up at her testily.

"I—I want—may I speak to you?"

"A moment, madam. I shall be free in a moment."

The sparkler leaned toward her. "What can I do for you, Mrs. Ravenal?"

"I just wanted to speak to this gentleman——"

"But I can assist you, I'm sure, as well as——"

She glanced at him and he was a row of teeth, all white and even, ready to bite. She shook her head miserably; glanced appealingly at the old man. The sparkler's eyebrows came up. He gave the effect of stepping back, courteously, without actually doing so. Now that the old clerk faced her, questioningly, she almost regretted her choice.

She blushed, stammered; her voice was little more than a whisper. "I . . . my husband . . . have been . . . he hasn't returned . . . worried . . . killed or . . . theatre . . ."

The old baby cupped one hand behind his ear. "What say?"

Her beautiful eyes, in their agony, begged the sparkler now to forgive her for having been rude. She needed him. She could not shout this. He stepped forward, but the teeth were hidden. After all, a chief clerk is a chief clerk. Miraculously, he had heard the whisper.

"You say your husband——?"

She nodded. She was terribly afraid that she was going to cry. She opened her eyes very wide and tried not to blink. If she so much as moved her lids she knew the mist that was making everything swim in a rainbow haze would crystallize into tears.

"He is terribly late. I—I've been so worried. We were going to the—to McVicker's—and dinner—and now it's after seven——"

"After eight," wheezed cotton whiskers, peering at the clock on the wall.

"—after eight," she echoed, wretchedly. There! She had winked. Two great drops plumped themselves down on the silk bosom of her bodice with the open-throated neck line. It seemed to her that she heard them splash.

"H'm!" cackled the old man.

The glittering one leaned toward her. She was enveloped in a waft of perfume. "Now, now, Mrs. Ravenal! There's absolutely nothing to worry about. Your husband has been delayed. That's all. Unavoidably delayed."

She snatched at this. "Do you think—? Are you sure? But he always is back by six, at the latest. Always. And we were going to dinner—and Mc——"

"You brides!" smiled the young man. He actually patted her hand, then. Just a touch. "Now you just have a bite of dinner, like a sensible little woman."

"Oh, I couldn't eat a bite! I couldn't!"

"A cup of tea. Let me send up a cup of tea."

The old one made a sucking sound with tongue and teeth, rubbed his chin, and proffered his suggestion in a voice that seemed to Magnolia to echo and reëcho through the hotel lobby. "Why'n't you send a messenger around for him, madam?"

"Messenger? Around? Where?"

Sparkler made a little gesture—a tactful gesture. "Perhaps he's having a little game of—uh—cards; and you know how time flies. I've done the same thing myself. Look up at the clock and first thing you know it's eight. Now if I were you, Mrs. Ravenal——"

She knew, then. There was something so sure about this young man; and so pitying. And suddenly she, too, was sure. She recalled in a flash that time when they were playing Paducah, and he had not come. They had held the curtain until after eight. Ralph had searched for him. He had been playing poker in a waterfront saloon. Send around for him! Not she. The words of a popular sentimental song of the day went through her mind, absurdly.

Father, dear father, come home with me now.
The clock in the steeple strikes one.

She drew herself up, now. The actress. She even managed a smile,
as even and sparkling and toothy as the sparkler's own. "Of course. I'm
very silly. Thank you so . . . I'll just have a bit of supper in my
room. . . ." She turned away with a little gracious bow. The eyes very
wide again.

"H'm!" The old man. Translated it meant, "Little idiot!"

She took off the dress with the two dark spots on the silk of the
basque. She put away his linen and his shiny shoes. She took up some
sewing. But the mist interfered with that. She threw herself on the bed.
An agony of tears. That was better. Ten o'clock. She fell asleep, the
gas lights burning. At a little before midnight he came in. She awoke
with a little cry. Queerly enough, the first thing she noticed was that
he had not his cane—the richly mottled malacca stick that he always
carried. She heard herself saying, ridiculously, half awake, half asleep,
"Where's your cane?"

His surprise at this matter-of-fact reception made his expression almost ludicrous. "Cane! Oh, that's so. Why I left it. Must have left it."

In the years that followed she learned what the absence of the malacca
stick meant. It had come to be a symbol in every pawnshop on Clark
Street. Its appearance was bond for a sum a hundred times its actual
value. Gaylord Ravenal always paid his debts.

She finished undressing, in silence. Her face was red and swollen.
She looked young and helpless and almost ugly. He was uncomfortable
and self-reproachful. "I'm sorry, Nola. I was detained. We'll go to the
theatre to-morrow night."

She almost hated him then. Being, after all, a normal woman, there
followed a normal scene—tears, reproaches, accusations, threats, pleadings, forgiveness. Then:

"Uh—Nola, will you let me take your ring—just for a day or two?"

"Ring?" But she knew.

"You'll have it back. This is Wednesday. You'll have it by Saturday.
I swear it."

The clear white diamond had begun its travels with the malacca
stick.

He had spoken the truth when he said that he had been unavoidably
detained.

She had meant not to sleep. She had felt sure that she would not
sleep. But she was young and healthy and exhausted from emotion. She
slept. As she lay there by his side she thought, before she slept, that life

was very terrible—but fascinating. Even got from this a glow of discovery. She felt old and experienced and married and tragic. She thought of her mother. She was much, much older and more married, she decided, than her mother ever had been.

They returned to Thebes in February. Magnolia longed to be near her father. She even felt a pang of loneliness for her mother. The little white cottage near the river, at Thebes, looked like a toy house. Her bedroom was doll-size. The town was a miniature village, like a child's Christmas set. Her mother's bonnet was a bit of grotesquerie. Her father's face was etched with lines that she did not remember having seen there when she left. The home-cooked food, prepared by Parthy's expert hands, was delicious beyond belief. She was a traveller returned from a far place.

Captain Andy had ordered a new boat. He talked of nothing else. The old *Cotton Blossom*, bought from Pegram years before, was to be discarded. The new boat was to be lighted by some newfangled gas arrangement instead of the old kerosene lamps. Carbide or some such thing Andy said it was. There were to be special footlights, new scenery, improved dressing and sleeping rooms. She was being built at the St. Louis shipyards.

"She's a daisy!" squeaked Andy, capering. He had just returned from a trip to the place of the *Cotton Blossom's* imminent birth. Of the two impending accouchements—that which was to bring forth a grandchild and that which was to produce a new show boat—it was difficult to say which caused him keenest anticipation. Perhaps, secretly, it was the boat, much as he loved Magnolia. He was, first, the river man; second, the showman; third, the father.

"Like to know what you want a new boat for!" Parthy scolded. "Take all the money you've earned these years past with the old tub and throw it away on a new one."

"Old one a'n't good enough."

"Good enough for the riff-raff we get on it."

"Now, Parthy, you know's well's I do you couldn't be shooed off the rivers now you've got used to 'em. Any other way of living'd seem stale to you."

"I'm a woman loves her home and asks for nothing better."

"Bet you wouldn't stay ashore, permanent, if you had the chance." He won the wager, though he had to die to do it.

The new *Cotton Blossom* and the new grandchild had a trial by flood on their entrance into life. The Mississippi, savage mother that she was, gave them both a baptism that threatened for a time to make their entrance into and their exit from the world a simultaneous act.

But both, after some perilous hours, were piloted to safety; the one by old Windy, who swore that this was his last year on the rivers; the other by a fat midwife and a frightened young doctor. Through storm and flood was heard the voice of Parthenia Ann Hawks, the scold, berating Captain Hawks her husband, and Magnolia Ravenal her daughter, as though they, and not the elements, were responsible for the predicament in which they now found themselves.

There followed four years of war and peace. The strife was internal. It raged between Parthy and her son-in-law. The conflict of the two was a chemical thing. Combustion followed inevitably upon their meeting. The biting acid of Mrs. Hawks' discernment cut relentlessly through the outer layers of the young man's charm and grace and melting manner and revealed the alloy. Ravenal's nature recoiled at sight of a woman who employed none of the arts of her sex and despised and penetrated those of the opposite sex. She had no vanity, no coquetry, no reticences, no respect for the reticence of others; treated compliment as insult, met flattery with contempt.

A hundred times during those four years he threatened to leave the *Cotton Blossom*, yet he was held to his wife Magnolia and to the child Kim by too many tender ties. His revolt usually took the form of a gambling spree ashore during which he often lost every dollar he had saved throughout weeks of enforced economy. There was no opportunity to spend money legitimately in the straggling hamlets to whose landings the *Cotton Blossom* was so often fastened. Then, too, the easy indolence of the life was beginning to claim him—its effortlessness, its freedom from responsibility. Perhaps a new part to learn at the beginning of the season—that was all. River audiences liked the old plays. Came to see them again and again. It was Ravenal who always made the little speech in front of the curtain. Wish to thank you one and all . . . always glad to come back to the old . . . to-morrow night that thrilling comedy-drama entitled . . . each and every one . . . concert after the show . . .

Never had the *Cotton Blossom* troupe so revelled in home-baked cakes, pies, cookies; home-brewed wine; fruits of tree and vine. The female population of the river towns from the Great Lakes to the Gulf beheld in him the lover of their secret dreams and laid at his feet burnt offerings and shewbread. Ravenal, it was said by the *Cotton Blossom* troupe, could charm the gold out of their teeth.

Perhaps, with the passing of the years, he might have grown quite content with this life. Sometimes the little captain, when the two men were conversing quietly apart, dropped a word about the future.

"When I'm gone—you and Magnolia—the boat'll be yours, of course."

Ravenal would laugh. Little Captain Andy looked so very much alive, his bright brown eyes glancing here and there, missing nothing on land or shore, his brown paw scratching the whiskers that showed so little of gray, his nimble legs scampering from texas to gangplank, never still for more than a minute.

"No need to worry about that for another fifty years," Ravenal assured him.

The end had in it, perhaps, a touch of the ludicrous, as had almost everything the little capering captain did. The *Cotton Blossom*, headed upstream on the Mississippi, bound for St. Louis, had struck a snag in Cahokia Bend, three miles from the city. It was barely dawn, and a dense fog swathed the river. The old *Cotton Blossom* probably would have sunk midstream. The new boat stood the shock bravely. In the midst of the pandemonium that followed the high shrill falsetto of the little captain's voice could be heard giving commands which he, most of all, knew he had no right to give. The pilot only was to be obeyed under such conditions. The crew understood this, as did the pilot. It was, in fact, a legend that more than once in a crisis Captain Andy on the upper deck had screamed his orders in a kind of dramatic frenzy of satisfaction, interspersing these with picturesque and vivid oaths during which he had capered and bounced his way right off the deck and into the river, from which damp station he had continued to screech his orders and profanities in cheerful unconcern until fished aboard again. Exactly this happened. High above the clamour rose the voice of Andy. His little figure whirled like that of a dervish. Up, down, fore, aft —suddenly he was overboard unseen in the dimness, in the fog, in the savage swift current of the Mississippi, wrapped in the coils of the old yellow serpent, tighter, tighter, deeper, deeper, until his struggles ceased. She had him at last.

"The river," Magnolia had said, over and over. "The river. The river."

XII

"THEBES?" echoed Parthenia Ann Hawks, widow. The stiff crêpe of her weeds seemed to bristle. "I'll do nothing of the kind, miss! If you and that fine husband of yours think to rid yourself of me *that* way——"

"But, Mama, we're not trying to rid ourselves of you. How can you think of such things! You've always said you hated the boat. Always. And now that Papa—now that you needn't stay with the show any longer, I thought you'd want to go back to Thebes to live."

"Indeed! And what's to become of the *Cotton Blossom*, tell me that, Maggie Hawks!"

"I don't know," confessed Magnolia, miserably. "I don't—know. That's what I think we ought to talk about." The *Cotton Blossom*, after her tragic encounter with the hidden snag in the Mississippi, was in for repairs. The damage to the show boat had been greater than they had thought. The snag had, after all, inflicted a jagged wound. So, too, had it torn and wounded something deep and hidden in Magnolia's soul. Suddenly she had a horror of the great river whose treacherous secret fangs had struck so poisonously. The sight of the yellow turbid flood sickened her; yet held her hypnotized. Now she thought that she must run from it, with her husband and her child, to safety. Now she knew that she never could be content away from it. She wanted to flee. She longed to stay. This, if ever, was her chance. But the river had Captain Andy. Somewhere in its secret coils he lay. She could not leave him. On the rivers the three great mysteries—Love and Birth and Death—had been revealed to her. All that she had known of happiness and tragedy and tranquillity and adventure and romance and fulfilment was bound up in the rivers. Their willow-fringed banks framed her world. The motley figures that went up and down upon them or that dwelt on their shores were her people. She knew them; was of them. The Mississippi had her as surely as it had little Andy Hawks.

"Well, we're talking about it, ain't we?" Mrs. Hawks now demanded.

"I mean—the repairs are going to be quite expensive. She'll be laid up for a month or more, right in the season. Now's the time to decide whether we're going to try to run her ourselves just as if Papa were still——"

"I can see you've been talking things over pretty hard and fast with Ravenal. Well, I'll tell you what we're going to do, miss. We're going to run her ourselves—leastways, I am."

"But, Mama!"

"Your pa left no will. Hawks all over. I've as much say-so as you have. More. I'm his widow. You won't see me willing to throw away the good-will of a business that it's taken years to build up. The boat's insurance'll take care of the repairs. Your pa's life insurance is paid up, and quite a decent sum—for him. I saw to that. You'll get your share, I'll get mine. The boat goes on like it always has. No Thebes for me. You'll go on playing ingénue leads: Ravenal juvenile. Kim——"

"No!" cried Magnolia much as Parthy had, years before. "Not Kim."

"Why not?"

There was about the Widow Hawks a terrifying and invincible energy. Her black habiliments of woe billowed about her like the sable wings of a destroying angel. With Captain Andy gone, she would appoint herself commander of the Cotton Blossom Floating Palace Theatre. Magnolia knew that. Who, knowing Parthy, could imagine it otherwise? She would appoint herself commander of their lives. Magnolia was no weakling. She was a woman of mettle. But no mettle could withstand the sledge-hammer blows of Parthy Ann Hawks' iron.

It was impossible that such an arrangement could hold. From the first Ravenal rejected it. But Magnolia's pleadings for at least a trial won him over, but grudgingly.

"It won't work, Nola, I tell you. We'll be at each other's throats. She's got all kinds of plans. I can see them whirling around in her eye."

"But you will try to be patient, won't you, Gay? For my sake and Kim's?"

But they had not been out a week before mutiny struck the *Cotton Blossom*. The first to go was Windy. Once his great feet were set toward the gangplank there was no stopping him. He was over seventy now, but he looked not an hour older than when he had come aboard the *Cotton Blossom* almost fifteen years before. To the irate widow he spoke briefly but with finality.

"You're Hawks' widow. That's why I said I'd take her same's if Andy was alive. I thought Nollie's husband would boss this boat, but seems you're running it. Well, ma'am, I ain't no petticoat-pilot. I'm off the end of this trip down. Young Tanner'll come aboard there and pilot you."

"Tanner! Who's he? How d'you know I want him? I'm running this boat."

"You better take him, Mrs. Hawks, ma'am. He's young, and not set in his ways, and likely won't mind your nagging. I'm too old. Lost my taste for the rivers, anyway, since Cap went. Lost my nerve, too, seems like. . . . Well, ma'am, I'm going."

And he went.

Changes came then, tripping on each other's heels. Mis' Means stayed, and little weak-chested Mr. Means. Frank had gone after Magnolia's marriage. Ralph left.

Parthy met these difficulties and defeats with magnificent generalship. She seemed actually to thrive on them. Do this. Do that. Ravenal's right eyebrow was cocked in a perpetual circumflex of disdain. One could feel the impact of opposition whenever the two came together. Every fibre of Ravenal's silent secretive nature was taut in rejection of this managerial mother-in-law. Every nerve and muscle of that energetic female's frame tingled with enmity toward this suave soft-spoken contemptuous husband of her daughter.

Finally, "Choose," said Gaylord Ravenal, "between your mother and me."

Magnolia chose. Her decision met with such terrific opposition from Parthy as would have shaken any woman less determined and less in love.

"Where you going with that fine husband of yours? Tell me that!"

"I don't know."

"I'll warrant you don't. No more does he. Why're you going? You've got a good home on the boat."

"Kim . . . school . . ."

"Fiddlesticks!"

Magnolia took the plunge. "We're not—I'm not—Gay's not happy any more on the rivers."

"You'll be a sight unhappier on land before you're through, make no mistake about that, young lady. Where'll you go? Chicago, h'm? What'll you do there? Starve, and worse. I know. Many's the time you'll wish yourself back here."

Magnolia, nervous, apprehensive, torn, now burst into sudden rebellion against the iron hand that had gripped her all these years.

"How do you know? How can you be so sure? And even if you are right, what of it? You're always trying to keep people from doing the things they want to do. You're always wanting people to live cautiously. You fought to keep Papa from buying the *Cotton Blossom* in the first place, and made his life a hell. And now you won't leave it. You didn't want me to act. You didn't want me to marry Gay. You didn't want me to have Kim. Maybe you were right. Maybe I shouldn't have done any of those things. But how do you know? You can't twist people's lives around like that, even if you twist them right. Because how do you know that even when you're right you mayn't be wrong? If Papa had listened to you, we'd be living in Thebes. He'd be alive, probably. I'd be married to the butcher, maybe. You can't do it. Even God lets people have their own way, though they have to fall down and break their necks to find out they were wrong. . . . You can't do it . . . and you're glad when it turns out badly . . ."

She was growing incoherent.

Back of Parthy's opposition to their going was a deep relief of which even she was unaware, and whose existence she would have denied had she been informed of it. Her business talent, so long dormant, was leaping into life. Her energy was cataclysmic. One would almost have said she was happy. She discharged actors, crew; engaged actors, crew. Ordered supplies. Spoke of shifting to an entirely new territory the following year—perhaps to the rivers of North Carolina and Maryland. She actually did this, though not until much later. Magnolia, years afterward reading her mother's terse and maddening letters, would be seized with a nostalgia not for the writer but for the lovely-sounding places of which she wrote—though they probably were as barren and unpicturesque as the river towns of the Mississippi and Ohio and Big Sandy and Kanawha. "We're playing the town of Bath, on the Pamlico River," Parthy's letter would say. Or, "We had a good week at Queenstown, on the Sassafras."

Magnolia, looking out into the gray Chicago streets, slippery with black ice, thick with the Lake Michigan fog, would repeat the names over to herself. Bath on the Pamlico. Queenstown on the Sassafras.

Mrs. Hawks, at parting, was all for Magnolia's retaining her financial share in the *Cotton Blossom*, the money accruing therefrom to be paid at regular intervals. In this she was right. She knew Ravenal. In her hard and managing way she loved her daughter; wished to insure her best interests. But Magnolia and Ravenal preferred to sell their share outright if she would buy. Ravenal would probably invest it in some business, Magnolia said.

"Yes—monkey business," retorted Mrs. Hawks. Then added, earnestly, "Now mind, don't you come snivelling to me when it's gone and you and your child haven't a penny to bless yourselves with. For that's what it'll come to in the end. Mark my words. I don't say I wouldn't be happy to see you and Kim back. But not him. When he's run through every penny of your money, he needn't look to me for more. You can come back to the boat; you and Kim. I'll look for you. But him! Never!"

The two women faced each other, and they were no longer mother and daughter but two forces opposing each other with all the strength that lay in the deep and powerful nature of both.

Magnolia made one of those fine speeches. "I wouldn't come to you for help—not if I were starving to death, and Kim too."

"Oh, there's worse things than starving to death."

"I wouldn't come to you no matter what."

"You will, just the same. I'd take my oath on that."

"I never will."

Secretly she was filled with terror at leaving the rivers; for the rivers, and the little inaccessible river towns, and the indolent and naïve people of those towns whose very presence in them confessed them failures, had with the years taken on in Magnolia's eyes the friendly aspect of the accustomed. Here was comfort assured; here were friends; here the ease

that goes with familiarity. Even her mother's bristling generalship had
in it a protective quality. The very show boat was a second mother,
shielding her from the problems and cares that beset the land-dweller.
The *Cotton Blossom* had been a little world in itself on which life was a
thing detached, dream-like, narcotic.

As Magnolia Ravenal, with her husband and her child, turned from
this existence of ease to the outside world of which she already had had
one bitter taste, she was beset by hordes of fears and doubts. Yet opposing these, and all but vanquishing them, was the strong love of
adventure—the eager curiosity about the unknown—which had always
characterized her and her dead father, the little captain, and caused
them both to triumph, thus far, over the clutching cautious admonitions
of Parthenia Ann Hawks.

Fright and anticipation; nostalgia and curiosity; a soaring sense of
freedom at leaving her mother's too-protective wing; a pang of com-
punction that she should feel this unfilial surge of relief.

They were going. You saw the three of them scrambling up the steep
river bank to the levee (perhaps for the last time, Magnolia thought
with a great pang. And within herself a voice cried no! no!) Ravenal
slim, cool, contained; Magnolia whiter than usual, and frankly tearful;
the child Kim waving an insouciant farewell with both small fists. They
carried no bundles, no parcels, no valises. Ravenal disdained to carry
parcels; he did not permit those of his party to carry them. Two Negroes
in tattered and faded blue overalls made much of the luggage, stowing
it inefficiently under the seats and over the floor of the livery rig which
had been hired to take the three to the nearest railway station, a good
twelve miles distant.

The *Cotton Blossom* troupe was grouped on the forward deck to see
them off. The *Cotton Blossom* lay, smug, safe, plump, at the water's
edge. A passing side-wheeler, flopping ponderously downstream, sent
little flirty waves across the calm waters to her, and set her to palpitating
coyly. Good-bye! Good-bye! Write, now. Mis' Means' face distorted in a
ridiculous pucker of woe. Ravenal in the front seat with the driver.
Magnolia and Kim in the back seat with the luggage protruding at
uncomfortable angles all about them. Parthenia Ann Hawks, the better
to see them, had stationed herself on the little protruding upper deck,
forward—the deck that resembled a balcony much like that on the old
Cotton Blossom. The livery nags started with a lurch up the dusty
village street. They clattered across the bridge toward the upper road.
Magnolia turned for a last glimpse through her tears. There stood
Parthenia Ann Hawks, silhouetted against sky and water, a massive and
almost menacing figure in her robes of black—tall, erect, indomitable.

Her face was set. The keen eyes gazed, unblinking, across the sunlit waters. One arm was raised in a gesture of farewell. Ruthless, unconquerable, headstrong, untamed, terrible.

"She's like the River," Magnolia thought, through her grief, in a sudden flash of vision. "She's the one, after all, who's like the Mississippi."

A bend in the upper road. A clump of sycamores. The river, the show boat, the silent black-robed figure were lost to view.

XIII

THE most casual onlooker could gauge the fluctuations of the Ravenal fortunes by any one of three signs. There was Magnolia Ravenal's sealskin sacque; there was Magnolia Ravenal's diamond ring; there was Gaylord Ravenal's malacca cane. Any or all of these had a way of vanishing and reappearing in a manner that would have been baffling to one not an habitué of South Clark Street, Chicago. Of the three, the malacca stick, though of almost no tangible value, disappeared first and oftenest, for it came to be recognized as an I O U by every reputable Clark Street pawnbroker. Deep in a losing game of faro at Jeff Hankins' or Mike McDonald's, Ravenal would summon a Negro boy to him. He would hand him the little ivory-topped cane. "Here—take this down to Abe Lipman's, corner Clark and Monroe. Tell him I want two hundred dollars. Hurry." Or: "Run over to Goldsmith's with this. Tell him a hundred."

The black boy would understand. In ten minutes he would return minus the stick and bearing a wilted sheaf of ten-dollar bills. If Ravenal's luck turned, the cane was redeemed. If it still stayed stubborn, the diamond ring must go; that failing, then the sealskin sacque. Ravenal, contrary to the custom of his confrères, wore no jewellery; possessed none. There were certain sinister aspects of these outward signs, as when, for example, the reigning sealskin sacque was known to skip an entire winter.

Perhaps none of these three symbols was as significant a betrayal of the Ravenal finances as was Gay Ravenal's choice of a breakfasting place. He almost never breakfasted at home. This was a reversion to one of the habits of his bachelor days; was, doubtless, a tardy rebellion, too, against the years spent under Mrs. Hawks' harsh régime. He always had hated those *Cotton Blossom* nine o'clock family breakfasts ominously presided over by Parthy in cap and curl papers.

Since their coming to Chicago Gay liked to breakfast between eleven and twelve, and certainly never rose before ten. If the Ravenal luck was high, the meal was eaten in leisurely luxury at Billy Boyle's Chop House between Clark and Dearborn streets. This was most agreeable, for at Billy Boyle's, during the noon hour, you encountered Chicago's sporting blood—political overlords, gamblers, jockeys, actors, reporters—these last mere nobodies—lean and somewhat morose young fellows vaguely known as George Ade, Brand Whitlock, John McCutcheon, Pete Dunne. Here the news and gossip of the day went round. Here you saw the Prince Albert coat, the silk hat, the rattling cuffs, the glittering collar, the diamond stud of the professional gamester. Old Carter Harrison, Mayor of Chicago, would drop in daily, a good twenty-five-cent cigar waggling between his lips as he greeted this friend and that. In came the brokers from the Board of Trade across the way. Smoke-blue air. The rich heavy smell of thick steaks cut from prime Western beef. Massive glasses of beer through which shone the pale amber of light brew, or the seal-brown of dark. The scent of strong black coffee. Rye bread pungent with caraway. Little crisp round breakfast rolls sprinkled with poppy-seed.

Calories, high blood pressure, vegetable luncheons, golf, were words not yet included in the American everyday vocabulary. Fried potatoes were still considered a breakfast dish, and a meatless meal was a snack.

Here it was, then, that Gay Ravenal, slim, pale, quiet, elegant, liked best to begin his day; listening charmingly and attentively to the talk that swirled about him—talk of yesterday's lucky winners in Gamblers' Alley, at Prince Varnell's place, or Jeff Hankins' or Mike McDonald's; of the Washington Park racetrack entries; of the new blonde girl at Hetty Chilson's, of politics in their simplest terms. Occasionally he took part in this talk, but like most professional gamblers, his was not the conversational gift. He was given credit for the astuteness he did not possess merely on the strength of his cool evasive glance, his habit of listening and saying little, and his bland poker face.

"Ravenal doesn't say much but there's damned little he misses. Watch him an hour straight and you can't make out from his face whether he's cleaning up a thousand or losing his shirt." An enviable Clark Street reputation.

Still, this availed him nothing when funds were low. At such times he eschewed Billy Boyle's and breakfasted meagrely instead at the Cock-eyed Bakery just east of Clark. That famous refuge for the temporarily insolvent was so named because of the optical peculiarity of the lady who owned it and who dispensed its coffee and sinkers. This refreshment cost ten cents. The coffee was hot, strong, revivifying; the sinkers crisp and fresh. Every Clark Street gambler was, at one time or another, through the vagaries of Lady Luck, to be found moodily munching the plain fare that made up the limited menu to be had at the Cockeyed Bakery. For that matter lacking even the modest sum required for this sustenance, he knew that there he would be allowed to "throw up a tab" until luck should turn.

Many a morning Gaylord Ravenal, dapper, nonchalant, sartorially exquisite, fared forth at eleven with but fifty cents in the pocket of his excellently tailored pants. Usually, on these occasions, the malacca stick was significantly absent. Of the fifty cents, ten went for the glassy shoeshine; twenty-five for a boutonnière; ten for coffee and sinkers at the Cockeyed Bakery. The remaining five cents stayed in his pocket as a sop to the superstition that no coin breeds no more coins. Stopping first to look in a moment at Weeping Willy Mangler's, or at Reilly's pool room for a glance at the racing chart, or to hear a bit of the talk missed through his enforced absence from Boyle's, he would end at Hankins' or McDonald's, there to woo fortune with nothing at all to offer as oblation. But affairs did not reach this pass until after the first year.

It was incredible that Magnolia Ravenal could so soon have adapted herself to the life in which she now moved. Yet it was explicable, perhaps, when one took into consideration her inclusive nature. She was interested, alert, eager—and still in love with Gaylord Ravenal. Her life on the rivers had accustomed her to all that was bizarre in humanity. Queenie and Jo had been as much a part of her existence as Elly and Schultzy. The housewives in the little towns, the Negroes lounging on the wharves, the gamblers in the river-front saloons, the miners of the coal belt, the Northern fruit-pickers, the boatmen, the Southern poor whites, the Louisiana aristocracy, all had passed in fantastic parade before her ambient eyes. And she, too, had marched in a parade, a figure as gorgeous, as colourful as the rest.

Now, in this new life, she accepted everything, enjoyed everything with a naïveté that was, perhaps, her greatest charm. It was, doubtless, the thing that held the roving Ravenal to her. Nothing shocked her; this was her singularly pure and open mind. She brought to this new life an interest and a curiosity as fresh as that which had characterized the little girl who had so eagerly and companionably sat with Mr. Pepper, the pilot, in the bright cosy glass-enclosed pilot house atop the old *Creole Belle* on that first enchanting trip down the Mississippi to New Orleans.

To him she had said, "What's around that bend? . . . Now what's

coming? . . . How deep is it here? . . . What used to be there? . . .
What island is that?"

Mr. Pepper, the pilot, had answered her questions amply and with a
feeling of satisfaction to himself as he beheld her childish hunger for
knowledge being appeased.

Now she said to her husband with equal eagerness: "Who is that stout
woman with the pretty yellow-haired girl? What queer eyes they have!
. . . What does it mean when it says odds are two to one? . . . Why
do they call him Bath House John? . . . Who is that large woman in
the victoria, with the lovely sunshade? How rich her dress is, yet it's
plain. Why don't you introduce me to—— Oh! That! Hetty Chilson!
Oh! . . . Why do they call him Bad Jimmy Connerton? . . . But why
do they call it the Levee? It's really Clark Street, and no water anywhere
near, so why do they call it the Levee? . . . What's a percentage game?
. . . Hieronymus! What a funny word! . . . Mike McDonald? That!
Why, he looks like a farmer, doesn't he? A farmer in his Sunday-best
black clothes that don't fit him. The Boss of the Gamblers. Why do
they call his place 'The Store'? . . . Oh, Gay darling, I wish you
wouldn't. . . . Now don't frown like that. I just mean I—when I think
of Kim, I get scared because, how about Kim—I mean when she grows
up? . . . Why are they called owl cars? . . . But I don't understand
why Lipman lets you have money just for a cane that isn't worth more
than ten or twenty . . . How do pawnbrokers . . . Mont Tennes—what
a queer name! . . . Al Hankins? Oh, you're joking now. Really killed
by having a folding bed close up on him! Oh, I'll never again sleep in a
. . . Boiler Avenue? . . . Hooley's Theatre? . . . Cinquevalli? . . .
Fanny Davenport? . . . Derby Day? . . . Weber and Fields? . . . Sauterne? . . . Rector's? . . .

Quite another world about which to be curious—a world as sordid
and colourful and crude and passionate and cruel and rich and varied as
that other had been.

It had taken Ravenal little more than a year to dissipate the tidy fortune which had been Magnolia's share of Captain Andy's estate, including the *Cotton Blossom* interest. He had, of course, meant to double
the sum—to multiply it many times so that the plump thousands should
increase to tens—to hundreds of thousands. Once you had money—a
really respectable amount of it—it was simple enough to manipulate
that money so as to make it magically produce more and more money.

They had made straight for Chicago, at that period the gamblers'
paradise. When Ravenal announced this step, a little look of panic had
come into Magnolia's eyes. She was reluctant to demur at his plans. It
was the thing her mother always had done when her father had pro-

posed a new move. Always Captain Andy's enthusiasm had suffered the
cold douche of Parthy's disapproval. At the prospect of Chicago, the old
haunts, congenial companions, the restaurants, the theatres, the races,
Ravenal had been more elated than she had ever seen him. He had become almost loquacious. He could even be charming to Mrs. Hawks, now
that he was so nearly free of her. That iron woman had regarded him
as her enemy to the last and, in making over to Magnolia the goodish
sum of money which was due her, had uttered dire predictions, all of
which promptly came true.

That first year in Chicago was a picture so kaleidoscopic, so extrava-
gant, so ridiculous that even the child Kim retained in her memory's
eye something of its colour and pageantry. This father and mother in
their twenties seemed really little older than their child. Certainly there
was something pathetically childish in their evident belief that they
could at once spend their money and keep it intact. Just a fur coat—
what was that! Bonnets. A smart high yellow trap. Horses. The races.
Suppers. A nursemaid for Kim. Magnolia knew nothing of money. She
never had had any. On the *Cotton Blossom* money was a commodity of
which one had little need.

On coming to Chicago they had gone directly to the Sherman House.
Compared with this, that first visit to Chicago before Kim's birth had
been a mere picnic jaunt. Ravenal was proud of his young wife and of
his quiet, grave big-eyed child; of the nursemaid in a smart uniform; of
the pair of English hackneys which he sometimes allowed Magnolia to
drive, to her exquisite delight. Magnolia had her first real evening dress,
cut décolleté; tasted champagne; went to the races at the Washington
Park race track; sat in a box at Hooley's; was horrified at witnessing the
hootchie-kootchie dance on the Midway Plaisance at the World's Fair.

The first fur coat was worthy of note. The wives of the well-to-do wore
sealskin sacques as proof of their husband's prosperity. Magnolia descended to these later. But the pelts which warmed her during that first
winter of Chicago lake blasts and numbing cold had been cunningly
matched in Paris, and French fingers had fashioned them into a wrap.

Ravenal had selected it for her, of course. He always accompanied her
on her shopping trips. He liked to loll elegantly at ease like a pasha while
the keen-eyed saleswomen brought out this gown and that for his expert
inspection. To these alert ladies it was plain to see that Magnolia knew
little enough about chic attire. The gentleman, though—he knew what
was what. Magnolia had been aghast at the cost of that first fur coat,
but then, how should she know of such things? Between them, she and
Parthy had made most of the costumes she had worn in her *Cotton
Blossom* days, both for stage and private use. The new coat was a black

astrakhan jacket; the fur lay in large smooth waves known as baby lamb. Magnolia said it made her feel like a cannibal to wear a thing like that. The salesladies did not smile at this, but that was all right because Magnolia had not intended that they should. The revers and cuffs were of Russian sable, dark and rich and deep; and it had large mutton-leg sleeves—large enough to contain her dress sleeves comfortably, with a little expert aid in the way of stuffing. "Stuff my sleeves in," was one of the directions always given a gentleman when he assisted a lady with her wrap.

This royal garment had cost—— "Oh, Gay!" Magnolia had protested, in a low shocked voice (but not so low that the sharp-eared saleswomen failed to hear it)—"Oh, Gay! I honestly don't think we ought——"

"Mrs. Potter Palmer," spoke up the chief saleswoman in a voice at once sharp and suave, "has a coat identically similar. They are the only two of the kind in the whole country. To tell you the truth, I think the sable skins on this garment of madam's are just a little finer than Mrs. Palmer's. Though perhaps it's just that madam sets it off better, being so young and all."

He liked her to wear, nestling in the rich depths of the sable revers, a bunch of violets. For the theatre she had one of those new winged bonnets, representing a butterfly, cunningly contrived of mousseline de soie wired and brilliantly spangled so that it quivered and trembled with the movements of her head and sparkled enchantingly. Kim adored the smell of the violet-scented creature who kissed her good-night and swept out, glittering. The impression must have gone deep, deep into the childish mind, for twenty years later she still retained a sort of story-book mental picture of this black-haired creamy mother who would come in late of a winter afternoon laughing and bright-eyed after a drive up Grand Boulevard in the sleigh behind the swift English hackneys. This vision would seem to fill the warm room with a delightful mixture of violets, and fur, and cold fresh air and velvet and spangles and love and laughter. Kim would plunge her face deep into the soft scented bosom.

"Oh, Gay, do see how she loves the violets! You won't mind if I take them off and put them here in this glass so she—— No, you mustn't buy me any fresh ones. Please! I wish she didn't look quite so much like me . . . her mouth . . . but it's going to be a great wide one, like mine. . . . Oh, Bernhardt! Who wants her little girl to look like Bernhardt! Besides, Kim isn't going to be an actress."

At the end of a year or so of this the money was gone—simply gone. Of course, it hadn't been only the hackneys, and the races, and the trap, and the furs, and the suppers and the theatres and dresses and Gay's fine garments and the nurse and the hotel. For, as Ravenal explained, the hackneys hadn't even been pure-blooded, which would have brought them up to one thousand each. He had never been really happy about them, because of a slight blot on their family escutcheon which had brought them down to a mere six hundred apiece. This flaw was apparent, surely, to no one who was not an accredited judge at a horse show. Yet when Ravenal and Magnolia on Derby Day joined the gay stream of tallyhos, wagonettes, coaches, phaetons, tandems, cocking carts, and dog-carts sweeping up Michigan Avenue and Grand Boulevard toward the Washington Park race track he was likely to fall into one of his moody silences and to flick the hackneys with little contemptuous cuts of the long lithe whip in a way that only they—and Magnolia—understood. On such occasions he called them nags.

"Ah! That off nag broke again. That's because they're not thorough-breds."

"But, Gay, you're hurting their mouths, sawing like that."

"Please, Nola. This isn't a Mississippi barge I'm driving."

She learned many things that first year, and saw so much that part of what she saw was mercifully soon forgotten. You said Darby Day, very English. You pretended not to mind when your husband went down to speak to Hetty Chilson and her girls in their box. For that matter, you pretended not to see Hetty Chilson and her girls at all, though they had driven out in a sort of private procession of victorias, landaus, broughams, and were by far the best-dressed women at the races. They actually set the styles, Gay had told her. Hetty Chilson's girls wore rich, quiet, almost sedate clothes; and no paint on their faces. They seemed an accepted part of the world in which Gaylord Ravenal moved. Even in the rough life of the rivers, Magnolia had always understood that women of Hetty Chilson's calling simply did not exist in the public sense. They were not of the substance of everyday life, but were shadows, sinister, menacing, evil. But with this new life of Magnolia's came the startling knowledge that these ladies played an important part in the social and political life of this huge sprawling Mid-western city. This stout, blonde, rather handsome woman who carried herself with an air of prosperous assurance; whose shrewd keen glance and hearty laugh rather attracted you—this one was Hetty Chilson. The horsewomen you saw riding in the Lincoln Park bridle path, handsomely habited in black close-fitting riding clothes, were, likely as not, Hetty Chilson's girls. She was actually a power in her way. When strangers were shown places of interest in Chicago—the Potter Palmer castle on Lake Shore Drive, the Art Museum, the Stockyards, the Auditorium Hotel, the great mansions of Phil Armour and his son on Michigan Avenue, with the garden embracing an entire city block—Hetty Chilson's place, too, was pointed out (with a lowering of the voice, of course, and a little leer, and perhaps an elbow dug into the ribs). A substantial brick house on Clark Street, near Polk, with two lions, carved in stone, absurdly guarding its profane portals.

"Hetty Chilson's place," Gay explained to his wide-eyed young wife, "is like a club. You're likely to find every prominent politician in Chicago there, smoking and having a sociable drink. And half the political plots that you read about in the newspapers later are hatched at Hetty's. She's as smart as they make 'em. Bought a farm, fifteen acres, out at Ninetieth and State, for her father and mother. And she's got a country place out on the Kankakee River, near Momence—about sixty miles south of here —that's known to have one of the finest libraries in the country. Cervantes—Balzac—rare editions. Stable full of horses—rose garden——"

"But, Gay dear!"

You saw Hetty driving down State Street during the shopping hour in her Kimball-made Victoria, an equipage such as royalty might have used, its ebony body fashioned by master craftsmen, its enamel as rich and deep and shining as a piano top. Her ample skirts would be spread upon the plum-coloured cushions. If it was summer the lace ruffles of her sunshade would plume gently in the breeze. In winter her mink coat swathed her full firm figure. One of her girls sat beside her, faultlessly dressed, pale, unvivacious. Two men in livery on the box. Harness that shone with polished metal and jingled splendidly. Two slim, quivering, high-stepping chestnuts. Queen of her world—Chicago's underworld.

"But, Gay dear!"

"Well, how about France!"

"France?"

"How about the women you used to read about—learned about them in your history books, for that matter, at school? Pompadour and Maintenon and Du Barry! Didn't they mix up in the politics of their day— and weren't they recognized? Courtesans, every one of them. You think just because they wore white wigs and flowered silk hoops and patches——"

A little unaccustomed flush surged over Magnolia's pallor—the deep, almost painful red of indignation. She was an inexperienced woman, but she was no fool. These last few months had taught her many things. Also the teachings of her school-teacher mother had not, after all, been quite forgotten, it appeared.

"She's a common woman of the town, Gaylord Ravenal. All the wigs and patches and silks in the world wouldn't make her anything else. She's no more a Du Barry than your Hinky Dink is a—uh—Mazarin."

It was as though he took a sort of perverse pleasure in thus startling her. It wasn't that she was shocked in the prim sense of the word. She was bewildered and a little frightened. At such times the austere form and the grim visage of Parthenia Ann Hawks would rise up before her puzzled eyes. What would Parthy have said of these unsavoury figures now passing in parade before Magnolia's confused vision—Hetty Chilson, Doc Haggerty, Mike McDonald, "Prince" Varnell, Effie Hankins? Uneasy though she was, Magnolia could manage to smile at the thought of her mother's verbal destruction of this raffish crew. There were no half tones in Parthy's vocabulary. A hussy was a hussy; a rake a rake. But her father, she thought, would have been interested in all this, and more than a little amused. His bright brown eyes would have missed nothing; the little nimble figure would have scampered inquisitively up and down the narrow and somewhat sinister lane that lay between Washington and Madison streets, known as Gamblers' Alley; he would have taken a turn at faro; appraised the Levee ladies at their worth; visited Sam T. Jack's Burlesque Show over on Madison, and Kohl & Middleton's Museum, probably, and Hooley's Theatre certainly. Nothing in Chicago's Levee life would have escaped little Captain Andy, and nothing would have changed him.

"See it all, Nollie," he had said to her in the old *Cotton Blossom* days, when Parthy would object to their taking this or that jaunt ashore between shows. "Don't you believe 'em when they say that what you don't know won't hurt you. Biggest lie ever was. See it all and go your own way and nothing'll hurt you. If what you see ain't pretty, what's the odds! See it anyway. Then next time you don't have to look."

Magnolia, gazing about her, decided that she was seeing it all.

The bulk of the money had gone at faro. The suckers played roulette, stud poker, hazard, the bird-cage, chuck-a-luck (the old army game). But your gambler played faro. Faro was Gaylord Ravenal's game, and he played at Hankins'—not at George Hankins' where they catered to the cheap trade who played percentage games—but at Jeff Hankins' or Mike McDonald's where were found the highest stakes in Chicago. Faro was not a game with Ravenal—it was for him at once his profession, his science, his drug, his drink, his mistress. He had, unhappily, as was so often the case with your confirmed gambler, no other vice. He rarely drank, and then abstemiously; smoked little and then a mild cigar, ate sparingly and fastidiously; eschewed even the diamond ring and shirt-stud of his kind.

The two did not, of course, watch the money go, or despair because it would soon be gone. There seemed to be plenty of it. There always would be enough. Next week they would invest it securely. Ravenal had inside tips on the market. He had heard of a Good Thing. This was not the right time, but They would let him know when the magic moment was at hand. In the meantime there was faro. And there were the luxurious hotel rooms with their soft thick carpets, and their big comfortable beds; ice water tinkling at the door in answer to your ring; special dishes to tempt the taste of Mr. Ravenal and his lady. The sharp-eyed gentleman in evening clothes who stood near the little ticket box as you entered the theatre said, "Good-evening, Mr. Ravenal," when they went to Hooley's or McVicker's or the Grand Opera House, or Kohl and Castle's. The heads of departments in Mandel's or Carson Pirie's or even Marshall Field's said, "I have something rather special to show you, Mrs. Ravenal. I thought of you the minute it came in."

Sometimes it seemed to Magnolia that the *Cotton Blossom* had been only a phantom ship—the rivers a dream—a legend.

It was all very pleasant and luxurious and strange. And Magnolia tried not to mind the clang of Clark Street by day and by night. The hideous cacophony of noise invaded their hotel apartment and filled its every corner. She wondered why the street-car motormen jangled their warning bells so persistently. Did they do it as an antidote to relieve their own jangled nerves? *Pay*-pes! MO'-nin' *pay*-pes! Crack! Crack! Crackcrackcrack! The shooting gallery across the street. Someone passing the bedroom door, walking heavily and clanking the metal disk of his room key. The sound of voices, laughter, from the street, and the unceasing shuffle of footsteps on stone. Whee-e-e-e-e! Whoop-a! Ye-e-eow! A drunkard. She knew about that, too. Part of her recently acquired knowledge. Ravenal had told her about Big Steve Rowan, the three-hundred-pound policeman, who, partly because of his goatee and moustache, and partly because of his expert manipulation of his official weapon, was called the Jack of Clubs.

"You'll never see Big Steve arrest a drunk at night," Gay had explained to her, laughing. "No, sir! Nor any other Clark Street cop if he can help it. If they arrest a man they have to appear against him next morning at the nine o'clock police court. That means getting up early. So if he's able to navigate at all, they pass him on down the street from corner to corner until they get him headed west somewhere, or north across the bridge. Great system."

All this was amusing and colourful, perhaps, but scarcely conducive to tranquillity and repose. Often Magnolia, lying awake by the side of the sleeping man, or lying awake awaiting his late return, would close her stinging eyelids the better to visualize and sense the deep velvet silence of the rivers of her girlhood—the black velvet nights, quiet, quiet. The lisping cluck-suck of the water against the hull.

Clang! MO'-nin' *pay*-pes! Crack! E-e-eee-yow!

And then, suddenly, one day: "But, Gay dear, how do you mean you haven't one hundred dollars? It's for that bronze-green velvet that you like so much, though I always think it makes me look sallow. You did urge me to get it, you know, dear. And now this is the third time they've sent the bill. So if you'll give me the money—or write a check, if you'd rather."

"I tell you I haven't got it, Nola."

"Oh, well, to-morrow'll do. But please be sure to-morrow, because I hate——"

"I can't be any surer to-morrow than I am to-day. I haven't got a hundred dollars in the world. And that's a fact."

Even after he had finished explaining, she did not understand; could not believe it; continued to stare at him with those great dark startled eyes.

Bad luck. At what? Faro. But, Gay—thousands! Well, thousands don't last for ever. Took a flyer. Flyer? Yes. A tip on the market. Market? The stock market. Stock? Oh, you wouldn't understand. But all of it, Gay? Well, some of it lost at faro. Where? Hankins'. How much? What does it matter?—it's gone. But, Gay, how much at faro? Oh, a few thousands. Five? Y-y-yes. Yes, five. More than that? Well, nearer ten, probably.

She noticed then that the malacca cane was gone. She slipped her diamond ring off her finger. Gave it to him. With the years, that became an automatic gesture.

Thus the change in their mode of living did not come about gradually. They were wafted, with Cinderella-like celerity, from the coach-and-four to the kitchen ashes. They left the plush and ice water and fresh linen and rich food and luxurious service of the Sherman House for a grubby little family hotel that was really a sort of actors' boarding house, on the north side, just across the Clark Street bridge, on Ontario Street. It was, Ravenal said, within convenient walking distance of places.

"What places?" Magnolia asked. But she knew. A ten minutes' saunter brought you to Gamblers' Alley. In the next fifteen years there was never a morning when Gaylord Ravenal failed to prove this interesting geographical fact.

XIV

THE Ravenal reverses, if they were noticed at all in Gamblers' Alley, went politely unremarked.

There was a curious and definite code of honour among the frequenters of Chicago's Levee. You paid your gambling debts. You never revealed your own financial status by way of conversation. You talked little. You maintained a certain physical, sartorial, and social standard in the face of all reverses. There were, of course, always unmistakable signs to be read even at the most passing glance. You drew your conclusions; made no comment. If you were seen to breakfast for days—a week—two weeks—at the Cockeyed Bakery, you were greeted by your confrères with the same suavity that would have been accorded you had you been standing treat at Billy Boyle's or the Palmer House. Your shoe might be cracked, but it must shine. Your linen might be frayed, but it must be clean. Your cheeks were perhaps a trifle hollow, but they must be shaven and smell pleasantly of bay rum. You might dine at Burkey and Milan's (Full Meal 15c.) with ravenous preliminary onslaughts upon the bread-and-butter and piccalilli. But you consumed, delicately and fastidiously, just so much and no more of the bountiful and rich repast spread out for your taking at Jeff Hankins' or at Mike McDonald's. Though your suit was shabby, it must bear the mark of that tailor to the well-dressed sporting man—Billy McLean. If you were too impecunious for Hetty Chilson's you disdained the window-tapping dives on Boiler Avenue and lower Clark Street and State; the sinister and foul shanties of Big Maud and her ilk. You bathed, shaved, dressed, ate, smoked with the same exotic care when you were broke as when luck was running your way. Your cigar was a mild one (also part of the code), and this mild one usually a dead one as you played. And no one is too broke for one cigar a day. Twelve o'clock—noon—found you awake. Twelve o'clock—midnight—found you awake. Somewhere between those hours you slept the deep sweet sleep of the abstemious. You were, in short, a gambler—and a gentleman.

Thus, when the Ravenals moved, perforce, from the comfort of the Sherman to the threadbare shabbiness of the Ontario Street boarding house, there was nothing in Gaylord Ravenal's appearance to tell the

tale. If his cronies knew of his financial straits, they said nothing. Magnolia had no women friends. During the year or more of their residence
in Chicago she had been richly content with Kim and Gay. The child
had a prim and winning gravity that gave her a curiously grown-up air.

"Do you know, Gay," Magnolia frequently said, "Kim sometimes
makes me feel so gawky and foolish and young. When she looks at me
after I've been amused about something, or am enthusiastic or excited
or—you know—anyway, she looks at me out of those big eyes of hers,
very solemn, and I feel—— Oh, Gay, you don't think she resembles—that
is—do you think she is much like Mama?"

"God forbid!" ejaculated Ravenal, piously.

Kim had been Magnolia's delight during the late morning hours and
the early afternoon. In company with the stolid nurse, they had fared
forth in search of such amusement as the city provided for a child
brought up amidst the unnatural surroundings of this one. The child
had grown accustomed to seeing her nurse stand finger on lips, eyes
commanding silence, before the closed door of her parents' room at ten
in the morning—at eleven, even—and she got it into her baby head that
this attitude, then, was the proper and normal one in which to approach
the closed door of that hushed chamber. Late one morning Magnolia,
in nightgown and silken wrapper, had opened this door suddenly to find
the child stationed there, silent, grave-eyed, admonitory, while in one
corner, against the door case, reposed the favourite doll of her collection
—a lymphatic blonde whose eyes had met with some unfortunate interior mishap which gave them a dying-calf look. This sprawling and inert lady was being shushed in a threatening and dramatic manner by the
sternly maternal Kim. There was, at sight of this, that which brought the
quick sting of tears to Magnolia's eyes. She gathered the child up in her
arms, kissed her passionately, held her close, brought her to Ravenal as
he lay yawning.

"Gay, look at her! She was standing by the door telling her doll not
to make any noise. She's only a baby. We don't pay enough attention
to her. Do you think I neglect her? Standing there by the door! And
it's nearly noon. Oh, Gay, we oughtn't to be living here. We ought to
be living in a house—a little house where it's quiet and peaceful and she
can play."

"Lovely," said Gay. "Thebes, for example. Now don't get dramatic,
Nola, for God's sake. I thought we'd finished with that."

With the change in their fortunes the English nurse had vanished
with the rest. She had gone, together with the hackneys, the high smart
yellow cart, the violets, the green velvets, the box seats at the theatre,
the champagne. She, or her counterpart, never returned, but many of

the lost luxuries did, from time to time. There were better days to come, and worse. Their real fortune gone, there now was something almost humdrum and methodical about the regularity of their ups and downs. There rarely was an intermediate state. It was feast or famine, always. They actually settled down to the life of a professional gambler and his family. Ravenal would have a run of luck at faro. Presto! Rooms at the Palmer House. A box at the races. The theatre. Supper at Rector's after the theatre. Hello, Gay! Evening, Mrs. Ravenal. Somebody's looking mighty lovely to-night. A new sealskin sacque. Her diamond ring on her finger. Two new suits of clothes for Ravenal, made by Billy Mc-Lean. A little dinner for Gay's friends at Cardinal Bemis's famous place on Michigan Avenue. You couldn't fool the Cardinal.

He would ask suavely, "What kind of a dinner, Mr. Ravenal?"

If Gay replied, "Oh—uh—a cocktail and a little red wine," Cardinal Bemis knew that luck was only so-so, and that the dinner was to be good, but plainish. But if, in reply to the tactful question, Gay said, magnificently, "A cocktail, Cardinal; claret, sauterne, champagne, and liqueurs," Bemis knew that Ravenal had had a real run of luck and prepared the canvasbacks boiled in champagne; or there were squabs or plover, with all sorts of delicacies, and the famous frozen watermelon that had been plugged, filled with champagne, put on ice for a day, and served in such chunks of scarlet fragrance as made the nectar and ambrosia of the gods seem poor, flavourless fare indeed.

Magnolia, when luck was high, tried to put a little money by as she had instinctively been prompted to do during those first months of their marriage, when they still were on the *Cotton Blossom*. But she rarely had money of her own. Gay, when he had ready cash, was generous—but not with the handing over of the actual coin itself.

"Buy yourself some decent clothes, Nola; and the kid. Tell them to send me the bill. That thing you're wearing is a terrible sight. It seems to me you haven't worn anything else for months." Which was true enough. There was something fantastic about the magnificence with which he ignored the reason for her not having worn anything else for months. It had been, certainly, her one decent garment during the lean period just passed, and she had cleaned and darned and refurbished to keep it so. Her experience in sewing during the old *Cotton Blossom* days stood her in good stead now.

There were times when even the Ontario Street hotel took on the aspect of unattainable luxury. That meant rock bottom. Then it was that the Ravenals took a room at three dollars a week in a frowzy rooming house on Ohio or Indiana or Erie; the Bloomsbury of Chicago. There you saw unshaven men, their coat collars turned up in artless at-

tempt to conceal the absence of linen, sallying forth, pail in hand, at ten
or eleven in the morning in search of the matutinal milk and rolls to accompany the coffee that was even now cooking over the gas jet. Morning
was a musty jade on these streets; nothing fresh and dewy and sparkling
about her. The ladies of the neighbourhood lolled huge, unwieldy,
flaccid, in wrappers. In the afternoon you saw them amazingly transformed into plump and pinkly powdered persons, snugly corseted, high-
heeled, rustling in silk petticoats, giving out a heady scent. They were
friendly voluble ladies who beamed on the pale slim Magnolia, and
said, "Won't you smile for me just a little bit? H'm?" to the sedate and
solemn-eyed Kim.

Magnolia, too, boiled coffee and eggs over the gas jet in these lean
times. Gravely she counted out the two nickels that would bring her
and Kim home from Lincoln Park on the street car. Lincoln Park was an
oasis—a life-giving breathing spot to the mother and child. They sallied
forth in the afternoon; left the gas jet, the three-dollar room, the musty
halls, the stout females behind them. There was the zoo; there was the
lake; there was the grass. If the lake was their choice it led inevitably to
tales of the rivers. It was in this way that the background of her mother's
life was first etched upon Kim's mind. The sight of the water always
filled Magnolia with a nostalgia so acute as to amount to an actual
physical pain.

The childish treble would repeat the words as the two sat on a park
bench facing the great blue sea that was Lake Michigan.

"You remember the boat, don't you, Kim?"

"Do I?" Kim's diction was curiously adult, due, doubtless, to the fact
that she had known almost no children.

"Of course you do, darling. Don't you remember the river, and
Grandma and Grandpa——"

"Cap'n!"

"Yes! I knew you remembered. And all the little darkies on the landing. And the band. And the steam organ. You used to put your hands
over your ears and run and hide, because it frightened you. And Jo and
Queenie."

"Tell me about it."

And Magnolia would assuage her own longing by telling and retelling
the things she liked to remember. The stories, with the years, became a
saga. Figures appeared, vanished, reappeared. The rivers wound through
the whole. Elly, Schultzy, Julie, Steve; the man in the box with the gun;
the old *Creole Belle* and Magnolia's first trip on the Mississippi; Mr.
Pepper and the pilot house; all these became familiar and yet legendary
figures and incidents to the child. They were her Three Bears, her Bo-

peep, her Red Riding Hood, her Cinderella. Magnolia must have painted these stories with the colour of life itself, for the child never wearied of them.

"Tell me the one about the time you were a little girl and Gra'ma locked you in the bedroom because she didn't want you to see the show and you climbed out of the window in your nightie . . ."

Kim Ravenal was probably the only white child north of the Mason and Dixon line who was sung to sleep to the tune of those plaintive, wistful Negro plantation songs which later were to come into such vogue as spirituals. They were the songs that Magnolia had learned from black Jo and from Queenie, the erstwhile rulers of the *Cotton Blossom* galley. Swing Low Sweet Chariot, she sang. O, Wasn't Dat a Wide River! And, of course, All God's Chillun Got Wings. Kim loved them. When she happened to be ill with some childhood ailment, they soothed her. Magnolia sang these songs, always, as she had learned to sing them in unconscious imitation of the soft husky Negro voice of her teacher. Through the years of Kim's early childhood, Magnolia's voice might have been heard thus wherever the shifting Ravenal fortunes had tossed the three, whether the red-plush luxury of the Sherman House, the respectable dulness of the family hotel, or the sordid fustiness of the cheap rooming house. Once, when they were living at the Sherman, Magnolia, seated in a rocking chair with Kim in her arms, had stopped suddenly in her song at a curious sound in the corridor. She had gone swiftly to the door, had opened it, and had been unable to stifle a little shriek of surprise and terror mingled. There stood a knot of black faces, teeth gleaming, eyes rolling. Attracted by the songs so rarely heard in the North, the Sherman House bell boys and waiters had eagerly gathered outside the closed door in what was, perhaps, as flattering and sincere a compliment as ever a singer received.

Never did child know such ups and downs as did this daughter of the Chicago gambler and the show-boat actress. She came to take quite for granted sudden and complete changes that would have disorganized any one more conventionally bred. One week she would find herself living in grubby quarters where the clammy fetid ghost of cabbage lurked always in the halls; the next would be a gay panorama of whisking waiters, new lace petticoats, drives along the lake front, ice cream for dessert, front seats at the matinée. The theatre bulked large in the life of the Ravenals. Magnolia loved it without being possessed of much discrimination with regard to it. Farce, comedy, melodrama—the whole gamut as outlined by Polonius—all held her interested, enthralled. Ravenal was much more critical than she. You saw him smoking in the lobby, bored, dégagé. It might be the opening of the rebuilt Lincoln Theatre on Clark

near Division, with Gustave Frohman's company playing The Charity
Ball.

"Oh, Gay, isn't it exciting!"

"I don't think much of it. Cheap-looking theatre, too, isn't it? They
might better have left it alone after it burned down."

Kim's introduction to the metropolitan theatre was when she was
taken, a mere baby, to see the spectacle America at the Auditorium. Before she was ten she had seen everyone from Julia Marlowe to Anna
Held; from Bernhardt to Lillian Russell. Gravely she beheld the antics
of the Rogers Brothers. As gravely saw Klaw and Erlanger's company
in Foxey Quiller.

"It isn't that she doesn't see the joke," Magnolia confided to Ravenal,
almost worriedly. "She actually doesn't seem to approve. Of course, I
suppose I ought to be glad that she prefers the more serious things, but
I wish she wouldn't seem quite so grown-up at ten. By the time she's
twenty she'll probably be spanking me and putting me to bed."

Certainly Magnolia was young enough for two. She was the sort of
theatre-goer who clutches the hand of her neighbour when stirred. When
Ravenal was absent Kim learned to sustain her mother at such emotional moments. They two frequently attended the theatre together.
Their precarious mode of living cut them off from sustained human
friendships. But the theatre was always there to stimulate them, to
amuse them, to make them forget or remember. There were long after-
noons to be filled, and many evenings as Ravenal became more and
more deeply involved in the intricacies of Chicago's night world.

There was, curiously enough, a pendulum-like regularity about his irregular life. His comings and goings could be depended on almost as
though he were a clerk or a humdrum bookkeeper. Though his fortunes
changed with bewildering rapidity, his habits remained the same. Indeed, he felt these changes much less than did Magnolia and Kim. No
matter what their habitation—cheap rooming house or expensive hotel
—he left at about the same hour each morning, took the same leisurely
course toward town, returned richer or poorer—but unruffled—well after
midnight. On his off nights he and Magnolia went to the theatre. Curiously, they seemed always to have enough money for that.

Usually they dwelt somewhere north, just the other side of the Chicago River, at that time a foul-smelling and viscid stream, with no drainage canal to deodorize it. Ravenal, in lean times, emerging from his
dingy hotel or rooming house on Ontario or Ohio, was as dapper, as
suave, as elegant as that younger Ravenal had been who, leaning against
the packing case on the wharf at New Orleans, had managed to triumph
over the handicap of a cracked boot. He would stand a moment, much

as he had stood that southern spring morning, coolly surveying the world about him. That his viewpoint was the dingy front stoop of a run-down Chicago rooming house and his view the sordid street that held it, apparently disturbed his equanimity not at all. On rising he had observed exactly the same niceties that would have been his had he enjoyed the services of a hotel valet. He bathed, shaved, dressed meticulously. Magnolia had early learned that the slatternly morning habits which she had taken for granted in the *Cotton Blossom* wives—Julie, Mis' Means, Mrs. Soaper, even the rather fastidious Elly—would be found inexcusable in the wife of Ravenal. The sternly utilitarian undergarments of Parthy's choosing had soon enough been done away with, to be replaced with a froth of lace and tucks and embroidery and batiste. The laundering of these was a pretty problem when faro's frown decreed Ohio Street.

Ravenal was spared these worrisome details. Once out of the dingy boarding house, he could take his day in his two hands and turn it over, like a bright, fresh-minted coin. Each day was a new start. How could you know that you would not break the bank! It had been done on a dollar.

Down the street Ravenal would stroll past the ship chandlers' and commission houses south of Ontario, to the swinging bridge that spanned the slimy river. There he would slacken his already leisurely pace, or even pause a moment, perhaps, to glance at the steamers tied up at the docks. There was an occasional sailboat. A three-masted schooner, *The Finney*, a grain boat, was in from up North. Over to Clark and Lake. You could sniff in the air the pleasant scent of coffee. That was Reid & Murdock's big warehouse a little to the east. He sometimes went a block out of his way just to sniff this delicious odour. A glittering shoeshine at the Sherman House or the Tremont.

"Good-morning, George."

"Mawnin' Mist' Ravenal! Mawnin'! Papah, suh?"

"Ah—n-n-no. No. H'm!" His fifty cents, budgeted, did not include the dispensing of those extra pennies for the *Times-Herald*, the *Inter-Ocean*, or the *Tribune*. They could be seen at McDonald's for nothing. A fine Chicago morning. The lake mist had lifted. That was one of the advantages of never rising early. Into the Cockeyed Bakery for breakfast. To-morrow it would be Boyle's. Surely his bad luck would break to-day. He felt it. Had felt it the moment he opened his eyes.

"Terrapin and champagne to-morrow, Nola. Feel it in my bones. I woke up with my palm itching, and passed a hunchback at Clark and Randolph last night."

"Why don't you let me give you your coffee and toast here this morning, Gay dear? It'll only take a minute. And it's so much better than the coffee you get at the—uh—downtown."

Ravenal, after surveying his necktie critically in the mirror of the crazy little bureau, would shrug himself into his well-made coat. "You know I never eat in a room in which I have slept."

Past the Court House; corner of Washington reached. Cut flowers in the glass case outside the basement florist's. A tapping on the glass with a coin, or a rapping on the pavement with his stick—if the malacca stick was in evidence. "Heh, Joe!"

Joe clattering up the wooden steps.

"Here you are, sir. All ready for you. Just came in fresh." A white carnation. Ravenal would sniff the spicy bloom, snap the brittle stem, thrust it through the buttonhole of his lapel.

A fine figure of a man from his boots to his hat. Young, handsome, well-dressed, leisurely. Joe, the Greek florist, pocketing his quarter, would reflect gloomily on luck—his own and that of others.

Ravenal might drop in a moment at Weeping Willy Mangler's, thence to Reilly's pool room near Madison, for a look at the racing odds. But no matter how low his finances, he scorned the cheaper gambling rooms that catered to the clerks and the working men. There was a great difference between Jeff Hankins' place and that of his brother, George. At George's place, and others of that class, barkers stood outside. "Game upstairs, gentlemen! Game upstairs! Come in and try your luck! Ten cents can make you a millionaire."

At George Hankins' the faro checks actually were ten cents. You saw there labouring men with their tin dinner pails, their boots lime-spattered, their garments reeking of cheap pipe tobacco. There, too, you found stud poker, roulette, hazard—percentage games. None of these for Ravenal. He played a gentleman's game, broke or flush.

This game he found at Mike McDonald's "The Store." Here he was at home. Here were excitement, luxury, companionship. Here he was Gaylord Ravenal. Fortune lurked just around the corner. At McDonald's his credit always was good for enough to start the play. On the first floor was the saloon, with its rich walnut panelling, its great mirrors, its tables of teakwood and ivory inlay, its paintings of lolling ladies. Chicago's saloons and gambling resorts vied with each other in rich and massive decoration. None of your soap-scrawled mirrors and fancy bottle structures for these. "Prince" Varnell's place had, for years, been famous for its magnificent built-in mantel of Mexican onyx, its great marble statue of the death of Cleopatra, its enormous Sèvres vases.

The second floor was Ravenal's goal. He did not even glance at the whirling of the elaborately inlaid roulette wheels. He nodded to the dealers and his greeting was deferentially returned. It was said that most of these men had come of fine old Southern families. They dressed the part. But McDonald himself looked like a farmer. His black clothes, though well made, never seemed to fit him. His black string tie never varied. Thin, short, gray-haired, Mike McDonald the Boss of the gamblers would have passed anywhere for a kindly rustic.

"Playing to-day, Mr. Ravenal?"

"Why, yes. Yes, I thought I'd play a while."

"Anything we can do to make you comfortable?"

"Well—uh—yes——"

McDonald would raise a benevolent though authoritative hand. His finger would summon a menial. "Dave, take care of Mr. Ravenal."

Ravenal joined the others then, a gentleman gambler among gentleman gamblers. A group smartly dressed like himself, well groomed, quiet, almost elegant. Most of them wore jewellery—a diamond scarf pin, a diamond ring, sometimes even a diamond stud, though this was frowned on by players of Ravenal's class. A dead cigar in the mouth of each. Little fine lines etched about their eyes. They addressed each other as "sir." Thank you, sir. . . . Yours I believe, sir. . . . They were quiet, quiet. Yet there was an electric vibration in the air above and about the faro table. Only the dealer seemed remote, detached, unmoved. An hour passed; two, three, four, five. The Negro waiters in very white starched aprons moved deferentially from group to group. One would have said that no favouritism was being shown, but they knew the piker from the plunger. Soft-voiced, coaxing: "Something to drink, suh? A little whisky, suh? Cigar? Might be you'd relish a little chicken white meat and a bottle of wine?"

Ravenal would glance up abstractedly. "Time is it?"

"Pushin' six o'clock, suh."

Ravenal might interrupt his game to eat something, but this was not his rule. He ate usually after he had finished his play for the day. It was understood that he and others of his stamp were the guests of McDonald or of Hankins. Twenty-five-cent cigars were to be had for the taking. Drinks of every description. Hot food of the choicest sort and of almost any variety could be ordered and eaten as though this were one's own house, and the servants at one's command. Hot soups and broths. Steaks. Chops. Hot birds. You could eat this at a little white-spread table alone, or with your companions, or you could have it brought to you as you played. On long tables in the adjoining room were spread the cold viands—roast chickens, tongue, sausages, cheese, joints of roast beef, salads. Everything about the place gave to its habitués the illusion of plenty, of ease, of luxury. Soft red carpets; great prism-hung chandeliers; the clink of ice; the scent of sappy cigars and rich food; the soft slap-slap of the cards; the low voices of the dealers. It was all friendly, relaxed, soothing. Yet when the dealer opened the little drawer that was so cleverly concealed under his side of the table—the money drawer with its orderly stacks of yellow-backs, and green-backs and gold and silver—you saw, if your glance was quick and sharp enough, the gleam of still another metal: the glittering, sinister blue-gray of steel.

A hundred superstitions swayed their play. Luck was a creature to be wooed, flattered, coaxed, feared. No jungle voodoo worshipper ever lent himself to simpler or more childish practices and beliefs than did these hard-faced men.

Sometimes Ravenal left the faro table penniless or even deeper in Mike McDonald's debt. His face at such times was not more impassive than the bucolic host's own. "Better luck next time, Mr. Ravenal."

"She's due to turn to-morrow, Mike. Watch out for me to-morrow. I'll probably clean you."

And if not to-morrow, to-morrow. Luck must turn, sooner or later. There! Five hundred! A thousand! Five thousand! Did you hear about Ravenal? Yes, he had a wonderful run. It happened in an hour. He walked out with ten thousand. More, some say.

On these nights Ravenal would stroll coolly home as on losing nights. Up Clark Street, the money in neat rolls in his pocket. There were almost no street robberies in those simpler Chicago days. If you were, like Ravenal, a well-dressed sporting looking man, strolling up Clark Street at midnight or thereabouts, you were likely to be stopped for the price of a meal. You gave it as a matter of course, unwrapping a bill, perhaps, from the roll you carried in your pocket.

They might be living in modest comfort at the Revere House on Clark and Austin. They might be living in decent discomfort at the little theatrical boarding house on Ontario. They might be huddled in actual discomfort in the sordid room of the Ohio Street rooming house. Be that as it may, Ravenal would take highhanded possession, but in a way so blithe, so gay, so charming that no one could have withstood him, least of all his wife who, though she knew him and understood him as well as any one could understand this secretive and baffling nature, frequently despised him, often hated him, still was in love with him and always would be.

The child would be asleep in her corner, but Magnolia would be wide awake, reading or sewing or simply sitting there waiting. She never reproached him for the hours he kept. Though they quarrelled frequently it was never about this. Sometimes, as she sat there, half dozing, her mind would go back to the rivers and gently float there. An hour—two hours—would slip by. Now the curtain would be going down on the last act. Now the crowd staying for the after-piece and concert would be moving down to occupy the seats nearer the stage. A song number by the ingénue, finishing with a clog or a soft-shoe dance. The comic tramp. The character team in a patter act, with a song. The after-piece now; probably Red Hot Coffee, or some similar stand-by. Now the crowd was leaving. The band struck up its last number. Up the river bank scrambled the last straggler. You never threw me my line at all. There I was like a stuck pig. Well, how did I know you was going to leave out that business with the door. Why'n't you tell me? Say, Ed, will you go over my song with me a minute? You know, that place where it goes TUM-ty-ty TUM-ty-ty TUM-TUM-TUM and then I vamp. It kind of went sour to-night, seemed to me. A bit of supper. Coffee cooked over a spirit lamp. Lumps of yellow cheese, a bite of ham. Relaxation after strain. A daubing with cold cream. A sloshing of water. Quieter. More quiet. Quiet. Darkness. Security. No sound but that of the river flowing by. Sometimes if she dozed she was wakened by the familiar hoot of a steamer whistle—some big lake boat, perhaps, bound for Michigan or Minnesota; or a river barge or tug on the Chicago River near by. She would start up, bewildered, scarcely knowing whether she had heard this hoarse blast or whether it was only, after all, part of her dream about the river and the *Cotton Blossom.*

Ravenal coming swiftly up the stairs. Ravenal's quick light tread in the hall.

"Come on, Nola! We're leaving this rat's nest."

"Gay, dear! Not now. You don't mean to-night."

"Now! It'll only take a minute. I'll wake up the slavey. She'll help."

"No. No! I'd rather do it myself. Oh, Gay, Kim's asleep. Can't we wait until morning?"

But somehow the fantastic procedure appealed tremendously to her love of the unexpected. Packing up and moving on. The irresponsible gaiety of it. The gas turned high. Out tumbled the contents of bureau drawers and boxes and trunks. Finery saved from just such another lucky day. Froth and foam of lace and silk strewn incongruously about this murky little chamber with its frayed carpet and stained walls and crazy chairs. They spoke in half whispers so as not to wake the child. They were themselves like two children, eager, excited, laughing.

"Where are we going, Gay?"

"Sherman. Or how would you like to try the Auditorium for a change? Rooms looking out over the lake."

"Gay!" Her hands clasped as she knelt in front of a trunk.

"Next week we'll run down to West Baden. Do us good. During the day we can walk and drive or ride. You ought to learn to ride, Nola. In the evening we can take a whirl at Sam Maddock's layout."

"Oh, don't play there—not much, I mean. Let's try to keep what we have for a little while."

"After all, we may as well give Sam a chance to pay our expenses. Remember the last time we were down I won a thousand at roulette alone—and roulette isn't my game."

He awoke the landlady and paid his bill in the middle of the night. She did not resent being thus disturbed. Women rarely resented Gaylord Ravenal's lack of consideration. They were off in a hack fetched by Ravenal from the near-by cab stand. It was no novelty for Kim to fall asleep in the dingy discomfort of a north side rooming house and to wake up amidst the bright luxuriousness of a hotel suite, without ever having been conscious of the events which had wrought this change. Instead of milk out of the bottle and an egg cooked over the gas jet, there was a shining breakfast tray bearing mysterious round-domed dishes whose covers you whipped off to disclose what not of savoury delights! Crisp curls of bacon, parsley-decked; eggs baked and actually bubbling in a brown crockery container; hot golden buttered toast. And her mother calling gaily in from the next room, "Drink your milk with your breakfast, Kim darling! Don't gulp it all down in one swallow at the end."

It was easy enough for Kim to believe in those fairy tales that had to do with kindly sprites who worked miracles overnight. A whole staff of such good creatures seemed pretty regularly occupied with the Ravenal affairs.

Once a month there came a letter from Mrs. Hawks. No more and no less. That indomitable woman was making a great success of her business. Her letters bristled with complaint, but between the lines Magnolia could read satisfaction and even a certain grim happiness. She was boss of her world, such as it was. Her word was final. The modern business woman had not yet begun her almost universal battle against the male in his own field. She was considered unique. Tales of her prowess became river lore. Parthy Ann Hawks, owner and manager of the Cotton Blossom Floating Palace Theatre, strong, erect, massive, her eyebrows black above her keen cold eyes, her abundant hair scarcely touched with gray, was now a well-known and important figure on the rivers. She ran her boat like a pirate captain. He who displeased her walked the plank. It was said that the more religious rivermen who hailed from the Louisiana parishes always crossed themselves fearfully at her approach and considered a meeting with the *Cotton Blossom* a bad omen. The towering black-garbed form standing like a

ship's figurehead, grim and portentous, as the boat swept downstream,
had been known to give a really devout Catholic captain a severe and
instantaneous case of chills and fever.

Her letters to Magnolia were characteristic:

Well, Maggie, I hope you and the child are in good health. Often
and often I think land knows what kind of a bringing up she is getting
with the life you are leading. I can imagine. Well, you made your own
bed and now you can lie in it. I have no doubt that he has run through
every penny of your money that your poor father worked so hard to get
as I predicted he would. I suppose you heard all about French's *New
Sensation*. French has the worst luck it does seem. She sank six weeks
ago at Medley's just above New Madrid. The fault of the pilot it was.
Carelessness if ever I heard it. He got caught in the down draft of a
gravel bar and snagged her they say. I think of your poor pa and how he
met his end. It took two weeks to raise her though she was only in six
feet of water. On top of that his other boat the *Golden Rod* you remember went down about four weeks ago in the Illinois near Hardin.
A total loss. Did you ever hear of such luck. Business is pretty good.
I can't complain. But I have to be right on hand every minute or they
would steal me blind and that's the truth. I have got a new heavy. No
great shakes as an actor but handy enough and a pretty good black face
in the concert and they seem to like him. We had a pretty rough
audience all through the coal country but whenever it looked like a
fight starting I'd come out in front and stand there a minute and say
if anybody started anything I would have the boat run out into the
middle of the river and sink her. That I'd never had a fight on my
boat and wasn't going to begin any such low life shenanigans now.

(Magnolia got a swift mental picture of this menacing, black-garbed
figure standing before the gay crude curtain, the footlights throwing
grim shadows on her stern face. That implacable woman was capable of
cowering even a tough coal-belt audience bent on a fight.)

Crops are pretty good so business is according. I put up grape jell
last week. A terrible job but I can't abide this store stuff made of
gelatine or something and no real grapes in it. Well I suppose you are
too stylish for the *Cotton Blossom* by now and Kim never hears of it.
I got the picture you sent. I think she looks kind of peaked. Up all
hours of the night I suppose and no proper food. What kind of an
education is she getting? You wrote about how you were going to send
her to a convent school. I never heard of such a thing. Well I will
close as goodness knows I have enough to do besides writing letters
where they are probably not wanted. Still I like to know how you and
the child are doing and all.

Your mother,
PARTHENIA ANN HAWKS.

These epistles always filled Magnolia with an emotion that was a poisonous mixture of rage and tenderness and nostalgia. She knew that her mother, in her harsh way, loved her, loved her grandchild, often longed to see both of them. Parthy's perverse and inhibited nature would not permit her to confess this. She would help them with money, Magnolia knew, if they needed help. But first she must know the grisly satisfaction of having them say so. This Magnolia would not do, though there were many times when her need was great. There was Kim, no longer a baby. This feverish and irregular life could not go on for her. Magnolia's letters to her mother, especially in lean times, were triumphs of lying pride. Sentimental Tommy's mother, writing boastfully home about her black silks and her gold chain, was never more stiff-necked than she.

Gay is more than good to me. . . . I have only to wish for a thing . . . Everyone says Kim is unusually tall and bright for her age. . . . He speaks of a trip to Europe next year . . . new fur coat . . . never an unkind word . . . very happy . . .

Still, if Magnolia was clever at reading between the lines of her mother's bald letters, so, too, was Parthenia at hers. In fact, Parthy took many a random shot that struck home, as when once she wrote, tartly, "Fur coat one day and none the next I'll be bound."

XV

THE problem of Kim's education, of Kim's future, was more and more insistently borne in upon her. She wanted money—money of her own with which to provide security for the child. Ravenal's improvident method was that of Paddy and the leaky roof. When luck was high and he was showering her and Kim with luxuries, he would say, "But, good God, haven't you got everything you want? There's no satisfying you any more, Nola."

When he had nothing he would throw out his hands, palms upward, in a gesture of despair. "I haven't got it, I tell you. I give you everything I can think of when I am flush. And now, when I'm broke, you nag me."

"But, Gay, that's just it. Everything one day and nothing the next. Couldn't we live like other people, in between? Enough, and none of this horrible worrying about to-morrow. I can't bear it."

"You should have married a plumber."

She found herself casting about in her mind for ways in which she could earn money of her own. She took stock of her talents: a slim array. There was her experience on the show-boat stage. She could play the piano a little. She could strum the banjo (relic of Jo's and Queenie's days in the old *Cotton Blossom* low-raftered kitchen). She had an untrained, true, and rather moving voice of mediocre quality.

Timidly, with a little nervous spot of red showing in either cheek, she broached this to Ravenal one fine afternoon when they were driving out to the Sunnyside Hotel for dinner. Gaylord had had a run of luck the week before. Two sleek handsome chestnuts seemed barely to flick the road with their hoofs as they flew along. The smart high cart glittered with yellow varnish. None of your cheap livery rigs for Ravenal. Magnolia was exhilarated, happy. Above all else she loved to drive into the country or the suburbs behind a swift pair of horses. Ravenal was charming; pleased with himself; with his handsome, well-dressed young wife; with the cart, the horses, the weather, the prospect of one of Old Man Dowling's excellent dinners. They sped through Lincoln Park. Their destination was a two-hours' drive north, outside the city limits: a favourite rendezvous for Chicago's sporting world. At Dowling's one had supper at a dollar a head—and such a supper! The beefsteak could be cut with a fork. Old Man Dowling bred his own fine fat cattle. Old Lady Dowling raised the plump broilers that followed the beefsteak. There was green corn grown in the Dowling garden; fresh-plucked tomatoes, young onions. There was home-made ice cream. There was a huge chocolate cake, each slice a gigantic edifice alternating layers of black and white.

"Can't I drive a while, Gay dear?"

"They're pretty frisky. You'd better wait till we get out a ways, where there aren't so many rigs." The fine cool late summer day had brought out all manner of vehicles. "By that time the nags'll have some of the skittishness worked out of them, too."

"But I like to have them when they're skittish. Papa always used to let me take them."

"Yes—well, these aren't canal-boat mules, you know. Why can't you be content just to sit back and enjoy the drive? You're getting to be like one of those bloomer girls they joke about. You'll be wanting to wear the family pants next."

"I am enjoying it, only——"

"Only don't be like your mother, Nola."

She lapsed into silence. During one of their many sojourns at the Ontario Street hotel she had struck up a passing acquaintance with a large, over-friendly blonde actress with green-gold hair and the tightest of black bodices stretched over an imposing shelf of bosom. This one had surveyed the Ravenal ménage with a shrewd and kindly though slightly bleary eye, and had given Magnolia some sound advice.

"Why'n't you go out more, dearie?" she had asked one evening when she herself was arrayed for festivity in such a bewilderment of flounces, bugles, jets, plumes, bracelets, and chains as to give the effect of a lighted Christmas tree in the narrow dim hallway. She had encountered Magnolia in the corridor and Nola had returned the woman's gusty greeting with a shy and faintly wistful smile. "Out more, evenin's. Young thing like you. I notice you're home with the little girl most the time. I guess you think that run, run is about all I do."

Magnolia resented this somewhat. But she reflected instantly this was a friendly and well-meaning creature. She reminded her faintly of Elly, somehow; Elly as she might be now, perhaps; blowsy, over-blown, middle-aged. "Oh, I go out a great deal," she said, politely.

"Husband home?" demanded the woman, bluntly. She was engaged in the apparently hopeless task of pulling a black kid glove over her massive arm.

Magnolia's fine eyebrows came up in a look of hauteur that she unconsciously had borrowed from Ravenal. "Mr. Ravenal is out." And started on toward her room.

The woman caught her hand. "Now don't get huffy, dear. I'm a older woman than you and I've seen a good deal. You stay home with the kid and your husband goes out, and will he like you any better for it? Nit! Now leave me tell you when he asks you to go out somewheres with him you go, want to or not, because if you don't there's those that will, and pretty soon he'll quit asking you."

She had waddled stiffly down the hallway then, in her absurdly high-heeled slippers, leaving a miasma of perfume in the passage. Magnolia had been furious, then amused, then thoughtful, then grateful. In the last few years she had met or seen the wives of professional gamblers. It was strange: they were all quiet, rather sad-faced women, home-loving and usually accompanied by a well-dressed and serious child. Much like herself and Kim, she thought. Sometimes she met them on Ohio Street. She thought she could recognize the wife of a gambler by the look in her face.

Frequently she saw them coming hurriedly out of one of the many pawnshops on North Clark, near the river. The windows of these shops fascinated her. They held, often, such intimate, revealing, and mutely appealing things—a doll, a wedding ring, a cornet, a meerschaum pipe, a Masonic emblem, a Bible, a piece of lace, a pair of gold-rimmed spectacles.

She thought of these things now as she sat so straight and smartly dressed beside Ravenal in the high yellow cart. She stole a glance at him. The colour was high in his cheeks. His box-cut covert coat with the big pearl buttons was a dashingly becoming garment. In the buttonhole bloomed a great pompon of a chrysanthemum. He looked very handsome. Magnolia's head came up spiritedly.

"I don't want to wear the pants. But I would like to have some say-so about things. There's Kim. She isn't getting the right kind of schooling. Half the time she goes to private schools and half the time to public and half the time to no school at all—oh, well, I know there aren't three halves, but anyway . . . and it isn't fair. It's because half the time we've got money and half the time we haven't any."

"Oh, God, here we are, driving out for pleasure——"

"But, Gay dear, you've got to think of those things. And so I thought —I wondered—Gay, I'd like to earn some money of my own."

Ravenal cut the chestnuts sharply with his whip.

"Pooh!" thought Magnolia. "He can't scare me that way. How like a man—to take it out on the horses just because he's angry." She slipped her hand through his arm.

"Don't! Don't jerk my arm like that. You'll have them running away in a minute."

"I should think they would, after the way you slashed them. Sometimes I think you don't care about horses—as horses—any more than you do about——" She stopped, aghast. She had almost said, "than you do about me as a wife." A long breath. Then, "Gay darling, I'd like to go back on the stage. I'd like to act again. Here, I mean. In Chicago."

She was braced for a storm and could have weathered it. But his shouts of laughter startled and bewildered her and the sensitive chestnuts as well. At this final affront they bolted, and for the next fifteen minutes Magnolia clutched the little iron rod at the end of the seat with one hand and clung to her hat with the other as the outraged horses stretched their length down the rutty country road, eyes flaming, nostrils distended, hoofs clattering, the light high cart rocking and leaping behind them. Ravenal's slender weight was braced against the footboard. The veins in his wrists shone blue against dead white. With a tearing sound his right sleeve ripped from his coat. Little beads of moisture stood out about his mouth and chin. Magnolia, white-lipped, tense, and terribly frightened, magnificently uttered no sound. If she had been one of your screamers there probably would have been a sad end. Slowly, gradually, the chestnuts slowed a trifle, slackened, resumed a normal pace, stood panting as Ravenal drew up at the side of the road. They actually essayed to nibble innocently at some sprigs of grass growing by the roadside while Ravenal wiped his face and neck and hands, slowly, with his fine perfumed linen handkerchief. He took off his black derby hat and mopped his forehead and the headband of his hat's splendid white satin lining. He fell to swearing, softly, this being the form in which the male, relieved after fright, tries to deny that he has been frightened.

He turned to look at her, his eyes narrow. She turned to look at him, her great eyes wide. She leaned toward him a little, her hand over her heart. And then, suddenly, they both began to laugh, so that the chestnuts pricked up their ears again and Ravenal grabbed the reins. They laughed because they were young, and had been terribly frightened, and were now a little hysterical following the strain. And because they loved each other, so that their fear of injury and possible death had been for each a double horror.

"That's what happens when you talk about going on the stage," said Ravenal. "Even the horses run at the thought. I hope this will be a lesson to you." He gathered up the reins.

"A person would think I'd never been an actress and knew nothing of the stage."

"You don't think that catch-as-catch-can performance was acting, do you? Or that hole in the wall a stage! Or that old tub a theatre! Or those plays—— Good God! Do you remember . . . 'Sue, if he loves yuh, go with him. Ef he ain't good to yuh——'"

"But I do!" cried Magnolia. "I do think so. I loved it. Everybody in the company was acting because they liked it. They'd rather do it than anything in the world. Maybe we weren't very good but the audiences thought we were; and they cried in the places where they were supposed to cry, and laughed when they should have laughed, and believed it all, and were happy, and if that isn't the theatre then what is?"

"Chicago isn't a river dump; and Chicago audiences aren't rubes. You've seen Modjeska and Mansfield and Bernhardt and Jefferson and Ada Rehan since then. Surely you know the difference."

"That's the funny part of it. I don't, much. Oh, I don't mean they haven't got genius. And they've been beautifully directed. And the scenery and costumes and all. But—I don't know—they do exactly the same things—do them better, but the same things that Schultzy told us to do—and the audiences laugh at the same things and cry at the same things—and they go trouping around the country, on land instead of water, but trouping just the same. They play heroes and heroines in plays all about love and adventure; and the audiences go out blinking with the same kind of look on their faces that the river-town audiences used to have, as though somebody had just waked them up."

"Don't be silly, darling. . . . Ah, here we are!"

And here they were. They had arrived in ample time, so that Magnolia chatted shyly and Ravenal chatted charmingly with Pa and Ma Dowling; and Magnolia was reminded of Thebes as she examined the shells and paper roses and china figurines in the parlour. The dinner was excellent, abundant, appetizing. Scarcely were they seated at the long table near the window when there was heard a great fanfare and hullabaloo outside. Up the winding driveway swept a tallyho, and out of it spilled a party of Chicago bloods in fawn covert coats and derby hats and ascot ties and shiny pointed shoes; and they gallantly assisted the very fashionable ladies who descended the perilous steps with much shrill squealing and shrieking and maidenly clutching at skirts, which clutchings failed satisfactorily of their purpose. Some of the young men carried banjos and mandolins. The four horses jangled their metal-trimmed harness and curveted magnificently. Up the steps swarmed the gay young men and the shrill young women. On closer sight Magnolia noticed that some of these were not, after all, so young.

"Good God!" Ravenal had exclaimed; and had frowned portentously.

"Do you know them, Gay?"

"It's Bliss Chapin's gang. He's giving a party. He's going to be married day after to-morrow. They're making a night of it."

"Really! How lovely! Which one's the girl he's to marry? Point her out."

And for the second time Ravenal said, "Don't be silly, darling."

They entered the big dining room on a wave of sound and colour. They swarmed the table. They snatched up bits of bread and pickles and celery, and munched them before they were seated. They caught sight of Ravenal.

"Gay! Well, I'm damned! Gay, you old Foxey Quiller, so that's why you wouldn't come out! Heh, Blanche, look! Here's Gay, the bad boy. Look who's here!"

"I thought you were going out to Cramp's place," Gay said, sullenly, in a low voice, to one of the men.

He chose the wrong confidant, the gentleman being neither reticent nor ebriate. He raised his voice to a shout. "That's a good 'un! Listen! Foxey Gay thought we were going out to Cramp's place, so what does he do? He brings his lady here. Heh, Blanche, d'you hear that? Now you know why he couldn't come." He bent upon Magnolia a look of melting admiration. "And can you blame him? All together! NO!"

"You go to hell," said the lady named Blanche from the far end of the table, though without anger; rather in the manner of one who is ready with a choice bit of repartee. Indeed it must have been so considered, for at its utterance Mr. Bliss Chapin's pre-nuptial group uttered shouts of approbation.

"Shut up, you jackass," said Ravenal then, sotto voce.

And "Oho!" bellowed the teaser. "Little Gay's afraid he'll get in trouble with his lady friend."

Gay's lady friend now disproved for all time her gentleman friend's recent accusation that she knew nothing about the art of acting. She raised her head and gazed upon the roistering crew about the long table. Her face was very white, her dark eyes were enormous; she was smiling.

"Won't you introduce me to your friends, Gay?" she said, in her clear and lovely voice.

"Don't be a fool," whispered Ravenal, at her side.

The host, Bliss Chapin, stood up rather red-faced and fumbling with his napkin. He was not sober, but his manner was formal—deferential, even. "Mrs.—uh—Rav'nal—I—uh—charmed. I rem'ber seeing you— someone pointed you out in a box at th—th—th—" he gave it up and decided to run the two words together—"ththeatre. Chapin's my name. Bliss Chapin. Call me Bliss. Ever'body calls me Bliss. Uh—" he decided to do the honours. He indicated each guest with a graceful though vague wave of the hand. "'S Tantine . . . Fifi . . . Gerty . . . Vi'let . . . Blanche . . . Mignon. Lovely girls. Lovely. But—we'll let that pass. Uh . . . Georgie Skiff. . . . Tom Haggerty . . . Billy Little—Li'l' Billee we call him. Pretty cute, huh? . . . Know what I mean? . . . Dave Lansing . . . Jerry Darling—that's his actu-al name. Can you 'mazhine what the girls can do with name like that! Boys 'n girls, this's Mrs. Gay-lord Ravenal, wife of the well-known faro expert. An' a lucky dog he is, too. No offense, I hope. Jus' my rough way. I'm going to be married to-morr'. An'thing goes 'sevening."

Prolonged applause and shouting. A twanging of mandolins and banjos.

"Speech!" shouted the man who had first called attention to Magnolia. "Speech by Mrs. Ravenal!"

They took it up shrilly, hoarsely, the Fifis, the Violets, the Billys, the Gertys, the Jerrys. Speech! Speech!

Ravenal got to his feet. "We've got to go," he began. "Sorry——"

"Sit down! Throw him out! Foxey Gay! Shut up, Gay!"

Ravenal turned to Magnolia. "We'll have to get out of this," he said. He put a hand on her arm. His hand was trembling. She turned her head slowly and looked up at him, her eyes blank, the smile still on her face. "Oh, no," she said, and shook her head. "Oh, no. I like it here, Gay dear."

"Speech!" yelled the Tantines, the Mignons, the Daves, beating on their plates with their spoons.

Magnolia brought one hand up to her throat in a little involuntary gesture that betokened breathlessness. There was nothing else to indicate how her heart was hammering. "I—I can't make a speech," she began in her lovely voice.

"Speech! Speech!"

She looked at Ravenal. She felt a little sorry for him.

"But I'll sing you a song if you'll lend me a banjo, someone."

She took the first of a half-dozen instruments thrust toward her.

"Magnolia!"

"Do sit down, Gay dear, and stop fidgeting about so. It's all right. I'm glad to entertain your friends." She still wore the little set smile. "I'm going to sing a song I learned from the Negroes when I was a little girl and lived on a show boat on the Mississippi River." She bent her head above the banjo and began to thumb it softly. Then she threw her head back slightly. One foot tapped emphasis to the music's cadence. Her lids came down over her eyes—closed down over them. She swayed a little, gently. It was an unconscious imitation of old Jo's attitude. "It's called Deep River. It doesn't mean—anything. It's just a song the niggers used to——" She began to sing, softly. "Deep——river——"

When she had finished there was polite applause.

"I think it's real sweet," announced the one they called Violet. And began to snivel, unbecomingly.

Mr. Tom Haggerty now voiced the puzzlement which had been clouding his normally cheerful countenance.

"You call that a coon song and maybe it is. I don't dispute you, mind. But I never heard any song like *that* called a coon song, and I heard a good many coon songs in my day. I Want Them Presents Back, and A Hot Time, and Mistah Johnson, Turn Me Loose."

"Sing another," they said, still more politely. "Maybe something not quite so sad. You'll have us thinking we're at prayer meeting next. First thing you know Violet here will start to repent her sins."

So she sang All God's Chillun Got Wings. They wagged their heads and tapped their feet to that. I got a wings. You got a wings. All o' God's chillun got a wings. When I get to heab'n I'm goin' to put on my wings, I'm goin' to fly all ovah God's heab'n . . . heab'n . . .

Well, that, they agreed, was better. That was more like it. The red-faced cut-up rose on imaginary wings to show how he, too, was going to fly all over God's heab'n. The forthright Blanche refused to be drawn into the polite acclaim. "If you ask me," she announced, moodily, "I think they're rotten." "I like somepin' a little more lively, myself," said the girl they called Fifi. "Do you know What! Marry Dat Gal! I heard May Irwin sing it. She was grand."

"No," said Magnolia. "That's the only kind of song I know, really." She stood up. "I think we must be going now." She looked across the table, her great dark eyes fixed on the red-faced bridegroom. "I hope you will be very happy."

"A toast to the Ravenals! To Gaylord Ravenal and Mrs. Ravenal!" She acknowledged that too, charmingly. Ravenal bowed stiffly and glowered and for the second time that day wiped his forehead and chin and wrists with his fine linen handkerchief.

The chestnuts were brought round. Bliss Chapin's crew crowded out to the veranda off the dining room. Magnolia stepped lightly up to the seat beside Ravenal in the high dog-cart. It was dusk. A sudden sharpness had come into the evening air as always, toward autumn, in that Lake Michigan region. Magnolia shivered a little and drew about her the little absurd flounced shoulder cape so recently purchased. The crowd on the veranda had caught the last tune and were strumming it now on their banjos and mandolins. The kindly light behind them threw their foolish faces into shadow. You heard their voices, plaintive, even sweet; the raucous note fled for the moment. Fifi's voice and Jerry's; Gerty's voice and little Billee's. I got a wings. You got a wings. All God's chillun got a wings. When I get to heab'n I'm goin' to put on my wings, I'm goin' to fly . . .

Magnolia turned to wave to them as the chestnuts made the final curve in the driveway and stretched eagerly toward home.

Silence between the two for a long half hour. Then Ravenal, almost humbly: "Well—I suppose I'm in for it, Nola. Shoot!"

But she had been thinking, "I must take things in hand now. I have been like a foolish young girl when I'm really quite an old married woman. I suppose being bossed by Mama so much did that. I must take Kim in hand now. What a fool I've been. 'Don't be silly, darling.' He was right. I have been——" Aloud she said, only half conscious that he had spoken, "What did you say?"

"You know very well what I said. I suppose I'm in for one of your mother's curtain lectures. Go on. Shoot and get it over."

"Don't be silly, darling," said Magnolia, a trifle maliciously. "What a lovely starlight night it is! . . ." She laughed a little. "Do you know, those dough-faced Fifis and Tantines and Mignons were just like the Ohio and Illinois farm girls, dressed up. The ignorant girls who used to come to see the show. I'll bet that when they were on the farm, barefooted, poor things, they were Annie and Jenny and Tillie and Emma right enough."

XVI

"AND this," said Sister Cecilia, "is the chapel." She took still another key from the great bunch on her key chain and unlocked the big gloomy double doors. It was incredible that doors and floors and wainscotings so shining with varnish could still diffuse such an atmosphere of gloom. She entered ahead of them with the air of a cicerone. It seemed to Magnolia that the corridors were tunnels of murk. It was like a prison. Magnolia took advantage of this moment to draw closer still to Kim. She whispered hurriedly in her ear:

"Kim darling, you don't need to stay. If you don't like it we'll slip away and you needn't come back. It's so gloomy."

"But I do like it," said Kim in her clear, decisive voice. "It's so shiny and clean and quiet." In spite of her lovely Ravenal features, which still retained something of their infantile curves, she looked at that moment startlingly like her grandmother, Parthenia Ann Hawks. They followed Sister Cecilia into the chapel. Magnolia shivered a little.

In giving Kim a convent education it was not in Magnolia's mind to prepare her for those Sunday theatrical page interviews beginning, "I was brought up by the dear Sisters in the Convent." For that matter, the theatre as having any part in Kim's future never once entered Magnolia's mind. Why this should have been true it is difficult to say, considering the child's background, together with the fact that she was seeing Camille and Ben Hur, and the Rogers Brothers in Central Park at an age when other little girls were barely permitted to go to cocoa parties in white muslin and blue sashes where they might, if they were lucky, see the funny man take the rabbit out of the hat.

The non-sectarian girls' schools of good standing looked askance at would-be entrants whose parentage was as socially questionable, not to say bizarre, as that represented by Ravenal mère and père. The daughter of a professional gambler and an ex-show-boat actress would have received short shrift at the hands of the head mistress of Miss Dignam's School for Girls at Somethingorother-on-the-Hudson. The convent school, then, opened its gloomy portals to as motley a collection of jeunes filles as could be imagined under one roof. In the prim dim corridors and cubicles of St. Agatha's on Wabash Avenue, south, you might see a score of girlish pupils who, in spite of the demure face, the sleek braids, the severe uniform, the modest manner, the prunes-and-prism expression, still resembled in a startling degree this or that vivacious lady whose name was associated with the notorious Everleigh Club, or with the music halls and museums thriving along Clark Street or Madison or Dearborn. Visiting day at St. Agatha's saw an impressive line of smart broughams outside the great solemn brick building; and the ladies who emerged therefrom, while invariably dressed in garments of sombre colour and restrained cut, still produced the effect of being attired in what is known as fast black. They gave forth a heady musky scent. And the mould of their features, even when transformed by the expression that crept over them as they gazed upon those girlish faces so markedly resembling their own, had a look as though the potter had used a heavy thumb.

The convent had been Magnolia's idea. Ravenal had laughed when she broached the subject to him. "She'll be well fed and housed and generally cared for there," he agreed. "And she'll learn French and embroidery and deportment and maybe some arithmetic, if she's lucky. But every t—uh—every shady lady on Clark Street sends her daughter there."

"She's got to go somewhere, Gay. This pillar-to-post life we're leading is terrible for a child."

"What about your own life when you were a child? I suppose you led a prissy existence."

"It was routine compared to Kim's. When I went to bed in my little room on the *Cotton Blossom* I at least woke up in it next morning. Kim goes to sleep on North Clark and wakes up on Michigan Avenue. She never sees a child her own age. She knows more bell boys and chambermaids and waiters than a travelling man. She thinks a dollar bill is something to buy candy with and that when a stocking has a hole in it you throw it away. She can't do the simplest problem in arithmetic, and yesterday I found her leaning over the second floor rotunda rail spitting on the heads of people in the——"

"Did she hit anybody?"

"It isn't funny, Gay."

"It is, too. I've always wanted to do it."

"Well, so have I—but, anyway, it won't be funny five years from now."

St. Agatha's occupied half of one of Chicago's huge square blocks. Its great flight of front steps was flush with the street, but at the back was a garden discreetly protected by a thick brick wall fully ten feet high and belligerently spiked. St. Agatha herself and a whole host of attendant cherubim looked critically down upon Magnolia and Kim as they ascended the long broad flight of steps that led to the elaborately (and lumpily) carved front door. Of the two Magnolia was the more terrified. The windows glittered so sharply. The stairs were so clean. The bell, as they rang it, seemed to echo so hollowly through endless unseen halls and halls and halls. The hand that opened the door had been preceded by no sound of human footsteps. The door had loomed before them seemingly as immovable as the building itself. There was the effect of black magic in its sudden and noiseless opening. The great entrance hall waited still and dim. The black-robed figure before them was vaguely surmounted by a round white face that had the look of being no face at all but a flat circular surface on which features had been clumsily daubed.

"I came to see about placing my little girl in school."

The flat surface broke up surprisingly into a smile. She was no longer a mysterious and sombre figure but a middle-aged person, kindly, but not especially bright. "This way."

This way led to a small and shiny office presided over by another flat circular surface. This, in turn, gave way to a large and almost startlingly sunny room, one flight up, where sat at a desk a black-robed figure different from the rest. A large pink face. Penetrating shrewd blue eyes behind gold-rimmed spectacles. A voice that was deep without resonance. A woman with the look of the ruler. Parthy, practically, in the garb of a Mother Superior.

"Oh, my goodness!" thought Magnolia, in a panic. She held Kim's cool little hand tight in her own agitated fingers. Of the two, she was incalculably the younger. The classrooms. The sewing room. Sister This. Sister That. The garden. Little hard benches. Prim gravel paths. Holy figures in stone brooding down upon the well-kept flower beds. Saints and angels and apostles. When all those glittering windows were dark, and the black-robed figures within lay in slumber, their hands (surely) crossed on their barren breasts and the flat circular surfaces reposed exactly in the centre of the hard pillows, and the moonlight flooded this cloistered garden spot with the same wanton witchery that enveloped a Sicilian bower, did these pious stone images turn suddenly into fauns and nymphs and dryads, Magnolia wondered, wickedly.

Aloud: "I see . . . I see . . . Oh, the refectory . . . I see. . . . Prayers . . . seven o'clock . . . dark blue dresses . . . every Thursday from two to five . . . and sewing and music and painting as well. . . ."

And this was the chapel. I see. And this was her bedroom to be shared with another pupil. But she has always had her own. It is the rule. I see. I'll let you know. It's Kim. I know it is, but that's her name, really. It's—she was born—in Kentucky and Illinois and Missouri—that is—yes, it does sound—no, I don't think she'd like to have you call her anything else, she's so used—I'll let you know, may I? I'd like to talk it over with her to see if she thinks she'd be happy . . .

In the garden, in various classrooms, in the corridors, and on the stairs they had encountered girls from ten to sixteen or even eighteen years of age, and they were all dressed exactly alike, and they had all flashed a quick prim look at the visitors from beneath demure lids. Magnolia had sensed a curious undercurrent of plot, of mischief. Hidden secret thoughts scurried up the bare varnished halls, lurked grinning in the stairway niches.

They were back in the big sunny second-floor room after their tour of inspection. The pink-faced Parthy person was regarding them with level brows. Magnolia was clinging more tightly than ever to Kim's hand. It was as though the child were supporting her, not she the child.

"But I know now whether I like it or not," Kim had spoken up, astonishingly. "I like it."

Magnolia was horrified to find that she had almost cried, "Oh, no! No, Kim!" aloud. She said, instead, "Are you sure, darling? You needn't stay unless you want to. Mother just brought you to see if you might like it."

"I do," repeated Kim, patiently, as one speaks to an irritating child.

Magnolia was conscious of a sinking sense of disappointment. She had hoped, perversely enough, that Kim would stamp her feet, throw herself screaming on the floor, and demand to be carried out of the bare clean orderly place back to the delightful welter of Clark Street. She could not overcome the feeling that in thus bestowing upon Kim a ladylike education and background she was depriving her of something rich and precious and colourful. She thought of her own childhood. She shut her eyes so as to see more clearly the pictures passing in her mind. Deep rivers. Wide rivers. Willows by the water's edge trailing gray-green. Dogwood in fairy bloom. Darkies on the landing. Plinketty-plunk-plunk-plunk, plinketty-plunk-plunk-plunk. Cotton bales. Sweating black bodies. Sue, ef he loves yuh, go with him. To-morrow night, ladies and gentlemen, that magnificent comedy-drama, Honest Hearts and Willing Hands. The band, red-coated, its brass screaming defiance at the noon-day sun.

The steely blue eyes in the pink face surrounded by the white wimple and the black coif seemed to be boring into her own eyes. "If you yourself would rather not have her here with us we would prefer not to take her."

"Oh, but I would! I do!" Magnolia cried hastily.

So it was arranged. Next week. Monday. Half a dozen woollen this. Half a dozen cotton that.

Descending the great broad flight of outside steps Magnolia said, like a child, "From now until Monday we'll do things, shall we? Fun. What would you like to do?"

"Oh, a matinée on Saturday——" began Kim eagerly. Magnolia was enormously relieved. She had been afraid that this brief glimpse into the more spiritual life might already have had a chastening effect upon the cosmopolitan Kim.

Thus the child was removed from the pernicious atmosphere of the Chicago Levee just when the Levee itself began to feel the chastening hand of reform. Suddenly, overnight, Chicago went civic. For a quarter of a century she had been a strident, ample-bosomed, loud-mouthed Rabelaisian giantess in red satin and diamonds, who kept open house day and night and welcomed all comers. There were food and drink and cheer. Her great muscular arms embraced ranchers from Montana and farmers from Indiana and bankers from New York. At Bath House John's Workingmen's Exchange you got a tub of beer for a nickel; the stubble-faced bums lined the curb outside his ceaselessly swinging door on Clark Street. The visiting ranchers and farmers and bankers were told to go over to the Palmer House and see the real silver dollars sunk in the tiled floor of that hostelry's barroom. The garrulous Coughlin, known as The Bath, and the silent little Hinky Dink Mike Kenna were Chicago's First Ward aldermen and her favourite naughty sons. The roulette wheels in Gamblers' Alley spun merrily by day and by night. The Mayor of the city called a genial, "Hope you're all winning, boys!" as he dropped in for a sociable drink and a look at the play; or even to take a hand. "What'll you have?" was Chicago's greeting, and "Don't care if I do," her catch phrase. Hetty Chilson was the recognized leader of her sinister world, and that this world happened to be prefaced by the quali-fying word, "under" made little difference in Chicago's eyes. Pawnshops, saloons, dives, and gambling houses lined Clark Street from Twelfth to the river, and dotted the near-by streets for blocks around. The wind-burned ranchmen in bearskin coats and sombreros at Polk and Clark were as common a sight as the suave white-fingered gentry in Prince Alberts and diamonds at Clark and Madison. It was all one to Chicago. "Game upstairs, gentlemen! Game upstairs!"

New York, eyeing her Western cousin through disapproving lorgnettes, said, "What a crude and vulgar person!"

"Me!" blustered Chicago, dabbing futilely at the food and wine spots on her broad satin bosom. "Me! I'll learn you I'm a lady."

The names of University of Chicago professors (Economics Department) began to appear on the lists of aldermanic candidates. Earnest young men and women with notebooks and fountain pens knocked at barred doors, stated that they were occupied in compiling a Survey, and asked intimate questions. Down came whole blocks of rats' nests on Clark and Dearborn, with the rats scuttling frantically to cover. Up went office buildings that actually sneered down upon the Masonic Temple's boasted height. Brisk gentlemen in eyeglasses and sack suits whisked in and out of these chaste edifices. The clicking sound to be heard on Clark Street was no longer that of the roulette wheel but of the stock market ticker and the Western Union transmitter.

It was rumoured that they were going to close Jeff Hankins'. They were going to close Mike McDonald's. They were going to banish the Washington Park race track.

"They can't do it," declared Gaylord Ravenal.

"Oh, can't we!" sneered the reformers. Snick-snack, went the bars on Hankins' doors and on Mike McDonald's. It actually began to be difficult to find an open game. It began to be well-nigh impossible. It came to such a pass that you had to know the signal knock. You had to submit to a silent scrutiny from unseen eyes peering through a slit somewhere behind a bland closed door. The Prince Alberts grew shiny. The fine linen showed frayed edges. The diamonds reposed unredeemed for longer and longer periods at Lipman's or Goldsmith's. The Ravenal ring and the succession of sealskin sacques seemed permanently to have passed out of the Ravenal possession. The malacca stick, on the other hand, was now a fixture. It had lost its magic. It was no longer a symbol of security. The day was past when its appearance at Lipman's or Goldsmith's meant an I O U for whatever sum Gay Ravenal's messenger might demand. There actually were mornings when even the Cockeyed Bakery represented luxury. As for breakfast at Billy Boyle's! An event.

The Ravenals' past experience in Chicago seemed, in comparison with their present precarious position, a secure and even humdrum existence. Ohio and Ontario streets knew them for longer and longer periods. Now when Magnolia looked into the motley assemblage of objects in the more obscure pawnshop windows, she was likely to avert her eyes quickly at recognition of some object not only intimate but familiar. Magnolia thought of Kim, safe, secure, comfortable, in the convent on Wabash Avenue.

"I must have felt this thing coming," she said to Ravenal. "Felt it in my bones. She's out of all this. It makes me happy just to think of it; to think of her there."

"How're you going to keep her there?" demanded Ravenal, gloomily.

"I'm strapped. You might as well know it, if you don't already. I've had the damnedest run of luck."

Magnolia's eyes grew wide with horror. "Keep her there! Gay! We've got to. I wouldn't have her knocking around here with us. Gay, can't you do something? Something real, I mean. Some kind of work like other—I mean, you're so wonderful. Aren't there things—positions—you know—with banks or—uh—those offices where they buy stocks and sell them and make money in wheat and—wheat and things?" Lamely.

Ravenal kissed her. "What a darling you are, Nola. A darling simpleton."

It was a curious and rather terrible thing, this love bond between them. All that Parthy had grimly predicted had come to pass. Magnolia knew him for what he was. Often she hated him. Often he hated her. Often he hated her because she shamed him with her gaiety, her loyalty, her courage, her tenderness. He was not true to her. She knew this now. He knew she knew this. She was a one-man woman. Frequently they quarrelled hideously. Tied to you. . . . Tied! God knows I'd be happier without you. You've never brought me anything but misery. . . . Always finding fault. . . . Put on those fine lady airs with me. What'd I take you out of! . . . An honest living, anyway. Look people in the face. Accusations. Bitterness. Longing. Passion. The long periods of living in sordid surroundings made impossible most of the finer reticences. Garments washed out in the basin. Food cooked over the gas jet. One room. One bed. Badly balanced meals. Reproaches. Tears. Sneers. Laughter. Understanding. Reconciliation.

They loved each other. Over and above and through and beneath it all, thick and thin, warp and woof, they loved each other.

It was when their fortunes were at lowest ebb; when the convent tuition had now been two terms unpaid; when the rent on the Ontario Street lodgings was overdue; when even Ravenal, handsome and morose, was forced to content himself with the coffee and rolls of the bedroom breakfast; when a stroll up Clark Street meant meeting a dozen McLean suits as shabby as his own—it was at this unpropitious time that Parthenia Ann Hawks was seized with the idea of visiting her daughter, her son-in-law, and her grandchild in Chicago. Her letters always came to the Sherman House—had been called for there through these years though the fluctuations of fortune had carried the Ravenals away from the hotel and back again with a tide-like regularity. Twice Magnolia had taken Kim to see her grim grandmama at Thebes when the *Cotton Blossom* was in for repairs during the winter season. These visits had always been timed when the Ravenal tide was high. Magnolia and Kim had come back to Thebes on the crest of a wave foaming with silks and laces and plumes and furs. The visits could not, however, be said to have been a success. Magnolia always came prepared to be the fond and dutiful daughter. Invariably she left seething between humorous rage and angry laughter.

"It wasn't anything she actually did," she would explain afterward, ruefully, to Ravenal. "It's just that she treats me with such disrespect." She pondered this a moment. "I honestly think Mama's the vainest woman I have ever met."

Strangely enough, Kim and her grandmother did not get on very satisfactorily, either. It dawned on Magnolia that the two were much alike. Their methods were different, but the result was the same. Each was possessed of an iron determination; boundless vitality; enormous resistance; canny foresight; definite ambition. Parthy was the blustering sort; Kim the quietly stubborn. When the two met in opposition they stood braced, horn to horn, like bulls.

On both occasions these visits had terminated abruptly in less than a week. The bare, wind-swept little town, winter-locked, had seemed unspeakably dreary to Magnolia. In the chill parlour of the cottage there was a wooden portrait of her father done in crayon. It was an enlargement which Parthy had had done from a small photograph of Andy in his blue coat and visored cap and baggy wrinkled pants. An atrocious thing, but the artist, clumsy though he was, had somehow happened to catch the alert and fun-loving brightness of the keen brown eyes. The mutton-chop whiskers looked like tufts of dirty cotton; the cheeks were pink as a chorus girl's. But the eyes were Andy's. Magnolia wandered into the parlour to stand before this picture, looking up at it with a smile. She wandered, too, down to the river to gaze at the sluggish yellow flood thick now with ice, but as enthralling as ever to her. She stood on the river bank in her rich furs, a lonely, wind-swept figure, gazing down the river, down the river, and her eyes that had grown so weary with looking always at great gray buildings and grim gray streets and swarming gray crowds now lost their look of strain, of unrepose, as they beheld in the far still distance the lazy Southern wharves, the sleepy Southern bayous—Cairo, Memphis, Vicksburg, Natchez, New Orleans—Queenie, Jo, Elly, Schultzy, Andy, Julie, Steve.

She took Kim eagerly to the water's edge—gave her the river with a sweep of her arm. Kim did not like it.

"Is that the river?" she asked.

"Why, yes, darling. Don't you remember! The river!"

"The river you told me about?"

"Of course!"

"It's all dirty and ugly. You said it was beautiful."

"Oh, Kim, isn't it?"

"No."

She showed her the picture of Captain Andy.

"Grampa?"

"Yes."

"Cap'n?"

"Yes, dear. He used to laugh so when you called him that when you were a little baby. Look at his eyes, Kim. Aren't they nice? He's laughing."

"He's funny-looking," said Kim.

Parthy asked blunt questions. "Sherman House? What do you go living in a hotel for all these years, with the way they charge for food and all! You and that husband of yours must have money to throw away. Why don't you live in a house, with your own things, like civilized people?"

"Gay likes hotels."

"Shiftless way to live. It must cost a mint of money."

"It does," agreed Magnolia, amiably.

"Like to know where you get it, that's what."

"Gay is very successful."

A snort as maddening as it was expressive from Parthy. The widow Hawks did not hesitate to catechize the child in the temporary absence of her mother. From these sessions Parthy must have gained some knowledge of the Ohio and Ontario street interludes, for she emerged from them with a look of grim satisfaction.

And now Parthenia Ann Hawks was coming to Chicago. She had never seen it. The letter announced her arrival as two weeks distant. The show-boat season was at an end. She would stay at the Sherman House where they were, if it wasn't too expensive. They were not to pay. She wouldn't be beholden to any one. She might stay a week, she might stay two weeks or longer, if she liked it. She wanted to see the Stockyards, the Grand Opera House, the Masonic Temple, Marshall Field's, Lincoln Park, and the Chicago River.

"My God!" said Gaylord Ravenal, almost piously. "My GOD!"

Stricken, they looked at each other. Stared. It was a thing beyond laughter. Every inch of space about them spelled failure. Just such failure as had been predicted for them by the woman who was now coming, and whose coming would prove to her the triumph of that prediction. They were living in a huddle of discomfort on Ontario Street. Magnolia, on her visits to Kim at the convent, was hard put to it to manage the little surprise gift planned to bring to the girl's face the flashing look of gay expectancy. A Henrici cake elaborately iced, to share with her intimates; a book; a pair of matinée tickets as a special treat; flowers for the Mother Superior; chocolates. Now the Christmas holidays were approaching. Kim would expect to spend them with her parents. But where? They would not bring her to this sordid lodging. And somehow, before the new term began, the unpaid tuition fee must be got together. Still, the Ravenals had faced such problems as these before now. They could have met them, they assured each other, as they always had. Luck always turned when things looked blackest. Life did that to tease you. But this was different. Gaylord Ravenal's world was crumbling. And Parthy! Parthy! Here was a situation fraught with what of horror! Here was humiliation. Here was acknowledged defeat.

"Borrow," suggested Magnolia.

"On what security?"

"I don't mean that kind of—I don't mean businesslike borrowing. I mean borrowing from friends. Friends. All these men——"

"Men! What men?"

"The men at the—at the places." She had always pretended that she did not actually know he came by his livelihood as he did. She never said, "Gamblers' Alley." She refused to admit that daily he had disappeared within the narrow slit of lane that was really a Clark Street alley; that he had spent the hours there watching bits of pasteboard for a living. "The men you have known so many years."

Grimly: "They've all been trying to borrow of me."

"But Mike McDonald. Hankins. Varnell." She cast pretense aside now. "Thousands. They've had thousands of dollars. All the money we brought with us to Chicago. Won't they give some of it back?"

This he found engaging rather than irritating, as well he might have. He shouted with laughter as he always did at a fresh proof of her almost incredible naïveté. At times such as these he invariably would be impelled to caress her much as one laughs at a child and then fondles it delightedly after it has surprised one with an unexpected and charming trick. He would kiss the back of her neck and then her wide, flexible mouth, and she would push him away, bewildered and annoyed that this should be his reaction to what she had meant so seriously.

"Nola, you're priceless! You're a darling. There's no one like you." He went off again into a shout of laughter. "Give it back! McDonald, h'm? There's an idea for you."

"How can you act like that when you know how serious it is!"

"Serious! Why, damn it, it's desperate. I tell you I'll never have her come here and see us living like this. We'll get out, first. . . . Say, Nola, what's to prevent us getting out, anyway? Chicago's no good any more. Why not get out of this! I'm sick of this town."

"We haven't any money to get out with, for one reason. And Kim's at school and she's going to stay there. She's going to stay there if I have to——"

"Have to what?"

"Ask Mama for the money." She said this mischievously, troubled though she was. Out he flew into a rage.

"I'll see her in—— I've been in deeper holes than this and managed to crawl out." He sat a moment in silence, staring with unseeing eyes at the shabby sticks of furniture that emphasized the room's dreariness. Magnolia, seated as quietly opposite him, sewing on a petticoat for Kim, suddenly let her hands sink in her lap. She realized, with a sort of fright, that he was as completely outside the room as though his body had been wafted magically through the window. And for him she, too, had vanished. He was deep in thought. The mask was off. She sat looking at him. She saw, clearly, the man her mother had so bitterly fought her marrying. The face of this man now in his late thirties was singularly unlined. Perhaps that was what you missed in it. The skin and hair and eyes, the set of the shoulders, the lead of the hand from the wrist, bespoke a virile man. But vigour—vigorous—no, he was not that. This was a fencer, not a fighter. But he had fought for her, years ago. The shambling preacher in the little river town whose name she had forgotten. That simple ignorant soul who preached hell fire and thought that play actors were damned. He had not expected to be knocked down in his own musty little shop. Not much of a victory, that. Gay had opposed that iron woman, her mother. But the soft life since then. Red plush, rich food, Clark Street. Weak. What was it? No lines about the mouth. Why was it weak? Why was it weak now if it had not been twelve years ago? A handsome man. Hard. But you couldn't be hard and weak at the same time, could you? What was he thinking of so intently? His face was so exposed, so defenceless, as sometimes when she awoke in the early morning and looked at him, asleep. Almost ashamed to look at his face, so naked was it of the customary daytime covering.

Now resolve suddenly tightened it. He stood up. He adjusted the smart and shabby hat at an angle that defied its shabbiness. He reached for the malacca stick. It was nine o'clock in the evening. They had had a frugal and unappetizing meal at a little near-by lunch room. Ravenal had eaten nothing. He had, for the most part, stared at the dishes with a detached and slightly amused air as though they had been served him by mistake and soon would be apologetically reclaimed by the slovenly waitress who had placed them before him.

She had never been one to say, "Where are you going?" Yet now her face was so moving in its appeal that he answered its unspoken question.

"Cheer up, old girl! I know somebody."

"Who? Who, Gay?"

"Somebody I've done favours for. She owes me a good turn." He was thinking aloud.

"She?"

"Never mind."

"She, Gay?"

"Did I say—now never mind, Nola. I'll do the worrying."

He was off.

She had become accustomed, through these years, to taking money without question when there was money; to doing without, uncomplainingly, when there was none. They had had to scheme before now, and scurry this way and that, seeking a way out of a tight corner. They had had to borrow as they had often lent. It had all been part of the Clark Street life—the gay, wasteful, lax, improvident sporting life of a crude new Mid-west city. But that life was vanishing now. That city was vanishing with it. In its place a newer, harder, more sophisticated metropolis was rearing its ambitious head.

Magnolia, inured to money crises, realized that the situation to-night was different. This was not a crisis. It was an impasse.

"Let's get out of here," Gay had said. There was no way out. The men from whom he had borrowed in the past were themselves as harried as he. The sources from which he had gained his precarious livelihood were drying up; had almost ceased to exist, except furtively. I know somebody. Somebody who would like to do me a favour. Somebody—who—would—like—— A horrid suspicion darted through her mind, released from the subconscious. Appalled at its ugliness, she tried to send it back to its hiding place. It would not go. It stayed there before her mind's eye, grinning, evil, unspeakably repulsive. She took up her sewing again. She endeavoured to fix her mind on Kim. Kim asleep in the cold calm quiet of the great walled convent on South Wabash. French and embroidery and deportment and china painting and wimples and black wings and long dark shining halls and round white faces and slim white tapers and statues of the saints that turned into fauns and why was that not surprising? A clatter. One of the saints had dropped her rosary on the bare shining floor. It wasn't a rosary. It was an anchor ringing against the metal stanchion of the *Cotton Blossom*.

Magnolia awoke. Her sewing scissors had fallen from her lap. Her face felt stiff and drawn. She hugged herself a little, and shivered, and looked about her. Her little gold watch on the dresser—no, of course not. That was gone. She folded her sewing. It was late, she knew. She was accustomed to being up until twelve, one, two. But this was later.

Something told her that this was later. The black hush of the city outside. The feel of the room in which she sat. The sinister quiet of the very walls about her. The cheap clock on the shelf had stopped. The hands said twenty minutes after two. Twenty-one minutes after, she told herself in a foolish triumph of precision.

She took down her fine long black hair. Brushed it. Plaited it. One of the lacy nightgowns so absurd in the sordid shabbiness of the rooming-house bedroom; so alien to the coarse gray sheets. She had no other kind. She went to bed. She fell asleep.

It was just before dawn when he returned. The black of the window panes showed the promise of gray. His step had an unaccustomed sound. He fumbled for the gas jet. His very presence was strange in the dark. The light flared blue, but she knew; she knew even before it illumined his face that bore queer slack lines she had never before seen there. For the first time in their life together Gaylord Ravenal was drunk.

She sat up; reached for her wrapper at the foot of the bed and bunched it about her shivering shoulders. He was immensely serious and dignified. He swayed a little. The slack look on his face. That was all.

"I'll do the worrying," he said, as though continuing the conversation that had held them at nine o'clock. He placed the malacca stick carefully in its corner. He removed his coat, keeping his hat on. The effect was startlingly rowdy, perhaps because he had always so meticulously observed the niceties. Standing thus, weaving back and forth ever so slightly, he pulled from his left vest pocket, where it fitted much too snugly, a plump bill-folder. Custom probably cautioned him to retain this, merely widening its open side to reveal the sheaf of notes within. But his condition, and all that had gone to bring it about, caused him to forego his cunning. With a vague, but successful, gesture, and a little lurch as he stood, he tossed the leather folder to the counterpane. "Coun' it!" he commanded, very distinctly. "Ten one hun'er' dollar bills and ten one hun'er' dollar bills makes twen'y one hun'er' dollar bills an' anybody says it doesn' is a liar. Two thousan' dollars. Would you kin'ly count 'em, Mrs. Rav'nal? I believe"—with businesslike dignity—"I b'lieve you'll find that correc'."

Magnolia Ravenal in her nightgown with her wrapper hunched about her shoulders sat staring at the little leather booklet on the bed. Its gaping mouth mocked her. She did not touch it.

"Two thousand dollars?" she said.

"I b'lieve you'll fin' tha's correc'." He seemed to be growing less distinct.

"Where did you get this, Gay?"

"Never min'. I'll do th' worrying."

He unbuttoned his vest with some difficulty. Yawned prodigiously, like one who has earned his rest after a good day's work.

She looked at him. She was like a drawing in French ink—her face so white, her eyes so enormous, her hair so black.

"You got this from Hetty Chilson."

His collar came off with a crack-snap. He held it in the hand that pointed toward the money. He seemed offended at something. Not angry, but hurt. "How can you say that, M'nolia! I got one thousan' from good ol' Het and not cen' more. Wha' do I do then! Marsh up to Sheedy's and win a thousan' more at roulette. Ha! That's a great joke on Sheedy because, look, roulette isn' my game. Nev' has been. Faro's my game. Tha's a gen'leman's game, faro. One thousan' Hetty, and marsh ri' up . . . roulette . . . win . . . 'nother . . . thous . . ." He lurched to the bed.

He was asleep at once, heavily, deeply, beside her on the bed, his fine long head lolling off the pillow. She knelt in her place and tried to lift the inert figure to a more comfortable position; succeeded, finally, after some tugging. She drew the lumpy coverlet over him. Then she sat as before, hunched in her nightgown and the wrapper, staring at the open wallet with its many leaves. It was dawn now. The room was gray with it. She ought to turn out the gas. She arose. She picked up the wallet. Before extinguishing the light she counted out ten one-hundred-dollar bills from the sheaf within the wallet. One thousand dollars. Her fingers touched the bills gingerly, fastidiously, and a little wrinkle of disgust curled her lip. She placed the bills on the dresser. She folded the leather holder and tucked it, with its remaining contents, under his pillow. He did not waken. She turned out the light then, and coming back to the bedside drew on the slippers that lay on the floor. She got her shirtwaist—a fresh white one with a Gibson tuck—from the drawer, and her skirt and jacket from the hooks covered over with a protecting length of calico against the wall. She heated a little water, and washed; combed and dressed her hair; put on her clothes, laid her hat on the dresser. Then she sat in the one comfortable chair that the room afforded—a crazy and decayed armchair done in dingy red plush, relic of some past grandeur—and waited. She even slept a little there in the sagging old chair, with the morning light glaring pitilessly in upon her face. When she awoke it must have been nearly noon. A dour day, but she had grown accustomed to the half-lights of the Chicago fogs. She glanced sharply at him. He had not moved. He had not stirred. He looked, somehow, young, helpless, innocent, pathetic. She busied herself in making a cup of coffee as quietly as might be. This might rouse him, but it would make little difference. She knew what she had to do. She drank the hot revivifying liquid in great gulps. Then she put on her jacket, pinned on her hat, took up the bills and placed them neatly in her handbag. She glanced at herself in the mirror.

"My, you're plain!" she thought, meaninglessly. She went down the dim stairway. The fusty landlady was flapping a gray rag in the outer doorway as her contribution to the grime of the street.

"What's taking you out so bright and early, Mis' Ravenal? Business or pleasure?" She liked her little joke.

"Business," said Magnolia.

XVII

THE knell had sounded for the red brick house with the lions guarding its portals. The Chicago soot hung like a pall over it. The front steps sagged. Even the stone lions had a mangy look. The lemon-water sunshine of a Chicago winter day despoiled the dwelling of any sinister exterior aspect. That light, filtering through the lake mist, gave to the house-front the look of a pock-marked, wrinkled, and evil old hag who squats in the market place with her face to the sun and thinks of her purple past and does not regret it.

It was half-past one. Magnolia Ravenal had figured this out nicely. That part of Clark Street would be astir by now. As she approached the house on Clark, near Polk, her courage had momentarily failed her, and she had passed it, hurriedly. She had walked a block south, wretchedly. But the feel of the bills in her bag gave her new resolve. She opened the handbag to look at them, turned and walked swiftly back to the house. She rang the bell this time, firmly, demandingly; stood looking down at its clean-scrubbed doorstep and tried to ignore the prickling sensation that ran up and down her spine and the weak and trembling feeling in her legs. The people passing by could see her. She was knocking at Hetty Chilson's notorious door, and the people passing by could see her: Magnolia Ravenal. Well, what of it! Don't be silly. She rang again.

The door was opened by a Negro in a clean starched white house coat. Magnolia did not know why the sight of this rather sad-eyed looking black man should have reassured her; but it did. She knew exactly what she wanted to say.

"My name is Mrs. Ravenal. I want to speak to Hetty Chilson."

"Mis' Chilson is busy, ma'am," he said, as though repeating a lesson. Still, something about the pale, well-dressed, earnest woman evidently impressed him. Of late, when he opened the door there had been frequent surprises for him in the shape of similar earnest and well-dressed young women who, when you refused them admittance, flashed an official-looking badge, whipped out notebook and pencil and insisted pleasantly but firmly that he make quite sure Miss Chilson was not in. "You-all one them Suhveys?"

Uncomprehending, she shook her head. He made as though to shut the door, gently. Magnolia had not spent years in the South for nothing. "Don't you shut that door on me! I want to see Hetty Chilson."

The man recognized the tone of white authority. "Wha' you want?"

Magnolia recovered herself. After all, this was not the front door of a home, but of a House. "Tell her Mrs. Gaylord Ravenal wants to speak to her. Tell her that I have one thousand dollars that belongs to her, and I want to give it to her." Foolishly she opened her bag and he saw the neat sheaf of bills. His eyes popped a little.

"Yes'm. Ah tell huh. Step in, ma'am."

Magnolia entered Hetty Chilson's house. She was frightened. The trembling had taken hold of her knees again. But she clutched the handbag and looked about her, frankly curious. A dim hallway, richly carpeted, its walls covered with a red satin brocade. There were deep soft cushioned chairs, and others of carved wood, high-backed. A lighted lamp on the stairway newel post cast a rosy glow over the whole. Huge Sèvres vases stood in the stained-glass window niches. It was an entrance hall such as might have been seen in the Prairie Avenue or Michigan Avenue house of a new rich Chicago packer. The place was quiet. Now and then you heard a door shut. There was the scent of coffee in the air. No footfall on the soft carpet, even though the tread were heavy. Hetty Chilson descended the stairs, a massive, imposing figure in a black-and-white patterned foulard dress. She gave the effect of activity hampered by some physical impediment. Her descent was one of impatient deliberateness. One hand clung to the railing. She appeared a stout, middle-aged, well-to-do householder summoned from some domestic task abovestairs. She had aged much in the last ten years. Magnolia, startled, realized that the distortion of her stout figure was due to a tumour.

"How do you do?" said Hetty Chilson. Her keen eyes searched her visitor's face. The Negro hovered near by in the dim hallway. "Are you Mrs. Ravenal?"

"Yes."

"What is it, please?"

Magnolia felt like a schoolgirl interrogated by a stern but well-intentioned preceptress. Her cheeks were burning as she opened her handbag, took out the sheaf of hundred-dollar bills, tendered them to this woman. "The money," she stammered, "the money you gave my—you gave my husband. Here it is."

Hetty Chilson looked at the bills. "I didn't give it to him. I loaned it to him. He said he'd pay it back and I believe he will. Ravenal's got the name for being square."

Magnolia touched Hetty Chilson's hand with the folded bills; pressed them on her so that the hand opened automatically to take them. "We don't want it."

"Don't want it! Well, what'd he come asking me for it for, then? I'm no bank that you can take money out and put money in."

"I'm sorry. He didn't know. I can't—we don't—I can't take it."

Hetty Chilson looked down at the bills. Her eyeglasses hung on the bodice of her dress, near the right shoulder, attached to a patent gold chain. This she pulled out now with a businesslike gesture and adjusted the eyeglasses to her nose. "Oh, you're that kind, huh?" She counted the bills once and then again; folded them. "Does your husband know about this?" Magnolia did not answer. She looked dignified and felt foolish. The very matter-of-factness of this world-hardened woman made this thing Magnolia had done seem overdramatic and silly. Hetty Chilson glanced over her shoulder to where the white-coated Negro stood. "Mose, tell Jule I want her. Tell her to bring her receipt book and a pen." Mose ran up the soft-carpeted stairs. You heard a deferential rap at an upper door; voices. Hetty turned again to Magnolia. "You'll want a receipt for this. Anyway, you'll have that to show him when he kicks up a fuss." She moved ponderously to the foot of the stairway; waited a moment there, looking up. Magnolia's eyes followed her gaze. Mose had vanished, evidently, down some rear passage and stairway, for he again appeared mysteriously at the back of the lower hall though he had not descended the stairway up which he had gone a moment before. Down this stair came a straight slim gray-haired figure. Genteel, was the word that popped into Magnolia's mind. A genteel figure in decent black silk, plain and good. It rustled discreetly. A white fine turnover collar finished it at the throat. Narrow cuffs at the wrist. It was difficult to see her face in the dim light. She paused a moment in the glow of the hall lamp as Hetty Chilson instructed her. A white face—no, not white—ivory. Like something dead. White hair still faintly streaked with black. In this clearer light the woman seemed almost gaunt. The eyes were incredibly black in that ivory face; like dull coals, Magnolia thought, staring at her, fascinated. Something in her memory stirred at sight of this woman in the garb of a companion-secretary and with a face like burned-out ashes. Perhaps she had seen her with Hetty Chilson at the theatre or the races. She could not remember.

"Make out a receipt for one thousand dollars received from Mrs. Gaylord Ravenal. R-a-v-e-n-a-l. Yes, that's right. Here; I'll sign it." Hetty Chilson penned her name swiftly as the woman held the book for her. She turned to Magnolia. "Excuse me," she said. "I have to be at the bank at two. Jule, give this receipt to Mrs. Ravenal. Come up as soon as you're through."

With a kind of ponderous dignity this strange and terrible woman ascended her infamous stairway. Magnolia stood, watching her. Her plump, well-shaped hand clung to the railing. An old woman, her sins heavy upon her. She had somehow made Magnolia feel a fool.

The companion tore the slip of paper from the booklet, advanced to Magnolia and held it out to her. "One thousand dollars," she said. Her voice was deep and rich and strange. "Mrs. Gaylord Ravenal. Correct?" Magnolia put out her hand, blindly. Unaccountably she was trembling again. The slip of paper dropped from her hand. The woman uttered a little exclamation of apology. They both stooped to pick it up as the paper fluttered to the floor. They bumped awkwardly, actually laughed a little, ruefully, and straightening, looked at each other, smiling. And as Magnolia smiled, shyly, she saw the smile on the face of the woman freeze into a terrible contortion of horror. Horror stamped itself on her every feature. Her eyes were wild and enormous with it; her mouth gaped with it. So the two stood staring at each other for one hideous moment. Then the woman turned, blindly, and vanished up the stairs like a black ghost. Magnolia stood staring after her. Then, with a little cry, she made as though to follow her up the stairway. Strangely she cried, "Julie! Julie, wait for me!" Mose, the Negro, came swiftly forward. "This way out, miss," he said, deferentially. He held the street door open. Magnolia passed through it, down the steps of the brick house with the lions couchant, into the midday brightness of Clark Street. Suddenly she was crying, who so rarely wept. South Clark Street paid little attention to her, inured as it was to queer sights. And if a passer-by had stopped and said, "What is it? Can I help you?" she would have been at a loss to reply. Certainly she could not have said, "I think I have just seen the ghost of a woman I knew when I was a little girl—a woman I first saw when I was swinging on the gate of our house at Thebes, and she went by in a long-tailed flounced black dress and a lace veil tied around her hat. And I last saw her—oh, I can't be sure. I can't be sure. It might not——"

Clark Street, even if it had understood (which is impossible), would not have been interested. And presently, as she walked along, she composed herself. She dabbed at her face with her handkerchief and pulled down her neat veil. She had still another task to perform. But the day seemed already so old. She was not sleepy, but her mind felt thick and slow. The events of the past night and of the morning did not stand out clearly. It was as if they had happened long ago. Perhaps she should eat something. She had had only that cup of coffee; had eaten almost nothing the night before.

She had a little silver in her purse. She counted it as it lay next to the carefully folded thousand-dollar receipt signed in Hetty Chilson's firm businesslike hand. Twenty-five—thirty-five—forty—fifty—seventy-three cents. Ample. She stopped at a lunch room on Harrison, near Wabash; ate a sandwich and drank two cups of coffee. She felt much better. On leaving she caught a glimpse of herself in a wall mirror—a haggard woman with a skin blotched from tears, and a shiny nose and with little untidy wisps of hair showing beneath her hat. Her shoes—she remembered having heard or read somewhere that neat shoes were the first requisite for an applicant seeking work. Furtively and childishly she rubbed the toe of either shoe on the back of each stocking. She decided to go to one of the department-store rest rooms for women and there repair her toilette. Field's was the nicest; the Boston store the nearest. She went up State Street to Field's. The white marble mirrored room was full of women. It was warm and bright and smelled pleasantly of powder and soap and perfume. Magnolia took off her hat, bathed her face, tidied her hair, powdered. Now she felt less alien to these others about her—these comfortable chattering shopping women; wives of husbands who worked in offices, who worked in shops, who worked in factories. She wondered about them. She was standing before a mirror adjusting her veil, and a woman was standing beside her, peering into the same glass, each seemingly oblivious of the other. "I wonder," Magnolia thought, fancifully, "what she would say if I were to turn to her and tell her that I used to be a show-boat actress, and that my father was drowned in the Mississippi, and my mother, at sixty, runs a show boat all alone, and that my husband is a gambler and we have no money, and that I have just come from the most notorious brothel in Chicago, where I returned a thousand dollars my husband had got there, and that I'm on my way to try to get work in a variety theatre." She was smiling a little at this absurd thought. The other woman saw the smile, met it with a frozen stare of utter respectability, and walked away.

There were few theatrical booking offices in Chicago and these were of doubtful reputation. Magnolia knew nothing of their location, though she thought, vaguely, that they probably would be somewhere in the vicinity of Clark, Madison, Randolph. She was wise enough in the ways of the theatre to realize that these shoddy agencies could do little for her. She had heard Ravenal speak of the variety houses and museums on State Street and Clark and Madison. The word "vaudeville" was just coming into use. In company with her husband she had even visited Kohl & Middleton's Museum—that smoke-filled comfortable shabby variety house on Clark, where the admission was ten cents. It had been during that first Chicago trip, before Kim's birth. Women seldom were seen in the audience, but Ravenal, for some reason, had wanted her to get a glimpse of this form of theatrical entertainment. Here Weber and Fields had played for fifteen dollars a week. Here you saw the funny Irishman, Eddie Foy; and May Howard had sung and danced.

"They'll probably build big expensive theatres some day for variety shows," Ravenal had predicted.

The performance was, Magnolia thought, much like that given as the concert after the evening's bill on the *Cotton Blossom*. "A whole evening of that?" she said. Years later the Masonic Temple Roof was opened for vaudeville.

"There!" Ravenal had triumphantly exclaimed. "What did I tell you! Some of those people get three and four hundred a week, and even more." Here the juggling Agoust family threw plates and lighted lamps and tables and chairs and ended by keeping aloft a whole dinner service and parlour suite, with lamps, soup tureens, and plush chairs passing each other affably in midair without mishap. Jessie Bartlett Davis sang, sentimentally, Tuh-rue LOVE, That's The Simple Charm That Opens Every Woman's Heart.

At the other end of the scale were the all-night restaurants with a stage at the rear where the waiters did an occasional song and dance, or where some amateur tried to prove his talent. Between these were two or three variety shows of decent enough reputation though frequented by the sporting world of Chicago. Chief of these was Jopper's Varieties, a basement theatre on Wabash supposed to be copied after the Criterion in London. There was a restaurant on the ground floor. A flight of marble steps led down to the underground auditorium. Here new acts were sometimes tried out. Lillian Russell, it was said, had got her first hearing at Jopper's. For some reason, Magnolia had her mind fixed on this place. She made straight for it, probably as unbusinesslike a performer as ever presented herself for a hearing. It was now well on toward mid-afternoon. Already the early December dusk was gathering, aided by the Chicago smoke and the lake fog. Her fright at Hetty Chilson's door was as nothing compared to the sickening fear that filled her now. She was physically and nervously exhausted. The false energy of the morning had vanished. She tried to goad herself into fresh courage by thoughts of Kim at the convent; of Parthy's impending visitation. As she approached the place on Wabash she resolved not to pass it, weakly. If she passed it but once she never would have the bravery to turn and go in. She and Ravenal had driven by many times on their way to the South Side races. It was in this block. It was four doors away. It was here. She wheeled stiffly, like a soldier, and went in. The restaurant was dark and deserted. One dim light showed at the far end. The tablecloths were white patches in the grayness. But a yellow path of light flowed up the stairway that led to the basement, and she heard the sound of a piano. She descended the swimming marble steps, aware of the most alarming sensation in her legs—rather, of no sensation in them. It was as though no solid structure of bone and flesh and muscle lay in the region between her faltering feet and her pounding heart.

There was a red-carpeted foyer; a little ticket window; the doors of the auditorium stood open. She put out a hand, blindly, to steady herself against the door jamb. She looked into the theatre; the badly lighted empty theatre, with its rows and rows of vacant seats; its stage at the far end, the curtain half raised, the set a crudely painted interior. As she looked there came over her—flowed over her like balm—a feeling of security, of peace, of home-coming. Here were accustomed surroundings. Here were the very sights and smells and sounds she knew best. Those men with their hats on the backs of their heads and their cigars waggling comfortably and their feet on the chair in front of them might have been Schultzy, Frank, Ralph, Pa Means. Evidently a song was being tried out in rehearsal. The man at the piano was hammering it and speaking the words in a voice as hoarse and unmusical as a boat whistle coming through the fog. It was a coon song full of mah babys and choo-choos and Alabam's.

Magnolia waited quietly until he had come to a full stop.

A thin pale young man in a striped shirt and a surprising gray derby who had been sitting with his wooden kitchen chair tipped up against the proscenium now brought his chair down on all fours.

"You was with Haverly's, you say?"

"I cer'nly was. Ask Jim. Ask Sam. Ask anybody."

"Well, go back to 'em is what I say. If you ever was more than a singin' waiter then I'm new to the show business." He took his coat from where it lay on top of the piano. "That's all for to-day, ain't it, Jo?" He addressed a large huddle whose thick shoulders and round head could just be seen above the back of a second-row centre seat. The fat huddle rose and stretched and yawned, and grunted an affirmative.

Magnolia came swiftly down the aisle. She looked up at the thin young man; he stared at her across the footlight gutter.

"Will you let me try some songs?" she said.

"Who're you?" demanded the young man.

"My name is Magnolia Ravenal."

"Never heard of it. What do you do?"

"I sing. I sing Negro songs with a banjo."

"All right," said the thin young man, resignedly. "Get out your banjo and sing us one."

"I haven't got one."

"Haven't got one what?"

"One—a banjo."

"Well, you said you—didn' you just say you sung nigger songs with a banjo!"

"I haven't got it with me. Isn't there one?" Actually, until this moment, she had not given the banjo a thought. She looked about her in the orchestra pit.

"Well, for God's sakes!" said the gray derby.

The hoarse-voiced singer who had just met with rebuff and who was shrugging himself into a shabby overcoat now showed himself a knight. He took an instrument case from the piano top. "Here," he said. "Take mine, sister."

Magnolia looked to left, to right. "There." The fat man in the second row jerked a thumb toward the right stage box back of which was the stage door. Magnolia passed swiftly up the aisle; was on the stage. She was quite at ease, relaxed, at home. She seated herself in one of the deal chairs; crossed her knees.

"Take your hat off," commanded the pasty young man.

She removed her veil and hat. A sallow big-eyed young woman, too thin, in a well-made suit and a modish rather crumpled shirtwaist and nothing of the look of the stage about her. She thumbed the instrument again. She remembered something dimly, dimly, far, far back; far back and yet very recent; this morning. "Don't smile too often. But if you ever want anything . . ."

She smiled. The thin young man did not appear overwhelmed. She threw back her head then as Jo had taught her, half closed her eyes, tapped time with the right foot, smartly. Imitative in this, she managed, too, to get into her voice that soft and husky Negro quality which for years she had heard on river boats, bayous, landings. I got a wings. You got a wings. All God's chillun got a wings.

"Sing another," said the old young man. She sang the one she had always liked best.

> "*Go down, Moses,*
> *'Way down in Egypt land,*
> *Tell ole Pharaoh,*
> *To let my people go.*"

Husky, mournful, melodious voice. Tapping foot. Rolling eye. Silence.

"What kind of a coon song do you call that?" inquired the gray derby.

"Why, it's a Negro melody—they sing them in the South."

"Sounds like a church hymn to me." He paused. His pale shrewd eyes searched her face. "You a nigger?"

The unaccustomed red surged into Magnolia's cheeks, dyed her forehead, her throat, painfully. "No, I'm not a—nigger."

"Well, you cer'nly sing like one. Voice and—I don't know—way you sing. Ain't that right, Jo?"

"Cer'nly is," agreed Jo.

The young man appeared a trifle embarrassed, which made him look all the younger. Years later, in New York, Kim was to know him as one of the most powerful theatrical producers of his day. And he was to say to Kim, "Ravenal, h'm? Why, say, I knew your mother when she was better-looking than you'll ever be. And smart! Say, she tried to sell me a coon song turn down in Jopper's in the old days, long before your time. I thought they were hymns and wouldn't touch them. Seems they're hot stuff now. Spirituals, they call them. You hear 'em in every show on Broadway. 'S fact! Got to go to church to get away from 'em. Well, live and learn's what I say."

It was through this shrewd, tough, stage-wise boy that Magnolia had her chance. He did not understand or like her Negro folk songs then, but he did recognize the quality she possessed. And it was due to this precociousness in him that Magnolia, a little more than a year later, was singing American coon songs in the Masonic Roof bill, her name on the programme with those of Cissie Loftus and Marshall Wilder and the Four Cohans.

But now she stood up, the scarlet receding from her face, leaving it paler than before. Silently she handed the husky singer his banjo; tried to murmur a word of thanks; choked. She put on her hat, adjusted her veil.

"Here, wait a minute, sister. No offense. I've seen 'em lighter'n you. Your voice sounds like a—ain't that the truth, Jo?" Actually distressed, he appealed again to his unloquacious ally in the third row.

"Sure does," agreed Jo.

The unfortunate hoarse-voiced man who had loaned her the banjo now departed. He seemed to bear no rancour. Magnolia, seeing this, tried again to smile on the theory that, if he could be game, then so, too, could she. And this time, it was the real Magnolia Ravenal smile of which the newspapers made much in the years to come. The ravishing Ravenal smile, they said (someone having considered that alliterative phrase rather neat).

Seeing it now the young showman exclaimed, without too much elegance, "Lookit that, Jo!" Then, to Magnolia: "Listen, sister. You won't get far with those. Your songs are too much like church tunes, see? They're for a funeral, not a theaytre. And that's a fact. But I like the way you got of singing them. How about singing me a real coon song? You know. Hello, Mah Baby! or something like that."

"I don't know any. These are the only songs I know."

"Well, for——! Listen. You learn some real coon songs and come back, see, in a week. Here. Try these over at home, see." He selected some song sheets from the accommodating piano top. She took them, numbly.

She was again in the cold moist winter street. Quite dark now. She walked over to State Street and took a northbound car. The door of their room on the third floor was locked, and when she had opened it she felt that the room was empty. Not empty merely; deserted. Before she had lighted the gas jet she had an icy feeling of desolation, of impending and piled-up tragedy at the close of a day that already toppled with it. Her gaze went straight to the dresser.

An envelope was there. Her name on it in Ravenal's neat delicate hand. Magnolia. Darling, I am going away for a few weeks . . . return when your mother is gone . . . or send for you . . . six hundred dollars for you on shelf under clock . . . Kim . . . convent . . . enough . . . weeks . . . darling . . . love . . . best . . . always . . .

She never saw him again.

She must have been a little light-headed by this time, for certainly no deserted wife in her right senses would have followed the course that Magnolia Ravenal now took. She read the note again, her lips forming some of the words aloud. She walked to the little painted shelf over the wash stand. Six hundred. That was right. Six hundred. Perhaps this really belonged to that woman, too. She couldn't go there again. Even if it did, she couldn't go there again.

She left the room, the gas flaring. She hurried down Clark Street, going a few blocks south. Into one of the pawnshops. That was nothing new. The man actually greeted her by name. "Good-evening, Mrs. Ravenal. And what can I do for you?"

"A banjo."

"What?"

"I want to buy a banjo."

She bargained for it, shrewdly. When she tendered a hundred-dollar bill in payment the man's face fell. "Oh, now, Mrs. Ravenal, I gave you that special price because you——"

"I'll go somewhere else."

She got it. Hurried back with it. Into her room again. She had not even locked the door. Five of the six one-hundred-dollar bills lay as she had tossed them on the dresser. A little crazy, certainly. Years, years afterward she actually could relate the fantastic demoniac events of this day that had begun at four in the morning and ended almost twenty hours later. It made a very good story, dramatic, humorous, tragic. Kim's crowd thought it was wonderful.

She took off her veil and hat and jacket. Her black hair lay in loose limp ugly loops about her face. She opened one of the sheets of music— Whose Black Baby Are You?—and propped it up against the centre section of the old-fashioned dresser. She crossed her knees. Cradled the banjo. One foot tapped the time rhythmically. An hour. Two hours.

A knock at the door. The landlady, twelve hours fustier than she had been that morning. "It ain't me, Mis' Ravenal, but Downstairs says she can't sleep for the noise. She's that sickly one. She says she pounded but you didn't——"

"I'll stop. I didn't hear her. I'm sorry."

"For me you could go on all night." The landlady leaned bulkily and sociably against the door. "I'm crazy about music. I never knew you was musical."

"Oh, yes," said Magnolia. "Very."

XVIII

"I was educated," began Kim Ravenal, studying her reflection in the mirror, and deftly placing a dab of rouge on either ear lobe, "in Chicago, by the dear Sisters there in St. Agatha's Convent."

She then had the grace to snigger, knowing well what the young second assistant dramatic critic would say to that. She was being interviewed in her dressing room at the Booth between the second and third acts of Needles and Pins. She had opened in this English comedy in October. Now it was April. Her play before this had run a year. Her play before that had run two years. Her play—well, there was nothing new to be said in an interview with Kim Ravenal, no matter how young or how dramatic the interviewer. There was, therefore, a touch of mischievous malice in this trite statement of hers. She knew what the bright young man would say in protest.

He said it. He said: "Oh, now, Pete's sake, Miss Ravenal! Quit kidding."

"But I was. I can't help it. I was! Ask my mother. Ask my husband. Ask anybody. Educated by the dear Sisters in the con——"

"Oh, I know it! So does everybody else who reads the papers. And you know as well as I do that that educated-in-a-convent stuff is rubber-stamp. It ceased to be readable publicity when Mrs. Siddons was a gal. Now be reasonable. Kaufman wants a bright piece about you for the Sunday page."

"All right. You ask intelligent questions and I'll answer them." Kim then leaned forward to peer intently at her own reflection in the dressing-room mirror with its brilliant border of amber lights. She reached for the rabbit's foot and applied to her cheeks that nervous and redundant film of rouge which means that the next curtain is four minutes away.

He was a very cagey New York second assistant dramatic critic, who did not confine his talents to second-assistant dramatic criticism. The pages of Vanity Fair and The New Yorker (locally known as the Fly Papers) frequently accepted first (assistant dramatic) aid from his pen. And, naturally, he had written one of those expressionistic plays so daringly different that three intrepid managers had decided not to put it on after all. Embittered, the second assistant dramatic critic threatened sardonically to get a production through the ruse of taking up residence in Prague or Budapest, changing his name to Capek or Vajda, and sending his manuscript back to New York as a foreign play for them to fight over.

Though she had now known New York for many years, there were phases of its theatrical life that still puzzled Kim's mother, Magnolia Ravenal; and this was one of them. "The critics all seem to write plays," she complained. "It makes the life of a successful actress like Kim so complicated. And the actors and actresses all lecture on the Trend of the Modern Drama at League Luncheons given at the Astor. I went to one once, with Kim. Blue voile ladies from Englewood. In my day critics criticized and actors acted."

Her suave and gifted son-in-law, Kenneth Cameron, himself a producer of plays of the more precious pattern (The Road to Sunrise, 1921;

Jock o' Dreams, 1924), teased her gently about this attitude of intolerance. "Why, Nola! And you a famous stage mama! You ought to know that even Kim occasionally has to do things for publicity."

"In my *Cotton Blossom* days we were more subtle. The band marched down Main Street and played on the corner and Papa gave out handbills. That was our publicity. I didn't have to turn handsprings up the levee."

There was little that the public did not know about Kim Ravenal. There was nothing that the cagey young assistant critic did not know. He now assumed a tone of deep bitterness.

"All right, my fine lady. I'll go back and write a pattern piece. Started in stock in Chicago. Went to New York National Theatre School. Star pupil and Teacher's Pet while there. Got a bit in—uh—Mufti, wasn't it? —and walked away with the play just like the aspiring young actress in a bum short story. Born on a show boat in Kentucky and Illinois and Missouri simultaneously—say, explain that to me some time, will you? —hence name of Kim. Also mother was a show-boat actress and later famous singer of coon—— Say, where is your mother these days, anyway? Gosh, I think she's grand! I'm stuck on her. She's the burning passion of my youth. No kidding. I don't know. She's got that kind of haunted hungry et-up look, like Bernhardt or Duse or one of them. You've got a little of it, yourself."

"Oh, sir!" murmured Kim, gratefully.

"Cultivate it, is my advice. And when she smiles! . . . Boy! I work like a dawg to get her to smile whenever I see her. She thinks I'm one of those cut-ups. I'm really a professional suicide at heart, but I'd wiggle my ears if it would win one of those slow, dazzling——"

"Listen! Who—or whom—are you interviewing, young man? Me or my mama?"

"She around?"

"No. She's at the Shaw opening with Ken."

"Well, then, you'll do."

"Just for that I think I'll turn elegant on you and not grant any more interviews. Maude Adams never did. Look at Mrs. Fiske! And Duse. Anyway, interviews always sound so dumb when they appear in print. Dignified silence is the thing. Mystery. Everybody knows too much about the stage, nowadays."

"Believe me, *I* do!" said the young second assistant dramatic critic, in a tone of intense acerbity.

A neat little triple tap at the dressing-room door. "Curtain already!" exclaimed Kim in a kind of panic. You would have thought this was her first stage summons. Another hasty application with the rabbit's foot.

A mulatto girl in black silk so crisp, and white batiste cap and apron so correct that she might have doubled as stage and practical maid, now opened the door outside which she had been discreetly stationed. "Curtain, Blanche?"

"Half a minute more, Miss Ravenal. Telegram." She handed a yellow envelope to Kim.

As Kim read it there settled over her face the rigidity of shock, so plain that the second assistant dramatic critic almost was guilty of, "No bad news, I hope?" But as though he had said it Kim Ravenal handed him the slip of paper.

"They've misspelled it," she said, irrelevantly. "It ought to be Parthenia."

He read:

Mrs. Parthna A. Hawks died suddenly eight o'clock before evening show Cotton Blossom playing Cold Spring Tennessee advise sympathy company.

CHAS. K. BARNATO.

"Hawks?"

"My grandmother."

"I'm sorry." Lamely. "Is there anything——"

"I haven't seen her in years. She was very old—over eighty. I can't quite realize. She was famous on the rivers. A sort of legendary figure. She owned and managed the *Cotton Blossom*. There was a curious kind of feud between her and Mother and my father. She was really a pretty terrible—I wonder—Mother——"

"Curtain, Miss Ravenal!"

She went swiftly toward the door.

"Can I do anything? Fetch your mother from the theatre?"

"She'll be back here with Ken after the play. Half an hour. No use——"

He followed her as she went swiftly toward the door from which she made her third-act entrance. "I don't want to be offensive, Miss Ravenal. But if there's a story in this—your grandmother, I mean—eighty, you know——"

Over her shoulder, in a whisper, "There is. See Ken." She stood a moment; seemed to set her whole figure; relaxed it then; vanished. You heard her lovely but synthetic voice as the American wife of the English husband in the opening lines of the third act:

"I'm so sick of soggy British breakfast. Devilled kidneys! Ugh! Who but the English could face food so visceral at nine A. M.!"

She was thinking as she played the third act for the three hundredth time that she must tuck the telegram under a cold cream jar or back of her mirror as soon as she returned to her dressing room. What if Magnolia should take it into her head to leave the Shaw play early and find it there on her dressing table! She must tell her gently. Magnolia never had learned to take telegrams calmly. They always threw her into a panic. Ever since that one about Gaylord Ravenal's death in San Francisco. Gaylord Ravenal. A lovely name. What a tin-horn sport he must have been. Charming though, probably.

Curtain. Bows. Curtain. Bows. Curtain. Bows. Curtain.

She was back in her dressing room, had removed her make-up, was almost dressed when Ken returned with her mother. She had made desperate haste, aided expertly by her maid.

The two entered laughing, talking, bickering good-naturedly. Kim heard her husband's jejune plangent voice outside her dressing-room door.

"I'm going to tell your daughter on you, Nola! Yes, I am."

"I don't care. He started it."

Kim looked round at them. Why need they be so horribly high-spirited just to-night? It was like comedy relief in a clumsily written play, put in to make the tragedy seem deeper. Still, this news was hardly tragic. Yet her mother might——

For years, now, Kim Ravenal had shielded her mother; protected her; spoiled her, Magnolia said, almost resentfully.

She stood now with her son-in-law in the cruel glare of the dressing-room lights. Her face was animated, almost flushed. Her fine head rose splendidly from the furred frame of her luxurious coat collar. Her breast and throat were firm and creamy above the square-cut décolletage of her black gown. Her brows looked the blacker and more startling for the wing of white that crossed the black of her straight thick hair. There was about this woman past middle age a breath-taking vitality. Her distinguished young son-in-law appeared rather anæmic in contrast.

"How was the play?" Kim asked, possibly in the hope of changing their ebullient mood.

"Nice production," said Cameron. "Lunt was flawless. Fontanne's turned just a shade cute on us. She'd better stop that. Shaw, revived, tastes a little mouldy. Westley yelled. Simonson's sets were—uh—meticulous I think the word is. . . . And I want to inform you, my dear Mrs. C., that your mama has been a very naughty girl."

This would never do, thought Kim, her mind on the yellow envelope. She put an arm about her mother. "Kiss me and I'll forgive you," she said.

"You don't know what she's done."

"Whatever it is——"

"Woollcott started it, anyway," protested Magnolia Ravenal, lighting her cigarette. "I should think a man who's dramatic critic of the New York *World* would have more consideration for the dignity of his——"

Cameron took up the story. "Our seats turned out to be next to his. Nola sat between us. You know how she always clutches somebody's hand during the emotional scenes."

"The last time I went to the theatre with Woollcott he said he'd slap my hands hard if I ever again——" put in Magnolia. But Cameron once more interrupted.

"Then in the second act she clutched him instead of me and he slapped her hand——"

"And pinched——"

"And Nola gave him a sharp dig in the stomach, I'm afraid, with her elbow, and there was quite a commotion. Mothers-in-law are a terrible responsibility."

"Mother *dear!* A first night of a Shaw revival at the National!"

"He started it. And anyway, you've brought me up wrong."

There was about her suddenly a curious effect of weariness. It was as though, until now, she had been acting, and had discarded her rôle. She stood up. "Ken, if you'll get me a taxi I'll run along home. I'm tired. You two are going to the Swopes', aren't you? That means three o'clock."

"I'm not going," said Kim. "Wait a minute, Ken." She came over to Magnolia. "Mother, I just got a telegram."

"Mama?" She uttered the word as though she were a little girl.

"Yes."

"Where is it?"

Kim indicated it. "There, Ken. Get it for me, will you? Under the make-up tray."

"Dead?" Magnolia had not unfolded the yellow slip.

"Yes."

She read it. She looked up. The last shadow had vanished of that mood in which she had entered ten minutes earlier. She looked, suddenly, sallow and sixty. "Let me see. Tennessee. Trains."

"But not to-night, Mother!"

"Yes. Ken, there's something to St. Louis—Memphis—I'm sure. And then from there to-morrow morning."

"Ken will go with you."

"No!" sharply. "No!"

She had her way in the end; left that night, and alone, over Kim's protests and Ken's. "If I need you, Ken dear, I'll telegraph. All those people in the troupe, you know. Some of them have been with her for ten years—fifteen."

All sorts of trains before you reached this remote little town. Little dusty red-plush trains with sociable brakemen and passengers whose clothes and bearing now seemed almost grotesque to the eyes that once had looked upon them without criticism. A long, hard, trying journey. Little towns at which you left this train and waited long hours for the next. Cinder-strewn junctions whose stations were little better than sheds.

Mile after mile the years had receded as New York was left behind. The sandy soil of the South. Little straggling villages. Unpainted weather-stained cabins, black as the faces that peered from their door-ways. When Magnolia Ravenal caught the first gleam of April dogwood flashing white in the forest depths as the train bumbled by, her heart gave a great leap. In a curious and dreamlike way the years of her life with Ravenal in Chicago, the years following Ravenal's desertion of her there, the years of Magnolia's sudden success in New York seemed to fade into unreality; they became unimportant fragmentary interludes. This was her life. She had never left it. They would be there—Julie, and Steve, and Windy, and Doc, and Parthy, and Andy, and Schultzy —somehow, they would be there. They were real. The others were dream people: Mike McDonald, Hankins, Hetty Chilson, all that raffish Chicago crew; the New York group—Kim's gay, fly, brittle brilliant crowd with which Magnolia had always assumed an ease she did not feel.

She decided, sensibly, that she was tired, a little dazed, even. She had slept scarcely at all the night before. Perhaps this news of her mother's death had been, after all, more of a shock than she thought. She would not pretend to be grief-stricken. The breach between her and the indomitable old woman had been a thing of many years' standing, and it had grown wider and wider with the years following that day when, descending upon her daughter in Chicago, Mrs. Hawks had learned that the handsome dashing Gaylord Ravenal had flown. She had been unable to resist her triumphant, "What did I tell you!" It had been the last straw.

She had wondered, vaguely, what sort of conveyance she might hire to carry her to Cold Spring, for she knew no railroad passed through this little river town. But when she descended from the train at this, the last stage but one in her wearisome journey, there was a little group at the red brick station to meet her. A man came toward her (he turned out to be the Chas. K. Barnato of the telegram). He was the general manager and press agent. Doc's old job, modernized. "How did you know me?" she had asked, and was startled when he replied:

"You look like your ma." Then, before she could recover from this: "But Elly told me it was you."

A rather amazing old lady came toward her. She looked like the ancient ruins of a bisque doll. Her cheeks were pink, her eyes bright, her skin parchment, her hat incredible.

"Don't you remember me, Nollie?" she said. And pouted her withered old lips. Then, as Magnolia stared, bewildered, she had chirped like an annoyed cockatoo, "Elly Chipley—Lenore La Verne."

"But it isn't possible!" Magnolia had cried.

This had appeared to annoy Miss Chipley afresh. "Why not, I'd like to know! I've been back with the *Cotton Blossom* the last ten years. Your ma advertised in the *Billboard* for a general utility team. My husband answered the ad, giving his name——"

"Not——?"

"Schultzy? Oh, no, dearie. I buried poor Schultzy in Douglas, Wyoming, twenty-two years ago. Yes, indeed. Clyde!" She wheeled briskly. "Clyde!" The man came forward. He was, perhaps, fifty. Surely twenty years younger than the erstwhile ingénue lead. A sheepish, grizzled man whose mouth looked as if a drawstring had been pulled out of it, leaving it limp and sprawling. "Meet my husband, Mr. Clyde Mellhop. This is Nollie. Mrs. Ravenal, it is, ain't it? Seems funny, you being married and got a famous daughter and all. Last time I saw you you was just a skinny little girl, dark-complected—— Well, your ma was hoity-toity with me when she seen it was me was the other half of the Mellhop General Utility Team. Wasn't going to let me stay, would you believe it! Well, she was glad enough to have me, in the end."

This, Magnolia realized, must be stopped. She met the understanding look of the man Barnato. He nodded. "I guess you must be pretty tuckered out, Mrs. Ravenal. Now, if you'll just step over to the car there." He indicated an important-looking closed car that stood at the far end of the station platform.

Gratefully Magnolia moved toward it. She was a little impressed with its appearance. "Your car! That was thoughtful of you. I was wondering how I'd get——"

"No, ma'am. That ain't mine. I got a little car of my own, but this is your ma's—that is—well, it's yours, now, I reckon." He helped her into the back seat with Elly. He seated himself before the wheel, with Mellhop beside him. He turned to her, solemnly. "I suppose you'd like to go right over to see your—to view the remains. She's—they're at Breitweiler's Undertaking Parlours. I kind of tended to everything, like your son-in-law's telegram said. I hope everything will suit you. Of course, if you'd like to go over to the hotel first. I took a room for you—best

they had. It's real comfortable. To-morrow morning we take her—we
go to Thebes on the ten-fifteen——"

"The hotel!" cried Magnolia. "But I want to sleep on the boat to-
night. I want to go back to the boat."

"It's a good three-quarters of an hour run from here, even in this
car."

"I know it. But I want to stay on the boat to-night."

"It's for you to say, ma'am."

The main business street of the little town was bustling and prosper-
ous-looking. Where, in her childhood river-town days the farm wagons
and buggies had stood hitched at the curb, she now saw rows of automobiles parked, side by side. Five-and-Ten-Cent Stores. Motion Pictures. Piggly-Wiggly. Popular magazines in the drug-store window. She
had thought that everything would be the same.

Breitweiler's Undertaking Parlours. Quite a little throng outside; and
within an actual crowd, close-packed. They made way respectfully for
Barnato and his party. "What is it?" whispered Magnolia. "What are
all these people here for? What has happened?"

"Your ma was quite a famous person in these parts, Mrs. Ravenal.
Up and down the rivers and around she was quite a character. I've saved
the pieces for you in the paper."

"You don't mean these people—all these people have come here to
see——"

"Yes, ma'am. In state. I hope you don't object, ma'am. I wouldn't
want to feel I'd done something you wouldn't like."

She felt a little faint. "I'd like them to go away now."

Parthenia Ann Hawks in her best black silk. Her strong black eyebrows punctuated the implacable old face with a kind of surprised resentment. She had not succumbed to the Conqueror without a battle.
Magnolia, gazing down upon the stern waxen features, the competent
hands crossed in unwilling submission upon her breast, could read the
message of revolt that was stamped, even in death, upon that strong and
terrible brow. Here! I'm mistress of this craft. You can't do this to me!
I'm Parthenia Ann Hawks! Death? Fiddlesticks and nonsense! For
others, perhaps. But not for me.

Presently they were driving swiftly out along the smooth asphalt road
toward Cold Spring. Elly Chipley was telling her tale with relish, palpably for the hundredth time.

". . . seven o'clock in the evening or maybe a few minutes past and
her standing in front of the looking-glass in her room doing her hair.
Clyde and me, we had the room next to hers, for'ard, the last few years,
on account I used to do for her, little ways. Not that she was feeble or

like that. But she needed somebody younger to do for her, now and then"—with the bridling self-consciousness of a girlish seventy, as compared to Parthy's eighty and over. "Well, I was in the next room, and just thinking I'd better be making up for the evening show when I hear a funny sound, and then a voice I didn't hardly recognize sort of squeaks, 'Elly! A stroke!' And then a crash."

Magnolia was surprised to find herself weeping: not for grief; in almost unwilling admiration of this powerful mind and will that had recognized the Enemy even as he stole up on her and struck the blow from behind.

"There, there!" cooed Elly Chipley, pleased that her recital had at last moved this handsome silent woman to proper tears. "There, there!" She patted her hand. "Look, Nollie dear. There's the boat. Seems funny not to see her lighted up for the show this time of night."

Magnolia peered through the dusk, a kind of dread in her heart. Would this, too, be changed beyond recognition? A great white long craft docked at the water's edge. Larger, yes. But much the same. In the gloom she could just make out the enormous letters painted in black against the white upper deck.

COTTON BLOSSOM FLOATING PALACE THEATRE
Parthenia Ann Hawks, Prop.

And there was the River. It was high with the April rains and the snows that nourished it from all the hundreds of miles of its vast domain—the Mississippi Basin.

Vaguely she heard Barnato—"Just started out and promised to be the biggest paying season we had for years. Yessir! Crops what they were last fall, and the country so prosperous. . . . Course, we don't aim to bother you with such details now. . . . Troupe wondering—ain't no more'n natural—what's to become of 'em now. . . . Finest show boat on the rivers. . . . Our own electric power plant. . . . Ice machine. . . . Seats fifteen hundred, easy. . . ."

And there was the River. Broad, yellow, turbulent. Magnolia was trembling. Down the embankment, across the gangplank, to the lower forward deck that was like a comfortable front porch. The bright semicircle of the little ticket window. A little group of Negro loungers and dock-hands making way respectfully, gently for the white folks. The sound of a banjo tinkling somewhere ashore, or perhaps on an old sidewheeler docked a short distance downstream. A playbill in the lobby. She stared at it. Tempest and Sunshine. The letters began to go oddly askew. A voice, far away—"Look out! She's going to faint!"

A tremendous effort. "No, I'm not. I'm—all right. I don't think I've eaten anything since early morning."

She was up in the bedroom. Dimity curtains at the windows, fresh and crisp. Clean. Shining. Orderly. Quiet. "Now you just get into bed. A hot-water bag. We'll fix you a tray and a good cup of tea. To-morrow morning you'll be feeling fine again. We got to get an early start."

She ate, gratefully. Anything I can do for you now, Nollie? No, nothing, thanks. Well, I'm kind of beat, myself. It's been a day, I can tell you. Good-night. Good-night. Now I'll leave my door open, so's if you call me——

Nine o'clock. Ten. The hoarse hoot of a boat whistle. The clank of anchor chains. Swish. Swash. Fainter. Cluck-suck against the hull. Quieter. More quiet. Quiet. Black velvet. The River. Home.

XIX

KIM RAVENAL's tenth letter to her mother was the decisive one. It arrived late in May, when the Cotton Blossom Floating Palace Theatre was playing Lulu, Mississippi. From where the show boat lay just below the landing there was little enough to indicate that a town was situated near by. Lulu, Mississippi, in May, was humid and drowsy and dusty and fly-ridden. The Negroes lolled in the shade of their cabins and loafed at the water's edge. Thick-petalled white flowers amidst glossy dark green foliage filled the air with a drugging sweetness, and scarlet-petalled flowers stuck their wicked yellow tongues out at the passer-by.

Magnolia, on the *Cotton Blossom* upper deck that was like a cosy veranda, sat half in the shade and half in the sun and let the moist heat envelop her. The little nervous lines that New York had etched about her eyes and mouth seemed to vanish magically under the languorous touch of the saturant Southern air. She was again like the lovely creamy blossom for which she had been named; a little drooping, perhaps; a little faded; but Magnolia.

Elly Chipley, setting to rights her privileged bedroom on the boat's port side, came to the screen door in cotton morning frock and boudoir cap. The frock was a gay gingham of girlish cut, its colour a delicate pink. The cap was a trifle of lace and ribbon. From this frame her withered life-scarred old mask looked out, almost fascinating in its grotesquerie.

"Beats me how you can sit out there in the heat like a lizard or a cat or something and not get a stroke. Will, too, one these fine days."

Magnolia, glancing up from the perusal of her letter, stretched her arms above her head luxuriously. "I love it."

Elly Chipley's sharp old eyes snapped at the typewritten sheets of the letter in Magnolia's hand. "Heard from your daughter again, did you?"

"Yes."

"I never seen anybody such a hand at writing letters. You got one about every stand since you started with the boat, seems. I was saying to Clyde only yesterday, I says, what's she find to write about!"

This, Magnolia knew, was not a mere figure of speech. In some mysterious way the knowledge had seeped through the *Cotton Blossom* company that in these frequent letters between mother and daughter a battle was being waged. They sensed, too, that in the outcome of this battle lay their own future.

The erstwhile ingénue now assumed an elaborate carelessness of manner which, to the doubting onlooker, would forever have decided the question of her dramatic ability. "What's she got to say, h'm? What——" here she giggled in shrill falsetto appreciation of her own wit—"what news on the Rialto?"

Magnolia glanced down again at the letter. "I think Kim may come down for a few days to visit us, in June. With her husband."

The ribbons of Elly's cap trembled. The little withered well-kept hand in which she still took such pride went to her lips that were working nervously. "You don't say! Well, that'll be nice." After which triumph of simulated casualness you heard her incautious steps clattering down the stairs and up the aisle to the lesser dressing rooms and bedrooms at the rear of the stage.

Magnolia picked up the letter again. Kim hated to write letters. The number that she had written her mother in the past month testified her perturbation.

Nola darling, you've just gone gaga, that's all. What do you mean by staying down there in that wretched malarial heat! Now listen to me. We close June first. They plan to open in Boston in September, then Philadelphia, Chicago. My contract, of course, doesn't call for the road. Cruger offered me an increase and a house percentage if I'd go when the road season opens, but you know how I hate touring. You're the trouper of this family. Besides, I wouldn't leave Andy. He misses you as much as Ken and I do. If he could talk, he would demand his grand-

mother's immediate presence. If you aren't in New York by June third
I shall come and get you. I mean this. Ken and I sail on the *Olympic*
June tenth. There's a play in London that Cruger wants me to see for
next season. You know. Casualty. We'll go to Paris, Vienna, Budapest,
and back August first. Come along or stay in the country with Andy.
Nate Fried says he'll settle up your business affairs if that's what's
bothering you. What is there to do except sell the old tub or give it
away or something, and take the next train for New York? Your bookings say Lazare, Mississippi, June fourth, fifth and sixth. Nate looked
it up and reports it's twenty miles from a railroad. Now, Nola, that's
just too mad. Come on home.

KIM.

The hand that held the letter dropped to her lap again. Magnolia lay
relaxed in the low deck chair and surveyed through half-closed lids the
turgid, swift-flowing stream that led on to Louisiana and the sea. Above
the clay banks that rose from the river lay the scrubby little settlement
shimmering in the noonday heat. A mule team toiled along the river
road drawing a decrepit cart on whose sagging seat a Negro sat slumped,
the rope lines slack in his listless hands, his body swaying with the motion of the vehicle. From the cook's galley, aft, came the yee-yah-yah-yah
of Negro laughter. Then a sudden crash of piano, drum, horn, and
cymbals. The band was rehearsing. The porcine squeal and bleat and
grunt of the saxophone. Mississippi Blues they were playing. Ort Han-
ley, of the Character Team, sang it in the concert after the show. I got
the blues. I said the blues. I got the M-i-s-, I said the s-i-s, I said the s-i-
pp-i, Mississippi, I got them Miss-is-*sippi blu*-hoo-hoos.

The heat and the music and the laughter and the squeak of the mule
cart up the road blended and made a colourful background against
which the woman in the chair viewed the procession of the last twenty-
five years.

It had turned out well enough. She had gone on, blindly, and it had
turned out well enough. Kim. Kim was different. Nothing blind about
Kim. She had emerged from the cloistral calm of the Chicago convent
with her competent mind quite made up. I am going to be an actress.
Oh, no, Kim! Not you! But Kim had gone about it as she went about
everything. Clearheaded. Thoughtful. Deliberate. But actresses were not
made in this way, Magnolia argued. Oh, yes, they were. Five years in
stock on Chicago's North Side. A tiny part in musical comedy. Kim
decided that she knew nothing. She would go to the National Theatre
School of Acting in New York and start all over again. Magnolia's vaudeville days were drawing to an end. A middle-aged woman, still able to
hold her audience, still possessing a haunting kind of melancholy beauty.

But more than this was needed to hold one's head above the roaring tide of ragtime jazz-time youngsters surging now toward the footlights. She had known what it was to be a headliner, but she had never commanded the fantastic figures of the more spectacular acts. She had been thrifty, though, and canny. She easily saw Kim through the National Theatre School. The idea of Kim in a school of acting struck her as being absurd, though Kim gravely explained to her its uses. Finally she took a tiny apartment in New York so that she and Kim might have a home together. Kim worked slavishly, ferociously. The idea of the school did not amuse Magnolia as much as it had at first.

Fencing lessons. Gymnastic dancing. Interpretive dancing. Singing lessons. Voice placing. French lessons.

"Are you studying to be an acrobat or a singer or a dancer? I can't make it out."

"Now, Nola, don't be an old-fashioned frumpy darling. Spend a day at the school and you'll know what I'm getting at."

The dancing class. A big bright bare room. A phonograph. Ten girls bare-legged, bare-footed, dressed in wisps. A sturdy, bare-legged woman teacher in a hard-worked green chiffon wisp. They stood in a circle, perhaps five feet apart, and jumped on one foot and swung the other leg behind them, and kept this up, alternating right leg and left, for ten minutes. It looked ridiculously simple. Magnolia tried it when she got home and found she couldn't do it at all. Bar work. Make a straight line of that leg. Back! Back! Stretch! Stretch! Stretch! Some of it was too precious. The girls in line formation and the green chiffon person facing them, saying, idiotically, and suiting actions to words:

"Reach down into the valley! Gather handfuls of mist. Up, up, facing the sun! Oh, how lovely!"

The Voice class. The Instructor, wearing a hat with an imposing façade and clanking with plaques of arts-and-crafts jewellery, resembled, as she sat at her table fronting the seated semi-circle of young men and women, the chairman of a woman's club during the business session of a committee meeting.

Her voice was "placed." Magnolia, listening and beholding, would not have been surprised to see her remove her voice, an entity, from her throat and hold it up for inspection. It was a thing so artificial, so studied, so manufactured. She articulated carefully and with great elegance.

"I don't need to go into the wide-open throat to-day. We will start with the jaw exercises. Down! To the side! Side! Rotate!"

With immense gravity and earnestness twelve young men and women took hold of their respective jaws and pulled these down; from side to side; around. They showed no embarrassment.

"Now then! The sound of *b*. Bub-ub-ub-ub. *They bribed Bob with a bib.* Sound of *t*. *It isn't a bit hot.* Sound of *d*. *Dad did the deed.* Sound of *n*. *None of the nine nuns came at noon.*"

Singly and en masse they disposed of Bob and Dad and the nine nuns. Pharynx resonance. Say, "Clear and free, Miss Ravenal." Miss Ravenal said clear-and-free, distinctly. No, no, no! Not clear-and-free, but clear—and free. Do you see what I mean? Good. Now take it again. Miss Ravenal took it again. Clear—and free. *That's* better.

Now then. Words that differ in the *wh* sound. Mr. Karel, let us hear your list. Mr. Karel obliges. Whether-weather, when-wen, whinny-winnow, whither-wither; why do you spell it with a y?

Miss Rogers, *l* sounds. Miss Rogers, enormously solemn (fated for Lady Macbeth at the lightest)—level, loyal, lull, lily, lentil, love, lust, liberty, boil, coral——

Now then! The nerve vitalizing breath! We'll all stand. Hold the breath. Stretch out arms. Arms in—and IN—AND IN—out—in—head up—mouth open——

Shades of Modjeska, Duse, Rachel, Mrs. Siddons, Bernhardt! Was this the way an actress was made!

"You wait and see," said Kim, grimly. Dancing, singing, fencing, voice, French. One year. Two. Three. Magnolia had waited, and she had seen.

Kim had had none of those preliminary hardships and terrors and temptations, then, that are supposed to beset the path of the attractive young woman who would travel the road to theatrical achievement. Her success actually had been instantaneous and sustained. She had been given the part of the daughter of a worldly mother in a new piece by Ford Salter and had taken the play away from the star who did the mother. Her performance had been clear-cut, modern, deft, convincing. She was fresh, but finished.

She was intelligent, successful, workmanlike, intuitive, vigorous, adaptable. She was almost the first of this new crop of intelligent, successful, deft, workmanlike, intuitive, vigorous, adaptable young women of the theatre. There was about her—or them—nothing of genius, of greatness, of the divine fire. But the dramatic critics of the younger school who were too late to have seen past genius in its heyday and for whom the theatrical genius of their day was yet to come, viewed her performance and waxed hysterical, mistaking talent and intelligence and hard work and ambition for something more rare. It became the thing to proclaim each smart young woman the Duse of her day if she had a decent feeling for stage tempo, could sustain a character throughout three acts, speak the English language intelligibly, cross a stage or sit in a chair naturally. By the time Kim had been five years out of the National Theatre School there were Duses by the dozen, and a Broadway Bernhardt was born at least once a season.

These gave, invariably, what is known as a fine performance. As you stood in the lobby between the acts, smoking your cigarette, you said, "She's giving a fine performance."

"A fine performance!" Magnolia echoed one evening, rather irritably, after she and Kim had returned from the opening of a play in which one of Kim's friends was featured. "But she doesn't act. Everything she did and everything she said was right. And I was as carried out of myself as though I were listening to a clock strike. When I go to the theatre I want to care. In the old days maybe they didn't know so much about tempo and rhythm, but in the audience strong men wept and women fainted——"

"Now listen, Nola darling. One of your old-day gals would last about four seconds on Broadway. I've heard about Clara Morris and Mrs. Siddons, and Modjeska, and Bernhardt all my life. If the sentimental old dears were to come back in an all-star revival to-day the intelligent modern theatre-going audience would walk out on them."

The new-school actresses went in for the smarter teas, eschewed cocktails, visited the art exhibits, had their portraits painted in the new manner, never were seen at night clubs, were glimpsed coming out of Scribner's with a thick volume of modern biography, used practically no make-up when in mufti, kept their names out of the New York telephone directory, wore flat-heeled shoes and woollen stockings while walking briskly in Central Park, went to Symphony Concerts; were, in short, figures as glamorous and romantic as a pint of milk. Everything they did on the stage was right. Intelligent, well thought out, and right. Watching them, you knew it was right—tempo, tone, mood, character. Right. As right as an engineering blueprint. Your pulses, as you sat in the theatre, were normal.

Usually, their third season, you saw them unwisely lunching too often at the Algonquin Round Table and wise-cracking with the critics there. The fourth they took a bit in that new English comedy just until O'Neill should have finished the play he was doing for them. The fifth they married that little Whatshisname. The sixth they said, mysteriously, that they were Writing.

Kim kept away from the Algonquin, did not attend first nights with Woollcott or Broun, had a full-page Steichen picture in *Vanity Fair*, and married Kenneth Cameron. She went out rarely. Sunday night dinners, sometimes; or she had people in (ham *à la* Queenie part of the cold buffet). Her list of Sunday night guests or engagements read like a roster of the New York Telephone Company's Exchanges. Stuyvesant, Beekman, Bleeker, Murray, Rhinelander, Vanderbilt, Jerome, Wadsworth, Tremont. She learned to say, "It's just one of those things——" She finished an unfinished sentence with, "I *mean*——!" and a throwing up of the open palms.

Kenneth Cameron. Her marriage with Kenneth Cameron was successful and happy and very nice. Separate bedrooms and those lovely negligées—velvet with Venetian sleeves and square neck-line. Excellent friends. Nothing sordid. Personal liberty and privacy of thought and action—those were the things that made for happiness in marriage. Magnolia wondered, sometimes, but certainly it was not for her to venture opinion. Her own marriage had been no such glittering example of perfection. Yet she wondered, seeing this well-ordered and respectful union, if Kim was not, after all, missing something. Wasn't marriage, like life, unstimulating and unprofitable and somewhat empty when too well ordered and protected and guarded? Wasn't it finer, more splendid, more nourishing, when it was, like life itself, a mixture of the sordid and the magnificent; of mud and stars; of earth and flowers; of love and hate and laughter and tears and ugliness and beauty and hurt? She was wrong, of course. Ken's manner toward Kim was polite, tender, thoughtful. Kim's manner toward Ken was polite, tender, thoughtful. Are you free next Thursday, dear? The Paynes are having those Russians. It might be rather interesting. . . . Sorry. Ken's voice. Soft, light. It was the—well, Magnolia never acknowledged this, even to herself, but it was what she called the male interior decorator's voice. You heard it a good deal at teas, and at the Algonquin, and in the lobby between the acts on first nights and in those fascinating shops on Madison Avenue where furniture and old glass and brasses and pictures were shown you by slim young men with delicate hands. I *mean*——! It's just one of those things. . . .

There was no Mississippi in Kim. Kim was like the Illinois River of Magnolia's childhood days. Kim's life flowed tranquilly between gentle green-clad shores, orderly, well regulated, dependable.

"For the land's sakes, Magnolia Hawks, you sitting out there yet! Here it's after three and nearly dinner time!" Elly Chipley at the screen door. "And in the blazing sun, too. You need somebody to look after you worse than your ma did."

Elly was justified, for Magnolia had a headache that night.

Kim and Ken arrived unexpectedly together on June second, clattering up to the boat landing in a scarecrow Ford driven by a stout Negro in khaki pants, puttees, and an army shirt.

Kim was breathless, but exhilarated. "He says he drove in France in '17, and I believe it. Good God! Every bolt, screw, bar, nut, curtain, and door in the thing rattled and flapped and opened and fell in and fell out. I've been working like a Swiss bell-ringer trying to keep things together there in the back seat. Nola darling, what do you mean by staying down in this miserable hole all these weeks! Ken, dear, take another aspirin and a pinch of bicarb and lie down a minute. . . . Ken's got a headache from the heat and the awful trip. . . . We're going back tonight, and we sail on the tenth, and, Nola darling, for heaven's sake . . ."

They had a talk. The customary four o'clock dinner was delayed until nearly five because of it. They sat in Magnolia's green-shaded bedroom with its frilled white bedspread and dimity curtains—rather, Kim and Magnolia sat and Ken sprawled his lean length on the bed, looking a little yellow and haggard, what with the heat and the headache. And in the cook's galley, and on the stage, and in the little dressing rooms that looked out on the river, and on deck, and in the box office, the company and crew of the Cotton Blossom Floating Palace Theatre lounged and waited, played pinochle and waited, sewed and napped and read and wondered and waited.

"You can't mean it, Nola darling. Flopping up and down these muddy wretched rivers in this heat! You could be out at the Bay with Andy. Or in London with Ken and me—Ken, dear, isn't it any better?—or even in New York, in the lovely airy apartment, it's cooler than——"

Magnolia sat forward.

"Listen, Kim. I love it. The rivers. And the people. And the show boat. And the life. I don't know why. It's bred in me, I suppose. Yes, I do know why. Your grandpa died when you were too little to remember him, really. Or you'd know why. Now, if you two are set on going back on the night train, you'll have to listen to me for a minute. I went over things with the lawyer and the banker in Thebes when we took Mama back there. Your grandmother left a fortune. I don't mean a few thousand dollars. She left half a million, made out of this boat in the last twenty-five years. I'm giving it to you, Kim, and Ken."

Refusal, of course. Protest. Consideration. Acquiescence. Agreement. Acceptance. Ken was sitting up now, pallidly. Kim was lyric. "Half a million! Mother! Ken! It means the plays I want, and Ken to produce them. It means that I can establish a real American theatre in New York. I can do the plays I've been longing to do—Ibsen and Hauptmann, and Werfel, and Schnitzler, and Molnar, and Chekhov, and Shakespeare even. Ken! We'll call it the American Theatre!"

"The American Theatre," Magnolia repeated after her, thoughtfully. And smiled then. "The American Theatre." She looked a trifle uncomfortable, as one who has heard a good joke, and has no one with whom to share it.

A loud-tongued bell clanged and reverberated through the show boat's length. Dinner.

Kim and Ken pretended not to notice the heat and flies and the molten state of the butter. They met everyone from the captain to the cook; from the ingénue lead to the drum.

"Well, Miss Ravenal, this is an—or Mrs. Cameron, I suppose I should say—an honour. We know all about you, even if you don't know about us." Not one of them had ever seen her.

A little tour of the show boat after dinner. Ken, still pale, but refreshed by tea, was moved to exclamations of admiration. Look at that, Kim! Ingenious. Oh, say, we must stay over and see a performance. I'd no idea! And these combination dressing rooms and bedrooms, eh? Well, I'll be damned!

Elly Chipley was making up in her special dressing room, infinitesimal in size, just off the stage. Her part for to-night was that of a grande dame in black silk and lace cap and fichu. The play was The Planter's Daughter. She had been rather sniffy in her attitude toward the distinguished visitors. They couldn't patronize *her*. She applied the rouge to her withered cheeks in little pettish dabs, and leaned critically forward to scrutinize her old mask of a face. What did she see there? Kim wondered, watching her, fascinated.

"Mother tells me you played Juliet, years ago. How marvellous!"

Elly Chipley tossed her head skittishly. "Yes, indeed! Played Juliet, and was known as the Western Favourite. I wasn't always on a show boat, I promise you."

"What a thrill—to play Juliet when you were so young! Usually we have to wait until we're fifty. Tell me, dear Miss La Verne"—elaborately polite, and determined to mollify this old harridan—"tell me, who was your Romeo?"

And then Life laughed at Elly Chipley (Lenore La Verne on the bills) and at Kim Ravenal, and the institution known as the Stage. For Elly Chipley tapped her cheek thoughtfully with her powder puff, and blinked her old eyes, and screwed up her tremulous old mouth, and pondered, and finally shook her head. "My Romeo? Let me see. Let—me—see. Who *was* my Romeo?"

They must go now. Oh, Nola darling, half a million! It's too fantastic. Mother, I can't bear to leave you down in this God-forsaken hole. Flies and Negroes and mud and all this yellow terrible river that you love more than me. Stand up there—high up—where we can see you as long as possible.

The usual crowd was drifting down to the landing as the show-boat lights began to glow. Twilight was coming on. On the landing, up the river bank, sauntering down the road, came the Negroes, and the hangers-on, the farm-hands, the river folk, the curious, the idle, the amusement-hungry. Snatches of song. Feet shuffling upon the wharf boards. A banjo twanging.

They were being taken back to the nearest railroad connection, but not in the Ford that had brought them. They sat luxuriously in the car that had been Parthy's and that was Magnolia's now.

"Mother, dearest, you'll be back in New York in October or November at the latest, won't you? Promise me. When the boat closes? You will!"

Kim was weeping. The car started smoothly. She turned for a last glimpse through her tears. "Oh, Ken, do you think I ought to leave her like this?"

"She'll be all right, dear. Look at her! Jove!"

There stood Magnolia Ravenal on the upper deck of the Cotton Blossom Floating Palace Theatre, silhouetted against sunset sky and water—tall, erect, indomitable. Her mouth was smiling but her great eyes were wide and sombre. They gazed, unwinking, across the sunlit waters. One arm was raised in a gesture of farewell.

"Isn't she splendid, Ken!" cried Kim, through her tears. "There's something about her that's eternal and unconquerable—like the River."

A bend in the upper road. A clump of sycamores. The river, the show boat, the straight silent figure were lost to view.

SO BIG

I

UNTIL he was almost ten the name stuck to him. He had literally to
fight his way free of it. From So Big (of fond and infantile derivation)
it had been condensed into Sobig. And Sobig DeJong, in all its con-
sonantal disharmony, he had remained until he was a ten-year-old school-
boy in that incredibly Dutch district southwest of Chicago known first
as New Holland and later as High Prairie. At ten, by dint of fists, teeth,
copper-toed boots, and temper, he earned the right to be called by his
real name, Dirk DeJong. Now and then, of course, the nickname bobbed
up and had to be subdued in a brief and bitter skirmish. His mother,
with whom the name had originated, was the worst offender. When she
lapsed he did not, naturally, use schoolyard tactics on her. But he sulked
and glowered portentously and refused to answer, though her tone,
when she called him So Big, would have melted the heart of any but
that natural savage, a boy of ten.

The nickname had sprung from the early and idiotic question invariably put to babies and answered by them, with infinite patience,
through the years of their infancy.

Selina DeJong, darting expertly about her kitchen, from washtub to
baking board, from stove to table, or, if at work in the fields of the
truck farm, straightening the numbed back for a moment's respite from
the close-set rows of carrots, turnips, spinach, or beets over which she
was labouring, would wipe the sweat beads from nose and forehead
with a quick duck of her head in the crook of her bent arm. Those great
fine dark eyes of hers would regard the child perched impermanently on
a little heap of empty potato sacks, one of which comprised his costume.
He was constantly detaching himself from the parent sack heap to dig
and burrow in the rich warm black loam of the truck garden. Selina
DeJong had little time for the expression of affection. The work was always hot at her heels. You saw a young woman in a blue calico dress,
faded and earth-grimed. Between her eyes was a driven look as of one

who walks always a little ahead of herself in her haste. Her dark abundant hair was skewered into a utilitarian knob from which soft loops and strands were constantly escaping, to be pushed back by that same harried ducking gesture of head and bent arm. Her hands, for such use, were usually too crusted and inground with the soil into which she was delving. You saw a child of perhaps two years, dirt-streaked, sunburned, and generally otherwise defaced by those bumps, bites, scratches, and contusions that are the common lot of the farm child of a mother harried by work. Yet, in that moment, as the woman looked at the child there in the warm moist spring of the Illinois prairie land, or in the cluttered kitchen of the farmhouse, there quivered and vibrated between them and all about them an aura, a glow, that imparted to them and their surroundings a mystery, a beauty, a radiance.

"How big is baby?" Selina would demand, senselessly. "How big is my man?"

The child would momentarily cease to poke plump fingers into the rich black loam. He would smile a gummy though slightly weary smile and stretch wide his arms. She, too, would open her tired arms wide, wide. Then they would say in a duet, his mouth a puckered pink petal, hers quivering with tenderness and a certain amusement, "So-o-o-o big!" with the voice soaring on the prolonged vowel and dropping suddenly with the second word. Part of the game. The child became so habituated to this question that sometimes, if Selina happened to glance round at him suddenly in the midst of her task, he would take his cue without the familiar question being put and would squeal his "So-o-o-o big!" rather absently, in dutiful solo. Then he would throw back his head and laugh a triumphant laugh, his open mouth a coral orifice. She would run to him, and swoop down upon him, and bury her flushed face in the warm moist creases of his neck, and make as though to devour him. "So big!"

But of course he wasn't. He wasn't as big as that. In fact, he never became as big as the wide-stretched arms of her love and imagination would have had him. You would have thought she should have been satisfied when, in later years, he was the Dirk DeJong whose name you saw (engraved) at the top of heavy cream linen paper, so rich and thick and stiff as to have the effect of being starched and ironed by some costly American business process; whose clothes were made by Peter Peel, the English tailor; whose roadster ran on a French chassis; whose cabinet held mellow Italian vermouth and Spanish sherry; whose wants were served by a Japanese houseman; whose life, in short, was that of the successful citizen of the Republic. But she wasn't. Not only was she dissatisfied: she was at once remorseful and indignant, as though she,

Selina DeJong, the vegetable pedler, had been partly to blame for this success of his, and partly cheated by it.

When Selina DeJong had been Selina Peake she had lived in Chicago with her father. They had lived in many other cities as well. In Denver during the rampant '8os. In New York when Selina was twelve. In Milwaukee briefly. There was even a San Francisco interlude which was always a little sketchy in Selina's mind and which had ended in a departure so hurried as to bewilder even Selina who had learned to accept sudden comings and abrupt goings without question. "Business," her father always said. "Little deal." She never knew until the day of his death how literally the word deal was applicable to his business transactions. Simeon Peake, travelling the country with his little daughter, was a gambler by profession, temperament, and natural talents. When in luck they lived royally, stopping at the best hotels, eating strange, succulent sea-viands, going to the play, driving in hired rigs (always with two horses. If Simeon Peake had not enough money for a two-horse equipage he walked). When Fortune hid her face they lived in boarding houses, ate boarding-house meals, wore the clothes bought when Fortune's breath was balmy. During all this time Selina attended schools, good, bad, private, public, with surprising regularity considering her nomadic existence. Deep-bosomed matrons, seeing this dark-eyed serious child seated alone in a hotel lobby or boarding-house parlour, would bend over her in solicitous questioning.

"Where is your mamma, little girl?"

"She is dead," Selina would reply, politely and composedly.

"Oh, my poor little dear!" Then, with a warm rush, "Don't you want to come and play with my little girl? She loves little girls to play with. H'm?" The "m" of the interrogation held hummingly, tenderly.

"No, thank you very much. I'm waiting for my father. He would be disappointed not to find me here."

These good ladies wasted their sympathy. Selina had a beautiful time. Except for three years, to recall which was to her like entering a sombre icy room on leaving a warm and glowing one, her life was free, interesting, varied. She made decisions usually devolving upon the adult mind. She selected clothes. She ruled her father. She read absorbedly books found in boarding-house parlours, in hotels, in such public libraries as the times afforded. She was alone for hours a day, daily. Frequently her father, fearful of loneliness for her, brought her an armful of books and she had an orgy, dipping and swooping about among them in a sort of gourmand's ecstasy of indecision. In this way, at fifteen, she knew the writings of Byron, Jane Austen, Dickens, Charlotte Brontë, Felicia Hemans. Not to speak of Mrs. E. D. E. N. Southworth, Bertha M. Clay, and that good fairy of the scullery, the *Fireside Companion*, in whose pages factory girls and dukes were brought together as inevitably as steak and onions. These last were, of course, the result of Selina's mode of living, and were loaned her by kind-hearted landladies, chambermaids, and waitresses all the way from California to New York.

Her three dark years—from nine to twelve—were spent with her two maiden aunts, the Misses Sarah and Abbie Peake, in the dim, prim Vermont Peake house from which her father, the black sheep, had run away when a boy. After her mother's death Simeon Peake had sent his little daughter back east in a fit of remorse and temporary helplessness on his part and a spurt of forgiveness and churchly charity on the part of his two sisters. The two women were incredibly drawn in the pattern of the New England spinster of fiction. Mitts, preserves, Bible, chilly best room, solemn and kittenless cat, order, little-girls-mustn't. They smelled of apples—of withered apples that have rotted at the core. Selina had once found such an apple in a corner of a disorderly school-desk, had sniffed it, regarded its wrinkled, sapless pink cheek, and had bitten into it adventuresomely, only to spit out the mouthful in an explosive and unladylike spray. It had been all black and mouldy at its heart.

Something of this she must have conveyed, in her desperation, to her father in an uncensored letter. Without warning he had come for her, and at sight of him she had been guilty of the only fit of hysteria that marked her life, before or after the episode.

So, then, from twelve to nineteen she was happy. They had come to Chicago in 1885, when she was sixteen. There they remained. Selina attended Miss Fister's Select School for Young Ladies. When her father brought her there he had raised quite a flutter in the Fister breast—so soft-spoken was he, so gentle, so sad-appearing, so winning as to smile. In the investment business, he explained. Stocks and that kind of thing. A widower. Miss Fister said, yes, she understood.

Simeon Peake had had nothing of the look of the professional gambler of the day. The wide slouch hat, the flowing mustache, the glittering eye, the too-bright boots, the gay cravat, all were missing in Simeon Peake's makeup. True, he did sport a singularly clear white diamond pin in his shirt front; and his hat he wore just a little on one side. But then, these both were in the male mode and quite commonly seen. For the rest he seemed a mild and suave man, slim, a trifle diffident, speaking seldom and then with a New England drawl by which he had come honestly enough, Vermont Peake that he was.

Chicago was his meat. It was booming, prosperous. Jeff Hankins's red plush and mirrored gambling house, and Mike McDonald's, too, both on Clark Street, knew him daily. He played in good luck and bad, but he managed somehow to see to it that there was always the money to pay for the Fister schooling. His was the ideal poker face—bland, emotionless, immobile. When he was flush they ate at the Palmer House, dining off chicken or quail and thick rich soup and the apple pie for which the hostelry was famous. Waiters hovered solicitously about Simeon Peake, though he rarely addressed them and never looked at them. Selina was happy. She knew only such young people—girls—as she met at Miss Fister's school. Of men, other than her father, she knew as little as a nun—less. For those cloistered creatures must, if only in the conning of their Bible, learn much of the moods and passions that sway the male. The Songs of Solomon alone are a glorious sex education. But the Bible was not included in Selina's haphazard reading, and the Gideonite was not then a force in the hotel world.

Her chum was Julie Hempel, daughter of August Hempel, the Clark Street butcher. You probably now own some Hempel stock, if you're lucky; and eat Hempel bacon and Hempel hams cured in the hickory, for in Chicago the distance from butcher of 1885 to packer of 1890 was only a five-year leap.

Being so much alone developed in her a gift for the make-believe. In a comfortable, well-dressed way she was a sort of mixture of Dick Swiveller's Marchioness and Sarah Crewe. Even in her childhood she extracted from life the double enjoyment that comes usually only to the creative mind. "Now I'm doing this. Now I'm doing that," she told herself while she was doing it. Looking on while she participated. Perhaps her theatre-going had something to do with this. At an age when most little girls were not only unheard but practically unseen, she occupied a grown-up seat at the play, her rapt face, with its dark serious eyes, glowing in a sort of luminous pallor as she sat proudly next her father. Simeon Peake had the gambler's love of the theatre, himself possessing the dramatic quality necessary to the successful following of his profession.

In this way Selina, half-hidden in the depths of an orchestra seat, wriggled in ecstatic anticipation when the curtain ascended on the grotesque rows of Haverly's minstrels. She wept (as did Simeon) over the agonies of The Two Orphans when Kitty Blanchard and McKee Rankin came to Chicago with the Union Square Stock Company. She witnessed that startling innovation, a Jewish play, called Samuel of Posen. She saw Fanny Davenport in Pique. Simeon even took her to a performance of that shocking and delightful form of new entertainment, the Extravaganza. She thought the plump creature in tights and spangles, descending the long stairway, the most beautiful being she had ever seen.

"The thing I like about plays and books is that anything can happen. Anything! You never know," Selina said, after one of these evenings.

"No different from life," Simeon Peake assured her. "You've no idea the things that happen to you if you just relax and take them as they come."

Curiously enough, Simeon Peake said this, not through ignorance, but deliberately and with reason. In his way and day he was a very modern father. "I want you to see all kinds," he would say to her. "I want you to realize that this whole thing is just a grand adventure. A fine show. The trick is to play in it and look at it at the same time."

"What whole thing?"

"Living. All mixed up. The more kinds of people you see, and the more things you do, and the more things that happen to you, the richer you are. Even if they're not pleasant things. That's living. Remember, no matter what happens, good or bad, it's just so much"—he used the gambler's term, unconsciously—"just so much velvet."

But Selina, somehow, understood. "You mean that anything's better than being Aunt Sarah and Aunt Abbie."

"Well—yes. There are only two kinds of people in the world that really count. One kind's wheat and the other kind's emeralds."

"Fanny Davenport's an emerald," said Selina, quickly, and rather surprised to find herself saying it.

"Yes. That's it."

"And—and Julie Hempel's father—he's wheat."

"By golly, Sele!" shouted Simeon Peake. "You're a shrewd little tyke!"

It was after reading "Pride and Prejudice" that she decided to be the Jane Austen of her time. She became very mysterious and enjoyed a brief period of unpopularity at Miss Fister's owing to her veiled allusions to her "work"; and an annoying way of smiling to herself and tapping a ruminative toe as though engaged in visions far too exquisite for the common eye. Her chum Julie Hempel, properly enough, became enraged at this and gave Selina to understand that she must make her choice between revealing her secret or being cast out of the Hempel heart. Selina swore her to secrecy.

"Very well, then. Now I'll tell you. I'm going to be a novelist." Julie was palpably disappointed, though she said, "Selina!" as though properly impressed, but followed it up with: "Still, I don't see why you had to be so mysterious about it."

"You just don't understand, Julie. Writers have to study life at first hand. And if people know you're studying them they don't act natural. Now, that day you were telling me about the young man in your father's shop who looked at you and said——"

"Selina Peake, if you dare to put that in your book I'll never speak——"

"All right. I won't. But that's what I mean. You see!"

Julie Hempel and Selina Peake, both finished products of Miss Fister's school, were of an age—nineteen. Selina, on this September day, had been spending the afternoon with Julie, and now, adjusting her hat preparatory to leaving, she clapped her hands over her ears to shut out the sounds of Julie's importunings that she stay to supper. Certainly the prospect of the usual Monday evening meal in Mrs. Tebbitt's boarding house (the Peake luck was momentarily low) did not present sufficient excuse for Selina's refusal. Indeed, the Hempel supper as sketched dish for dish by the urgent Julie brought little greedy groans from Selina.

"It's prairie chickens—three of them—that a farmer west of town brought Father. Mother fixes them with stuffing, and there's currant jell. Creamed onions and baked tomatoes. And for dessert, apple roll."

Selina snapped the elastic holding her high-crowned hat under her chignon of hair in the back. She uttered a final and quavering groan. "On Monday nights we have cold mutton and cabbage at Mrs. Tebbitt's. This is Monday."

"Well then, silly, why not stay!"

"Father comes home at six. If I'm not there he's disappointed."

Julie, plump, blonde, placid, forsook her soft white blandishments and tried steel against the steel of Selina's decision.

"He leaves you right after supper. And you're alone every night until twelve and after."

"I don't see what that has to do with it," Selina said, stiffly.

Julie's steel, being low-grade, melted at once and ran off her in rivulets. "Of course it hasn't, Selie dear. Only I thought you might leave him just this once."

"If I'm not there he's disappointed. And that terrible Mrs. Tebbitt makes eyes at him. He hates it there."

"Then I don't see why you stay. I never could see. You've been there four months now, and I think it's horrid and stuffy; and oilcloth on the stairs."

"Father has had some temporary business setbacks."

Selina's costume testified to that. True, it was modish, and bustled, and basqued, and flounced; and her high-crowned, short-rimmed hat, with its trimming of feathers and flowers and ribbons had come from New York. But both were of last spring's purchasing, and this was September.

In the course of the afternoon they had been looking over the pages of Godey's *Ladies' Book* for that month. The disparity between Selina's costume and the creations pictured there was much as the difference

between the Tebbitt meal and that outlined by Julie. Now Julie, fond
though defeated, kissed her friend good-bye.

Selina walked quickly the short distance from the Hempel house to
Tebbitt's, on Dearborn Avenue. Up in her second-floor room she took
off her hat and called to her father, but he had not yet come in. She
was glad of that. She had been fearful of being late. She regarded her
hat now with some distaste, decided to rip off the faded spring roses,
did rip a stitch or two, only to discover that the hat material was more
faded than the roses, and that the uncovered surface showed up a dark
splotch like a wall-spot when a picture, long hung, is removed. So she
got a needle and prepared to tack the offending rose in its accustomed
place.

Perched on the arm of a chair near the window, taking quick deft
stitches, she heard a sound. She had never heard that sound before—
that peculiar sound—the slow, ominous tread of men laden with a heavy
inert burden; bearing with infinite care that which was well beyond
hurting. Selina had never heard that sound before, and yet, hearing it,
she recognized it by one of those pangs, centuries old, called woman's
instinct. Thud—shuffle—thud—shuffle—up the narrow stairway, along
the passage. She stood up, the needle poised in her hand. The hat fell to
the floor. Her eyes were wide, fixed. Her lips slightly parted. The listening look. She knew.

She knew even before she heard the hoarse man's voice saying, "Lift
'er up there a little on the corner, now. Easy—e-e-easy." And Mrs.
Tebbitt's high shrill clamour: "You can't bring it in there! You hadn't
ought to bring it in here like this!"

Selina's suspended breath came back. She was panting now. She
had flung open the door. A flat still burden partially covered with an
overcoat carelessly flung over the face. The feet, in their square-toed
boots, wobbled listlessly. Selina noticed how shiny the boots were. He
was always very finicking about such things.

Simeon Peake had been shot in Jeff Hankins's place at five in the
afternoon. The irony of it was that the bullet had not been intended for
him at all. Its derelict course had been due to feminine aim. Sped by
one of those over-dramatic ladies who, armed with horsewhip or pistol
in tardy defence of their honour, spangled Chicago's dull '80s with their
doings, it had been meant for a well-known newspaper publisher
usually mentioned (in papers other than his own) as a bon vivant.
The lady's leaden remonstrance was to have been proof of the fact
that he had been more vivacious than bon.

It was, perhaps, because of this that the matter was pretty well hushed
up. The publisher's paper—which was Chicago's foremost—scarcely

mentioned the incident and purposely misspelled the name. The lady, thinking her task accomplished, had taken truer aim with her second bullet, and had saved herself the trouble of trial by human jury.

Simeon Peake left his daughter Selina a legacy of two fine clear blue-white diamonds (he had had the gambler's love of them) and the sum of four hundred and ninety-seven dollars in cash. Just how he had managed to have a sum like this put by was a mystery. The envelope containing it had evidently once held a larger sum. It had been sealed, and then slit. On the outside was written, in Simeon Peake's fine, almost feminine hand: "For my little daughter Selina Peake in case anything should happen to me." It bore a date seven years old. What the original sum had been no one ever knew. That any sum remained was evidence of the almost heroic self-control practised by one to whom money—ready money in any sum at all—meant only fuel to feed the flames of his gaming fever.

To Selina fell the choice of earning her own living or of returning to the Vermont village and becoming a withered and sapless dried apple, with black fuzz and mould at her heart, like her aunts, the Misses Sarah and Abbie Peake. She did not hesitate.

"But what kind of work?" Julie Hempel demanded. "What kind of work can you do?" Women—that is, the Selina Peakes—did not work.

"I—well, I can teach."

"Teach what?"

"The things I learned at Miss Fister's."

Julie's expression weighed and discredited Miss Fister. "Who to?" Which certainly justified her expression.

"To children. People's children. Or in the public schools."

"You have to do something first—go to Normal, or teach in the country, don't you?—before you can teach in the public schools. They're mostly old. Twenty-five or even thirty—or more!" with nineteen's incapacity to imagine an age beyond thirty.

That Julie was taking the offensive in this conversation, and Selina the defensive, was indicative of the girl's numbed state. Selina did not then know the iron qualities her friend was displaying in being with her at all. Mrs. Hempel had quite properly forbidden Julie ever to see the dead dissolute gambler's daughter again. She had even sent a note to Miss Fister expressing her opinion of a school which would, by admitting such unselected ladies to its select circle, expose other pupils to contamination.

Selina rallied to Julie's onslaught. "Then I'll just teach a country school. I'm good at arithmetic. You know that." Julie should have known it, having had all her Fister sums solved by Selina. "Country schools are just arithmetic and grammar and geography."

"You! Teaching a country school!"

She looked at Selina.

She saw a misleadingly delicate face, the skull small and exquisitely formed. The cheek bones rather high—or perhaps they looked so because of the fact that the eyes, dark, soft, and luminous, were unusually deep-set in their sockets. The face, instead of narrowing to a soft curve at the chin, developed unexpected strength in the jaw line. That line, fine, steel-strong, sharp and clear, was of the stuff of which pioneer women are made. Julie, inexperienced in the art of reading the human physiognomy, did not decipher the meaning of it. Selina's hair was thick, long, and fine, so that she piled it easily in the loops, coils, and knots that fashion demanded. Her nose, slightly pinched at the nostrils, was exquisite. When she laughed it had the trick of wrinkling just a little across the narrow bridge; very engaging, and mischievous. She was thought a rather plain little thing, which she wasn't. But the eyes were what you marked and remembered. People to whom she was speaking had a way of looking into them deeply. Selina was often embarrassed to discover that they were not hearing what she had to say. Perhaps it was this velvety softness of the eyes that caused one to overlook the firmness of the lower face. When the next ten years had done their worst to her, and Julie had suddenly come upon her stepping agilely out of a truck gardener's wagon on Prairie Avenue, a tanned, weather-beaten, toil-worn woman, her abundant hair skewered into a knob and held by a long gray hairpin, her full calico skirt grimed with the mud of the wagon wheel, a pair of men's old side-boots on her slim feet, a grotesquely battered old felt hat (her husband's) on her head, her arms full of ears of sweet corn, and carrots, and radishes, and bunches of beets; a woman with bad teeth, flat breasts, a sagging pocket in her capacious skirt—even then Julie, staring, had known her by her eyes. And she had run to her in her silk suit and her fine silk shirtwaist and her hat with the plume and had cried, "Oh, Selina! My dear! My dear!"—with a sob of horror and pity—"My dear." And had taken Selina, carrots, beets, corn, and radishes, in her arms. The vegetables lay scattered all about them on the sidewalk in front of Julie Hempel Arnold's great stone house on Prairie Avenue. But strangely enough it had been Selina who had done the comforting, patting Julie's silken shoulder and saying, over and over, "There, there! It's all right, Julie. It's all right. Don't cry. What's there to cry for! Sh! . . . It's all right."

SELINA had thought herself lucky to get to the Dutch school at High Prairie, ten miles outside Chicago. Thirty dollars a month! She was to board at the house of Klaas Pool, the truck farmer. It was August Hempel who had brought it all about; or Julie, urging him. Now, at forty-five, August Hempel, the Clark Street butcher, knew every farmer and stockman for miles around, and hundreds besides scattered throughout Cook County and the State of Illinois.

To get the Dutch school for Selina Peake was a simple enough matter for him. The High Prairie district school teacher had always, heretofore, been a man. A more advantageous position presenting itself, this year's prospective teacher had withdrawn before the school term had begun. This was in September. High Prairie school did not open until the first week in November. In that region of truck farms every boy and girl over six was busy in the fields throughout the early autumn. Two years of this, and Selina would be qualified for a city grade. August Hempel indicated that he could arrange that, too, when the time came. Selina thought this shrewd red-faced butcher a wonderful man, indeed. Which he was.

At forty-seven, single-handed, he was to establish the famous Hempel Packing Company. At fifty he was the power in the yards, and there were Hempel branches in Kansas City, Omaha, Denver. At sixty you saw the name of Hempel plastered over packing sheds, factories, and canning plants all the way from Honolulu to Portland. You read:

Don't Say Ham: Say Hempel's.

Hempel products ranged incredibly from pork to pineapple; from grease to grape-juice. An indictment meant no more to Hempel, the packer, than an injunction for speeding to you. Something of his character may be gleaned from the fact that farmers who had known the butcher at forty still addressed this millionaire, at sixty, as Aug. At sixty-five he took up golf and beat his son-in-law, Michael Arnold, at it. A magnificent old pirate, sailing the perilous commercial seas of the American '90s before commissions, investigations, and inquisitive senate insisted on applying whitewash to the black flag of trade.

Selina went about her preparations in a singularly clear-headed fashion, considering her youth and inexperience. She sold one of the blue-white diamonds, and kept one. She placed her inheritance of four hundred and ninety-seven dollars, complete, in the bank. She bought stout sensible boots, two dresses, one a brown lady's-cloth which she made herself, finished with white collars and cuffs, very neat (the cuffs to be protected by black sateen sleevelets, of course, while teaching); and a wine-red cashmere (mad, but she couldn't resist it) for best.

She eagerly learned what she could of this region once known as New Holland. Its people were all truck gardeners, and as Dutch as the Netherlands from which they or their fathers had come. She heard stories of wooden shoes worn in the wet prairie fields; of a red-faced plodding Cornelius Van der Bilt living in placid ignorance of the existence of his distinguished New York patronymic connection; of sturdy, phlegmatic, industrious farmers in squat, many-windowed houses patterned after the north Holland houses of their European memories. Many of them had come from the town of Schoorl, or near it. Others from the lowlands outside Amsterdam. Selina pictured it another Sleepy Hollow, a replica of the quaint settlement in Washington Irving's delightful tale. The deserting schoolmaster had been a second Ichabod Crane, naturally; the farmer at whose house she was to live a modern Mynheer Van Tassel, pipe, chuckle, and all. She and Julie Hempel read the tale over together on an afternoon when Julie managed to evade the maternal edict. Selina, picturing mellow golden corn fields; crusty crullers, crumbling oly-koeks, toothsome wild ducks, sides of smoked beef, pumpkin pies; country dances, apple-cheeked farmer girls, felt sorry for poor Julie staying on in the dull gray commonplaceness of Chicago.

The last week in October found her on the way to High Prairie, seated beside Klaas Pool in the two-horse wagon with which he brought his garden stuff to the Chicago market. She sat perched next him on the high seat like a saucy wren beside a ruminant Holstein. So they jolted up the long Halsted road through the late October sunset. The prairie land just outside Chicago had not then been made a terrifying and epic thing of slag-heaps, smoke-stacks, and blast furnaces like a Pennell drawing. To-day it stretched away and away in the last rays of the late autumn sunlight over which the lake mist was beginning to creep like chiffon covering gold. Mile after mile of cabbage fields, jade-green against the earth. Mile after mile of red cabbage, a rich plummy Burgundy veined with black. Between these, heaps of corn were piled-up sunshine. Against the horizon an occasional patch of woods showed the last russet and bronze of oak and maple. These things Selina saw with her beauty-loving eye, and she clasped her hands in their black cotton gloves.

"Oh, Mr. Pool!" she cried. "Mr. Pool! How beautiful it is here!"

Klaas Pool, driving his team of horses down the muddy Halsted road, was looking straight ahead, his eyes fastened seemingly on an invisible spot between the off-horse's ears. His was not the kind of brain that acts quickly, nor was his body's mechanism the sort that quickly responds to that brain's message. His eyes were china-blue in a round red face that was covered with a stubble of stiff golden hairs. His round moon of a head was set low and solidly between his great shoulders, so that as he began to turn it now, slowly, you marvelled at the process and waited fearfully to hear a creak. He was turning his head toward Selina, but keeping his gaze on the spot between his horse's ears. Evidently the head and the eyes revolved by quite distinct processes. Now he faced Selina almost directly. Then he brought his eyes around, slowly, until they focussed on her cameo-like face all alight now with her enjoyment of the scene around her; with a certain elation at this new venture into which she was entering; and with excitement such as she used to feel when the curtain rose with tantalizing deliberateness on the first act of a play which she was seeing with her father. She was well bundled up against the sharp October air in her cloak and muffler, with a shawl tucked about her knees and waist. The usual creamy pallor of her fine clear skin showed an unwonted pink, and her eyes were wide, dark, and bright. Beside this sparkling delicate girl's face Klaas Pool's heavy features seemed carved from the stuff of another clay and race. His pale blue eyes showed incomprehension.

"Beautiful?" he echoed, in puzzled interrogation. "What is beautiful?"

Selina's slim arms flashed out from the swathings of cloak, shawl, and muffler and were flung wide in a gesture that embraced the landscape on which the late afternoon sun was casting a glow peculiar to that lake region, all rose and golden and mist-shimmering.

"This! The—the cabbages."

A slow-dawning film of fun crept over the blue of Klaas Pool's stare. This film spread almost imperceptibly so that it fluted his broad nostrils, met and widened his full lips, reached and agitated his massive shoulders, tickled the round belly, so that all Klaas Pool, from his eyes to his waist, was rippling and shaking with slow, solemn, heavy Dutch mirth.

"Cabbages is beautiful!" his round pop eyes staring at her in a fixity of glee. "Cabbages is beautiful!" His silent laughter now rose and became audible in a rich throaty chortle. It was plain that laughter, with Klaas Pool, was not a thing to be lightly dismissed, once raised. "Cabbages——" he choked a little, and spluttered, overcome. Now he began to shift his gaze back to his horses and the road, by the same process of turning his head first and then his eyes, so that to Selina the mirthful tail of his right eye and his round red cheek with the golden fuzz on it gave him an incredibly roguish brownie look.

Selina laughed, too, even while she protested his laughter. "But they are!" she insisted. "They *are* beautiful. Like jade and Burgundy. No, like —uh—like—what's that in—like chrysoprase and porphyry. All those fields of cabbages and the corn and the beet-tops together look like Persian patches."

Which was, certainly, no way for a new school teacher to talk to a Holland truck gardener driving his team along the dirt road on his way to High Prairie. But then, Selina, remember, had read Byron at seventeen.

Klaas Pool knew nothing of chrysoprase and porphyry. Nor of Byron. Nor, for that matter, of jade and Burgundy. But he did know cabbages, both green and red. He knew cabbage from seed to sauerkraut; he knew and grew varieties from the sturdy Flat Dutch to the early Wakefield. But that they were beautiful; that they looked like jewels; that they lay like Persian patches, had never entered his head, and rightly. What has the head of a cabbage, or, for that matter, of a robust, soil-stained, toiling Dutch truck farmer to do with nonsense like chrysoprase, with jade, with Burgundy, with Persian patterns!

The horses clopped down the heavy country road. Now and again the bulk beside Selina was agitated silently, as before. And from between the golden fuzz of stubble beard she would hear, "Cabbages! Cabbages is——" But she did not feel offended. She could not have been offended at anything to-day. For in spite of her recent tragedy, her nineteen years, her loneliness, the terrifying thought of this new home to which she was going, among strangers, she was conscious of a warm little thrill of elation, of excitement—of adventure! That was it. "The whole thing's just a grand adventure," Simeon Peake had said. Selina gave a little bounce of anticipation. She was doing a revolutionary and daring thing; a thing that the Vermont and now, fortunately, inaccessible Peakes would have regarded with horror. For equipment she had youth, curiosity, a steel-strong frame; one brown lady's-cloth, one wine-red cashmere; four hundred and ninety-seven dollars; and a gay, adventuresome spirit that was never to die, though it led her into curious places and she often found, at the end, only a trackless waste from which she had to retrace her steps, painfully. But always, to her, red and green cabbages were to be jade and Burgundy, chrysoprase and porphyry. Life has no weapons against a woman like that.

So now, as they bumped and jolted along the road Selina thought herself lucky, though she was a little terrified. She turned her gaze from the flat prairie land to the silent figure beside her. Hers was a lively, volatile nature, and his uncommunicativeness made her vaguely uncomfortable. Yet there was nothing glum about his face. Upon it there even lingered, in the corners of his eyes and about his mouth, faint shadows of merriment.

Klaas Pool was a school director. She was to live at his house. Perhaps she should not have said that about the cabbages. So now she drew herself up primly and tried to appear the school teacher, and succeeded in looking as severe as a white pansy.

"Ahem!" (or nearly that). "You have three children, haven't you, Mr. Pool? They'll all be my pupils?"

Klaas Pool ruminated on this. He concentrated so that a slight frown marred the serenity of his brow. In this double question of hers, an attempt to give the conversation a dignified turn, she had apparently created some difficulty for her host. He was trying to shake his head two ways at the same time. This gave it a rotary motion. Selina saw, with amazement, that he was attempting to nod negation and confirmation at once.

"You mean you haven't—or they're not?—or——?"

"I have got three children. All will not be your pupils." There was something final, unshakable in his delivery of this.

"Dear me! Why not? Which ones won't?"

This fusillade proved fatal. It served permanently to check the slight trickle of conversation which had begun to issue from his lips. They jogged on for perhaps a matter of three miles, in silence. Selina told herself then, sternly, that she must not laugh. Having told herself this, sternly, she began to laugh because she could not help it; a gay little sound that flew out like the whir of a bird's wing on the crisp autumnal sunset air. And suddenly this light sound was joined by a slow rumbling that swelled and bubbled a good deal in the manner of the rich glubby sounds that issue from a kettle that has been simmering for a long time. So they laughed together, these two; the rather scared young thing who was trying to be prim, and the dull, unimaginative truck farmer because this alert, great-eyed, slim white creature perched birdlike on the wagon seat beside him had tickled his slow humour-sense.

Selina felt suddenly friendly and happy. "Do tell me which ones will and which won't."

"Geertje goes to school. Jozina goes to school. Roelf works by the farm."

"How old is Roelf?" She was being school teacherly again.

"Roelf is twelve."

"Twelve! And no longer at school! But why not!"

"Roelf he works by the farm."

"Doesn't Roelf like school?"

"But sure."

"Don't you think he ought to go to school?"

"But sure."

Having begun, she could not go back. "Doesn't your wife want Roelf to go to school any more?"

"Maartje? But sure."

She gathered herself together; hurled herself behind the next question. "Then why *doesn't* he go to school, for pity's sake!"

Klaas Pool's pale blue eyes were fixed on the spot between the horse's ears. His face was serene, placid, patient.

"Roelf he works by the farm."

Selina subsided, beaten.

She wondered about Roelf. Would he be a furtive, slinking boy, like Smike? Geertje and Jozina. Geertje—Gertrude, of course. Jozina? Josephine. Maartje?—m-m-m-m—Martha, probably. At any rate, it was going to be interesting. It was going to be wonderful! Suppose she had gone to Vermont and become a dried apple!

Dusk was coming on. The lake mist came drifting across the prairie and hung, a pearly haze, over the frost-nipped stubble and the leafless trees. It caught the last light in the sky, and held it, giving to fields, trees, black earth, to the man seated stolidly beside the girl, and to the face of the girl herself an opalescent glow very wonderful to see. Selina, seeing it, opened her lips to exclaim again; and then, remembering, closed them. She had learned her first lesson in High Prairie.

III

The Klaas Pools lived in a typical High Prairie house. They had passed a score like it in the dusk. These sturdy Holland-Americans had built here in Illinois after the pattern of the squat houses that dot the lowlands about Amsterdam, Haarlem, and Rotterdam. A row of pollards stood stiffly by the roadside. As they turned in at the yard Selina's eye was caught by the glitter of glass. The house was many-windowed, the panes the size of pocket-handkerchiefs. Even in the dusk Selina thought she had never seen windows sparkle so. She did not then know that spotless window-panes were a mark of social standing in High Prairie. Yard and dwelling had a geometrical neatness like that of a toy house in a set of playthings. The effect was marred by a clothes-line hung with a dado of miscellaneous wash—a pair of faded overalls, a shirt, socks, a man's drawers carefully patched and now bellying grotesquely in the breeze like a comic tramp turned bacchanal. Selina was to know this frieze of nether garments as a daily decoration in the farm-wife's yard.

Peering down over the high wheel she waited for Klaas Pool to assist her in alighting. He seemed to have no such thought. Having jumped down, he was throwing empty crates and boxes out of the back of the wagon. So Selina, gathering her shawls and cloak about her, clambered down the side of the wheel and stood looking about her in the dim light, a very small figure in a very large world. Klaas had opened the barn door. Now he returned and slapped one of the horses smartly on the flank. The team trotted obediently off to the barn. He picked up her little hide-bound trunk. She took her satchel. The yard was quite dark now. As Klaas Pool opened the kitchen door the red mouth that was the open draught in the kitchen stove grinned a toothy welcome at them.

A woman stood over the stove, a fork in her hand. The kitchen was clean, but disorderly, with the disorder that comes of pressure of work. There was a not unpleasant smell of cooking. Selina sniffed it hungrily. The woman turned to face them. Selina stared.

This, she thought, must be some other—an old woman—his mother perhaps. But: "Maartje, here is school teacher," said Klaas Pool. Selina put out her hand to meet the other woman's hand, rough, hard, calloused. Her own, touching it, was like satin against a pine board. Maartje smiled, and you saw her broken discoloured teeth. She pushed back the sparse hair from her high forehead, fumbled a little, shyly, at the collar of her clean blue calico dress.

"Pleased to meet you," Maartje said, primly. "Make you welcome." Then, as Pool stamped out to the yard, slamming the door behind him, "Pool he could have come with you by the front way, too. Lay off your things." Selina began to remove the wrappings that swathed her—the muffler, the shawl, the cloak. Now she stood, a slim, incongruously elegant little figure in that kitchen. The brown lady's-cloth was very tight and basqued above, very flounced and bustled below. "My, how you are young!" cried Maartje. She moved nearer, as if impelled, and fingered the stuff of Selina's gown. And as she did this Selina suddenly saw that she, too, was young. The bad teeth, the thin hair, the careless dress, the littered kitchen, the harassed frown—above all these, standing out clearly, appeared the look of a girl.

"Why, I do believe she's not more than twenty-eight!" Selina said to herself in a kind of panic. "I do believe she's not more than twenty-eight."

She had been aware of the two pigtailed heads appearing and vanishing in the doorway of the next room. Now Maartje was shooing her into this room. Evidently her hostess was distressed because the school teacher's formal entrance had not been made by way of parlour instead of kitchen. She followed Maartje Pool into the front room. Behind the stove, tittering, were two yellow-haired little girls. Geertje and Jozina, of course. Selina went over to them, smiling. "Which is Geertje?" she asked. "And which Jozina?" But at this the titters became squeals. They retired behind the round black bulwark of the wood-burner, overcome. There was no fire in this shining ebon structure, though the evening was sharp. Above the stove a length of pipe, glittering with polish as was the stove itself, crossed the width of the room and vanished through a queer little perforated grating in the ceiling. Selina's quick glance encompassed the room. In the window were a few hardy plants in pots on a green-painted wooden rack. There were geraniums, blossomless; a cactus with its thick slabs of petals like slices of gangrenous ham set up for beauty in a parlour; a plant called Jacob's ladder, on a spindling trellis. The bony scaffolding of the green-painted wooden stand was turned toward the room. The flowers blindly faced the dark square of the window. There was a sofa with a wrinkled calico cover; three rocking chairs; some stark crayons of incredibly hard-featured Dutch ancients on the wall. It was all neat, stiff, unlovely. But Selina had known too many years of boarding-house ugliness to be offended at this.

Maartje had lighted a small glass-bowled lamp. The chimney of this sparkled as had the window-panes. A steep, uncarpeted stairway, enclosed, led off the sitting room. Up this Maartje Pool, talking, led the way to Selina's bedroom. Selina was to learn that the farm woman, often inarticulate through lack of companionship, becomes a torrent of talk when opportunity presents itself. They made quite a little procession. First, Mrs. Pool with the lamp; then Selina with the satchel; then, tap-tap, tap-tap, Jozina and Geertje, their heavy hob-nailed shoes creating a great clatter on the wooden stairs, though they were tip-toeing in an effort to make themselves unheard by their mother. There evidently had been an arrangement on the subject of their invisibility. The procession moved to the accompaniment of Maartje's, "Now you stay downstairs didn't I tell you!" There was in her tone a warning; a menace. The two pigtails would hang back a moment, only to come tap-tapping on again, their saucer eyes at once fearful and mischievous.

A narrow, dim, close-smelling hallway, uncarpeted. At the end of it a door opening into the room that was to be Selina's. As its chill struck her to the marrow three objects caught her eye. The bed, a huge and not unhandsome walnut mausoleum, reared its sombre height almost to the room's top. Indeed, its apex of grapes did actually seem to achieve a meeting with the whitewashed ceiling. The mattress of straw and corn-husks was unworthy of this edifice, but over it Mrs. Pool had mercifully placed a feather bed, stitched and quilted, so that Selina lay soft and warm through the winter. Along one wall stood a low chest so richly brown as to appear black. The front panel of this was curiously carved. Selina stooped before it and for the second time that day said: "How beautiful!" then looked quickly round at Maartje Pool as though fearful of finding her laughing as Klaas Pool had laughed. But Mrs. Pool's face reflected the glow in her own. She came over to Selina and stooped with her over the chest, holding the lamp so that its yellow flame lighted up the scrolls and tendrils of the carved surface. With one discoloured fore-finger she traced the bold flourishes on the panel. "See? How it makes out letters?"

Selina peered closer. "Why, sure enough! This first one's an S!"

Maartje was kneeling before the chest now. "Sure an S. For Sophia. It is a Holland bride's chest. And here is K. And here is big D. It makes Sophia Kroon DeVries. It is anyways two hundred years. My mother she gave it to me when I was married, and her mother she gave it to her when she was married, and her mother gave it to her when she was married, and her——"

"I should think so!" exclaimed Selina, rather meaninglessly; but stemming the torrent. "What's in it? Anything? There ought to be bride's clothes in it, yellow with age."

"It is!" cried Maartje Pool and gave a little bounce that imperilled the lamp.

"No!" The two on their knees sat smiling at each other, wide-eyed, like schoolgirls. The pigtails, emboldened, had come tap-tapping nearer and were peering over the shoulders of the women before the chest.

"Here—wait." Maartje Pool thrust the lamp into Selina's hand, raised the lid of the chest, dived expertly into its depths amidst a great rustling of old newspapers and emerged red-faced with a Dutch basque and voluminous skirt of silk; an age-yellow cap whose wings, stiff with embroidery, stood out grandly on either side; a pair of wooden shoes, stained terra-cotta like the sails of the Vollendam fishing boats, and

carved from toe to heel in a delicate and intricate pattern. A bridal gown,
a bridal cap, bridal shoes.

"Well!" said Selina, with the feeling of a little girl in a rich attic on
a rainy day. She clasped her hands. "May I dress up in it some time?"

Maartje Pool, folding the garments hastily, looked shocked and horrified. "Never must anybody dress up in a bride's dress only to get
married. It brings bad luck." Then, as Selina stroked the stiff silken folds
of the skirt with a slim and caressing forefinger: "So you get married to
a High Prairie Dutchman I let you wear it." At this absurdity they both
laughed again. Selina thought that this school-teaching venture was starting out very well. She would have *such* things to tell her father—then
she remembered. She shivered a little as she stood up now. She raised
her arms to take off her hat, feeling suddenly tired, cold, strange in this
house with this farm woman, and the two staring little girls, and the
great red-faced man. There surged over her a great wave of longing for
her father—for the gay little dinners, for the theatre treats, for his humorous philosophical drawl, for the Chicago streets, and the ugly
Chicago houses; for Julie; for Miss Fister's school; for anything and any
one that was accustomed, known, and therefore dear. Even Aunt Abbie
and Aunt Sarah had a not unlovely aspect, viewed from this chill farmhouse bedroom that had suddenly become her home. She had a horrible
premonition that she was going to cry, began to blink very fast, turned
a little blindly in the dim light and caught sight of the room's third
arresting object. A blue-black cylinder of tin sheeting, like a stove and yet
unlike. It was polished like the length of pipe in the sitting room below.
Indeed, it was evidently a giant flower of this stem.

"What's that?" demanded Selina, pointing.

Maartje Pool, depositing the lamp on the little wash-stand preparatory
to leaving, smiled pridefully. "Drum."

"Drum?"

"For heat your room." Selina touched it. It was icy. "When there is
fire," Mrs. Pool added, hastily. In her mind's eye Selina traced the tin
tube below running along the ceiling in the peaceful and orderly path
of a stove-pipe, thrusting its way through the cylindrical hole in the ceiling and here bursting suddenly into swollen and monstrous bloom like
an unthinkable goitre on a black neck. Selina was to learn that its heating
powers were mythical. Even when the stove in the sitting room was
blazing away with a cheerful roar none of the glow communicated itself to the drum. It remained as coolly indifferent to the blasts breathed
upon it as a girl hotly besieged by an unwelcome lover. This was to
influence a number of Selina's habits, including nocturnal reading and
matutinal bathing. Selina was a daily morning bather in a period which

looked upon the daily bath as an eccentricity, or, at best, an affectation. It would be charming to be able to record that she continued the practice in the Pool household; but a morning bath in the arctic atmosphere of an Illinois prairie farmhouse would not have been eccentric merely, but mad, even if there had been an available kettle of hot water at 6.30 A. M., which there emphatically was not. Selina was grateful for an occasional steaming basin of water at night and a hurried piecemeal bath by the mythical heat of the drum.

"Maartje!" roared a voice from belowstairs. The voice of the hungry male. There was wafted up, too, a faint smell of scorching. Then came sounds of a bumping and thumping along the narrow stairway.

"Og heden!" cried Maartje, in a panic, her hands high in air. She was off, sweeping the two pigtails with her in her flight. There were sounds of scuffling on the stairway, and Maartje's voice calling something that sounded like hookendunk to Selina. But she decided that that couldn't be. The bumping now sounded along the passage outside her room. Selina turned from her satchel to behold a gnome in the doorway. Below, she saw a pair of bow-legs; above, her own little hide-bound trunk; between, a broad face, a grizzled beard, a lack-lustre eye in a weather-beaten countenance.

"Jakob Hoogendunk," the gnome announced, briefly, peering up at her from beneath the trunk balanced on his back.

Selina laughed delightedly. "Not really! Do come in. This is a good place, don't you think? Along the wall? Mr.—Mr. Hoogendunk?"

Jakob Hoogendunk grunted and plodded across the room, the trunk lurching perilously above his bow-legged stride. He set it down with a final thump, wiped his nose with the back of his hand—sign of a task completed—and surveyed the trunk largely, as if he had made it. "Thank you, Mr. Hoogendunk," said Selina, and put out her hand. "I'm Selina Peake. How"—she couldn't resist it—"how did you leave Rip?"

It was characteristic of her that in this grizzled hired man, twisted with rheumatism, reeking of mould and manure, she should see a direct descendant of those gnarled and bearded bowlers so mysteriously encountered by Rip Van Winkle on that fatal day in the Kaatskills. The name, too, appealed to her in its comic ugliness. So she laughed a soft little laugh; held out her hand. The man was not offended. He knew that people laughed when they were introduced. So he laughed, too, in a mixture of embarrassment and attempted ease, looking down at the small hand extended to him. He blinked at it curiously. He wiped his two hands down his thighs, hard; then shook his great grizzled head. "My hand is all muck. I ain't washed up yet," and lurched off, leaving Se-

lina looking rather helplessly down at her own extended hand. His clatter
on the wooden stairway sounded like cavalry on a frozen road.

Left alone in her room Selina unlocked her trunk and took from it
two photographs—one of a mild-looking man with his hat a little on one
side, the other of a woman who might have been a twenty-five-year-old
Selina, minus the courageous jaw-line. Looking about for a fitting place
on which to stand these leather-framed treasures she considered the top
of the chill drum, humorously, then actually placed them there, for lack
of better refuge, from which vantage point they regarded her with politely interested eyes. Perhaps Jakob Hoogendunk would put up a shelf
for her. That would serve for her little stock of books and for the pictures
as well. She was enjoying that little flush of exhilaration that comes to a
woman, unpacking. There was about her trunk, even though closed but
this very day, the element of surprise that gilds familiar objects when
disclosed for the first time in unfamiliar surroundings. She took out her
neat pile of warm woollen underwear, her stout shoes. She shook out
the crushed folds of the wine-coloured cashmere. Now, if ever, she
should have regretted its purchase. But she didn't. No one, she reflected,
as she spread it rosily on the bed, possessing a wine-coloured cashmere
could be altogether downcast.

The wine cashmere on the bed, the photographs on the drum, her
clothes hanging comfortably on wall-hooks with a calico curtain on a cord
protecting them, her stock of books on the closed trunk. Already the
room wore the aspect of familiarity.

From belowstairs came the hiss of frying. Selina washed in the chill
water of the basin, took down her hair and coiled it again before the
swimmy little mirror over the wash-stand. She adjusted the stitched
white bands of the severe collar and patted the cuffs of the brown lady's-
cloth. The tight basque was fastened with buttons from throat to waist.
Her fine long head rose above this trying base with such grace and dignity as to render the stiff garment beautiful. The skirt billowed and
puffed out behind, and was drawn in folds across the front. It was a day
of appalling bunchiness and equally appalling tightness in dress; of pan-
niers, galloons, plastrons, reveres, bustles, and all manner of lumpy
bedevilment. That Selina could appear in this disfiguring garment a creature still graceful, slim, and pliant was a sheer triumph of spirit over
matter.

She blew out the light now and descended the steep wooden stairway
to the unlighted parlour. The door between parlour and kitchen was
closed. Selina sniffed sensitively. There was pork for supper. She was
to learn that there always was pork for supper. As the winter wore on she
developed a horror of this porcine fare, remembering to have read some-

where that one's diet was in time reflected in one's face; that gross eating made one gross looking. She would examine her features fearfully in the swimmy mirror—the lovely little white nose—was it coarsening? The deep-set dark eyes—were they squinting? The firm sweet lips—were they broadening? But the reflection in the glass reassured her.

She hesitated a moment there in the darkness. Then she opened the kitchen door. There swam out at her a haze of smoke, from which emerged round blue eyes, guttural talk, the smell of frying grease, of stable, of loam, and of woollen wash freshly brought in from the line. With an inrush of cold air that sent the blue haze into swirls the outer kitchen door opened. A boy, his arm piled high with stove-wood, entered; a dark, handsome sullen boy who stared at Selina over the armload of wood. Selina stared back at him. There sprang to life between the boy of twelve and the woman of nineteen an electric current of feeling.

"Roelf," thought Selina; and even took a step toward him, inexplicably drawn.

"Hurry then with that wood there!" fretted Maartje at the stove. The boy flung the armful into the box, brushed his sleeve and coat-front mechanically, still looking at Selina. A slave to the insatiable maw of the wood-box.

Klaas Pool, already at table, thumped with his knife. "Sit down! Sit down, teacher." Selina hesitated, looked at Maartje. Maartje was holding a frying pan aloft in one hand while with the other she thrust and poked a fresh stick of wood into the open-lidded stove. The two pigtails seated themselves at the table, set with its red-checked cloth and bone-handled cutlery. Jakob Hoogendunk, who had been splashing, snorting, and puffing porpoise-fashion in a corner over a hand-basin whose cubic contents were out of all proportion to the sounds extracted therefrom, now seated himself. Roelf flung his cap on a wall-hook and sat down. Only Selina and Maartje remained standing. "Sit down! Sit down!" Klaas Pool said again, jovially. "Well, how is cabbages?" He chuckled and winked. Jakob Hoogendunk snorted. A duet of titters from the pigtails. Maartje at the stove smiled; but a trifle grimly, one might have thought, watching her. Evidently Klaas had not hugged his joke in secret. Only the boy Roelf remained unsmiling. Even Selina, feeling the red mounting her cheeks, smiled a little, nervously, and sat down with some suddenness.

Maartje Pool now thumped down on the table a great bowl of potatoes fried in grease; a platter of ham. There was bread cut in chunks. The coffee was rye, roasted in the oven, ground, and taken without sugar or cream. Of this food there was plenty. It made Mrs. Tebbitt's

Monday night meal seem ambrosial. Selina's visions of chickens, oly-
koeks, wild ducks, crusty crullers, and pumpkin pies vanished, never to
return. She had been very hungry, but now, as she talked, nodded,
smiled, she cut her food into infinitesimal bites, did not chew them so
very well, and despised herself for being dainty. A slight, distinctive little
figure there in the yellow lamplight, eating this coarse fare bravely,
turning her soft dark glance on the woman who was making countless
trips from stove to table, from table to stove; on the sullen handsome
boy with his purplish chapped hands and his sombre eyes; on the two
round-eyed, red-cheeked little girls; on the great red-faced full-lipped
man eating his supper noisily and with relish; on Jakob Hoogendunk,
grazing greedily. . . .

"Well," she thought, "it's going to be different enough, that's certain.
. . . This is a vegetable farm, and they don't eat vegetables. I wonder
why. . . . What a pity that she lets herself look like that, just because
she's a farm woman. Her hair screwed into that knob, her skin rough
and neglected. That hideous dress. Shapeless. She's not bad looking,
either. A red spot on either cheek, now; and her eyes so blue. A little
like those women in the Dutch pictures Father took me to see in—
where?—where?—New York, years ago?—yes. A woman in a kitchen, a
dark sort of room with pots of brass on a shelf; a high mullioned window. But that woman's face was placid. This one's strained. Why need
she look like that, frowsy, harried, old! . . . The boy is, somehow, foreign looking—Italian. Queer. . . . They talk a good deal like some
German neighbours we had in Milwaukee. They twist sentences. Literal
translations from the Dutch, I suppose." . . .

Jakob Hoogendunk was talking. Supper over, the men sat relaxed,
pipe in mouth. Maartje was clearing the supper things, with Geertje
and Jozina making a great pretense at helping. If they giggled like that
in school, Selina thought, she would, in time, go mad, and knock their
pigtailed heads together.

"You got to have rich bottom land," Hoogendunk was saying, "else
you get little tough stringy stuff. I seen it in market Friday, laying. Stick
to vegetables that is vegetables and not new-fangled stuff. Celery!
What is celery! It ain't rightly a vegetable, and it ain't a yerb. Look
how Voorhees he used as much as one hundred fifty pounds nitrate
of sody, let alone regular fertilizer, and what comes from it? Little stringy
stuff. You got to have rich bottom land."

Selina was interested. She had always thought that vegetables grew.
You put them in the ground—seeds or something—and pretty soon
things came popping up—potatoes, cabbages, onions, carrots, beets. But
what was this thing called nitrate of soda? It must have had something

to do with the creamed cabbage at Mrs. Tebbitt's. And she had never known it. And what was regular fertilizer? She leaned forward.

"What's a regular fertilizer?"

Klaas Pool and Jakob Hoogendunk looked at her. She looked at them, her fine intelligent eyes alight with interest. Pool then tipped back his chair, lifted a stove-lid, spat into the embers, replaced the lid and rolled his eyes in the direction of Jakob Hoogendunk. Hoogendunk rolled his slow gaze in the direction of Klaas Pool. Then both turned to look at this audacious female who thus interrupted men's conversation.

Pool took his pipe from his mouth, blew a thin spiral, wiped his mouth with the back of his hand. "Regular fertilizer is—regular fertilizer."

Jakob Hoogendunk nodded his solemn confirmation of this.

"What's in it?" persisted Selina.

Pool waved a huge red hand as though to waft away this troublesome insect. He looked at Maartje. But Maartje was slamming about her work. Geertje and Jozina were absorbed in some game of their own behind the stove. Roelf, at the table, sat reading, one slim hand, chapped and gritty with rough work, outspread on the cloth. Selina noticed, without knowing she noticed, that the fingers were long, slim, and the broken nails thin and fine. "But what's in it?" she said again. Suddenly life in the kitchen hung suspended. The two men frowned. Maartje half turned from her dishpan. The two little girls peered out from behind the stove. Roelf looked up from his book. Even the collie, lying in front of the stove half asleep, suddenly ran his tongue out, winked one eye. But Selina, all sociability, awaited her answer. She could not know that in High Prairie women did not brazenly intrude thus on men's weighty conversation. The men looked at her, unanswering. She began to feel a little uncomfortable. The boy Roelf rose and went to the cupboard in the kitchen corner. He took down a large green-bound book, and placed it in Selina's hand. The book smelled terribly. Its covers were greasy with handling. On the page margins a brown stain showed the imprint of fingers. Roelf pointed at a page. Selina followed the line with her eye.

GOOD BASIC FERTILIZER FOR
MARKET-GARDEN CROPS.

Then, below:

Nitrate of soda.
Ammonium sulfate.
Dried blood.

Selina shut the book and handed it back to Roelf, gingerly. Dried blood! She stared at the two men. "What does it mean by dried blood?"

Klaas answered stubbornly, "Dried blood is dried blood. You put in the field dried blood and it makes grow. Cabbages, onions, squash." At the sight of her horrified face he grinned. "Well, cabbages is anyway beautiful, huh?" He rolled a facetious eye around at Jakob. Evidently this joke was going to last him the winter.

Selina stood up. She wasn't annoyed; but she wanted, suddenly, to be alone in her room—in the room that but an hour before had been a strange and terrifying chamber with its towering bed, its chill drum, its ghostly bride's chest. Now it had become a refuge, snug, safe, infinitely desirable. She turned to Mrs. Pool. "I—I think I'll go up to my room. I'm very tired. The ride, I suppose. I'm not used . . ." Her voice trailed off.

"Sure," said Maartje, briskly. She had finished the supper dishes and was busy with a huge bowl, flour, a baking board. "Sure go up. I got my bread to set yet and what all."

"If I could have some hot water——"

"Roelf! Stop once that reading and show school teacher where is hot water. Geertje! Jozina! Never in my world did I see such." She cuffed a convenient pigtail by way of emphasis. A wail arose.

"Never mind. It doesn't matter. Don't bother." Selina was in a sort of panic now. She wanted to be out of the room. But the boy Roelf, with quiet swiftness, had taken a battered tin pail from its hook on the wall, had lifted an iron slab at the back of the kitchen stove. A mist of steam arose. He dipped the pail into the tiny reservoir thus revealed. Then, as Selina made as though to take it, he walked past her. She heard him ascending the wooden stairway. She wanted to be after him. But first she must know the name of the book over which he had been poring. But between her and the book outspread on the table were Pool, Hoogendunk, dog, pigtails, Maartje. She pointed with a determined forefinger. "What's that book Roelf was reading?"

Maartje thumped a great ball of dough on the baking board. Her arms were white with flour. She kneaded and pummelled expertly. "Woorden boek."

Well. That meant nothing. Woorden boek. Woorden b—— Dimly the meaning of the Dutch words began to come to her. But it couldn't be. She brushed past the men in the tipped-back chairs, stepped over the collie, reached across the table. Woorden—word. Boek—book. Word book. "He's reading the dictionary!" Selina said, aloud. "He's reading the dictionary!" She had the horrible feeling that she was going to laugh and cry at once; hysteria.

Mrs. Pool glanced around. "School teacher he gave it to Roelf time he quit last year for spring planting. A word book. In it is more as a hundred thousand words, all different."

Selina flung a good-night over her shoulder and made for the stairway. He should have all her books. She would sent to Chicago for books. She would spend her thirty dollars a month buying books for him. He had been reading the dictionary!

Roelf had placed the pail of hot water on the little wash-stand, and had lighted the glass lamp. He was intent on replacing the glass chimney within the four prongs that held it firm. Downstairs, in the crowded kitchen, he had seemed quite the man. Now, in the yellow lamplight, his profile sharply outlined, she saw that he was just a small boy with tousled hair. About his cheeks, his mouth, his chin one could even see the last faint traces of soft infantile roundness. His trousers, absurdly cut down from a man's pair by inexpert hands, hung grotesquely about his slim shanks.

"He's just a little boy," thought Selina, with a quick pang. He was about to pass her now, without glancing at her, his head down. She put out her hand; touched his shoulder. He looked up at her, his face startlingly alive, his eyes blazing. It came to Selina that until now she had not heard him speak. Her hand pressed the thin stuff of his coat sleeve.

"Cabbages—fields of cabbages—what you said—they *are* beautiful," he stammered. He was terribly in earnest. Before she could reply he was out of the room, clattering down the stairs.

Selina stood, blinking a little.

The glow that warmed her now endured while she splashed about in the inadequate basin; took down the dark soft masses of her hair; put on the voluminous long-sleeved, high-necked nightgown. Just before she blew out the lamp her last glimpse was of the black drum stationed like a patient eunuch in the corner; and she could smile at that; even giggle a little, what with weariness, excitement, and a general feeling of being awake in a dream. But once in the vast bed she lay there utterly lost in the waves of terror and loneliness that envelop one at night in a strange house amongst strange people. She lay there, tensed and tight, her toes curled with nervousness, her spine hunched with it, her leg muscles taut. She peeked over the edge of the covers looking a good deal like a frightened brownie, if one could have seen her; her eyes very wide, the pupils turned well toward the corners with the look of listening and distrust. The sharp November air cut in from the fields that were fertilized with dried blood. She shivered, and wrinkled up her lovely little nose and seemed to sniff this loathsome taint in the air. She listened to the noises that came from belowstairs; voices gruff, unaccustomed; shrill, high.

These ceased and gave place to others less accustomed to her city-bred ears; a dog's bark and an answering one; a far-off train whistle; the dull thud of hoofs stamping on the barn floor; the wind in the bare tree branches outside the window.

Her watch—a gift from Simeon Peake on her eighteenth birthday— with the gold case all beautifully engraved with a likeness of a gate, and a church, and a waterfall and a bird, linked together with spirals and flourishes of the most graceful description, was ticking away companionably under her pillow. She felt for it, took it out and held it in her palm, under her cheek, for comfort.

She knew she would not sleep that night. She knew she would not sleep——

She awoke to a clear, cold November dawn; children's voices; the neighing of horses; a great sizzling and hissing, and scent of frying bacon; a clucking and squawking in the barnyard. It was six o'clock. Selina's first day as a school teacher. In a little more than two hours she would be facing a whole roomful of round-eyed Geertjes and Jozinas and Roelfs. The bedroom was cruelly cold. As she threw the bedclothes heroically aside Selina decided that it took an appalling amount of courage—this life that Simeon Peake had called a great adventure.

IV

Every morning throughout November it was the same. At six o'clock: "Miss Peake! Oh, Miss Peake!"

"I'm up!" Selina would call in what she meant to be a gay voice, through chattering teeth.

"You better come down and dress where is warm here by the stove."

Peering down the perforations in the floor-hole through which the parlour chimney swelled so proudly into the drum, Selina could vaguely descry Mrs. Pool stationed just below, her gaze upturned.

That first morning, on hearing this invitation, Selina had been rocked between horror and mirth. "I'm not cold, really. I'm almost dressed. I'll be down directly."

Maartje Pool must have sensed some of the shock in the girl's voice; or, perhaps, even some of the laughter. "Pool and Jakob are long out already cutting. Here back of the stove you can dress warm."

Shivering and tempted though she was, Selina had set her will against it. A little hardening of the muscles around her jaw so that they stood out whitely beneath the fine-grained skin. "I won't go down," she said to herself, shaking with the cold. "I won't come down to dressing behind the kitchen stove like a—like a peasant in one of those dreadful Russian novels. . . . That sounds stuck up and horrid. . . . The Pools are good and kind and decent. . . . But I *won't* come down to huddling behind the stove with a bundle of underwear in my arms. Oh, *dear*, this corset's like a casing of ice."

Geertje and Jozina had no such maidenly scruples. Each morning they gathered their small woollen garments in a bundle and scudded briskly to the kitchen for warmth, though their bedroom just off the parlour had by no means the degree of refrigeration possessed by Selina's clammy chamber. Not only that, the Misses Pool slept snugly in the woollen nether garments that invested them by day and so had only mounds of woollen petticoats, woollen stockings, and mysterious grimy straps, bands, and fastenings with which to struggle. Their intimate flannels had a cactus quality that made the early martyrs' hair shirts seem, in comparison, but a fleece-lined cloud. Dressing behind the kitchen stove was a natural and universal custom in High Prairie.

By the middle of December as Selina stuck her nose cautiously out of the covers into the midnight blackness of early morning you might have observed, if it had been at all light, that the tip of that elegant and erstwhile alabaster feature had been encarmined during the night by a mischievous brush wielded by that same wight who had been busy painting fronds and lacy ferns and gorgeous blossoms of silver all over the bedroom window. Slowly, inch by inch, that bedroom window crept down, down. Then, too, the Pools objected to the icy blasts which swept the open stairway and penetrated their hermetically sealed bedrooms below. Often the water in the pitcher on her washstand was frozen when Selina awoke. Her garments, laid out the night before so that their donning next morning might occupy a minimum of time, were mortuary to the touch. Worst of all were the steel-stiffened, unwieldy, and ridiculous stays that encased the female form of that day. As Selina's numbed fingers struggled with the fastenings of this iciest of garments her ribs shrank from its arctic embrace.

"But I won't dress behind the kitchen stove!" declared Selina, glaring meanwhile at that hollow pretense, the drum. She even stuck her tongue out at it (only nineteen, remember!). For that matter, it may as well be known that she brought home a piece of chalk from school and sketched a demon face on the drum's bulging front, giving it a personal and horrid aspect that afforded her much satisfaction.

When she thought back, years later, on that period of her High Prairie experience, stoves seemed to figure with absurd prominence in her memory. That might well be. A stove changed the whole course of her life.

From the first, the schoolhouse stove was her bête noir. Out of the welter of that first year it stood, huge and menacing, a black tyrant. The High Prairie schoolhouse in which Selina taught was a little more than a mile up the road beyond the Pool farm. She came to know that road in all its moods—ice-locked, drifted with snow, wallowing in mud. School began at half-past eight. After her first week Selina had the mathematics of her early morning reduced to the least common denominator. Up at six. A plunge into the frigid garments; breakfast of bread, cheese, sometimes bacon, always rye coffee without cream or sugar. On with the cloak, muffler, hood, mittens, galoshes. The lunch box in bad weather. Up the road to the schoolhouse, battling the prairie wind that whipped the tears into the eyes, ploughing the drifts, slipping on the hard ruts and icy ridges in dry weather. Excellent at nineteen. As she flew down the road in sun or rain, in wind or snow, her mind's eye was fixed on the stove. The schoolhouse reached, her numbed fingers wrestled with the rusty lock. The door opened, there smote her the schoolroom smell— a mingling of dead ashes, kerosene, unwashed bodies, dust, mice, chalk, stove-wood, lunch crumbs, mould, slate that has been washed with saliva. Into this Selina rushed, untying her muffler as she entered. In the little vestibule there was a box piled with chunks of stove-wood and another heaped with dried corn-cobs. Alongside this a can of kerosene. The cobs served as kindling. A dozen or more of these you soaked with kerosene and stuffed into the maw of the rusty iron pot-bellied stove. A match. Up flared the corn-cobs. Now was the moment for a small stick of wood; another to keep it company. Shut the door. Draughts. Dampers. Smoke. Suspense. A blaze, then a crackle. The wood has caught. In with a chunk now. A wait. Another chunk. Slam the door. The schoolhouse fire is started for the day. As the room thawed gradually Selina removed layers of outer garments. By the time the children arrived the room was livable.

Naturally, those who sat near this monster baked; those near the windows froze. Sometimes Selina felt she must go mad beholding the writhings and contortions of a roomful of wriggling bodies scratching at backs, legs, and sides as the stove grew hotter and flesh rebelled against the harsh contact with the prickling undergarments of an over-cautious day.

Selina had seen herself, dignified, yet gentle, instructing a roomful of Dutch cherubs in the simpler elements of learning. But it is difficult to be dignified and gracious when you are suffering from chilblains. Selina fell victim to this sordid discomfort, as did every child in the room. She sat at the battered pine desk or moved about, a little ice-wool shawl around her shoulders when the wind was wrong and the stove balky. Her white little face seemed whiter in contrast with the black folds of this sombre garment. Her slim hands were rough and chapped. The oldest child in the room was thirteen, the youngest four and a half. From eight-thirty until four Selina ruled this grubby domain; a hot-and-cold roomful of sneezing, coughing, wriggling, shuffling, dozing children, toe scuffling on agonized heel, and heel scrunching on agonized toe, in a frenzy of itching.

"Aggie Vander Sijde, parse this sentence: The ground is wet because it has rained."

Miss Vander Sijde, eleven, arises with a switching of skirts and a tossing of pigtail. "'Ground' the subject; 'is wet' the predicate; 'because' . . ."

Selina is listening with school-teacherly expression indicative of encouragement and approval. "Jan Snip, parse this sentence: The flower will wither if it is picked."

Brown lady's-cloth; ice-wool shawl; chalk in hand. Just a phase; a brief chapter in the adventure. Something to remember and look back on with a mingling of amusement and wonder. Things were going to happen. Such things, with life and life and life stretching ahead of her! In five years—two—even one, perhaps, who knows but that she might be lying on lacy pillows on just such a bleak winter morning, a satin coverlet over her, the morning light shaded by soft rose-coloured hangings. (Early influence of the *Fireside Companion*.)

"What time is it, Celeste?"

"It is now eleven o'clock, madame."

"Is that all!"

"Would madame like that I prepare her bath now, or later?"

"Later, Celeste. My chocolate now. My letters."

". . . and if is the conjunction modifying . . ."

Early in the winter Selina had had the unfortunate idea of opening the ice-locked windows at intervals and giving the children five minutes of exercise while the fresh cold air cleared brains and room at once. Arms waved wildly, heads wobbled, short legs worked vigorously. At the end of the week twenty High Prairie parents sent protests by note or word of mouth. Jan and Cornelius, Katrina and Aggie went to school to learn reading and writing and numbers, not to stand with open windows in the winter.

On the Pool farm the winter work had set in. Klaas drove into Chi-

cago with winter vegetables only once a week now. He and Jakob and
Roelf were storing potatoes and cabbages underground; repairing fences;
preparing frames for the early spring planting; sorting seedlings. It had
been Roelf who had taught Selina to build the schoolhouse fire. He had
gone with her on that first morning, had started the fire, filled the water
pail, initiated her in the rites of corn-cobs, kerosene, and dampers. A
shy, dark, silent boy. She set out deliberately to woo him to friendship.
"Roelf, I have a book called 'Ivanhoe.' Would you like to read it?"
"Well, I don't get much time."
"You wouldn't have to hurry. Right there in the house. And there's
another called 'The Three Musketeers'."

He was trying not to look pleased; to appear stolid and Dutch, like
the people from whom he had sprung. Some Dutch sailor ancestor,
Selina thought, or fisherman, must have touched at an Italian port or
Spanish and brought back a wife whose eyes and skin and feeling for
beauty had skipped layer on layer of placid Netherlanders to crop out
now in this wistful sensitive boy.

Selina had spoken to Jakob Hoogendunk about a shelf for her books
and her photographs. He had put up a rough bit of board, very crude
and ugly, but it had served. She had come home one snowy afternoon
to find this shelf gone and in its place a smooth and polished one, with
brackets intricately carved. Roelf had cut, planed, polished, and carved
it in many hours of work in the cold little shed off the kitchen. He had
there a workshop of sorts, fitted with such tools and implements as he
could devise. He did man's work on the farm, yet often at night Selina
could faintly hear the rasp of his handsaw after she had gone to bed.
He had built a doll's house for Geertje and Jozina that was the black
envy of every pigtail in High Prairie. This sort of thing was looked upon
by Klaas Pool as foolishness. Roelf's real work in the shed was the making and mending of coldframes and hotbeds for the early spring plants.
Whenever possible Roelf neglected this dull work for some fancy of his
own. To this Klaas Pool objected as being "dumb." For that matter,
High Prairie considered Pool's boy "dumb like." He said such things.
When the new Dutch Reformed Church was completed after gigantic
effort—red brick, and the first brick church in High Prairie—bright yellow painted pews—a red and yellow glass window, most handsome—the
Reverend Vaarwerk brought from New Haarlem to preach the first sermon—Pool's Roelf was heard to hint darkly to a group of High Prairie
boys that some night he was going to burn the church down. It was
ugly. It hurt you to look at it, just.

Certainly, the boy was different. Selina, none too knowledgeous herself, still recognized that here was something rare, something precious to be fostered, shielded, encouraged.

"Roelf, stop that foolishness, get your ma once some wood. Carving on that box again instead finishing them coldframes. Some day, by golly, I show you. I break every stick . . . dumb as a Groningen . . ."

Roelf did not sulk. He seemed not to mind, particularly, but he came back to the carved box as soon as chance presented itself. Maartje and Klaas Pool were not cruel people, nor unkind. They were a little bewildered by this odd creature that they, inexplicably enough, had produced. It was not a family given to demonstration of affection. Life was too grim for the flowering of this softer side. Then, too, they had sprung from a phlegmatic and unemotional people. Klaas toiled like a slave in the fields and barn; Maartje's day was a treadmill of cooking, scrubbing, washing, mending from the moment she arose (four in the summer, five in the winter) until she dropped with a groan in her bed often long after the others were asleep. Selina had never seen her kiss Geertje or Jozina. But once she had been a little startled to see Maartje, on one of her countless trips between stove and table, run her hand through the boy's shock of black hair, down the side of his face to his chin which she tipped up with an indescribably tender gesture as she looked down into his eyes. It was a movement fleeting, vague, yet infinitely compassionate. Sometimes she even remonstrated when Klaas berated Roelf. "Leave the boy be, then, Klaas. Leave him be, once."

"She loves him best," Selina thought. "She'd even try to understand him if she had time."

He was reading her books with such hunger as to cause her to wonder if her stock would last him the winter. Sometimes, after supper, when he was hammering and sawing away in the little shed Selina would snatch Maartje's old shawl off the hook, and swathed in this against draughty chinks, she would read aloud to him while he carved, or talk to him above the noise of his tools. Selina was a gay and volatile person. She loved to make this boy laugh. His dark face would flash into almost dazzling animation. Sometimes Maartje, hearing their young laughter, would come to the shed door and stand there a moment, hugging her arms in her rolled apron and smiling at them, uncomprehending but companionable.

"You make fun, h'm?"

"Come in, Mrs. Pool. Sit down on my box and make fun, too. Here, you may have half the shawl."

"Og heden! I got no time to sit down." She was off.

Roelf slid his plane slowly, more slowly, over the surface of a satin-smooth oak board. He stopped, twined a curl of shaving about his finger. "When I am a man, and earning, I am going to buy my mother a silk dress like I saw in a store in Chicago and she should put it on every day, not only for Sunday; and sit in a chair and make little fine stitches like Widow Paarlenberg."

"What else are you going to do when you grow up?" She waited, certain that he would say something delightful.

"Drive the team to town alone to market."

"Oh, Roelf!"

"Sure. Already I have gone five times—twice with Jakob and three times with Pop. Pretty soon, when I am seventeen or eighteen, I can go alone. At five in the afternoon you start and at nine you are in the Haymarket. There all night you sleep on the wagon. There are gas lights. The men play dice and cards. At four in the morning you are ready when they come, the commission men and the pedlers and the grocery men. Oh, it's fine, I tell you!"

"Roelf!" She was bitterly disappointed.

"Here. Look." He rummaged around in a dusty box in a corner and, suddenly shy again, laid before her a torn sheet of coarse brown paper on which he had sketched crudely, effectively, a mêlée of great-haunched horses; wagons piled high with garden truck; men in overalls and corduroys; flaring gas torches. He had drawn it with a stub of pencil exactly as it looked to him. The result was as startling as that achieved by the present-day disciple of the impressionistic school.

Selina was enchanted.

Many of her evenings during November were spent thus. The family life was lived in a kitchen blue with pipe smoke, heavy with the smell of cooking. Sometimes—though rarely—a fire was lighted in the parlour stove. Often she had school papers to correct—grubby sheaves of arithmetic, grammar, or spelling lessons. Often she longed to read; wanted to sew. Her bedroom was too cold. The men sat in the kitchen or tramped in and out. Geertje and Jozina scuffled and played. Maartje scuttled about like a harried animal, heavy-footed but incredibly swift. The floor was always gritty with the sandy loam tracked in by the men's heavy boots.

Once, early in December, Selina went into town. The trip was born of sudden revolt against her surroundings and a great wave of nostalgia for the dirt and clamour and crowds of Chicago. Early Saturday morning Klaas drove her to the railway station five miles distant. She was to stay until Sunday. A letter had been written Julie Hempel ten days before, but there had been no answer. Once in town she went straight to the Hempel house. Mrs. Hempel, thin-lipped, met her in the hall and said that Julie was out of town. She was visiting her friend Miss Arnold, in Kansas City. Selina was not asked to stay to dinner. She was not asked to sit down. When she left the house her great fine eyes seemed larger and more deep-set than ever, and her jaw-line was set hard against the invasion of tears. Suddenly she hated this Chicago that wanted none of her; that brushed past her, bumping her elbow and offering no apology; that clanged, and shrieked, and whistled, and roared in her ears now grown accustomed to the prairie silence.

"I don't care," she said, which meant she did. "I don't care. Just you wait. Some day I'm going to be—oh, terribly important. And people will say, 'Do you know that wonderful Selina Peake? Well, they say she used to be a country school teacher and slept in an ice-cold room and ate pork three times a . . .' There! I know what I'm going to do. I'm going to have luncheon and I'll order the most delicious things. I think I'll go to the Palmer House where Father and I . . . no, I couldn't stand that. I'll go to the Auditorium Hotel restaurant and have ice cream; and chicken broth in a silver cup; and cream puffs, and all kinds of vegetables and little lamb chops in paper panties. And orange pekoe tea."

She actually did order all these things and had a group of amazed waiters hovering about her table waiting to see her devour this meal, much as a similar group had stared at David Copperfield when he was innocent of having bolted the huge dinner ordered in the inn on his way to London.

She ate the ice cream and drank the orange pekoe (mainly because she loved the sound of its name; it made her think of chrysanthemums and cherry blossoms, spices, fans, and slant-eyed maidens). She devoured a crisp salad with the avidity of a canary pecking at a lettuce leaf. She flirted with the lamb chops. She remembered the size of her father's generous tips and left a sum on the table that temporarily dulled the edge of the waiter's hatred of women diners. But the luncheon could not be said to have been a success. She thought of dinner, and her spirit quailed. She spent the time between one and three buying portable presents for the entire Pool household—including bananas for Geertje and Jozina, for whom that farinaceous fruit had the fascination always held for the farm child. She caught a train at four thirty-five and actually trudged the five miles from the station to the farm, arriving half frozen, weary, with aching arms and nipped toes, to a great welcome of the squeals, grunts, barks, and gutturals that formed the expression of the Pool household. She was astonished to find how happy she was to return to the kitchen stove, to the smell of frying pork, to her own room with the walnut bed and the book shelf. Even the grim drum had taken on the dear and comforting aspect of the accustomed.

V

HIGH PRAIRIE swains failed to find Selina alluring. She was too small, too pale and fragile for their robust taste. Naturally, her coming had been an event in this isolated community. She would have been surprised to know with what eagerness and curiosity High Prairie gathered crumbs of news about her; her appearance, her manner, her dress. Was she stuck up? Was she new fangled? She failed to notice the agitation of the parlour curtains behind the glittering windows of the farmhouses she passed on her way to school. With no visible means of communication news of her leaped from farm to farm as flame leaps the gaps in a forest fire. She would have been aghast to learn that High Prairie, inexplicably enough, knew all about her from the colour of the ribbon that threaded her neat little white corset covers to the number of books on her shelf. She thought cabbage fields beautiful; she read books to that dumb-acting Roelf Pool; she was making over a dress for Maartje after the pattern of the stylish brown lady's-cloth she wore (foolishly) to school. Now and then she encountered a team on the road. She would call a good-day. Sometimes the driver answered, tardily, as though surprised. Sometimes he only stared. She almost never saw the High Prairie farm women, busy in their kitchens.

On her fifth Sunday in the district she accompanied the Pools to the morning service at the Dutch Reformed Church. Maartje seldom had the time for such frivolity. But on this morning Klaas hitched up the big farm wagon with the double seat and took the family complete—Maartje, Selina, Roelf, and the pigtails. Maartje, out of her kitchen calico and dressed in her best black, with a funereal bonnet made sadder by a sparse and drooping feather whose listless fronds emerged surprisingly from a faded red cotton rose, wore a new strange aspect to Selina's eyes, as did Klaas in his clumsy sabbaticals. Roelf had rebelled against going, had been cuffed for it, and had sat very still all through the service, gazing at the red and yellow glass church window. Later he confided to Selina that the sunlight filtering through the crude yellow panes had imparted a bilious look to the unfortunates seated within its range, affording him much secret satisfaction.

Selina's appearance had made quite a stir, of which she was entirely unaware. As the congregation entered by twos and threes she thought they resembled startlingly a woodcut in an old illustrated book she once had seen. The men's Sunday trousers and coats had a square stiff angularity, as though chopped out of a block. The women, in shawls and bonnets of rusty black, were incredibly cut in the same pattern. The unmarried girls, though, were plump, red-cheeked, and not uncomely, with high round cheek bones on which sat a spot of brick-red which imparted no glow to the face. Their foreheads were prominent and meaningless.

In the midst of this drab assemblage there entered late and rustlingly a tall, slow-moving woman in a city-bought cloak and a bonnet quite unlike the vintage millinery of High Prairie. As she came down the aisle Selina thought she was like a full-sailed frigate. An ample woman, with a fine fair skin and a ripe red mouth; a high firm bosom and great thighs that moved rhythmically, slowly. She had thick, insolent eyelids. Her hands, as she turned the leaves of her hymn book, were smooth and white. As she entered there was a little rustle throughout the congregation; a craning of necks. Though she was bustled and flounced and panniered, you thought, curiously enough, of those lolling white-fleshed and unconventional ladies whom the sixteenth century painters were always portraying as having their toe nails cut with nothing on.

"Who's that?" whispered Selina to Maartje.

"Widow Paarlenberg. She is rich like anything."

"Yes?" Selina was fascinated.

"Look once how she makes eyes at him."

"At him? Who? Who?"

"Pervus DeJong. By Gerrit Pon he is sitting with the blue shirt and sad looking so."

Selina craned, peered. "The—oh—he's very good looking, isn't he?"

"Sure. Widow Paarlenberg is stuck on him. See how she—Sh-sh-sh!— Reverend Dekker looks at us. I tell you after."

Selina decided she'd come to church oftener. The service went on, dull, heavy. It was in English and Dutch. She heard scarcely a word of it. The Widow Paarlenberg and this Pervus DeJong occupied her thoughts. She decided, without malice, that the widow resembled one of the sleekest of the pink porkers rooting in Klaas Pool's barnyard, waiting to be cut into Christmas meat.

The Widow Paarlenberg turned and smiled. Her eyes were slippery (Selina's term). Her mouth became loose and wide with one corner sliding down a trifle into something very like a leer.

With one surge the Dutch Reformed congregation leaned forward to see how Pervus DeJong would respond to this public mark of favour.

His gaze was stern, unsmiling. His eyes were fixed on that extremely dull gentleman, the Reverend Dekker.

"He's annoyed," thought Selina, and was pleased at the thought. "Well, I may not be a widow, but I'm sure that's not the way." And then: "Now I wonder what it's like when *he* smiles."

According to fiction as Selina had found it in the *Fireside Companion* and elsewhere, he should have turned at this moment, irresistibly drawn by the magnetism of her gaze, and smiled a rare sweet smile that lighted up his stern young face. But he did not. He yawned suddenly and capaciously. The Reformed Dutch congregation leaned back feeling cheated. Handsome, certainly, Selina reflected. But then, probably Klaas Pool, too, had been handsome a few years ago.

The service ended, there was much talk of the weather, seedlings, stock, the approaching holiday season. Maartje, her Sunday dinner heavy on her mind, was elbowing her way up the aisle. Here and there she introduced Selina briefly to a woman friend. "Mrs. Vander Sijde, meet school teacher."

"Aggie's mother?" Selina would begin, primly, only to be swept along by Maartje on her way to the door. "Mrs. Von Mijnen, meet school teacher. Is Mrs. Von Mijnen." They regarded her with a grim gaze. Selina would smile and nod rather nervously, feeling young, frivolous, and somehow guilty.

When, with Maartje, she reached the church porch Pervus DeJong was unhitching the dejected horse that was harnessed to his battered and lopsided cart. The animal stood with four feet bunched together in a drooping and pathetic attitude and seemed inevitably meant for mating with this decrepit vehicle. DeJong untied the reins quickly, and was about to step into the sagging conveyance when the Widow Paarlenberg sailed down the church steps with admirable speed for one so amply proportioned. She made straight for him, skirts billowing, flounces flying, plumes waving. Maartje clutched Selina's arm. "Look how she makes! She asks him to eat Sunday dinner I bet you! See once how he makes with his head no."

Selina—and the whole congregation unashamedly watching—could indeed see how he made with his head no. His whole body seemed set in negation—the fine head, the broad patient shoulders, the muscular powerful legs in their ill-fitting Sunday blacks. He shook his head, gathered up the reins, and drove away, leaving the Widow Paarlenberg to carry off with such bravado as she could muster this public flouting in full sight of the Dutch Reformed congregation of High Prairie. It must be said that she actually achieved this feat with a rather magnificent composure. Her round pink face, as she turned away, was placid;

her great cowlike eyes mild. Selina abandoned the pink porker simile
for that of a great Persian cat, full-fed and treacherous, its claws all
sheathed in velvet. The widow stepped agilely into her own neat phaeton
with its sleek horse and was off down the hard snowless road, her head
high.

"Well!" exclaimed Selina, feeling as though she had witnessed the
first act of an exciting play. And breathed deeply. So, too, did the watching congregation, so that the widow could be said to have driven off
in quite a gust.

As they jogged home in the Pool farm wagon Maartje told her tale
with a good deal of savour.

Pervus DeJong had been left a widower two years before. Within a
month of that time Leendert Paarlenberg had died, leaving to his widow
the richest and most profitable farm in the whole community. Pervus
DeJong, on the contrary, through inheritance from his father, old
Johannes, possessed a scant twenty-five acres of the worst lowland—
practically the only lowland—in all High Prairie. The acreage was
notoriously barren. In spring, the critical time for seedlings and early
vegetable crops, sixteen of the twenty-five were likely to be under water.
Pervus DeJong patiently planted, sowed, gathered crops, hauled them
to market; seemed still never to get on in this thrifty Dutch community
where getting on was so common a trait as to be no longer thought a
virtue. Luck and nature seemed to work against him. His seedlings
proved unfertile; his stock was always ailing; his cabbages were worm-
infested; snout-beetle bored his rhubarb. When he planted largely of
spinach, hoping for a wet spring, the season was dry. Did he turn the
following year to sweet potatoes, all auguries pointing to a dry spring and
summer, the summer proved the wettest in a decade. Insects and fungi
seemed drawn to his fields as by a malevolent force. Had he been small,
puny, and insignificant his bad luck would have called forth contemptuous pity. But there was about him the lovableness and splendour of the
stricken giant. To complete his discomfort, his household was inadequately ministered by an elderly and rheumatic female connection whose
pies and bread were the scandal of the neighbouring housewives.

It was on this Pervus DeJong, then, that the Widow Paarlenberg of
the rich acres, the comfortable farmhouse, the gold neck chain, the silk
gowns, the soft white hands and the cooking talents, had set her affec-
tions. She wooed him openly, notoriously, and with a Dutch vehemence
that would have swept another man off his feet. It was known that she
sent him a weekly baking of cakes, pies, and bread. She urged upon him
choice seeds from her thriving fields; seedlings from her hotbeds; plants,
all of which he steadfastly refused. She tricked, cajoled, or nagged him

into eating her ample meals. She even asked his advice—that subtlest form of flattery. She asked him about sub-soiling, humus, rotation—she whose rich land yielded, under her shrewd management, more profitably to the single acre than to any ten of Pervus's. One Jan Bras managed her farm admirably under her supervision.

DeJong's was a simple mind. In the beginning, when she said to him, in her deep, caressing voice, "Mr. DeJong, could I ask you a little advice about something? I'm a woman alone since I haven't got Leendert any more, and strangers what do they care how they run the land! It's about my radishes, lettuce, spinach, and turnips. Last year, instead of tender, they were stringy and full of fibre on account that Jan Bras. He's for slow growing. Those vegetables you've got to grow quick. Bras says my fertilizer is the fault, but I know different. What you think?"

Jan Bras, getting wind of this, told it abroad with grim humour. Masculine High Prairie, meeting Pervus DeJong on the road, greeted him with: "Well, DeJong, you been giving the Widow Paarlenberg any good advice here lately about growing?"

It had been a particularly bad season for his fields. As High Prairie poked a sly thumb into his ribs thus he realized that he had been duped by the wily widow. A slow Dutch wrath rose in him against her; a male resentment at being manipulated by a woman. When next she approached him, cajolery in her voice, seeking guidance about tillage, drainage, or crops, he said, bluntly: "Better you ask Harm Tien his advice." Harm Tien was the district idiot, a poor witless creature of thirty with the mind of a child.

Knowing well that the entire community was urging him toward this profitable match with the plump, rich, red-lipped widow, Pervus set his will like a stubborn steer and would have none of her. He was uncomfortable in his untidy house; he was lonely, he was unhappy. But he would have none of her. Vanity, pride, resentment were all mixed up in it.

The very first time that Pervus DeJong met Selina he had a chance to protect her. With such a start, the end was inevitable. Then, too, Selina had on the wine-coloured cashmere and was trying hard to keep the tears back in full view of the whole of High Prairie. Urged by Maartje (and rather fancying the idea) Selina had attended the great meeting and dance at Adam Ooms's hall above the general store near the High Prairie station. Farmer families for miles around were there. The new church organ—that time-hallowed pretext for sociability—was the excuse for this gathering. There was a small admission charge. Adam Ooms had given them the hall. The three musicians were playing without fee. The women were to bring supper packed in boxes or baskets, these to be raffled off to the highest bidder whose privilege it then was to sup with the fair whose basket he had bought. Hot coffee could be had at so much the cup. All the proceeds were to be devoted to the organ. It was understood, of course, that there was to be no lively bidding against husbands. Each farm woman knew her own basket as she knew the countenance of her children, and each farmer, as that basket came up at auction, named a cautious sum which automatically made him the basket's possessor. The larger freedom had not come to High Prairie in 1890. The baskets and boxes of the unwed women were to be the fought-for prizes. Maartje had packed her own basket at noon and had driven off at four with Klaas and the children. She was to serve on one of those bustling committees whose duties ranged from coffee making to dish washing. Klaas and Roelf were to be pressed into service. The pigtails would slide up and down the waxed floor of Ooms's hall with other shrieking pigtails of the neighbourhood until the crowd began to arrive for the auction and supper. Jakob Hoogendunk would convey Selina to the festivities when his chores were done. Selina's lunch basket was to be a separate and distinct affair, offered at auction with those of the Katrinas and Linas and Sophias of High Prairie. Not a little apprehensive, she was to pack this basket herself. Maartje, departing, had left copious but disjointed instructions.

"Ham . . . them big cookies in the crock . . . pickles . . . watch how you don't spill . . . plum preserves . . ."

Maartje's own basket was of gigantic proportions and staggering content. Her sandwiches were cubic blocks; her pickles clubs of cucumber; her pies vast plateaus.

The basket provided for Selina, while not quite so large, still was of appalling size as Selina contemplated it. She decided, suddenly, that she would have none of it. In her trunk she had a cardboard box such as shoes come in. Certainly this should hold enough lunch for two, she thought. She and Julie Hempel had used such boxes for picnic lunches on their Saturday holidays. She was a little nervous about the whole thing; rather dreaded the prospect of eating her supper with a High Prairie swain unknown to her. Suppose no one should bid for her box! She resolved to fill it after her own pattern, disregarding Maartje's heavy provender.

She had the kitchen to herself. Jakob was in the fields or out-houses. The house was deliciously quiet. Selina rummaged for the shoe box, lined it with a sheet of tissue paper, rolled up her sleeves, got out mixing bowl, flour, pans. Cup cakes were her ambition. She baked six of them. They came out a beautiful brown but somewhat leaden. Still, anything was better than a wedge of soggy pie, she told herself. She boiled eggs very hard, halved them, devilled their yolks, filled the whites neatly with this mixture and clapped the halves together again, skewering them with a toothpick. Then she rolled each egg separately in tissue paper twisted at the ends. Daintiness, she had decided, should be the keynote of her supper box. She cut bread paper-thin and made jelly sandwiches, scorning the ubiquitous pork. Bananas, she knew, belonged in a lunch box, but these were unobtainable. She substituted two juicy pippins, polished until their cheeks glittered. The food neatly packed she wrapped the box in paper and tied it with a gay red ribbon yielded by her trunk. At the last moment she whipped into the yard, twisted a brush of evergreen from the tree at the side of the house, and tucked this into the knot of ribbon atop the box. She stepped back and thought the effect enchanting.

She was waiting in her red cashmere and her cloak and hood when Hoogendunk called for her. They were late arrivals, for outside Ooms's hall were hitched all manner of vehicles. There had been a heavy snowfall two days before. This had brought out bob-sleds, cutters, sleighs. The horse sheds were not large enough to shelter all. Late comers had to hitch were they could. There was a great jangling of bells as the horses stamped in the snow.

Selina, balancing her box carefully, opened the door that led to the wooden stairway. The hall was on the second floor. The clamour that struck her ears had the effect of a physical blow. She hesitated a moment, and if there had been any means of returning to the Pool farm, short of walking five miles in the snow, she would have taken it. Up the stairs and into the din. Evidently the auctioning of supper baskets was even now in progress. The roar of voices had broken out after the sale of a basket and now was subsiding under the ear-splitting cracks of the auctioneer's hammer. Through the crowded doorway Selina could catch a glimpse of him as he stood on a chair, the baskets piled before him. He used a barrel elevated on a box as his pulpit. The auctioneer was Adam Ooms who himself had once been the High Prairie school teacher. A fox-faced little man, bald, falsetto, the village clown with a solid foundation of shrewdness under his clowning and a tart layer of malice over it.

High and shrill came his voice. "What am I bid! What am I bid! Thirty cents! Thirty-five! Shame on you, gentlemen. What am I bid! Who'll make it forty!"

Selina felt a little thrill of excitement. She looked about for a place on which to lay her wraps. Every table, chair, hook, and rack in the hallway was piled with clothing. She espied a box that appeared empty, rolled her cloak, muffler, and hood into a neat bundle and, about to cast it into the box, saw, upturned to her from its depths, the round pink faces of the sleeping Kuyper twins, aged six months. From the big hall now came a great shouting, clapping of hands, stamping, cat-calls. Another basket had been disposed of. Oh, dear! In desperation Selina placed her bundle on the floor in a corner, smoothed down the red cashmere, snatched up her lunch box and made for the doorway with the childish eagerness of one out of the crowd to be in it. She wondered where Maartje and Klaas Pool were in this close-packed roomful; and Roelf. In the doorway she found that broad black-coated backs shut off sight and ingress. She had written her name neatly on her lunch box. Now she was at a loss to find a way to reach Adam Ooms. She eyed the great-shouldered expanse just ahead of her. In desperation she decided to dig into it with a corner of her box. She dug, viciously. The back winced. Its owner turned. "Here! What——!"

Selina looked up into the wrathful face of Pervus DeJong. Pervus DeJong looked down into the startled eyes of Selina Peake. Large enough eyes at any time; enormous now in her fright at what she had done.

"I'm sorry! I'm—sorry. I thought if I could—there's no way of getting my lunch box up there—such a crowd——"

A slim, appealing, lovely little figure in the wine-red cashmere, amidst all those buxom bosoms, and overheated bodies, and flushed faces. His gaze left her reluctantly, settled on the lunch box, became, if possible, more bewildered. "That? Lunch box?"

"Yes. For the raffle. I'm the school teacher. Selina Peake."

He nodded. "I saw you in church Sunday."

"You did! I didn't think you. . . . Did you?"

"Wait here. I'll come back. Wait here."

He took the shoe box. She waited. He ploughed his way through the crowd like a Juggernaut, reached Adam Ooms's platform and placed the box inconspicuously next a colossal hamper that was one of a dozen grouped awaiting Adam's attention. When he had made his way back to Selina he again said, "Wait," and plunged down the wooden stairway. Selina waited. She had ceased to feel distressed at her inability to find the Pools in the crowd, a-tiptoe though she was. When presently he came back he had in his hand an empty wooden soap-box. This he up-ended in the doorway just behind the crowd stationed there. Selina mounted it; found her head a little above the level of his. She could survey the room from end to end. There were the Pools. She waved to Maartje; smiled at Roelf. He made as though to come toward her; did come part way, and was restrained by Maartje catching at his coat tail.

Selina wished she could think of something to say. She looked down at Pervus DeJong. The back of his neck was pink, as though with effort. She thought, instinctively, "My goodness, he's trying to think of something to say, too." That, somehow, put her at her ease. She would wait until he spoke. His neck was now a deep red. The crowd surged back at some disturbance around Adam Ooms's elevation. Selina teetered perilously on her box, put out a hand blindly, felt his great hard hand on her arm, steadying her.

"Quite a crowd, ain't it?" The effort had reached its apex. The red of his neck began to recede.

"Oh, quite!"

"They ain't all High Prairie. Some of 'em's from Low Prairie way. New Haarlem, even."

"Really!"

A pause. Another effort.

"How goes it school teaching?"

"Oh—it goes pretty well."

"You are little to be school teacher, anyway, ain't you?"

"Little!" She drew herself up from her vantage point of the soap-box. "I'm bigger than you are."

They laughed at that as at an exquisite piece of repartee.

Adam Oom's gavel (a wooden potato masher) crashed for silence. "Ladies!" [Crash!] "And gents!" [Crash!] "Gents! Look what basket we've got here!"

Look indeed. A great hamper, grown so plethoric that it could no longer wear its cover. Its contents bellied into a mound smoothly covered with a fine white cloth whose glistening surface proclaimed it damask. A Himalaya among hampers. You knew that under that snowy crust lay gold that was fowl done crisply, succulently; emeralds in the form of gherkins; rubies that melted into strawberry preserves; cakes frosted like diamonds; to say nothing of such semi-precious jewels as potato salad; cheeses; sour cream to be spread on rye bread and butter; coffee cakes; crullers.

Crash! "The Widow Paarlenberg's basket, ladies—*and* gents! The Widow Paarlenberg! I don't know what's in it. You don't know what's in it. We don't have to know what's in it. Who has eaten Widow Paarlenberg's chicken once don't have to know. Who has eaten Widow Paarlenberg's cake once don't have to know. What am I bid on Widow Paarlenberg's basket! What am I bid! WhatmIbidwhatmIbidwhatmIbid!" [Crash!]

The widow herself, very handsome in black silk, her gold neck chain rising and falling richly with the little flurry that now agitated her broad bosom, was seated in a chair against the wall not five feet from the auctioneer's stand. She bridled now, blushed, cast down her eyes, cast up her eyes, succeeded in looking as unconscious as a complaisant Turkish slave girl on the block.

Adam Ooms's glance swept the hall. He leaned forward, his fox-like face fixed in a smile. From the widow herself, seated so prominently at his right, his gaze marked the young blades of the village; the old bucks; youths and widowers and bachelors. Here was the prize of the evening. Around, in a semi-circle, went his keen glance until it reached the tall figure towering in the doorway—reached it, and rested there. His gimlet eyes seemed to bore their way into Pervus DeJong's steady stare. He raised his right arm aloft, brandishing the potato masher. The whole room fixed its gaze on the blond head in the doorway. "Speak up! Young men of High Prairie! Heh, you, Pervus DeJong! WhatmIbidwhatmIbidwhatmIbid!"

"Fifty cents!" The bid came from Gerrit Pon at the other end of the hall. A dashing offer, as a start, in this district where one dollar often represented the profits on a whole load of market truck brought to the city.

Crash! went the potato masher. "Fifty cents I'm bid. Who'll make it seventy-five? Who'll make it seventy-five?"

"Sixty!" Johannes Ambuul, a widower, his age more than the sum of his bid.

"Seventy!" Gerrit Pon.

Adam Ooms whispered it—hissed it. "S-s-s-seventy. Ladies and gents, I wouldn't repeat out loud sucha figger. I would be ashamed. Look at this basket, gents, and then you can say . . . s-s-seventy!"

"Seventy-five!" the cautious Ambuul.

Scarlet, flooding her face, belied the widow's outward air of composure. Pervus DeJong, standing beside Selina, viewed the proceedings with an air of detachment. High Prairie was looking at him expectantly, openly. The widow bit her red lip, tossed her head. Pervus DeJong returned the auctioneer's meaning smirk with the mild gaze of a disinterested outsider. High Prairie, Low Prairie, and New Haarlem sat tense, like an audience at a play. Here, indeed, was drama being enacted in a community whose thrills were all too rare.

"Gents!" Adam Ooms's voice took on a tearful note—the tone of one who is more hurt than angry. "Gents!" Slowly, with infinite reverence, he lifted one corner of the damask cloth that concealed the hamper's contents—lifted it and peered within as at a treasure. At what he saw there he started back dramatically, at once rapturous, despairing, amazed. He rolled his eyes. He smacked his lips. He rubbed his stomach. The sort of dumb show that, since the days of the Greek drama, has been used to denote gastronomic delight.

"Eighty!" was wrenched suddenly from Goris Von Vuuren, the nineteen-year-old fat and gluttonous son of a prosperous New Haarlem farmer.

Adam Ooms rubbed brisk palms together. "Now then! A dollar! A dollar! It's an insult to this basket to make it less than a dollar." He lifted the cover again, sniffed, appeared overcome. "Gents, if it wasn't for Mrs. Ooms sitting there I'd make it a dollar myself and a bargain. A dollar! Am I bid a dollar!" He leaned far forward over his improvised pulpit. "Did I hear you say a dollar, Pervus DeJong?" DeJong stared, immovable, unabashed. His very indifference was contagious. The widow's bountiful basket seemed to shrink before one's eyes. "Eighty-eighty-eighty-eighty—gents! I'm going to tell you something. I'm going to whisper a secret." His lean face was veined with craftiness. "Gents. Listen. It isn't chicken in this beautiful basket. It isn't chicken. It's"— a dramatic pause—"it's *roast duck!*" He swayed back, mopped his brow with his red handkerchief, held one hand high in the air. His last card.

"Eighty-five!" groaned the fat Goris Von Vuuren.

"Eighty-five! Eighty-five! Eightyfiveeightyfiveeightyfive eighty-five! Gents! Gen-tle-men! Eighty-five once! Eighty-five—twice!" [Crash!] "Gone to Goris Von Vuuren for eighty-five."

A sigh went up from the assemblage; a sigh that was the wind before the storm. There followed a tornado of talk. It crackled and thundered. The rich Widow Paarlenberg would have to eat her supper with Von Vuuren's boy, the great thick Goris. And there in the doorway, talking to teacher as if they had known each other for years, was Pervus DeJong with his money in his pocket. It was as good as a play.

Adam Ooms was angry. His lean, fox-like face became pinched with spite. He prided himself on his antics as auctioneer; and his chef d'œuvre had brought a meagre eighty-five cents, besides doubtless winning him the enmity of that profitable store customer, the Widow Paarlenberg. Goris Von Vuuren came forward to claim his prize amidst shouting, clapping, laughter. The great hamper was handed down to him; an ample, rich-looking burden, its handle folded comfortably over its round stomach, its white cover so glistening with starch and ironing that it gave back the light from the big lamp above the auctioneer's stand. As Goris Von Vuuren lifted it his great shoulders actually sagged. Its contents promised satiety even to such a feeder as he. A grin, half sheepish, half triumphant, creased his plump pink face.

Adam Ooms scuffled about among the many baskets at his feet. His nostrils looked pinched and his skinny hands shook a little as he searched for one small object.

When he stood upright once more he was smiling. His little eyes gleamed. His wooden sceptre pounded for silence. High in one hand, balanced daintily on his finger tips, he held Selina's little white shoe box, with its red ribbon binding it, and the plume of evergreen stuck in the ribbon. Affecting great solicitude he brought it down then to read the name written on it; held it aloft again, smirking.

He said nothing. Grinning, he held it high. He turned his body at the waist from side to side, so that all might see. The eyes of those before him still held a mental picture of the huge hamper, food-packed, that had just been handed down. The contrast was too absurd, too cruel. A ripple of laughter swept the room; rose; swelled to a roar. Adam Ooms drew his mouth down solemnly. His little finger elegantly crooked, he pendulumed the box to right and left. He swerved his beady eyes from side to side. He waited with a nice sense of the dramatic until the laughter had reached its height, then held up a hand for silence. A great scraping "Ahem!" as he cleared his throat threatened to send the crowd off again.

"Ladies—*and* gents! Here's a dainty little tid-bit. Here's something not only for the inner man, but a feast for the eye. Well, boys, if the last lot was too much for you this lot ought to be just about right. If the food ain't quite enough for you, you can tie the ribbon in the lady's hair and put the posy in your buttonhole and there you are. *There* you are! What's more, the lady herself goes with it. You don't get a country girl with this here box, gents. A city girl, you can tell by looking at it, just. And who is she? Who did up this dainty little box just big enough for two?" He inspected it again, solemnly, and added, as an after-thought, "If you ain't feeling specially hungry. Who?——" He looked about, apishly.

Selina's cheeks matched her gown. Her eyes were wide and dark with the effort she was making to force back the hot haze threatening them. Why had she mounted this wretched soap-box! Why had she come to this hideous party! Why had she come to High Prairie! Why! . . .

"Miss Selina Peake, that's who. Miss Se-li-na Peake!"

A hundred balloon faces pulled by a single cord turned toward her as she stood there on the box for all to see. They swam toward her. She put up a hand to push them back.

"What'm I bid! What'm I bid! What'm I bid for this here lovely little toothful, gents! Start her up!"

"Five cents!" piped up old Johannes Ambuul, with a snicker. The tittering crowd broke into a guffaw. Selina was conscious of a little sick feeling at the pit of her stomach. Through the haze she saw the widow's face, no longer sulky, but smiling now. She saw Roelf's dear dark head. His face was set, like a man's. He was coming toward her, or trying to, but the crowd wedged him in, small as he was among those great bodies. She lost sight of him. How hot it was! how hot . . . An arm at her waist. Some one had mounted the little box and stood teetering there beside her, pressed against her slightly, reassuringly. Pervus DeJong. Her head was on a level with his great shoulder now. They stood together in the doorway, on the soap-box, for all High Prairie to see.

"Five cents I'm bid for this lovely little mouthful put up by the school teacher's own fair hands. Five cents! Five——"

"One dollar!" Pervus DeJong.

The balloon faces were suddenly punctured with holes. High Prairie's jaw dropped with astonishment. Its mouth stood open.

There was nothing plain about Selina now. Her dark head was held high, and his fair one beside it made a vivid foil. The purchase of the wine-coloured cashmere was at last justified.

"And ten!" cackled old Johannes Ambuul, his rheumy eyes on Selina.

Art and human spitefulness struggled visibly for mastery in Adam Ooms's face—and art won. The auctioneer triumphed over the man. The term "crowd psychology" was unknown to him, but he was artist enough to sense that some curious magic process, working through this roomful of people, had transformed the little white box, from a thing despised and ridiculed, into an object of beauty, of value, of infinite desirability. He now eyed it in a catalepsy of admiration.

"One-ten I'm bid for this box all tied with a ribbon to match the gown of the girl who brought it. Gents, you get the ribbon, the lunch, *and* the girl. And only one-ten bid for all that. Gents! Gents! Remember, it ain't only a lunch—it's a picture. It pleases the eye. Do I hear one——"

"Five bits!" Barend DeRoo, of Low Prairie, in the lists. A strapping young Dutchman, the Brom Bones of the district. Aaltje Huff, in a fit of pique at his indifference, had married to spite him. Cornelia Vinke, belle of New Haarlem, was said to be languishing for love of him. He drove to the Haymarket with his load of produce and played cards all night on the wagon under the gas torches while the street girls of the neighbourhood assailed him in vain. Six feet three, his red face shone now like a harvest moon above the crowd. A merry, mischievous eye that laughed at Pervus DeJong and his dollar bid.

"Dollar and a half!" A high clear voice—a boy's voice. Roelf.

"Oh, no!" said Selina aloud. But she was unheard in the gabble. Roelf had once confided to her that he had saved three dollars and fifty cents in the last three years. Five dollars would purchase a set of tools that his mind had been fixed on for months past. Selina saw Klaas Pool's look of astonishment changing to anger. Saw Maartje Pool's quick hand on his arm, restraining him.

"Two dollars!" Pervus DeJong.

"Twotwotwotwotwotwo!" Adam Ooms in a frenzy of salesmanship.

"And ten." Johannes Ambuul's cautious bid.

"Two and a quarter." Barend DeRoo.

"Two-fifty!" Pervus DeJong.

"Three dollars!" The high voice of the boy. It cracked a little on the last syllable, and the crowd laughed.

"Three-three-three-three-threethreethree. Three once——"

"And a half." Pervus DeJong.

"Three sixty."

"Four!" DeRoo.

"And ten."

The boy's voice was heard no more.

"I wish they'd stop," whispered Selina.

"Five!" Pervus DeJong.

"Six!" DeRoo, his face very red.

"And ten."

"Seven!"

"It's only jelly sandwiches," said Selina to DeJong, in a panic.

"Eight!" Johannes Ambuul, gone mad.

"Nine!" DeRoo.

"Nine! Nine I'm bid! Nine-nine-nine! Who'll make it——"

"Let him have it. The cup cakes fell a little. Don't——"

"Ten!" said Pervus DeJong.

Barend DeRoo shrugged his great shoulders.

"Ten-ten-ten. Do I hear eleven? Do I hear ten-fifty! Ten-ten-ten tententententententen! Gents! Ten once. Ten twice! Gone!—for ten dollars to Pervus DeJong. And a bargain." Adam Ooms mopped his bald head and his cheeks and the damp spot under his chin.

Ten dollars. Adam Ooms knew, as did all the countryside, this was not the sum of ten dollars merely. No basket of food, though it contained nightingales' tongues, the golden apple of Atalanta, wines of rare vintage, could have been adequate recompense for these ten dollars. They represented sweat and blood; toil and hardship; hours under the burning prairie sun at mid-day; work doggedly carried on through the drenching showers of spring; nights of restless sleep snatched an hour at a time under the sky in the Chicago market place; miles of weary travel down the rude corduroy road between High Prairie and Chicago, now up to the hubs in mud, now blinded by dust and blowing sand.

A sale at Christie's, with a miniature going for a million, could not have met with a deeper hush, a more dramatic babble following the hush.

They ate their lunch together in one corner of Adam Ooms's hall. Selina opened the box and took out the devilled eggs, and the cup cakes that had fallen a little, and the apples, and the sandwiches sliced very, very thin. The coldly appraising eye of all High Prairie, Low Prairie, and New Haarlem watched this sparse provender emerge from the ribbon-tied shoe box. She offered him a sandwich. It looked infinitesimal in his great paw. Suddenly all Selina's agony of embarrassment was swept away, and she was laughing, not wildly or hysterically, but joyously and girlishly. She sank her little white teeth into one of the absurd sandwiches and looked at him, expecting to find him laughing, too. But he wasn't laughing. He looked very earnest, and his blue eyes were fixed hard on the bit of bread in his hand, and his face was very red and clean-shaven. He bit into the sandwich and chewed it solemnly. And Selina thought: "Why, the dear thing! The great big dear thing! And he might have been eating breast of duck . . . Ten dollars!" Aloud she said, "What made you do it?"

"I don't know. I don't know." Then, "You looked so little. And they were making fun. Laughing." He looked very earnest, and his blue eyes were fixed hard on the sandwich, and his face was very red.

"That's a very foolish reason for throwing away ten dollars," Selina said, severely.

He seemed not to hear her; bit ruminantly into one of the cup cakes. Suddenly: "I can't hardly write at all, only to sign my name and like that."

"Read?"

"Only to spell out the words. Anyways I don't get time for reading. But figuring I wish I knew. 'Rithmetic. I can figger some, but those fellows in Haymarket they are too sharp for me. They do numbers in their head—like that, so quick."

Selina leaned toward him. "I'll teach you. I'll teach you."

"How do you mean, teach me?"

"Evenings."

He looked down at his great calloused palms, then up at her. "What would you take for pay?"

"Pay! I don't want any pay." She was genuinely shocked.

His face lighted up with a sudden thought. "Tell you what. My place is just this side the school, next to Bouts's place. I could start for you the fire, mornings, in the school. And thaw the pump and bring in a pail of water. This month, and January and February and part of March, even, now I don't go to market on account it's winter, I could start you the fire. Till spring. And I could come maybe three times a week, evenings, to Pool's place, for lessons." He looked so helpless, so humble, so huge; and the more pathetic for his hugeness.

She felt a little rush of warmth toward him that was at once impersonal and maternal. She thought again, "Why, the dear thing! The great helpless big thing! How serious he is! And funny." He was indeed both serious and funny, with the ridiculous cup cake in his great hand, his eyes wide and ruminant, his face ruddier than ever, his forehead knotted with earnestness. She laughed, suddenly, a gay little laugh, and he, after a puzzled pause, joined her companionably.

"Three evenings a week," repeated Selina, then, from the depths of her ignorance. "Why, I'd love to. I'd—love to."

VI

THE evenings turned out to be Tuesdays, Thursdays, and Saturdays. Supper was over by six-thirty in the Pool household. Pervus was there by seven, very clean as to shirt, his hair brushed till it shone; shy, and given to dropping his hat and bumping against chairs, and looking solemn. Selina was torn between pity and mirth. If only he had blustered. A blustering big man puts the world on the defensive. A gentle giant disarms it.

Selina got out her McBride's Grammar and Duffy's Arithmetic, and together they started to parse verbs, paper walls, dig cisterns, and extract square roots. They found study impossible at the oilcloth-covered kitchen table, with the Pool household eddying about it. Jakob built a fire in the parlour stove and there they sat, teacher and pupil, their feet resting cosily on the gleaming nickel railing that encircled the wood burner.

On the evening of the first lesson Roelf had glowered throughout supper and had disappeared into the work-shed, whence issued a great sound of hammering, sawing, and general clatter. He and Selina had got into the way of spending much time together, in or out of doors. They skated on Vander Sijde's pond; together with the shrieking pigtails they coasted on the little slope that led down from Kuyper's woods to the main road, using sleds that had been put together by Roelf. On bad days they read or studied. Not Sundays merely, but many week-day evenings were spent thus. Selina was determined that Roelf should break away from the uncouth speech of the countryside; that he should at least share with her the somewhat sketchy knowledge gained at Miss Fister's select school. She, the woman of almost twenty, never talked down to this boy of twelve. The boy worshipped her inarticulately. She had early discovered that he had a feeling for beauty—beauty of line, texture, colour, and grouping—that was rare in one of his years. The feel of a satin ribbon in his fingers; the orange and rose of a sunset; the folds of the wine-red cashmere dress; the cadence of a spoken line, brought a look to his face that startled her. She had a battered volume of Tenny-son. When first she read him the line beginning, "Elaine the fair, Elaine the lovable, Elaine, the lily maid of Astolat——" he had uttered a little exclamation. She, glancing up from her book, had found his eyes wide, bright, and luminous in his lean dark face.

"What is it, Roelf?"

He had flushed. "I didn't say nothing—anything. Start over again how it goes, 'Elaine——' "

She had begun again the fragrant lines, "Elaine the fair, Elaine the lovable . . ."

Since the gathering at Ooms's hall he had been moody and sullen; had refused to answer when she spoke to him of his bid for her basket. Urged, he would only say, "Oh, it was just fun to make old Ooms mad."

Now, with the advent of Pervus DeJong, Roelf presented that most touching and miserable of spectacles, a small boy jealous and helpless in his jealousy. Selina had asked him to join the tri-weekly evening lessons; had, indeed, insisted that he be a pupil in the class round the parlour stove. Maartje had said, on the night of Pervus DeJong's first visit, "Roelf, you sit, too, and learn. Is good for you to learn out of books the way teacher says." Klaas Pool, too, had approved the plan, since it would cost nothing and, furthermore, would in no way interfere with Roelf's farm work. "Sure; learn," he said, with a large gesture.

Roelf would not. He behaved very badly; slammed doors, whistled, scuffled on the kitchen floor, made many mysterious trips through the parlour up the stairs that led off that room, ascending with a clatter; in-cited Geertje and Jozina to quarrels and tears; had the household in a hubbub; stumbled over Dunder, the dog, so that that anguished animal's yelps were added to the din.

Selina was frantic. Lessons were impossible amidst this uproar. "It has never been like this before," she assured Pervus, almost tearfully. "I don't know what's the matter. It's awful."

Pervus had looked up from his slate. His eyes were calm, his lips smiling. "Is all right. In my house is too still, evenings. Next time it goes better. You see."

Next time it did go better. Roelf disappeared into his work-shed after supper; did not emerge until after DeJong's departure.

There was something about the sight of this great creature bent laboriously over a slate, the pencil held clumsily in his huge fingers, that moved Selina strangely. Pity wracked her. If she had known to what emotion this pity was akin she might have taken away the slate and given him a tablet, and the whole course of her life would have been different. "Poor lad," she thought. "Poor lad." Chided herself for being amused at his childlike earnestness.

He did not make an apt pupil, though painstaking. Usually the top draught of the stove was open, and the glow of the fire imparted to his face and head a certain roseate glory. He was very grave. His brow wore a troubled frown. Selina would go over a problem or a sentence again and again, patiently, patiently. Then, suddenly, like a hand passed over his face, his smile would come, transforming it. He had white strong teeth, too small, and perhaps not so white as they seemed because of his russet blondeur. He would smile like a child, and Selina should have been warned by the warm rush of joy that his smile gave her. She would smile, too. He was as pleased as though he had made a fresh and wonderful discovery.

"It's easy," he would say, "when you know it once." Like a boy.

He usually went home by eight-thirty or nine. Often the Pools went to bed before he left. After he had gone Selina was wakeful. She would heat water and wash; brush her hair vigorously; feeling at once buoyant and depressed.

Sometimes they fell to talking. His wife had died in the second year of their marriage, when the child was born. The child, too, had died. A girl. He was unlucky, like that. It was the same with the farm.

"Spring, half of the land is under water. My piece, just. Bouts's place, next to me, is high and rich. Bouts, he don't even need deep ploughing. His land is quick land. It warms up in the spring early. After rain it works easy. He puts in fertilizer, any kind, and his plants jump, like. My place is bad for garden truck. Wet. All the time, wet; or in summer baked before I can loosen it again. Muckland."

Selina thought a moment. She had heard much talk between Klaas and Jakob, winter evenings. "Can't you do something to it—fix it—so that the water will run off? Raise it, or dig a ditch or something?"

"We-e-ell, maybe. Maybe you could. But it costs money, draining."

"It costs money not to, doesn't it?"

He considered this, ruminatively. "Guess it does. But you don't have to have ready cash to let the land lay. To drain it you do."

Selina shook her head impatiently. "That's a very foolish, short-sighted way to reason."

He looked helpless as only the strong and powerful can look. Selina's heart melted in pity. He would look down at the great calloused hands; up at her. One of the charms of Pervus DeJong lay in the things that his eyes said and his tongue did not. Women always imagined he was about to say what he looked, but he never did. It made otherwise dull conversation with him most exciting.

His was in no way a shrewd mind. His respect for Selina was almost reverence. But he had this advantage: he had married a woman, had lived with her for two years. She had borne him a child. Selina was a girl in experience. She was a woman capable of a great deal of passion, but she did not know that. Passion was a thing no woman possessed, much less talked about. It simply did not exist, except in men, and then was something to be ashamed of, like a violent temper, or a weak stomach.

By the first of March he could speak a slow, careful, and fairly grammatical English. He could master simple sums. By the middle of March the lessons would cease. There was too much work to do about the farm—night work as well as day. She found herself trying not to think about the time when the lessons should cease. She refused to look ahead to April.

One night, late in February, Selina was conscious that she was trying to control something. She was trying to keep her eyes away from something. She realized that she was trying not to look at his hands. She wanted, crazily, to touch them. She wanted to feel them about her throat. She wanted to put her lips on his hands—brush the backs of them, slowly, moistly, with her mouth, lingeringly. She was terribly frightened. She thought to herself: "I am going crazy. I am losing my mind. There is something the matter with me. I wonder how I look. I must look queer."

She said something to make him look up at her. His glance was mild, undismayed. So this hideous thing did not show in her face. She kept her eyes resolutely on the book. At half-past eight she closed her book suddenly. "I'm tired. I think it's the spring coming on." She smiled a little wavering smile. He rose and stretched himself, his great arms high above his head. Selina shivered.

"Two more weeks," he said, "is the last lesson. Well, do you think I have done pretty good—well?"

"Very well," Selina replied, evenly. She felt very tired.

The first week in March he was ill, and did not come. A rheumatic affliction to which he was subject. His father, old Johannes DeJong, had had it before him. Working in the wet fields did it, they said. It was the curse of the truck farmer. Selina's evenings were free to devote to Roelf, who glowed again. She sewed, too; read; helped Mrs. Pool with the housework in a gust of sympathy and found strange relief therein; made over an old dress; studied; wrote all her letters (few enough), even one to the dried-apple aunts in Vermont. She no longer wrote to Julie Hempel. She had heard that Julie was to be married to a Kansas man named Arnold. Julie herself had not written. The first week in March passed. He did not come. Nor did he come the following Tuesday or Thursday. After a terrific battle with herself Selina, after school on Thursday, walked past his house, busily, as though bent on an errand. Despised herself for doing it, could not help herself, found a horrible and tortuous satisfaction in not looking at the house as she passed it.

She was bewildered, frightened. All that week she had a curious feeling—or succession of feelings. There was the sensation of suffocation followed by that of emptiness—of being hollow—boneless—bloodless. Then, at times, there was a feeling of physical pain; at others a sense of being disembowelled. She was restless, listless, by turns. Period of furious activity followed by days of inertia. It was the spring, Maartje said. Selina hoped she wasn't going to be ill. She had never felt like that before. She wanted to cry. She was irritable to the point of waspishness with the children in the schoolroom.

On Saturday—the fourteenth of March—he walked in at seven. Klaas, Maartje, and Roelf had driven off to a gathering at Low Prairie, leaving Selina with the pigtails and old Jakob. She had promised to make taffy for them, and was in the midst of it when his knock sounded at the kitchen door. All the blood in her body rushed to her head; pounded there hotly. He entered. There slipped down over her a complete armour of calmness, of self-possession; of glib how do you do Mr. De-Jong and how are you feeling and won't you sit down and there's no fire in the parlour we'll have to sit here.

He took part in the taffy pulling. Selina wondered if Geertje and Jozina would ever have done squealing. It was half-past eight before she bundled them off to bed with a plate of clipped taffy lozenges between them. She heard them scuffling and scrimmaging about in the rare freedom of their parents' absence.

"Now, children!" she called. "You know what you promised your mother and father."

She heard Geertje's tones mimicking her mincingly, "You know what you promised your mother and father." Then a cascade of smothered giggles.

Pervus had been to town, evidently, for he now took from his coat
pocket a bag containing half a dozen bananas—that delicacy of delicacies to the farm palate. She half peeled two and brought them in to the
pigtails. They ate them thickly rapturous, and dropped off to sleep immediately, surfeited.

Pervus DeJong and Selina sat at the kitchen table, their books spread
out before them on the oilcloth. The sweet heavy scent of the fruit
filled the room. Selina brought the parlour lamp into the kitchen, the
better to see. It was a nickel-bellied lamp with a yellow glass shade that
cast a mellow golden glow.

"You didn't go to the meeting," primly. "Mr. and Mrs. Pool went."

"No. No, I didn't go."

"Why not?"

She saw him swallow. "I got through too late. I went to town, and I
got through too late. We're fixing to sow tomato seeds in the hotbeds
to-morrow."

Selina opened McBride's Grammar. "Ahem!" a school-teacherly
cough. "Now, then, we'll parse this sentence: Blucher arrived on the
field of Waterloo just as Wellington was receiving the last onslaught of
Napoleon. 'Just' may be treated as a modifier of the dependent clause.
That is: 'Just' means: at the time *at which*. Well. *Just* here modified
at the time. And Wellington is the . . ."

This for half an hour. Selina kept her eyes resolutely on the book. His
voice went on with the dry business of parsing and its deep resonance
struck a response from her as a harp responds when a hand is swept over
its strings. Upstairs she could hear old Jakob clumping about in his preparations for bed. Then there was only stillness overhead. Selina kept her
eyes resolutely on the book. Yet she saw, as though her eyes rested on
them, his large, strong hands. On the backs of them was a fine golden
down that deepened at his wrists. Heavier and darker at the wrists. She
found herself praying a little for strength—for strength against this horror and wickedness. This sin, this abomination that held her. A terrible,
stark, and pitiful prayer, couched in the idiom of the Bible.

Oh, God, keep my eyes and my thoughts away from him. Away from
his hands. Let me keep my eyes and my thoughts away from the golden
hairs on his wrists. Let me not think of his wrists. . . . "The owner of
the southwest ¼ sells a strip 20 rods wide along the south side of his
farm. How much does he receive at $150 per acre?"

He triumphed in this transaction, began the struggle with the square
root of 576. Square roots agonized him. She washed the slate clean with
her little sponge. He was leaning close in his effort to comprehend the

fiendish little figures that marched so tractably under Selina's masterly
pencil.

She took it up, glibly. "The remainder must contain twice the product
of the tens by the units plus the square of the units." He blinked. Utterly bewildered. "*And*," went on Selina, blithely, "twice the tens, times
the units, plus the square of the units, is the same as the sum of twice
the tens, and the units, times the units. *Therefore*"—with a flourish—
"add 4 units to the 40 and multiply the result by 4. *Therefore*"—in final
triumph—"the square root of 576 is 24."

She was breathing rather fast. The fire in the kitchen stove snapped
and cracked. "Now, then, suppose you do that for me. We'll wipe it out.
There! What must the remainder contain?"

He took it up, slowly, haltingly. The house was terribly still except
for the man's voice. "The remainder . . . twice . . . product . . . tens
. . . units . . ." A something in his voice—a note—a timbre. She felt
herself swaying queerly, as though the whole house were gently rocking.
Little delicious agonizing shivers chased each other, hot and cold, up
her arms, down her legs, over her spine. . . . "plus the square of the
units is the same as the sum twice the tens . . . twice . . . the tens
. . . the tens . . ." His voice stopped.

Selina's eyes leaped from the book to his hands, uncontrollably. Something about them startled her. They were clenched into fists. Her eyes
now leaped from those clenched fists to the face of the man beside her.
Her head came up, and back. Her wide startled eyes met his. His were
a blaze of blinding blue in his tanned face. Some corner of her mind that
was still working clearly noted this. Then his hands unclenched. The
blue blaze scorched her, enveloped her. Her cheek knew the harsh cool
feel of a man's cheek. She sensed the potent, terrifying, pungent odour
of close contact—a mixture of tobacco smoke, his hair, freshly laundered
linen, an indefinable body smell. It was a mingling that disgusted and
attracted her. She was at once repelled and drawn. Then she felt his
lips on hers and her own, incredibly, responding eagerly, wholly to that
pressure.

THEY were married the following May, just two months later. The High Prairie school year practically ended with the appearance of the first tender shoots of green that meant onions, radishes, and spinach above the rich sandy loam. Selina's classes broke, dwindled, shrank to almost nothing. The school became a kindergarten of five-year-old babies who wriggled and shifted and scratched in the warm spring air that came from the teeming prairie through the open windows. The schoolhouse stove stood rusty-red and cold. The drum in Selina's bedroom was a black genie deprived of his power now to taunt her.

Selina was at once bewildered and calm; rebellious and content. Overlaying these emotions was something like grim amusement. Beneath them, something like fright. High Prairie, in May, was green and gold and rose and blue. The spring flowers painted the fields and the roadside with splashes of yellow, of pink, of mauve, and purple. Violets, buttercups, mandrakes, marsh-marigolds, hepatica. The air was soft and cool from the lake. Selina had never known spring in the country before. It made her ache with an actual physical ache. She moved with a strange air of fatality. It was as if she were being drawn inexorably, against her will, her judgment, her plans, into something sweet and terrible. When with Pervus she was elated, gay, voluble. He talked little; looked at her dumbly, worshippingly. When he brought her a withered bunch of trilliums, the tears came to her eyes. He had walked to Updike's woods to get them because he had heard her say she loved them, and there were none nearer. They were limp and listless from the heat, and from being held in his hand. He looked up at her from where he stood on the kitchen steps, she in the doorway. She took them, laid her hand on his head. It was as when some great gentle dog brings in a limp and bedraggled prize dug from the yard and, laying it at one's feet, looks up at one with soft asking eyes.

There were days when the feeling of unreality possessed her. She, a truck farmer's wife, living in High Prairie the rest of her days! Why, no! No! Was this the great adventure that her father had always spoken of? She, who was going to be a happy wayfarer down the path of life —any one of a dozen things. This High Prairie winter was to have been only an episode. Not her life! She looked at Maartje. Oh, but she'd never be like that. That was stupid, unnecessary. Pink and blue dresses in the house, for her. Frills on the window curtains. Flowers in bowls.

Some of the pangs and terrors with which most prospective brides are assailed she confided to Mrs. Pool while that active lady was slamming about the kitchen.

"Did you ever feel scared and—and sort of—scared when you thought about marrying, Mrs. Pool?"

Maartje Pool's hands were in a great batch of bread dough which she pummelled and slapped and kneaded vigorously. She shook out a handful of flour on the baking board while she held the dough mass in the other hand, then plumped it down and again began to knead, both hands doubled into fists.

She laughed a short little laugh. "I ran away."

"You did! You mean you really ran—but why? Didn't you lo—like Klaas?"

Maartje Pool kneaded briskly, the colour high in her cheeks, what with the vigorous pummelling and rolling, and something else that made her look strangely young for the moment—girlish, almost. "Sure I liked him. I liked him."

"But you ran away?"

"Not far. I came back. Nobody ever knew I ran, even. But I ran. I knew."

"Why did you come back?"

Maartje elucidated her philosophy without being in the least aware that it could be called by any such high-sounding name. "You can't run away far enough. Except you stop living you can't run away from life."

The girlish look had fled. She was world-old. Her strong arms ceased their pounding and thumping for a moment. On the steps just outside Klaas and Jakob were scanning the weekly reports preparatory to going into the city late that afternoon.

Selina had the difficult task of winning Roelf to her all over again. He was like a trusting little animal, who, wounded by the hand he has trusted, is shy of it. She used blandishments on this boy of thirteen such as she had never vouchsafed the man she was going to marry. He had asked her, bluntly, one day: "Why are you going to marry with him?" He never spoke the name.

She thought deeply. What to say? The answer ready on her tongue would have little meaning for this boy. There came to her a line from Lancelot and Elaine. She answered, "To serve him, and to follow him through the world." She thought that rather fine-sounding until Roelf promptly rejected it. "That's no reason. An answer out of a book. Anyway, to follow him through the world is dumb. He stays right here in High Prairie all his life."

"How do you know!" Selina retorted, almost angrily. Startled, too.

"I know. He stays."

Still, he could not withstand her long. Together they dug and planted flower beds in Pervus's dingy front yard. It was too late for tulips now. Pervus had brought her some seeds from town. They ranged all the way from poppies to asters; from purple iris to morning glories. The last named were to form the back-porch vine, of course, because they grew quickly. Selina, city-bred, was ignorant of varieties, but insisted she wanted an old-fashioned garden—marigolds, pinks, mignonette, phlox. She and Roelf dug, spaded, planted. The DeJong place was markedly ugly even in that community of squat houses. It lacked the air of sparkling cleanliness that saved the other places from sordidness. The house, even then, was thirty years old—a gray, weather-beaten frame box with a mansard roof and a flat face staring out at the dense willows by the roadside. It needed paint; the fences sagged; the window curtains were awry. The parlour was damp, funereal. The old woman who tended the house for Pervus slopped about all day with a pail and a wet gray rag. There was always a crazy campanile of dirty dishes stacked on the table, and the last meal seemed never to catch up with the next. About the whole house there was a starkness, a bareness that proclaimed no woman who loved it dwelt therein.

Selina told herself (and Pervus) that she would change all that. She saw herself going about with a brush and a can of white paint, leaving beauty in her wake, where ugliness had been.

Her trousseau was of the scantiest. Pervus's household was already equipped with such linens as they would need. The question of a wedding gown troubled her until Maartje suggested that she be married in the old Dutch wedding dress that lay in the bride's chest in Selina's bedroom.

"A real Dutch bride," Maartje said. "Your man will think that is fine." Pervus was delighted. Selina basked in his love like a kitten in the sun. She was, after all, a very lonely little bride with only two photographs on the shelf in her bedroom to give her courage and counsel. The old Dutch wedding gown was many inches too large for her. The skirt-band overlapped her slim waist; her slender little bosom did not fill out the generous width of the bodice; but the effect of the whole was amazingly quaint as well as pathetic. The wings of the stiffly embroidered coif framed the white face from which the eyes looked out, large and dark. She had even tried to wear the hand-carved shoes, but had to give that up. In them her feet were as lost as minnows in a rowboat. She had much difficulty with the queer old buttons and fastenings. It was as though the dead and gone Sophia Kroon were trying, with futile ghostly fingers, to prevent this young thing from meeting the fate that was to be hers.

They were married at the Pools'. Klaas and Maartje had insisted on furnishing the wedding supper—ham, chickens, sausages, cakes, pickles, beer. The Reverend Dekker married them and all through the ceremony Selina chided herself because she could not keep her mind on his words in the fascination of watching his short stubby beard as it waggled with every motion of his jaw. Pervus looked stiff, solemn, and uncomfortable in his wedding blacks—not at all the handsome giant of the everyday corduroys and blue shirt. In the midst of the ceremony Selina had her moment of panic when she actually saw herself running shrieking from this company, this man, this house, down the road, on, on toward—toward what? The feeling was so strong that she was surprised to find herself still standing there in the Dutch wedding gown answering "I do" in the proper place.

The wedding gifts were few. The Pools had given them a "hanging lamp," coveted of the farmer's wife; a hideous atrocity in yellow, with pink roses on its shade and prisms dangling and tinkling all around the edge. It was intended to hang suspended from the parlour ceiling, and worked up and down on a sort of pulley chain. From the Widow Paarlenberg came a water set in red frosted glass shading to pink—a fat pitcher and six tumblers. Roelf's gift, the result of many weeks' labour in the work-shed, was a bride's chest copied from the fine old piece that had saved Selina's room from sheer ugliness. He had stained the wood, polished it. Had carved the front of it with her initials—very like those that stood out so boldly on the old chest upstairs—S. P. D. And the year—1890. The whole was a fine piece of craftsmanship for a boy of thirteen—would not have discredited a man of any age. It was the one beautiful gift among Selina's clumsy crude wedding things. She had thanked him with tears in her eyes. "Roelf, you'll come to see me often, won't you? Often!" Then, as he had hesitated, "I'll need you so. You're all I've got." A strange thing for a bride to say.

"I'll come," the boy had said, trying to make his voice casual, his tone careless. "Sure, I'll come oncet in a while."

"Once, Roelf. *Once* in a while."

He repeated it after her, dutifully.

After the wedding they went straight to DeJong's house. In May the vegetable farmer cannot neglect his garden even for a day. The house had been made ready for them. The sway of the old housekeeper was over. Her kitchen bedroom was empty.

Throughout the supper Selina had had thoughts which were so foolish and detached as almost to alarm her.

"Now I am married. I am Mrs. Pervus DeJong. That's a pretty name.
It would look quite distinguished on a calling card, very spidery and
fine:

MRS. PERVUS DEJONG
At Home Fridays

She recalled this later, grimly, when she was Mrs. Pervus DeJong, at
home not only Fridays, but Saturdays, Sundays, Mondays, Tuesdays,
Wednesdays, and Thursdays.

They drove down the road to DeJong's place. Selina thought, "Now
I am driving home with my husband. I feel his shoulder against mine. I
wish he would talk. I wish he would say something. Still, I'm not
frightened."

Pervus's market wagon was standing in the yard, shafts down. He
should have gone to market to-day; would certainly have to go to-morrow, starting early in the afternoon so as to get a good stand in the
Haymarket. By the light of his lantern the wagon seemed to Selina to
be a symbol. She had often seen it before, but now that it was to be a
part of her life—this the DeJong market wagon and she Mrs. DeJong—
she saw clearly what a crazy, disreputable, and poverty-proclaiming old
vehicle it was, in contrast with the neat strong wagon in Klaas Pool's
yard, smart with green paint and red lettering that announced, "Klaas
Pool, Garden Produce." With the two sleek farm horses the turnout
looked as prosperous and comfortable as Klaas himself.

Pervus swung her down from the seat of the buggy, his hand about
her waist, and held her so for a moment, close. Selina said, "You must
have that wagon painted, Pervus. And the seat-springs fixed and the
sideboard mended."

He stared. "Wagon!"

"Yes. It looks a sight."

The house was tidy enough, but none too clean. Old Mrs. Voorhees
had not been minded to keep house too scrupulously for a man who
would be unlikely to know whether or not it was clean. Pervus lighted
the lamps. There was a fire in the kitchen stove. It made the house seem
stuffy on this mild May night. Selina thought that her own little bedroom at the Pools', no longer hers, must be deliciously cool and still
with the breeze fanning fresh from the west. Pervus was putting the
horse into the barn. The bedroom was off the sitting room. The window
was shut. This last year had taught Selina to prepare the night before for
next morning's rising, so as to lose the least possible time. She did this

now, unconsciously. She took off her white muslin underwear with its frills and embroidery—the three stiff petticoats, and the stiffly starched corset-cover, and the high-bosomed corset and put them into the bureau drawer that she herself had cleaned and papered neatly the week before. She brushed her hair, laid out to-morrow's garments, put on her high-necked, long-sleeved nightgown and got into this strange bed. She heard Pervus DeJong shut the kitchen door; the latch clicked, the lock turned. Heavy quick footsteps across the bare kitchen floor. This man was coming into her room . . . "You can't run far enough," Maartje Pool had said. "Except you stop living you can't run away from life."

Next morning it was dark when he awakened her at four. She started up with a little cry and sat up, straining her ears, her eyes. "Is that you, Father?" She was little Selina Peake again, and Simeon Peake had come in, gay, debonair, from a night's gaming.

Pervus DeJong was already padding about the room in stocking feet. "What—what time is it? What's the matter, Father? Why are you up? Haven't you gone to bed . . ." Then she remembered.

Pervus DeJong laughed and came toward her. "Get up, little lazy bones. It's after four. All yesterday's work I've got to do, and all to-day's. Breakfast, little Lina, breakfast. You are a farmer's wife now."

VIII

By October High Prairie housewives told each other that Mrs. Pervus DeJong was "expecting." Dirk DeJong was born in the bedroom off the sitting room on the fifteenth day of March, of a bewildered, somewhat resentful, but deeply interested mother; and a proud, foolish, and vainglorious father whose air of achievement, considering the really slight part he had played in the long, tedious, and racking business, was disproportionate. The name Dirk had sounded to Selina like something tall, straight, and slim. Pervus had chosen it. It had been his grandfather's name.

Sometimes, during those months, Selina would look back on her first winter in High Prairie—that winter of the icy bedroom, the chill black drum, the schoolhouse fire, the chilblains, the Pool pork—and it seemed a lovely dream; a time of ease, of freedom, of careless happiness. That icy room had been her room; that mile of road traversed on bitter winter mornings a mere jaunt; the schoolhouse stove a toy, fractious but fascinating.

Pervus DeJong loved his pretty young wife, and she him. But young love thrives on colour, warmth, beauty. It becomes prosaic and inarticulate when forced to begin its day at four in the morning by reaching blindly, dazedly, for limp and obscure garments dangling from bedpost or chair, and to end that day at nine, numb and sodden with weariness, after seventeen hours of physical labour.

It was a wet summer. Pervus's choice tomato plants, so carefully set out in the hope of a dry season, became draggled gray spectres in a waste of mire. Of fruit the field bore one tomato the size of a marble.

For the rest, the crops were moderately successful on the DeJong place. But the work necessary to make this so was heartbreaking. Pervus and his hired helper, Jan Steen, used the hand sower and hand cultivator. It seemed to Selina that they were slaves to these buds, shoots, and roots that clamoured with a hundred thousand voices, "Let me out! Let me out!" She had known, during her winter at the Pools', that Klaas, Roelf, and old Jakob worked early and late, but her months there had encompassed what is really the truck farmer's leisure period. She had arrived in November. She had married in May. From May until October it was necessary to tend the fields with a concentration amounting to fury. Selina had never dreamed that human beings toiled like that for sustenance. Toil was a thing she had never encountered until coming to High Prairie. Now she saw her husband wrenching a living out of the earth by sheer muscle, sweat, and pain. During June, July, August, and September the good black prairie soil for miles around was teeming, a hotbed of plenty. There was born in Selina at this time a feeling for the land that she was never to lose. Perhaps the child within her had something to do with this. She was aware of a feeling of kinship with the earth; an illusion of splendour, of fulfilment. Sometimes, in a moment's respite from her work about the house, she would stand in the kitchen doorway, her flushed face turned toward the fields. Wave on wave of green, wave on wave, until the waves melted into each other and became a verdant sea.

As cabbages had been cabbages, and no more, to Klaas Pool, so, to Pervus, these carrots, beets, onions, turnips, and radishes were just so much produce, to be planted, tended, gathered, marketed. But to Selina, during that summer, they became a vital part in the vast mechanism of a living world. Pervus, earth, sun, rain, all elemental forces that laboured to produce the food for millions of humans. The sordid, grubby little acreage became a kingdom; the phlegmatic Dutch-American truck farmers of the region were high priests consecrated to the service of the divinity, Earth. She thought of Chicago's children. If they had red cheeks, clear eyes, nimble brains it was because Pervus brought them the food that made them so. It was before the day when glib talk of irons, vitamines, arsenic entered into all discussion pertaining to food. Yet Selina sensed something of the meaning behind these toiling, patient figures, all unconscious of meaning, bent double in the fields for miles throughout High Prairie. Something of this she tried to convey to Pervus. He only stared, his blue eyes wide and unresponsive.

"Farm work grand! Farm work is slave work. Yesterday, from the load of carrots in town I didn't make enough to bring you the goods for the child so when it comes you should have clothes for it. It's better I feed them to the livestock."

Pervus drove into the Chicago market every other day. During July and August he sometimes did not have his clothes off for a week. Together he and Jan Steen would load the wagon with the day's garnering. At four he would start on the tedious trip into town. The historic old Haymarket on west Randolph Street had become the stand for market gardeners for miles around Chicago. Here they stationed their wagons in preparation for the next day's selling. The wagons stood, close packed, in triple rows, down both sides of the curb and in the middle of the street. The early comer got the advantageous stand. There was no regular allotment of space. Pervus tried to reach the Haymarket by nine at night. Often bad roads made a detour necessary and he was late. That usually meant bad business next day. The men, for the most part, slept on their wagons, curled up on the wagonseat or stretched out on the sacks. Their horses were stabled and fed in near-by sheds, with more actual comfort than the men themselves. One could get a room for twenty-five cents in one of the ramshackle rooming houses that faced the street. But the rooms were small, stuffy, none too clean; the beds little more comfortable than the wagons. Besides, twenty-five cents! You got twenty-five cents for half a barrel of tomatoes. You got twenty-five cents for a sack of potatoes. Onions brought seventy-five cents a sack. Cabbages went a hundred heads for two dollars, and they were five-pound heads. If you drove home with ten dollars in your pocket it represented a profit of exactly zero. The sum must go above that. No; one did not pay out twenty-five cents for the mere privilege of sleeping in a bed.

One June day, a month or more after their marriage, Selina drove into Chicago with Pervus, an incongruous little figure in her bride's finery perched on the seat of the vegetable wagon piled high with early garden stuff. They had started before four that afternoon, and reached

the city at nine, though the roads were still heavy from the late May
rains. It was, in a way, their wedding trip, for Selina had not been
away from the farm since her marriage. The sun was bright and hot. Selina held an umbrella to shield herself from the heat and looked about
her with enjoyment and interest. She chattered, turned her head this
way and that, exclaimed, questioned. Sometimes she wished that Pervus
would respond more quickly to her mood. A gay, volatile creature, she
frisked about him like a friendly bright-eyed terrier about a stolid, ponderous St. Bernard.

As they jogged along now she revealed magnificent plans that had
been forming in her imagination during the past four weeks. It had not
taken her four weeks—or days—to discover that this great broad-shouldered man she had married was a kindly creature, tender and good, but
lacking any vestige of initiative, of spirit. She marvelled, sometimes, at
the memory of his boldness in bidding for her lunch box that evening
of the raffle. It seemed incredible now, though he frequently referred
to it, wagging his head doggishly and grinning the broadly complacent
grin of the conquering male. But he was, after all, a dull fellow, and
there was in Selina a dash of fire, of wholesome wickedness, of adventure, that he never quite understood. For her flashes of flame he had a
mingled feeling of uneasiness and pride.

In the manner of all young brides, Selina started bravely out to make
her husband over. He was handsome, strong, gentle; slow, conservative,
morose. She would make him keen, daring, successful, buoyant. Now,
bumping down the Halsted road, she sketched some of her plans in
large dashing strokes.

"Pervus, we must paint the house in October, before the frost sets in,
and after the summer work is over. White would be nice, with green
trimmings. Though perhaps white isn't practical. Or maybe green with
darker green trimmings. A lovely background for the hollyhocks." (Those
that she and Roelf had planted showed no signs of coming up.) "Then
that west sixteen. We'll drain it."

"Yeh, drain," Pervus muttered. "It's clay land. Drain and you have
got yet clay. Hard clay soil."

Selina had the answer to that. "I know it. You've got to use tile drainage. And—wait a minute—humus. I know what humus is. It's decayed
vegetables. There's always a pile by the side of the barn; and you've
been using it on the quick land. All the west sixteen isn't clay. Part of
it's muckland. All it needs is draining and manure. With potash, too,
and phosphoric acid."

Pervus laughed a great hearty laugh that Selina found surprisingly infuriating. He put one great brown hand patronizingly on her flushed cheek; pinched it gently.

"Don't!" said Selina, and jerked her head away. It was the first time she had ever resented a caress from him.

Pervus laughed again. "Well, well, well! School teacher is a farmer now, huh? I bet even Widow Paarlenberg don't know as much as my little farmer about"—he exploded again—"about this, now, potash and —what kind of acid? Tell me, little Lina, from where did you learn all this about truck farming?"

"Out of a book," Selina said, almost snappishly. "I sent to Chicago for it."

"A book! A book!" He slapped his knee. "A vegetable farmer out of a book."

"Why not! The man who wrote it knows more about vegetable farming than anybody in all High Prairie. He knows about new ways. You're running the farm just the way your father ran it."

"What was good enough for my father is good enough for me."

"It isn't!" cried Selina, "It isn't! The book says clay loam is all right for cabbages, peas, and beans. It tells you how. It tells you how!" She was like a frantic little fly darting and pricking him on to accelerate the stolid sluggishness of his slow plodding gait.

Having begun, she plunged on. "We ought to have two horses to haul the wagon to market. It would save you hours of time that you could spend on the place. Two horses, and a new wagon, green and red, like Klaas Pool's."

Pervus stared straight ahead down the road between his horse's ears much as Klaas Pool had done so maddeningly on Selina's first ride on the Halsted road. "Fine talk. Fine talk."

"It isn't talk. It's plans. You've got to plan."

"Fine talk. Fine talk."

"Oh!" Selina beat her knee with an impotent fist.

It was the nearest they had ever come to quarrelling. It would seem that Pervus had the best of the argument, for when two years had passed the west sixteen was still a boggy clay mass, and unprolific; and the old house stared out shabby and paintless, at the dense willows by the roadside.

They slept that night in one of the twenty-five-cent rooming houses. Rather, Pervus slept. The woman lay awake, listening to the city noises that had become strange in her ears; staring out into the purple-black oblong that was the open window, until that oblong became gray. She wept a little, perhaps. But in the morning Pervus might have noted (if he had been a man given to noting) that the fine jaw-line was set as

determinedly as ever with an angle that spelled inevitably paint, drainage, humus, potash, phosphoric acid, and a horse team.

She rose before four with Pervus, glad to be out of the stuffy little
room with its spotted and scaly green wall paper, its rickety bed and
chair. They had a cup of coffee and a slice of bread in the eating house
on the first floor. Selina waited while he tended the horse. The night-
watchman had been paid another twenty-five cents for watching the
wagonload through the night as it stood in a row with the hundreds of
others in the Haymarket. It was scarcely dawn when the trading began.
Selina, watching it from the wagon seat, thought that this was a ridiculously haphazard and perilous method of distributing the food for whose
fruition Pervus had toiled with aching back and tired arms. But she said
nothing.

She kept, perforce, to the house that first year, and the second. Pervus
declared that his woman should never work in the fields as did many of
the High Prairie wives and daughters. Of ready cash there was almost
none. Pervus was hard put to it to pay Jan Steen his monthly wage
during May, June, July, and August, when he was employed on the
DeJong place, though Steen got but a pittance, being known as a poor
hand, and "dumb." Selina learned much that first year, and the second,
but she said little. She kept the house in order—rough work, and endless
—and she managed, miraculously, to keep herself looking fresh and
neat. She understood now Maartje Pool's drab garments, harassed face,
heavily swift feet, never at rest. The idea of flowers in bowls was abandoned by July. Had it not been for Roelf's faithful tending, the flower
beds themselves, planted with such hopes, would have perished for lack
of care.

Roelf came often to the house. He found there a tranquillity and
peace never known in the Pool place, with its hubbub and clatter. In
order to make her house attractive Selina had actually rifled her precious
little bank hoard—the four hundred and ninety-seven dollars left her
by her father. She still had one of the clear white diamonds. She kept
it sewed in the hem of an old flannel petticoat. Once she had shown
it to Pervus.

"If I sell this maybe we could get enough money to drain and tile."

Pervus took the stone, weighed it in his great palm, blinked as he
always did when discussing a subject of which he was ignorant. "How
much could you get for it? Fifty dollars, maybe. Five hundred is what I
would need."

"I've got that. I've got it in the bank!"

"Well, maybe next spring. Right now I got my hands full, and more."

To Selina that seemed a short-sighted argument. But she was too newly married to stand her ground; too much in love; too ignorant still of farm conditions.

The can of white paint and the brush actually did materialize. For weeks it was dangerous to sit, lean, or tread upon any paintable thing in the DeJong farmhouse without eliciting a cry of warning from Selina. She would actually have tried her hand at the outside of the house with a quart can and three-inch brush if Pervus hadn't intervened. She hemmed dimity curtains, made slip-covers for the hideous parlour sofa and the ugliest of the chairs. Subscribed for a magazine called *House and Garden*. Together she and Roelf used to pore over this fascinating periodical. Terraces, lily-pools, leaded casements, cretonne, fireplaces, yew trees, pergolas, fountains—they absorbed them all, exclaimed, admired, actually criticized. Selina was torn between an English cottage with timbered porch, bay window, stone flagging, and an Italian villa with a broad terrace on which she would stand in trailing white with a Russian wolf-hound. If High Prairie had ever overheard one of these conversations between the farm woman who would always be a girl and the farm boy who had never been quite a child, it would have raised palms high in an "Og heden!" of horror. But High Prairie never heard, and wouldn't have understood if it had. She did another strange thing: She placed the fine hand-carved oak chest Roelf had given her in a position so that her child should see it as soon as he opened his eyes in the morning. It was the most beautiful thing she possessed. She had, too, an incomplete set of old Dutch lustre ware. It had belonged to Pervus's mother, and to her mother before her. On Sunday nights Selina used this set for supper, though Pervus protested. And she always insisted that Dirk drink his milk out of one of the lovely jewel-like cups. Pervus thought this a piece of madness.

Selina was up daily at four. Dressing was a swift and mechanical covering of the body. Breakfast must be ready for Pervus and Jan when they came in from the barn. The house to clean, the chickens to tend, sewing, washing, ironing, cooking. She contrived ways of minimizing her steps, of lightening her labour. And she saw clearly how the little farm was mismanaged through lack of foresight, imagination, and—she faced it squarely—through stupidity. She was fond of this great, kindly, blundering, stubborn boy who was her husband. But she saw him with amazing clearness through the mists of her love. There was something prophetic about the way she began to absorb knowledge of the farm work, of vegetable culture, of marketing. Listening, seeing, she learned about soil, planting, weather, selling. The daily talk of the house and fields was of nothing else. About this little twenty-five-acre garden patch there was nothing of the majesty of the Iowa, Illinois, and Kansas grain farms, with their endless billows of wheat and corn, rye, alfalfa, and barley rolling away to the horizon. Everything was done in diminutive here. An acre of this. Two acres of that. A score of chickens. One cow. One horse. Two pigs. Here was all the drudgery of farm life with none of its bounteousness, fine sweep, or splendour. Selina sensed that every inch of soil should have been made to yield to the utmost. Yet there lay the west sixteen, useless during most of the year; reliable never. And there was no money to drain it or enrich it; no ready cash for the purchase of profitable neighbouring acreage. She did not know the term intensive farming, but this was what she meant. Artificial protection against the treacherous climate of the Great Lakes region was pitifully lacking in Pervus's plans. Now it would be hot with the humid, withering, sticky heat of the district. The ground was teeming, smoking, and the green things seemed actually to be pushing their way out of the earth so that one could almost see them growing, as in some absurd optical illusion. Then, without warning, would come the icy Lake Michigan wind, nipping the tender shoots with fiendish fingers. There should have been hotbeds and coldframes, forcing-hills, hand-boxes. There were almost none.

These things Selina saw, but not quite clearly. She went about her housework, now dreamily, now happily. Her physical condition swayed her mood. Sometimes, in the early autumn, when the days became cooler, she would go to where Pervus and Jan were working in the fields in the late afternoon gathering the produce for that night's trip to market. She would stand there, a bit of sewing in her hand, perhaps, the wind ruffling her hair, whipping her skirts, her face no longer pale, tilted a little toward the good sun like a lovely tawny flower. Sometimes she sat perched on a pile of empty sacks, or on an up-ended crate, her sewing in her hand. She was happiest at such times—most content—except for the pang she felt at sight of the great dark splotch on the blue of Pervus's work-shirt where the sweat stained it.

She had come out so one autumn afternoon. She was feeling particularly gay, buoyant. In one of his rare hours of leisure Roelf Pool had come to help her with her peony roots which Pervus had brought her from Chicago for fall planting. Roelf had dug the trench, deep and wide, mulched it with cow-manure, banked it. They were to form a double row up the path to the front of the house, and in her mind's eye Selina already saw them blooming when spring should come, shaggy balls of luscious pink. Now Roelf was lending a hand to Pervus and Jan as they bent over the late beets and radishes. It was a day all gold and blue and scarlet; warm for the season with a ripe mellow warmth like yellow chartreuse. There were stretches of seal-black loam where the vegetables had been uprooted. Bunches of them, string-tied, lay ready for gathering into baskets. Selina's eye was gladdened by the clear coral of radishes flung against the rich black loam.

"A jewel, Pervus!" she cried. "A jewel in an Ethiop's ear!"

"What?" said Pervus, looking up, amiable but uncomprehending. But the boy smiled. Selina had left him that book for his own when she went away. Suddenly Selina stooped and picked up one of the scarlet and green clusters tied with its bit of string. Laughing, she whipped out a hairpin and fastened the bunch in her hair just behind her ear. An absurd thing to do, and childish. It should have looked as absurd as it was, but it didn't. Instead it was like a great crimson flower there. Her cheeks were flushed with the hot sun. Her fine dark hair was wind-blown and a little loosened, her dress open at the throat. Her figure was fuller, her breast had a richer curve, for the child was four months on the way. She was laughing. At a little exclamation from Roelf, Pervus looked up, as did Jan. Selina took a slow rhythmic step, and another, her arms upraised, a provocative lovely bacchic little figure there in the fields under the hot blue sky. Jan Steen wiped the sweat from his brown face, a glow in his eyes.

"You are like the calendar!" cried Roelf, "on the wall in the parlour." A cheap but vivid and not unlovely picture of a girl with cherries in her hair. It hung in the Pool farmhouse.

Pervus DeJong showed one of his rare storms of passion. Selina had not seen that blaze of blue in his eyes since the night, months ago, in the Pools' kitchen. But that blaze had been a hot and burning blue, like the sky of to-day. This was a bitter blue, a chill and freezing thing, like the steel-blue of ice in the sun.

"Take them things out of your hair now! Take shame to yourself!" He strode over to her and snatched the things from her hair and threw them down and ground them into the soft earth with his heavy heel. A long coil of her fine dark hair came rippling over her shoulder as he did so. She stood looking at him, her eyes wide, dark, enormous in her face now suddenly white.

His wrath was born of the narrow insular mind that fears gossip. He knew that the hired man would tell through the length and width of High Prairie how Pervus DeJong's wife pinned red radishes in her hair and danced in the fields like a loose woman.

Selina had turned, fled to the house. It was their first serious quarrel. For days she was hurt, ashamed, moody. They made it up, of course. Pervus was contrite, abject almost. But something that belonged to her girlhood had left her that day.

During that winter she was often hideously lonely. She never got over her hunger for companionship. Here she was, a gregarious and fun-loving creature, buried in a snow-bound Illinois prairie farmhouse with a husband who looked upon conversation as a convenience, not a pastime. She learned much that winter about the utter sordidness of farm life. She rarely saw the Pools; she rarely saw any one outside her own little household. The front room—the parlour—was usually bitterly cold but sometimes she used to slip in there, a shawl over her shoulders, and sit at the frosty window to watch for a wagon to go by, or a chance pedestrian up the road. She did not pity herself, nor regret her step. She felt, physically, pretty well for a child-bearing woman; and Pervus was tender, kindly, sympathetic, if not always understanding. She struggled gallantly to keep up the small decencies of existence. She loved the glow in Pervus's eyes when she appeared with a bright ribbon, a fresh collar, though he said nothing and perhaps she only fancied that he noticed. Once or twice she had walked the mile and a half of slippery road to the Pools', and had sat in Maartje's warm bright bustling kitchen for comfort. It seemed to her incredible that a little more than a year ago she had first stepped into this kitchen in her modish brown lady's-cloth dress, muffled in wraps, cold but elated, interested, ready for adventure, surprise, discomfort—anything. And now here she was in that same kitchen, amazingly, unbelievably Mrs. Pervus DeJong, truck farmer's wife, with a child soon to be born. And where was adventure now? And where was life? And where the love of chance bred in her by her father?

The two years following Dirk's birth were always somewhat vague in Selina's mind, like a dream in which horror and happiness are inextricably blended. The boy was a plump hardy infant who employed himself cheerfully in whatever spot Selina happened to deposit him. He had his father's blond exterior, his mother's brunette vivacity. At two he was a child of average intelligence, sturdy physique, and marked good humour. He almost never cried.

He was just twelve months old when Selina's second child—a girl—was born dead. Twice during those two years Pervus fell victim to his so-called rheumatic attacks following the early spring planting when he was often forced to stand in water up to his ankles. He suffered intensely and during his illness was as tractable as a goaded bull. Selina understood why half of High Prairie was bent and twisted with rheumatism—why the little Dutch Reformed church on Sunday mornings resembled a shrine to which sick and crippled pilgrims creep.

High Prairie was kind to the harried household. The farm women sent Dutch dainties. The men lent a hand in the fields, though they were hard put to it to tend their own crops at this season. The Widow Paarlenberg's neat smart rig was frequently to be seen waiting under the

willows in the DeJong yard. The Paarlenberg, still widow, still Paarlenberg, brought soups and chickens and cakes which never stuck in Selina's
throat because she refused to touch them. The Widow Paarlenberg
was what is known as good-hearted. She was happiest when some one
else was in trouble. Hearing of an illness, a catastrophe, "Og heden!"
she would cry, and rush off to the scene with sustaining soup. She was
the sort of lady bountiful who likes to see her beneficiaries benefit before
her very eyes. If she brought them soup at ten in the morning she wanted
to see that soup consumed.

"Eat it all," she would urge. "Take it now, while it is hot. See, you
are looking better already. Just another spoonful."

In the DeJongs' plight she found a grisly satisfaction, cloaked by
commiseration. Selina, white and weak following her tragic second confinement, still found strength to refuse the widow's sustaining potions.
The widow, her silks making a gentle susurrus in the bare little bedroom, regarded Selina with eyes in which pity and triumph made horrid
conflict. Selina's eyes, enormous now in her white face, were twin pools
of Peake pride.

"It's most kind of you, Mrs. Paarlenberg, but I don't like soup."

"A whole chicken boiled in it."

"Especially chicken soup. Neither does Pervus. But I'm sure Mrs.
Voorhees will enjoy it." This being Pervus's old housekeeper pressed
now into temporary emergency service.

It was easy to see why the DeJong house still was unpainted two
years after Selina's rosy plans began to form; why the fences still sagged,
the wagon creaked, the single horse hauled the produce to market.

Selina had been married almost three years when there came to her
a letter from Julie Hempel, now married. The letter had been sent to the
Klaas Pool farm and Jozina had brought it to her. Though she had not
seen it since her days at Miss Fister's school, Selina recognized with a
little hastening heart-beat the spidery handwriting with the shading
and curleycues. Seated on her kitchen steps in her calico dress she read
it.

DARLING SELINA:—

I thought it was so queer that you didn't answer my letter and now
I know you must have thought it queer that I did not answer yours.
I found your letter to me, written long ago, when I was going over
Mother's things last week. It was the letter you must have written
when I was in Kansas City. Mother had never given it to me. I am not
reproaching her. You see, I had written you from Kansas City, but had
sent my letter to Mamma to mail because I never could remember that
funny address of yours in the country.

Mamma died three weeks ago. Last week I was going over her things—a trying task, you may imagine—and there were your two letters addressed to me. She had never destroyed them. Poor Mamma . . .

Well, dear Selina, I suppose you don't even know that I am married. I married Michael Arnold of Kansas City. The Arnolds were in the packing business there, you know. Michael has gone into business with Pa here in Chicago and I suppose you have heard of Pa's success. Just all of a sudden he began to make a great deal of money after he left the butcher business and went into the yards—the stockyards, you know. Poor Mamma was so happy these last few years, and had everything that was beautiful. I have two children. Eugene and Pauline.

I am getting to be quite a society person. You would laugh to see me. I am on the Ladies' Entertainment Committee of the World's Fair. We are supposed to entertain all the visiting big bugs—that is the lady bugs. There! How is that for a joke?

I suppose you know about the Infanta Eulalie. Of Spain, you know. And what she did about the Potter Palmer ball. . . .

Selina, holding the letter in her work-stained hand, looked up and across the fields and away to where the prairie met the sky and closed in on her; her world. The Infanta Eulalie of Spain. . . . She went back to the letter.

Well, she came to Chicago for the Fair and Mrs. Potter Palmer was to give a huge reception and ball for her. Mrs. P. is head of the whole committee, you know, and I must say she looks queenly with her white hair so beautifully dressed and her diamond dog-collar and her black velvet and all. Well, at the very last minute the Infanta refused to attend the ball because she had just heard that Mrs. P. was an innkeeper's wife. Imagine! The Palmer House, of course.

Selina, holding the letter in her hand, imagined.

It was in the third year of Selina's marriage that she first went into the fields to work. Pervus had protested miserably, though the vegetables were spoiling in the ground.

"Let them rot," he said. "Better the stuff rots in the ground. DeJong women folks they never worked in the fields. Not even in Holland. Not my mother or my grandmother. It isn't for women."

Selina had regained health and vigour after two years of wretchedness. She felt steel-strong and even hopeful again, sure sign of physical well-being. Long before now she had realized that this time must inevitably come. So she answered briskly, "Nonsense, Pervus. Working in the field's no harder than washing or ironing or scrubbing or standing over a hot stove in August. Women's work! Housework's the hardest work in the world. That's why men won't do it."

She would often take the boy Dirk with her into the fields, placing him on a heap of empty sacks in the shade. He invariably crawled off this lowly throne to dig and burrow in the warm black dirt. He even made as though to help his mother, pulling at the rooted things with futile fingers, and sitting back with a bump when a shallow root did unexpectedly yield to his tugging.

"Look! He's a farmer already," Pervus would say.

But within Selina something would cry, "No! No!"

During May, June, and July Pervus worked not only from morning until night, but by moonlight as well, and Selina worked with him. Often their sleep was a matter of three hours only, or four.

So two years went—three years—four. In the fourth year of Selina's marriage she suffered the loss of her one woman friend in all High Prairie. Maartje Pool died in childbirth, as was so often the case in this region where a Gampish midwife acted as obstetrician. The child, too, had not lived. Death had not been kind to Maartje Pool. It had brought neither peace nor youth to her face, as it so often does. Selina, looking down at the strangely still figure that had been so active, so bustling, realized that for the first time in the years she had known her she was seeing Maartje Pool at rest. It seemed incredible that she could lie there, the infant in her arms, while the house was filled with people and there were chairs to be handed, space to be cleared, food to be cooked and served. Sitting there with the other High Prairie women Selina had a hideous feeling that Maartje would suddenly rise up and take things in charge; rub and scratch with capable fingers the spatters of dried mud on Klaas Pool's black trousers (he had been in the yard to see to the horses); quiet the loud wailing of Geertje and Jozina; pass her gnarled hand over Roelf's wide-staring tearless eyes; wipe the film of dust from the parlour table that had never known a speck during her régime.

"You can't run far enough," Maartje had said. "Except you stop living you can't run away from life."

Well, she had run far enough this time.

Roelf was sixteen now, Geertje twelve, Jozina eleven. What would this household do now, Selina wondered, without the woman who had been so faithful a slave to it? Who would keep the pigtails—no longer giggling—in clean ginghams and decent square-toed shoes? Who, when Klaas broke out in rumbling Dutch wrath against what he termed Roelf's "dumb" ways, would say, "Og, Pool, leave the boy alone once. He does nothing." Who would keep Klaas himself in order; cook his meals, wash his clothes, iron his shirts, take pride in the great ruddy childlike giant?

Klaas answered these questions just nine months later by marrying the Widow Paarlenberg. High Prairie was rocked with surprise. For months this marriage was the talk of the district. They had gone to Niagara Falls on a wedding trip; Pool's place was going to have this improvement and that; no, they were going to move to the Widow Paarlenberg's large farmhouse (they would always call her that); no, Pool was putting in a bathroom with a bathtub and running water; no, they were going to buy the Stikker place between Pool's and Paarlenberg's and make one farm of it, the largest in all High Prairie, Low Prairie, or New Haarlem. Well, no fool like an old fool.

So insatiable was High Prairie's curiosity that every scrap of fresh news was swallowed at a gulp. When the word went round of Roelf's flight from the farm, no one knew where, it served only as sauce to the great dish of gossip.

Selina had known. Pervus was away at the market when Roelf had knocked at the farmhouse door one night at eight, had turned the knob and entered, as usual. But there was nothing of the usual about his appearance. He wore his best suit—his first suit of store clothes, bought at the time of his mother's funeral. It never had fitted him; now was grotesquely small for him. He had shot up amazingly in the last eight or nine months. Yet there was nothing of the ridiculous about him as he stood before her now, tall, lean, dark. He put down his cheap yellow suitcase.

"Well, Roelf."

"I am going away. I couldn't stay."

She nodded. "Where?"

"Away. Chicago maybe." He was terribly moved, so he made his tone casual. "They came home last night. I have got some books that belong to you." He made as though to open the suitcase.

"No, no! Keep them."

"Good-bye."

"Good-bye, Roelf." She took the boy's dark head in her two hands and, standing on tiptoe, kissed him. He turned to go. "Wait a minute. Wait a minute." She had a few dollars—in quarters, dimes, half dollars —perhaps ten dollars in all—hidden away in a canister on the shelf. She reached for it. But when she came back with the box in her hand he was gone.

IX

DIRK was eight; Little Sobig DeJong, in a suit made of bean-sacking sewed together by his mother. A brown blond boy with mosquito bites on his legs and his legs never still. Nothing of the dreamer about this lad. The one-room schoolhouse of Selina's day had been replaced by a two-story brick structure, very fine, of which High Prairie was vastly proud. The rusty iron stove had been dethroned by a central heater. Dirk went to school from October until June. Pervus protested that this was foolish. The boy could be of great help in the fields from the beginning of April to the first of November, but Selina fought savagely for his schooling, and won.

"Reading and writing and figgering is what a farmer is got to know," Pervus argued. "The rest is all foolishness. Constantinople is the capital of Turkey he studies last night and uses good oil in the lamp. What good does it do a truck farmer when he knows Constantinople is the capital of Turkey? That don't help him raise turnips."

"Sobig isn't a truck farmer."

"Well, he will be pretty soon. Time I was fifteen I was running our place."

Verbally Selina did not combat this. But within her every force was gathering to fight it when the time should come. Her Sobig a truck farmer, a slave to the soil, bent by it, beaten by it, blasted by it, so that he, in time, like the other men of High Prairie, would take on the very look of the rocks and earth among which they toiled!

Dirk, at eight, was a none too handsome child, considering his father and mother—or his father and mother as they had been. He had, though, a "different" look. His eyelashes were too long for a boy. Wasted, Selina said as she touched them with a fond forefinger, when a girl would have been so glad of them. He had developed, too, a slightly aquiline nose, probably a long-jump inheritance from some Cromwellian rapscallion of the English Peakes of a past century. It was not until he was seventeen or eighteen that he was to metamorphose suddenly into a graceful and aristocratic youngster with an indefinable look about him of distinction and actual elegance. It was when Dirk was thirty that Peter Peel the English tailor (of Michigan Avenue north) said he was the only man

in Chicago who could wear English clothes without having them look
like Halsted Street. Dirk probably appeared a little startled at that, as
well he might, west Halsted Street having loomed up so large in his
background.

Selina was a farm woman now, nearing thirty. The work rode her as it
had ridden Maartje Pool. In the DeJong yard there was always a dado of
washing, identical with the one that had greeted Selina's eye when first
she drove into the Pool yard years before. Faded overalls, a shirt, socks,
a boy's drawers grotesquely patched and mended, towels of rough sacking. She, too, rose at four, snatched up shapeless garments, invested
herself with them, seized her great coil of fine cloudy hair, twisted it
into a utilitarian knob and skewered it with a hairpin from which the
varnish had long departed, leaving it a dull gray; thrust her slim feet into
shapeless shoes, dabbed her face with cold water, hurried to the kitchen
stove. The work was always at her heels, its breath hot on her neck. Baskets of mending piled up, threatened to overwhelm her. Overalls, woollen
shirts, drawers, socks. Socks! They lay coiled and twisted in an old
market basket. Sometimes as she sat late at night mending them, in and
out, in and out, with quick fierce stabs of the needle in her work-scarred
hand, they seemed to writhe and squirm and wriggle horribly, like
snakes. One of her bad dreams was that in which she saw herself overwhelmed, drowned, swallowed up by a huge welter and boiling of un-
darned, unmended nightshirts, drawers, socks, aprons, overalls.

Seeing her thus one would have thought that the Selina Peake of the
wine-red cashmere, the fun-loving disposition, the high-spirited courage,
had departed forever. But these things still persisted. For that matter,
even the wine-red cashmere clung to existence. So hopelessly old-
fashioned now as to be almost picturesque, it hung in Selina's closet like
a rosy memory. Sometimes when she came upon it in an orgy of cleaning
she would pass her rough hands over its soft folds and by that magic
process Mrs. Pervus DeJong vanished in a pouf and in her place was the
girl Selina Peake perched a-tiptoe on a soap-box in Adam Ooms's hall
while all High Prairie, open-mouthed, looked on as the impecunious
Pervus DeJong threw ten hard-earned dollars at her feet. In thrifty moments she had often thought of cutting the wine-red cashmere into rag-
rug strips; of dyeing it a sedate brown or black and remodelling it for
a much-needed best dress; of fashioning it into shirts for Dirk. But she
never did.

It would be gratifying to be able to record that in these eight or nine
years Selina had been able to work wonders on the DeJong farm; that
the house glittered, the crops thrived richly, the barn housed sleek cattle.
But it could not be truthfully said. True, she had achieved some changes,

but at the cost of terrific effort. A less indomitable woman would have
sunk into apathy years before. The house had a coat of paint—lead-
gray, because it was cheapest. There were two horses—the second a
broken-down old mare, blind in one eye, that they had picked up for five
dollars after it had been turned out to pasture for future sale as horse-
carcass. Piet Pon, the mare's owner who drove a milk route, had hoped
to get three dollars for the animal, dead. A month of rest and pasturage
restored the mare to usefulness. Selina had made the bargain, and
Pervus had scolded her roundly for it. Now he drove the mare to market,
saw that she pulled more sturdily than the other horse, but had never
retracted. It was no quality of meanness in him. Pervus merely was
like that.

But the west sixteen! That had been Selina's most heroic achievement.
Her plan, spoken of to Pervus in the first month of her marriage, had
taken years to mature; even now was but a partial triumph. She had
even descended to nagging.

"Why don't we put in asparagus?"

"Asparagus!" considered something of a luxury, and rarely included
in the High Prairie truck farmer's products. "And wait three years for a
crop!"

"Yes, but then we'd have it. And a plantation's good for ten years,
once it's started."

"Plantation! What is that? An asparagus plantation? Asparagus I've
always heard of in beds."

"That's the old idea. I've been reading up on it. The new way is to
plant asparagus in rows, the way you would rhubarb or corn. Plant six
feet apart, and four acres anyway."

He was not even sufficiently interested to be amused. "Yeh, four
acres where? In the clay land, maybe." He did laugh then, if the short
bitter sound he made could be construed as indicating mirth. "Out of a
book."

"In the clay land," Selina urged, crisply. "And out of a book. Every
farmer in High Prairie raises cabbage, turnips, carrots, beets, beans,
onions, and they're better quality than ours. That west sixteen isn't
bringing you anything, so what difference does it make if I am wrong!
Let me put my own money into it, I've thought it all out, Pervus. Please.
We'll under-drain the clay soil. Just five or six acres, to start. We'll
manure it heavily—as much as we can afford—and then for two years
we'll plant potatoes there. We'll put in our asparagus plants the third
spring—one-year-old seedlings. I'll promise to keep it weeded—Dirk and
I. He'll be a big boy by that time."

"How much manure?"

"Oh, twenty to forty tons to the acre——"

He shook his head in slow Dutch opposition.

"—but if you'll let me use humus I won't need that much. Let me try it, Pervus. Let me try."

In the end she had her way, partly because Pervus was too occupied with his own endless work to oppose her; and partly because he was, in his undemonstrative way, still in love with his vivacious, nimble-witted, high-spirited wife, though to her frantic goadings and proddings he was as phlegmatically oblivious as an elephant to a pin prick. Year in, year out, he maintained his slow-plodding gait, content to do as his father had done before him; content to let the rest of High Prairie pass him on the road. He rarely showed temper. Selina often wished he would. Sometimes, in a sort of hysteria of hopelessness, she would rush at him, ruffle up his thick coarse hair, now beginning to be threaded with gray; shake his great impassive shoulders.

"Pervus! Pervus! if you'd only get mad—real mad! Fly into a rage. Break things! Beat me! Sell the farm! Run away!" She didn't mean it, of course. It was the vital and constructive force in her resenting his apathy, his acceptance of things as they were.

"What is that for dumb talk?" He would regard her solemnly through a haze of smoke, his pipe making a maddening putt-putt of sleepy content.

Though she worked as hard as any woman in High Prairie, had as little, dressed as badly, he still regarded her as a luxury; an exquisite toy which, in a moment of madness, he had taken for himself. "Little Lina"—tolerantly, fondly. You would have thought that he spoiled her, pampered her. Perhaps he even thought he did.

When she spoke of modern farming, of books on vegetable gardening, he came very near to angry impatience, though his amusement at the idea saved him from it. College agricultural courses he designated as foolishness. Of Linnæus he had never heard. Burbank was, for him, non-existent, and he thought head-lettuce a silly fad. Selina sometimes talked of raising this last named green as a salad, with marketing value. Everyone knew that regular lettuce was leaf lettuce which you ate with vinegar and a sprinkling of sugar, or with hot bacon and fat sopping its wilted leaves.

He said, too, she spoiled the boy. Back of this may have been a lurking jealousy. "Always the boy; always the boy," he would mutter when Selina planned for the child; shielded him; took his part (sometimes unjustly). "You will make a softy of him with your always babying." So from time to time he undertook to harden Dirk. The result was generally disastrous. In one case the process terminated in what was perilously near to tragedy. It was during the midsummer school vacation. Dirk was eight. The woody slopes about High Prairie and the sand hills beyond were covered with the rich blue of huckleberries. They were dead ripe. One shower would spoil them. Geertje and Jozina Pool were going huckleberrying and had consented to take Dirk—a concession, for he was only eight and considered, at their advanced age, a tagger. But the last of the tomatoes on the DeJong place were also ripe and ready for picking. They hung, firm, juicy scarlet globes, prime for the Chicago market. Pervus meant to haul them to town that day. And this was work in which the boy could help. To Dirk's, "Can I go berrying? The huckleberries are ripe. Geert and Jozina are going," his father shook a negative head.

"Yes, well, tomatoes are ripe, too, and that comes before huckleberries. There's the whole patch to clean up this afternoon by four."

Selina looked up, glanced at Pervus's face, at the boy's, said nothing. The look said, "He's a child. Let him go, Pervus."

Dirk flushed with disappointment. They were at breakfast. It was barely daybreak. He looked down at his plate, his lip quivered, his long lashes lay heavy on his cheeks. Pervus got up, wiped his mouth with the back of his hand. There was a hard day ahead of him. "Time I was your age, Sobig, I would think it was an easy day when all I had to do was pick a tomato patch clean."

Dirk looked up then, quickly. "If I get it all picked can I go?"

"It's a day's job."

"But if I do pick the patch—if I get through early enough—can I go?"

In his mind's eye Pervus saw the tomato patch, more scarlet than green, so thick hung the fruit upon the bushes. He smiled. "Yes. You pick them tomatoes and you can go. But no throwing into the baskets and getting 'em all softed up."

Secretly Selina resolved to help him, but she knew that this could not be until afternoon. The berry patches were fully three miles from the DeJong farm. Dirk would have to finish by three o'clock, at the latest, to get there. Selina had her morning full with the housework.

He was in the patch before six; fell to work, feverishly. He picked, heaped the fruit into hillocks. The scarlet patches glowed, blood-red, in the sun. The child worked like a machine, with an economy of gesture calculated to the fraction of an inch. He picked, stooped, heaped the mounds in the sultry heat of the August morning. The sweat stood out on his forehead, darkened his blond hair, slid down his cheeks that were pink, then red, then tinged with a purplish tone beneath the summer tan. When dinner time came he gulped a dozen alarming mouthfuls and was out again in the broiling noonday glare. Selina left her dinner dishes unwashed on the table to help him, but Pervus intervened. "The boy's got to do it alone," he insisted.

"He'll never do it, Pervus. He's only eight."

"Time I was eight——"

He actually had cleared the patch by three. He went to the well and took a huge draught of water; drank two great dippersful, lipping it down thirstily, like a colt. It was cool and delicious beyond belief. Then he sloshed a third and a fourth dipperful over his hot head and neck, took an empty lard pail for berries and was off down the dusty road and across the fields, running fleetly in spite of the quivering heat waves that seemed to dance between fiery heaven and parched earth. Selina stood in the kitchen doorway a moment, watching him. He looked very small and determined.

He found Geertje and Jozina, surfeited with fruit, berry stained and bramble torn, lolling languidly in Kuyper's woods. He began to pick the plump blue balls but he ate them listlessly, though thriftily, because that was what he had come for and his father was Dutch. When Geertje and Jozina prepared to leave not an hour after he had come he was ready to go, yet curiously loath to move. His lard pail was half filled. He trotted home laboriously through the late afternoon, feeling giddy and sick, with horrid pains in his head. That night he tossed in delirium, begged not to be made lie down, came perilously near to death.

Selina's heart was an engine pumping terror, hate, agony through her veins. Hate for her husband who had done this to the boy.

"You did it! You did it! He's a baby and you made him work like a man. If anything happens to him! If anything happens to him!——"

"Well, I didn't think the kid would go for to do it. I didn't ask him to pick and then go berrying. He said could he and I said yes. If I had said no it would have been wrong, too, maybe."

"You're all alike. Look at Roelf Pool! They tried to make a farmer of him, too. And ruined him."

"What's the matter with farming? What's the matter with a farmer? You said farm work was grand work, once."

"Oh, I did. It is. It could be. It—— Oh, what's the use of talking like that now! Look at him! Don't, Sobig! Don't, baby. How hot his head is! Listen! Is that Jan with the doctor? No. No, it isn't. Mustard plasters. Are you sure that's the right thing?"

It was before the day of the omnipresent farmhouse telephone and the farmhouse Ford. Jan's trip to High Prairie village for the doctor and back to the farm meant a delay of hours. But within two days the boy was again about, rather pale, but otherwise seeming none the worse for his experience.

That was Pervus. Thrifty, like his kind, but unlike them in shrewdness. Penny wise, pound foolish; a characteristic that brought him his death. September, usually a succession of golden days and hazy opalescent evenings on the Illinois prairie land, was disastrously cold and rainy that year. Pervus's great frame was racked by rheumatism. He was forty now, and over, still of magnificent physique, so that to see him suffering gave Selina the pangs of pity that one has at sight of the very strong or the very weak in pain. He drove the weary miles to market three times a week, for September was the last big month of the truck farmer's season. After that only the hardier plants survived the frosts —the cabbages, beets, turnips, carrots, pumpkins, squash. The roads in places were morasses of mud into which the wheels were likely to sink to the hubs. Once stuck you had often to wait for a friendly passing team to haul you out. Pervus would start early, detour for miles in order to avoid the worst places. Jan was too stupid, too old, too inexpert to be trusted with the Haymarket trading. Selina would watch Pervus drive off down the road in the creaking old market wagon, the green stuff protected by canvas, but Pervus wet before ever he climbed into the seat. There never seemed to be enough waterproof canvas for both.

"Pervus, take it off those sacks and put it over your shoulders."

"That's them white globe onions. The last of 'em. I can get a fancy price for them but not if they're all wetted down."

"Don't sleep on the wagon to-night, Pervus. Sleep in. Be sure. It saves in the end. You know the last time you were laid up for a week."

"It'll clear. Breaking now over there in the west."

The clouds did break late in the afternoon; the false sun came out hot and bright. Pervus slept out in the Haymarket, for the night was close and humid. At midnight the lake wind sprang up, cold and treacherous, and with it came the rain again. Pervus was drenched by morning, chilled, thoroughly miserable. A hot cup of coffee at four and another at ten when the rush of trading was over stimulated him but little. When he reached home it was mid-afternoon. Beneath the bronze wrought by the wind and sun of many years the gray-white of sickness shone dully, like silver under enamel. Selina put him to bed against his half-hearted protests. Banked him with hot water jars, a hot iron wrapped in flannel at his feet. But later came fever instead of the expected relief of perspiration. Ill though he was he looked more ruddy and hale than most men in health; but suddenly Selina, startled, saw black lines like gashes etched under his eyes, about his mouth, in his cheeks.

In a day when pneumonia was known as lung fever and in a locality that advised closed windows and hot air as a remedy, Pervus's battle was lost before the doctor's hooded buggy was seen standing in

the yard for long hours through the night. Toward morning the doctor
had Jan Steen stable the horse. It was a sultry night, with flashes of heat
lightning in the west.

"I should think if you opened the windows," Selina said to the old
High Prairie doctor over and over, emboldened by terror, "it would help
him to breathe. He—he's breathing so—he's breathing so——" She
could not bring herself to say so terribly. The sound of the words wrung
her as did the sound of his terrible breathing.

X

PERHAPS the most poignant and touching feature of the days that followed was not the sight of this stricken giant, lying majestic and aloof
in his unwonted black; nor of the boy Dirk, mystified but elated, too,
with the unaccustomed stir and excitement; nor of the shabby little farm
that seemed to shrink and dwindle into further insignificance beneath
the sudden publicity turned upon it. No; it was the sight of Selina,
widowed, but having no time for decent tears. The farm was there; it
must be tended. Illness, death, sorrow—the garden must be tended, the
vegetables pulled, hauled to market, sold. Upon the garden depended
the boy's future, and hers.

For the first few days following the funeral one or another of the
neighbouring farmers drove the DeJong team to market, aided the blundering Jan in the fields. But each his hands full with his own farm
work. On the fifth day Jan Steen had to take the garden truck to Chicago, though not without many misgivings on Selina's part, all of which
were realized when he returned late next day with half the load still on
his wagon and a sum of money representing exactly zero in profits. The
wilted left-over vegetables were dumped behind the barn to be used later
as fertilizer.

"I didn't do so good this time," Jan explained, "on account I didn't get
no right place in the market."

"You started early enough."

"Well, they kind of crowded me out, like. They see I was a new hand
and time I got the animals stabled and come back they had the wagon
crowded out, like."

Selina was standing in the kitchen doorway, Jan in the yard with the team. She turned her face toward the fields. An observant person (Jan Steen was not one of these) would have noted the singularly determined and clear-cut jaw-line of this drably calicoed farm woman.

"I'll go myself Monday."

Jan stared. "Go? Go where, Monday?"

"To market."

At this seeming pleasantry Jan Steen smiled uncertainly, shrugged his shoulders, and was off to the barn. She was always saying things that didn't make sense. His horror and unbelief were shared by the rest of High Prairie when on Monday Selina literally took the reins in her own slim work-scarred hands.

"To market!" argued Jan as excitedly as his phlegmatic nature would permit. "A woman she don't go to market. A woman——"

"This woman does." Selina had risen at three in the morning. Not only that, she had got Jan up, grumbling. Dirk had joined them in the fields at five. Together the three of them had pulled and bunched a wagon load. "Size them," Selina ordered, as they started to bunch radishes, beets, turnips, carrots. "And don't leave them loose like that. Tie them tight at the heads, like this. Twice around with the string, and through. Make bouquets of them, not bunches. And we're going to scrub them."

High Prairie washed its vegetables desultorily; sometimes not at all. Higgledy piggledy, large and small, they were bunched and sold as vegetables, not objets d'art. Generally there was a tan crust of good earth coating them which the housewife could scrub off at her own kitchen sink. What else had housewives to do!

Selina, scrubbing the carrots vigorously under the pump, thought they emerged from their unaccustomed bath looking like clustered spears of pure gold. She knew better, though, than to say this in Jan's hearing. Jan, by now, was sullen with bewilderment. He refused to believe that she actually intended to carry out her plan. A woman—a High Prairie farmer's wife—driving to market like a man! Alone at night in the market place—or at best in one of the cheap rooming houses! By Sunday somehow, mysteriously, the news had filtered through the district. High Prairie attended the Dutch Reformed church with a question hot on its tongue and Selina did not attend the morning services. A fine state of things, and she a widow of a week! High Prairie called at the DeJong farm on Sunday afternoon and was told that the widow was over in the wet west sixteen, poking about with the boy Dirk at her heels.

The Reverend Dekker appeared late Sunday afternoon on his way to evening service. A dour dominie, the Reverend Dekker, and one whose

talents were anachronistic. He would have been invaluable in the days
when New York was New Amsterdam. But the second and third generations of High Prairie Dutch were beginning to chafe under his old-world
régime. A hard blue eye, had the Reverend Dekker, and a fanatic one.

"What is this talk I hear, Mrs. DeJong, that you are going to the
Haymarket with the garden stuff, a woman alone?"

"Dirk goes with me."

"You don't know what you are doing, Mrs. DeJong. The Haymarket
is no place for a decent woman. As for the boy! There is card-playing,
drinking—all manner of wickedness—daughters of Jezebel on the street,
going among the wagons."

"Really!" said Selina. It sounded thrilling, after twelve years on the
farm.

"You must not go."

"The vegetables are rotting in the ground. And Dirk and I must live."

"Remember the two sparrows. 'One of them shall not fall on the
ground without'—Matthew X-29."

"I don't see," replied Selina, simply, "what good that does the sparrow, once it's fallen."

By Monday afternoon the parlour curtains of every High Prairie farmhouse that faced the Halsted road were agitated as though by a brisk
wind between the hours of three and five, when the market wagons were
to be seen moving toward Chicago. Klaas Pool at dinner that noon had
spoken of Selina's contemplated trip with a mingling of pity and disapproval.

"It ain't decent a woman should drive to market."

Mrs. Klaas Pool (they still spoke of her as the Widow Paarlenberg)
smiled her slippery crooked smile. "What could you expect! Look how
she's always acted."

Klaas did not follow this. He was busy with his own train of thought.
"It don't seem hardly possible. Time she come here school teacher I
drove her out and she was like a little robin or what, set up on the seat.
She says, I remember like yesterday, cabbages was beautiful. I bet she
learned different by this time."

But she hadn't. So little had Selina learned in these past eleven years
that now, having loaded the wagon in the yard she surveyed it with
more sparkle in her eye than High Prairie would have approved in a
widow of little more than a week. They had picked and bunched only
the best of the late crop—the firmest reddest radishes, the roundest
juiciest beets; the carrots that tapered a good seven inches from base to
tip; kraut cabbages of the drumhead variety that were flawless green
balls; firm juicy spears of cucumber; cauliflower (of her own planting;

Pervus had opposed it) that looked like a bride's bouquet. Selina stepped back now and regarded this riot of crimson and green, of white and gold and purple.

"Aren't they beautiful! Dirk, aren't they beautiful!"

Dirk, capering in his excitement at the prospect of the trip before him, shook his head impatiently. "What? I don't see anything beautiful. What's beautiful?"

Selina flung out her arms. "The—the whole wagon load. The cabbages."

"I don't know what you mean," said Dirk. "Let's go, Mother. Aren't we going now? You said as soon as the load was on."

"Oh, Sobig, you're just exactly like your——" She stopped.

"Like my what?"

"We'll go now, son. There's cold meat for your supper, Jan, and potatoes all sliced for frying and half an apple pie left from noon. Wash your dishes—don't leave them cluttering around the kitchen. You ought to get in the rest of the squash and pumpkins by evening. Maybe I can sell the lot instead of taking them in by the load. I'll see a commission man. Take less, if I have to."

She had dressed the boy in his home-made suit cut down from one of his father's. He wore a wide-brimmed straw hat which he hated. Selina had made him an overcoat of stout bean-sacking and this she tucked under the wagon seat, together with an old black fascinator, for though the September afternoon was white-hot she knew that the evenings were likely to be chilly, once the sun, a great crimson Chinese balloon, had burned itself out in a blaze of flame across the prairie horizon. Selina herself, in a full-skirted black-stuff dress, mounted the wagon agilely, took up the reins, looked down at the boy seated beside her, clucked to the horses. Jan Steen gave vent to a final outraged bellow.

"Never in my life did I hear of such a thing!"

Selina turned the horses' heads toward the city. "You'd be surprised, Jan, to know of all the things you're going to hear of some day that you've never heard of before." Still, when twenty years had passed and the Ford, the phonograph, the radio, and the rural mail delivery had dumped the world at Jan's plodding feet he liked to tell of that momentous day when Selina DeJong had driven off to market like a man with a wagon load of hand-scrubbed garden truck and the boy Dirk perched beside her on the seat.

If, then, you had been travelling the Halsted road, you would have seen a decrepit wagon, vegetable-laden, driven by a too-thin woman, sallow, bright-eyed, in a shapeless black dress, a battered black felt hat that looked like a man's old "fedora" and probably was. Her hair was un-

becomingly strained away from the face with its high cheek bones, so
that unless you were really observant you failed to notice the exquisite
little nose or the really fine eyes so unnaturally large now in the anxious
face. On the seat beside her you would have seen a farm boy of nine or
thereabouts—a brown freckle-faced lad in a comically home-made suit of
clothes and a straw hat with a broken and flopping brim which he was
forever jerking off only to have it set firmly on again by the woman who
seemed to fear the effects of the hot afternoon sun on his close-cropped
head. But in the brief intervals when the hat was off you must have
noted how the boy's eyes were shining.

At their feet was the dog Pom, a mongrel whose tail bore no relation
to his head, whose ill-assorted legs appeared wholly at variance with his
sturdy barrel of a body. He dozed now, for it had been his duty to
watch the wagon load at night, while Pervus slept.

A shabby enough little outfit, but magnificent, too. Here was Selina
DeJong driving up the Halsted road toward the city instead of sitting,
black-robed, in the farm parlour while High Prairie came to condole. In
Selina, as they jogged along the hot dusty way, there welled up a feeling
very like elation. Conscious of this, the New England strain in her took
her to task. "Selina Peake, aren't you ashamed of yourself! You're a
wicked woman! Feeling almost gay when you ought to be sad. . . .
Poor Pervus . . . the farm . . . Dirk . . . and you can feel almost gay!
You ought to be ashamed of yourself!"

But she wasn't, and knew it. For even as she thought this the little
wave of elation came flooding over her again. More than ten years ago
she had driven with Klaas Pool up that same road for the first time, and
in spite of the recent tragedy of her father's death, her youth, her loneliness, the terrifying thought of the new home to which she was going, a
stranger among strangers, she had been conscious of a warm little thrill
of elation, of excitement—of adventure! That was it. "The whole thing's
just a grand adventure," her father, Simeon Peake, had said. And now the
sensations of that day were repeating themselves. Now, as then, she was
doing what was considered a revolutionary and daring thing; a thing
that High Prairie regarded with horror. And now, as then, she took
stock. Youth was gone, but she had health, courage; a boy of nine;
twenty-five acres of wornout farm land; dwelling and out-houses in a
bad state of repair; and a gay adventuresome spirit that was never to
die, though it led her into curious places and she often found, at the
end, only a trackless waste from which she had to retrace her steps painfully. But always, to her, red and green cabbages were to be jade and
burgundy, chrysoprase and porphyry. Life has no weapons against a
woman like that.

And the wine-red cashmere. She laughed aloud.

"What are you laughing at, Mom?"

That sobered her. "Oh, nothing, Sobig. I didn't know I was laughing. I was just thinking about a red dress I had when I first came to High Prairie a girl. I've got it yet."

"What's that to laugh at?" He was following a yellow-hammer with his eyes.

"Nothing. Mother said it was nothing."

"Wisht I'd brought my sling-shot." The yellow-hammer was perched on the fence by the roadside not ten feet away.

"Sobig, you promised me you wouldn't throw at any more birds, ever."

"Oh, I wouldn't hit it. I would just like to aim at it."

Down the hot dusty country road. She was serious enough now. The cost of the funeral to be paid. The doctor's bills. Jan's wage. All the expenses, large and small, of the poor little farm holding. Nothing to laugh at, certainly. The boy was wiser than she.

"There's Mrs. Pool on her porch, Mom. Rocking."

There, indeed, was the erstwhile Widow Paarlenberg on her porch, rocking. A pleasant place to be in mid-afternoon of a hot September day. She stared at the creaking farm wagon, vegetable laden; at the boy perched on the high seat; at the sallow shabby woman who was charioteer for the whole crazy outfit. Mrs. Klaas Pool's pink face creased in a smile. She sat forward in her chair and ceased to rock.

"Where you going this hot day, Mis' DeJong?"

Selina sat up very straight. "To Bagdad, Mrs. Pool."

"To—Where's that? What for?"

"To sell my jewels, Mrs. Pool. And to see Aladdin, and Harun-al-Rashid and Ali Baba. And the Forty Thieves."

Mrs. Pool had left her rocker and had come down the steps. The wagon creaked on past her gate. She took a step or two down the path, and called after them. "I never heard of it. Bag—How do you get there?"

Over her shoulder Selina called out from the wagon seat. "You just go until you come to a closed door. And you say 'Open Sesame!' and there you are."

Bewilderment shadowed Mrs. Pool's placid face. As the wagon lurched on down the road it was Selina who was smiling and Mrs. Pool who was serious.

The boy, round eyed, was looking up at his mother. "That's out of *Arabian Nights*, what you said. Why did you say that?" Suddenly excitement tinged his voice. "That's out of the book. Isn't it? Isn't it! We're not really——"

She was a little contrite, but not very. "Well, not really, perhaps. But 'most any place is Bagdad if you don't know what will happen in it. And this is an adventure, isn't it, that we're going on? How can you tell! All kind of things can happen. All kinds of people. People in disguise in the Haymarket. Caliphs, and princes, and slaves, and thieves, and good fairies, and witches."

"In the Haymarket! That Pop went to all the time! That is just dumb talk."

Within Selina something cried out, "Don't say that, Sobig! Don't say that!"

On down the road. Here a head at a front room window. There a woman's calicoed figure standing in the doorway. Mrs. Vander Sijde on the porch, fanning her flushed face with her apron; Cornelia Snip in the yard pretending to tie up the drooping stalks of the golden-glow and eyeing the approaching team with the avid gossip's gaze. To these Selina waved, bowed, called.

"How d'you do, Mrs. Vander Sijde!"

A prim reply to this salutation. Disapproval writ large on the farm-wife's flushed face.

"Hello, Cornelia!"

A pretended start, notable for its bad acting. "Oh, is it you, Mrs. DeJong! Sun's in my eyes. I couldn't think it was you like that."

Women's eyes, hostile, cold, peering.

Five o'clock. Six. The boy climbed over the wheel, filled a tin pail with water at a farmhouse well. They ate and drank as they rode along, for there was no time to lose. Bread and meat and pickles and pie. There were vegetables in the wagon, ripe for eating. There were other varieties that Selina might have cooked at home in preparation for this meal— German celery root boiled tender and soaked in vinegar; red beets, pickled; onions; coleslaw; beans. They would have regarded these with an apathetic eye all too familiar with the sight of them. Selina knew now why the Pools' table, in her school-teacher days, had been so lacking in the green stuff she had craved. The thought of cooking the spinach which she had planted, weeded, spaded, tended, picked, washed, bunched, filled her with a nausea of distaste such as she might have experienced at the contemplation of cannibalism.

The boy had started out bravely enough in the heat of the day, sitting up very straight beside his mother, calling to the horses, shrieking and waving his arms at chickens that flew squawking across the road. Now he began to droop. Evening was coming on. A cool blanket of air from the lake on the east enveloped them with the suddenness characteristic of the region, and the mist began to drift across the prairie, softening the autumn stubble, cooling the dusty road, misting the parched willows by the roadside, hazing the shabby squat farmhouses.

She brushed away the crumbs, packed the remaining bread and meat thriftily into the basket and covered it with a napkin against the boy's future hunger should he waken in the night.

"Sleepy, Sobig?"

"No. Should say not." His lids were heavy. His face and body, relaxed, took on the soft baby contours that come with weariness. The sun was low. Sunset gloried the west in a final flare of orange and crimson. Dusk. The boy drooped against her heavy, sagging. She wrapped the old black fascinator about him. He opened his eyes, tugged at the wrapping about his shoulders. "Don't want the old thing . . . fas'nator . . . like a girl . . ." drooped again with a sigh and found the soft curve where her side just cushioned his head. In the twilight the dust gleamed white on weeds, and brush, and grass. The far-off mellow sonance of a cowbell. Horses' hoofs clopping up behind them, a wagon passing in a cloud of dust, a curious backward glance, or a greeting exchanged.

One of the Ooms boys, or Jakob Boomsma. "You're never going to market, Mis' DeJong!" staring with china-blue eyes at her load.

"Yes, I am, Mr. Boomsma."

"That ain't work for a woman, Mis' DeJong. You better stay home and let the men folks go."

Selina's men folks looked up at her—one with the asking eyes of a child, one with the trusting eyes of a dog. "My men folks are going," answered Selina. But then, they had always thought her a little queer, so it didn't matter much.

She urged the horses on, refusing to confess to herself her dread of the destination which they were approaching. Lights now, in the houses along the way, and those houses closer together. She wrapped the reins around the whip, and holding the sleeping boy with one hand reached beneath the seat with the other for the coat of sacking. This she placed around him snugly, folded an empty sack for a pillow, and lifting the boy in her arms laid him gently on the lumpy bed formed by the bags of potatoes piled up just behind the seat in the back of the wagon. So the boy slept. Night had come on.

The figure of the woman drooped a little now as the old wagon creaked on toward Chicago. A very small figure in the black dress and a shawl over her shoulders. She had taken off her old black felt hat. The breeze ruffled her hair that was fine and soft, and it made a little halo about the white face that gleamed almost luminously in the darkness as she turned it up toward the sky.

"I'll sleep out with Sobig in the wagon. It won't hurt either of us. It

will be warm in town, there in the Haymarket. Twenty-five cents—maybe
fifty for the two of us, in the rooming house. Fifty cents just to sleep.
It takes hours of work in the fields to make fifty cents."

She was sleepy now. The night air was deliciously soft and soothing.
In her nostrils was the smell of the fields, of grass dew-wet, of damp
dust, of cattle; the pungent prick of goldenrod, and occasionally a
scented wave that meant wild phlox in a near-by ditch. She sniffed all
this gratefully, her mind and body curiously alert to sounds, scents, forms
even, in the darkness. She had suffered much in the past week; had eaten
and slept but little. Had known terror, bewilderment, agony, shock. Now
she was relaxed, receptive, a little light-headed perhaps, what with under-
feeding and tears and over-work. The racking process had cleared brain
and bowels; had washed her spiritually clean; had quickened her per-
ceptions abnormally. Now she was like a delicate and sensitive electric
instrument keyed to receive and register; vibrating to every ether wave.

She drove along in the dark, a dowdy farm woman in shapeless garments; just a bundle on the rickety seat of a decrepit truck wagon. The
boy slept on his hard lumpy bed like the little vegetable that he was. The
farm lights went out. The houses were blurs in the black. The lights of
the city came nearer. She was thinking clearly, if disconnectedly, without
bitterness, without reproach.

"My father was wrong. He said that life was a great adventure—a fine
show. He said the more things that happen to you the richer you are,
even if they're not pleasant things. That's living, he said. No matter
what happens to you, good or bad, it's just so much—what was that
word he used?—so much—oh, yes—'velvet.' Just so much velvet. Well, it
isn't true. He had brains, and charm, and knowledge and he died in a
gambling house, shot while looking on at some one else who was to
have been killed. . . . Now we're on the cobblestones. Will Dirk wake
up? My little So Big. . . . No, he's asleep. Asleep on a pile of potato
sacks because his mother thought that life was a grand adventure—a
fine show—and that you took it as it came. A lie! I've taken it as it came
and made the best of it. That isn't the way. You take the best, and make
the most of it . . . Thirty-fifth Street, that was. Another hour and a half
to reach the Haymarket. . . . I'm not afraid. After all, you just sell your
vegetables for what you can get. . . . Well, it's going to be different with
him. I mustn't call him Sobig any more. He doesn't like it. Dirk. That's
a fine name. Dirk DeJong. . . . No drifting along for him. I'll see that
he starts with a plan, and follows it. He'll have every chance. Every
chance. Too late for me, now, but he'll be different. . . . Twenty-second
Street . . . Twelfth . . . Look at all the people! . . . I'm enjoying this.
No use denying it. I'm enjoying this. Just as I enjoyed driving along

with Klaas Pool that evening, years and years ago. Scared, but enjoying it. Perhaps I oughtn't to be—but that's hypocritical and sneaking. Why not, if I really do enjoy it! I'll wake him. . . . Dirk! Dirk, we're almost there. Look at all the people, and the lights. We're almost there."

The boy awoke, raised himself from his bed of sacking, looked about, blinked, sank back again and curled into a ball. "Don't want to see the lights . . . people . . ."

He was asleep again. Selina guided the horses skilfully through the downtown streets. She looked about with wide ambient eyes. Other wagons passed her. There was a line of them ahead of her. The men looked at her curiously. They called to one another, and jerked a thumb in her direction, but she paid no heed. She decided, though, to have the boy on the seat beside her. They were within two blocks of the Haymarket, on Randolph Street.

"Dirk! Come, now. Come up here with mother." Grumbling, he climbed to the seat, yawned, smacked his lips, rubbed his knuckles into his eyes.

"What are we here for?"

"So we can sell the garden truck and earn money."

"What for?"

"To send you to school to learn things."

"That's funny. I go to school already."

"A different school. A big school."

He was fully awake now, and looking about him interestedly. They turned into the Haymarket. It was a tangle of horses, carts, men. The wagons were streaming in from the German truck farms that lay to the north of Chicago as well as from the Dutch farms that lay to the southwest, whence Selina came. Fruits and vegetables—tons of it—acres of it—piled in the wagons that blocked the historic square. An unarmed army bringing food to feed a great city. Through this little section, and South Water Street that lay to the east, passed all the verdant growing things that fed Chicago's millions. Something of this came to Selina as she manœuvred her way through the throng. She felt a little thrill of significance, of achievement. She knew the spot she wanted for her own. Since that first trip to Chicago with Pervus in the early days of her marriage she had made the journey into town perhaps not more than a dozen times, but she had seen, and heard, and remembered. A place near the corner of Des Plaines, not at the curb, but rather in the double line of wagons that extended down the middle of the road. Here the purchasing pedlers and grocers had easy access to the wagons. Here Selina could display her wares to the best advantage. It was just across the way from Chris Spanknoebel's restaurant, rooming house, and saloon. Chris knew her; had known Pervus for years and his father before him; would be kind to her and the boy in case of need.

Dirk was wide awake now; eager, excited. The lights, the men, the horses, the sound of talk, and laughter, and clinking glasses from the eating houses along the street were bewilderingly strange to his country-bred eyes and ears. He called to the horses; stood up in the wagon; but clung closer to her as they found themselves in the thick of the mêlée.

On the street corners where the lights were brightest there were stands at which men sold chocolate, cigars, collar buttons, suspenders, shoe strings, patent contrivances. It was like a fair. Farther down the men's faces loomed mysteriously out of the half light. Stolid, sunburned faces now looked dark, terrifying, the whites of the eyes very white, the mustaches very black, their shoulders enormous. Here was a crap game beneath the street light. There stood two girls laughing and chatting with a policeman.

"Here's a good place, Mother. Here! There's a dog on that wagon like Pom."

Pom, hearing his name, stood up, looked into the boy's face, quivered, wagged a nervous tail, barked sharply. The Haymarket night life was an old story to Pom, but it never failed to stimulate him. Often he had guarded the wagon when Pervus was absent for a short time. He would stand on the seat ready to growl at any one who so much as fingered a radish in Pervus's absence.

"Down, Pom! Quiet, Pom!" She did not want to attract attention to herself and the boy. It was still early. She had made excellent time. Pervus had often slept in snatches as he drove into town and the horses had lagged, but Selina had urged them on to-night. They had gained a good half hour over the usual time. Halfway down the block Selina espied the place she wanted. From the opposite direction came a truck farmer's cart obviously making for the same stand. For the first time that night Selina drew the whip out of its socket and clipped sharply her surprised nags. With a start and a shuffle they broke into an awkward lope. Ten seconds too late the German farmer perceived her intention, whipped up his own tired team, arrived at the spot just as Selina, blocking the way, prepared to back into the vacant space.

"Heh, get out of there you——" he roared; then, for the first time, perceived in the dim light of the street that his rival was a woman. He faltered, stared open-mouthed, tried other tactics. "You can't go in there, missus."

"Oh, yes, I can." She backed her team dexterously.

"Yes, we can!" shouted Dirk in an attitude of fierce belligerence.

From the wagons on either side heads were lifted. "Where's your man?" demanded the defeated driver, glaring.

"Here," replied Selina; put her hand on Dirk's head.

The other, preparing to drive on, received this with incredulity. He assumed the existence of a husband in the neighbourhood—at Chris Spanknoebel's probably, or talking prices with a friend at another wagon when he should be here attending to his own. In the absence of this, her natural protector, he relieved his disgruntled feelings as he gathered up the reins. "Woman ain't got no business here in Haymarket, anyway. Better you're home night time in your kitchen where you belong."

This admonition, so glibly mouthed by so many people in the past few days, now was uttered once too often. Selina's nerves snapped. A surprised German truck farmer found himself being harangued from the driver's seat of a vegetable wagon by an irate and fluent woman in a mashed black hat.

"Don't talk to me like that, you great stupid! What good does it do a woman to stay home in her kitchen if she's going to starve there, and her boy with her! Staying home in my kitchen won't earn me any money. I'm here to sell the vegetables I helped raise and I'm going to do it. Get out of my way, you. Go along about your business or I'll report you to Mike, the street policeman."

Now she clambered over the wagon wheel to unhitch the tired horses. It is impossible to tell what interpretation the dumfounded north-sider put upon her movements. Certainly he had nothing to fear from this small gaunt creature with the blazing eyes. Nevertheless as he gathered up his reins terror was writ large on his rubicund face.

"*Teufel!* What a woman!" Was off in a clatter of wheels and hoofs on the cobblestones.

Selina unharnessed swiftly. "You stay here, Dirk, with Pom. Mother'll be back in a minute." She marched down the street driving the horses to the barns where, for twenty-five cents, the animals were to be housed in more comfort than their owner. She returned to find Dirk deep in conversation with two young women in red shirtwaists, plaid skirts that swept the ground, and sailor hats tipped at a saucy angle over pyramidal pompadours.

"I can't make any sense out of it, can you, Elsie? Sounds like Dirt to me, but nobody's going to name a kid that, are they? Stands to reason."

"Oh, come on. Your name'll be mud first thing you know. Here it's after nine already and not a——" she turned and saw Selina's white face.

"There's my mother," said Dirk, triumphantly, pointing. The three women looked at each other. Two saw the pathetic hat and the dowdy clothes, and knew. One saw the red shirtwaists and the loose red lips, and knew.

"We was just talking to the kid," said the girl who had been puzzled by Dirk's name. Her tone was defensive. "Just asking him his name, and like that."

"His name is Dirk," said Selina, mildly. "It's a Dutch name—Holland, you know. We're from out High Prairie way, south. Dirk DeJong. I'm Mrs. DeJong."

"Yeh?" said the other girl. "I'm Elsie. Elsie from Chelsea, that's me. Come on, Mabel. Stand gabbin' all night." She was blonde and shrill. The other was older, dark-haired. There was about her a paradoxical wholesomeness.

Mable, the older one, looked at Selina sharply. From the next wagon came loud snores issuing from beneath the seat. From down the line where a lantern swung from the tailboard of a cart came the rattle of dice. "What you doing down here, anyway?"

"I'm here to sell my stuff to-morrow morning. Vegetables. From the farm."

Mabel looked around. Hers was not a quick mind. "Where's your man?"

"My husband died a week ago." Selina was making up their bed for the night. From beneath the seat she took a sack of hay, tight-packed, shook out its contents, spread them evenly on the floor of the wagon, at the front, first having unhinged the seat and clapped it against the wagon side as a headboard. Over the hay she spread empty sacking. She shook out her shawl, which would serve as cover. The girl Mabel beheld these preparations. Her dull eyes showed a gleam of interest which deepened to horror.

"Say, you ain't never going to sleep out here, are you? You and the kid. Like that!"

"Yes."

"Well, for——" She stared, turned to go, came back. From her belt that dipped so stylishly in the front hung an arsenal of jangling metal articles—purse, pencil, mirror, comb—a chatelaine, they called it. She opened the purse now and took from it a silver dollar. This she tendered Selina, almost roughly. "Here. Get the kid a decent roost for the night. You and the kid, see."

Selina stared at the shining round dollar; at Mabel's face. The quick sting of tears came to her eyes. She shook her head, smiled. "We don't mind sleeping out here. Thank you just the same—Mabel."

The girl put her dollar plumply back into her purse. "Well, takes all kinds, I always say. I thought I had a bum deal but, say, alongside of

what you got I ain't got it so worse. Place to sleep in, anyways, even if
it is—well, good-night. Listen to that Elsie, hollering for me. I'm comin'!
Shut up!"

You heard the two on their way up the street, arm in arm, laughing.
"Come Dirk."

"Are we going to sleep here!" He was delighted.

"Right here, all snug in the hay, like campers."

The boy lay down, wriggling, laughing. "Like gypsies. Ain't it, Mom?"

" 'Isn't it,' Dirk—not 'ain't it'." The school teacher.

She lay down beside him. The boy seemed terribly wide awake. "I
liked the Mabel one best, didn't you? She was the nicest, h'm?"

"Oh, much the nicest," said Selina, and put one arm around him and
drew him to her, close. And suddenly he was asleep, deeply. The street
became quieter. The talking and laughter ceased. The lights were dim
at Chris Spanknoebel's. Now and then the clatter of wheels and horses'
hoofs proclaimed a late comer seeking a place, but the sound was not
near by, for this block and those to east and west were filled by now.
These men had been up at four that morning, must be up before four
the next.

The night was cool, but not cold. Overhead you saw the wide strip
of sky between the brick buildings on either side of the street. Two men
came along singing. "Shut up!" growled a voice from a wagon along the
curb. The singers subsided. It must be ten o'clock and after, Selina
thought. She had with her Pervus's nickel watch, but it was too dark to
see its face, and she did not want to risk a match. Measured footsteps
that passed and repassed at regular intervals. The night policeman.

She lay looking up at the sky. There were no tears in her eyes. She
was past tears. She thought, "Here I am, Selina Peake, sleeping in a
wagon, in the straw, like a bitch with my puppy snuggled beside me. I
was going to be like Jo in Louisa Alcott's book. On my feet are boots
and on my body a dyed dress. How terribly long it is going to be until
morning . . . I must try to sleep. . . . I must try to sleep . . ."

She did sleep, miraculously. The September stars twinkled brightly
down on them. As she lay there, the child in her arms, asleep, peace
came to the haggard face, relaxed the tired limbs. Much like another
woman who had lain in the straw with her child in her arms almost two
thousand years before.

XI

It would be enchanting to be able to record that Selina, next day, had phenomenal success, disposing of her carefully bunched wares to great advantage, driving smartly off up Halsted Street toward High Prairie with a goodly profit jingling in her scuffed leather purse. The truth is that she had a day so devastating, so catastrophic, as would have discouraged most men and certainly any woman less desperate and determined.

She had awakened, not to daylight, but to the three o'clock blackness. The street was already astir. Selina brushed her skirt to rid it of the clinging hay, tidied herself as best she could. Leaving Dirk still asleep, she called Pom from beneath the wagon to act as sentinel at the dashboard, and crossed the street to Chris Spanknoebel's. She knew Chris, and he her. He would let her wash at the faucet at the rear of the eating house. She would buy hot coffee for herself and Dirk to warm and revivify them. They would eat the sandwiches left from the night before.

Chris himself, a pot-paunched Austrian, blond, benevolent, was standing behind his bar, wiping the slab with a large moist cloth. With the other hand he swept the surface with a rubber-tipped board about the size of a shingle. This contrivance gathered up such beads of moisture as might be left by the cloth. Two sweeps of it rendered the counter dry and shining. Later Chris allowed Dirk to wield this rubber-tipped contrivance—a most satisfactory thing to do, leaving one with a feeling of perfect achievement.

Spanknoebel seemed never to sleep, yet his colour was ruddy, his blue eyes clear. The last truckster coming in at night for a beer or a cup of coffee and a sandwich was greeted by Chris, white-aproned, pink-cheeked, wide awake, swabbing the bar's shining surface with the thirsty cloth, swishing it with the sly rubber-tipped board. "Well, how goes it all the while?" said Chris. The earliest morning trader found Chris in a fresh white apron crackling with starch and ironing. He would swab the bar with a gesture of welcome, of greeting. "Well, how goes it all the while?"

As Selina entered the long room now there was something heartening, reassuring about Chris's clean white apron, his ruddy colour, the very sweep of his shirt-sleeved arm as it encompassed the bar-slab. From the kitchen at the rear came the sounds of sizzling and frying, and the gracious scent of coffee and of frying pork and potatoes. Already the market men were seated at the tables eating huge and hurried breakfasts: hunks of ham; eggs in pairs; potatoes cut in great cubes; cups of steaming coffee and chunks of bread that they plastered liberally with butter.

Selina approached Chris. His round face loomed out through the smoke like the sun in a fog. "Well, how goes it all the while?" Then he recognized her. "*Um Gottes!*—why, it's Mis' DeJong!" He wiped his great hand on a convenient towel, extended it in sympathy to the widow. "I heerd," he said, "I heerd." His inarticulateness made his words doubly effective.

"I've come in with the load, Mr. Spanknoebel. The boy and I. He's still asleep in the wagon. May I bring him over here to clean him up a little before breakfast?"

"Sure! Sure!" A sudden suspicion struck him. "You ain't slept in the wagon, Mis' DeJong! *Um Gottes!*——"

"Yes. It wasn't bad. The boy slept the night through. I slept, too, quite a little."

"Why you didn't come here! Why——" At the look in Selina's face he knew then. "For nothing you and the boy could sleep here."

"I knew that! That's why."

"Don't talk dumb, Mrs. DeJong. Half the time the rooms is vacant. You and the boy chust as well—twenty cents, then, and pay me when you got it. But any way you don't come in reg'lar with the load, do you? That ain't for womans."

"There's no one to do it for me, except Jan. And he's worse than nobody. Just through September and October. After that, maybe——" Her voice trailed off. It is hard to be hopeful at three in the morning, before breakfast.

She went to the little wash room at the rear, felt better immediately she had washed vigorously, combed her hair. She returned to the wagon to find a panic-stricken Dirk sure of nothing but that he had been deserted by his mother. Fifteen minutes later the two were seated at a table on which was spread what Chris Spanknoebel considered an adequate breakfast. A heartening enough beginning for the day, and a deceptive.

The Haymarket buyers did not want to purchase its vegetables from Selina DeJong. It wasn't used to buying of women, but to selling to them. Pedlers and small grocers swarmed in at four—Greeks, Italians,

Jews. They bought shrewdly, craftily, often dishonestly. They sold their wares to the housewives. Their tricks were many. They would change a box of tomatoes while your back was turned; filch a head of cauliflower. There was little system or organization.

Take Luigi. Luigi peddled on the north side. He called his wares through the alleys and side streets of Chicago, adding his raucous voice to the din of an inchoate city. A swarthy face had Luigi, a swift brilliant smile, a crafty eye. The Haymarket called him Loogy. When prices did not please Luigi he pretended not to understand. Then the Haymarket would yell, undeceived, "Heh, Loogy, what de mattah! Spika da Engleesh!" They knew him.

Selina had taken the covers off her vegetables. They were revealed crisp, fresh, colourful. But Selina knew they must be sold now, quickly. When the leaves began to wilt, when the edges of the cauliflower heads curled ever so slightly, turned brown and limp, their value decreased by half, even though the heads themselves remained white and firm.

Down the street came the buyers—little black-eyed swarthy men; plump, shirt-sleeved, greasy men; shrewd, tobacco-chewing men in overalls. Stolid red Dutch faces, sunburned. Lean dark foreign faces. Shouting, clatter, turmoil.

"Heh! Get your horse outta here! What the hell!"

"How much for the whole barrel?"

"Got any beans? No, don't want no cauliflower. Beans!"

"Tough!"

"Well, keep 'em. I don't want 'em."

"Quarter for the sack."

"G'wan, them ain't five-pound heads. Bet they don't come four pounds to the head."

"Who says they don't!"

"Gimme five bushels them."

Food for Chicago's millions. In and out of the wagons. Under horses' hoofs. Bare-footed children, baskets on their arms, snatching bits of fallen vegetables from the cobbles. Gutter Annie, a shawl pinned across her pendulous breasts, scavenging a potato there, an onion fallen to the street, scraps of fruit and green stuff in the ditch. Big Kate buying carrots, parsley, turnips, beets, all slightly wilted and cheap, which she would tie into bunches with her bit of string and sell to the real grocers for soup greens.

The day broke warm. The sun rose red. It would be a humid September day such as frequently came in the autumn to this lake region. Garden stuff would have to move quickly this morning. Afternoon would find it worthless.

Selina stationed herself by her wagon. She saw the familiar faces of a half dozen or more High Prairie neighbours. These called to her, or came over briefly to her wagon, eyeing her wares with a calculating glance. "How you making out, Mis' DeJong? Well, you got a good load there. Move it along quick this morning. It's going to be hot I betcha." Their tone was kindly, but disapproving, too. Their look said, "No place for a woman. No place for a woman."

The pedlers looked at her bunched bouquets, glanced at her, passed her by. It was not unkindness that prompted them, but a certain shyness, a fear of the unaccustomed. They saw her pale fine face with its great sombre eyes; the slight figure in the decent black dress; the slim brown hands clasped so anxiously together. Her wares were tempting but they passed her by with the instinct that the ignorant have against that which is unusual.

By nine o'clock trading began to fall off. In a panic Selina realized that the sales she had made amounted to little more than two dollars. If she stayed there until noon she might double that, but no more. In desperation she harnessed the horses, threaded her way out of the swarming street, and made for South Water Street farther east. Here were the commission houses. The district was jammed with laden carts and wagons exactly as the Haymarket had been, but trading was done on a different scale. She knew that Pervus had sometimes left his entire load with an established dealer here, to be sold on commission. She remembered the name—Talcott—though she did not know the exact location.

"Where we going now, Mom?" The boy had been almost incredibly patient and good. He had accepted his bewildering new surroundings with the adaptability of childhood. He had revelled richly in Chris Spanknoebel's generous breakfast. He had thought the four dusty artificial palms that graced Chris's back room luxuriantly tropical. He had been fascinated by the kitchen with its long glowing range, its great tables for slicing, paring, cutting. He liked the ruddy cheer of it, the bustle, the mouth-watering smells. At the wagon he had stood sturdily next his mother, had busied himself vastly assisting her in her few pitiful sales; had plucked wilted leaves, brought forward the freshest and crispest vegetables. But now she saw that he was drooping a little as were her wares, with the heat and the absence from accustomed soil. "Where we going now, Mom?"

"To another street, Sobig——"

"Dirk!"

"—Dirk, where there's a man who'll buy all our stuff at once—maybe. Won't that be fine! Then we'll go home. You help mother find his name over the store. Talcott—T-a-l-c-o-double t."

South Water Street was changing with the city's growth. Yankee names they used to be—Flint—Keen—Rusk—Lane. Now you saw Cuneo—Meleges—Garibaldi—Campagna. There it was: William Talcott. Fruits and Vegetables.

William Talcott, standing in the cool doorway of his great deep shed-like store, was the antithesis of the feverish crowded street which he so calmly surveyed. He had dealt for forty years in provender. His was the unruffled demeanour of a man who knows the world must have what he has to sell. Every week-day morning at six his dim shaded cavern of a store was packed with sacks, crates, boxes, barrels from which peeped ruffles and sprigs of green; flashes of scarlet, plum-colour, orange. He bought the best only; sold at high prices. He had known Pervus, and Pervus's father before him, and had adjudged them honest, admirable men. But of their garden truck he had small opinion. The Great Lakes boats brought him choice Michigan peaches and grapes; refrigerator cars brought him the products of California's soil in a day when out-of-season food was a rare luxury. He wore neat pepper-and-salt pants and vest; shirt sleeves a startling white in that blue-shirted overalled world; a massive gold watch chain spanning his middle; square-toed boots; a straw fedora set well back; a pretty good cigar, unlighted, in his mouth. Shrewd blue eyes he had; sparse hair much the colour of his suit. Like a lean laconic god he stood in his doorway niche while toilers offered for his inspection the fruits of the earth.

"Nope. Can't use that lot, Jake. Runty. H'm. Wa-a-al, guess you'd better take them farther up the street, Tunis. Edges look kind of brown. Wilty."

Stewards from the best Chicago hotels of that day—the Sherman House, the Auditorium, the Palmer House, the Wellington, the Stratford—came to Will Talcott for their daily supplies. The grocers who catered to the well-to-do north-side families and those in the neighbourhood of fashionable Prairie Avenue on the south bought of him.

Now, in his doorway, he eyed the spare little figure that appeared before him all in rusty black, with its strained anxious face, its great deep-sunk eyes.

"DeJong, eh? Sorry to hear about your loss, ma'am. Pervus was a fine lad. No great shakes at truck farming, though. His widow, h'm? Hm." Here, he saw, was no dull-witted farm woman; no stolid Dutch woman truckster. He went out to her wagon, tweaked the boy's brown cheek. "Wa-al now, Mis' DeJong, you got a right smart lot of garden stuff here and it looks pretty good. Yessir, pretty good. But you're too late. Ten, pret' near."

"Oh, no!" cried Selina. "Oh, no! Not too late!" And at the agony in her voice he looked at her sharply.

"Tell you what, mebbe I can move half of 'em along for you. But stuff don't keep this weather. Turns wilty and my trade won't touch it . . . First trip in?"

She wiped her face that was damp and yet cold to the touch. "First —trip in." Suddenly she was finding it absurdly hard to breathe.

He called from the sidewalk to the men within: "George! Ben! Hustle this stuff in. Half of it. The best. Send you check to-morrow, Mis' DeJong. Picked a bad day, didn't you, for your first day?"

"Hot, you mean?"

"Wa-al, hot, yes. But I mean a holiday like this pedlers mostly ain't buying."

"Holiday?"

"You knew it was a Jew holiday, didn't you? Didn't!—Wa-al, my sakes! Worst day in the year. Jew pedlers all at church to-day and all the others not pedlers bought in Saturday for two days. Chicken men down the street got empty coops and will have till to-morrow. Yessir. Biggest chicken eaters, Jews are, in the world . . . Hm . . . Better just drive along home and just dump the rest that stuff, my good woman."

One hand on the seat she prepared to climb up again—did step to the hub. You saw her shabby, absurd side-boots that were so much too big for the slim little feet. "If you're just buying my stuff because you're sorry for me——" The Peake pride.

"Don't do business that way. Can't afford to, ma'am. My da'ter she's studying to be a singer. In Italy now, Car'line is, and costs like all get-out. Takes all the money I can scrape together, just about."

There was a little colour in Selina's face now. "Italy! Oh, Mr. Tal-cott!" You'd have thought she had seen it, from her face. She began to thank him, gravely.

"Now, that's all right, Mis' DeJong. I notice your stuff's bunched kind of extry, and all of a size. Fixin' to do that way right along?"

"Yes. I thought—they looked prettier that way—of course vegetables aren't supposed to look pretty, I expect——" she stammered, stopped.

"You fix 'em pretty like that and bring 'em in to me first thing, or send 'em. My trade, they like their stuff kind of special. Yessir."

As she gathered up the reins he stood again in his doorway, cool, remote, his unlighted cigar in his mouth, while hand-trucks rattled past him, barrels and boxes thumped to the sidewalk in front of him, wheels and hoofs and shouts made a great clamour all about him.

"We going home now?" demanded Dirk. "We going home now? I'm hungry."

"Yes, lamb." Two dollars in her pocket. All yesterday's grim toil, and all to-day's, and months of labour behind those two days. Two dollars in the pocket of her black calico petticoat. "We'll get something to eat when we drive out a ways. Some milk and bread and cheese."

The sun was very hot. She took the boy's hat off, passed her tender work-calloused hand over the damp hair that clung to his forehead. "It's been fun, hasn't it?" she said. "Like an adventure. Look at all the kind people we've met. Mr. Spanknoebel, and Mr. Talcott——"

"And Mabel."

Startled, "And Mabel."

She wanted suddenly to kiss him, knew he would hate it with all the boy and all the Holland Dutch in him, and did not.

She made up her mind to drive east and then south. Pervus had sometimes achieved a late sale to outlying grocers. Jan's face if she came home with half the load still on the wagon! And what of the unpaid bills? She had, perhaps, thirty dollars, all told. She owed four hundred. More than that. There were seedlings that Pervus had bought in April to be paid for at the end of the growing season, in the fall. And now fall was here.

Fear shook her. She told herself she was tired, nervous. That terrible week. And now this. The heat. Soon they'd be home, she and Dirk. How cool and quiet the house would seem. The squares of the kitchen tablecloth. Her own neat bedroom with the black walnut bed and dresser. The sofa in the parlour with the ruffled calico cover. The old chair on the porch with the cane seat sagging where warp and woof had become loosened with much use and stuck out in ragged tufts. It seemed years since she had seen all this. The comfort of it, the peace of it. Safe, desirable, suddenly dear. No work for a woman, this. Well, perhaps they were right.

Down Wabash Avenue, with the L trains thundering overhead and her horses, frightened and uneasy with the unaccustomed roar and clang-our of traffic, stepping high and swerving stiffly, grotesque and angular in their movements. A dowdy farm woman and a sunburned boy in a rickety vegetable wagon absurdly out of place in this canyon of cobble-stones, shops, street-cars, drays, carriages, bicycles, pedestrians. It was terribly hot.

The boy's eyes popped with excitement and bewilderment.

"Pretty soon," Selina said. The muscles showed white beneath the skin of her jaw. "Pretty soon. Prairie Avenue. Great big houses, and lawns, all quiet." She even managed a smile.

"I like it better home."

Prairie Avenue at last, turning in at Sixteenth Street. It was like calm after a storm. Selina felt battered, spent.

There were groceries near Eighteenth, and at the other cross-streets—Twenty-second, Twenty-sixth, Thirty-first, Thirty-fifth. They were passing the great stone houses of Prairie Avenue of the '90s. Turrets and towers, cornices and cupolas, hump-backed conservatories, porte-cochères, bow windows—here lived Chicago's rich that had made their riches in pork and wheat and dry goods; the selling of necessities to a city that clamoured for them.

"Just like me," Selina thought, humorously. Then another thought came to her. Her vegetables, canvas covered, were fresher than those in the near-by markets. Why not try to sell some of them here, in these big houses? In an hour she might earn a few dollars this way at retail prices slightly less than those asked by the grocers of the neighbourhood.

She stopped her wagon in the middle of the block on Twenty-fourth Street. Agilely she stepped down the wheel, gave the reins to Dirk. The horses were no more minded to run than the wooden steeds on a carrousel. She filled a large market basket with the finest and freshest of her stock and with this on her arm looked up a moment at the house in front of which she had stopped. It was a four-story brownstone, with a hideous high stoop. Beneath the steps were a little vestibule and a door that was the tradesmen's entrance. The kitchen entrance, she knew, was by way of the alley at the back, but this she would not take. Across the sidewalk, down a little flight of stone steps, into the vestibule under the porch. She looked at the bell—a brass knob. You pulled it out, shoved it in, and there sounded a jangling down the dim hallway beyond. Simple enough. Her hand was on the bell. "Pull it!" said the desperate Selina. "I can't! I can't!" cried all the prim dim Vermont Peakes, in chorus. "All right. Starve to death and let them take the farm and Dirk, then."

At that she pulled the knob hard. Jangle went the bell in the hall. Again. Again.

Footsteps up the hall. The door opened to disclose a large woman, high cheek-boned, in a work apron; a cook, apparently.

"Good morning," said Selina. "Would you like some fresh country vegetables?"

"No." She half shut the door, opening it again to ask, "Got any fresh eggs or butter?" At Selina's negative she closed the door, bolted it. Selina, standing there, basket on arm, could hear her heavy tread down the passageway toward the kitchen. Well, that was all right. Nothing so terrible about that, Selina told herself. Simply hadn't wanted any vegetables. The next house. The next house, and the next, and the next. Up one side of the street, and down the other. Four times she refilled her basket. At one house she sold a quarter's worth. Fifteen at another. Twenty cents here. Almost fifty there. "Good morning," she always said at the door in her clear, distinct way. They stared, usually. But they were curious, too, and did not often shut the door in her face.

"Do you know of a good place?" one kitchen maid said. "This place ain't so good. She only pays me three dollars. You can get four now. Maybe you know a lady wants a good girl."

"No," Selina answered. "No."

At another house the cook had offered her a cup of coffee, noting the white face, the look of weariness. Selina refused it, politely. Twenty-first Street—Twenty-fifth—Twenty-eighth. She had over four dollars in her purse. Dirk was weary now and hungry to the point of tears. "The last house," Selina promised him, "the very last one. After this one we'll go home." She filled her basket again. "We'll have something to eat on the way, and maybe you'll go to sleep with the canvas over you, high, fastened to the seat like a tent. And we'll be home in a jiffy."

The last house was a new gray stone one, already beginning to turn dingy from the smoke of the Illinois Central suburban trains that puffed along the lake front a block to the east. The house had large bow windows, plump and shining. There was a lawn, with statues, and a conservatory in the rear. Real lace curtains at the downstairs windows with plush hangings behind them. A high iron grille ran all about the property giving it an air of aloofness, of security. Selina glanced at this wrought-iron fence. And it seemed to bar her out. There was something forbidding about it—menacing. She was tired, that was it. The last house. She had almost five dollars, earned in the last hour. "Just five minutes," she said to Dirk, trying to make her tone bright, her voice gay. Her arms full of vegetables which she was about to place in the basket at her feet she heard at her elbow:

"Now, then, where's your license?"

She turned. A policeman at her side. She stared up at him. How enormously tall, she thought; and how red his face. "License?"

"Yeh, you heard me. License. Where's your pedler's license? You got one, I s'pose."

"Why, no. No." She stared at him, still.

His face grew redder. Selina was a little worried about him. She thought, stupidly, that if it grew any redder——

"Well, say, where d'ye think you are, peddlin' without a license! A good mind to run you in. Get along out of here, you and the kid. Leave me ketch you around here again!"

"What's the trouble, Officer?" said a woman's voice. A smart open carriage of the type known as a victoria, with two chestnut horses whose harness shone with metal. Spanking, was the word that came to Selina's mind, which was acting perversely certainly; crazily. A spanking team. The spankers disdainfully faced Selina's comic bony nags which were grazing the close-cropped grass that grew in the neat little lawn-squares between curb and sidewalk. "What's the trouble, Reilly?"

The woman stepped out of the victoria. She wore a black silk Eton suit, very modish, and a black hat with a plume.

"Woman peddling without a license, Mrs. Arnold. You got to watch 'em like a hawk. . . . Get along wid you, then." He put a hand on Selina's shoulder and gave her a gentle push.

There shook Selina from head to foot such a passion, such a storm of outraged sensibilities, as to cause street, victoria, silk-clad woman, horses, and policeman to swim and shiver in a haze before her eyes. The rage of a fastidious woman who had had an alien male hand put upon her. Her face was white. Her eyes glowed black, enormous. She seemed tall, majestic even.

"Take your hand off me!" Her speech was clipped, vibrant. "How dare you touch me! How dare you! Take your hand!——" The blazing eyes in the white mask. He took his hand from her shoulder. The red surged into her face. A tanned weather-beaten toil-worn woman, her abundant hair skewered into a knob and held by a long gray-black hairpin, her full skirt grimed with the mud of the wagon wheel, a pair of old side-boots on her slim feet, a grotesquely battered old felt hat (her husband's) on her head, her arms full of ears of sweet corn, and carrots, and radishes and bunches of beets; a woman with bad teeth, flat breasts —even then Julie had known her by her eyes. And she had stared and then run to her in her silk dress and her plumed hat, crying, "Oh, Selina! My dear! My dear!" with a sob of horror and pity. "My dear!" And had taken Selina, carrots, beets, corn, and radishes in her arms. The vegetables lay scattered all about them on the sidewalk in front of Julie Hempel Arnold's great stone house on Prairie Avenue. But strangely enough it had been Selina who had done the comforting, patting Julie's plump silken shoulder and saying, over and over, soothingly, as to a child, "There, there! It's all right, Julie. It's all right. Don't cry. What's there to cry for! Sh-sh! It's all right."

Julie lifted her head in its modish black plumed hat, wiped her eyes, blew her nose. "Get along with you, do," she said to Reilly, the policeman, using his very words to Selina. "I'm going to report you to Mr. Arnold, see if I don't. And you know what that means."

"Well, now, Mrs. Arnold, ma'am, I was only doing my duty. How

cud I know the lady was a friend of yours. Sure, I——" He surveyed
Selina, cart, jaded horses, wilted vegetables. "Well, how *cud* I, now, Mrs.
Arnold, ma'am!"

"And why not!" demanded Julie with superb unreasonableness.
"Why not, I'd like to know. Do get along with you."

He got along, a defeated officer of the law, and a bitter. And now it
was Julie who surveyed Selina, cart, Dirk, jaded horses, wilted left-
over vegetables. "Selina, whatever in the world! What are you doing
with——" She caught sight of Selina's absurd boots then and she began
to cry again. At that Selina's overwrought nerves snapped and she began
to laugh, hysterically. It frightened Julie, that laughter. "Selina, don't!
Come in the house with me. What are you laughing at! Selina!"

With shaking finger Selina was pointing at the vegetables that lay
tumbled at her feet. "Do you see that cabbage, Julie? Do you remember
how I used to despise Mrs. Tebbitt's because she used to have boiled
cabbage on Monday nights?"

"That's nothing to laugh at, is it? Stop laughing this minute, Selina
Peake!"

"I'll stop. I've stopped now. I was just laughing at my ignorance.
Sweat and blood and health and youth go into every cabbage. Did you
know that, Julie? One doesn't despise them as food, knowing that.
. . . Come, climb down, Dirk. Here's a lady mother used to know—oh,
years and years ago, when she was a girl. Thousands of years ago."

XII

THE best thing for Dirk. The best thing for Dirk. It was the phrase
that repeated itself over and over in Selina's speech during the days that
followed. Julie Arnold was all for taking him into her gray stone house,
dressing him like Lord Fauntleroy and sending him to the north-side
private school attended by Eugene, her boy, and Pauline, her girl. In
this period of bewilderment and fatigue Julie had attempted to take
charge of Selina much as she had done a dozen years before at the
time of Simeon Peake's dramatic death. And now, as then, she pressed
into service her wonder-working father and bounden slave, August
Hempel. Her husband she dismissed with affectionate disregard.

"Michael's all right," she had said on that day of their first meeting, "if you tell him what's to be done. He'll always do it. But Pa's the one that thinks of things. He's like a general, and Michael's the captain. Well, now, Pa'll be out to-morrow and I'll probably come with him. I've got a committee meeting, but I can easily——"

"You said—did you say your father would be out to-morrow! Out where?"

"To your place. Farm."

"But why should he? It's a little twenty-five-acre truck farm, and half of it under water a good deal of the time."

"Pa'll find a use for it, never fear. He won't say much, but he'll think of things. And then everything will be all right."

"It's miles. Miles. Way out in High Prairie."

"Well, if you could make it with those horses, Selina, I guess we can with Pa's two grays that hold a record for a mile in three minutes or three miles in a minute, I forget which. Or in the auto, though Pa hates it. Michael is the only one in the family who likes it."

A species of ugly pride now possessed Selina. "I don't need help. Really I don't, Julie dear. It's never been like to-day. Never before. We were getting on very well, Pervus and I. Then after Pervus's death so suddenly like that I was frightened. Terribly frightened. About Dirk. I wanted him to have everything. Beautiful things. I wanted his life to be beautiful. Life can be so ugly, Julie. You don't know. You don't know."

"Well, now, that's why I say. We'll be out to-morrow, Pa and I. Dirk's going to have everything beautiful. We'll see to that."

It was then that Selina had said, "But that's just it. I want to do it myself, for him. I can. I want to give him all these things myself."

"But that's selfish."

"I don't mean to be. I just want to do the best thing for Dirk."

It was shortly after noon that High Prairie, hearing the unaccustomed chug of a motor, rushed to its windows or porches to behold Selina DeJong in her mashed black felt hat and Dirk waving his battered straw wildly, riding up the Halsted road toward the DeJong farm in a bright red automobile that had shattered the nerves of every farmer's team it had met on the way. Of the DeJong team and the DeJong dog Pom, and the DeJong vegetable wagon there was absolutely no sign. High Prairie was rendered unfit for work throughout the next twenty-four hours.

The idea had been Julie's, and Selina had submitted rather than acquiesced, for by now she was too tired to combat anything or any one. If Julie had proposed her entering High Prairie on the back of an elephant with a mahout perched between his ears Selina would have agreed—rather, would have been unable to object.

"It'll get you home in no time," Julie had said, energetically. "You look like a ghost and the boy's half asleep. I'll telephone Pa and he'll have one of the men from the barns drive your team out so it'll be there by six. Just you leave it all to me. Haven't you ever ridden in one! Why, there's nothing to be scared of. I like the horses best, myself. I'm like Pa. He says if you use horses you get there."

Dirk had accepted the new conveyance with the adaptability of childhood, had even predicted, grandly, "I'm going to have one when I grow up that'll go faster 'n this, even."

"Oh, you wouldn't want to go faster than this, Dirk," Selina had protested breathlessly as they chugged along at the alarming rate of almost fifteen miles an hour.

Jan Snip had been rendered speechless. Until the actual arrival of the team and wagon at six he counted them as mysteriously lost and DeJong's widow clearly gone mad. August Hempel's arrival next day with Julie seated beside him in the light spider-phaeton drawn by two slim wild-eyed quivering grays made little tumult in Jan's stunned mind by now incapable of absorbing any fresh surprises.

In the twelve years' transition from butcher to packer Aug Hempel had taken on a certain authority and distinction. Now, at fifty-five, his hair was gray, relieving the too-ruddy colour of his face. He talked almost without an accent; used the idiomatic American speech he heard about the yards, where the Hempel packing plant was situated. Only his d's were likely to sound like t's. The letter j had a slightly ch sound. In the last few years he had grown very deaf in one ear, so that when you spoke to him he looked at you intently. This had given him a reputation for keenness and great character insight, when it was merely the protective trick of a man who does not want to confess that he is hard of hearing. He wore square-toed shoes with soft tips and square-cut gray clothes and a large gray hat with a chronically inadequate sweatband. The square-cut boots were expensive, and the square-cut gray clothes and the large gray hat, but in them he always gave the effect of being dressed in the discarded garments of a much larger man.

Selina's domain he surveyed with a keen and comprehensive eye.

"You want to sell?"

"No."

"That's good." (It was nearly goot as he said it.) "Few years from now this land will be worth money." He had spent a bare fifteen minutes taking shrewd valuation of the property from fields to barn, from barn to house. "Well, what *do* you want to do, heh, Selina?"

They were seated in the cool and unexpectedly pleasing little parlour, with its old Dutch lustre set gleaming softly in the cabinet, its three rows of books, its air of comfort and usage.

Dirk was in the yard with one of the Van Ruys boys, surveying the grays proprietorially. Jan was rooting in the fields. Selina clasped her hands tightly in her lap—those hands that, from much grubbing in the soil, had taken on something of the look of the gnarled things they tended. The nails were short, discoloured, broken. The palms rough, calloused. The whole story of the last twelve years of Selina's life was written in her two hands.

"I want to stay here, and work the farm, and make it pay. I can. By next spring my asparagus is going to begin to bring in money. I'm not going to grow just the common garden stuff any more—not much, anyway. I'm going to specialize in the fine things—the kind the South Water Street commission men want. I want to drain the low land. Tile it. That land hasn't been used for years. It ought to be rich growing land by now, if once it's properly drained. And I want Dirk to go to school. Good schools. I never want my son to go to the Haymarket. Never. Never."

Julie stirred with a little rustle and click of silk and beads. Her gentle amiability was vaguely alarmed by the iron quality of determination in the other's tone.

"Yes, but what about you, Selina?"

"Me?"

"Yes, of course. You talk as though you didn't count. Your life. Things to make you happy."

"My life doesn't count, except as something for Dirk to use. I'm done with anything else. Oh, I don't mean that I'm discouraged, or disappointed in life, or anything like that. I mean I started out with the wrong idea. I know better now. I'm here to keep Dirk from making the mistakes I made."

Here Aug Hempel, lounging largely in his chair and eyeing Selina intently, turned his gaze absently through the window to where the grays, a living equine statue, stood before the house. His tone was one of meditation, not of argument. "It don't work out that way, seems. About mistakes it's funny. You got to make your own; and not only that, if you try to keep people from making theirs they get mad." He whistled softly through his teeth following this utterance and tapped the chair seat with his fingernails.

"It's beauty!" Selina said then, almost passionately. Aug Hempel and Julie plainly could make nothing of this remark so she went on, eager, explanatory. "I used to think that if you wanted beauty—if you wanted it hard enough and hopefully enough—it came to you. You just waited, and lived your life as best you could, knowing that beauty might be just around the corner. You just waited, and then it came."

"Beauty!" exclaimed Julie, weakly. She stared at Selina in the evident belief that this work-worn haggard woman was bemoaning her lack of personal pulchritude.

"Yes. All the worth-while things in life. All mixed up. Rooms in candle-light. Leisure. Colour. Travel. Books. Music. Pictures. People— all kinds of people. Work that you love. And growth—growth and watching people grow. Feeling very strongly about things and then developing that feeling to—to make something fine come of it." The word self-expression was not in cant use then, and Selina hadn't it to offer them. They would not have known what she meant if she had. She threw out her hands now in a futile gesture. "That's what I mean by beauty. I want Dirk to have it."

Julie blinked and nodded with the wise amiable look of comprehension assumed by one who has understood no single word of what has been said. August Hempel cleared his throat.

"I guess I know what you're driving at, Selina, maybe. About Julie I felt just like that. She should have everything fine. I wanted her to have everything. And she did, too. Cried for the moon she had it."

"I never did have it Pa, any such thing!"

"Never cried for it, I know of."

"For pity's sake!" pleaded Julie, the literal, "let's stop talking and do something. My goodness, anybody with a little money can have books and candles and travel around and look at pictures, if that's all. So let's *do* something. Pa, you've probably got it all fixed in your mind long ago. It's time we heard it. Here Selina was one of the most popular girls in Miss Fister's school, and lots of people thought the prettiest. And now just look at her!"

A flicker of the old flame leaped up in Selina. "Flatterer!" she murmured.

Aug Hempel stood up. "If you think giving your whole life to making the boy happy is going to make him happy you ain't so smart as I took you for. You go trying to live somebody else's life for them."

"I'm not going to live his life for him. I want to show him how to live it so that he'll get full value out of it."

"Keeping him out of the Haymarket if the Haymarket's the natural place for him to be won't do that. How can you tell! Monkeying with what's to be. I'm out at the yards every day, in and out of the cattle pens, talking to the drovers and herders, mixing in with the buyers. I can tell the weight of a hog and what he's worth just by a look at him, and a steer, too. My son-in-law Michael Arnold sits up in the office all day in our plant, dictating letters. His clothes they never stink of the pens like mine do. . . . Now I ain't saying anything against him, Julie. But I bet my grandson Eugene"—he repeated it, stressing the name so that you sensed his dislike of it—"Eugene, if he comes into the business at all when he grows up, won't go within smelling distance of the yards. His office I bet will be in a new office building on, say Madison Street, with a view of the lake. Life! You'll be hoggin' it all yourself and not know it."

"Don't pay any attention to him," Julie interposed. "He goes on like that. Old yards!"

August Hempel bit off the end of a cigar, was about to spit out the speck explosively, thought better of it and tucked it in his vest pocket. "I wouldn't change places with Mike, not——"

"Please don't call him Mike, Pa."

"Michael, then. Not for ten million. And I need ten million right now."

"And I suppose," retorted Selina, spiritedly, "that when your son-in-law Michael Arnold is your age he'll be telling Eugene how he roughed it in an office over at the yards in the old days. These will be the old days."

August Hempel laughed good-humouredly. "That can be, Selina. That can be." He chewed his cigar and settled to the business at hand. "You want to drain and tile. Plant high-grade stuff. You got to have a man on the place that knows what's what, not this Rip Van Winkle we saw in the cabbage field. New horses. A wagon." His eyes narrowed speculatively. Shrewd wrinkles radiated from their corners. "I betcha we'll see the day when you truck farmers will run into town with your stuff in big automobile wagons that will get you there in under an hour. It's bound to come. The horse is doomed, that's chust what." Then, abruptly, "I will get you the horses, a bargain, at the yards." He took out a long flat check book. He began writing in it with a pen that he took from his pocket—some sort of marvellous pen that seemed already filled with ink and that you unscrewed at the top and then screwed at the bottom. He squinted through his cigar smoke, the check book propped on his knee. He tore off the check with a clean rip. "For a starter," he said. He held it out to Selina.

"There now!" exclaimed Julie, in triumphant satisfaction. That was more like it. Doing something.

But Selina did not take the check. She sat very still in her chair, her hands folded. "That isn't the regular way," she said.

August Hempel was screwing the top on his fountain pen again. "Regular way? for what?"

"I'm borrowing this money, not taking it. Oh, yes, I am! I couldn't get along without it. I realize that now, after yesterday. Yesterday! But in five years—seven—I'll pay it back." Then, at a half-uttered protest from Julie, "That's the only way I'll take it. It's for Dirk. But I'm going to earn it—and pay it back. I want a——" she was being enormously businesslike, and unconsciously enjoying it—— "a—an I. O. U. A promise to pay you back just as—as soon as I can. That's business, isn't it? And I'll sign it."

"Sure," said Aug Hempel, and unscrewed his fountain pen again. "Sure that's business." Very serious, he scribbled again, busily, on a piece of paper. A year later, when Selina had learned many things, among them that simple and compound interest on money loaned are not mere problems devised to fill Duffy's Arithmetic in her school-teaching days, she went to August Hempel between laughter and tears.

"You didn't say one word about interest, that day. Not a word. What a little fool you must have thought me."

"Between friends," protested August Hempel.

But—"No," Selina insisted. "Interest."

"I guess I better start me a bank pretty soon if you keep on so businesslike."

Ten years later he was actually the controlling power in the Yards & Rangers' Bank. And Selina had that original I. O. U. with its "Paid In Full. Aug Hempel," carefully tucked away in the carved oak chest together with other keepsakes that she foolishly treasured—ridiculous scraps that no one but she would have understood or valued—a small school slate such as little children use (the one on which she had taught Pervus to figure and parse); a dried bunch of trilliums; a bustled and panniered wine-red cashmere dress, absurdly old-fashioned; a letter telling about the Infanta Eulalie of Spain, and signed Julie Hempel Arnold; a pair of men's old side-boots with mud caked on them; a crude sketch, almost obliterated now, done on a torn scrap of brown paper and showing the Haymarket with the wagons vegetable-laden and the men gathered beneath the street-flares, and the patient farm horses—Roelf's childish sketch.

Among this rubbish she rummaged periodically in the years that followed. Indeed, twenty years later Dirk, coming upon her smoothing out the wrinkled yellow creases of the I. O. U. or shaking the camphor-laden folds of the wine-red cashmere, would say, "At it again! What a sentimental generation yours was, Mother. Pressed flowers! They went out

with the attic, didn't they? If the house caught fire you'd probably run
for the junk in that chest. It isn't worth two cents, the lot of it."

"Perhaps not," Selina said, slowly. "Still, there'd be some money value,
I suppose, in an early original signed sketch by Rodin."

"Rodin! You haven't got a——"

"No, but here's one by Pool—Roelf Pool—signed. At a sale in New
York last week one of his sketches—not a finished thing at all—just a
rough drawing that he'd made of some figures in a group that went into
the Doughboy statue—brought one thous——"

"Oh, well, that—yes. But the rest of the stuff you've got there—funny
how people will treasure old stuff like that. Useless stuff. It isn't even
beautiful."

"Beautiful!" said Selina, and shut the lid of the old chest. "Why, Dirk
—Dirk! You don't even know what beauty is. You never will know."

XIII

IF THOSE vague characteristics called (variously) magnetism, manner,
grace, distinction, attractiveness, fascination, go to make up that nebu-
lous quality known as charm; and if the possessor of that quality is accounted fortunate in his equipment for that which the class-day orators
style the battle of life, then Dirk DeJong was a lucky lad and life lay
promisingly before him. Undoubtedly he had it; and undoubtedly it
did. People said that things "came easy" for Dirk. He said so himself,
not boastfully, but rather shyly. He was not one to talk a great deal.
Perhaps that was one of his most charming qualities. He listened so
well. And he was so quietly effortless. He listened while other people
talked, his fine head inclined just a little to one side and bent toward
you. Intent on what you were saying, and evidently impressed by it. You
felt him immensely intelligent, appreciative. It was a gift more valuable
than any other social talent he might have possessed. He himself did not
know how precious an attribute this was to prove in a later day when to
be allowed to finish a sentence was an experience all too rare. Older
men especially said he was a smart young feller and would make his
mark. This, surprisingly enough, after a conversation to which he had

contributed not a word other than "Yes," or "No," or, "Perhaps you're right, sir," in the proper places.

Selina thought constantly of Dirk's future. A thousand other thoughts might be racing through her mind during the day—plans for the farm, for the house—but always, over and above and through all these, like the steady beat of a drum penetrating sharper and more urgent sounds —was the thought of Dirk. He did well enough at high school. Not a brilliant student, nor even a very good one. But good enough. Average. And well liked.

It was during those careless years of Dirk's boyhood between nine and fifteen that Selina changed the DeJong acres from a worn-out and down-at-heel truck farm whose scant products brought a second-rate price in a second-rate market to a prosperous and blooming vegetable garden whose output was sought a year in advance by the South Water Street commission merchants. DeJong asparagus with firm white thick stalk bases tapering to a rich green streaked with lavender at the tips. DeJong hothouse tomatoes in February, plump, scarlet, juicy. You paid for a pound a sum Pervus had been glad to get for a bushel.

These six or seven years of relentless labour had been no showy success with Selina posing grandly as the New Woman in Business. No, it had been a painful, grubbing, heart-breaking process as is any project that depends on the actual soil for its realization. She drove herself pitilessly. She literally tore a living out of the earth with her two bare hands. Yet there was nothing pitiable about this small energetic woman of thirty-five or forty with her fine soft dark eyes, her clean-cut jaw-line, her shabby decent clothes that were so likely to be spattered with the mud of the road or fields, her exquisite nose with the funny little wrinkle across the bridge when she laughed. Rather, there was something splendid about her; something rich, prophetic. It was the splendour and richness that achievement imparts.

It is doubtful that she ever could have succeeded without the money borrowed from August Hempel; without his shrewd counsel. She told him this, sometimes. He denied it. "Easier, yes. But you would have found a way, Selina. Some way. Julie, no. But you, yes. You are like that. Me, too. Say, plenty fellers that was butchers with me twenty years ago over on North Clark Street are butchers yet, cutting off a steak or a chop. 'Good morning, Mrs. Kruger. What'll it be to-day?'"

The Hempel Packing Company was a vast monster now stretching great arms into Europe, into South America. In some of the yellow journals that had cropped up in the last few years you even saw old Aug himself portrayed in cartoons as an octopus with cold slimy eyes and a hundred writhing reaching tentacles. These bothered Aug a little, though he pretended to laugh at them. "What do they want to go to work and make me out like that for? I sell good meat for all I can get for it. That's business, ain't it?"

Dirk had his tasks on the farm. Selina saw to that. But they were not heavy. He left for school at eight in the morning, driving, for the distance was too great for walking. Often it was dark on his return in the late afternoon. Between these hours Selina had accomplished the work of two men. She had two field-helpers on the place now during the busy season and a woman in the house, the wife of Adam Bras, one of the labourers. Jan Snip, too, still worked about the place in the barn, the sheds, tending the coldframes and hothouses, doing odd jobs of carpentering. He distrusted Selina's new-fangled methods, glowered at any modern piece of machinery, predicted dire things when Selina bought the twenty acres that comprised the old Bouts place adjoining the De-Jong farm.

"You bit off more as you can chaw," he told her. "You choke yet. You see."

By the time Dirk returned from school the rough work of the day was over. His food was always hot, appetizing, plentiful. The house was neat, comfortable. Selina had installed a bathroom—one of the two bathrooms in High Prairie. The neighbourhood was still rocking with the shock of this when it was informed by Jan that Selina and Dirk ate with candles lighted on the supper table. High Prairie slapped its thigh and howled with mirth.

"Cabbages is beautiful," said old Klaas Pool when he heard this. "Cabbages is beautiful I betcha."

Selina, during the years of the boy's adolescence, had never urged him to a decision about his future. That, she decided, would come. As the farm prospered and the pressure of necessity lifted she tried, in various ingenious ways, to extract from him some unconscious sign of definite preference for this calling, that profession. As in her leanest days she had bought an occasional book at the cost of much-needed shoes for herself so now she bought many of them with money that another woman would have used for luxury or adornments. Years of personal privation had not killed her love of fine soft silken things, mellow colouring, exquisite workmanship. But they had made it impossible for her to covet these things for herself. She loved to see them, to feel them. Could not wear them. Years later, when she could well afford a French hat in one of the Michigan Avenue millinery shops, she would look at the silk and satin trifles blooming in the windows like gay brilliant flowers in a conservatory—and would buy an untrimmed "shape" for $2.95 in Field's basement. The habit of a lifetime is strong. Just once she

made herself buy one of these costly silk-and-feather extravagances, going
about the purchase deliberately and coldly as a man gets drunk once for
the experience. The hat had cost twenty-two dollars. She never had
worn it.

Until Dirk was sixteen she had been content to let him develop as
naturally as possible, and to absorb impressions unconsciously from the
traps she so guilefully left about him. Books on the lives of great men—
lives of Lincoln, of Washington, Gladstone, Disraeli, Voltaire. History.
Books on painting, charmingly illustrated. Books on architecture; law;
medicine, even. She subscribed to two of the best engineering magazines. There was a shed which he was free to use as a workshop, fitted
up with all sorts of tools. He did not use it much, after the first few
weeks. He was pleasantly and mildly interested in all these things; held
by none of them. Selina had thought of Roelf when they were fitting
up the workshop. The Pools had heard from Roelf just once since his
flight from the farm. A letter had come from France. In it was a sum of
money for Geertje and Jozina—a small sum to take the trouble to send
all the way from an outlandish country, the well-to-do Pool household
thought. Geertje was married now to Vander Sijde's son Gerrit and
living on a farm out Low Prairie way. Jozina had a crazy idea that she
wanted to go into the city as a nurse. Roelf's small gift of money made
little difference in their day. They never knew the struggle that the
impecunious young Paris art student had had to save it sou by sou. Selina had never heard from him. But one day years later she had come
running to Dirk with an illustrated magazine in her hand.

"Look!" she had cried, and pointed to a picture. He had rarely seen
her so excited, so stirred. The illustration showed a photographic repro-
duction of a piece of sculpture—a woman's figure. It was called The
Seine. A figure sinuous, snake-like, graceful, revolting, beautiful, terrible.
The face alluring, insatiable, generous, treacherous, all at once. It was
the Seine that fed the fertile valley land; the Seine that claimed a thousand bloated lifeless floating Things; the red-eyed hag of 1793; the dimpling coquette of 1650. Beneath the illustration a line or two—Roelf
Pool . . . Salon . . . American . . . future . . .

"It's Roelf!" Selina had cried. "Roelf. Little Roelf Pool!" Tears in her
eyes. Dirk had been politely interested. But then he had never known
him, really. He had heard his mother speak of him, but——

Selina showed the picture to the Pools, driving over there one evening
to surprise them with it. Mrs. Klaas Pool had been horrified at the picture of a nude woman's figure; had cried "Og heden!" in disgust, and
had seemed to think that Selina had brought it over in a spirit of spite.
Was she going to show it to the rest of High Prairie!

Selina understood High Prairie folk better now, though not altogether, even after almost twenty years of living amongst them. A cold people, yet kindly. Suspicious, yet generous. Distrustful of all change, yet progressing by sheer force of thrift and unceasing labour. Unimaginative for generations, only to produce—a Roelf Pool.

She tried now to explain the meaning of the figure Roelf had moulded so masterfully. "You see, it's supposed to represent the Seine. The River Seine that flows through Paris into the countryside beyond. The whole history of Paris—of France—is bound up in the Seine; intertwined with it. Terrible things, and magnificent things. It flows just beneath the Louvre. You can see it from the Bastille. On its largest island stands Notre Dame. The Seine has seen such things, Mrs. Pool!——"

"What *dom* talk!" interrupted the late widow. "A river can't see. Anybody knows that."

At seventeen Dirk and Selina talked of the year to come. He was going to a university. But to what university? And what did he want to study? We-e-ll, hard to say. Kind of a general course, wasn't there? Some languages—little French or something—and political economy, and some literature and maybe history.

"Oh," Selina had said. "Yes. General. Of course, if a person wanted to be an architect, why, I suppose Cornell would be the place. Or Harvard for law. Or Boston Tech for engineering, or——"

Oh, yeh, if a fellow wanted any of those things. Good idea, though, to take a kind of general course until you found out exactly what you wanted to do. Languages and literature and that kind of thing.

Selina was rather delighted than otherwise. That, she knew, was the way they did it in England. You sent your son to a university not to cram some technical course into him, or to railroad him through a book-knowledge of some profession. You sent him so that he might develop in an atmosphere of books, of learning; spending relaxed hours in the companionship of men who taught for the love of teaching; whose informal talks before a study fire were more richly valuable than whole courses of classroom lectures. She had read of these things in English novels. Oxford. Cambridge. Dons. Ivy. Punting. Prints. Mullioned windows. Books. Discussion. Literary clubs.

This was England. An older civilization, of course. But there must be something of that in American universities. And if that was what Dirk wanted she was glad. Glad! A reaching after true beauty.

You heard such wonderful things about Midwest University, in Chicago. On the south side. It was new, yes. But those Gothic buildings gave an effect, somehow, of age and permanence (the smoke and cinders from the Illinois Central suburban trains were largely responsible for that, as well as the soft coal from a thousand neighbouring chimneys). And there actually was ivy. Undeniable ivy, and mullioned windows.

Dirk had suggested it, not she. The entrance requirements were quite mild. Harvard? Yale? Oh, those fellows all had wads of money. Eugene Arnold had his own car at New Haven.

In that case, they decided, Midwest University, in Chicago, on the south side near the lake, would do splendidly. For a general course, sort of. The world lay ahead of Dirk. It was like the childhood game of counting buttons.

> Rich man, poor man, beggar-man, thief.
> Doctor, lawyer, merchant, chief.

Together they counted Dirk's mental buttons but it never came out twice the same. It depended on the suit you happened to be wearing, of course. Eugene Arnold was going to take law at Yale. He said it would be necessary if he was going into the business. He didn't put it just that way, when talking to Dirk. He said the damned old hog business. Pauline (she insisted that they call her Paula now) was at a girls' school up the Hudson—one of those schools that never advertise even in the front of the thirty-five-cent magazines.

So, at eighteen, it had been Midwest University for Dirk. It was a much more economical plan than would have resulted from the choice of an eastern college. High Prairie heard that Dirk DeJong was going away to college. A neighbour's son said, "Going to Wisconsin? Agricultural course there?"

"My gosh, no!" Dirk had answered. He told this to Selina, laughing. But she had not laughed.

"I'd like to take that course myself, if you must know. They say it's wonderful." She looked at him, suddenly. "Dirk, you wouldn't like to take it, would you? To go to Madison, I mean. Is that what you'd like?"

He stared. "Me! No! . . . Unless you want me to, Mother. Then I would, gladly. I hate your working like this, on the farm, while I go off to school. It makes me feel kind of rotten, having my mother working for me. The other fellows——"

"I'm doing the work I'm interested in, for the person I love best in the world. I'd be lost—unhappy—without the farm. If the city creeps up on me here, as they predict it will, I don't know what I shall do."

But Dirk had a prediction of his own to make. "Chicago'll never grow this way, with all those steel mills and hunkies to the south of us. The north side is going to be the place to live. It is already."

"The place for whom?"

"For the people with money."

She smiled then so that you saw the funny little wrinkle across her nose. "Well, then the south section of Chicago is going to be all right for us yet a while."

"Just you wait till I'm successful. Then there'll be no more working for you."

"What do you mean by 'successful', Sobig?" She had not called him that in years. But now the old nickname came to her tongue perhaps because they were speaking of his future, his success. "What do you mean by 'successful', Sobig?"

"Rich. Lots of money."

"Oh, no, Dirk! No! That's not success. Roelf—the thing Roelf does —that's success."

"Oh, well, if you have money enough you can buy the things he makes, and have 'em. That's almost as good, isn't it?"

Midwest University had sprung up almost literally overnight on the property that had been the site of the Midway Plaisance during the World's Fair in Chicago in '93. One man's millions had been the magic wand that, waved over a bare stretch of prairie land, had produced a seat of learning. The university guide book spoke of him reverently as the Founder, capitalizing the word as one does the Diety. The student body spoke of him with somewhat less veneration. They called him Coal-Oil Johnny. He had already given thirty millions to the university and still the insatiable maw of this institute of learning yawned for more. When oil went up a fraction of a cent they said, "Guess Coal-Oil Johnny's fixing to feed us another million."

Dirk commenced his studies at Midwest University in the autumn of 1909. His first year was none too agreeable, as is usually the case in first years. He got on well, though. A large proportion of the men students were taking law, which accounts for the great number of real-estate salesmen and insurance agents now doing business in and about Chicago. Before the end of the first semester he was popular. He was a natural-born floor committeeman and badges bloomed in his buttonhole. Merely by donning a ready-made dress suit he could give it a made-to-order air. He had great natural charm of manner. The men liked him, and the girls, too. He learned to say, "Got Pol Econ at ten," which meant that he took Political Economy at that hour; and "I'd like to cut Psyk," meant that he was not up on his approaching lesson in Applied Psychology. He rarely "cut" a class. He would have felt that this was unfair and disloyal to his mother. Some of his fellow students joked about this faithfulness to his classes. "Person would think you were an Unclassified," they said.

The Unclassifieds were made up, for the most part, of earnest and rather middle-aged students whose education was a delayed blooming. They usually were not enrolled for a full course, or were taking double work feverishly. The Classifieds, on the other hand, were the regularly enrolled students, pretty well of an age (between seventeen and twenty-three) who took their education with a sprinkling of sugar. Of the Unclassified students the University catalogue said:

> Persons at least twenty-one years of age, not seeking a degree, may be admitted through the office of the University Examiner to the courses of instruction offered in the University, as unclassified students. They shall present evidence of successful experience as a teacher or *other valuable educative experience in practical life.* . . . They are ineligible for public appearance. . . .

You saw them the Cinderellas and the Smikes of this temple of learning.

The Classifieds and the Unclassifieds rarely mixed. Not age alone, but purpose separated them. The Classifieds, boys and girls, were, for the most part, slim young lads with caps and pipes and sweaters, their talk of football, baseball, girls; slim young girls in sheer shirtwaists with pink ribbons run through the corset covers showing beneath, pleated skirts that switched delightfully as they strolled across the campus arm in arm, their talk of football games, fudge, clothes, boys. They cut classes whenever possible. The Student Body. Midwest turned them out by the hundreds—almost by the link, one might say, as Aug Hempel's sausage factory turned out its fine plump sausages, each one exactly like the one behind and the one ahead of it. So many hundreds graduated in this year's class. So many more hundreds to be graduated in next year's class. Occasionally an unruly sausage burst its skin and was discarded. They attended a university because their parents—thrifty shop-keepers, manufacturers, merchants, or professional men and their good wives—wanted their children to have an education. Were ambitious for them. "I couldn't have it myself, and always regretted it. Now I want my boy (or girl) to have a good education that'll fit 'em for the battle of life. This is an age of specialization, let me tell you."

Football, fudge, I-said-to-Jim, I-said-to-Bessie.

The Unclassifieds would no more have deliberately cut a class than they would have thrown their sparse weekly budget-allowance into the gutter. If it had been physically possible they would have attended two classes at once, listened to two lectures, prepared two papers simultaneously. Drab and earnest women between thirty and forty-eight, their hair not an ornament, but something to be pinned up quickly out of the way, their clothes a covering, their shoes not even smartly "sensible," but just shoes, scuffed, patched, utilitarian. The men were serious, shabby, often spectacled; dandruff on their coat collars; their lined, anxious faces in curious contrast to the fresh, boyish, care-free countenances of the Classifieds. They said, carefully, almost sonorously, "Political Economy. Applied Psychology." Most of them had worked ten years, fifteen years for this deferred schooling. This one had had to support a mother; that one a family of younger brothers and sisters. This plump woman of thirty-nine, with the jolly kindly face, had had a paralyzed father. Another had known merely poverty, grinding, sordid poverty, with fifteen years of painful penny savings to bring true this gloriously realized dream of a university education. Here was one studying to be a trained Social Service Worker. She had done everything from housework as a servant girl to clerking in a 5- and 10-cent store. She had studied evenings; saved pennies, nickels, dimes, quarters. *Other valuable educative experience in practical life.* They had had it, God knows.

They regarded the university at first with the love-blind eyes of a bridegroom who looks with the passionate tenderness of possession upon his mistress for whom he has worked and waited through the years of his youth. The university was to bring back that vanished youth—and something more. Wisdom. Knowledge. Power. Understanding. They would have died for it—they almost had, what with privation, self-denial, work.

They came with love clasped close in their two hands, an offertory. "Take me!" they cried. "I come with all I have. Devotion, hope, desire to learn, a promise to be a credit to you. I have had experience, bittersweet experience. I have known the battle. See, here are my scars. I can bring to your classrooms much that is valuable. I ask only for bread—the bread of knowledge."

And the University gave them a stone.

"Get on to the hat!" said the Classifieds, humorously, crossing the campus. "A fright!"

The professors found them a shade too eager, perhaps; too inquiring; demanding too much. They stayed after class and asked innumerable questions. They bristled with interrogation. They were prone to hold forth in the classroom, "Well, I have found it to be the case in my experience that——"

But the professor preferred to do the lecturing himself. If there was to be any experience related it should come from the teacher's platform, not the student's chair. Besides, this sort of thing interfered with the routine; kept you from covering ground fast enough. The period bell rang, and there you were, halfway through the day's prescribed lesson.

In his first year Dirk made the almost fatal mistake of being rather friendly with one of these Unclassifieds—a female Unclassified. She was in his Pol Econ class and sat next to him. A large, good-humoured, plump girl, about thirty-eight, with a shiny skin which she never powdered and thick hair that exuded a disagreeable odour of oil. She was sympathetic and jolly, but her clothes were a fright, the Classifieds would have told you, and no matter how cold the day there was always a half-moon of stain showing under her armpits. She had a really fine mind, quick, eager, balanced, almost judicial. She knew just which references were valuable, which useless. Just how to go about getting information for next day's class; for the weekly paper to be prepared. Her name was Schwengauer—Mattie Schwengauer. Terrible!

"Here," she would say good-naturedly, to Dirk. "You don't need to read all those. My, no! I'll tell you. You'll get exactly what you want by reading pages 256 to 273 in Blaine's; 549 to 567 in Jaeckel; and the first eleven—no, twelve—pages of Trowbridge's report. That'll give you practically everything you need."

Dirk was grateful. Her notes were always copious, perfect. She never hesitated to let him copy them. They got in the way of walking out of the classroom together, across the campus. She told him something of herself.

"Your people farmers!" Surprised, she looked at his well-cut clothes, his slim, strong, unmarked hands, his smart shoes and cap. "Why, so are mine. Iowa." She pronounced it Ioway. "I lived on the farm all my life till I was twenty-seven. I always wanted to go away to school, but we never had the money and I couldn't come to town to earn because I was the oldest, and Ma was sickly after Emma—that's the youngest—there are nine of us—was born. Ma was anxious I should go and Pa was willing, but it couldn't be. No fault of theirs. One year the summer would be so hot, with no rain hardly from spring till fall, and the corn would just dry up on the stalks, like paper. The next year it would be so wet the seed would rot in the ground. Ma died when I was twenty-six. The kids were all pretty well grown up by that time. Pa married again in a year and I went to Des Moines to work. I stayed there six years but I didn't save much on account of my brother. He was kind of wild. He had come to Des Moines, too, after Pa married. He and Aggie —that's the second wife—didn't get along. I came to Chicago about five years ago. . . . I've done all kinds of work, I guess, except digging in a coal mine. I'd have done that if I'd had to."

She told him all this ingenuously, simply. Dirk felt drawn toward her, sorry for her. His was a nature quick to sympathy. Something she said now stirred him while it bewildered him a little, too.

"You can't have any idea what it means to me to be here . . . All those years! I used to dream about it. Even now it seems to me it can't be true. I'm conscious of my surroundings all the time and yet I can't believe them. You know, like when you are asleep and dream about something beautiful, and then wake up and find it's actually true. I get a thrill out of just being here. 'I'm crossing the campus,' I say to myself. 'I'm a student—a girl student—in Midwest University and now I'm cross-ing the campus of my university to go to a class.' "

Her face was very greasy and earnest and fine.

"Well, that's great," Dirk replied, weakly. "That's cer'nly great."

He told his mother about her. Usually he went home on Friday nights to stay until Monday morning. His first Monday-morning class was not until ten. Selina was deeply interested and stirred. "Do you think she'd spend some Saturday and Sunday here with us on the farm? She could come with you on Friday and go back Sunday night if she wanted to. Or stay until Monday morning and go back with you. There's the spare room, all quiet and cool. She could do as she liked. I'd give her cream and all the fresh fruit and vegetables she wanted. And Meena would bake one of her fresh cocoanut cakes. I'd have Adam bring a fresh cocoa-nut from South Water Street."

Mattie came one Friday night. It was the end of October, and Indian summer, the most beautiful time of the year on the Illinois prairie. A mellow golden light seemed to suffuse everything. It was as if the very air were liquid gold, and tonic. The squash and pumpkins next the good brown earth gave back the glow, and the frost-turned leaves of the ma-ples in the sun. About the countryside for miles was the look of boun-teousness, of plenty, of prophecy fulfilled as when a beautiful and fertile woman having borne her children and found them good, now sits serene-eyed, gracious, ample-bosomed, satisfied.

Into the face of Mattie Schwengauer there came a certain glory. When she and Selina clasped hands Selina stared at her rather curiously, as though startled. Afterward she said to Dirk, aside, "But I thought you said she was ugly!"

"Well, she is, or—well, isn't she?"

"Look at her!"

Mattie Schwengauer was talking to Meena Bras, the houseworker. She was standing with her hands on her ample hips, her fine head thrown back, her eyes alight, her lips smiling so that you saw her strong square teeth. A new cream separator was the subject of their conversation. Something had amused Mattie. She laughed. It was the laugh of a young girl, care-free, relaxed, at ease.

For two days Mattie did as she pleased, which meant she helped pull vegetables in the garden, milk the cows, saddle the horses; rode them without a saddle in the pasture. She tramped the road. She scuffled through the leaves in the woods, wore a scarlet maple leaf in her hair, slept like one gloriously dead from ten until six; ate prodigiously of cream, fruits, vegetables, eggs, sausage, cake.

"It got so I hated to do all those things on the farm," she said, laughing a little shamefacedly. "I guess it was because I had to. But now it comes back to me and I enjoy it because it's natural to me, I suppose. Anyway, I'm having a grand time, Mrs. DeJong. The grandest time I ever had in my life." Her face was radiant and almost beautiful.

"If you want me to believe that," said Selina, "you'll come again."

But Mattie Schwengauer never did come again.

Early the next week one of the university students approached Dirk. He was a Junior, very influential in his class, and a member of the fraternity to which Dirk was practically pledged. A decidedly desirable frat.

"Say, look here, DeJong, I want to talk to you a minute. Uh, you've got to cut out that girl—Swinegour or whatever her name is—or it's all off with the fellows in the frat."

"What d'you mean! Cut out! What's the matter with her!"

"Matter! She's Unclassified, isn't she! And do you know what the story is? She told it herself as an economy hint to a girl who was working her way through. She bathes with her union suit and white stockings on to save laundry soap. Scrubs 'em on her! 'S the God's truth."

Into Dirk's mind there flashed a picture of this large girl in her tight knitted union suit and her white stockings sitting in a tub half full of water and scrubbing them and herself simultaneously. A comic picture, and a revolting one. Pathetic, too, but he would not admit that.

"Imagine!" the frat brother-to-be was saying. "Well, we can't have a fellow who goes around with a girl like that. You got to cut her out, see! Completely. The fellahs won't stand for it."

Dirk had a mental picture of himself striking a noble attitude and saying, "Won't stand for it, huh! She's worth more than the whole caboodle of you put together. And you can all go to hell!"

Instead he said, vaguely, "Oh. Well. Uh——"

Dirk changed his seat in the classroom, avoided Mattie's eye, shot out of the door the minute class was over. One day he saw her coming toward him on the campus and he sensed that she intended to stop and speak to him—chide him laughingly, perhaps. He quickened his pace, swerved a little to one side, and as he passed lifted his cap and nodded, keeping his eyes straight ahead. Out of the tail of his eye he could see her standing a moment irresolutely in the path.

He got into the fraternity. The fellahs liked him from the first. Selina said once or twice, "Why don't you bring that nice Mattie home with you again some time soon? Such a nice girl—woman, rather. But she seemed so young and care-free while she was here, didn't she? A fine mind, too, that girl. She'll make something of herself. You'll see. Bring her next week, h'm?"

Dirk shuffled, coughed, looked away. "Oh, I dunno. Haven't seen her lately. Guess she's busy with another crowd, or something."

He tried not to think of what he had done, for he was honestly ashamed. Terribly ashamed. So he said to himself, "Oh, what of it!" and hid his shame. A month later Selina again said, "I wish you'd invite Mattie for Thanksgiving dinner. Unless she's going home, which I doubt. We'll have turkey and pumpkin pie and all the rest of it. She'll love it."

"Mattie?" He had actually forgotten her name.

"Yes, of course. Isn't that right? Mattie Schwengauer?"

"Oh, her. Uh—well—I haven't been seeing her lately."

"Oh, Dirk, you haven't quarrelled with that nice girl!"

He decided to have it out. "Listen, Mother. There are a lot of different crowds at the U, see? And Mattie doesn't belong to any of 'em. You wouldn't understand, but it's like this. She—she's smart and jolly and everything but she just doesn't belong. Being friends with a girl like that doesn't get you anywhere. Besides, she isn't a girl. She's a middle-aged woman, when you come to think of it."

"Doesn't get you anywhere!" Selina's tone was cool and even. Then, as the boy's gaze did not meet hers: "Why, Dirk DeJong, Mattie Schwengauer is one of my reasons for sending you to a university. She's what I call part of a university education. Just talking to her is learning something valuable. I don't mean that you wouldn't naturally prefer pretty young girls of your own age to go around with, and all. It would be queer if you didn't. But this Mattie—why, she's life. Do you remember that story of when she washed dishes in the kosher restaurant over on Twelfth Street and the proprietor used to rent out dishes and cutlery for Irish and Italian neighbourhood weddings where they had pork and goodness knows what all, and then use them next day in the restaurant again for the kosher customers?"

Yes, Dirk remembered. Selina wrote Mattie, inviting her to the farm for Thanksgiving, and Mattie answered gratefully, declining. "I shall always remember you," she wrote in that letter, "with love."

XIV

THROUGHOUT Dirk's Freshman year there were, for him, no heartening, informal, mellow talks before the wood-fire in the book-lined study of some professor whose wisdom was such a mixture of classic lore and modernism as to be an inspiration to his listeners. Midwest professors delivered their lectures in the classroom as they had been delivering them in the past ten or twenty years and as they would deliver them until death or a trustees' meeting should remove them. The younger professors and instructors in natty gray suits and bright-coloured ties made a point of being unpedantic in the classroom and rather overdid it. They posed as being one of the fellows; would dashingly use a bit of slang to create a laugh from the boys and an adoring titter from the girls. Dirk somehow preferred the pedants to these. When these had to give an informal talk to the men before some university event they would start by saying, "Now listen, fellahs——" At the dances they were not above "rushing" the pretty co-eds.

Two of Dirk's classes were conducted by women professors. They were well on toward middle age, or past it; desiccated women. Only their eyes were alive. Their clothes were of some indefinite dark stuff, brown or drab-gray; their hair lifeless; their hands long, bony, unvital. They had seen classes and classes and classes. A roomful of fresh young faces that appeared briefly only to be replaced by another roomful of fresh young faces like round white pencil marks manipulated momentarily on a slate, only to be sponged off to give way to other round white marks. Of the two women one—the elder—was occasionally likely to flare into sudden life; a flame in the ashes of a burned-out grate. She had humour and a certain caustic wit, qualities that had managed miraculously to survive even the deadly and numbing effects of thirty years in the classroom. A fine mind, and iconoclastic, hampered by the restrictions of a conventional community and the soul of a congenital spinster.

Under the guidance of these Dirk chafed and grew restless. Miss Euphemia Hollingswood had a way of emphasizing every third or fifth syllable, bringing her voice down hard on it, thus:

"In the *consideration* of *all* the facts in the *case* presented be*fore* us we must *first* review the *history* and at*tempt* to analyze the *out-standing*——"

He found himself waiting for that emphasis and shrinking from it as from a sledge-hammer blow. It hurt his head.

Miss Lodge droned. She approached a word with a maddening uh-uh-uh-uh. In the uh-uh-uh face of the uh-uh-uh-uh geometrical situation of the uh-uh-uh-uh——

He shifted restlessly in his chair, found his hands clenched into fists, and took refuge in watching the shadow cast by an oak branch outside the window on a patch of sunlight against the blackboard behind her.

During the early spring Dirk and Selina talked things over again, seated before their own fireplace in the High Prairie farmhouse. Selina had had that fireplace built five years before and her love of it amounted to fire-worship. She had it lighted always on winter evenings and in the spring when the nights were sharp. In Dirk's absence she would sit before it at night long after the rest of the weary household had gone to bed. Old Pom, the mongrel, lay stretched at her feet enjoying such luxury in old age as he had never dreamed of in his bastard youth. High Prairie, driving by from some rare social gathering or making a late trip to market as they sometimes were forced to do, saw the rosy flicker of Mrs. DeJong's fire dancing on the wall and warmed themselves by it even while they resented it.

"A good heater in there and yet anyway she's got to have a fire going in a grate. Always she does something funny like that. I should think she'd be lonesome sitting there like that with her dog only."

They never knew how many guests Selina entertained there before her fire those winter evenings—old friends and new. Sobig was there, the plump earth-grimed baby who rolled and tumbled in the fields while his young mother wiped the sweat from her face to look at him with fond eyes. Dirk DeJong of ten years hence was there. Simeon Peake, dapper, soft-spoken, ironic, in his shiny boots and his hat always a little on one side. Pervus DeJong, a blue-shirted giant with strong tender hands and little fine golden hairs on the backs of them. Fanny Davenport, the actress-idol of her girlhood came back to her, smiling, bowing; and the gorgeous spangled creatures in the tights and bodices of the old Extravaganzas. In strange contrast to these was the patient, tireless figure of Maartje Pool standing in the doorway of Roelf's little shed, her arms tucked in her apron for warmth. "You make fun, huh?" she said, wistfully, "you and Roelf. You make fun." And Roelf, the dark vivid boy, misunderstood. Roelf, the genius. He was always one of the company.

Oh, Selina DeJong never was lonely on these winter evenings before her fire.

She and Dirk sat there one fine sharp evening in early April. It was
Saturday. Of late Dirk had not always come to the farm for the week-
end. Eugene and Paula Arnold had been home for the Easter holidays.
Julie Arnold had invited Dirk to the gay parties at the Prairie Avenue
house. He had even spent two entire week-ends there. After the bro-
caded luxury of the Prairie Avenue house his farm bedroom seemed
almost startlingly stark and bare. Selina frankly enjoyed Dirk's somewhat fragmentary accounts of these visits; extracted from them as much
vicarious pleasure as he had had in the reality—more, probably.

"Now tell me what you had to eat," she would say, sociably, like a
child. "What did you have for dinner, for example? Was it grand? Julie
tells me they have a butler now. Well! I can't wait till I hear Aug Hempel
on the subject."

He would tell her of the grandeurs of the Arnold ménage. She would
interrupt and exclaim: "Mayonnaise! On fruit! Oh, I don't believe I'd
like *that*. You did! Well, I'll have it for you next week when you come
home. I'll get the recipe from Julie."

He didn't think he'd be home next week. One of the fellows he'd
met at the Arnolds' had invited him to their place out north, on the
lake. He had a boat.

"That'll be lovely!" Selina exclaimed, after an almost unnoticeable
moment of silence—silence with panic in it. "I'll try not to fuss and be
worried like an old hen every minute of the time I think you're on the
water. . . . Now do go on, Sobig. First fruit with mayonnaise, h'm?
What kind of soup?"

He was not a naturally talkative person. There was nothing surly
about his silence. It was a taciturn streak inherited from his Dutch ancestry. This time, though, he was more voluble than usual. "Paula . . ."
came again and again into his conversation. "Paula . . . Paula . . ." and
again ". . . Paula." He did not seem conscious of the repetition, but
Selina's quick ear caught it.

"I haven't seen her," Selina said, "since she went away to school the
first year. She must be—let's see—she's a year older than you are. She's
nineteen going on twenty. Last time I saw her I thought she was a
dark scrawny little thing. Too bad she didn't inherit Julie's lovely gold
colouring and good looks, instead of Eugene, who doesn't need 'em."

"She isn't!" said Dirk, hotly. "She's dark and slim and sort of—uh—
sensuous"—Selina started visibly, and raised her hand quickly to her
mouth to hide a smile—"like Cleopatra. Her eyes are big and kind of
slanting—not squinty I don't mean, but slanting up a little at the corners.
Cut out, kind of, so that they look bigger than most people's."

"My eyes used to be considered rather fine," said Selina, mischievously; but he did not hear.

"She makes all the other girls look sort of blowzy." He was silent a moment. Selina was silent, too, and it was not a happy silence. Dirk spoke again, suddenly, as though continuing aloud a train of thought, "—all but her hands."

Selina made her voice sound natural, not sharply inquisitive. "What's the matter with her hands, Dirk?"

He pondered a moment, his brows knitted. At last, slowly, "Well, I don't know. They're brown, and awfully thin and sort of—grabby. I mean it makes me nervous to watch them. And when the rest of her is cool they're hot when you touch them."

He looked at his mother's hands that were busy with some sewing. The stuff on which she was working was a bit of satin ribbon; part of a hood intended to grace the head of Geertje Pool Vander Sijde's second baby. She had difficulty in keeping her rough fingers from catching on the soft surface of the satin. Manual work, water, sun, and wind had tanned those hands, hardened them, enlarged the knuckles, spread them, roughened them. Yet how sure they were, and strong, and cool and reliable—and tender. Suddenly, looking at them, Dirk said, "Now your hands. I love your hands, Mother."

She put down her work hastily, yet quietly, so that the sudden rush of happy grateful tears in her eyes should not sully the pink satin ribbon. She was flushed, like a girl. "Do you, Sobig?" she said.

After a moment she took up her sewing again. Her face looked young, eager, fresh, like the face of the girl who had found cabbages so beautiful that night when she bounced along the rutty Halsted road with Klaas Pool, many years ago. It came into her face, that look, when she was happy, exhilarated, excited. That was why those who loved her and brought that look into her face thought her beautiful, while those who did not love her never saw the look and consequently considered her a plain woman.

There was another silence between the two. Then: "Mother, what would you think of my going East next fall, to take a course in architecture?"

"Would you like that, Dirk?"

"Yes, I think so—yes."

"Then I'd like it better than anything in the world. I—it makes me happy just to think of it."

"It would—cost an awful lot."

"I'll manage. I'll manage. . . . What made you decide on architecture?"

"I don't know, exactly. The new buildings at the university—Gothic, you know—are such a contrast to the old. Then Paula and I were talking the other day. She hates their house on Prairie—terrible old lumpy gray stone pile, with the black of the I. C. trains all over it. She wants her father to build north—an Italian villa or French château. Something of that sort. So many of her friends are moving to the north shore, away from these hideous south-side and north-side Chicago houses with their stoops, and their bay windows, and their terrible turrets. Ugh!"

"Well, now, do you know," Selina remonstrated mildly, "I like 'em. I suppose I'm wrong, but to me they seem sort of natural and solid and unpretentious, like the clothes that old August Hempel wears, so square-cut and baggy. Those houses look dignified to me, and fitting. They may be ugly—probably are—but anyway they're not ridiculous. They have a certain rugged grandeur. They're Chicago. Those French and Italian gimcracky things they—they're incongruous. It's as if Abraham Lincoln were to appear suddenly in pink satin knee breeches and buckled shoes, and lace ruffles at his wrists."

Dirk could laugh at that picture. But he protested, too. "But there's no native architecture, so what's to be done! You wouldn't call those smoke-blackened old stone and brick piles with their iron fences and their conservatories and cupolas and gingerbread exactly native, would you?"

"No," Selina admitted, "but those Italian villas and French châteaux in north Chicago suburbs are a good deal like a lace evening gown in the Arizona desert. It wouldn't keep you cool in the daytime, and it wouldn't be warm enough at night. I suppose a native architecture is evolved from building for the local climate and the needs of the community, keeping beauty in mind as you go. We don't need turrets and towers any more than we need draw-bridges and moats. It's all right to keep them, I suppose, where they grew up, in a country where the feudal system meant that any day your next-door neighbour might take it into his head to call his gang around him and sneak up to steal your wife and tapestries and gold drinking cups."

Dirk was interested and amused. Talks with his mother were likely to affect him thus. "What's your idea of a real Chicago house, Mother?"

Selina answered quickly, as if she had thought often about it; as if she would have liked just such a dwelling on the site of the old DeJong farmhouse in which they now were seated so comfortably. "Well, it would need big porches for the hot days and nights so's to catch the prevailing southwest winds from the prairies in the summer—a porch that would be swung clear around to the east, too—or a terrace or another porch east so that if the precious old lake breeze should come up just when you think you're dying of the heat, as it sometimes does, you could catch that, too. It ought to be built—the house, I mean—rather squarish and tight and solid against our cold winters and north-easters. Then sleeping porches, of course. There's a grand American institution for you! England may have its afternoon tea on the terrace, and Spain may have its patio, and France its courtyard, and Italy its pergola, vine-covered; but America's got the sleeping porch—the screened-in open-air sleeping porch, and I shouldn't wonder if the man who first thought of that would get precedence, on Judgment Day, over the men who invented the aeroplane, the talking machine, and the telephone. After all, he had nothing in mind but the health of the human race." After which grand period Selina grinned at Dirk, and Dirk grinned at Selina and the two giggled together there by the fireplace, companionably.

"Mother, you're simply wonderful!—only your native Chicago dwelling seems to be mostly porch."

Selina waved such carping criticism away with a careless hand. "Oh, well, any house that has enough porches, and two or three bathrooms and at least eight closets can be lived in comfortably, no matter what else it has or hasn't got."

Next day they were more serious. The eastern college and the architectural career seemed to be settled things. Selina was content, happy. Dirk was troubled about the expense. He spoke of it at breakfast next morning (Dirk's breakfast; his mother had had hers hours before and now as he drank his coffee, was sitting with him a moment and glancing at the paper that had come in the rural mail delivery). She had been out in the fields overseeing the transplanting of young tomato seedlings from hotbed to field. She wore an old gray sweater buttoned up tight, for the air was still sharp. On her head was a battered black felt soft hat (an old one of Dirk's) much like the one she had worn to the Haymarket that day ten years ago. Selina's cheeks were faintly pink from her walk across the fields in the brisk morning air.

She sniffed. "That coffee smells wonderful. I think I'll just——" She poured herself a half cup with the air of virtue worn by one who really longs for a whole cup and doesn't take it.

"I've been thinking," he began, "the expense——"

"Pigs," said Selina, serenely.

"Pigs!" He looked around, bewildered; stared at his mother.

"Pigs'll do it," Selina explained, calmly. "I've been wanting to put them in for three or four years. It's August Hempel's idea. Hogs, I should have said."

Again, as before, he echoed, "Hogs!" rather faintly.

"High-bred hogs. They're worth their weight in silver this minute, and will be for years to come. I won't go in for them extensively. Just enough to make an architect out of Mr. Dirk DeJong." Then, at the expression in his face: "Don't look so pained, son. There's nothing revolting about a hog—not my kind, brought up in a pen as sanitary as a tiled bathroom and fed on corn. He's a handsome, impressive-looking animal, the hog, when he isn't treated like one."

He looked dejected. "I'd rather not go to school on—hogs."

She took off the felt hat and tossed it over to the old couch by the window; smoothed her hair back with the flat of her palm. You saw that the soft dark hair was liberally sprinkled with gray now, but the eyes were bright and clear as ever.

"You know, Sobig, this is what they call a paying farm—as vegetable farms go. We're out of debt, the land's in good shape, the crop promises well if we don't have another rainy cold spring like last year's. But no truck garden is going to make its owner rich these days, with labour so high and the market what it is, and the expense of hauling and all. Any truck farmer who comes out even thinks he's come out ahead."

"I know it." Rather miserably.

"Well. I'm not complaining, son. I'm just telling you. I'm having a grand time. When I see the asparagus plantation actually yielding, that I planted ten years ago, I'm as happy as if I'd stumbled on a gold mine. I think, sometimes, of the way your father objected to my planting the first one. April, like this, in the country, with everything coming up green and new in the rich black loam—I can't tell you. And when I know that it goes to market as food—the best kind of food, that keeps people's bodies clean and clear and flexible and strong! I like to think of babies' mothers saying: 'Now eat your spinach, every scrap, or you can't have any dessert! . . . Carrots make your eyes bright. . . . Finish your potato. Potatoes make you strong!' "

Selina laughed, flushed a little.

"Yes, but how about hogs? Do you feel that way about hogs?"

"Certainly!" said Selina, briskly. She pushed toward him a little blue-and-white platter that lay on the white cloth near her elbow. "Have a bit more bacon, Dirk. One of these nice curly slivers that are so crisp."

"I've finished my breakfast, Mother." He rose.

The following autumn saw him a student of architecture at Cornell. He worked hard, studied even during his vacations. He would come home to the heat and humidity of the Illinois summers and spend hours each day in his own room that he had fitted up with a long work table and a drawing board. His T-square was at hand; two triangles—a 45 and a 60; his compass; a pair of dividers. Selina sometimes stood behind him watching him as he carefully worked on the tracing paper. His contempt for the local architecture was now complete. Especially did he hold forth on the subject of the apartment-houses that were mushrooming on every street in Chicago from Hyde Park on the south to Evanston on the north. Chicago was very elegant in speaking of these; never called them "flats"; always apartments. In front of each of these (there were usually six to a building) was stuck a little glass-enclosed cubicle known as a sun-parlour. In these (sometimes you heard them spoken of, grandly, as solariums) Chicago dwellers took refuge from the leaden skies, the heavy lake atmosphere, the gray mist and fog and smoke that so frequently swathed the city in gloom. They were done in yellow or rose cretonnes. Silk lamp shades glowed therein, and flower-laden boxes. In these frank little boxes Chicago read its paper, sewed, played bridge, even ate its breakfast. It never pulled down the shades.

"Terrible!" Dirk fumed. "Not only are they hideous in themselves, stuck on the front of those houses like three pairs of spectacles; but the lack of decent privacy! They do everything but bathe in 'em. Have they never heard the advice given people who live in glass houses!"

By his junior year he was talking in a large way about the Beaux Arts. But Selina did not laugh at this. "Perhaps," she thought. "Who can tell! After a year or two in an office here, why not another year of study in Paris if he needs it."

Though it was her busiest time on the farm Selina went to Ithaca for his graduation in 1913. He was twenty-two and, she was calmly sure, the best-looking man in his class. Undeniably he was a figure to please the eye; tall, well-built, as his father had been, and blond, too, like his father, except for his eyes. These were brown—not so dark as Selina's, but with some of the soft liquid quality of her glance. They strengthened his face, somehow; gave him an ardent look of which he was not conscious. Women, feeling the ardour of that dark glance turned upon them, were likely to credit him with feelings toward themselves of which he was quite innocent. They did not know that the glance and its effect were mere matters of pigmentation and eye-conformation. Then, too, the gaze of a man who talks little is always more effective than that of one who is loquacious.

Selina, in her black silk dress, and her plain black hat, and her sensible shoes was rather a quaint little figure amongst all those vivacious, bevoiled, and beribboned mammas. But a distinctive little figure, too. Dirk need not be ashamed of her. She eyed the rather paunchy, prosperous, middle-aged fathers and thought, with a pang, how much handsomer Pervus would have been than any of these, if only he could have lived to see this day. Then, involuntarily, she wondered if this day would ever have occurred, had Pervus lived. Chided herself for thinking thus.

When he returned to Chicago, Dirk went into the office of Hollis & Sprague, Architects. He thought himself lucky to work with this firm, for it was doing much to guide Chicago's taste in architecture away from the box car. Already Michigan Boulevard's skyline soared somewhat above the grimly horizontal. But his work there was little more than that of draughtsman, and his weekly stipend could hardly be dignified by the term of salary. But he had large ideas about architecture and he found expression for his suppressed feelings on his week-ends spent with Selina at the farm. "Baroque" was the word with which he dismissed the new Beachside Hotel, north. He said the new Lincoln Park band-stand looked like an igloo. He said that the city council ought to order the Potter Palmer mansion destroyed as a blot on the landscape, and waxed profane on the subject of the east face of the Public Library Building, down town.

"Never mind," Selina assured him, happily. "It was all thrown up so hastily. Remember that just yesterday, or the day before, Chicago was an Indian fort, with tepees where towers are now, and mud wallows in place of asphalt. Beauty needs time to perfect it. Perhaps we've been waiting all these years for just such youngsters as you. And maybe some day I'll be driving down Michigan Boulevard with a distinguished visitor —Roelf Pool, perhaps. Why not? Let's say Roelf Pool, the famous sculptor. And he'll say, 'Who designed that building—the one that is so strong and yet so light? So gay and graceful, and yet so reticent!' And I'll say, 'Oh, that! That's one of the earlier efforts of my son, Dirk DeJong.'"

But Dirk pulled at his pipe moodily; shook his head. "Oh, you don't know, Mother. It's so damned slow. First thing you know I'll be thirty. And what am I! An office boy—or little more than that—at Hollis's."

During his university years Dirk had seen much of the Arnolds, Eugene and Paula, but it sometimes seemed to Selina that he avoided these meetings—these parties and week-ends. She was content that this should be so, for she guessed that the matter of money held him back. She thought it was well that he should realize the difference now. Eugene had his own car—one of five in the Arnold garage. Paula, too, had hers. She had been one of the first Chicago girls to drive a gas car; had breezed about Chicago's boulevards in one when she had been little more than a child in short skirts. At the wheel she was dexterous, dare-devil, incredibly relaxed. Her fascination for Dirk was strong. Selina knew that, too. In the last year or two he had talked very little of Paula and that, Selina knew, meant that he was hard hit.

Sometimes Paula and Eugene drove out to the farm, making the distance from their new north-shore house to the DeJong place far south in some breath-taking number of minutes. Eugene would appear in rakish cap, loose London coat, knickers, queer brogans with an English look about them, a carefully careless looseness about the hang and fit of his jacket. Paula did not affect sports clothes for herself. She was not the type, she said. Slim, dark, vivacious, she wore slinky clothes—crêpes, chiffons. Her feet were slim in sheer silk stockings and slippers with buckles. Her eyes were languorous, lovely. She worshipped luxury and said so.

"I'll have to marry money," she declared. "Now that they've finished calling poor Grandpa a beef-baron and taken I don't know how many millions away from him, we're practically on the streets."

"You look it!" from Dirk; and there was bitterness beneath his light tone.

"Well, it's true. All this silly muckraking in the past ten years or more. Poor Father! Of course Grand-dad was pur-ty rough, let me tell you. I read some of the accounts of that last indictment—the 1910 one—and I must say I gathered that dear old Aug made Jesse James look like a philanthropist. I should think, at his age, he'd be a little scared. After all, when you're over seventy you're likely to have some doubts and fears about punishment in the next world. But not a grand old pirate like Grandfather. He'll sack and burn and plunder until he goes down with the ship. And it looks to me as if the old boat had a pretty strong list to starboard right now. Father says himself that unless a war breaks, or something, which isn't at all likely, the packing industry is going to spring a leak."

"Elaborate figure of speech," murmured Eugene. The four of them—Paula, Dirk, Eugene, and Selina—were sitting on the wide screened porch that Selina had had built at the southwest corner of the house. Paula was, of course, in the couch-swing. Occasionally she touched one slim languid foot to the floor and gave indolent impetus to the couch.

"It is, rather, isn't it? Might as well finish it, then. Darling Aug's been the grand old captain right through the vi'age. Dad's never been more than a pretty bum second mate. And as for you, Gene my love, cabin boy would be, y'understand me, big." Eugene had gone into the business a year before.

"What can you expect," retorted Eugene, "of a lad that hates salt pork? And every other kind of pig meat?" He despised the yards and all that went with it.

Selina now got up and walked to the end of the porch. She looked out across the fields, shading her eyes with her hand. "There's Adam coming in with the last load for the day. He'll be driving into town now.

Cornelius started an hour ago." The DeJong farm sent two great loads to the city now. Selina was contemplating the purchase of one of the large automobile trucks that would do away with the plodding horses and save hours of time on the trip. She went down the steps now on her way to oversee the loading of Adam Bras's wagon. At the bottom of the steps she turned. "Why can't you two stay to supper? You can quarrel comfortably right through the meal and drive home in the cool of the evening."

"I'll stay," said Paula, "thanks. If you'll have all kinds of vegetables, cooked and uncooked. The cooked ones smothered in cream and oozing butter. And let me go out into the fields and pick 'em myself like Maud Muller or Marie Antoinette or any of those make-believe rustic gals."

In her French-heeled slippers and her filmy silk stockings she went out into the rich black furrows of the fields, Dirk carrying the basket.

"Asparagus," she ordered first. Then, "But where is it? Is *that* it!"

"You dig for it, idiot," said Dirk, stooping, and taking from his basket the queerly curved sharp knife or spud used for cutting the asparagus shoots. "Cut the shoots three or four inches below the surface."

"Oh, let me do it!" She was down on her silken knees in the dirt, ruined a goodly patch of the fine tender shoots, gave it up and sat watching Dirk's expert manipulation of the knife. "Let's have radishes, and corn, and tomatoes and lettuce and peas and artichokes and——"

"Artichokes grow in California, not Illinois." He was more than usually uncommunicative, and noticeably moody.

Paula remarked it. "Why the Othello brow?"

"You didn't mean that rot, did you? about marrying a rich man."

"Of course I meant it. What other sort of man do you think I ought to marry?" He looked at her, silently. She smiled. "Yes, wouldn't I make an ideal bride for a farmer!"

"I'm not a farmer."

"Well, architect then. Your job as draughtsman at Hollis & Sprague's must pay you all of twenty-five a week."

"Thirty-five," said Dirk, grimly. "What's that got to do with it!"

"Not a thing, darling." She stuck out one foot. "These slippers cost thirty."

"I won't be getting thirty-five a week all my life. You've got brains enough to know that. Eugene wouldn't be getting that much if he weren't the son of his father."

"The grandson of his grandfather," Paula corrected him. "And I'm not so sure he wouldn't. Gene's a born mechanic if they'd just let him work at it. He's crazy about engines and all that junk. But no—'Millionaire Packer's Son Learns Business from Bottom Rung of Ladder.' Picture

of Gene in workman's overalls and cap in the Sunday papers. He drives
to the office on Michigan at ten and leaves at four and he doesn't know
a steer from a cow when he sees it."

"I don't care a damn about Gene. I'm talking about you. You were
joking, weren't you?"

"I wasn't. I'd hate being poor, or even just moderately rich. I'm used
to money—loads of it. I'm twenty-four. And I'm looking around."

He kicked an innocent beet-top with his boot. "You like me better
than any man you know."

"Of course I do. Just my luck."

"Well, then!"

"Well, then, let's take these weggibles in and have 'em cooked in
cream, as ordered."

She made a pretense of lifting the heavy basket. Dirk snatched it
roughly out of her hand so that she gave a little cry and looked ruefully
down at the red mark on her palm. He caught her by the shoulder—even
shook her a little. "Look here, Paula. Do you mean to tell me you'd
marry a man simply because he happened to have a lot of money!"

"Perhaps not simply because he had a lot of money. But it certainly
would be a factor, among other things. Certainly he would be preferable
to a man who knocked me about the fields as if I were a bag of potatoes."

"Oh, forgive me. But—listen, Paula—you know I'm—gosh!—— And
there I am stuck in an architect's office and it'll be years before I——"

"Yes, but it'll probably be years before I meet the millions I require,
too. So why bother? And even if I do, you and I can be just as good
friends."

"Oh, shut up. Don't pull that ingénue stuff on me, please. Remember
I've known you since you were ten years old."

"And you know just how black my heart is, don't you, what? You
want, really, some nice hearty lass who can tell asparagus from peas
when she sees 'em, and who'll offer to race you from here to the
kitchen."

"God forbid!"

Six months later Paula Arnold was married to Theodore A. Storm,
a man of fifty, a friend of her father's, head of so many companies,
stockholder in so many banks, director of so many corporations that
even old Aug Hempel seemed a recluse from business in comparison.
She never called him Teddy. No one ever did. Theodore Storm was a
large man—not exactly stout, perhaps, but flabby. His inches saved him
from grossness. He had a large white serious face, fine thick dark hair,
graying at the temples, and he dressed very well except for a leaning
toward rather effeminate ties. He built for Paula a town house on the

Lake Shore drive in the region known as the Gold Coast. The house looked like a restrained public library. There was a country place beyond Lake Forest far out on the north shore, sloping down to the lake and surrounded by acres and acres of fine woodland, expertly parked. There were drives, ravines, brooks, bridges, hothouses, stables, a race-track, gardens, dairies, fountains, bosky paths, keeper's cottage (twice the size of Selina's farmhouse). Within three years Paula had two children, a boy and a girl. "There! That's done," she said. Her marriage was a great mistake and she knew it. For the war, coming in 1914, a few months after her wedding, sent the Hempel-Arnold interests sky-rocketing. Millions of pounds of American beef and pork were shipped to Europe. In two years the Hempel fortune was greater than it ever had been. Paula was up to her eyes in relief work for Bleeding Belgium. All the Gold Coast was. The Beautiful Mrs. Theodore A. Storm in her Gift Shop Conducted for the Relief of Bleeding Belgium.

Dirk had not seen her in months. She telephoned him unexpectedly one Friday afternoon in his office at Hollis & Sprague's.

"Come out and spend Saturday and Sunday with us, won't you? We're running away to the country this afternoon. I'm so sick of Bleeding Belgium, you can't imagine. I'm sending the children out this morning. I can't get away so early. I'll call for you in the roadster this afternoon at four and drive you out myself."

"I am going to spend the week-end with Mother. She's expecting me."

"Bring her along."

"She wouldn't come. You know she doesn't enjoy all that velvet-footed servitor stuff."

"Oh, but we live quite simply out there, really. Just sort of rough it. Do come, Dirk. I've got some plans to talk over with you . . . How's the job?"

"Oh, good enough. There's very little building going on, you know."

"Will you come?"

"I don't think I——"

"I'll call for you at four. I'll be at the curb. Don't keep me waiting, will you? The cops fuss so if you park in the Loop after four."

XV

"RUN along!" said Selina, when he called her on the farm telephone. "It'll do you good. You've been as grumpy as a gander for weeks. How about shirts? And you left one pair of flannel tennis pants out here last fall—clean ones. Won't you need . . ."

In town he lived in a large front room and alcove on the third floor of a handsome old-fashioned three-story-and-basement house in Deming Place. He used the front room as a living room, the alcove as a bedroom. He and Selina had furnished it together, discarding all of the room's original belongings except the bed, a table, and one fat comfortable faded old armchair whose brocade surface hinted a past grandeur. When he had got his books ranged in open shelves along one wall, soft-shaded lamps on table and desk, the place looked more than livable; lived in. During the process of furnishing Selina got into the way of coming into town for a day or two to prowl the auction rooms and the second-hand stores. She had a genius for this sort of thing; hated the spick-and-span varnish and veneer of the new furniture to be got in the regular way.

"Any piece of furniture, I don't care how beautiful it is, has got to be lived with, and kicked about, and rubbed down, and mistreated by servants, and repolished, and knocked around and dusted and sat on or slept in or eaten off of before it develops its real character," Selina said. "A good deal like human beings. I'd rather have my old maple table, mellow with age and rubbing, that Pervus's father put together himself by hand seventy years ago, than all the mahogany library slabs on Wabash Avenue."

She enjoyed these rare trips into town; made a holiday of them. Dirk would take her to the theatre and she would sit entranced. Her feeling for this form of entertainment was as fresh and eager as it had been in the days of the Daly Stock Company when she, a little girl, had been seated in the parquet with her father, Simeon Peake. Strangely enough, considering the lack of what the world calls romance and adventure in her life, she did not like the motion pictures. "All the difference in the world," she would say, "between the movies and the thrill I get out of a play at the theatre. My, yes! Like fooling with paper dolls when you could be playing with a real live baby."

She developed a mania for nosing into strange corners of the huge sprawling city; seemed to discover a fresh wonder on each visit. In a short time she was more familiar with Chicago than was Dirk—for that matter, than old Aug Hempel who had lived in it for over half a century but who never had gone far afield in his pendulum path between the yards and his house, his house and the yards.

The things that excited her about Chicago did not seem to interest Dirk at all. Sometimes she took a vacant room for a day or two in Dirk's boarding house. "What do you think!" she would say to him, breathlessly, when he returned from the office in the evening. "I've been way over on the northwest side. It's another world. It's—it's Poland. Cathedrals and shops and men sitting in restaurants all day long reading papers and drinking coffee and playing dominoes or something like it. And what do you think I found out! Chicago's got the second largest Polish population of any city in the world. In the *world!*"

"Yeh?" Dirk would reply, absently.

There was nothing absent-minded about his tone this afternoon as he talked to his mother on the telephone. "Sure you don't mind? Then I'll be out next Saturday. Or I may run out in the middle of the week to stay over night . . . Are you all right?"

"I'm fine. Be sure and remember all about Paula's new house so's you can tell me about it. Julie says it's like the kind you read of in the novels. She says old Aug saw it just once and now won't go near it even to visit his grandchildren."

The day was marvellously mild for March in Chicago. Spring, usually so coy in this region, had flung herself at them head first. As the massive revolving door of Dirk's office building fanned him into the street he saw Paula in her long low sporting roadster at the curb. She was dressed in black. All feminine fashionable and middle-class Chicago was dressed in black. All feminine fashionable and middle-class America was dressed in black. Two years of war had robbed Paris of its husbands, brothers, sons. All Paris walked in black. America, untouched, gayly borrowed the smart habiliments of mourning and now Michigan Boulevard and Fifth Avenue walked demurely in the gloom of crêpe and chiffon; black hats, black gloves, black slippers. Only black was "good" this year.

Paula did not wear black well. She was a shade too sallow for these sombre swathings even though relieved by a pearl strand of exquisite colour, flawlessly matched; and a new sly face-powder. Paula smiled up at him, patted the leather seat beside her with one hand that was absurdly thick-fingered in its fur-lined glove.

"It's cold driving. Button up tight. Where'll we stop for your bag? Are you still in Deming Place?"

He was still in Deming Place. He climbed into the seat beside her— a feat for the young and nimble. Theodore Storm never tried to double his bulk into the jack-knife position necessary to riding in his wife's roadster. The car was built for speed, not comfort. One sat flat with the length of one's legs stretched out. Paula's feet, pedalling brake and clutch so expertly, were inadequately clothed in sheer black silk stockings and slim buckled patent-leather slippers.

"You're not dressed warmly enough," her husband would have said. "Those shoes are idiotic for driving." And he would have been right.

Dirk said nothing.

Her manipulation of the wheel was witchcraft. The roadster slid in and out of traffic like a fluid thing, an enamel stream, silent as a swift current in a river. "Can't let her out here," said Paula. "Wait till we get past Lincoln Park. Do you suppose they'll ever really get rid of this terrible Rush Street bridge?" When his house was reached, "I'm coming up," she said. "I suppose you haven't any tea?"

"Gosh, no! What do you think I am! A young man in an English novel!"

"Now, don't be provincial and Chicago-ish, Dirk." They climbed the three flights of stairs. She looked about. Her glance was not disapproving. "This isn't so bad. Who did it? She did! Very nice. But of course you ought to have your own smart little apartment, with a Jap to do you up. To do that for you, for example."

"Yes," grimly. He was packing his bag—not throwing clothes into it, but folding them deftly, neatly, as the son of a wise mother packs. "My salary'd just about keep him in white linen house-coats."

She was walking about the living room, picking up a book, putting it down, fingering an ash tray, gazing out of the window, examining a photograph, smoking a cigarette from the box on his table. Restless, nervously alive, catlike. "I'm going to send you some things for your room, Dirk."

"For God's sake don't!"

"Why not?"

"Two kinds of women in the world. I learned that at college. Those who send men things for their rooms and those that don't."

"You're very rude."

"You asked me. There! I'm all set." He snapped the lock of his bag. "I'm sorry I can't give you anything. I haven't a thing. Not even a glass of wine and a—what is it they say in books?—oh, yeh—a biscuit."

In the roadster again they slid smoothly out along the drive, along Sheridan Road, swung sharply around the cemetery curve into Evanston, past the smug middle-class suburban neatness of Wilmette and Win-

netka. She negotiated expertly the nerve-racking curves of the Hubbard
Woods hills, then maintained a fierce and steady speed for the remainder
of the drive.

"We call the place Stormwood," Paula told him. "And nobody outside the dear family knows how fitting that is. Don't scowl. I'm not going
to tell you my marital woes. And don't you say I asked for it. . . . How's
the job?"

"Rotten."

"You don't like it? The work?"

"I like it well enough, only—well, you see we leave the university
architectural course thinking we're all going to be Stanford Whites or
Cass Gilberts, tossing off a Woolworth building and making ourselves
famous overnight. I've spent all yesterday and to-day planning how to
work in space for toilets on every floor of the new office building, six
stories high and shaped like a drygoods box, that's going up on the
corner of Milwaukee Avenue and Ashland, west."

"And ten years from now?"

"Ten years from now maybe they'll let me do the plans for the drygoods box all alone."

"Why don't you drop it?"

He was startled. "Drop it! How do you mean?"

"Chuck it. Do something that will bring you quick results. This isn't
an age of waiting. Suppose, twenty years from now, you do plan a grand
Gothic office building to grace this new and glorified Michigan Boulevard they're always shouting about! You'll be a middle-aged man living
in a middle-class house in a middle-class suburb with a middle-class
wife."

"Maybe"—slightly nettled. "And maybe I'll be the Sir Christopher
Wren of Chicago."

"Who's he?"

"Good G——, how often have you been in London?"

"Three times."

"Next time you find yourself there you might cast your eye over a very
nice little structure called St. Paul's Cathedral. I've never seen it but it
has been very well spoken of."

They turned in at the gates of Stormwood. Though the trees and
bushes were gaunt and bare the grass already showed stretches of vivid
green. In the fading light one caught glimpses through the shrubbery
of the lake beyond. It was a dazzling sapphire blue in the sunset. A final
turn of the drive. An avenue of trees. A house, massive, pillared,
porticoed. The door opened as they drew up at the entrance. A maid
in cap and apron stood in the doorway. A man appeared at the side of

the car, coming seemingly from nowhere, greeted Paula civilly and drove the car off. The glow of an open fire in the hall welcomed them. "He'll bring up your bag," said Paula. "How're the babies, Anna? Has Mr. Storm got here?"

"He telephoned, Mrs. Storm. He says he won't be out till late—maybe ten or after. Anyway, you're not to wait dinner."

Paula, from being the limp, expert, fearless driver of the high-powered roadster was now suddenly very much the mistress of the house, quietly observant, giving an order with a lift of the eyebrow or a nod of the head. Would Dirk like to go to his room at once? Perhaps he'd like to look at the babies before they went to sleep for the night, though the nurse would probably throw him out. One of those stern British females. Dinner at seven-thirty. He needn't dress. Just as he liked. Everything was very informal here. They roughed it. (Dirk had counted thirteen servants by noon next day and hadn't been near the kitchen, laundry, or dairy.)

His room, when he reached it, he thought pretty awful. A great square chamber with narrow leaded windows, deep-set, on either side. From one he could get a glimpse of the lake, but only a glimpse. Evidently the family bedrooms were the lake rooms. In the DeJong code and class the guest had the best but evidently among these moneyed ones the family had the best and the guest was made comfortable, but was not pampered. It was a new angle for Dirk. He thought it startling but rather sensible. His bag had been brought up, unpacked, and stowed away in a closet before he reached his room. "Have to tell that to Selina," he thought, grinning. He looked about the room, critically. It was done in a style that he vaguely defined as French. It gave him the feeling that he had stumbled accidentally into the chamber of a Récamier and couldn't get out. Rose brocade with gold net and cream lace and rosebuds. "Swell place for a man," he thought, and kicked a footstool—a *fauteuil* he supposed it was called, and was secretly glad that he could pronounce it faultlessly. Long mirrors, silken hangings, cream walls. The bed was lace hung. The coverlet was rose satin, feather-light. He explored his bathroom. It actually was a room, much larger than his alcove bedroom on Deming Place—as large as his own bedroom at home on the farm. The bath was done dazzlingly in blue and white. The tub was enormous and as solid as if the house had been built around it. There were towels and towels and towels in blue and white, ranging in size all the way from tiny embroidered wisps to fuzzy all-enveloping bath towels as big as a carpet.

He was much impressed.

He decided to bathe and change into dinner clothes and was glad of this when he found Paula in black chiffon before the fire in the great beamed room she had called the library. Dirk thought she looked very beautiful in that diaphanous stuff, with the pearls. Her heart-shaped face, with its large eyes that slanted a little at the corners; her long slim throat; her dark hair piled high and away from her little ears. He decided not to mention it.

"You look extremely dangerous," said Paula.

"I am," replied Dirk, "but it's hunger that brings this look of the beast to my usually mild Dutch features. Also, why do you call this the library?" Empty shelves gaped from the wall on all sides. The room was meant to hold hundreds of volumes. Perhaps fifty or sixty in all now leaned limply against each other or lay supine.

Paula laughed. "They do look sort of sparse, don't they? Theodore bought this place, you know, as is. We've books enough in town, of course. But I don't read much out here. And Theodore!—I don't believe he ever in his life read anything but detective stories and the newspapers."

Dirk told himself that Paula had known her husband would not be home until ten and had deliberately planned a tête-à-tête meal. He would not, therefore, confess himself a little nettled when Paula said, "I've asked the Emerys in for dinner; and we'll have a game of bridge afterward. Phil Emery, you know, the Third. He used to have it on his visiting card, like royalty."

The Emerys were drygoods; had been drygoods for sixty years; were accounted Chicago aristocracy; preferred England; rode to hounds in pink coats along Chicago's prim and startled suburban prairies. They had a vast estate on the lake near Stormwood. They arrived a trifle late. Dirk had seen pictures of old Phillip Emery ("Phillip the First," he thought, with an inward grin) and decided, looking at the rather anæmic third edition, that the stock was running a little thin. Mrs. Emery was blonde, statuesque, and unmagnetic. In contrast Paula seemed to glow like a sombre jewel. The dinner was delicious but surprisingly simple; little more than Selina would have given him, Dirk thought, had he come home to the farm this week-end. The talk was desultory and rather dull. And this chap had millions, Dirk said to himself. Millions. No scratching in an architect's office for this lad. Mrs. Emery was interested in the correct pronunciation of Chicago street names.

"It's terrible," she said. "I think there ought to be a Movement for the proper pronunciation. The people ought to be taught; and the children in the schools. They call Goethe Street 'Gerty'; and pronounce all the s's in Des Plaines. Even Illinois they call 'Illinoise.'" She was very much in earnest. Her breast rose and fell. She ate her salad rapidly. Dirk thought that large blondes oughtn't to get excited. It made their faces red.

At bridge after dinner Phillip the Third proved to be sufficiently the son of his father to win from Dirk more money than he could conveniently afford to lose. Though Mrs. Phil had much to do with this, as Dirk's partner. Paula played with Emery, a bold shrewd game.

Theodore Storm came in at ten and stood watching them. When the guests had left the three sat before the fire. "Something to drink?" Storm asked Dirk. Dirk refused but Storm mixed a stiff highball for himself, and then another. The whiskey brought no flush to his large white impassive face. He talked almost not at all. Dirk, naturally silent, was loquacious by comparison. But while there was nothing heavy, unvital about Dirk's silence this man's was oppressive, irritating. His paunch, his large white hands, his great white face gave the effect of bleached bloodless bulk. "I don't see how she stands him," Dirk thought. Husband and wife seemed to be on terms of polite friendliness. Storm excused himself and took himself off with a word about being tired, and seeing them in the morning.

After he had gone: "He likes you," said Paula.

"Important," said Dirk, "if true."

"But it is important. He can help you a lot."

"Help me how? I don't want——"

"But I do. I want you to be successful. I want you to be. You can be. You've got it written all over you. In the way you stand, and talk, and don't talk. In the way you look at people. In something in the way you carry yourself. It's what they call force, I suppose. Anyway, you've got it."

"Has your husband got it?"

"Theodore! No! That is——"

"There you are. I've got the force, but he's got the money."

"You can have both." She was leaning forward. Her eyes were bright, enormous. Her hands—those thin dark hot hands—were twisted in her lap. He looked at her quietly. Suddenly there were tears in her eyes. "Don't look at me that way, Dirk." She huddled back in her chair, limp. She looked a little haggard and older, somehow. "My marriage is a mess, of course. You can see that."

"You knew it would be, didn't you?"

"No. Yes. Oh, I don't know. Anyway, what's the difference, now? I'm not trying to be what they call an Influence in your life. I'm just fond of you—you know that—and I want you to be great and successful. It's maternal, I suppose."

"I should think two babies would satisfy that urge."

"Oh, I can't get excited about two pink healthy lumps of babies. I love them and all that, but all they need is to have a bottle stuffed into their mouths at proper intervals and to be bathed, and dressed and aired and slept. It's a mechanical routine and about as exciting as a treadmill. I can't go round being maternal and beating my breast over two nice firm lumps of flesh."

"Just what do you want me to do, Paula?"

She was eager again, vitally concerned in him. "It's all so ridiculous. All these men whose incomes are thirty—forty—sixty—a hundred thousand a year usually haven't any qualities, really, that the five-thousand-a-year man hasn't. The doctor who sent Theodore a bill for four thousand dollars when each of my babies was born didn't do a thing that a country doctor with a Ford wouldn't do. But he knew he could get it and he asked it. Somebody has to get the fifty-thousand-dollar salaries—some advertising man, or bond salesman or—why, look at Phil Emery! He probably couldn't sell a yard of pink ribbon to a schoolgirl if he had to. Look at Theodore! He just sits and blinks and says nothing. But when the time comes he doubles up his fat white fist and mumbles, 'Ten million,' or 'Fifteen million,' and that settles it."

Dirk laughed to hide his own little mounting sensation of excitement. "It isn't quite as simple as that, I imagine. There's more to it than meets the eye."

"There isn't! I tell you I know the whole crowd of them. I've been brought up with this moneyed pack all my life, haven't I? Pork packers and wheat grabbers and pedlers of gas and electric light and dry goods. Grandfather's the only one of the crowd that I respect. He has stayed the same. They can't fool him. He knows he just happened to go into wholesale beef and pork when wholesale beef and pork was a new game in Chicago. Now look at him!"

"Still, you will admit there's something in knowing when," he argued.

Paula stood up. "If you don't know I'll tell you. Now is when. I've got Grandfather and Dad and Theodore to work with. You can go on being an architect if you want to. It's a fine enough profession. But unless you're a genius where'll it get you! Go in with them, and Dirk, in five years——"

"What!" They were both standing, facing each other, she tense, eager; he relaxed but stimulated.

"Try it and see what, will you? Will you, Dirk?"

"I don't know, Paula. I should say my mother wouldn't think much of it."

"What does she know! Oh, I don't mean that she isn't a fine, wonderful person. She is. I love her. But success! She thinks success is another acre of asparagus or cabbage; or a new stove in the kitchen now that they've brought gas out as far as High Prairie."

He had a feeling that she possessed him; that her hot eager hands held him though they stood apart and eyed each other almost hostilely.

As he undressed that night in his rose and satin room he thought, "Now what's her game? What's she up to? Be careful, Dirk, old boy." On coming into the room he had gone immediately to the long mirror and had looked at himself carefully, searchingly, not knowing that Paula, in her room, had done the same. He ran a hand over his close-shaved chin, looked at the fit of his dinner coat. He wished he had had it made at Peter Peel's, the English tailor on Michigan Boulevard. But Peel was so damned expensive. Perhaps next time . . .

As he lay in the soft bed with the satin coverlet over him he thought, "Now what's her lit-tle game!"

He awoke at eight, enormously hungry. He wondered, uneasily, just how he was going to get his breakfast. She had said his breakfast would be brought him in his room. He stretched luxuriously, sprang up, turned on his bath water, bathed. When he emerged in dressing gown and slippers his breakfast tray had been brought him mysteriously and its contents lay appetizingly on a little portable table. There were flocks of small covered dishes and a charming individual coffee service. The morning papers, folded and virgin, lay next this. A little note from Paula: "Would you like to take a walk at about half-past nine? Stroll down to the stables. I want to show you my new horse."

The distance from the house to the stables was actually quite a brisk little walk in itself. Paula, in riding clothes, was waiting for him. She looked boyish and young standing beside the sturdy bulk of Pat, the head stableman. She wore tan whipcord breeches, a coat of darker stuff, a little round felt hat whose brim curved away from her face.

She greeted him. "I've been out two hours. Had my ride."

"I hate people who tell you, first thing in the morning, that they've been out two hours."

"If that's the kind of mood you're in we won't show him the horse, will we, Pat?"

Pat thought they would. Pat showed him the new saddle mare as a mother exhibits her latest offspring, tenderly, proudly. "Look at her back," said Pat. "That's the way you tell a horse, sir. By the length of this here line. Lookut it! There's a picture for you, now!"

Paula looked up at Dirk. "You ride, don't you?"

"I used to ride the old nags, bareback, on the farm."

"You'll have to learn. We'll teach him, won't we, Pat?"

Pat surveyed Dirk's lean, flexible figure. "Easy."

"Oh, say!" protested Dirk.

"Then I'll have some one to ride with me. Theodore never rides. He never takes any sort of exercise. Sits in that great fat car of his."

They went into the coach house, a great airy whitewashed place with glittering harness and spurs and bridles like jewels in glass cases. There were ribbons, too, red and yellow and blue in a rack on the wall; and trophy cups. The coach house gave Dirk a little hopeless feeling. He had never before seen anything like it. In the first place, there were no motors in it. He had forgotten that people rode in anything but motors. A horse on Chicago's boulevards raised a laugh. The sight of a shining brougham with two sleek chestnuts driving down Michigan Avenue would have set that street to staring and sniggering as a Roman chariot drawn by zebras might have done. Yet here was such a brougham, glittering, spotless. Here was a smart cream surrey with a cream-coloured top hung with fringe. There were two-wheeled carts high and slim and chic. A victoria. Two pony carts. One would have thought, seeing this room, that the motor vehicle had never been invented. And towering over all, dwarfing the rest, out-glittering them, stood a tally-ho, a sheer piece of wanton insolence. It was in perfect order. Its cushions were immaculate. Its sides shone. Its steps glistened. Dirk, looking up at it, laughed outright. It seemed too splendid, too absurd. With a sudden boyish impulse he swung himself up the three steps that led to the box and perched himself on the fawn cushioned seat. He looked very handsome there. "A coach and four—isn't that what they call it? Got any Roman juggernauts?"

"Do you want to drive it?" asked Paula. "This afternoon? Do you think you can? Four horses, you know." She laughed up at him, her dark face upturned to his.

Dirk looked down at her. "No." He climbed down. "I suppose that at about the time they drove this hereabouts my father was taking the farm plugs into the Haymarket."

Something had annoyed him, she saw. Would he wait while she changed to walking things? Or perhaps he'd rather drive in the roadster. They walked up to the house together. He wished that she would not consult his wishes so anxiously. It made him sulky, impatient.

She put a hand on his arm. "Dirk, are you annoyed at me for what I said last night?"

"No."

"What did you think when you went to your room last night? Tell me. What did you think?"

"I thought: 'She's bored with her husband and she's trying to vamp me. I'll have to be careful.'"

Paula laughed delightedly. "That's nice and frank . . . What else?"
"I thought my coat didn't fit very well and I wished I could afford
to have Peel make my next one."
"You can," said Paula.

XVI

As it turned out, Dirk was spared the necessity of worrying about the
fit of his next dinner coat for the following year and a half. His coat,
during that period, was a neat olive drab as was that of some millions of
young men of his age, or thereabouts. He wore it very well, and with the
calm assurance of one who knows that his shoulders are broad, his waist
slim, his stomach flat, his flanks lean, and his legs straight. Most of that
time he spent at Fort Sheridan, first as an officer in training, then as an
officer training others to be officers. He was excellent at this job. Influence put him there and kept him there even after he began to chafe
at the restraint. Fort Sheridan is a few miles outside Chicago, north. No
smart North Shore dinner was considered complete without at least a
major, a colonel, two captains, and a sprinkling of first lieutenants. Their
boots shone so delightfully while dancing.

In the last six months of it (though he did not, of course, know that
it was to be the last six months) Dirk tried desperately to get to France.
He was suddenly sick of the neat job at home; of the dinners; of the
smug routine; of the olive-drab motor car that whisked him wherever he
wanted to go (he had a captaincy); of making them "snap into it"; of
Paula; of his mother, even. Two months before the war's close he succeeded in getting over; but Paris was his headquarters.

Between Dirk and his mother the first rift had appeared.

"If I were a man," Selina said, "I'd make up my mind straight about
this war and then I'd do one of two things. I'd go into it the way Jan
Snip goes at forking the manure pile—a dirty job that's got to be cleaned
up; or I'd refuse to do it altogether if I didn't believe in it as a job for
me. I'd fight, or I'd be a conscientious objector. There's nothing in between for any one who isn't old or crippled, or sick."

Paula was aghast when she heard this. So was Julie whose wailings had
been loud when Eugene had gone into the air service. He was in France

now, thoroughly happy. "Do you mean," demanded Paula, "that you actually want Dirk to go over there and be wounded or killed!"

"No. If Dirk were killed my life would stop. I'd go on living, I suppose, but my life would have stopped."

They all were doing some share in the work to be done.

Selina had thought about her own place in this war welter. She had wanted to do canteen work in France but had decided against this as being selfish. "The thing for me to do," she said, "is to go on raising vegetables and hogs as fast as I can." She supplied countless households with free food while their men were gone. She herself worked like a man, taking the place of the able-bodied helper who had been employed on her farm.

Paula was lovely in her Red Cross uniform. She persuaded Dirk to go into the Liberty Bond selling drive and he was unexpectedly effective in his quiet, serious way; most convincing and undeniably thrilling to look at in uniform. Paula's little air of possession had grown until now it enveloped him. She wasn't playing now; was deeply and terribly in love with him.

When, in 1918, Dirk took off his uniform he went into the bond department of the Great Lakes Trust Company in which Theodore Storm had a large interest. He said that the war had disillusioned him. It was a word you often heard uttered as a reason or an excuse for abandoning the normal. "Disillusioned."

"What did you think war was going to do?" said Selina. "Purify! It never has yet."

It was understood, by Selina at least, that Dirk's abandoning of his profession was a temporary thing. Quick as she usually was to arrive at conclusions, she did not realize until too late that this son of hers had definitely deserted building for bonds; that the only structures he would rear were her own castles in Spain. His first two months as a bond salesman netted him more than a year's salary at his old post at Hollis & Sprague's. When he told this to Selina, in triumph, she said, "Yes, but there isn't much fun in it, is there? This selling things on paper? Now architecture, that must be thrilling. Next to writing a play and seeing it acted by real people—seeing it actually come alive before your eyes— architecture must be the next most fun. Putting a building down on paper—little marks here, straight lines there, figures, calculations, blueprints, measurements—and then, suddenly one day, the actual building itself. Steel and stone and brick, with engines throbbing inside it like a heart, and people flowing in and out. Part of a city. A piece of actual beauty conceived by you! Oh, Dirk!" To see her face then must have given him a pang, it was so alive, so eager.

He found excuses for himself. "Selling bonds that make that building possible isn't so dull, either."

But she waved that aside almost contemptuously. "What nonsense, Dirk. It's like selling seats at the box office of a theatre for the play inside."

But Dirk had made many new friends in the last year and a half. More than that, he had acquired a new manner; an air of quiet authority, of assurance. The profession of architecture was put definitely behind him. There had been no building in all the months of the war; probably would be none in years. Materials were prohibitive, labour exorbitant. He did not say to Selina that he had put the other work from him. But after six months in his new position he knew that he would never go back.

From the start he was a success. Within one year he was so successful that you could hardly distinguish him from a hundred other successful young Chicago business and professional men whose clothes were made at Peel's; who kept their collars miraculously clean in the soot-laden atmosphere of the Loop; whose shoes were bench-made; who lunched at the Noon Club on the roof of the First National Bank where Chicago's millionaires ate corned-beef hash whenever that plebeian dish appeared on the bill of fare. He had had a little thrill out of his first meal at this club whose membership was made up of the "big men" of the city's financial circle. Now he could even feel a little flicker of contempt for them. He had known old Aug Hempel, of course, for years, as well as Michael Arnold, and, later, Phillip Emery, Theodore Storm, and others. But he had expected these men to be different.

Paula had said, "Theodore, why don't you take Dirk up to the Noon Club some day? There are a lot of big men he ought to meet."

Dirk went in some trepidation. The great grilled elevator, as large as a room, whisked them up to the roof of the fortress of gold. The club lounge furnished his first disappointment. It looked like a Pullman smoker. The chairs were upholstered in black leather or red plush. The woodwork was shiny red imitation mahogany. The carpet was green. There were bright shining brass cuspidors in the hall near the cigar counter. The food was well cooked. Man's food. Nine out of every ten of these men possessed millions. Whenever corned beef and cabbage appeared on the luncheon menu nine out of ten took it. These were not at all the American Big Business Man of the comic papers and of fiction —that yellow, nervous, dyspeptic creature who lunches off milk and pie. They were divided into two definite types. The older men of between fifty and sixty were great high-coloured fellows of full habit. Many of them had had a physician's warning of high blood pressure, hardening arteries, overworked heart, rebellious kidneys. So now they waxed cautious, taking time over their substantial lunches, smoking and talking. Their faces were impassive, their eyes shrewd, hard. Their talk was colloquial and frequently illiterate. They often said "was" for "were." "Was you going to see Baldwin about that South American stuff or is he going to ship it through without?" Most of them had known little of play in their youth and now they played ponderously and a little sadly and yet eagerly as does one to whom the gift of leisure had come too late. On Saturday afternoon you saw them in imported heather green golf stockings and Scotch tweed suits making for the links or the lake. They ruined their palates and livers with strong cigars, thinking cigarette smoking undignified and pipes common. "Have a cigar!" was their greeting, their password, their open sesame. "Have a cigar." Only a few were so rich, so assured as to smoke cheap light panatellas. Old Aug Hempel was one of these. Dirk noticed that when he made one of his rare visits to the Noon Club his entrance was met with a little stir, a deference. He was nearing seventy-five now; was still straight, strong, zestful of life; a magnificent old buccaneer among the pettier crew. His had been the direct and brutal method—swish! swash! and his enemies walked the plank. The younger men eyed him with a certain amusement and respect.

These younger men whose ages ranged from twenty-eight to forty-five were disciples of the new system in business. They were graduates of universities. They had known luxury all their lives. They were the second or third generation. They used the word "psychology." They practised restraint. They knew the power of suggestion. Where old Aug Hempel had flown the black flag they resorted to the periscope. Dirk learned that these men did not talk business during meal time except when they had met definitely for that purpose. They wasted a good deal of time, Dirk thought, and often, when they were supposed to be "in conference" or when their secretaries said primly that they were very busy and not to be disturbed until three, they were dozing off for a comfortable half hour in their private offices. They were the sons or grandsons of those bearded, rugged, and rather terrible old boys who, in 1835 or 1840, had come out of County Limerick or County Kilkenny or out of Scotland or the Rhineland to mold this new country in their strong hairy hands; those hands whose work had made possible the symphony orchestras, the yacht clubs, the golf clubs through which their descendants now found amusement and relaxation.

Dirk listened to the talk of the Noon Club.

"I made it in eighty-six. That isn't so bad for the Tippecanoe course."

". . . boxes are going pretty well but the Metropolitan grabs up all the big ones and the house wants names. Garden doesn't draw the way she used to, even in Chicago. It's the popular subscription that counts."

". . . grabbed the Century out of New York at two-forty-five and got back here in time to try out my new horse in the park. She's a little nervous for city riding but we're opening the house at Lake Forest next week——"

". . . pretty good show but they don't send the original companies here, that's the trouble . . ."

". . . in London. It's a neat shade of green, isn't it? You can't get ties like this over here, I don't know why. Got a dozen last time I was over. Yeh, Plumbridge in Bond Street."

Well, Dirk could talk like that easily enough. He listened quietly, nodded, smiled, agreed or disagreed. He looked about him carefully, appraisingly. Waist lines well kept in; carefully tailored clothes; shrewd wrinkles of experience radiating in fine sprays in the skin around the corners of their eyes. The president of an advertising firm lunching with a banker; a bond salesman talking to a rare book collector; a packer seated at a small table with Horatio Craft, the sculptor.

Two years and Dirk, too, had learned to "grab the Century" in order to save an hour or so of time between Chicago and New York. Peel said it was a pleasure to fit a coat to his broad, flat tapering back, and trousers to his strong sturdy legs. His colour, inherited from his red-cheeked Dutch ancestors brought up in the fresh sea-laden air of the Holland flats, was fine and clear. Sometimes Selina, in pure sensuous delight, passed her gnarled, work-worn hand over his shoulders and down his fine, strong, straight back. He had been abroad twice. He learned to call it "running over to Europe for a few days." It had all come about in a scant two years, as is the theatrical way in which life speeds in America.

Selina was a little bewildered now at this new Dirk whose life was so full without her. Sometimes she did not see him for two weeks, or three. He sent her gifts which she smoothed and touched delightedly and put away; fine soft silken things, hand-made—which she could not wear. The habit of years was too strong upon her. Though she had always been a woman of dainty habits and fastidious tastes the grind of her early married life had left its indelible mark. Now, as she dressed, you might have seen that her petticoat was likely to be black sateen and her plain, durable corset cover neatly patched where it had worn under the arms. She employed none of the artifices of a youth-mad day. Sun and wind and rain and the cold and heat of the open prairie had wreaked their vengeance on her flouting of them. Her skin was tanned, weather-beaten; her hair rough and dry. Her eyes, in that frame, startled you by their unexpectedness, they were so calm, so serene, yet so alive.

They were the beautiful eyes of a wise young girl in the face of a middle-aged woman. Life was still so fresh to her.

She had almost poignantly few personal belongings. Her bureau drawers were like a nun's; her brush and comb, a scant stock of plain white underwear. On the bathroom shelf her toothbrush, some vaseline, a box of talcum powder. None of those aids to artifice with which the elderly woman deludes herself into thinking that she is hoodwinking the world. She wore well-made walking oxfords now, with sensible heels—the kind known as Field's special; plain shirtwaists and neat dark suits, or a blue cloth dress. A middle-aged woman approaching elderliness; a woman who walked and carried herself well; who looked at you with a glance that was direct but never hard. That was all. Yet there was about her something arresting, something compelling. You felt it.

"I don't see how you do it!" Julie Arnold complained one day as Selina was paying her one of her rare visits in town. "Your eyes are as bright as a baby's and mine look like dead oysters." They were up in Julie's dressing room in the new house on the north side—the new house that was now the old house. Julie's dressing table was a bewildering thing. Selina DeJong, in her neat black suit and her plain black hat, sat regarding it and Julie seated before it, with a grim and lively interest.

"It looks," Selina said, "like Mandel's toilette section, or a hospital operating room just before a major operation." There were great glass jars that contained meal, white and gold. There were rows and rows of cream pots holding massage cream, vanishing cream, cleansing cream. There were little china bowls of scarlet and white and yellowish pastes. A perforated container spouted a wisp of cotton. You saw toilet waters, perfumes, atomizers, French soaps, unguents, tubes. It wasn't a dressing table merely, but a laboratory.

"This!" exclaimed Julie. "You ought to see Paula's. Compared to her toilette ceremony mine is just a splash at the kitchen sink." She rubbed cold cream now around her eyes with her two forefingers, using a practised upward stroke.

"It looks fascinating," Selina exclaimed. "Some day I'm going to try it. There are so many things I'm going to try some day. So many things I've never done that I'm going to do for the fun of it. Think of it, Julie! I've never had a manicure! Some day I'm going to have one. I'll tell the girl to paint my nails a beautiful bright vermilion. And I'll tip her twenty-five cents. They're so pretty with their bobbed hair and their queer bright eyes. I s'pose you'll think I'm crazy if I tell you they make me feel young."

Julie was massaging. Her eyes had an absent look. Suddenly: "Listen, Selina. Dirk and Paula are together too much. People are talking."

"Talking?" The smile faded from Selina's face.

"Goodness knows I'm not strait-laced. You can't be in this day and age. If I had ever thought I'd live to see the time when—— Well, since the war of course anything's all right, seems. But Paula has no sense. Everybody knows she's insane about Dirk. That's all right for Dirk, but how about Paula! She won't go anywhere unless he's invited. Of course Dirk is awfully popular. Goodness knows there are few enough young men like him in Chicago—handsome and successful and polished and all. Most of them dash off East just as soon as they can get their fathers to establish an Eastern branch or something. . . . They're together all the time, everywhere. I asked her if she was going to divorce Storm and she said no, she hadn't enough money of her own and Dirk wasn't earning enough. His salary's thousands, but she's used to millions. Well!"

"They were boy and girl together," Selina interrupted, feebly.

"They're not any more. Don't be silly, Selina. You're not as young as that."

No, she was not as young as that. When Dirk next paid one of his rare visits to the farm she called him into her bedroom—the cool, dim shabby bedroom with the old black walnut bed in which she had lain as Pervus DeJong's bride more than thirty years ago. She had on a little knitted jacket over her severe white nightgown. Her abundant hair was neatly braided in two long plaits. She looked somehow girlish there in the dim light, her great soft eyes gazing up at him.

"Dirk, sit down here at the side of my bed the way you used to."

"I'm dead tired, Mother. Twenty-seven holes of golf before I came out."

"I know. You ache all over—a nice kind of ache. I used to feel like that when I'd worked in the fields all day, pulling vegetables, or planting." He was silent. She caught his hand. "You didn't like that. My saying that. I'm sorry. I didn't say it to make you feel bad, dear."

"I know you didn't, Mother."

"Dirk, do you know what that woman who writes the society news in the Sunday *Tribune* called you today?"

"No. What? I never read it."

"She said you were one of the *jeunesse dorée*."

Dirk grinned. "Gosh!"

"I remember enough of my French at Miss Fister's school to know that that means gilded youth."

"Me! That's good! I'm not even spangled."

"Dirk!" her voice was low, vibrant. "Dirk, I don't want you to be a gilded youth, I don't care how thick the gilding. Dirk, that isn't what I worked in the sun and cold for. I'm not reproaching you; I didn't mind the work. Forgive me for even mentioning it. But, Dirk, I don't want my son to be known as one of the *jeunesse dorée*. No! Not my son!"

"Now, listen, Mother. That's foolish. If you're going to talk like that. Like a mother in a melodrama whose son's gone wrong. . . . I work like a dog. You know that. You get the wrong angle on things, stuck out here on this little farm. Why don't you come into town and take a little place and sell the farm?"

"Live with you, you mean?" Pure mischievousness.

"Oh, no. You wouldn't like that," hastily. "Besides, I'd never be there. At the office all day, and out somewhere in the evening."

"When do you do your reading, Dirk?"

"Why—uh——"

She sat up in bed, looking down at the thin end of her braid as she twined it round and round her finger. "Dirk, what is this you sell in that mahogany office of yours? I never did get the hang of it."

"Bonds, Mother. You know that perfectly well."

"Bonds." She considered this a moment. "Are they hard to sell? Who buys them?"

"That depends. Everybody buys them—that is . . ."

"I don't. I suppose because whenever I had any money it went back into the farm for implements, or repairs, or seed, or stock, or improvements. That's always the way with a farmer—even on a little truck farm like this." She pondered again a moment. He fidgeted, yawned. "Dirk DeJong—Bond Salesman."

"The way you say it, Mother, it sounds like a low criminal pursuit."

"Dirk, do you know sometimes I actually think that if you had stayed here on the farm——"

"Good God, Mother! What for!"

"Oh, I don't know. Time to dream. Time to—no, I suppose that isn't true any more. I suppose the day is past when the genius came from the farm. Machinery has cut into his dreams. He used to sit for hours on the wagon seat, the reins slack in his hands, while the horses plodded into town. Now he whizzes by in a jitney. Patent binders, ploughs, reapers —he's a mechanic. He hasn't time to dream. I guess if Lincoln had lived to-day he'd have split his rails to the tune of a humming, snarling patent wood cutter, and in the evening he'd have whirled into town to get his books at the public library, and he'd have read them under the glare of the electric light bulb instead of lying flat in front of the flickering wood fire. . . . Well. . . ."

She lay back, looked up at him. "Dirk, why don't you marry?"

"Why—there's no one I want to marry."

"No one who's free, you mean?"

He stood up. "I mean no one." He stooped and kissed her lightly. Her arms went round him close. Her hand with the thick gold wedding band on it pressed his head to her hard. "Sobig!" He was a baby again.

"You haven't called me that in years." He was laughing.

She reverted to the old game they had played when he was a child. "How big is my son! How big?" She was smiling, but her eyes were sombre.

"So big!" answered Dirk, and measured a very tiny space between thumb and forefinger. "So big."

She faced him, sitting up very straight in bed, the little wool shawl hunched about her shoulders. "Dirk, are you ever going back to architecture? The war is history. It's now or never with you. Pretty soon it will be too late. Are you ever going back to architecture? To your profession?"

A clean amputation. "No, Mother."

She gave an actual gasp, as though icy water had been thrown full in her face. She looked suddenly old, tired. Her shoulders sagged. He stood in the doorway, braced for her reproaches. But when she spoke it was to reproach herself. "Then I'm a failure."

"Oh, what nonsense, Mother. I'm happy. You can't live somebody else's life. You used to tell me, when I was a kid I remember, that life wasn't just an adventure, to be taken as it came, with the hope that something glorious was always hidden just around the corner. You said you had lived that way and it hadn't worked. You said——"

She interrupted him with a little cry. "I know I did. I know I did." Suddenly she raised a warning finger. Her eyes were luminous, prophetic. "Dirk, you can't desert her like that!"

"Desert who?" He was startled.

"Beauty! Self-expression. Whatever you want to call it. You wait! She'll turn on you some day. Some day you'll want her, and she won't be there."

Inwardly he had been resentful of this bedside conversation with his mother. She made little of him, he thought, while outsiders appreciated his success. He had said, "So big," measuring a tiny space between thumb and forefinger in answer to her half-playful question, but he had not honestly meant it. He thought her ridiculously old-fashioned now in her viewpoint, and certainly unreasonable. But he would not quarrel with her.

"You wait, too, Mother," he said now, smiling. "Some day your wayward son will be a real success. Wait till the millions roll in. Then we'll see."

She lay down, turned her back deliberately upon him, pulled the covers up about her.

"Shall I turn out your light, Mother, and open the windows?"

"Meena'll do it. She always does. Just call her. . . . Good-night."

He knew that he had come to be a rather big man in his world. Influence had helped. He knew that, too. But he shut his mind to much
of Paula's manœuvring and wire pulling—refused to acknowledge that
her lean, dark, eager fingers had manipulated the mechanism that ordered his career. Paula herself was wise enough to know that to hold
him she must not let him feel indebted to her. She knew that the debtor
hates his creditor. She lay awake at night planning for him, scheming
for his advancement, then suggested these schemes to him so deftly as
to make him think he himself had devised them. She had even realized
of late that their growing intimacy might handicap him if openly commented on. But now she must see him daily, or speak to him. In the
huge house on Lake Shore Drive her own rooms—sitting room, bedroom,
dressing room, bath—were as detached as though she occupied a separate
apartment. Her telephone was a private wire leading only to her own
bedroom. She called him the first thing in the morning; the last thing
at night. Her voice, when she spoke to him, was an organ transformed;
low, vibrant, with a timbre in its tone that would have made it un-
recognizable to an outsider. Her words were commonplace enough, but
pregnant and meaningful for her.

"What did you do to-day? Did you have a good day? . . . Why
didn't you call me? . . . Did you follow up that suggestion you made
about Kennedy? I think it's a wonderful idea, don't you? You're a wonderful man, Dirk; did you know that? . . . I miss you. . . . Do you?
. . . When? . . . Why not lunch? . . . Oh, not if you have a business
appointment . . . How about five o'clock? . . . No, not there . . . Oh,
I don't know. It's so public . . . Yes . . . Good-bye. . . . Good-night.
. . . Good-night. . . ."

They began to meet rather furtively, in out-of-the-way places. They
would lunch in department store restaurants where none of their friends
ever came. They spent off afternoon hours in the dim, close atmosphere
of the motion picture palaces, sitting in the back row, seeing nothing of
the film, talking in eager whispers that failed to annoy the scattered
devotees in the middle of the house. When they drove it was on obscure
streets of the south side, as secure there from observation as though they
had been in Africa, for to the north sider the south side of Chicago is
the hinterland of civilization.

Paula had grown very beautiful, her world thought. There was about
her the aura, the glow, the roseate exhalation that surrounds the woman
in love.

Frequently she irritated Dirk. At such times he grew quieter than ever; more reserved. As he involuntarily withdrew she advanced. Sometimes he thought he hated her—her hot eager hands, her glowing asking eyes, her thin red mouth, her sallow heart-shaped exquisite face, her perfumed clothing, her air of ownership. That was it! Her possessiveness. She clutched him so with her every look and gesture, even when she did not touch him. There was about her something avid, sultry. It was like the hot wind that sometimes blew over the prairie—blowing, blowing, but never refreshing. It made you feel dry, arid, irritated, parched. Sometimes Dirk wondered what Theodore Storm thought and knew behind that impassive flabby white mask of his.

Dirk met plenty of other girls. Paula was clever enough to see to that. She asked them to share her box at the opera. She had them at her dinners. She affected great indifference to their effect on him. She suffered when he talked to one of them.

"Dirk, why don't you take out that nice Farnham girl?"

"Is she nice?"

"Well, isn't she! You were talking to her long enough at the Kirks' dance. What were you talking about?"

"Books."

"Oh. Books. She's awfully nice and intelligent, isn't she? A lovely girl." She was suddenly happy. Books.

The Farnham girl was a nice girl. She was the kind of girl one should fall in love with and doesn't. The Farnham girl was one of many well-bred Chicago girls of her day and class. Fine, honest, clear-headed, frank, capable, good-looking in an indefinite and unarresting sort of way. Hair-coloured hair, good teeth, good enough eyes, clear skin, sensible medium hands and feet; skated well, danced well, talked well. Read the books you had read. A companionable girl. Loads of money but never spoke of it. Travelled. Her hand met yours firmly—and it was just a hand. At the contact no current darted through you, sending its shaft with a little zing to your heart.

But when Paula showed you a book her arm, as she stood next you, would somehow fit into the curve of yours and you were conscious of the feel of her soft slim side against you.

He knew many girls. There was a distinct type known as the North Shore Girl. Slim, tall, exquisite; a little fine nose, a high, sweet, slightly nasal voice, earrings, a cigarette, luncheon at Huyler's. All these girls looked amazingly alike, Dirk thought; talked very much alike. They all spoke French with a pretty good accent; danced intricate symbolic dances; read the new books; had the same patter. They prefaced, interlarded, concluded their remarks to each other with, "My deah!" It expressed, for them, surprise, sympathy, amusement, ridicule, horror, resig-

nation. "My *deah!* You should have seen her! My *deeah!*"—horror. Their
slang was almost identical with that used by the girls working in his
office. "She's a good kid," they said, speaking in admiration of another
girl. They made a fetish of frankness. In a day when everyone talked in
screaming headlines they knew it was necessary to red-ink their remarks
in order to get them noticed at all. The word rot was replaced by garbage
and garbage gave way to the ultimate swill. One no longer said "How
shocking!" but, "How perfectly obscene!" The words, spoken in their
sweet clear voices, fell nonchalantly from their pretty lips. All very fearless and uninhibited and free. That, they told you, was the main thing.
Sometimes Dirk wished they wouldn't work so hard at their play. They
were forever getting up pageants and plays and large festivals for charity;
Venetian fêtes, Oriental bazaars, charity balls. In the programme performance of these many of them sang better, acted better, danced better
than most professional performers, but the whole thing always lacked
the flavour, somehow, of professional performance. On these affairs they
lavished thousands in costumes and decorations, receiving in return
other thousands which they soberly turned over to the Cause. They
found nothing ludicrous in this. Spasmodically they went into business
or semi-professional ventures, defying the conventions. Paula did this,
too. She or one of her friends were forever opening blouse shops; starting Gifte Shoppes; burgeoning into tea rooms decorated in crude green
and vermilion and orange and black; announcing their affiliation with
an advertising agency. These adventures blossomed, withered, died. They
were the result of post-war restlessness. Many of these girls had worked
indefatigably during the 1917–1918 period; had driven service cars, managed ambulances, nursed, scrubbed, conducted canteens. They missed
the excitement, the satisfaction of achievement.

They found Dirk fair game, resented Paula's proprietorship. Susans
and Janes and Kates and Bettys and Sallys—plain old-fashioned names
for modern, erotic misses—they talked to Dirk, danced with him, rode
with him, flirted with him. His very unattainableness gave him piquancy.
That Paula Storm had him fast. He didn't care a hoot about girls.

"Oh, Mr. DeJong," they said, "your name's Dirk, isn't it? What a
slick name! What does it mean?"

"Nothing, I suppose. It's a Dutch name. My people—my father's people—were Dutch, you know."

"A dirk's a sort of sword, isn't it, or poniard? Anyway, it sounds very
keen and cruel and fatal—Dirk."

He would flush a little (one of his assets) and smile, and look at
them, and say nothing. He found that to be all that was necessary.

He got on enormously.

XVII

BETWEEN these girls and the girls that worked in his office there existed a similarity that struck and amused Dirk. He said, "Take a letter, Miss Roach," to a slim young creature as exquisite as the girl with whom he had danced the day before; or ridden or played tennis or bridge. Their very clothes were faultless imitations. They even used the same perfume. He wondered, idly, how they did it. They were eighteen, nineteen, twenty, and their faces and bodies and desires and natural equipment made their presence in a business office a paradox, an absurdity. Yet they were capable, too, in a mechanical sort of way. Theirs were mechanical jobs. They answered telephones, pressed levers, clicked buttons, tapped typewriters, jotted down names. They were lovely creatures with the minds of fourteen-year-old children. Their hair was shining, perfectly undulated, as fine and glossy and tenderly curling as a young child's. Their breasts were flat, their figures singularly sexless like that of a very young boy. They were wise with the wisdom of the serpent. They wore wonderful little sweaters and flat babyish collars and ridiculously sensible stockings and oxfords. Their legs were slim and sturdy. Their mouths were pouting, soft, pink, the lower lip a little curled back, petalwise, like the moist mouth of a baby that has just finished nursing. Their eyes were wide apart, empty, knowledgeous. They managed their private affairs like generals. They were cool, remote, disdainful. They reduced their boys to desperation. They were brigands, desperadoes, pirates, taking all, giving little. They came, for the most part, from sordid homes, yet they knew, in some miraculous way, all the fine arts that Paula knew and practised. They were corsetless, pliant, bewildering, lovely, dangerous. They ate lunches that were horrible mixtures of cloying sweets and biting acids yet their skin was like velvet and cream. Their voices were thin, nasal, vulgar; their faces like those in a Greuze or a Fragonard. They said, with a twang that racked the listener, "I wouldn't of went if I got an invite but he could of give me a ring, anyways. I called him right. I was sore."

"Yeh? Wha'd he say?"

"Oh, he laffed."

"Didja go?"

"Me! No! Whatcha think I yam, anyway?"

"Oh, he's a good kid."

Among these Dirk worked immune, aloof, untouched. He would have
been surprised to learn that he was known among them as Frosty. They
approved his socks, his scarfs, his nails, his features, his legs in their well-
fitting pants, his flat strong back in the Peel coat. They admired and
resented him. Not one that did not secretly dream of the day when he
would call her into his office, shut the door, and say, "Loretta" (their
names were burbankian monstrosities, born of grafting the original ap-
pellation onto their own idea of beauty in nomenclature—hence Loretta,
Imogene, Nadine, Natalie, Ardella), "Loretta, I have watched you for
a long, long time and you must have noticed how deeply I admire you."

It wasn't impossible. Those things happen. The movies had taught
them that.

Dirk, all unconscious of their pitiless, all-absorbing scrutiny, would
have been still further appalled to learn how fully aware they were of
his personal and private affairs. They knew about Paula, for example.
They admired and resented her, too. They were fair in granting her the
perfection of her clothes, drew immense satisfaction from the knowledge
of their own superiority in the matters of youth and colouring; despised
her for the way in which she openly displayed her feeling for him (how
they knew this was a miracle and a mystery, for she almost never came
into the office and disguised all her telephone talks with him). They
thought he was grand to his mother. Selina had been in his office twice,
perhaps. On one of these occasions she had spent five minutes chatting
sociably with Ethelinda Quinn who had the face of a Da Vinci cherub
and the soul of a man-eating shark. Selina always talked to everyone. She
enjoyed listening to street car conductors, washwomen, janitors, landladies, clerks, doormen, chauffeurs, policemen. Something about her
made them talk. They opened to her as flowers to the sun. They sensed
her interest, her liking. As they talked Selina would exclaim, "You don't
say! Well, that's terrible!" Her eyes would be bright with sympathy.

Selina had said, on entering Dirk's office, "My land! I don't see how
you can work among those pretty creatures and not be a sultan. I'm
going to ask some of them down to the farm over Sunday."

"Don't, Mother! They wouldn't understand. I scarcely see them.
They're just part of the office equipment."

Afterward, Ethelinda Quinn had passed expert opinion. "Say, she's
got ten times the guts that Frosty's got. I like her fine. Did you see her
terrible hat! But say, it didn't look funny on her, did it? Anybody else in
that getup would look comical, but she's the kind that could walk off
with anything. I don't know. She's got what I call an air. It beats style.

Nice, too. She said I was a pretty little thing. Can you beat it! At that she's right. I cer'nly yam."

All unconscious, "Take a letter, Miss Quinn," said Dirk half an hour later.

In the midst, then, of this fiery furnace of femininity Dirk walked unscorched. Paula, the North Shore girls, well-bred business and professional women he occasionally met in the course of business, the enticing little nymphs he encountered in his own office, all practised on him their warm and perfumed wiles. He moved among them cool and serene. Perhaps his sudden success had had something to do with this; and his quiet ambition for further success. For he really was accounted successful now, even in the spectacular whirl of Chicago's meteoric financial constellation. North-side mammas regarded his income, his career, and his future with eyes of respect and wily speculation. There was always a neat little pile of invitations in the mail that lay on the correct little console in the correct little apartment ministered by the correct little Jap on the correct north-side street near (but not too near) the lake, and overlooking it.

The apartment had been furnished with Paula's aid. Together she and Dirk had gone to interior decorators. "But you've got to use your own taste, too," Paula had said, "to give it the individual touch." The apartment was furnished in a good deal of Italian furniture, the finish a dark oak or walnut, the whole massive and yet somehow unconvincing. The effect was sombre without being impressive. There were long carved tables on which an ash tray seemed a desecration; great chairs roomy enough for lolling, yet in which you did not relax; dull silver candlesticks; vestments; Dante's saturnine features sneering down upon you from a correct cabinet. There were not many books. Tiny foyer, large living room, bedroom, dining room, kitchen, and a cubby-hole for the Jap. Dirk did not spend much time in the place. Sometimes he did not sit in a chair in the sitting room for days at a time, using the room only as a short cut in his rush for the bedroom to change from office to dinner clothes. His upward climb was a treadmill, really. His office, the apartment, a dinner, a dance. His contacts were monotonous, and too few. His office was a great splendid office in a great splendid office building in LaSalle Street. He drove back and forth in a motor car along the boulevards. His social engagements lay north. LaSalle Street bounded him on the west, Lake Michigan on the east, Jackson Boulevard on the south, Lake Forest on the north. He might have lived a thousand miles away for all he knew of the rest of Chicago—the mighty, roaring, sweltering, pushing, screaming, magnificent hideous steel giant that was Chicago.

Selina had had no hand in the furnishing of his apartment. When it was finished Dirk had brought her in triumph to see it. "Well," he had said, "what do you think of it, Mother?"

She had stood in the centre of the room, a small plain figure in the midst of these massive sombre carved tables, chairs, chests. A little smile had quirked the corner of her mouth. "I think it's as cosy as a cathedral."

Sometimes Selina remonstrated with him, though of late she had taken on a strange reticence. She no longer asked him about the furnishings of the houses he visited (Italian villas on Ohio Street), or the exotic food he ate at splendid dinners. The farm flourished. The great steel mills and factories to the south were closing in upon her but had not yet set iron foot on her rich green acres. She was rather famous now for the quality of her farm products and her pens. You saw "DeJong asparagus" on the menu at the Blackstone and the Drake hotels. Sometimes Dirk's friends twitted him about this and he did not always acknowledge that the similarity of names was not a coincidence.

"Dirk, you seem to see no one but just these people," Selina told him in one of her infrequent rebukes. "You don't get the full flavour of life. You've got to have a vulgar curiosity about people and things. All kinds of people. All kinds of things. You revolve in the same little circle, over and over and over."

"Haven't time. Can't afford to take the time."

"You can't afford not to."

Sometimes Selina came into town for a week or ten days at a stretch, and indulged in what she called an orgy. At such times Julie Arnold would invite her to occupy one of the guest rooms at the Arnold house, or Dirk would offer her his bedroom and tell her that he would be comfortable on the big couch in the living room, or that he would take a room at the University Club. She always declined. She would take a room in a hotel, sometimes north, sometimes south. Her holiday before her she would go off roaming gaily as a small boy on a Saturday morning, with the day stretching gorgeously and adventuresomely ahead of him, sallies down the street without plan or appointment, knowing that richness in one form or another lies before him for the choosing. She loved the Michigan Boulevard and State Street shop windows in which haughty waxed ladies in glittering evening gowns postured, fingers elegantly crooked as they held a fan, a rose, a programme, meanwhile smiling condescendingly out upon an envious world flattening its nose against the plate glass barrier. A sociable woman, Selina, savouring life, she liked the lights, the colour, the rush, the noise. Her years of grinding work, with her face pressed down to the very soil itself, had failed to kill her zest for living. She prowled into the city's foreign quarters—Italian,

Greek, Chinese, Jewish. She penetrated the Black Belt, where Chicago's vast and growing Negro population shifted and moved and stretched its great limbs ominously, reaching out and out in protest and overflowing the bounds that irked it. Her serene face and her quiet manner, her bland interest and friendly look protected her. They thought her a social worker, perhaps; one of the uplifters. She bought and read the *Independent*, the Negro newspaper in which herb doctors advertised magic roots. She even sent the twenty-five cents required for a box of these, charmed by their names—Adam and Eve roots, Master of the Woods, Dragon's Blood, High John the Conqueror, Jezebel Roots, Grains of Paradise.

"Look here, Mother," Dirk would protest, "you can't wander around like that. It isn't safe. This isn't High Prairie, you know. If you want to go round I'll get Saki to drive you."

"That would be nice," she said, mildly. But she never availed herself of this offer. Sometimes she went over to South Water Street, changed now, and swollen to such proportions that it threatened to burst its confines. She liked to stroll along the crowded sidewalks, lined with crates and boxes and barrels of fruits, vegetables, poultry. Swarthy foreign faces predominated now. Where the red-faced overalled men had been she now saw lean muscular lads in old army shirts and khaki pants and scuffed puttees wheeling trucks, loading boxes, charging down the street in huge rumbling auto vans. Their faces were hard, their talk terse. They moved gracefully, with an economy of gesture. Any one of these, she reflected, was more vital, more native, functioned more usefully and honestly than her successful son, Dirk DeJong.

"Where 'r' beans?"

"In th' ol' beanery."

"Tough."

"Best you can get."

"Keep 'em."

Many of the older men knew her, shook hands with her, chatted a moment friendlily. William Talcott, a little more dried up, more wrinkled, his sparse hair quite gray now, still leaned up against the side of his doorway in his shirt sleeves and his neat pepper-and-salt pants and vest, a pretty good cigar, unlighted, in his mouth, the heavy gold watch chain spanning his middle.

"Well, you certainly made good, Mrs. DeJong. Remember the day you come here with your first load?"

Oh, yes. She remembered.

"That boy of yours has made his mark, too, I see. Doing grand, ain't he? Wa-al, great satisfaction having a son turn out well like that. Yes, sirree! Why, look at my da'ter Car'line——"

Life at High Prairie had its savour, too. Frequently you saw strange visitors there for a week or ten days at a time—boys and girls whose city pallor gave way to a rich tan; tired-looking women with sagging figures who drank Selina's cream and ate her abundant vegetables and tender chickens as though they expected these viands to be momentarily snatched from them. Selina picked these up in odd corners of the city. Dirk protested against this, too. Selina was a member of the High Prairie school board now. She often drove about the roads and into town in a disreputable Ford which she manipulated with imagination and skill. She was on the Good Roads Committee and the Truck Farmers' Association valued her opinion. Her life was full, pleasant, prolific.

XVIII

PAULA had a scheme for interesting women in bond buying. It was a good scheme. She suggested it so that Dirk thought he had thought of it. Dirk was head now of the bond department in the Great Lakes Trust Company's magnificent new white building on Michigan Boulevard north. Its white towers gleamed pink in the lake mists. Dirk said it was a terrible building, badly proportioned, and that it looked like a vast vanilla sundae. His new private domain was more like a splendid bookless library than a business office. It was finished in rich dull walnut and there were great upholstered chairs, soft rugs, shaded lights. Special attention was paid to women clients. There was a room for their convenience fitted with low restful chairs and couches, lamps, writing desks, in mauve and rose. Paula had selected the furnishings for this room. Ten years earlier it would have been considered absurd in a suite of business offices. Now it was a routine part of the equipment.

Dirk's private office was almost as difficult of access as that of the nation's executive. Cards, telephones, office boys, secretaries stood between the caller and Dirk DeJong, head of the bond department. You asked for him, uttering his name in the ear of the six-foot statuesque detective who, in the guise of usher, stood in the centre of the marble rotunda eyeing each visitor with a coldly appraising gaze. This one padded softly ahead of you on rubber heels, only to give you over to the care of a glorified office boy who took your name. You waited. He returned. You waited. Presently there appeared a young woman with inquiring eyebrows. She conversed with you. She vanished. You waited. She reappeared. You were ushered into Dirk DeJong's large and luxurious inner office. And there formality fled.

Dirk was glad to see you; quietly, interestedly glad to see you. As you stated your business he listened attentively, as was his charming way. The volume of business done with women clients by the Great Lakes Trust Company was enormous. Dirk was conservative, helpful—and he always got the business. He talked little. He was amazingly effective. Ladies in the modish black of recent bereavement made quite a sombre procession to his door. His suggestions (often originating with Paula) made the Great Lakes Trust Company's discreet advertising rich in results. Neat little pamphlets written for women on the subjects of saving, investments. "You are not dealing with a soulless corporation," said these brochures. "May we serve you? You need more than friends. Before acting, you should have your judgment vindicated by an organization of investment specialists. You may have relatives and friends, some of whom would gladly advise you on investments. But perhaps you rightly feel that the less they know about your financial affairs, the better. To handle trusts, and to care for the securities of widows and orphans, is our business."

It was startling to note how this sort of thing mounted into millions. "Women are becoming more and more used to the handling of money," Paula said, shrewdly. "Pretty soon their patronage is going to be as valuable as that of men. The average woman doesn't know about bonds—about bond buying. They think they're something mysterious and risky. They ought to be educated up to it. Didn't you say something, Dirk, about classes in finance for women? You could make a sort of semi-social affair of it. Send out invitations and get various bankers—big men, whose names are known—to talk to these women."

"But would the women come?"

"Of course they'd come. Women will accept any invitation that's engraved on heavy cream paper."

The Great Lakes Trust had a branch in Cleveland now, and one in New York, on Fifth Avenue. The drive to interest women in bond buying and to instruct them in finance was to take on almost national proportions. There was to be newspaper and magazine advertising.

The Talks for Women on the Subject of Finance were held every two weeks in the crystal room of the Blackstone and were a great success. Paula was right. Much of old Aug Hempel's shrewdness and business foresight had descended to her. The women came—widows with money to invest; business women who had thriftily saved a portion of their salaries; moneyed women who wanted to manage their own property, or who resented a husband's interference. Some came out of curiosity. Others for lack of anything better to do. Others to gaze on the well-known banker or lawyer or business man who was scheduled to address the meeting. Dirk spoke three or four times during the winter and was markedly a favourite. The women, in smart crêpe gowns and tailored suits and small chic hats, twittered and murmured about him, even while they sensibly digested his well-thought-out remarks. He looked very handsome, clean-cut, and distinguished there on the platform in his admirably tailored clothes, a small white flower in his buttonhole. He talked easily, clearly, fluently; answered the questions put to him afterward with just the right mixture of thoughtful hesitation and confidence.

It was decided that for the national advertising there must be an illustration that would catch the eye of women, and interest them. The person to do it, Dirk thought, was this Dallas O'Mara whose queer hentrack signature you saw scrawled on half the advertising illustrations that caught your eye. Paula had not been enthusiastic about this idea.

"M-m-m, she's very good," Paula had said, guardedly, "but aren't there others who are better?"

"She!" Dirk had exclaimed. "Is it a woman? I didn't know. That name might be anything."

"Oh, yes, she's a woman. She's said to be very—very attractive."

Dirk sent for Dallas O'Mara. She replied, suggesting an appointment two weeks from that date. Dirk decided not to wait, consulted other commercial artists, looked at their work, heard their plans outlined, and was satisfied with none of them. The time was short. Ten days had passed. He had his secretary call Dallas O'Mara on the telephone. Could she come down to see him that day at eleven?

No: she worked until four daily at her studio.

Could she come to his office at four-thirty, then?

Yes, but wouldn't it be better if he could come to her studio where he could see something of the various types of drawings—oils, or black-and-white, or crayons. She was working mostly in crayons now.

All this relayed by his secretary at the telephone to Dirk at his desk. He jammed his cigarette-end viciously into a tray, blew a final infuriated wraith of smoke, and picked up the telephone connection on his own desk. "One of those damned temperamental near-artists trying to be grand," he muttered, his hand over the mouthpiece. "Here, Miss Rawlings—I'll talk to her. Switch her over."

"Hello, Miss—uh—O'Mara. This is Mr. DeJong talking. I much prefer that you come to my office and talk to me." (No more of this non-sense.)

Her voice: "Certainly, if you prefer it. I thought the other would save us both some time. I'll be there at four-thirty." Her voice was leisurely, low, rounded. An admirable voice. Restful.

"Very well. Four-thirty," said Dirk, crisply. Jerked the receiver onto the hook. That was the way to handle 'em. These females of forty with straggling hair and a bundle of drawings under their arm.

The female of forty with straggling hair and a bundle of drawings un-der her arm was announced at four-thirty to the dot. Dirk let her wait five minutes in the outer office, being still a little annoyed. At four-thirty-five there entered his private office a tall slim girl in a smart little broad-tail jacket, fur-trimmed skirt, and a black hat at once so daring and so simple that even a man must recognize its French nativity. She carried no portfolio of drawings under her arms.

Through the man's mind flashed a series of unbusinesslike thoughts such as: "Gosh! . . . Eyes! . . . That's way I like to see girl dress . . . Tired looking . . . No, guess it's her eyes—sort of fatigued. . . . Pretty . . . No, she isn't . . . yes, she . . ." Aloud he said, "This is very kind of you, Miss O'Mara." Then he thought that sounded pomp-ous and said, curtly, "Sit down."

Miss O'Mara sat down. Miss O'Mara looked at him with her tired deep blue eyes. Miss O'Mara said nothing. She regarded him pleasantly, quietly, composedly. He waited for her to say that usually she did not come to business offices; that she had only twenty minutes to give him; that the day was warm, or cold; his office handsome; the view over the river magnificent. Miss O'Mara said nothing, pleasantly. So Dirk began to talk, rather hurriedly.

Now, this was a new experience for Dirk DeJong. Usually women spoke to him first and fluently. Quiet women waxed voluble under his silence; voluble women chattered. Paula always spoke a hundred words to his one. But here was a woman more silent than he; not sullenly silent, nor heavily silent, but quietly, composedly, restfully silent.

"I'll tell you the sort of thing we want, Miss O'Mara." He told her. When he had finished she probably would burst out with three or four plans. The others had done that.

When he had finished she said, "I'll think about it for a couple of days while I'm working on something else. I always do. I'm doing an olive soap picture now. I can begin work on yours Wednesday."

"But I'd like to see it—that is, I'd like to have an idea of what you're planning to do with it." Did she think he was going to let her go ahead without consulting his judgment!

"Oh, it will be all right. But drop into the studio if you like. It will take me about a week, I suppose. I'm over on Ontario in that old studio building. You'll know it by the way most of the bricks have fallen out of the building and are scattered over the sidewalk." She smiled a slow wide smile. Her teeth were good but her mouth was too big, he thought. Nice big warm kind of smile, though. He found himself smiling, too, sociably. Then he became businesslike again. Very businesslike.

"How much do you—what is your—what would you expect to get for a drawing such as that?"

"Fifteen hundred dollars," said Miss O'Mara.

"Nonsense." He looked at her then. Perhaps that had been humour. But she was not smiling. "You mean fifteen hundred for a single drawing?"

"For that sort of thing, yes."

"I'm afraid we can't pay that, Miss O'Mara."

Miss O'Mara stood up. "That is my price." She was not at all embarrassed. He realized that he had never seen such effortless composure. It was he who was fumbling with the objects on his flat-topped desk—a pen, a sheet of paper, a blotter. "Good-bye, Mr.—DeJong." She held out a friendly hand. He took it. Her hair was gold—dull gold, not bright— and coiled in a single great knot at the back of her head, low. He took her hand. The tired eyes looked up at him.

"Well, if that's your price, Miss O'Mara. I wasn't prepared to pay any such—but of course I suppose you top-notchers do get crazy prices for your work."

"Not any crazier than the prices you top-notchers get."

"Still, fifteen hundred dollars is quite a lot of money."

"I think so, too. But then, I'll always think anything over nine dollars is quite a lot of money. You see, I used to get twenty-five cents apiece for sketching hats for Gage's."

She was undeniably attractive. "And now you've arrived. You're successful."

"Arrived! Heavens, no! I've started."

"Who gets more money than you do for a drawing?"

"Nobody, I suppose."

"Well, then?"

"Well, then, in another minute I'll be telling you the story of my life."

She smiled again her slow wide smile; turned to leave. Dirk decided that while most women's mouths were merely features this girl's was a decoration.

She was gone. Miss Ethelinda Quinn *et al.*, in the outer office, appraised the costume of Miss Dallas O'Mara from her made-to-order footgear to her made-in-France millinery and achieved a lightning mental reconstruction of their own costumes. Dirk DeJong in the inner office realized that he had ordered a fifteen-hundred-dollar drawing, sight unseen, and that Paula was going to ask questions about it.

"Make a note, Miss Rawlings, to call Miss O'Mara's studio on Thursday."

In the next few days he learned that a surprising lot of people knew a surprisingly good deal about this Dallas O'Mara. She hailed from Texas, hence the absurd name. She was twenty-eight—twenty-five—thirty-two—thirty-six. She was beautiful. She was ugly. She was an orphan. She had worked her way through art school. She had no sense of the value of money. Two years ago she had achieved sudden success with her drawings. Her ambition was to work in oils. She toiled like a galley-slave; played like a child; had twenty beaux and no lover; her friends, men and women, were legion and wandered in and out of her studio as though it were a public thoroughfare. You were likely to find there at any hour any one from Bert Colson, the blackface musical comedy star, to Mrs. Robinson Gilman of Lake Forest and Paris; from Leo Mahler, first violin with the Chicago Symphony Orchestra, to Fanny Whipple who designed dresses for Carson's. She supported an assortment of unlucky brothers and spineless sisters in Texas and points west.

Miss Rawlings made an appointment for Thursday at three. Paula said she'd go with him and went. She dressed for Dallas O'Mara and the result was undeniably enchanting. Dallas sometimes did a crayon portrait, or even attempted one in oils. Had got a prize for her portrait of Mrs. Robinson Gilman at last spring's portrait exhibit at the Chicago Art Institute. It was considered something of an achievement to be asked to pose for her. Paula's hat had been chosen in deference to her hair and profile, and the neck line of her gown in deference to hat, hair, and profile, and her pearls with an eye to all four. The whole defied competition on the part of Miss Dallas O'Mara.

Miss Dallas O'Mara, in her studio, was perched on a high stool before an easel with a large tray of assorted crayons at her side. She looked a sight and didn't care at all. She greeted Dirk and Paula with a cheerful friendliness and went right on working. A model, very smartly gowned, was sitting for her.

"Hello!" said Dallas O'Mara. "This is it. Do you think you're going to like it?"

"Oh," said Dirk. "Is that it?" It was merely the beginning of a drawing of the smartly gowned model. "Oh, that's it, is it?" Fifteen hundred dollars!

"I hope you didn't think it was going to be a picture of a woman buying bonds." She went on working. She squinted one eye, picked up a funny little mirror thing which she held to one side, looked into, and put down. She made a black mark on the board with a piece of crayon then smeared the mark with her thumb. She had on a faded all-enveloping smock over which French ink, rubber cement, pencil marks, crayon dust and wash were so impartially distributed that the whole blended and mixed in a rich mellow haze like the Chicago atmosphere itself. The collar of a white silk blouse, not especially clean, showed above this. On her feet were soft kid bedroom slippers, scuffed, with pompons on them. Her dull gold hair was carelessly rolled into that great loose knot at the back. Across one cheek was a swipe of black.

"Well," thought Dirk, "she looks a sight."

Dallas O'Mara waved a friendly hand toward some chairs on which were piled hats, odd garments, bristol board and (on the broad arm of one) a piece of yellow cake. "Sit down." She called to the girl who had opened the door to them: "Gilda, will you dump some of those things. This is Mrs. Storm, Mr. DeJong—Gilda Hanan." Her secretary, Dirk later learned.

The place was disorderly, comfortable, shabby. A battered grand piano stood in one corner. A great skylight formed half the ceiling and sloped down at the north end of the room. A man and a girl sat talking earnestly on the couch in another corner. A swarthy foreign-looking chap, vaguely familiar to Dirk, was playing softly at the piano. The telephone rang. Miss Hanan took the message, transmitted it to Dallas O'Mara, received the answer, repeated it. Perched atop the stool, one slippered foot screwed in a rung, Dallas worked on concentratedly, calmly, earnestly. A lock of hair straggled over her eyes. She pushed it back with her wrist and left another dark splotch on her forehead. There was something splendid, something impressive, something magnificent about her absorption, her indifference to appearance, her unawareness of outsiders, her concentration on the work before her. Her nose was shiny. Dirk hadn't seen a girl with a shiny nose in years. They were always taking out those little boxes and things and plastering themselves with the stuff in 'em.

"How can you work with all this crowd around?"

"Oh," said Dallas in that deep restful leisurely voice of hers, "there are always between twenty and thirty"—she slapped a quick scarlet line on the board, rubbed it out at once—"thousand people in and out of here every hour, just about. I like it. Friends around me while I'm slaving."

"Gosh!" he thought, "she's—— I don't know—she's——"

"Shall we go?" said Paula.

He had forgotten all about her. "Yes. Yes, I'm ready if you are."

Outside, "Do you think you're going to like the picture?" Paula asked. They stepped into her car.

"Oh, I don't know. Can't tell much about it at this stage, I suppose."

"Back to your office?"

"Sure."

"Attractive, isn't she?"

"Think so?"

So he was going to be on his guard, was he! Paula threw in the clutch viciously, jerked the lever into second speed. "Her neck was dirty."

"Crayon dust," said Dirk.

"Not necessarily," replied Paula.

Dirk turned sideways to look at her. It was as though he saw her for the first time. She looked brittle, hard, artificial—small, somehow. Not in physique but in personality.

The picture was finished and delivered within ten days. In that time Dirk went twice to the studio in Ontario Street. Dallas did not seem to mind. Neither did she appear particularly interested. She was working hard both times. Once she looked as he had seen her on her first visit. The second time she had on a fresh crisp smock of faded yellow that was glorious with her hair; and high-heeled beige kid slippers, very smart. She was like a little girl who has just been freshly scrubbed and dressed in a clean pinafore, Dirk thought.

He thought a good deal about Dallas O'Mara. He found himself talking about her in what he assumed to be a careless offhand manner. He liked to talk about her. He told his mother of her. He could let himself go with Selina and he must have taken advantage of this for she looked at him intently and said: "I'd like to meet her. I've never met a girl like that."

"I'll ask her if she'll let me bring you up to the studio some time when you're in town."

It was practically impossible to get a minute with her alone. That irritated him. People were always drifting in and out of the studio— queer, important, startling people; little, dejected, shabby people. An impecunious girl art student, red-haired and wistful, that Dallas was taking in until the girl got some money from home; a pearl-hung grand-opera singer who was condescending to the Chicago Opera for a fortnight. He did not know that Dallas played until he came upon her late one afternoon sitting at the piano in the twilight with Bert Colson, the blackface comedian. Colson sang those terrible songs about April showers bringing violets, and about mah Ma-ha-ha-ha-ha-ha-my but they didn't seem terrible when he sang them. There was about this lean, hollow-chested, sombre-eyed comedian a poignant pathos, a gorgeous sense of rhythm—a something unnameable that bound you to him, made you love him. In the theatre he came out to the edge of the runway and took the audience in his arms. He talked like a bootblack and sang like an angel. Dallas at the piano, he leaning over it, were doing "blues." The two were rapt, ecstatic. I got the blues—I said the blues—I got the this or that—the somethingorother—blue—hoo-hoos. They scarcely noticed Dirk. Dallas had nodded when he came in, and had gone on playing. Colson sang the cheaply sentimental ballad as though it were the folk-song of a tragic race. His arms were extended, his face rapt. As Dallas played the tears stood in her eyes. When they had finished, "Isn't it a terrible song?" she said. "I'm crazy about it. Bert's going to try it out to-night."

"Who—uh—wrote it?" asked Dirk politely.

Dallas began to play again. "H'm? Oh, I did." They were off once more. They paid no more attention to Dirk. Yet there was nothing rude about their indifference. They simply were more interested in what they were doing. He left telling himself that he wouldn't go there again. Hanging around a studio. But next day he was back.

"Look here, Miss O'Mara," he had got her alone for a second. "Look here, will you come out to dinner with me some time? And the theatre?"

"Love to."

"When?" He was actually trembling.

"To-night." He had an important engagement. He cast it out of his life.

"To-night! That's grand. Where do you want to dine? The Casino?" The smartest club in Chicago; a little pink stucco Italian box of a place on the Lake Shore Drive. He was rather proud of being in a position to take her there as his guest.

"Oh, no, I hate those arty little places. I like dining in a hotel full of all sorts of people. Dining in a club means you're surrounded by people who're pretty much alike. Their membership in the club means they're there because they are all interested in golf, or because they're university graduates, or belong to the same political party or write, or paint, or have incomes of over fifty thousand a year, or something. I like 'em mixed up, higgledy-piggledy. A dining room full of gamblers, and insurance agents, and actors, and merchants, thieves, bootleggers, lawyers, kept ladies, wives, flaps, travelling men, millionaires—everything. That's what I call dining out. Unless one is dining at a friend's house, of course." A rarely long speech for her.

"Perhaps," eagerly, "you'll dine at my little apartment some time. Just four or six of us, or even——"

"Perhaps."

"Would you like the Drake to-night?"

"It looks too much like a Roman bath. The pillars scare me. Let's go to the Blackstone. I'll always be sufficiently from Texas to think the Blackstone French room the last word in elegance."

They went to the Blackstone. The head waiter knew him. "Good evening, Mr. DeJong." Dirk was secretly gratified. Then, with a shock, he realized that the head waiter was grinning at Dallas and Dallas was grinning at the head waiter. "Hello, André," said Dallas.

"Good evening, Miss O'Mara." The text of his greeting was correct and befitting the head waiter of the French room at the Blackstone. But his voice was lyric and his eyes glowed. His manner of seating her at a table was an enthronement.

At the look in Dirk's eyes, "I met him in the army," Dallas explained, "when I was in France. He's a grand lad."

"Were you in—what did you do in France?"

"Oh, odd jobs."

Her dinner gown was very smart, but the pink ribbon strap of an under-garment showed untidily at one side. Her silk brassière, probably. Paula would have—but then, a thing like that was impossible in Paula's perfection of toilette. He loved the way the gown cut sharply away at the shoulder to show her firm white arms. It was dull gold, the colour of her hair. This was one Dallas. There were a dozen—a hundred. Yet she was always the same. You never knew whether you were going to meet the gamin of the rumpled smock and the smudged face or the beauty of the little fur jacket. Sometimes Dirk thought she looked like a Swede hired girl with those high cheek bones of hers and her deep-set eyes and her large capable hands. Sometimes he thought she looked like the splendid goddesses you saw in paintings—the kind with high pointed breasts and gracious gentle pose—holding out a horn of plenty. There was about her something genuine and earthy and elemental. He noticed that her nails were short and not well cared for—not glittering and pointed and cruelly sharp and horridly vermilion, like Paula's. That pleased him, too, somehow.

"Some oysters?" he suggested. "They're perfectly safe here. Or fruit cocktail? Then breast of guinea hen under glass and an artichoke——"

She looked a little worried. "If you—suppose you take that. Me, I'd like a steak and some potatoes au gratin and a salad with Russian——"

"That's fine!" He was delighted. He doubled that order and they consumed it with devastating thoroughness. She ate rolls. She ate butter. She made no remarks about the food except to say, once, that it was good and that she had forgotten to eat lunch because she had been so busy working. All this Dirk found most restful and refreshing. Usually, when you dined in a restaurant with a woman she said, "Oh, I'd love to eat one of those crisp little rolls!"

You said, "Why not?"

Invariably the answer to this was, "I daren't! Goodness! A half pound at least. I haven't eaten a roll with butter in a year."

Again you said, "Why not?"

"Afraid I'll get fat."

Automatically, "You! Nonsense. You're just right."

He was bored with these women who talked about their weight, figure, lines. He thought it in bad taste. Paula was always rigidly refraining from this or that. It made him uncomfortable to sit at the table facing her; eating his thorough meal while she nibbled fragile curls of Melba toast, a lettuce leaf, and half a sugarless grapefruit. It lessened his enjoyment of his own oysters, steak, coffee. He thought that she always eyed his food a little avidly, for all her expressed indifference to it. She was looking a little haggard, too.

"The theatre's next door," he said. "Just a step. We don't have to leave here until after eight."

"That's nice." She had her cigarette with her coffee in a mellow sensuous atmosphere of enjoyment. He was talking about himself a good deal. He felt relaxed, at ease, happy.

"You know I'm an architect—at least, I was one. Perhaps that's why I like to hang around your shop so. I get sort of homesick for the pencils and the drawing board—the whole thing."

"Why did you give it up, then?"

"Nothing in it."

"How do you mean—nothing in it?"

"No money. After the war nobody was building. Oh, I suppose if I'd hung on——"

"And then you became a banker, h'm? Well, there ought to be money enough in a bank."

He was a little nettled. "I wasn't a banker—at first. I was a bond salesman."

Her brows met in a little frown. Her eyebrows were thick and strongly marked and a little uneven and inclined to meet over her nose. Paula's brows were a mere line of black—a carefully traced half-parenthesis above her unmysterious dark eyes. "I'd rather," Dallas said, slowly, "plan one back door of a building that's going to help make this town beautiful and significant than sell all the bonds that ever floated a—whatever it is that bonds are supposed to float."

He defended himself. "I felt that way, too. But you see my mother had given me my education, really. She worked for it. I couldn't go dubbing along, earning just enough to keep me. I wanted to give her things. I wanted——"

"Did she want those things? Did she want you to give up architecture and go into bonds?"

"Well—she—I don't know that she exactly——" He was too decent—still too much the son of Selina DeJong—to be able to lie about that.

"You said you were going to let me meet her."

"Would you let me bring her in? Or perhaps you'd even—would you drive out to the farm with me some day. She'd like that so much."

"So would I."

He leaned toward her, suddenly. "Listen, Dallas. What do you think of me, anyway?" He wanted to know. He couldn't stand not knowing any longer.

"I think you're a nice young man."

That was terrible. "But I don't want you to think I'm a nice young man. I want you to like me—a lot. Tell me, what haven't I got that you think I ought to have? Why do you put me off so many times? I never feel that I'm really near you. What is it I lack?" He was abject.

"Well, if you're asking for it. I do demand of the people I see often that they possess at least a splash of splendour in their makeup. Some people are nine tenths splendour and one tenth tawdriness, like Gene Meran. And some are nine tenths tawdriness and one tenth splendour, like Sam Huebch. But some people are all just a nice even pink without a single patch of royal purple."

"And that's me, h'm?"

He was horribly disappointed, hurt, wretched. But a little angry, too. His pride. Why, he was Dirk DeJong, the most successful of Chicago's younger men; the most promising; the most popular. After all, what did she do but paint commercial pictures for fifteen hundred dollars apiece?

"What happens to the men who fall in love with you? What do they do?"

Dallas stirred her coffee thoughtfully. "They usually tell me about it."

"And then what?"

"Then they seem to feel better and we become great friends."

"But don't you ever fall in love with them?" Pretty damned sure of herself. "Don't you ever fall in love with them?"

"I almost always do," said Dallas.

He plunged. "I could give you a lot of things you haven't got, purple or no purple."

"I'm going to France in April. Paris."

"What d'you mean! Paris. What for?"

"Study. I want to do portraits. Oils."

He was terrified. "Can't you do them here?"

"Oh, no. Not what I need. I have been studying here. I've been taking life-work three nights a week at the Art Institute, just to keep my hand in."

"So that's where you are, evenings." He was strangely relieved. "Let me go with you some time, will you?" Anything. Anything.

She took him with her one evening, steering him successfully past the stern Irishman who guarded the entrance to the basement classrooms; to her locker, got into her smock, grabbed her brushes. She rushed down the hall. "Don't talk," she cautioned him. "It bothers them. I wonder what they'd think of my shop." She turned into a small, cruelly bright, breathlessly hot little room, its walls whitewashed. Every inch of the floor space was covered with easels. Before them stood men and women, brushes in hand, intent. Dallas went directly to her place, fell to work at once. Dirk blinked in the strong light. He glanced at the dais toward which they were all gazing from time to time as they worked. On it lay a nude woman.

To himself Dirk said in a sort of panic: "Why, say, she hasn't got any clothes on! My gosh! this is fierce. She hasn't got anything on!" He tried, meanwhile, to look easy, careless, critical. Strangely enough, he succeeded, after the first shock, not only in looking at ease, but feeling so. The class was doing the whole figure in oils.

The model was a moron with a skin like velvet and rose petals. She fell into poses that flowed like cream. Her hair was waved in wooden undulations and her nose was pure vulgarity and her earrings were drugstore pearls in triple strands but her back was probably finer than Helen's and her breasts twin snowdrifts peaked with coral. In twenty minutes Dirk found himself impersonally interested in tone, shadows, colours, line. He listened to the low-voiced instructor and squinted carefully to ascertain whether that shadow on the model's stomach really should be painted blue or brown. Even he could see that Dallas's canvas was almost insultingly superior to that of the men and women about her. Beneath the flesh on her canvas there were muscles, and beneath those muscles blood and bone. You felt she had a surgeon's knowledge of anatomy. That, Dirk decided, was what made her commercial pictures so attractive. The drawing she had done for the Great Lakes Trust Company's bond department had been conventional enough in theme. The treatment, the technique, had made it arresting. He thought that if she ever did portraits in oils they would be vital and compelling portraits. But oh, he wished she didn't want to do portraits in oils. He wished——

It was after eleven when they emerged from the Art Institute doorway and stood a moment together at the top of the broad steps surveying the world that lay before them. Dallas said nothing. Suddenly the beauty of the night rushed up and overwhelmed Dirk. Gorgeousness and tawdriness; colour and gloom. At the right the white tower of the Wrigley building rose wraithlike against a background of purple sky. Just this side of it a swarm of impish electric lights grinned their message in scarlet and white. In white:

TRADE AT

then blackness, while you waited against your will. In red:

THE FAIR

Blackness again. Then, in a burst of both colours, in bigger letters, and in a blaze that hurled itself at your eyeballs, momentarily shutting out tower, sky, and street:

SAVE MONEY

Straight ahead the hut of the Adams Street L station in midair was a Venetian bridge with the black canal of asphalt flowing sluggishly beneath. The reflection of cafeteria and cigar-shop windows on either side were slender shafts of light along the canal. An enchanting sight. Dirk thought suddenly that Dallas was a good deal like that—like Chicago. A mixture of grandeur and cheapness; of tawdriness and magnificence; of splendour and ugliness.

"Nice," said Dallas. A long breath. She was a part of all this.

"Yes." He felt an outsider. "Want a sandwich? Are you hungry?"

"I'm starved."

They had sandwiches and coffee at an all-night one-arm lunch room because Dallas said her face was too dirty for a restaurant and she didn't want to bother to wash it. She was more than ordinarily companionable that night; a little tired; less buoyant and independent than usual. This gave her a little air of helplessness—of fatigue—that aroused all his tenderness. Her smile gave him a warm rush of pure happiness—until he saw her smile in exactly the same way at the pimply young man who lorded it over the shining nickel coffee container, as she told him that his coffee was grand.

XIX

THE things that had mattered so vitally didn't seem to be important, somehow, now. The people who had seemed so desirable had become suddenly insignificant. The games he had played appeared silly games. He was seeing things through Dallas O'Mara's wise, beauty-loving eyes. Strangely enough, he did not realize that this girl saw life from much the same angle as that at which his mother regarded it. In the last few years his mother had often offended him by her attitude toward these rich and powerful friends of his—their ways, their games, their amusements, their manners. And her way of living in turn offended him. On his rare visits to the farm it seemed to him there was always some drab dejected female in the kitchen or living room or on the porch—a woman with broken teeth and comic shoes and tragic eyes—drinking great draughts of coffee and telling her woes to Selina—Sairey Gampish ladies smelling unpleasantly of peppermint and perspiration and poverty. "And he ain't had a lick of work since November——"

"You don't say! That's terrible!"

He wished she wouldn't.

Sometimes old Aug Hempel drove out there and Dirk would come upon the two snickering wickedly together about something that he knew concerned the North Shore crowd.

It had been years since Selina had said, sociably, "What did they have for dinner, Dirk? H'm?"

"Well—soup——"

"Nothing before the soup?"

"Oh, yeh. Some kind of a—one of those canape things, you know. Caviare."

"My! Caviare!"

Sometimes Selina giggled like a naughty girl at things that Dirk had taken quite seriously. The fox hunts, for example. Lake Forest had taken to fox hunting, and the Tippecanoe crowd kept kennels. Dirk had learned to ride—pretty well. An Englishman—a certain Captain Stokes-Beatty—had initiated the North Shore into the mysteries of fox hunting. Huntin'. The North Shore learned to say nec's'ry and conservat'ry. Captain Stokes-Beatty was a tall, bow-legged, and somewhat horse-faced young man, remote in manner. The nice Farnham girl seemed fated to marry him. Paula had had a hunt breakfast at Stormwood and it had been very successful, though the American men had balked a little at the devilled kidneys. The food had been patterned as far as possible after the pale flabby viands served at English hunt breakfasts and ruined in an atmosphere of lukewarm steam. The women were slim and perfectly tailored but wore their hunting clothes a trifle uneasily and self-consciously like girls in their first low-cut party dresses. Most of the men had turned stubborn on the subject of pink coats, but Captain Stokes-Beatty wore his handsomely. The fox—a worried and somewhat dejected-looking animal—had been shipped in a crate from the south and on being released had a way of sitting sociably in an Illinois corn field instead of leaping fleetly to cover. At the finish you had a feeling of guilt, as though you had killed a cockroach.

Dirk had told Selina about it, feeling rather magnificent. A fox hunt.

"A fox hunt! What for?"

"For! Why, what's any fox hunt for?"

"I can't imagine. They used to be for the purpose of ridding a fox-infested country of a nuisance. Have the foxes been bothering 'em out in Lake Forest?"

"Now, Mother, don't be funny." He told her about the breakfast.

"Well, but it's so silly, Dirk. It's smart to copy from another country the things that that country does better than we do. England does gardens and wood-fires and dogs and tweeds and walking shoes and pipes and leisure better than we do. But those luke-warm steamy breakfasts of theirs! It's because they haven't gas, most of them. No Kansas or Nebraska farmer's wife would stand for one of their kitchens—not for a minute. And the hired man would balk at such bacon." She giggled.

"Oh, well, if you're going to talk like that."

But Dallas O'Mara felt much the same about these things. Dallas, it appeared, had been something of a fad with the North Shore society crowd after she had painted Mrs. Robinson Gilman's portrait. She had been invited to dinners and luncheons and dances, but their doings, she told Dirk, had bored her.

"They're nice," she said, "but they don't have much fun. They're all trying to be something they're not. And that's such hard work. The women were always explaining that they lived in Chicago because their husband's business was here. They all do things pretty well—dance or paint or ride or write or sing—but not well enough. They're professional amateurs, trying to express something they don't feel; or that they don't feel strongly enough to make it worth while expressing."

She admitted, though, that they did appreciate the things that other people did well. Visiting and acknowledged writers, painters, lecturers, heroes, they entertained lavishly and hospitably in their Florentine or English or Spanish or French palaces on the north side of Chicago, Illinois. Especially foreign notables of this description. Since 1918 these had descended upon Chicago (and all America) like a plague of locusts, starting usually in New York and sweeping westward, devouring the pleasant verdure of greenbacks and chirping as they came. Returning to Europe, bursting with profits and spleen, they thriftily wrote of what they had seen and the result was more clever than amiable; bearing, too, the taint of bad taste.

North Shore hostesses vied for the honour of entertaining these notables. Paula—pretty, clever, moneyed, shrewd—often emerged from these contests the winner. Her latest catch was Emile Goguet—General Emile Goguet, hero of Champagne—Goguet of the stiff white beard, the empty left coat-sleeve, and the score of medals. He was coming to America ostensibly to be the guest of the American Division which, with Goguet's French troops, had turned the German onslaught at Champagne, but really, it was whispered, to cement friendly relations between his country and a somewhat diffident United States.

"And guess," trilled Paula, "guess who's coming with him, Dirk! That wonderful Roelf Pool, the French sculptor! Goguet's going to be my guest. Pool's going to do a bust, you know, of young Quentin Roosevelt from a photograph that Mrs. Theodore Roosevelt——"

"What d'you mean—French sculptor! He's no more French than I am. He was born within a couple of miles of my mother's farm. His people were Dutch truck farmers. His father lived in High Prairie until a year ago, when he died of a stroke."

When he told Selina she flushed like a girl, as she sometimes still did when she was much excited. "Yes, I saw it in the paper. I wonder," she added, quietly, "if I shall see him."

That evening you might have seen her sitting, cross-legged, before the old carved chest, fingering the faded shabby time-worn objects the saving of which Dirk had denounced as sentimental. The crude drawing of the Haymarket; the wine-red cashmere dress; some faded brittle flowers.

Paula was giving a large—but not too large—dinner on the second night. She was very animated about it, excited, gay. "They say," she told Dirk, "that Goguet doesn't eat anything but hard-boiled eggs and rusks. Oh, well, the others won't object to squabs and mushrooms and things. And his hobby is his farm in Brittany. Pool's stunning—dark and sombre and very white teeth."

Paula was very gay these days. Too gay. It seemed to Dirk that her

nervous energy was inexhaustible—and exhausting. Dirk refused to admit to himself how irked he was by the sallow heart-shaped exquisite
face, the lean brown clutching fingers, the air of ownership. He had
begun to dislike things about her as an unfaithful spouse is irritated by
quite innocent mannerisms of his unconscious mate. She scuffed her
heels a little when she walked, for example. It maddened him. She had
a way of biting the rough skin around her carefully tended nails when
she was nervous. "Don't *do* that!" he said.

Dallas never irritated him. She rested him, he told himself. He would
arm himself against her, but one minute after meeting her he would
sink gratefully and resistlessly into her quiet depths. Sometimes he
thought all this was an assumed manner in her.

"This calm of your—this effortlessness," he said to her one day, "is a
pose, isn't it?" Anything to get her notice.

"Partly," Dallas had replied, amiably. "It's a nice pose though, don't
you think?"

What are you going to do with a girl like that!

Here was the woman who could hold him entirely, and who never
held out a finger to hold him. He tore at the smooth wall of her indifference, though he only cut and bruised his own hands in doing it.

"Is it because I'm a successful business man that you don't like me?"

"But I do like you."

"That you don't find me attractive, then."

"But I think you're an awfully attractive man. Dangerous, that's wot."

"Oh, don't be the wide-eyed ingénue. You know damned well what
I mean. You've got me and you don't want me. If I had been a successful
architect instead of a successful business man would that have made any
difference?" He was thinking of what his mother had said just a few
years back, that night when they had talked at her bedside. "Is that it?
He's got to be an artist, I suppose, to interest you."

"Good Lord, no! Some day I'll probably marry a horny-handed son of
toil, and if I do it'll be the horny hands that will win me. If you want
to know, I like 'em with their scars on them. There's something about
a man who has fought for it—I don't know what it is—a look in his
eye—the feel of his hand. He needn't have been successful—though he
probably would be. I don't know. I'm not very good at this analysis
stuff. I only know he—well, you haven't a mark on you. Not a mark. You
quit being an architect, or whatever it was, because architecture was an
uphill disheartening job at the time. I don't say that you should have
kept on. For all I know you were a bum architect. But if you had kept
on—if you had loved it enough to keep on—fighting, and struggling,
and sticking it out—why, that fight would show in your face to-day—in

your eyes and your jaw and your hands and in your way of standing and walking and sitting and talking. Listen. I'm not criticizing you. But you're all smooth. I like 'em bumpy. That sounds terrible. It isn't what I mean at all. It isn't——"

"Oh, never mind," Dirk said, wearily. "I think I know what you mean." He sat looking down at his hands—his fine strong unscarred hands. Suddenly and unreasonably he thought of another pair of hands —his mother's—with the knuckles enlarged, the skin broken—expressive —her life written on them. Scars. She had them. "Listen, Dallas. If I thought—I'd go back to Hollis & Sprague's and begin all over again at forty a week if I thought you'd——"

"Don't."

XX

GENERAL GOGUET and Roelf Pool had been in Chicago one night and part of a day. Dirk had not met them—was to meet them at Paula's dinner that evening. He was curious about Pool but not particularly interested in the warrior. Restless, unhappy, wanting to see Dallas (he admitted it, bitterly) he dropped into her studio at an unaccustomed hour almost immediately after lunch and heard gay voices and laughter. Why couldn't she work alone once in a while without that rabble around her!

Dallas in a grimy smock and the scuffed kid slippers was entertaining two truants from Chicago society—General Emile Goguet and Roelf Pool. They seemed to be enjoying themselves immensely. She introduced Dirk as casually as though their presence were a natural and expected thing—which it was. She had never mentioned them to him. Yet now: "This is Dirk DeJong—General Emile Goguet. We were campaigners together in France. Roelf Pool. So were we, weren't we, Roelf?"

General Emile Goguet bowed formally, but his eyes were twinkling. He appeared to be having a very good time. Roelf Pool's dark face had lighted up with such a glow of surprise and pleasure as to transform it. He strode over to Dirk, clasped his hand. "Dirk DeJong! Not—why, say, don't you know me? I'm Roelf Pool!"

"I ought to know you," said Dirk.

"Oh, but I mean I'm—I knew you when you were a kid. You're Selina's Dirk. Aren't you? My Selina. I'm driving out to see her this afternoon. She's one of my reasons for being here. Why, I'm——" He was laughing, talking excitedly, like a boy. Dallas, all agrin, was enjoying it immensely.

"They've run away," she explained to Dirk, "from the elaborate programme that was arranged for them this afternoon. I don't know where the French got their reputation for being polite. The General is a perfect boor, aren't you? And scared to death of women. He's the only French general in captivity who ever took the trouble to learn English."

General Goguet nodded violently and roared. "And you?" he said to Dirk in his careful and perfect English. "You, too, are an artist?"

"No," Dirk said, "not an artist."

"What, then?"

"Why—uh—bonds. That is, the banking business. Bonds."

"Ah, yes," said General Goguet, politely. "Bonds. A very good thing, bonds. We French are very fond of them. We have great respect for American bonds, we French." He nodded and twinkled and turned away to Dallas.

"We're all going," announced Dallas, and made a dash for the stuffy little bedroom off the studio.

Well, this was a bit too informal. "Going where?" inquired Dirk. The General, too, appeared bewildered.

Roelf explained, delightedly. "It's a plot. We're all going to drive out to your mother's. You'll go, won't you? You simply must."

"Go?" now put in General Goguet. "Where is it that we go? I thought we stayed here, quietly. It is quiet here, and no reception committees." His tone was wistful.

Roelf attempted to make it clear. "Mr. DeJong's mother is a farmer. You remember I told you all about her in the ship coming over. She was wonderful to me when I was a kid. She was the first person to tell me what beauty was—is. She's magnificent. She raises vegetables."

"Ah! A farm! But yes! I, too, am a farmer. Well!" He shook Dirk's hand again. He appeared now for the first time to find him interesting.

"Of course I'll go. Does Mother know you're coming? She has been hoping she'd see you but she thought you'd grown so grand——"

"Wait until I tell her about the day I landed in Paris with five francs in my pocket. No, she doesn't know we're coming, but she'll be there, won't she? I've a feeling she'll be there, exactly the same. She will, won't she?"

"She'll be there." It was early spring; the busiest of seasons on the farm.

Dallas emerged in greatcoat and a new spring hat. She waved a hand to the faithful Gilda Hanan. "Tell any one who inquires for me that I've felt the call of spring. And if the boy comes for that clay pack picture tell him to-morrow was the day."

They were down the stairs and off in the powerful car that seemed to be at the visitors' disposal. Through the Loop, up Michigan Avenue, into the south side. Chicago, often lowering and gray in April, was wearing gold and blue to-day. The air was sharp but beneath the brusqueness of it was a gentle promise. Dallas and Pool were very much absorbed in Paris plans, Paris reminiscences. "And do you remember the time we . . . only seven francs among the lot of us and the dinner was . . . you're surely coming over in June, then . . . oils . . . you've got the thing, I tell you . . . you'll be great, Dallas . . . remember what Vibray said . . . study . . . work . . ."

Dirk was wretched. He pointed out objects of interest to General Goguet. Sixty miles of boulevard. Park system. Finest in the country. Grand Boulevard. Drexel Boulevard. Jackson Park. Illinois Central trains. Terrible, yes, but they were electrifying. Going to make 'em run by electricity, you know. Things wouldn't look so dirty, after that. Halsted Street. Longest street in the world.

And, "Ah, yes," said the General, politely. "Ah, yes. Quite so. Most interesting."

The rich black loam of High Prairie. A hint of fresh green things just peeping out of the earth. Hothouses. Coldframes. The farm.

It looked very trim and neat. The house, white with green shutters (Selina's dream realized), smiled at them from among the willows that were already burgeoning hazily under the wooing of a mild and early spring.

"But I thought you said it was a small farm!" said General Goguet, as they descended from the car. He looked about at the acreage.

"It is small," Dirk assured him. "Only about forty acres."

"Ah, well, you Americans. In France we farm on a very small scale, you understand. We have not the land. The great vast country." He waved his right arm. You felt that if the left sleeve had not been empty he would have made a large and sweeping gesture with both arms.

Selina was not in the neat quiet house. She was not on the porch, or in the yard. Meena Bras, phlegmatic and unflustered, came in from the kitchen. Mis' DeJong was in the fields. She would call her. This she proceeded to do by blowing three powerful blasts and again three on a horn which she took from a hook on the wall. She stood in the kitchen doorway facing the fields, blowing, her red cheeks puffed outrageously. "That brings her," Meena assured them; and went back to her work. They came out on the porch to await Selina. She was out on the west sixteen—the west sixteen that used to be unprolific, half-drowned muckland. Dirk felt a little uneasy, and ashamed that he should feel so.

Then they saw her coming, a small dark figure against the background of sun and sky and fields. She came swiftly yet ploddingly, for the ground was heavy. They stood facing her, the four of them. As she came nearer they saw that she was wearing a dark skirt pinned up about her ankles to protect if from the wet spring earth and yet it was spattered with a border of mud spots. A rough heavy gray sweater was buttoned closely about the straight slim body. On her head was a battered soft black hat. Her feet, in broad-toed sensible boots, she lifted high out of the soft clinging soil. As she came nearer she took off her hat and holding it a little to one side against the sun, shaded her eyes with it. Her hair blew a little in the gentle spring breeze. Her cheeks were faintly pink. She was coming up the path now. She could distinguish their faces. She saw Dirk; smiled, waved. Her glance went inquiringly to the others—the bearded man in uniform, the tall girl, the man with the dark vivid face. Then she stopped, suddenly, and her hand went to her heart as though she had felt a great pang, and her lips were parted, and her eyes enormous. As Roelf came forward swiftly she took a few quick running steps toward him like a young girl. He took the slight figure in the mud-spattered skirt, the rough gray sweater, and the battered old hat into his arms.

XXI

They had had tea in the farm sitting room and Dallas had made a little moaning over the beauty of the Dutch lustre set. Selina had entertained them with the shining air of one who is robed in silk and fine linen. She and General Goguet had got on famously from the start, meeting on the common ground of asparagus culture.

"But how thick?" he had demanded, for he, too, had his pet asparagus beds on the farm in Brittany. "How thick at the base?"

Selina made a circle with thumb and forefinger. The General groaned with envy and despair. He was very comfortable, the General. He partook largely of tea and cakes. He flattered Selina with his eyes. She actually dimpled, flushed, laughed like a girl. But it was to Roelf she turned; it was on Roelf that her eyes dwelt and rested. It was with him she walked when she was silent and the others talked. It was as though he were her one son, and had come home. Her face was radiant, beautiful.

Seated next to Dirk, Dallas said, in a low voice: "There, that's what I mean. That's what I mean when I say I want to do portraits. Not portraits of ladies with a string of pearls and one lily hand half hidden in the folds of a satin skirt. I mean character portraits of men and women who are really distinguished looking—distinguishedly American, for example—like your mother."

Dirk looked up at her quickly, half smiling, as though expecting to find her smiling, too. But she was not smiling. "My mother!"

"Yes, if she'd let me. With that fine splendid face all lit up with the light that comes from inside; and the jaw-line like that of the women who came over in the *Mayflower*; or crossed the continent in a covered wagon; and her eyes! And that battered funny gorgeous bum old hat and the white shirtwaist—and her hands! She's beautiful. She'd make me famous at one leap. You'd see!"

Dirk stared at her. It was as though he could not comprehend. Then he turned in his chair to stare at his mother. Selina was talking to Roelf.

"And you've done all the famous men of Europe, haven't you, Roelf! To think of it! You've seen the world, and you've got it in your hand. Little Roelf Pool. And you did it all alone. In spite of everything."

Roelf leaned toward her. He put his hand over her rough one. "Cabbages are beautiful," he said. Then they both laughed as at some exquisite joke. Then, seriously: "What a fine life you've had, too, Selina. A full life, and a rich one and successful."

"I!" exclaimed Selina. "Why, Roelf, I've been here all these years, just where you left me when you were a boy. I think the very hat and dress I'm wearing might be the same I wore then. I've been nowhere, done nothing, seen nothing. When I think of all the places I was going to see! All the things I was going to do!"

"You've been everywhere in the world," said Roelf. "You've seen all the places of great beauty and light. You remember you told me that your father had once said, when you were a little girl, that there were only two kinds of people who really mattered in the world. One kind was wheat and the other kind emeralds. You're wheat, Selina."

"And you're emerald," said Selina, quickly.

The General was interested but uncomprehending. He glanced now

at the watch on his wrist and gave a little exclamation. "But the dinner!
Our hostess, Madame Storm! It is very fine to run away but one must
come back. Our so beautiful hostess." He had sprung to his feet.

"She is beautiful, isn't she?" said Selina.

"No," Roelf replied, abruptly. "The mouth is smaller than the eyes.
With Mrs. Storm from here to here"—he illustrated by turning to Dallas,
touching her lips, her eyes, lightly with his slender powerful brown
fingers—"is smaller than from here to here. When the mouth is smaller
than the eyes there is no real beauty. Now Dallas here——"

"Yes, me," scoffed Dallas, all agrin. "There's a grand mouth for you.
If a large mouth is your notion of beauty then I must look like Helen
of Troy to you, Roelf."

"You do," said Roelf, simply.

Inside Dirk something was saying, over and over, "You're nothing
but a rubber stamp, Dirk DeJong. You're nothing but a rubber stamp."
Over and over.

"These dinners!" exclaimed the General. "I do not wish to seem un-
gracious, but these dinners! Much rather would I remain here on this
quiet and beautiful farm."

At the porch steps he turned, brought his heels together with a sharp
smack, bent from the waist, picked up Selina's rough work-worn hand
and kissed it. And then, as she smiled a little, uncertainly, her left hand
at her breast, her cheeks pink, Roelf, too, kissed her hand tenderly.

"Why," said Selina, and laughed a soft tremulous little laugh, "Why,
I've never had my hand kissed before."

She stood on the porch steps and waved at them as they were whirled
swiftly away, the four of them. A slight straight little figure in the plain
white blouse and the skirt spattered with the soil of the farm.

"You'll come out again?" she had said to Dallas. And Dallas had said
yes, but that she was leaving soon for Paris, to study and work.

"When I come back you'll let me do your portrait?"

"*My* portrait!" Selina had exclaimed, wonderingly.

Now as the four were whirled back to Chicago over the asphalted
Halsted road they were relaxed, a little tired. They yielded to the narcotic
of spring that was in the air.

Roelf Pool took off his hat. In the cruel spring sunshine you saw that
the black hair was sprinkled with gray. "On days like this I refuse to
believe that I'm forty-five. Dallas, tell me I'm not forty-five."

"You're not forty-five," said Dallas in her leisurely caressing voice.

Roelf's lean brown hand reached over frankly and clasped her strong
white one. "When you say it like that, Dallas, it sounds true."

"It is true," said Dallas.

They dropped Dallas first at the shabby old Ontario Street studio, then Dirk at his smart little apartment, and went on.

Dirk turned his key in the lock. Saki, the Japanese houseman, slid silently into the hall making little hissing noises of greeting. On the correct little console in the hall there was a correct little pile of letters and invitations. He went through the Italian living room and into his bedroom. The Jap followed him. Dirk's correct evening clothes (made by Peel the English tailor on Michigan Boulevard) were laid correctly on his bed—trousers, vest, shirt, coat; fine, immaculate.

"Messages, Saki?"

"Missy Stlom telephone."

"Oh. Leave any message?"

"No. Say s'e call 'gain."

"All right, Saki." He waved him away and out of the room. The man went and closed the door softly behind him as a correct Jap servant should. Dirk took off his coat, his vest, threw them on a chair near the bed. He stood at the bedside looking down at his Peel evening clothes, at the glossy shirtfront that never bulged. A bath, he thought, dully, automatically. Then, quite suddenly, he flung himself on the fine silk-covered bed, face down, and lay there, his head in his arms, very still. He was lying there half an hour later when he heard the telephone's shrill insistence and Saki's gentle deferential rap at the bedroom door.

CIMARRON

To My Mother
JULIA FERBER

ACKNOWLEDGMENT

FOR certain descriptive passages in the portion of this book concerned with the Opening of Oklahoma in 1889 acknowledgment is made to HANDS UP, by Fred E. Sutton and A. B. MacDonald, published and copyright MCMXXVII by the Bobbs-Merrill Company.

FOREWORD

ONLY the more fantastic and improbable events contained in this book are true. There is no attempt to set down a literal history of Oklahoma. All the characters, the towns, and many of the happenings contained herein are imaginary. But through reading the scant available records, documents, and histories (including the Oklahoma State Historical Library collection) and through many talks with men and women who have lived in Oklahoma since the day of the Opening, something of the spirit, the color, the movement, the life of that incredible commonwealth has, I hope, been caught. Certainly the Run, the Sunday service in the gambling tent, the death of Isaiah and of Arita Red Feather, the catching of the can of nitroglycerin, many of the shooting affrays, most descriptive passages, all of the oil phase, and the Osage Indian material complete—these are based on actual happenings. In many cases material entirely true was discarded as unfit for use because it was so melodramatic, so absurd as to be too strange for the realm of fiction.

There is no city of Osage, Oklahoma. It is a composite of, perhaps, five existent Oklahoma cities. The Kid is not meant to be the notorious Billy the Kid of an earlier day. There was no Yancey Cravat—he is a blending of a number of dashing Oklahoma figures of a past and present day. There is no Sabra Cravat, but she exists in a score of bright-eyed, white-haired, intensely interesting women of sixty-five or thereabouts who told me many strange things as we talked and rocked on an Oklahoma front porch (tree-shaded now).

Anything can have happened in Oklahoma. Practically everything has.

EDNA FERBER.

I

ALL the Venables sat at Sunday dinner. All those handsome inbred Venable faces were turned, enthralled, toward Yancey Cravat, who was talking. The combined effect was almost blinding, as of incandescence; but Yancey Cravat was not bedazzled. A sun surrounded by lesser planets, he gave out a radiance so powerful as to dim the luminous circle about him.

Yancey had a disconcerting habit of abruptly concluding a meal—for himself, at least—by throwing down his napkin at the side of his plate, rising, and striding about the room, or even leaving it. It was not deliberate rudeness. He ate little. His appetite satisfied, he instinctively ceased to eat; ceased to wish to contemplate food. But the Venables sat hours at table, leisurely shelling almonds, sipping sherry; Cousin Dabney Venable peeling an orange for Cousin Bella French Vian with the absorbed concentration of a sculptor molding his clay.

The Venables, dining, strangely resembled one of those fertile and dramatic family groups portrayed lolling unconventionally at meat in the less spiritual of those Biblical canvases that glow richly down at one from the great gallery walls of Europe. Though their garb was sober enough, being characteristic of the time—1889—and the place—Kansas —it yet conveyed an impression as of purple and scarlet robes enveloping these gracile shoulders. You would not have been surprised to see, moving silently about this board, Nubian blacks in loincloths, bearing aloft golden vessels piled with exotic fruits or steaming with strange pasties in which nightingales' tongues figured prominently. Blacks, as a matter of fact, did move about the Venable table, but these, too, wore the conventional garb of the servitor.

This branch of the Venable family tree had been transplanted from Mississippi to Kansas more than two decades before, but the mid-west had failed to set her bourgeois stamp upon them. Straitened though it was, there still obtained in that household, by some genealogical miracle, many of those charming ways, remotely Oriental, that were of the South whence they had sprung. The midday meal was, more often than not, a sort of tribal feast at which sprawled hosts of impecunious kin, mysteriously sprung up at the sound of the dinner bell and the scent of baking meats. Unwilling émigrés, war ruined, Lewis Venable and his wife Felice had brought their dear customs with them into exile, as well as the superb mahogany oval at which they now sat, and the war-salvaged silver which gave elegance to the Wichita, Kansas, board. Certainly the mahogany had suffered in transit; and many of their Southern ways, transplanted to Kansas, seemed slightly silly—or would have, had they not been tinged with pathos. The hot breads of the South, heaped high at every meal, still wrought alimentary havoc. The frying pan and the deep-fat kettle (both, perhaps, as much as anything responsible for the tragedy of '64) still spattered their deadly fusillade in this household. Indeed, the creamy pallor of the Venable women, so like that of a magnolia petal in their girlhood, and tending so surely toward the ocherous in middle age, was less a matter of pigment than of liver. Impecunious though the family now was, three or four negro servants went about the house, soft-footed, slack, charming. "Rest yo' wrap?" they suggested, velvet voiced and hospitable, as you entered the wide hallway that was at once so bare and so cluttered. And, "Beat biscuit, Miss Adeline?" as they proffered a fragrant plate.

Even that Kansas garden was of another latitude. Lean hounds drowsed in the sun-drenched untidiness of the doorway, and that untidiness was hidden and transformed by a miracle of color and scent and bloom. Here were passion flower and wisteria and even Bougainvillea in season. Honeysuckle gave out its swooning sweetness. In the early spring lilies of the valley thrust the phantom green of their spears up through the dead brown banking the lilac bushes. That coarse vulgarian, the Kansas sunflower, was a thing despised of the Venables. If one so much as showed its broad face among the scented élégantes of that garden it suffered instant decapitation. On one occasion Felice Venable had been known to ruin a pair of very fine-tempered embroidery scissors while impetuously acting as headsman. She had even been heard to bewail the absence of Spanish moss in this northerly climate. A neighboring mid-west matron, miffed, resented this.

"But that's a parasite! And real creepy, almost. I was in South Carolina and saw it. Kind of floating, like ghosts. And no earthly good."

"Do even the flowers have to be useful in Kansas?" drawled Felice Venable. She was not very popular with the bustling wives of Wichita. They resented her ruffled and trailing white wrappers of cross-barred dimity; her pointed slippers, her arched instep, her indifference to all that went on outside the hedge that surrounded the Venable yard; they resented the hedge itself, symbol of exclusiveness in that open-faced

Kansas town. Sheathed in the velvet of Felice Venable's languor was a sharp-edged poniard of wit inherited from her French forbears, the old Marcys of St. Louis; Missouri fur traders of almost a century earlier. You saw the Marcy mark in the black of her still bountiful hair, in the curve of the brows above the dark eyes—in the dark eyes themselves, so alive in the otherwise immobile face.

As the family now sat at its noonday meal it was plain that while two decades of living in the Middle West had done little to quicken the speech or hasten the movements of Lewis Venable and his wife Felice (they still "you-alled"; they declared to goodness; the eighteenth letter of the alphabet would forever be ah to them) it had made a noticeable difference in the younger generation. Up and down the long table they ranged, sons and daughters, sons-in-law and daughters-in-law; grandchildren; remoter kin such as visiting nieces and nephews and cousins, offshoots of this far-flung family. As the more northern-bred members of the company exclaimed at the tale they now were hearing you noted that their vowels were shorter, their diction more clipped, the turn of the head, the lift of the hand less leisurely. In all those faces there was a resemblance, one to the other. Perhaps the listening look which all of them now wore served to accentuate this.

It was late May, and unseasonably hot for the altitude. Then, too, there had been an early pest of moths and June flies this spring. High above the table, and directly over it, on a narrow board suspended by rods from the lofty ceiling sat perched Isaiah, the little black boy. With one hand he clung to the side rods of his precarious roost; with the other he wielded a shoo-fly of feathery asparagus ferns cut from the early garden. Its soft susurrus as he swished it back and forth was an obbligato to the music of Yancey Cravat's golden voice. Clinging thus aloft the black boy looked a simian version of one of Raphael's ceilinged angels. His round head, fuzzed with little tight tufts, as of woolly astrachan through which the black of his poll gleamed richly, was cocked at an impish angle the better to catch the words that flowed from the lips of the speaker. His eyes, popping with excitement, were fixed in an entrancement on the great lounging figure of Yancey Cravat. So bewitched was the boy that frequently his hand fell limp and he forgot altogether his task of bestirring with his verdant fan the hot moist air above the food-laden table. An impatient upward glance from Felice Venable's darting black eyes, together with a sharply admonitory "Ah-saiah!" would set him to swishing vigorously until the enchantment again stayed his arm.

The Venables saw nothing untoward in this remnant of Mississippi feudalism. Dozens of Isaiah's forbears had sat perched thus, bestirring

the air so that generations of Mississippi Venables might the more
agreeably sup and eat and talk. Wichita had first beheld this phenome-
non aghast; and even now, after twenty years, it was a subject for local
tongue waggings.

Yancey Cravat was talking. He had been talking for the better part
of an hour. This very morning he had returned from the Oklahoma
country—the newly opened Indian Territory where he had made the
Run that marked the settling of this vast tract of virgin land known
colloquially as the Nation. Now, as he talked, the faces of the others
had the rapt look of those who listen to a saga. It was the look that
Jason's listeners must have had, and Ulysses'; and the eager crowd that
gathered about Francisco Vasquez de Coronado before they learned that
his search for the Seven Cities of Cibolo had been in vain.

The men at table leaned forward, their hands clasped rather loosely
between their knees or on the cloth before them, their plates pushed
away, their chairs shoved back. Now and then the sudden white ridge
of a hard-set muscle showed along the line of a masculine jaw. Their
eyes were those of men who follow a game in which they would fain
take part. The women listened, a little frightened, their lips parted. They
shushed their children when they moved or whimpered, or, that failing,
sent them, with a half-tender, half-admonitory slap behind, to play in
the sunny dooryard. Sometimes a woman's hand reached out posses-
sively, remindingly, and was laid on the arm or the hand of the man
seated beside her. "I am here," the hand's pressure said. "Your place is
with me. Don't listen to him like that. Don't believe him. I am your
wife. I am safety. I am security. I am comfort. I am habit. I am convention. Don't listen like that. Don't look like that."

But the man would shake off the hand, not roughly, but with absent-
minded resentment.

Of all that circlet of faces, linked by the enchantment of the tale now
being unfolded before them, there stood out lambent as a flame the face
of Sabra Cravat as she sat there at table, her child Cim in her lap.
Though she, like her mother Felice Venable, was definitely of the olive-
skinned type, her face seemed luminously white as she listened to the
amazing, incredible, and slightly ridiculous story now being unfolded by
her husband. It was plain, too, that in her, as in her mother, the strain
of the pioneering French Marcys was strong. Her abundant hair was as
black, and her eyes; and the strong brows arched with a swooping curve
like the twin scimitars that hung above the fireplace in the company
room. Sabra was secretly ashamed of her heavy brows and given to surveying them disapprovingly in her mirror while running a forefinger
(slightly moistened by her tongue) along their sable curves. For the

rest, there was something more New England than Southern in the directness of her glance, the quick turn of her head, the briskness of her speech and manner. Twenty-one now, married at sixteen, mother of a four-year-old boy, and still in love with her picturesque giant of a husband, there was about Sabra Cravat a bloom, a glow, sometimes seen at that exquisite and transitory time in a woman's life when her chemical, emotional, and physical make-up attains its highest point and fuses.

It was easy to trace the resemblance, both in face and spirit, between this glowing girl and the sallow woman at the foot of the table. But to turn from her to old Lewis Venable was to find one's self baffled by the mysteries of paternity. Old Lewis Venable was not old, but aged; a futile, fumbling, gentle man, somewhat hag-ridden and rendered the more unvital by malaria. Face and hands had a yellow ivory quality born of generations subjected to hot breads, lowlands, bad liver, port wine. To say nothing of a resident unexplored bullet somewhere between the third and fifth ribs, got at Murfreesboro as a member of Stanford's Battery, Heavy Artillery, long long before Roentgen had conceived an eye like God's.

Lewis Venable, in his armchair at the head of the table, was as spellbound as black Isaiah in his high perch above it. Curiously enough, even the boy Cim had listened, or seemed to listen, as he sat in his mother's lap. Sabra had eaten her dinner over the child's head in absent-minded bites, her eyes always on her husband's face. She rarely had had to say, "Hush, Cim, hush!" or to wrest a knife or fork or forbidden tidbit from his clutching fingers. Perhaps it was the curiously musical quality of the story-teller's voice that lulled him. Sabra Venable's disgruntled suitors had said when she married Yancey Cravat, a stranger, mysterious, out of Texas and the Cimarron, that it was his voice that had bewitched her. They were in a measure right, for though Yancey Cravat was verbose, frequently even windy, and though much that he said was dry enough in actual content, he had those priceless gifts of the born orator, a vibrant and flexible voice, great sweetness and charm of manner, an hypnotic eye, and the power of making each listener feel that what was being said was intended for his ear alone. Something of the charlatan was in him, much of the actor, a dash of the fanatic.

Any tale told by Yancey Cravat was likely to contain enchantment, incredibility (though this last was not present while he was telling it), and a tinge of the absurd. Yancey himself, even at this early time, was a bizarre, glamorous, and slightly mythical figure. No room seemed big enough for his gigantic frame; no chair but dwindled beneath the breadth of his shoulders. He seemed actually to loom more than his six feet two. His black locks he wore overlong, so that they curled a little about his neck in the manner of Booth. His cheeks and forehead were, in places, deeply pitted, as with the pox. Women, perversely enough, found this attractive.

But first of all you noted his head, his huge head, like a buffalo's, so heavy that it seemed to loll of its own weight. It was with a shock of astonishment that you remarked about him certain things totally at variance with his bulk, his virility, his appearance of enormous power. His mouth, full and sensual, had still an expression of great sweetness. His eyelashes were long and curling, like a beautiful girl's, and when he raised his heavy head to look at you, beneath the long black locks and the dark lashes you saw with something of bewilderment that his eyes were a deep and unfathomable ocean gray.

Now, in the course of his story, and under the excitement of it, he left the table and sprang to his feet, striding about and talking as he strode. His step was amazingly light and graceful for a man of his powerful frame. Fascinated, you saw that his feet were small and arched like a woman's, and he wore, even in this year of 1889, Texas star boots of fine soft flexible calf, very high heeled, thin soled, and ornamented with cunningly wrought gold stars around the tops. His hands, too, were disproportionate to a man of his stature; slim, pliant, white. He used them as he talked, and the eye followed their movements, bewitched. For the rest, his costume was a Prince Albert of fine black broadcloth whose skirts swooped and spread with the vigor of his movements; a pleated white shirt, soft and of exquisite material; a black string tie; trousers tucked into the gay boot-tops; and, always, a white felt hat, broad-brimmed and rolling. On occasion he simply blubbered Shakespeare, the Old Testament, the Odyssey, the Iliad. His speech was spattered with bits of Latin, and with occasional Spanish phrases, relic of his Texas days. He flattered you with his fine eyes; he bewitched you with his voice; he mesmerized you with his hands. He drank a quart of whisky a day; was almost never drunk, but on rare occasions when the liquor fumes bested him he would invariably select a hapless victim and, whipping out the pair of mother-o'-pearl-handled six-shooters he always wore at his belt, would force him to dance by shooting at his feet—a pleasing fancy brought with him from Texas and the Cimarron. Afterward, sobered, he was always filled with shame. Wine, he quoted sadly, is a mocker, strong drink is raging. Yancey Cravat could have been (in fact was, though most of America never knew it) the greatest criminal lawyer of his day. It was said that he hypnotized a jury with his eyes and his hands and his voice. His law practice yielded him nothing, or less than that, for being sentimental and melodramatic he usually found himself out of pocket following his brilliant and successful defense of

some Dodge City dance-hall girl or roistering cowboy whose six-shooter
had been pointed the wrong way.

His past, before his coming to Wichita, was clouded with myths
and surmises. Gossip said this; slander whispered that. Rumor, romantic,
unsavory, fantastic, shifting and changing like clouds on a mountain
peak, floated about the head of Yancey Cravat. They say he has Indian
blood in him. They say he has an Indian wife somewhere, and a lot of
papooses. Cherokee. They say he used to be known as "Cimarron"
Cravat, hence his son's name, corrupted to Cim. They say his real name
is Cimarron Seven, of the Choctaw Indian family of Sevens; he was
raised in a tepee; a wickiup had been his bedroom, a blanket his robe.
It was known he had been one of the early Boomers who followed the
banner of the picturesque and splendidly mad David Payne in the first
wild dash of that adventurer into Indian Territory. He had dwelt, others
whispered, in that sinister strip, thirty-four miles wide and almost two
hundred miles long, called No-Man's-Land as early as 1854, and, later,
known as the Cimarron, a Spanish word meaning wild or unruly. Here,
in this strange unowned empire without laws and without a government,
a paradise for horse thieves, murderers, desperadoes it was rumored
he had spent at least a year (and for good reason). They said the evi-
dences of his Indian blood were plain; look at his skin, his hair, his
manner of walking. And why did he protest in his newspaper against the
government's treatment of those dirty, thieving, lazy, good-for-nothing
wards of a beneficent country! As for his newspaper—its very name was
a scandal: The Wichita *Wigwam.* And just below this: All the News.
Any Scandal Not Libelous. Published Once a week if Convenient. For
that matter, who ever heard of a practising lawyer who ran a newspaper
at the same time? Its columns were echoes of his own thundering oratory
in the courtroom or on the platform. He had started his paper in opposition to the old established Wichita *Eagle.* Wichita, roaring, said he
should have called his sheet the *Rooster.* The combination law and
newspaper office itself was a jumble and welter of pied type, unopened
exchanges, boiler plate, legal volumes, paste pots, loose tobacco, old
coats, and racing posters. Wichita, professing scorn of the *Wigwam,*
read it. Wichita perused his maiden editorial entitled Shall the Blue
Blood of the Decayed South Poison the Red Blood of the Great Middle
West? and saw him, two months later, carry off in triumph as his bride
Sabra Venable, daughter of that same Decay; Sabra Venable, whose
cerulean stream might have mingled with the more vulgarly sanguine
life fluid of any youth in Wichita. In spite of the garden hedge, the
parental pride, the arched insteps, the colored servants, and the general
air of what-would-you-varlet that pervaded the Venable household at

the entrance of a local male a-wooing, Sabra Venable, at sixteen, might have had her pick of the red-blooded lads of Kansas, all the way from Salina to Winfield. Not to mention more legitimate suitors of blue-blooded stock up from the South, such as Dabney Venable himself, Sabra's cousin, who resembled at once Lafayette and old Lewis, even to the premature silver of his hair, the length of the fine, dolichocephalic, slightly decadent head, and the black stock at sight of which Wichita gasped. When, from among all these eligibles, Sabra had chosen the romantic but mysterious Cravat, Wichita mothers of marriageable daughters felt themselves revenged of the Venable airs. Strangely enough, the marriageable daughters seemed more resentful than ever, and there was a noticeable falling off in the number of young ladies who had been wont to drop round at the *Wigwam* office with notices of this or that meeting or social event to be inserted in the columns of the paper.

During the course of the bountiful meal with which the Venable table was spread Yancey Cravat had eaten almost nothing. Here was an audience to his liking. Here was a tale to his taste. His story, wild, unbelievable, yet true, was of the opening of the Oklahoma country; of a wilderness made populous in an hour; of cities numbering thousands literally sprung up overnight, where the day before had been only prairie, coyotes, rattlesnakes, red clay, scrub oak, and an occasional nester hidden in the security of a weedy draw.

He had been a month absent. Like thousands of others he had gone in search of free land, and a fortune. Here was an empire to be had for the taking. He talked, as always, in the highfalutin terms of the speaker who is ever conscious of his audience. Yet, fantastic as it was, all that he said was woven of the warp and woof of truth. Whole scenes, as he talked, seemed to be happening before his listeners' eyes.

II

COAT tails swishing, eyes flashing, arms waving, voice soaring.

"Folks, there's never been anything like it since Creation. Creation! Hell! That took six days. This was done in one. It was History made in an hour—and I helped make it. Thousands and thousands of people from all over this vast commonwealth of ours" (he talked like that) "traveled hundreds of miles to get a bare piece of land for nothing. But what land! Virgin, except when the Indians had roamed it. 'Lands of lost gods, and godlike men!' They came like a procession—a crazy procession—all the way to the Border, covering the ground as fast as they could, by any means at hand—scrambling over the ground, pushing and shoving each other into the ditches to get there first. God knows why—for they all knew that once arrived there they'd have to wait like penned cattle for the firing of the signal shot that opened the promised land. As I got nearer the line it was like ants swarming on sugar. Over the little hills they came, and out of the scrub-oak woods and across the prairie. They came from Texas, and Arkansas and Colorado and Missouri. They came on foot, by God, all the way from Iowa and Nebraska! They came in buggies and wagons and on horseback and muleback. In prairie schooners and ox carts and carriages. I saw a surrey, honey colored, with a fringe around the top, and two elegant bays drawing it, still stepping high along those rutted clay roads as if out for a drive in the Presidio. There was a black boy driving it, brass buttons and all, and in the back seat was a dude in a light tan coat and a cigar in his mouth and a diamond in his shirtfront; and a woman beside him in a big hat and a pink dress laughing and urging the horses along the red dust that was halfway up to the wheel spokes and fit to choke you. They had driven like that from Denver, damned if they hadn't. I met up with one old homesteader by the roadside—a face dried and wrinkled as a nutmeg—who told me he had started weeks and weeks before, and had made the long trip as best he could, on foot or by rail and boat and wagon, just as kind-hearted people along the way would pick him up. I wonder if he ever got his piece of land in that savage rush—poor old devil."

He paused a moment, perhaps in retrospect, perhaps cunningly to whet the appetites of his listeners. He wrung a breathless, "Oh, Yancey, go on! Go on!" from Sabra.

"Well, the Border at last, and it was like a Fourth of July celebration on Judgment Day. The militia was lined up at the boundary. No one was allowed to set foot on the new land until noon next day, at the firing of the guns. Two million acres of land were to be given away for the grabbing. Noon was the time. They all knew it by heart. April twenty-second, at noon. It takes generations of people hundreds of years to settle a new land. This was going to be made livable territory over night—was made—like a miracle out of the Old Testament. Compared to this, the Loaves and the Fishes and the parting of the Red Sea were nothing—mere tricks."

"Don't be blasphemous, Yancey!" spoke up Aunt Cassandra Venable. Cousin Dabney Venable tittered into his stock.

"A wilderness one day—except for an occasional wandering band of Indians—an empire the next. If that isn't a modern miracle——"

"Indians, h'm?" sneered Cousin Dabney, meaningly.

"Oh, Dabney!" exclaimed Sabra, sharply. "Why do you interrupt? Why don't you just listen!"

Yancey Cravat raised a pacifying hand, but the great buffalo head was lowered toward Cousin Dabney, as though charging. The sweetest of smiles wreathed his lips. "It's all right, Sabra. Let Cousin Dabney speak. And why not? *Un cabello haze sombra.*"

Cousin Dabney's ivory face flushed a delicate pink. "What's that, Cravat? Cherokee talk?"

"Spanish, my lad. Spanish."

A little moment of silent expectation. Yancey did not explain. A plump and pretty daughter-in-law (not a Venable born) put the question.

"Spanish, Cousin Yancey! I declare! Whatever in the world does it mean? Something romantic, I do hope."

"Not exactly. A Spanish proverb. It means, literally, 'Even a hair casts a shadow.'"

Another second's silence. The pretty daughter-in-law's face became quite vacuous. "Oh. A hair—but I don't see what that's got to do with . . ."

The time had come for Felice Venable to take charge. Her drawling, querulous voice dripped its slow sweetness upon the bitter feud that lay, a poisonous pool, between the two men.

"Well, I must say I call it downright bad manners, I do indeed. Here we all are with our ears just a-flapping to hear the first sound of the militia guns at high noon on the Border, and here's Cousin Jouett Goforth all the way up from Louisiana the first time in fifteen years, and just a-quivering with curiosity, and what do we hear but chit-chat about Spanish proverbs and shadows." She broke off abruptly, cast a lightning glance aloft, and in a tone that would have been called a shout had it issued from the throat of any but a Venable, said, "Ahsaiah!"

The black boy's shoo-fly, hanging limp from his inert hand, took up its frantic swishing. The air was cleared. The figures around the table relaxed. Their faces again turned toward Yancey Cravat. Yancey glanced at Sabra. Sabra's lips puckered into a phantom kiss. They formed two words, unseen, unheard by the rest of the company. "Please, darling."

"*Cede Deo,*" said Yancey, with a little bow to her. Then, with a still slighter bow, he turned to Cousin Dabney. " 'Let there be no strife, I pray thee, between thee and me.' You may not recognize that either, Dabney. It's from the Old Testament."

Cousin Dabney Venable ran a finger along the top of his black silk stock, as though to ease his throat.

With a switch of his coat tails Yancey was off again, pausing only a moment at the sideboard to toss off three fingers of Spanish brandy, like burning liquid amber. He patted his lips with his fine linen handkerchief. "I've tasted nothing like that in a month, I can tell you. Raw corn whisky fit to tear your throat out. And as for the water! Red mud. There wasn't a drink of water to be had in the town after the first twenty-four hours. There we were, thousands and thousands of us, milling around the Border like cattle, with the burning sun baking us all day, nowhere to go for shade, and the thick red dust clogging eyes and nose and mouth. No place to wash, no place to sleep, nothing to eat. Queer enough, they didn't seem to mind. Didn't seem to notice. They were feeding on a kind of crazy excitement, and there was a wild light in their eyes. They laughed and joked and just milled around, all day and all night and until near noon next day. If you had a bit of food you divided it with someone. I finally got a cup of water for a dollar, after standing in line for three hours, and then a woman just behind me——"

"A woman!" Cousin Arminta Greenwood (of the Georgia Greenwoods). And Sabra Cravat echoed the words in a shocked whisper.

"You wouldn't believe, would you, that women would go it alone in a fracas like that. But they did. They were there with their husbands, some of them, but there were women who made the Run alone."

"What kind of women?" Felice Venable's tone was not one of inquiry but of condemnation.

"Women with iron in 'em. Women who wanted land and a home. Pioneer women."

From Aunt Cassandra Venable's end of the table there came a word that sounded like, "Hussies!"

Yancey Cravat caught the word beneath his teeth and spat it back. "Hussies, heh! The one behind me in the line was a woman of forty—or looked it—in a calico dress and a sunbonnet. She had driven across the prairies all the way from the north of Arkansas in a springless wagon. She was like the women who crossed the continent to California in '49. A gaunt woman, with a weather-beaten face; the terribly neglected skin"—he glanced at Sabra with her creamy coloring—"that means alkali water and sun and dust and wind. Rough hair, and unlovely hands, and boots with the mud caked on them. It's women like her who've made this country what it is. You can't read the history of the United States,

my friends" (all this he later used in an Oklahoma Fourth of July speech
when they tried to make him Governor) "without learning the great
story of those thousands of unnamed women—women like this one I've
described—women in mud-caked boots and calico dresses and sunbonnets, crossing the prairie and the desert and the mountains enduring
hardship and privation. Good women, with a terrible and rigid goodness
that comes of work and self-denial. Nothing picturesque or romantic
about them, I suppose—though occasionally one of them flashes—Belle
Starr the outlaw—Rose of the Cimarron—Jeannette Daisy who jumped
from a moving Santa Fé train to stake her claim—but the others—no,
their story's never really been told. But it's there, just the same. And if
it's ever told straight you'll know it's the sunbonnet and not the sombrero that has settled this country."

"Talking nonsense," drawled Felice Venable.

Yancey whirled on his high heels to face her, his fine eyes blazing.
"You're one of them. You came up from the South with your husband
to make a new home in this Kansas——"

"I am not!" retorted Felice Venable, with enormous dignity. "And I'll
thank you not to say any such thing. Sunbonnet indeed! I've never worn
a sunbonnet in my life. And as for my skin and hair and hands, they
were the toast of the South, as I can prove by anyone here, all the way
from Louisiana to Tennessee. And feet so small my slippers had to
be made to order. Calico and muddy boots indeed!"

"Oh, Mamma, Yancey didn't mean—he meant courage to leave your
home in the South and come up—he wasn't thinking of—— Yancey, do
get on with your story of the Run. You got a drink of water for a dollar
—dear me!—and shared it with the woman in the calico and the sunbonnet . . ."

He looked a little sheepish. "Well, matter of fact, it turned out she
didn't have a dollar to spare, or anywhere near it, but even if she had
it wouldn't have done her any good. The fellow selling it was a rat-
faced hombre with one eye and Mexican pants. The trigger finger of his
right hand had been shot away in some fracas or other, so he ladled
out water with that hand and toted his gun in his left. Bunged up he
was, plenty. A scar on his nose, healed up, but showing the marks of
where human teeth had bit him in a fight, as neat and clear as a dentist's
signboard. By the time I got to him there was one cup of water left
in the bucket. He tipped it while I held the dipper, and it trickled out,
just an even dipperful. The last cup of water on the Border. The crowd
waiting in line behind me gave a kind of sound between a groan and a
moan. The sound you hear a herd of cow animals give, out on the
prairie, when their tongues are hanging out for water in the dry spell. I

tipped up the dipper and had downed a big mouthful—filthy tasting
stuff it was, too. Gyp water. You could feel the alkali cake on your
tongue. Well, my head went back as I drank, and I got one look at
that woman's face. Her eyes were on me—on my throat, where the
Adam's apple had just given that one big gulp after the first swallow.
All bloodshot the whites of her eyes, and a look in them like a dying
man looks at a light. Her mouth was open, and her lips were all split
with the heat and the dust and the sun, and dry and flaky as ashes.
And then she shut her lips a little and tried to swallow nothing, and
couldn't. There wasn't any spit in her mouth. I couldn't down another
mouthful, parching as I was. I'd have seen her terrible face to the last
day of my life. So I righted it, and held it out to her and said, 'Here,
sister, take the rest of it. I'm through.'"

Cousin Jouett Goforth essayed his little joke. "Are you right sure
she was forty, Yancey, and weather-beaten? And that about her hair and
boots and hands?"

Cravat, standing behind his wife's chair, looked down at her; at the
fine white line that marked the parting of her thick black hair. With one
forefinger he touched her cheek, gently. He allowed the finger to slip
down the creamy surface of her skin, from cheek bone to chin. "Dead
sure, Jouett. I left out one thing, though." Cousin Jouett made a sound
signifying, ah, I thought so. "Her teeth," Yancey Cravat went on
thoughtfully. "Broken and discolored like those of a woman of seventy.
And most of them gone at the side."

Here Yancey could not resist charging up and down, flirting his coat
tails and generally ruining the fine flavor of his victory over the Venable
mind. The Venable mind (or the prospect of escaping it) had been
one of the reasons for his dash into the wild mêlée of the Run in the first
place. Now he stood surveying these handsome futile faces, and a great
impatience shook him, and a flame of rage shot through him, and a
tongue of malice flicked him. With these to goad him, and the knowledge of how he had failed, he plunged again into his story to the end.

"I had planned to try and get a place on the Santa Fé train that
was standing, steam up, ready to run into the Nation. But you couldn't
get on. There wasn't room for a flea. They were hanging on the cow-
catcher and swarming all over the engine, and sitting on top of the cars.
It was keyed down to make no more speed than a horse. It turned out
they didn't even do that. They went twenty miles in ninety minutes. I
decided I'd use my Indian pony. I knew I'd get endurance, anyway, if
not speed. And that's what counted in the end.

"There we stood, by the thousands, all night. Morning, and we began
to line up at the Border, as near as they'd let us go. Militia all along

to keep us back. They had burned the prairie ahead for miles into the Nation, so as to keep the grass down and make the way clearer. To smoke out the Sooners, too, who had sneaked in and were hiding in the scrub oaks, in the draws, wherever they could. Most of the killing was due to them. They had crawled in and staked the land and stood ready to shoot those of us who came in, fair and square, in the Run. I knew the piece I wanted. An old freighters' trail, out of use, but still marked with deep ruts, led almost straight to it, once you found the trail, all overgrown as it was. A little creek ran through the land, and the prairie rolled a little there, too. Nothing but blackjacks for miles around it, but on that section, because of the water, I suppose, there were elms and persimmons and cottonwoods and even a grove of pecans. I had noticed it many a time, riding the range."

(H'm! Riding the range! All the Venables made a quick mental note of that. It was thus, by stray bits and snatches, that they managed to piece together something of Yancey Cravat's past.)

"Ten o'clock, and the crowd was nervous and restless. Hundreds of us had been followers of Payne and had gone as Boomers in the old Payne colonies, and had been driven out, and had come back again. Thousands from all parts of the country had waited ten years for this day when the land-hungry would be fed. They were like people starving. I've seen the same look exactly on the faces of men who were ravenous for food.

"Well, eleven o'clock, and they were crowding and cursing and fighting for places near the Line. They shouted and sang and yelled and argued, and the sound they made wasn't human at all, but like thousands of wild animals penned up. The sun blazed down. It was cruel. The dust hung over everything in a thick cloud, blinding you and choking you. The black dust of the burned prairie was over everything. We were like a horde of fiends with our red eyes and our cracked lips and our blackened faces. Eleven-thirty. It was a picture straight out of hell. The roar grew louder. People fought for an inch of gain on the Border. Just next to me was a girl who looked about eighteen—she turned out to be twenty-five—and a beauty she was, too—on a coal-black thoroughbred."

"Aha!" said Cousin Jouett Goforth. He was the kind of man who says, "Aha."

"On the other side was an old fellow with a long gray beard—a plainsman, he was—a six-shooter in his belt, one wooden leg, and a flask of whisky. He took a pull out of that every minute or two. He was mounted on an Indian pony like mine. Every now and then he'd throw back his head and let out a yell that would curdle your blood, even in that chorus of fiends. As we waited we fell to talking, the three of us, though you couldn't hear much in that uproar. The girl said she had trained her thoroughbred for the race. He was from Kentucky, and so was she. She was bound to get her hundred and sixty acres, she said. She had to have it. She didn't say why, and I didn't ask her. We were all too keyed up, anyway, to make sense. Oh, I forgot. She had on a get-up that took the attention of anyone that saw her, even in that crazy mob. The better to cut the wind, she had shortened sail and wore a short skirt, black tights, and a skullcap."

Here there was quite a bombardment of sound as silver spoons and knives and forks were dropped from shocked and nerveless feminine Venable fingers.

"It turned out that the three of us, there in the front line, were headed down the old freighters' trail toward the creek land. I said, 'I'll be the first in the Run to reach Little Bear.' That was the name of the creek on the section. The girl pulled her cap down tight over her ears. 'Follow me,' she laughed. 'I'll show you the way.' Then the old fellow with the wooden leg and the whiskers yelled out, 'Whoop-ee! I'll tell 'em along the Little Bear you're both a-comin'.'

"There we were, the girl on my left, the old plainsman on my right. Eleven forty-five. Along the Border were the soldiers, their guns in one hand, their watches in the other. Those last five minutes seemed years long; and funny, they'd quieted till there wasn't a sound. Listening. The last minute was an eternity. Twelve o'clock. There went up a roar that drowned the crack of the soldiers' musketry as they fired in the air as the signal of noon and the start of the Run. You could see the puffs of smoke from their guns, but you couldn't hear a sound. The thousands surged over the Line. It was like water going over a broken dam. The rush had started, and it was devil take the hindmost. We swept across the prairie in a cloud of black and red dust that covered our faces and hands in a minute, so that we looked like black demons from hell. Off we went, down the old freight trail that was two wheel ruts, a foot wide each, worn into the prairie soil. The old man on his pony kept in one rut, the girl on her thoroughbred in the other, and I on my Whitefoot on the raised place in the middle. That first half mile was almost a neck-and-neck race. The old fellow was yelling and waving one arm and hanging on somehow. He was beating his pony with the flask on his flanks. Then he began to drop behind. Next thing I heard a terrible scream and a great shouting behind me. I threw a quick glance over my shoulder. The old plainsman's pony had stumbled and fallen. His bottle smashed into bits, his six-shooter flew in another direction, and he lay sprawling full length in the rut of the trail. The next instant he was hidden in a welter of pounding hoofs and flying dirt and cinders and wagon wheels."

A dramatic pause. Black Isaiah was hanging from his perch like a mon-

key on a branch. His asparagus shoo-fly was limp. The faces around the
table were balloons pulled by a single string. They swung this way and
that with Yancey Cravat's pace as he strode the room, his Prince Albert
coat tails billowing. This way—the faces turned toward the sideboard.
That way—they turned toward the windows. Yancey held the little moment of silence like a jewel in the circlet of faces. Sabra Cravat's voice,
high and sharp with suspense, cut the stillness.

"What happened? What happened to the old man?"

Yancey's pliant hands flew up in a gesture of inevitability. "Oh, he
was trampled to death in the mad mob that charged over him. Crazy.
They couldn't stop for a one-legged old whiskers with a quart flask."

Out of the well-bred murmur of horror that now arose about the
Venable board there emerged the voice of Felice Venable, sharp-edged
with disapproval. "And the girl. The girl with the black——" Unable to
say it. Southern.

"The girl and I—funny, I never did learn her name—were in the lead
because we had stuck to the old trail, rutted though it was, rather than
strike out across the prairie that by this time was beyond the burned
area and was covered with a heavy growth of blue stem grass almost six
feet high in places. A horse could only be forced through that at a slow
pace. That jungle of grass kept many a racer from winning his section
that day.

"The girl followed close behind me. That thoroughbred she rode was
built for speed, not distance. A race horse, blooded. I could hear him
blowing. He was trained to short bursts. My Indian pony was just getting
his second wind as her horse slackened into a trot. We had come nearly
sixteen miles. I was well in the lead by that time, with the girl following.
She was crouched low over his neck, like a jockey, and I could hear her
talking to him, low and sweet and eager, as if he were a human being.
We were far in the lead now. We had left the others behind, hundreds
going this way, hundreds that, scattering for miles over the prairie. Then
I saw that the prairie ahead was afire. The tall grass was blazing. Only
the narrow trail down which we were galloping was open. On either
side of it was a wall of flame. Some skunk of a Sooner, sneaking in ahead
of the Run, had set the blaze to keep the Boomers off, saving the land
for himself. The dry grass burned like oiled paper. I turned around. The
girl was there, her racer stumbling, breaking and going on, his head lolling now. I saw her motion with her hand. She was coming. I whipped
off my hat and clapped it over Whitefoot's eyes, gave him the spurs,
crouched down low and tight, shut my own eyes, and down the trail we
went into the furnace. Hot! It was hell! The crackling and snapping on
either side was like a fusillade. I could smell the singed hair on the flanks

of the mustang. My own hair was singeing. I could feel the flames licking my legs and back. Another hundred yards and neither the horse nor
I could have come through it. But we broke out into the open choking
and blinded and half suffocated. I looked down the lane of flame. The
girl hung on her horse's neck. Her skullcap was pulled down over her
eyes. She was coming through, game. I knew that my land—the piece
that I had come through hell for—was not more than a mile ahead. I
knew that hanging around here would probably get me a shot through
the head, for the Sooner that started that fire must be lurking somewhere
in the high grass ready to kill anybody that tried to lay claim to his
land. I began to wonder, too, if that girl wasn't headed for the same section that I was bound for. I made up my mind that, woman or no
woman, this was a race, and devil take the hindmost. My poor little
pony was coughing and sneezing and trembling. Her racer must have
been ready to drop. I wheeled and went on. I kept thinking how, when
I came to Little Bear Creek, I'd bathe my little mustang's nose and face
and his poor heaving flanks, and how I mustn't let him drink too much,
once he got his muzzle in the water.

"Just before I reached the land I was riding for I had to leave the
trail and cut across the prairie. I could see a clump of elms ahead. I
knew the creek was near by. But just before I got to it I came to one
of those deep gullies you find in the plains country. Drought does it—
a crack in the dry earth to begin with, widening with every rain until it
becomes a small cañon. Almost ten feet across this one was, and deep.
No way around it that I could see, and no time to look for one. I put
Whitefoot to the leap and, by God, he took it, landing on the other
side with hardly an inch to spare. I heard a wild scream behind me. I
turned. The girl on her spent racer had tried to make the gulch. He had
actually taken it—a thoroughbred and a gentleman, that animal—but he
came down on his knees just on the farther edge, rolled, and slid down
the gully side into the ditch. The girl had flung herself free. My claim
was fifty yards away. So was the girl, with her dying horse. She lay there
on the prairie. As I raced toward her—my own poor little mount was
nearly gone by this time—she scrambled to her knees. I can see her face
now, black with cinders and soot and dirt, her hair all over her shoulders,
her cheek bleeding where she had struck a stone in her fall, her black
tights torn, her little short skirt sagging. She sort of sat up and looked
around her. Then she staggered to her feet before I reached her and
stood there swaying, and pushing her hair out of her eyes like someone
who'd been asleep. She pointed down the gully. The black of her face
was streaked with tears.

" 'Shoot him!' she said. 'I can't. His two forelegs are broken. I heard them crack. Shoot him! For God's sake!'

"So I off my horse and down to the gully's edge. There the animal lay, his eyes all whites, his poor legs doubled under him, his flanks black and sticky with sweat and dirt. He was done for, all right. I took out my six-shooter and aimed right between his eyes. He kicked once, sort of leaped—or tried to, and then lay still. I stood there a minute, to see if he had to have another. He was so game that, some way, I didn't want to give him more than he needed.

"Then something made me turn around. The girl had mounted my mustang. She was off toward the creek section. Before I had moved ten paces she had reached the very piece I had marked in my mind for my own. She leaped from the horse, ripped off her skirt, tied it to her riding whip that she still held tight in her hand, dug the whip butt into the soil of the prairie—planted her flag—and the land was hers by right of claim."

Yancey Cravat stopped talking. There was a moment of stricken silence. Sabra Cravat staring, staring at her husband with great round eyes. Lewis Venable, limp, yellow, tremulous. Felice Venable, upright and quivering. It was she who spoke first. And when she did she was every inch the thrifty descendant of French forbears; nothing of the Southern belle about her.

"Yancey Cravat, do you mean that you let her have your quarter section on the creek that you had gone to the Indian Territory for! That you had been gone a month for! That you had left your wife and child for! That——"

"Now, Mamma!" You saw that all the Venable in Sabra was summoned to keep the tears from her eyes, and that thus denied they had crowded themselves into her trembling voice. "Now, Mamma!"

"Don't you 'now Mamma' me! What of the land that you were to have had! It was bad enough to think of your going to that wilderness, but to——" She paused. Her voice took on a new and more sinister note. "I don't believe a word of it." She whirled on Yancey, her black eyes blazing. "Why did you let that trollop in the black tights have that land?"

Yancey regarded this question with considerable judicial calm, but Felice, knowing him, might have been warned by the way his great head was lowered like that of a charging bull buffalo.

"If it had been a man I could have shot him. A good many had to, to keep the land they'd run fairly for. But you can't shoot a woman."

"Why not?" demanded the erstwhile Southern belle, sharply.

The Venables, as one man, gave a little jump. A nervous sound, that was half gasp and half shocked titter, went round the Venable board. A startled "Felice!" was wrung from Lewis Venable. "Why, Mamma!" said Sabra.

Yancey Cravat, enormously vital, felt rising within him the tide of irritability which this vitiated family always stirred in him. Something now about their shocked and staring faces, their lolling and graceful forms, roused in him an unreasoning rebellion. He suddenly hated them. He wanted to be free of them. He wanted to be free of them— of Wichita—of convention—of smooth custom—of—no, not of her. He now smiled his brilliant sweet smile which alone should have warned Felice Venable. But that intrepid matriarch was not one to let a tale go unpointed.

"I'm mighty pleased, for one, that it turned out as it did. Do you suppose I'd have allowed a daughter of mine—a Venable—to go traipsing down into the wilderness to live among drunken one-legged plainsmen, and toothless scrags in calico, and trollops in tights! Never! It's over now, and a mighty good thing, too. Perhaps now, Yancey, you'll stop this ramping up and down and be content to run that newspaper of yours and conduct your law practice—such as it is—with no more talk of this Indian Territory. A daughter of mine in boots and calico and sunbonnet, if you please, a-pioneering among savages. Reared as she was! No, indeed."

Yancey was strangely silent. He was surveying his fine white hands critically, interestedly, as though seeing them in admiration for the first time—another sign that should have warned the brash Felice. When he spoke it was with utter gentleness.

"I'm no farmer. I'm no rancher. I didn't want a section of farm land, anyway. The town's where I belong, and I should have made for the town sites. There were towns of ten thousand and over sprung up in a night during the Run. Wagallala—Sperry—Wawhuska—Osage. It's the last frontier in America, that new country. There isn't a newspaper in one of those towns—or wasn't, when I left. I want to go back there and help build a state out of prairie and Indians and scrub oaks and red clay. For it'll be a state some day—mark my words."

"That wilderness a state!" sneered Cousin Dabney Venable. "With an Osage buck or a Cherokee chief for governor, I suppose."

"Why not? What a revenge on a government that has cheated them and driven them like cattle from place to place and broken its treaties with them and robbed them of their land. Look at Georgia! Look at Mississippi! Remember the Trail of Tears!"

"Ho hum," yawned Cousin Jouett Goforth, and rose, fumblingly. "This has all been very interesting—odd, but interesting. But if you will excuse me now I shall have my little siesta. I am accustomed after dinner . . ."

Lewis Venable, so long silent, now too reached for his cane and prepared to rise. He was not quick enough. Felice Venable's hand, thin, febrile, darted out and clutched his coat sleeve—pressed him back so that he became at once prisoner and judge in his chair at the head of the table.

"Lewis Venable, you heard him! Are you going to sit there? He says he's going back. How about your daughter?" She turned blazing black eyes on her son-in-law. "Do you mean you're going back to that Indian country? Do you?"

"I'll be back there in two weeks. And remember, it's white man's country now."

Sabra stood up, the boy Cim grasped about his middle in her arms, so that he began to whimper, dangling there. Her eyes were startled, enormous. "Yancey! Yancey, you're not leaving me again!"

"Leaving you, my beauty!" He strode over to her. "Not by a long shot. This time you're going with me."

"And I say she's not!" Felice Venable rapped it out. "And neither are you, my fine fellow. You were tricked out of your land by a trollop in tights, and that ends it. You'll stay here with your wife and child."

He shook his great head gently. His voice was dulcet.

"I'm going back to the Oklahoma country; and Sabra and Cim with me."

Felice whirled on her husband. "Lewis! You can sit there and see your daughter dragged off to be scalped among savages!"

The sick man raised his fine white head. The faded blue eyes were turned on the girl. The child, sensing conflict, had buried his head in her shoulder. "You came with me, Felice, more than twenty years ago, and your mother thought you were going to the wilderness, too. You remember? She cried and made mourning for weeks."

"Sabra's different. Sabra's different."

The reedy voice of the sick man had the ghostly carrying quality of an echo. You heard it above the women's shrill clamor. "No, she isn't, Felice. She's more like you this minute than you are yourself. She favors those pioneer women Yancey was telling about in the old days. Look at her."

The Venable eye, from one end of the table to the other, turned like a single orb in its socket toward the young woman facing them with defiance in her bearing. Not defiance, perhaps, so much as resolve. Seeing her, head up, standing there beside her husband, one arm about the child, you saw that what her father said was indeed true. She was her mother, the Felice Venable of two decades ago; she was the woman in sunbonnet and calico to whom Yancey had given his cup of water; she was the women jolting endless miles in covered wagons, spinning in log cabins, cooking over crude fires; she was all women who have traveled American prairie and desert and mountain and plain. Here was that inner rectitude, that chastity of lip, that clearness of eye, that refinement of feature, that absence of allure that comes with cold white fire. The pioneer type, as Yancey had said. Potentially a more formidable woman than her mother.

Seeing something of this, Felice Venable said again, more loudly, as though to convince herself, "She's not to go."

Looking more than ever like her mother, Sabra met this stubbornly. "But I want to go, Mamma."

"I forbid it. You don't know what you want. You don't know what you're talking about. I say you'll stay here with your mother and father in decent civilization. I've heard enough. I hope this will serve a lesson to you, Yancey."

"I'm going back to the Nation," said Yancey, quite pleasantly.

Sabra stiffened. "I'm going with him." In her new resolve she must have squeezed the hand of the child Cim, for he gave a little yelp. The combined Venables, nerves on edge, leaped in their chairs and then looked at each other with some hostility.

"And I say you're not."

"But I want to go."

"You don't."

Perhaps Sabra had not realized until now how terribly she had counted on her husband's return as marking the time when she would be free to leave the Venable board, to break away from the Venable clan; no more to be handled, talked over, peered at by the Venable eye—and most of all by the maternal Venable eye. Twenty-one, and the yoke of her mother's dominance was beginning to gall her. Now, at her own inner rage and sickening disappointment, all the iron in her fused and hardened. It had gone less often to the fire than the older woman's had. For the first time this quality in her met that of her mother, and the metal of the older woman bent.

"I *will* go," said Sabra Cravat.

If anyone had been looking at Lewis Venable at that moment (which no one ever thought of doing) he could have seen a ghostly smile momentarily irradiating the transparent ivory face. But now it was Yancey Cravat who held their fascinated eye. With a cowboy yip he swung the defiant Sabra and the boy Cim high in the air in his great arms—tossed them up, so that Sabra screamed, and Cim squealed in mingled terror and delight. It was the kind of horseplay (her word) at which Felice Venable always shuddered. Altogether the three seemed suddenly an outrage in that seemly room with its mahogany and its decanters and its circle of staring high-bred faces.

"Week from to-morrow," announced Yancey, in something like a shout, so exulting it seemed. "We'll start on a Monday, fresh and fair. Two wagons. One with the printing outfit—you'll drive that, Sabra—and one with the household goods and bedding and camp stuff and the rest. We ought to make it in nine days. . . . Wichita!" His glance went round the room, and in that glance you saw not only Wichita! but Venables! "I've had enough of it. Sabra, my girl, we'll leave all the god-damned middle-class respectability of Wichita, Kansas, behind us. We're going out, by God, to a brand-new, two-fisted, rip-snorting country, full of Injuns and rattlesnakes and two-gun toters and gyp water and des-per-*ah*-dos! Whoop-*ee!*"

It was too much for black Isaiah in his perilous perch high above the table. He had long ago ceased to wield his asparagus fan. He had been leaning farther and farther forward, the better to hear and see all of the scene that was spread beneath him. Now, at Yancey's cowboy whoop, he started violently, his slight hold was loosed, and he fell like a great black grape from the vine directly into the midst of one of Felice Venable's white and virgin frosted silver cakes.

Shouts, screams, upleapings. Isaiah plucked, white-bottomed, out of the center of the vast pastry. The sudden grayish pallor of his face matched the silver tone of his pants' seat. Felice Venable, nerves strained to breaking, lifted her hand to cuff him smartly. But the black boy was too quick for her. With the swiftness of a wild thing he scuttled across the table to where Yancey Cravat stood with his wife and child, leaped nimbly to the floor, crept between the man's legs like a whimpering little dog, and lay there, locked in the safety of Yancey's great knees.

III

INDIANS were no novelty to the townspeople of Wichita. Sabra had seen them all her life. At the age of three Cim was held up in his father's arms to watch a great band of them go by on one of their annual pilgrimages. He played Indian, of course, patting his lips to simulate the Indian yodeling yell. He had a war bonnet made of chicken feathers sewed to the edge of a long strip of red calico.

Twice a year, chaperoned by old General "Bull" Plummer, the Indians swept through the streets of Wichita in their visiting regalia—feathers, beads, blankets, chains—a brilliant sight. Ahead of them and behind them was the reassuring blue of United States army uniforms worn by the Kansas regiment from Fort Riley. All Wichita, accustomed to them though it was, rushed out to gaze at them from store doorways and offices and kitchens. Bucks, braves, chiefs, squaws, papooses; tepees, poles, pots, dogs, ponies, the cavalcade swept through the quiet sunny streets of the mid-western town, a vivid frieze of color against the drab monotony of the prairies.

In late spring it was likely to be the Cheyennes going north from their reservation in the Indian Territory to visit their cousins the Sioux in Dakota. In the late autumn it was the Sioux riding south to return the visit of the Cheyennes. Both of these were horse Indians, and of the Plains tribes, great visitors among themselves, and as gossipy and highly gregarious as old women on a hotel veranda. Usually they called a halt in their journey to make camp for the night outside the town. Though watched over by martial eye, they usually managed to pilfer, in a friendly sort of way, anything they could lay hands on—chickens, wash unwisely left on the line, the very clothes off the scarecrows in the field.

Throughout the year there were always little groups of Indians to be seen on the streets of the town—Kaws, Osages, and Poncas. They came on ponies or in wagons from their reservations; bought bacon, calico, whisky if they could get it. You saw them squatting on their haunches in the dust of the sunny street, silent, sloe eyed, aloof. They seemed to be studying the townspeople passing to and fro. Only their eyes moved. Their dress was a mixture of savagery and civilization. The Osages, especially, clung to the blanket. Trousers, coat, and even hat might be in the conventional pattern of the whites. But over this the Osage wore his striped blanket of vivid orange and purple and red. It was as though he defied the whites to take from him that last insignia of race.

A cowed enough people they seemed by now; dirty, degraded. Since the Custer Massacre of '76 they had been pretty thoroughly beaten into submission. Only occasionally there seemed to emanate from a band of them a sullen, enduring hate. It had no definite expression. It was not in their bearing; it could not be said to look out from the dead black Indian eye, nor was it anywhere about the immobile parchment face. Yet somewhere black implacable resentment smoldered in the heart of this dying race.

In one way or another, at school, in books and newspapers of the time, in her father's talk with the men and women of his own generation, Sabra had picked up odds and ends of information about these silent, slothful, yet sinister figures. She had been surprised—even incredulous—at her husband's partisanship of the redskins. It was one of his absurdities. He seemed actually to consider them as human beings.

Tears came to his own eyes when he spoke of that blot on southern civilization, the Trail of Tears, in which the Cherokees, a peaceful and home-loving Indian tribe, were torn from the land which a government had given them by sworn treaty, to be sent far away on a march which, from cold, hunger, exposure, and heartbreak, was marked by bleaching bones from Georgia to Oklahoma. Yancey and old Lewis Venable had a long-standing feud on the subject of Mississippi's treatment of the Choctaws and Georgia's cruelty to the Cherokees.

"Oh, treaties!" sneered Yancey's father-in-law, outraged at some blistering editorial with which Yancey had enlivened the pages of the Wichita *Wigwam*. "One doesn't make treaties with savages—and expect to keep them."

"You call the Choctaws, the Creeks, the Chickasaws, the Cherokees and the Seminoles savages! They are the Five Civilized Tribes! They had their laws, they had their religion, they cultivated the land, they were peaceful, home-loving, wise. Would you call Chief Apushmataha a savage?"

"Certainly, sir! Most assuredly."

"How about Sequoyah? John Ross? Stand Waitie? Quanah Parker? They were wise men. Great men."

"Savages, with enough white blood in them to make them leaders of their dull-witted, full-blood brothers. The Creeks, sir" (he pronounced it "suh") "intermarried with niggers. And so did the Choctaws; and the Seminoles down in Florida."

Yancey smiled his winning smile. "I understand that while you Southerners didn't exactly marry——"

"Marriage, sir, is one thing. Nature, sir, is another. Far from signing treaties with these creatures and giving them valuable American land to call their own——"

"Which was their own before we took it away from them."

"—I would be in favor of extermination by some humane but effective process. They are a sore on the benign bosom of an otherwise healthy government."

"It is now being done as effectively as even you could wish, though perhaps lacking a little something on the humane side."

From her father and mother, too, Sabra had heard much of this sort of talk before Yancey had come into her life. She had heard of them at school, as well. Their savagery and trickiness had been emphasized; their tragedy had been glossed over or scarcely touched upon. Sabra, if she considered them at all, thought of them as dirty and useless two-footed animals. In her girlhood she had gone to a school conducted by the Sisters of Loretto, under the jurisdiction of the Jesuit Fathers. Early in the history of Kansas, long before Sabra's day, it had started as a Mission school, and the indefatigable Jesuit priests had traveled the country on horseback, riding the weary and dangerous miles over the prairies to convert the Indians. Mother Bridget, a powerful, heavy woman of past sixty now, shrewd, dominating, yet strangely childlike, had come to the Mission when a girl just past her novitiate, in the wild and woolly days of Kansas. She had seen the oxen haul the native yellow limestone of which the building was made; she had known the fear of the scalping knife; with her own big, capable, curiously masculine hands she had planted the first young fruit trees, the vegetable and flower garden that now flourished in the encircling Osage hedge; she had superintended the building of the great hedge itself, made of the tough yet supple wood that the exploring pioneer French had called *bois d'arc*, because in the early days the Indians had fashioned their bows of it. The Kansans had corrupted the word until now the wood was known as "bodark." The Mission had been an Indian school then, with a constantly fluctuating attendance. One day there would be forty pairs of curiously dead black Indian eyes intent on a primer of reading, writing, or arithmetic; the next there would be none. The tribe had gone on a visit to a neighboring friendly tribe. Bucks and squaws, ponies and dogs and children, they were off on society bent, the Osages visiting the Kaws, or the Kaws the Quapaws. At other times their absence might mean something more sinister—an uprising in the brewing, or an attack on an enemy tribe. Mother Bridget had terrible tales to tell. She could even make grim jokes about those early days. "Hair-raising times they were," she would tell you (it was her pet pun), "in more ways than one, as many a poor white settler could prove to you who'd had the scalp lifted off him by the knife." She had taught the Indian girls to sew, to exchange wigwams for cabins, and to wear sunbonnets and to speak about their souls and their earthly troubles as well to a Great Father named God who was much more powerful than the Sun and the Rain and the Wind to whom they attributed such potency. These things they did with gratifying docility for weeks at a time, or even months, after which it was discovered that they buried their dead under the cabins, removing enough of the puncheon floor to enable them to dig a grave, laying the timbers back neatly, and then deserting the cabins to live outdoors again, going back to the blanket at the same time and holding elaborate placating ceremonies to various gods of the elements. Mother Bridget (Sister Bridget then, red cheeked in her wimple, her beads clicking a stubborn race against the treachery of the savages) and the other Sisters of Loretto had it all to do over again from the start.

All this was past now. The Indians were herded on reservations in the Indian Territory. Mother Bridget and her helpers taught embroidery and music and kindred ladylike accomplishments to the bonneted and gloved young ladies of Wichita's gentry. The Osage hedge now shielded prim and docile misses where once it had tried to confine the wild things of the prairie. The wild things seemed tame enough now, herded together on their reservations, spirit broken, pride destroyed.

Sabra had her calico pony hitched to the phaëton (a matron now, it was no longer seemly to ride him as she used to, up and down the rutted prairie roads, her black hair in a long thick braid switching to the speed of the hard-bitten hoofs). Mother Bridget was in the Mission vegetable garden, superintending the cutting of great rosy stalks of late pie plant. The skirt of her habit was hitched up informally above her list shoes, muddied by the soft loam of the garden.

"Indian Territory! What does your ma say?"

"She's wild."

"Do you want to go?"

"Oh, yes, yes!" Then added hastily: "Of course, I hate to leave Mamma and Papa. But the Bible says, 'Whither thou——' "

"I know what the Bible says," interrupted the old nun shrewdly. "Why does he want to go—Cravat?"

Sabra glowed with pride. "Yancey says it's a chance to build an empire out of the last frontier in America. He says its lawmakers can profit by the mistakes of the other states, so that when the Indian Territory becomes a state some day it will know wherein the other states have failed, and knowing—uh—avoid the pitfalls——"

"Stuff!" interrupted Mother Bridget. "He's going for the adventure of it. They always have, no matter what excuse they've given, from the Holy Grail to the California gold fields. The difference in America is that the women have always gone along. When you read the history of France you're peeking through a bedroom keyhole. The history of England is a joust. The womenfolks were always Elaineish and anemic, seems. When Ladye Guinevere had pinned a bow of ribbon to her knight's sleeve, why, her job was done for the day. He could ride off to be killed while she stayed home and stitched at a tapestry. But here in this land, Sabra, my girl, the women, they've been the real hewers of wood and drawers of water. You'll want to remember that."

"But that's what Yancey said. Exactly."

"Did he now!" She stood up and released the full folds of her skirt from the waist cord that had served to loop it away from the moist earth. She lifted her voice in an order to the figure that stooped over the pie-plant bed. "Enough, Sister Norah, enough. Tell Sister Agnes plenty of sugar and not like the last pie, fit to pucker your mouth." She turned back to Sabra. "When do you start? How do you go?"

"Next Monday. Two wagons. One with the printing outfit, the other with the household goods and bedding. Yancey will have it that we've got to take along bedsprings for me, right out of our bed here and laid flat in the wagon."

Mother Bridget seemed not to hear. She looked out across the garden to where prairie met sky. Her eyes, behind the steel-rimmed spectacles, saw a pageant that Sabra had never known. "So. It's come to that. They've opened it to the whites after all—the land that was to belong to the Indians forever. 'As long as grass grows and the rivers flow.' That's what the treaty said. H'm. Well, what next!"

"Oh, Indians . . ." said Sabra. Her tone was that of one who speaks of prairie dogs, seven-year locusts, or any like Western nuisance.

"I know," said Mother Bridget. "You can't change them. Nobody knows better than I. I've had Indian girls here in the school for two years at a stretch. We'd teach them to wash themselves every day; they'd learn to sew, and embroider, and cook and read and write. They were taught worsted and coral work and drawing and even painting and vocal music. They learned the Gospel of the Son of God. They'd leave here as neat and pretty and well behaved as any girl you'd care to see. In two weeks I'd hear they'd gone back to the blanket. Say what you like, the full-blood Indian to-day is just about where he was before Joshua. Well——"

Sabra was a little bored by all this. She had not come out to the old Mission to hear about Indians. She had come to say farewell to Mother Bridget, and have a fuss made over her, and to be exclaimed over. Wasn't she going to be a pioneer woman such as you read about in the books?

"I must be going, dear Mother Bridget. I just came out—there's so much to do." She was vaguely disappointed in the dramatics of this visit.

"I've something for you. Come along." She led the way through the garden, across the sandstone flagging of the porch, into the dim cool mustiness of the Mission hall. She left Sabra there and went swiftly down the corridor. Sabra waited, grateful for this shady haven after the heat of the Kansas sun. She had known this hall, and the bare bright rooms that opened off it, all through her girlhood. The fragrance of pie crust, baking crisply, came to her nostrils: the shell, of course, that was to hold the succulent rhubarb. There was the sound of a heavy door opening, shutting, click, thud, somewhere down a turn in the corridor. She had never seen Mother Bridget's room. No one had. Sabra wondered about it. The Sisters of Loretto owned nothing. It was a rule of the Order. The possessive pronoun, first person, was never used by them. Sabra recalled how Sister Innocenta had come running in one morning in great distress. "Our rosary!" she had cried. "I have lost our rosary!" The string of devotional beads she always wore at her waist had somehow slipped or broken and was missing. They kept nothing for themselves. Strange and sometimes beautiful things came into their hands and were immediately disposed of. Sabra had seen Mother Bridget part with queer objects. Once it had been a scalping knife with brown stains on it that looked like rust and were not; another time an Osage papoose board with its gay and intricately beaded pocket in which some Indian woman had carried her babies strapped to her tireless back. There had been a crewel-work motto done in bright-colored wool threads by the fingers of some hopeful New England émigrée of years ago. Its curlycue letters announced: Music Hath Charms to Soothe the Savage Breast. It had been found hanging on the wall just above the prim little parlor organ in the cabin of a settler whose young wife and children had been killed during a sudden uprising of Indians in his absence.

Suddenly, as she waited there in the peace of the old building, there swept over Sabra a great wave of nostalgia for the very scenes she was leaving. It was as though she already had put behind her these familiar things of her girlhood: the calico pony and the little yellow phaëton; the oblong of Kansas sunshine and sky and garden seen through the Mission doorway; the scents and sounds and security of the solid stone building itself. She was shaken by terror. Indian Territory! Indian—why, she couldn't go there to live. To live forever, the rest of her life. Yancey Cravat, her husband, became suddenly remote, a stranger, terrible. She was Sabra Venable, Sabra Venable, here, safe from harm, in the Mission school. She wouldn't go. Her mother was right.

A door at the end of the corridor opened. The huge figure of Mother Bridget appeared, filling the oblong, blotting out the sunlight. In her arms was a thick roll of cloth. "Here," she said, and turned to let the light fall on it. It was a blanket or coverlet woven in a block pattern of white and a deep, brilliant blue. "It's to keep you and little Cim warm, in the wagon, on the way to the Indian Territory. I wove it myself, on a hand loom. There's no wear-out to it. The blue is Indian dye, and nothing can fade it. It's a wild country you'll be going to. But there's something in the blue of this makes any room fit to live in, no matter how bare and ugly. If they ask you out there what it is, tell 'em a Kansas tapestry."

She walked with Sabra to the phaëton and produced from a capacious pocket hidden in the folds of her habit a little scarlet June apple for the pony. Sabra kissed her on both plump cheeks quickly and stepped into the buggy, placing the blue and white blanket on the seat beside her. Her face was screwed up comically—the face of a little girl who is pretending not to be crying. "Good-bye," she said, and was surprised to find that her voice was no more than a whisper. And at that, feeling very sorry for herself, she began to cry, openly, even as she matter-of-factly gathered up the reins in her strong young fingers.

Mother Bridget stepped close to the wheel. "It'll be all right. There's no such thing as a new country for the people who come to it. They bring along their own ways and their own bits of things and make it like the old as fast as they can."

"I'm taking along my china dishes," breathed Sabra through her tears, "and my lovely linen and the mantel set that Cousin Dabney gave me for a wedding present, and my own rocker to sit in, and my wine-color silk-warp henrietta, and some slips from the garden, because Yancey says there isn't much growing."

Behind her spectacles the eyes of the wise old nun were soft with pity. "That'll be lovely." She watched the calico pony and the phaëton drive off up the dusty Kansas road. She turned toward the Mission house. The beads clicked. Hail, Mary, full of grace . . .

IV

THE child Cim had got it into his head that this was to be a picnic. He had smelled pies and cakes baking; had seen hampers packed. Certainly, except for the bizarre load that both wagons contained, this might have been one of those informal excursions into a nearby wood which Cim so loved, where they lunched in the open, camped near a stream, and he was allowed to run barefoot in the shadow of his aristocratic grandmother's cool disapproval. Felice Venable loathed all forms of bucolic diversion and could, with a glance, cause more discomfort at an al fresco luncheon than a whole battalion of red ants.

There was a lunatic week preceding their departure from Wichita. Felice fought their going to the last, and finally took to her bed with threats of impending dissolution which failed to achieve the desired effect owing to the preoccupation of the persons supposed to be stricken by her plight. From time to time, intrigued by the thumpings, scurryings, shouts, laughter, quarrels, and general upheaval attendant on the Cravats' departure, Felice rose from her bed and trailed wanly about the house, looking, in her white dimity wrapper, like a bilious and distracted ghost. She issued orders. Take this. Don't take that. It can't be that you're leaving those behind! Your own Aunt Sarah Moncrief du Tisne embroidered every inch of them with her own——

"But, Mamma, you don't understand. Yancey says there's very little society, and it's all quite rough and unsettled—wild, almost."

"That needn't prevent you from remembering you're a lady, I hope. Unless you are planning to be one of those hags in a sunbonnet and no teeth that Yancey seems to have taken such a fancy to."

So Sabra Cravat took along to the frontier wilderness such oddments and elegancies as her training, lack of experience, and Southern family tradition dictated. A dozen silver knives, forks, and spoons in the De-Grasse pattern; actually, too, a dozen silver after-dinner coffee spoons; a silver cake dish, very handsome, upheld by three solid silver cupids in care-free attitudes; linen that had been spun by hand and that bore vine-wreathed monograms; many ruffled and embroidered and starched white muslin petticoats to be sullied in the red clay of the Western muck; her heavy black grosgrain silk with the three box pleats on each side, and trimmed with black passementerie; her black hat with the five black plumes; her beautiful green nun's veiling; her tulle bonnet with the little pink flowers; forty jars of preserves; her own rocker, a lady's chair whose seat and back were upholstered fashionably with bright colored Brussels carpeting. There were two wagons, canvas covered and lumbering. Dishes, trunks, bedding, boxes were snugly stowed away in the capacious belly of one; the printing outfit, securely roped and lashed, went in the other. This wagon held the little hand press; two six-column forms; the case rack containing the type (cardboard was tacked snugly over this to keep the type from escaping); the rollers; a stock of paper; a can of printer's ink, tubes of job ink, a box of wooden quoins used in locking the forms.

There was, to the Wichita eye, nothing unusual in the sight of these huge covered freighters that would soon go lumbering off toward the horizon. Their like had worn many a track in the Kansas prairie. The wagon train had wound its perilous way westward since the day of the old Spanish trail, deeply rutted by the heavy wheels of Mexican carts. The very Indians who trafficked in pelts and furs and human beings had used the white man's trails for their trading. Yet in this small expedition faring forth there was something that held the poignancy of the tragic and the ridiculous. The man, huge, bizarre, impractical; the woman, tight lipped, terribly determined, her eyes staring with the fixed, unseeing gaze of one who knows that to blink but once is to be awash with tears; the child, out of hand with excitement and impatience to be gone. From the day of Yancey's recital of the Run, black Isaiah had begged to be taken along. Denied this, he had sulked for a week and now was nowhere to be found.

The wagons, packed, stood waiting before the Venable house. Perhaps never in the history of the settling of the West did a woman go a-pioneering in such a costume. Sabra had driven horses all her life; so now she stepped agilely from ground to hub, from hub to wheel top, perched herself on the high wagon seat and gathered up the reins with deftness and outward composure. Her eyes were enormous, her pale face paler. She wore last year's second best gray cheviot, lined, boned, basqued, and (though plain for its day) braided all the way down the front with an elaborate pattern of curlycues. Her gray straw bonnet was trimmed only with a puff of velvet and a bird. Her feet, in high buttoned shoes, were found to touch the wagon floor with difficulty, so at the last minute a footstool was snatched from the house and placed so that she might brace herself properly during the long and racking drive. This article of furniture was no more at variance with its surroundings than the driver herself. A plump round mahogany foot rest it was, covered with a gay tapestry that had been stitched by Sabra's grandmother on the distaff side. Its pattern of faded scarlet and yellow and blue represented what seemed to be a pair of cockatoos sparring in a rose bush. Yancey had swung Cim up to the calico-cushioned seat beside Sabra. His short legs, in their copper-toed boots, stuck straight out in front of him. His dark eyes were huge with excitement. "Why don't we go?" he demanded, over and over, in something like a scream. He shouted to the horses as he had heard teamsters do. "Giddap in 'ere! Gee-op! G'larng!" His grandmother and grandfather, gazing up with sudden agony in their faces at sight of this little expedition actually faring forth so absurdly into the unknown, had ceased to exist for Cim. As Sabra drove one wagon and Yancey the other, the boy pivoted between them through the long drive, spending the morning in the seat beside his mother, the afternoon beside his father, with intervals of napping curled up on the bedding at the back of the wagon. All through the first day they could do nothing with him. He yelled, "Giddap! Whoa! Gee-op!" until he was hoarse, pausing only to shoot imaginary bears, panthers, wildcats and Indians, and altogether working himself up into such a state of excitement and exhaustion that he became glittering eyed and feverish and subsequently had to be inconveniently dosed with castor oil.

Now, with a lurch and a rattle and a great clatter of hoofs the two wagons were off. Sabra had scarcely time for one final frantic look at her father and mother, at minor massed Venables, at the servants' black faces that seemed all rolling eyeballs. She was so busy with the horses, with Cim, so filled with a dizzy mixture of fright and exhilaration and a kind of terror-stricken happiness that she forgot to turn and look back, as she had meant to, like the heroine in a melodrama, at the big white house, at the hedge, at the lovely untidy garden, at the three great elms. Later she reproached herself for this. And she would say to the boy, in the bare treeless ugliness of the town that became their home, "Cim, do you remember the yellow and purple flags that used to come up first thing in the spring, in the yard?"

"What yard?"

"Granny's yard, back home."

"Nope."

"Oh, Cim!"

It was as though the boy's life had begun with this trip. The four previous years of his existence seemed to be sponged from his mind like yesterday's exercise from a slate. Perched beside his father on the high wagon seat his thirsty little mind drank in tales that became forever part of his consciousness and influenced his whole life.

They had made an early start. By ten the boy's eyes were heavy with sleep. He refused stubbornly to lie on the mattress inside the larger wagon; denied that he was sleepy. Sabra coaxed him to curl up on the wagon seat, his head in her lap. She held the reins in one hand; one arm was about the child. It was hot and still and drowsy. Noon came with surprising swiftness. They had brought along a precious keg of water and a food supply sufficient, they thought, to last through most of the trip— salt pork, mince and apple pies, bread, doughnuts—but their appetites were enormous. At midday they stopped and ate in the shade. Sabra prepared the meal while Yancey tended the horses. Cim, wide awake now and refreshed, ate largely with them of the fried salt pork and potatoes, the hard-boiled eggs, the mince pie. He was even given one of the precious oranges with which the journey had been provided by his grandparents. It was all very gay and comfortable and relaxed. Short as the morning had been, the afternoon stretched out, somehow, endless. Sabra began to be horribly tired, cramped. The boy whimpered. It was mid-afternoon and hot; it was late afternoon; then the brilliant Western sunset began to paint the sky. Yancey, in the wagon ahead, drew up, gazed about, got out, tied his team to one of a clump of cottonwoods.

"We'll camp here," he called to Sabra and came toward her wagon, prepared to lift her down, and the boy. She was stiff, utterly weary. She stared down at him, dully, then around the landscape.

"Camp?"

"Yes. For the night. Come, Cim." He lifted the boy down with a great swoop.

"You mean for the night? Sleep here?"

He was quite matter-of-fact. "Yes. It's a good place. Water and trees. I'll have a fire before you can say Jack Robinson. Where'd you think you were going to sleep? Back home?"

Somehow she had not thought. She had not believed it. To sleep out of doors like this, in the open, with only a wagon top as roof! All her neat conventional life she had slept in a four-poster bed with a dotted Swiss canopy and net curtains and linen sheets that smelled sweetly of the sun and the air.

Yancey began to make camp. Already the duties of this new manner of living had become familiar. There was wood to gather, a fire to start, water to be boiled. Cim, very wide awake now, trotted after his father, after his mother. Meat began to sizzle appetizingly in the pan. The exquisite scent of coffee revived them with its promise of stimulation.

"That roll of carpet," called Sabra, busy at the fire, to Yancey at the wagon. "Under the seat. I want Cim to sit on it . . . ground may be damp. . . ."

A sudden shout from Yancey. A squeal of terror from the bundle of carpeting in his arms—a bundle that suddenly was alive and wriggling. Yancey dropped it with an oath. The bundle lay on the ground a moment, heaving, then it began to unroll itself while the three regarded it with startling eyes. A black paw, a woolly head, a face all open mouth and whites of eyes. Black Isaiah. He had found a way to come with them to the Indian Territory.

V

By noon next day they were wondering how they had got on at all without him. He gathered wood. He started fires. He tended Cim like a nurse, played with him, sang to him, helped put him to bed, slept anywhere, like a little dog. He even helped Sabra to drive her team, change and change about, for after all there was little to it but the holding of the reins slackly in one's fingers while the horses plodded across the prairie, mile on mile, mile on mile.

Yancey pointed out the definiteness with which the land changed when they left Kansas and came into the Oklahoma country. "Oklahoma," he explained to Cim. "That's Choctaw. Okla—people. Humma —red. Red People. That's what they called it when the Indians came here to live."

Suddenly the land, too, had become red: red clay as far as the eye could see. The rivers and little creeks were sanguine with it, and at sunset the sky seemed to reflect it, so that sometimes Sabra's eyes burned with all this scarlet. When the trail led through a cleft in a hill the blood red of the clay on either side was like a gaping wound. Sabra shrank from it. She longed for the green of Kansas. The Oklahoma sky was not blue but steel color, and all through the day it was a brazen sheet of glittering tin over their heads. Its glare seared the eyeballs.

It was a hard trip for the child. He was by turns unruly and listless. He could not run about, except when they stopped to make camp. Sabra, curiously enough, had not the gift of amusing him as Yancey had, or even Isaiah. Isaiah told him tales that were negro folklore, handed down by word of mouth through the years. Like the songs he sang, these were primitive accounts of the sorrows and the tribulations of a wronged people and their inevitable reward in after life.

"An' de angel say to him, he say, 'Mose, come on up on dis'ya throne an' eat 'case yo' hongry, an' drink 'case yo' parch, and res' yo' weary an' achin' feet . . .'"

But when he rode with his father he heard thrilling tales. If it was just before his bedtime, after their early supper had been eaten, Yancey invariably began his story with the magic words, "It was on just such a night as this . . ."

There would follow a legend of buried treasure. Spanish conquistadores wandered weary miles over plains and prairie and desert, led, perhaps, by the false golden promises of some captured Indian eager to get back to the home of his own tribe far away. Like all newly settled countries, there were here hundreds of such tales. The sparsely settled land was full of them. The poorer the class the more glittering the treasure. These people, wresting a meager living from the barren plains, consoled themselves with tales of buried Spanish gold; of jewels. No hairy squatter or nester in his log cabin with his bony parchment-skinned wife and litter of barelegged brats but had some tale of long-sought treasure. Cim heard dozens of these tales as they dragged their way across the red clay of Oklahoma, as they forded rivers, passed little patches of blackjack or cottonwood. He was full of them. They became as real to him as the rivers and trees themselves.

During the day Yancey told him stories of the Indians. He taught him the names of the Five Civilized Tribes, and Cim remembered the difficult Indian words and repeated them—Cherokee, Choctaw, Creek, Seminole, and Chickasaw. He heard the Indian story, not in terms of raids, scalpings, tomahawk, and tom-tom, but as the saga of a tricked and wronged people. Yancey Cravat needed only a listener. That that listener was four, and quite incapable of comprehending the significance of what he heard, made no difference to Cravat. He told the boy the terrific story of the Trail of Tears—of the Cherokee Nation, a simple and unnomadic people, driven from their homes in Georgia, like cattle across hundreds of miles of plain and prairie to die by the thousands before they reached the Oklahoma land that had been allotted to them, with two thousand troops under General Winfield Scott to urge on their flagging footsteps.

"Why did they make the Indians go away?"

"They wanted the land for themselves."

"Why?"

"It had marble, and gold and silver and iron and lead, and great forests. So they took all this away from them and drove them out. They promised them things and then broke their promise."

Sabra was horrified at Cim's second-hand recital of this saga. He told her all about it as he later sat on the seat beside her. "Uncle Sam is a mean bad man. He took all the farms and the gold and the silver and the buff'-loes away from the Indians and made them go away and they didn't want to go and so they went and they died."

He knew more about David Payne than about Columbus. He was more familiar with Quanah Parker, the Comanche, with Elias Boudinot and General Stand Waitie, his brother, both full-blooded Cherokees, than he was with the names of Lincoln and Washington.

Sabra, in her turn, undertook to wipe this impression from the boy's mind. "Indians are bad people. They take little boys from their mammas and never bring them back. They burn down people's houses, and hurt them. They're dirty and lazy, and they steal."

She was unprepared for the hysterical burst of protest that greeted this. The boy grew white with rage. "They're not. You're a liar. I hate you. I won't ride with you."

He actually prepared to climb down over the wagon wheel. She clutched at him with one hand, shook him smartly, cuffed him. He kicked her. She stopped the team, wound the reins, took him over her knee and spanked him soundly. He announced, through his tears, that he was going to run away and join the Indians and never come back. If she could have known that his later life was to be shaped by Yancey's tales and this incident, certainly her protests would have been even more forceful than they were.

"Why can't you talk to him about something besides those dirty thieving Indians? There's enough to teach him about the history of his country, I should think. George Washington and Jefferson Davis and Captain John Smith . . ."

"The one who married Pocahontas, you mean?"

"I declare, Yancey, sometimes I wonder if——"

"What?"

"Oh—nothing."

But often the days were gay enough. They fell into the routine, adjusted themselves to the discomfort. At first Sabra had been so racked with the jolting of the wagon that she was a cripple by night. Yancey taught her how to relax; not to brace herself against the wagon's jolting but to sway easily with it. By the second day her young body had accustomed itself to the motion. She actually began to enjoy it, and at the journey's end missed it as a traveler at sea misses the roll and dip of a ship. By this time she had the second-best gray cheviot open at the throat and her hair in a long black braid. She looked like a schoolgirl. She had got out the sunbonnet which one of the less formidable Venables had jokingly given her at parting, and this she wore to shield her eyes from the pitiless glare of sky and plain. The gray straw bonnet, with its puff of velvet and its bird, reposed in its box in the back of the wagon. The sight of her in that prairie wilderness engaged in the domestic task of beating up a bowl of biscuit dough struck no one as being incongruous. The bread supply was early exhausted. She baked in a little portable tin oven that Yancey had fitted out for her.

As for Yancey himself, Sabra had never known him so happy. He was tireless, charming, varied. She herself was fascinated by his tales of hidden mines, of Spanish doubloons, of iron chests plowed up by some gaunt homesteader's hand plow hitched to a stumbling mule. Yancey roared snatches of cowboy songs:

> *When I was young I was a reckless lad,*
> *Lots of fun with the gals I had,*
> *I took one out each day fur a ride,*
> *An' I always had one by my side.*
> *I'd hug 'em an' kiss 'em just fur fun,*
> *An' I've proposed to more'n one,*
> *If there's a gal here got a kiss for me,*
> *She'll find me as young as I used to be.*
>
> *Hi rickety whoop ti do,*
> *How I love to sing to you.*
> *Oh, I could sing an' dance with glee,*
> *If I was as young as I used to be.*

Once they saw him whip a rattlesnake to death with his wagon whip. They had unhitched the horses to water them. Yancey, whip in hand, had taken them down to the muddy stream, Cim leaping and shouting at his side. His two guns, in their holsters, lay on the ground with the belt which he had just now unstrapped from about his waist. Sabra saw the thick coil, the wicked head. Perhaps she sensed it. She screamed horribly, stood transfixed. The boy's face was a mask of fright. Yancey lashed out once with his whip, the thing struck out, he lashed again, again, again, in a kind of fury. She turned away, sickened. The whip kept up its whistle, its snap. The coiled thing lay in ribbons. Isaiah, though ashen with fright, still had to be forcibly restrained from prowling among the mass for the rattlers which, with some combination of sunset and human saliva, were supposed to be a charm against practically every misfortune known to man. Cim had nightmares all that night and awoke screaming.

Once they saw the figure of a solitary horseman against the sunset sky. Inexplicably the figure dismounted, stood a moment, mounted swiftly and vanished.

"What was that?"

"That was an Indian."

"How could you tell?"

"He dismounted on the opposite side from a white man."

That night it was Sabra who did not sleep. She held the boy tight in her arms. Every snap of a twig, every stamp of a horse's hoof caused her to start up in terror.

Yancey tried in vain to reassure her. "Indian? What of it? Indians aren't anything to be scared of. Not any more."

She remembered something that Mother Bridget had said. "They're no different. They haven't changed since Joshua."

"Since what?" He was very sleepy.

"Joshua."

He could make nothing of this. He was asleep again, heavily, worn out with the day's journey.

The wind, at certain periods of the year, blows almost without ceasing in Oklahoma. And when it rains the roads become slithering bogs of greased red dough, so that a wagon will sink and slide at the same time. They had two days of rain during which they plodded miserably, inch by inch. Cim squalled, Isaiah became just a shivering black lump of misery, and Sabra thought of her dimity-hung bed back home in Wichita; of the garden in the cool of the evening; of the family gathered in the dining room; of the pleasant food, the easy talk, the luxurious ease. "Lak yo' breakfus' in bed, Miss Sabra? Mizzly mo'nin'."

At Pawnee Yancey saw fresh deer tracks. He saddled a horse and was off. They had, before this, caught bass in the streams, and Yancey had shot prairie chicken and quail, and Sabra had fried them delicately. But this was their first promise of big game. Sabra felt no fear at being left alone with the two children. It was midafternoon. She was happy, peaceful. There was about this existence a delightful detachment. Her prim girlhood, which, because she had continued to live in her parents' household, had lasted into her marriage, was now behind her. Ahead of her lay all manner of unknown terrors and strangeness, but here in the wilderness she was secure. She ruled her little world. Her husband was hers, alone. Her child, too. The little black boy Isaiah was as much her slave as though the Emancipation Proclamation had never been. Here, in the wide freedom of the prairie, she was, temporarily at least, suspended out of the reach of human interference.

Now she welcomed this unexpected halt. She and Isaiah carried water from the creek and washed a few bits of clothes and hung them to dry. She bathed Cim. She heated water for herself and bathed gratefully. She set Isaiah to gathering fuel for the evening meal, while Cim played in the shade of the clump of scrub oak. She was quite serene. She listened for the sound of horse's hoofs that would announce Yancey's triumphant return. She could hear Cim as he played under the trees, crooning to himself some snatch of song that Yancey had taught him. Vaguely she began to wonder if Yancey should not have returned by now. She brushed her hair thoroughly, enjoying the motion, throwing it over her head and bending far forward in that contortionistic attitude required by her task. After she had braided it she decided to leave it in a long thick plait down her back. Audaciously she tied it with a bright red ribbon, smiling to think of what Yancey would say. She tidied the wagon. She was frankly worried now. Nothing could happen. Of course nothing could happen. And in another part of her mind she thought that any one of a dozen dreadful things could happen. Indians. Why not? Some wild thing in the woods. Broken bones. A fall from his horse. He might lose his way. Suppose she had to spend the night alone here on the prairie with the two children. Here was the little clump of scrub oaks. The land just beyond showed a series of tiny hillocks that rolled gently away toward the horizon—rolled just enough to conceal what not of horror! A head perhaps even now peering craftily over the slope's edge to see what it could see.

In a sudden panic she stepped out of the wagon with the feeling that she must have her own human things near her—Cim, Isaiah—to talk to. Cim was not there playing with his bits of stone and twigs. He had gone off with Isaiah to gather fuel, though she had forbidden it. Isaiah, his long arms full of dead twigs and small branches, was coming toward the wagon now. Cim was not with him.

"Where's Cim?"

He dropped his load, looked around. "I lef' him playin' by hisself right hyah when Ah go fetch de wood. Ain' he in de wagon?"

"No. No."

"Might be he crep' in de print wagon."

"Wagon?" She ran to the other wagon, peered inside, called. He was not there.

Together they looked under the wagons, behind the trees. Cim! Cim! Cimarron Cravat, if you are hiding I shall punish you if you don't come out this minute. A shrill note of terror crept into her voice. She began to run up and down, calling him. She began to scream his name, her voice cracking grotesquely. Cim! Cim! She prayed as she ran, mumblingly. O God, help me find him. O God, don't let anything happen to him. Dear God, help me find him—Cim! Cim! Cim!

She had heard among pioneer stories that of the McAlastair wagon train crossing the continent toward California in '49. The Benson party had got separated perhaps a half day's journey from the front section when scouts brought news of Indians on the trail. Immediately they must break camp and hurry on to join the section ahead for mutual protection. In the midst of the bustle and confusion it was discovered that a child—a boy of three—was missing. The whole party searched at first confidently, then frenziedly, then despairingly. The parents of the missing child had three other small children and another on the way. Every second's delay meant possible death to every other member of the party. They must push on. They appealed to the mother. "I'll go on," she said, and the wagon train wound its dusty way across the plains. The woman sat ashen faced, stony, her eyes fixed in a kind of perpetual horror. She never spoke of the child again.

O God! whimpered Sabra, running this way and that. O God! Oh, Cim! Cim!

She came to a little mound that dipped suddenly and unexpectedly to a draw. And there, in a hollow, she came upon him, seated before a cave in the side of the hill, the front and roof ingeniously timbered to make a log cabin. One might pass within five feet of it and never find it. Four men were seated about the doorstep outside the rude cabin. Cim was perched on the knee of one of them, who was cracking nuts for him. They were laughing and talking and munching nuts and having altogether a delightful time of it. Sabra's knees suddenly became weak. She was trembling. She stumbled as she ran toward him. Her face worked queerly. The men sprang up, their hands at their hips.

"The man is cracking nuts for me," remarked Cim, sociably, and not especially glad to see her.

The man on whose knee he sat was a slim young fellow with a sandy mustache and a red handkerchief knotted cowboy fashion around his throat. He put the boy down gently as Sabra came up, and rose with a kind of easy grace.

"You ran away—you—we hunted every—Cim——" she stammered, and burst into tears of mingled anger and relief.

The slim young man seemed the spokesman, though the other three were obviously older than he.

"Why, I'm real sorry you was distressed, ma'am. We was going to bring the boy back safe enough. He wandered down here lookin' for his pa, he said." He was standing with one hand resting lightly, tenderly, on Cim's head, and looking down at Sabra with a smile of utter sweetness. His was the soft-spoken, almost caressing voice of the Southwestern cowman and ranger. At this Sabra's anger, born of fright, vanished. Besides, he was so young—scarcely more than a boy.

"Well," she explained, a little sheepishly, "I was worried. . . . My husband went off on the track of a deer . . . hours ago . . . he hasn't come back . . . then when Cim . . . I came out and he was gone. . . . I was so—so terribly . . ."

She looked very wan and schoolgirlish in her prim gray dress and with her hair in a braid tied with a bright red ribbon, and her tear-stained cheeks.

One of the men who had strolled off a little way with the appearance of utmost casualness returned to the group in time to hear this. "He'll be back any minute now," he announced. "He didn't get no deer."

"But how do you know?"

The soft-spoken young man shot a malignant look at the other, and the older man looked suddenly abashed. Sabra's question went unanswered. "Won't you sit and rest yourself, ma'am?" suggested the spokesman. The words were hospitable enough, yet there was that in the boy's tone which conveyed to Sabra the suggestion that she and Cim had better be gone. She took Cim's hand. Now that her fright was past she thought she must have looked very silly running down the draw with her tears and her pigtail and her screaming. She thanked them, using a little Southern charm and Southern drawl, which she often legitimately borrowed from the ancestral Venables for special occasions such as this.

"I'm ve'y grateful to you-all," she now said. "You've been mighty kind. If you would just drop around to our camp I'm sure my husband would be delighted to meet you."

The young man smiled more sweetly than ever, and the others looked at him, an inexplicable glint of humor in their weather-beaten faces.

"I sure thank you, ma'am. We're movin' on, my friends here and me. Pronto. Floyd, how about you getting a piece of deer meat for the lady, seeing she's been cheated of her supper. Now, if you and the little fella don't mind sittin' up behind and before, why, I'll take you back a ways. You probably run fu'ther than you expected, ma'am, scared as you was." She had, as a matter of fact, in her terror, run almost half a mile from camp.

He mounted first. His method of accomplishing this was something of a miracle. At one moment the horse was standing ready and he was at its side. The next there was a flash, and he was on its back. It was like an optical illusion in which he seemed to have been drawn to the saddle as a needle flies to the magnet. Cim he drew up to the pommel, holding him with one hand; Sabra, perched on the horse's rump, clung with both arms round the lad's slim waist. Something of a horsewoman, she noticed his fine Mexican saddle, studded with silver. From the sides of the saddle hung hair-covered pockets whose bulge was the outline of a gun. A slicker such as is carried by those who ride the trails made a compact ship-shape roll behind the saddle. The horse had a velvet gait, even with this triple load. Sabra found herself wishing that this exhilarating ride might go on for miles. Suddenly she noticed that the young rider wore gloves. The sight of them made her vaguely uneasy, as though some memory had been stirred. She had never seen a plainsman wearing gloves. It was absurd, somehow.

A hundred feet or so from the camp he reined in his horse abruptly, half turned in his saddle, and with his free hand swung Sabra gently to the ground, leaning far from his saddle and keeping a firm hold on Cim and reins as he did so. He placed the child in her upraised arms, wheeled, and was gone before she could open her lips to frame a word of thanks. The piece of deer meat, neatly wrapped, lay on the ground at her feet. She stood staring after the galloping figure, dumbly. She took Cim's hand. Together they ran toward the camp. Isaiah had a fire going, a pot of coffee bubbling. His greeting to Cim was sternly admonitory. Ten minutes later Yancey galloped in, empty handed.

"What a chase he led me! Twice I thought I had him. I'd have run him into Texas if I hadn't thought you'd be——"

Sabra, for the first time since her marriage, felt superior to him; was impatient of his tale of prowess. She had her own story to tell, spiced with indignation. She was not interested in his mythical deer. She had an actual piece of fresh deer meat to cook for their supper.

". . . and just when I was ready to die with fright, there he was, talking to those four men, and sitting on the knee of one of them as though he'd known him all his life eating nuts. . . . Anything might have happened to him and to me while you were off after your old deer."

Yancey seemed less interested in the part that she and Cim had played in the adventure than in the appearance and behavior of the four men in the draw, and especially the charming young man who had so gallantly brought them back.

"Thin faced, was he? And a youngster? About nineteen or twenty? What else?"

"Oh, a low voice, and kind of sweet, as though he sang tenor. And his teeth——"

Yancey interrupted. "Long, weren't they? The two at the side, I mean. Like a wolf's?"

"Yes. How did you—— Do you know him?"

"Sort of," Yancey answered, thoughtfully.

Sabra was piqued. "It was lucky for us it was someone who knows you, probably. Because you don't seem to care much about what happened to us—what might have happened."

"You said you wanted to go a-pioneering."

"Well?"

"This is it. Stir that fire, Isaiah. Sabra, get that deer meat a-frizzling that your friend gave you. Because we're moving on."

"Now? To-night? But it's late. I thought we were camping here for the night."

"We'll eat and get going. Moonlight to-night. I don't just like it here. There's been a lot of time lost this afternoon. We'll push on. In another day or so, with luck, we'll be in Osage, snug and safe."

They ate hurriedly. Yancey seemed restless, anxious to be off.

They jolted on. Cim slept, a little ball of weariness, in the back of the wagon. Isaiah drowsed beside Sabra, and she herself was half asleep, the reins slack in her hands. The scent of the sun-warmed prairie came up to her, and the pungent smell of the sagebrush. The Indians had swept over this plain in hordes; and buffalo by the millions. She wondered if the early Spaniards, in their lust for gold, had trod this ground—perhaps this very trail. Coronado, De Soto, Narváez. She had seen pictures of them, these dark-skinned élégantes in their cumbersome trappings of leather and heavy metal, tramping the pitiless plains of this vast Southwest, searching like children for cities of gold. . . . The steady clop-clop of the horses' feet, the rattle of the wagon, the squeak of the wheels, the smell of sun-baked earth . . .

She must have dozed off, for suddenly the sun's rays were sharply slanted, and she shivered with the cool of the prairie night air. Voices had awakened her. Three horsemen had dashed out of a little copse and stood in the path of Yancey's lead wagon. They were heavily armed. Their hands rested on their guns. Their faces were grim. They wore the mournful mustaches of the Western plainsman, their eyes were the eyes of men accustomed to great distances; their gaze was searing. All three wore the badge of United States marshals, but there was about them something that announced this even before the eye was caught by their badge of office. The leader addressed Yancey, his voice mild, even gentle.

"Howdy."

"Howdy."

"Where you bound for, pardner?"

"Osage."

The questioner's hand rested lightly on the butt of the six-shooter at his waist. "What might your name be?"

"Cravat—Yancey Cravat."

The spokesman's face lighted up with the slow, incredulous smile of a delighted child. "I'll be doggoned!" He turned his slow grin on the man at his right, on the man at his left. "Yancey Cravat!" he said again, as though they had not heard. "I sure am pleased to make your acquaintance. Heard about you till I feel like I knew you."

"Why, thanks," replied Yancey, unusually modest and laconic. Sabra knew then that Yancey was playing one of his rôles. He would talk as they talked. Be one of them.

"Aimin' to make quite a stay in Osage?"

"Aim to live there."

"Go on! I've a notion to swear you in as Deputy Marshal right now, darned if I ain't. Citizens like you is what we need, and no mistake. Lawy'in'?"

"I'm planning to take up my law practice in Osage, yes," Yancey answered, "and start a newspaper as well."

The three looked a little perturbed at this. They glanced at each other, then at Yancey, then away, uncomfortably. "Oh, newspaper, huh?" There was little enthusiasm in the marshal's voice. "Well, we did have a newspaper there for a little while in Osage, 'bout a week."

"A daily?"

"A weekly."

There was something sinister in this. "What became of it?"

"Well, seems the editor—name of Pegler—died."

There was a little silence. Sabra gathered up her reins and brought her team alongside Yancey's, the better to hear. The three mustached ones acknowledged her more formal presence by briefly touching their hat brims with the forefinger of the hand that had rested on their guns.

"Who killed him?"

A little shadow of pained surprise passed over the features of the marshal. "He was just found dead one morning on the banks of the Canadian. Bullet wounds. But bullets is all pretty much alike, out here. He might 'a' killed himself, plumb discouraged."

The silence fell again. Yancey broke it. "The first edition of the *Oklahoma Wigwam* will be off the press two weeks from to-morrow."

He gathered up the reins as though to end this chance meeting, however agreeable. "Well, gentlemen, good-evening. Glad to have met you."

The three did not budge. "What we stopped to ask you," said the spokesman, in his gentle drawl, "was, did you happen to glimpse four men anywhere on the road? They're nesting somewheres in here, the Kid and his gang. Stole four horses, robbed the bank at Red Fork, shot the cashier, and lit out for the prairie. Light complected, all of 'em. The Kid is a slim young fella, light hair, red handkerchief, soft spoken, and rides with gloves on. But then you know what he's like, Cravat, well's I do."

Yancey nodded in agreement. "Everybody's heard of the Kid. No, sir, I haven't seen him. Haven't seen anybody the last three days but a Kaw on a pony and a bunch of dirty Cheyennes in a wagon. Funny thing, I never yet knew a bad man who wasn't light complected—or, anyway, blue or gray eyes."

"Oh, say, now!" protested the marshal, stroking his sandy mustache.

"Fact. You take the Kid, and the James boys, and Tom O'Phalliard, and the whole Mullins gang."

"How about yourself? You're pretty good with the gun, from all accounts. And black as a crow."

Yancey lifted his great head and the heavy lids that usually drooped over the gray eyes and looked at the marshal. "That's so," said the other, as though in agreement at the end of an argument. "I reckon it goes fur killers and fur killers of killers. . . . Well, boys, we'll be lopin'. Good luck to you."

"Good luck to *you!*" responded Yancey, politely.

The three whirled their steeds spectacularly, raised their right hands in salute; the horses pivoted on their hind legs prettily; Cim crowed with delight. They were off in a cloud of red dust made redder by the last rays of the setting sun.

Yancey gathered up his reins. Sabra stared at him in bewildered indignation. "But the person who shields a criminal is just as bad as the criminal himself, isn't he?"

Yancey looked back at her around the side of his wagon top. His smile was mischievous, sparkling, irresistible. "Don't be righteous, Sabra. It's middle class—and a terrible trait in a woman."

Late next day, just before sunset, after pushing on relentlessly through the blistering sun of midday, Yancey pointed with his wagon whip to something that looked like a wallow of mud dotted with crazy shanties and tents. Theatrically he picked Cim up in his arms so that the child, too, might see. But he spoke to Sabra.

"There it is," he said. "That's our future home."

Sabra looked. And her brain seemed to have no order or reason about it, for she could think only of the green nun's veiling trimmed with ruchings of pink which lay so carefully folded, with its modish sleeves all stuffed out with soft paper, in the trunk under the canvas of the wagon.

VI

Long before the end of that first nightmarish day in Osage, Sabra had confronted her husband with blazing eyes. "I won't bring up my boy in a town like this!"

It had been a night and a day fantastic with untoward happenings. Their wagons had rumbled wearily down the broad main street of the settlement—a raw gash in the prairie. All about, on either side, were wooden shacks, and Indians and dried mud and hitching posts and dogs and crude wagons like their own. It looked like pictures Sabra had seen of California in '49. They had supped on ham and eggs, fried potatoes, and muddy coffee in a place labeled Ice Cream and Oyster Parlor. They spent that first night in a rooming house above one of the score of saloons that enlivened the main street—Pawhuska Avenue, it was called. It was a longish street, for the Osage town settlers seemed to have felt the need of huddling together for company in this wilderness. The street stopped abruptly at either end and became suddenly prairie.

"Pawhuska Avenue," said a tipsy sign tacked on the front of a false-front pine shack. Yancey chose this unfortunate time to impart a little Indian lore to Cim, wide eyed on the wagon seat beside his mother.

"That's Osage," he shouted to the boy. "Pawhu—that means hair. And scah, that means white. White Hair. Pawhuska—White Hair—was an old Osage Chief——"

"Yancey Cravat!" Sabra called in a shout that almost equaled his own, and in a tone startlingly like one of Felice Venable's best (she was, in fact, slightly hysterical, what with weariness and disappointment and fear), "Yancey Cravat, will you stop talking Indian history and find us a place to eat and sleep! Where's your sense? Can't you see he's ready to drop, and so am I?"

The greasy food set before them in the eating house sickened her. She shrank from the slatternly bold-faced girl who slammed the dishes down in front of them on the oilcloth-covered table. At this same table with them—there was only one, a long board accommodating perhaps twenty—sat red-faced men talking in great rough voices, eating with a mechanical and absent-minded thoroughness, shoveling potatoes, canned vegetables, pie into their mouths with knives. Cim was terribly wide awake and noisily unruly, excited by the sounds and strangeness about him.

"I'm an Indian!" he would yell, making a great clatter with his spoon on the table. "Ol' White Hair! Wa-wa-wa-wa-wa-wa-wa!" Being reprimanded, and having the spoon forcibly removed from his clutching fingers, he burst into tears and howls.

Sabra had taken him up to the bare and clean enough little room which was to be their shelter for the night. From wide-eyed wakefulness Cim had become suddenly limp with sleep. Yancey had gone out to see to the horses, to get what information he could about renting a house, and a shack for the newspaper. A score of plans were teeming in his mind.

"You'll be all right," he had said. "A good night's sleep and everything'll look rosy in the morning. Don't look so down in the mouth, honey. You're going to like it."

"It's horrible! It's—and those men! Those dreadful men."

" 'For my part, I had rather be the first man among these fellows than the second man in Rome.' " Yancey struck an attitude.

Sabra looked at him dully. "Rome?"

"Plutarch, my sweet." He kissed her; was gone with a great flirt of his coat tails. She heard his light step clattering down the flimsy wooden stairs. She could distinguish his beautiful vibrant voice among the raucous speech of the other men below.

The boy was asleep in a rude box bed drawn up beside theirs. Black Isaiah was bedded down somewhere in a little kennel outside. Sabra sank suspiciously down on the doubtful mattress. The walls of the room were wafer thin; mere pine slats with cracks between. From the street below came women's shrill laughter, the sound of a piano hammered horribly. Horses clattered by. Voices came up in jocose greeting; there were conversations and arguments excruciatingly prolonged beneath her window.

"I was sellin' a thousand beef steers one time—holdin' a herd of about three thousand—and me and my foreman, we was countin' the cattle as they come between us. Well, the steers was wild long-legged coasters— and run! Say, they come through between us like scairt wolves, and I lost the count . . ."

"Heard where the Mullins gang rode in there this morning and cleaned up the town—both banks—eleven thousand in one and nineteen thousand in the other, and when they come out it looked like the whole county'd rallied against 'em. . . ."

"Say, he's a bad hombre, that fella. Got a poisoned tongue, like a rattlesnake. . . . Spades trump?"

"No, hearts. Say, I would of known how to handle him. One time we was campin' on Amarillo Creek . . ."

A loud knock at the door opposite Sabra's room. The knock repeated. Then a woman's voice, metallic, high. "*Quien es? Quien es?*" The impatient rattle of a door knob, and a man's gruff voice.

A long-drawn wail in the street below, "Oh, Joe! He-e-e-ere's your mule!" followed by a burst of laughter.

Yet somehow she had fallen asleep in utter exhaustion, only to be awakened by pistol shots, a series of blood-curdling yells, the crash and tinkle of broken glass. Then came screams of women, the sound of horses galloping. She lay there, cowering. Cim stirred in his bed, sighed deeply, slept again. She was too terrified to go to the window. Her shivering seemed to shake the bed. She wanted to waken the child for comfort, for company. She summoned courage to go to the window; peered fearfully out into the dim street below. Nothing. No one in the street. Yancey's bleeding body was not lying in the road; no masked men. Nothing again but the clink of glasses and plates; the tinny piano, the slap of cards.

She longed with unutterable longing, not for the sweet security of her bed back in Wichita—that seemed unreal now—but for those nights in the wagon on the prairie with no sound but the rustle of the scrub oaks, the occasional stamp of horses' hoofs on dry clay, the rippling of a near-by stream. She looked at her little gold watch, all engraved with a bird and a branch and a waterfall and a church spire. It was only nine.

It was midnight when Yancey came in. She sat up in bed in her high-necked, long-sleeved nightgown. Her eyes, in her white face, were two black holes burned in a piece of paper.

"What was it? What was it?"

"What was what? Why aren't you asleep, sugar?"

"Those shots. And the screaming. And the men hollering."

"Shots?" He was unstrapping his broad leather belt with its twin six-shooters whose menacing heads peered just above their holsters. He wore it always now. It came, in time, to represent for her a sinister symbol of all the terrors, all the perils that lay waiting for them in this new existence. "Why, sugar, I don't recollect hearing any—— Oh—that!" He threw back his great head and laughed. "That was just a cowboy, feeling high, shooting out the lights over in Strap Turket's saloon. On his way home and having a little fun with the boys. Scare you, did it?"

He came over to her, put a hand on her shoulder. She shrugged away from him, furious. She pressed her hand frantically to her forehead. It was cold and wet. She was panting a little. "I won't bring my boy up in a

town like this. I won't. I'm going back. I'm going back home, I tell
you."

"Wait till morning, anyhow, won't you, honey?" he said, and took her
in his arms.

Next morning was, somehow, magically, next morning, with the terrors of the night vanished quite. The sun was shining. For a moment
Sabra had the illusion that she was again at home in her own bed at
Wichita. Then she realized that this was because she had been awakened
by a familiar sound. It was the sound of Isaiah's voice somewhere below
in the dusty yard. He was polishing Yancey's boots, spitting on them
industriously and singing as he rubbed. His husky sweet voice came up to
her as she lay there.

> Lis'en to de lambs, all a-cryin'
> Lis'en to de lambs, all a-cryin'
> Lis'en to de lambs, all a-cryin',
> Ah wanta go to heab'n when ah die.
> Come on, sister, wid yo' ups an' downs,
> Wanta go to heab'n when ah die,
> De angels waitin' fo' to gib yo' a crown,
> Wanta go to heab'n when ah die.

Lugubrious though the words were, Sabra knew he was utterly happy.

There was much to be done—a dwelling to be got somehow—a place
in which to house the newspaper plant. If necessary, Yancey said, they
could live in the rear and set up the printing and law office in the front.
Almost everyone who conducted a business in the town did this.
"Houses are mighty scarce," Yancey said, making a great masculine
snorting and snuffling at the wash bowl as they dressed. "It's take what
you can get or live in a tent. I heard last night that Doc Nisbett's got a
good house. Five rooms, and he'll furnish us with water. There're
a dozen families after it, and Doc's as independent as a hog on ice."

Sabra rather welcomed this idea of combining office and home. She
would be near him all day. As soon as breakfast was over she and Yancey
fared forth, leaving Cim in Isaiah's care (under many and detailed instructions from Sabra). She had put on her black grosgrain silk with
the three box pleats on each side, trimmed with the passementerie and
jet buttons—somewhat wrinkled from its long stay in the trunk—and her
modish hat with the five ostrich plumes and the pink roses that had cost
twelve dollars and fifty cents in Wichita, and her best black buttoned
kid shoes and her black kid gloves. In the tightly basqued black silk she
was nineteen inches round the waist and very proud of it. Her dark eyes,

slightly shadowed now, what with weariness, excitement, and loss of sleep, were enormous beneath the brim of the romantic black plumed hat.

Yancey, seeing her thus attired in splendor after almost a fortnight of the gray cheviot, struck an attitude of dazzlement. Blank verse leaped to his ready lips. " 'But who is this, what thing of land or sea,—female of sex it seems—that so bedeck'd, ornate, and gay, comes this way sailing, like a stately ship of Tarsus, bound for th' isles of Javan or Gadire, with all her bravery on. . . .' "

"Oh, now, Yancey, don't talk nonsense. It's only my second-best black grosgrain."

"You're right, my darling. Even Milton has no words for such beauty."

"Do hurry, dear. We've so much to do."

With his curling locks, his broad-brimmed white sombrero, his high-heeled boots, his fine white shirt, the ample skirts of his Prince Albert spreading and swooping with the vigor of his movements, Yancey was an equally striking figure, though perhaps not so unusual as she, in this day and place.

The little haphazard town lay broiling in the summer sun. The sky that Sabra was to know so well hung flat and glaring, a gray-blue metal disk, over the prairie.

"Well, Sabra honey, this isn't so bad!" exclaimed Yancey, and looked about him largely. " 'Now Morning saffron-robed arose from the streams of Ocean to bring light to gods and men.' "

"Ocean!" echoed Sabra, the literal. "Mighty little water I've seen around here—unless you call that desert prairie the ocean."

"And so it is, my pet. That's very poetic of you. The prairie's an ocean of land." He seemed enormously elated—jubilant, almost. His coat tails switched; he stepped high in his fine Texas star boots. She tucked her hand in her handsome husband's arm. The air was sweet, and they were young, and it was morning. Perhaps it was not going to be so dreadful, after all.

Somehow, she had yet no feeling that she, Sabra Cravat, was part of this thing. She was an onlooker. The first thing she noticed, as she stepped into the dust of the street in her modish dress and hat, caused her heart to sink. The few women to be seen scuttling about wore sun-bonnets and calico—the kind of garments in which Sabra had seen the women back home in Wichita hanging up the Monday wash to dry on the line in the back yard. Here they came out of butcher's shop or grocery store with the day's provisions in their arms; a packet of meat, tins of tomatoes or peaches, unwrapped. After sharp furtive glances at Sabra, they vanished into this little pine shack or that. Immediately afterward there was great agitation among the prim coarse window curtains in those dwellings boasting such elegance.

"But the others—the other kind of women——" Sabra faltered.

Yancey misunderstood. "Plenty of the other kind in a town like this, but they aren't stirring this time of day."

"Don't be coarse, Yancey. I mean ladies like myself—that I can talk to—who'll come calling—that is——"

He waved a hand this way and that. "Why, you just saw some women folks, didn't you?"

"Those!"

"Well, now, honey, you can't expect those ladies to be wearing their best bib and tucker mornings to do the housework in. Besides, most of the men came without their women folks. They'll send for them, and then you'll have plenty of company. It isn't every woman who'd have the courage you showed, roughing it out here. You're the stuff that Rachel was made of, and the mother of the Gracchi."

Rachel was, she knew, out of the Bible; she was a little hazy about the Gracchi, but basked serene in the knowledge that a compliment was intended.

There was the absurdly wide street—surely fifty feet wide—in this little one-street town. Here and there a straggling house or so branched off it. But the life of Osage seemed to be concentrated just here. There were tents still to be seen serving as dwellings. Houses and stores were built of unpainted wood. They looked as if they had been run up overnight, as indeed they had. They stared starkly out into the wide-rutted red clay road, and the muddy road glared back at them, and the brazen sky burned with fierce intensity down on both, with never a tree or bit of green to cheer the spirit or rest the eye. Tied to the crude hitching posts driven well into the ground were all sorts of vehicles: buckboards, crazy carts, dilapidated wagons, mule drawn; here and there a top buggy covered with the dust of the prairie; and everywhere, lording it, those four-footed kings without which life in this remote place could not have been sustained—horses of every size and type and color and degree. Indian ponies, pintos, pack horses, lean long-legged range horses, and occasionally a flashing-eyed creature who spurned the red clay with the disdainful hoof of one whose ancestors have known the mesas of Spain. Direct descendants, these, of the equine patricians who, almost four hundred years before, had been brought across the ocean by Coronado or Moscoso to the land of the Seven Cities of Gold.

There were the sounds of the hammer and the saw, the rattle of chains, the thud of hoofs, all very sharp and distinct, as though this mushroom town were pulling itself out of the red clay of the prairie by its own boot straps before one's very eyes. Crude and ugly though the scene was that now spread itself before Sabra and Yancey, it still was not squalid. It had vitality. You sensed that behind those bare boards people were planning and stirring mightily. There was life in the feel of it. The very names tacked up over the store fronts had bite and sting. Sam Pack. Mott Bixler. Strap Buckner. Ike Hawes. Clint Hopper. Jim Click.

Though they had come to town but the night before, it seemed to her that a surprising number of people knew Yancey and greeted him as they passed down the street. "H'are you, Yancey! Howdy, ma'am." Loungers in doorways stared at them curiously. Cowboys loping by gave her a long hard look that still had in it something of shyness—a boyish look, much like that with which the outlaws had greeted her down in the draw on the prairie when they learned that she was Cim's mother.

It struck Sabra suddenly with a little shock of discovery that the men really were doing nothing. They lounged in doorways and against hitching posts and talked; you heard their voices in animated conversation within saloon and store and office; they cantered by gracefully, and wheeled and whirled and cantered back again. She was to learn that many of these men were not builders but scavengers. The indomitable old '49ers were no kin of these. They were, frequently, soft, cruel, furtive, and avaricious. They had gathered here to pick up what they could and move on. Some were cowmen, full of resentment against a government that had taken the free range away from them and given it over to the homesteaders. Deprived of their only occupation, many of these became outlaws. Equipped with six-shooters, a deadly aim, and horsemanship that amounted to the miraculous, they took to the Gyp Hills, or the Osage, swooping down from their hidden haunts to terrorize a town, shoot up a bank, hold up a train, and dash out again, leaving blood behind them. They risked their lives for a few hundred dollars. Here was a vast domain without written laws, without precedent, without the customs of civilization; part of a great country, yet no part of its government. Here a horse was more valuable than a human life. A horse thief, caught, was summarily hanged to the nearest tree; the killer of a man often went free.

Down the street these two stepped in their finery, the man swaggering a little as a man should in a white sombrero and with a pretty woman on his arm; the woman looking about her interestedly, terrified at what she saw and determined not to show it. If two can be said to make a procession, then Yancey and Sabra Cravat formed quite a parade as they walked down Pawhuska Avenue in the blaze of the morning sun. Certainly they seemed to be causing a stir. Lean rangers in buckboards turned to stare. Loungers in doorways nudged each other, yawping. Cowboys clattering by whooped a greeting. It was unreal, absurd, grotesque.

"Hi, Yancey! Howdy, ma'am."

Past the Red Dog Saloon. A group in chairs tilted up against the wall or standing about in high-heeled boots and sombreros greeted Yancey now with a familiarity that astonished Sabra. "Howdy, Cim! Hello, Yancey!"

"He called you Cim!"

He ignored her surprised remark. Narrowly he was watching them as he passed. "Boys are up to something. If they try to get funny while you're here with me . . ."

Sabra, glancing at the group from beneath her shielding hat brim, did see that they were behaving much like a lot of snickering schoolboys who are preparing to let fly a bombardment of snowballs. There was nudging, there was whispering, an air of secret mischief afoot.

"Why are they—what do you think makes them——" Sabra began, a trifle nervously.

"Oh, they're probably fixing up a little initiation for me," Yancey explained, his tone light but his eye wary. "Don't get nervous. They won't dare try any monkeyshines while you're with me."

"But who are they?" He evaded her question. She persisted. "Who are they?"

"I can't say for sure. But I suspect they're the boys that did Pegler dirt."

"Pegler? Who is—oh, isn't that the man—the editor—the one who was found dead—shot dead on the banks of the—— Yancey! Do you mean they did it!"

"I don't say they did it—exactly. They know more than is comfortable, even for these parts. I was inquiring around last night, and everybody shut up like a clam. I'm going to find out who killed Pegler and print it in the first number of the *Oklahoma Wigwam*."

"Oh, Yancey! Yancey, I'm frightened!" She clung tighter to his arm. The grinning mirthless faces of the men on the saloon porch seemed to her like the fanged and snarling muzzles of wolves in a pack.

"Nothing to be frightened of, honey. They know me. I'm no Pegler they can scare. They don't like my white hat, that's the truth of it. Dared me last night down at the Sunny Southwest Saloon to wear it this morning. Just to try me out. They won't have the guts to come out in the open——"

The sentence never was finished. Sabra heard a curious buzzing sound past her ear. Something sang—zing! Yancey's white sombrero went spinning into the dust of the road.

Sabra's mouth opened as though she were screaming, but the sounds she would have made emerged, feebly, as a croak.

"Stay where you are," Yancey ordered, his voice low and even. "The dirty dogs." She stood transfixed. She could not have run if she had wanted to. Her legs seemed suddenly no part of her—remote, melting beneath her, and yet pricked with a thousand pins and needles. Yancey strolled leisurely over to where the white hat lay in the dust. He stooped carelessly, his back to the crowd on the saloon porch, picked up the hat, surveyed it, and reached toward his pocket for his handkerchief. At that movement there was a rush and a scramble on the porch. Tilted chairs leaped forward, heels clattered, a door slammed. The white-aproned proprietor who, tray in hand, had been standing idly in the doorway, vanished as though he had been blotted out by blackness. Of the group only three men remained. One of these leaned insolently against a porch post, a second stood warily behind him, and a third was edging prudently toward the closed door. There was nothing to indicate who had fired the shot that had sent Yancey's hat spinning.

Yancey, now half turned toward them, had taken his fine white handkerchief from his pocket, had shaken out its ample folds with a gesture of elegant leisure, and, hat in hand, was flicking the dust from his headgear. This done he surveyed the hat critically, seemed to find it little the worse for its experience unless, perhaps, one excepts the two neat round holes that were drilled, back and front, through the peak of its crown. He now placed it on his head again with a gesture almost languid, tossed the fine handkerchief into the road, and with almost the same gesture, or with another so lightning quick that Sabra's eye never followed it, his hand went to his hip. There was the crack of a shot. The man who was edging toward the door clapped his hand to his ear and brought his hand away and looked at it, and it was darkly smeared. Yancey still stood in the road, his hand at his thigh, one slim foot, in its fine high-heeled Texas star boot, advanced carelessly. His great head was lowered menacingly. His eyes, steel gray beneath the brim of the white sombrero, looked as Sabra had never before seen them look. They were terrible eyes, merciless, cold, hypnotic. She could only think of the eyes of the rattler that Yancey had whipped to death with the wagon whip on the trip across the prairie.

"A three-cornered piece, you'll find it, Lon. The Cravat sheep brand."

"Can't you take a joke, Yancey?" whined one of the three, his eyes on Yancey's gun hand.

"Joke—hell!" snarled the man who had been nicked. His hand was clapped over his ear. "God help you, Cravat."

"He always has," replied Yancey, piously.

"If your missus wasn't with you——" began the man whom Yancey had called Lon. Perhaps the rough joke would have ended grimly enough. But here, suddenly, Sabra herself took a hand in the proceedings. Her fright had vanished. These were no longer men, evil, sinister, to be feared, but mean little boys to be put in their place. She now advanced on them in the majesty of her plumes and her silk, her fine eyes flashing, her gloved forefinger admonishing them as if they were indeed naughty children. She was every inch the descendant of the Marcys of France and the very essence of that iron woman, Felice Venable.

"Don't you 'missus' me! You're a lot of miserable, good-for-nothing loafers, that's what you are! Shooting at people in the streets. You leave my husband alone. I declare, I've a notion to——"

For one ridiculous dreadful moment it looked as though she meant to slap the leathery bearded cheek of the bad man known as Lon Yountis. Certainly she raised her little hand in its neat black kid. The eyes of the three were popping. Lon Yountis ducked his head exactly like an urchin who is about to be smacked by the schoolmarm. Then, with a yelp of pure terror he fled into the saloon, followed by the other two.

Sabra stood a moment. It really looked as though she might make after them. But she thought better of it and sailed down the steps in triumph to behold a crushed, a despairing Yancey.

"Oh, my God, Sabra! What have you done to me!"

"What's the matter?"

"This time to-morrow it'll be all over the whole Southwest, from Mexico to Arkansas, that Yancey Cravat hid behind a woman's petticoats."

"But you didn't. They can't say so. You shot him very nicely in the ear, darling." Thus had a scant eighteen hours in the Oklahoma country twisted her normal viewpoint so askew that she did not even notice the grotesquerie of what she had just said.

"They're telling it now, in there. My God, a woman's got no call to interfere when men are having a little dispute."

"Dispute! Why, Yancey Cravat! He shot your hat right off your head!"

"What of it! Little friendly shooting."

The enormity of this example of masculine clannishness left her temporarily speechless with indignation. "Let's be getting on," Yancey continued, calmly. "If we're going to look at Doc Nisbett's house we'd better look at it. There are only two or three to be had in the whole town, and his is the pick of them. It's central" (Central! she thought, looking about her) "and according to what he said last night there's a room in the front big enough for getting out the paper. It'll have to be newspaper and law office in one. Then there are four rooms in the back to live in. Plenty."

"Oh, plenty," echoed Sabra, thinking of the nine or ten visiting Venables always comfortably tucked away in the various high-ceilinged bedrooms in the Wichita house.

They resumed their walk. Sabra wondered if she had imagined the shooting outside the Red Dog Saloon.

Doc Nisbett (veterinarian), shirt sleeved, shrewd, with generations of New England ancestry behind him, was seated in a chair tipped up against the front of his coveted property. Nothing of the brilliant Southwest sun had mellowed the vinegar of his chemical make-up. In the rush for Territory town sites at the time of the Opening he had managed to lay his gnarled hands on five choice pieces. On these he erected dwellings, tilted his chair up against each in turn, and took his pick of late-comers frantic for some sort of shelter they could call a home. That perjury, thieving, trickery, gun play, and murder had gone into the acquiring of these—as well as many other—sites was not considered important or, for that matter, especially interesting.

The dwelling itself looked like one of Cim's childish drawings of a house. The roof was an inverted V; there was a front door, a side door, and a spindling little porch. It was a box, a shelter merely, as angular and unlovely as the man who owned it. The walls were no more than partitions, the floor boards laid on dirt.

Taking her cue from Yancey—"Lovely," murmured Sabra, agonized. The mantel ornaments that had been Cousin Dabney's wedding present! The hand-woven monogrammed linen! The silver cake dish with the carefree cupids. The dozen solid silver coffee spoons! "Do very nicely. Perfectly comfortable. I see. I see. I see."

"There you are!" They stood again on the porch, the tour completed. Yancey clapped his hands together gayly, as though by so doing he had summoned a genie who had tossed up the house before their very eyes. In the discussion of monthly rental he had been a child in the hands of this lean and grasping New Englander. "There you are! That's all settled." He struck an attitude. " 'Survey our empire, and behold our home!' "

"Heh, hold on a minute," rasped Doc Nisbett. "How about water?"

"Sabra, honey, you settle these little matters between you—you and the Doc—will you? I've got to run down the street and see Jesse Rickey about putting up the press and setting up the type racks and helping me haul the form tables, and then we've got the furniture to buy for the house. Meet you down the street at Hefner's Furniture Store. Ten minutes."

He was off, with a flirt of his coat tails. She would have called, "Yancey! Don't leave me!" but for a prideful reluctance to show fear before this dour-visaged man with the tight lips and the gimlet eyes. From the first he had seemed to regard her with disfavor. She could not imagine why. It was, of course, his Puritan New England revulsion against her plumes, her silks, her faintly Latin beauty.

"Well, now," repeated Doc Nisbett, nasally, "about water."

"Water?"

"How much you going to need? Renting this house depends on how much water you think you going to need. How many barrels."

Sabra had always taken water for granted, like air and sunshine. It was one of the elements. It was simply there. But since leaving Wichita there was always talk of water. Yancey, on the prairie journey, made it the basis of their camping site.

"Oh, barrels," she now repeated, trying to appear intensely practical. "Well, let—me—see. There's cooking, of course, and all the cleaning around the house, and drinking, and bathing. I always give Cim his bath in the evening if I can. You wouldn't believe how dirty that child gets by the end of the day. His knees—oh, yes—well, I should think ten barrels a day would be enough."

"Ten barrels," said Doc Nisbett, in a flat voice utterly devoid of expression, "a day."

"I should think that would be ample," Sabra repeated, judiciously.

Doc Nisbett now regarded Sabra with a look of active dislike. Then he did a strange thing. He walked across the little porch, shut the front door, locked it, put the key in his pocket, seated himself in the chair and tilted it up against the wall at exactly the angle at which they had come upon him.

Sabra stood there. Seeing her, it would have been almost impossible to believe that anyone so bravely decked out in silk and plumes and pink roses could present a figure so bewildered, so disconsolate, so defeated. Literally, she did not know what to do. She had met and surmounted many strange experiences in these last ten days. But she had been born of generations of women to whom men had paid homage. Perhaps in all her life she had never encountered the slightest discourtesy in a man, much less this abysmal boorishness.

She looked at him, her face white, shocked. She looked up, in embarrassment, at the glaring steel sky; she looked down at the blinding red dust, she looked helplessly in the direction that Yancey had so blithely taken. She glanced again at Doc Nisbett, propped so woodenly against the wall of his hateful house. His eye was as cold, as glassy, as unseeing as the eye of a dead fish.

She should, of course, have gone straight up to him and said, "Do you mean that ten barrels are too much! I didn't know. I am new to all this. Whatever you say."

But she was young, and inexperienced, and full of pride, and terribly offended. So without another word she turned and marched down the dusty street. Her head in its plumed hat was high. On either cheek burned a scarlet patch. Her eyes, in her effort to keep back the hot tears, were blazing, liquid, enormous. She saw nothing. From the saloons that lined the street there came, even at this hour of the morning, yelps and the sound of music.

And then a fearful thing happened to Sabra Cravat.

Down the street toward her came a galloping cowboy in sombrero and chaps and six-shooters. Sabra was used to such as he. Full of her troubles, she was scarcely aware that she had glanced at him. How could she know that he was just up from the plains of Texas, that this raw town represented for him the height of effete civilization, that he was, in celebration of his arrival, already howling drunk as befits a cowboy just off the range, and that never before in his life (he was barely twenty-three) had he seen a creature so gorgeous as this which now came toward him, all silk, plumes, roses, jet, scarlet cheeks, and great liquid eyes. Up he galloped; stared, wheeled, flung himself off his horse, ran toward her in his high-heeled cowboy boots (strangely enough all that Sabra could recall about him afterward were those boots as he came toward her. The gay tops were of shiny leather, and alternating around them was the figure of a dancing girl with flaring skirts, and a poker hand of cards which later she learned was a royal flush, all handsomely embossed on the patent leather cuffs of the boots). She realized, in a flash of pure terror, that he was making straight for her. She stood, petrified. He came nearer, he stood before her, he threw his arms like steel bands about her, he kissed her full on the lips, released her, leaped on his horse, and was off with a blood-curdling yelp and a clatter and a whirl of dust.

She thought that she was going to be sick, there, in the road. Then she began to run, fleetly but awkwardly, in her flounced and bustled silken skirts. Hefner's Furniture Store. Hefner's Furniture Store. Hefner's Furniture Store. She saw it at last. Hefner's Furniture and Undertaking Parlors. A crude wooden shack, like the rest. She ran in. Yancey. Yancey! Everything looked dim to her bewildered and sun-blinded eyes. Someone came toward her. A large moist man, in shirt sleeves. Hefner, probably. My husband. My husband, Yancey Cravat. No. Sorry, ma'am. Ain't been in, I know of. Anything I can do for you, ma'am?

She blurted it, hysterically. "A man—a cowboy—I was walking along —he jumped off his horse—he—I never saw him b—— he kissed me— there on the street in broad daylight—a cowboy—he kissed——"

"Why, ma'am, don't take on so. Young fella off the range, prob'ly. Up from Texas, more'n likely, and never did see a gorgeous critter like yourself, if you'll pardon my mentioning it."

Her voice rose in her hysteria. "You don't understand! He kissed me. He k-k-k-k——" racking sobs.

"Now, now, lady. He was drunk, and you kind of went to his head. He'll ride back to Texas, and you'll be none the worse for it."

At this calloused viewpoint of a tragedy she broke down completely and buried her head on her folded arms atop the object nearest at hand. Her slim body shook with her sobs. Her tears flowed. She cried aloud like a child.

But at that a plaintive but firm note of protest entered Mr. Hefner's voice.

"Excuse me, ma'am, but that's velvet you're crying on, and water spots velvet something terrible. If you'd just lean on something else . . ."

She raised herself from the object on which she had collapsed, weeping, and looked at it with brimming eyes that widened in horror as she realized that she had showered her tears on that pride of Hefner's Furniture and Undertaking establishment, the newly arrived white velvet coffin (child's size) intended for show window purposes alone.

VII

From Doc Nisbett, Yancey received laconic information to the effect that the house had been rented by a family whose aquatic demands were more modest than Sabra's. Sabra was inconsolable, but Yancey did not once reproach her for her mistake. It was characteristic of him that he was most charming and considerate in crises which might have been expected to infuriate him. "Never mind, sugar. Don't take on like that. We'll find a house. And, anyway, we're here. That's the main thing. God, when I think of those years in Wichita!"

"Why, Yancey! I thought you were happy there."

"'A prison'd soul, lapped in Elysium.' Almost five years in one place —that's the longest stretch I've ever done, honey. Five years, back and forth like a trail horse; walking down to the *Wigwam* office in the morning, setting up personal and local items and writing editorials for a smug citizenry interested in nothing but the new waterworks. Walking back to dinner at noon, sitting on the veranda evenings, looking at the vegetables in the garden or the Venables in the house until I couldn't tell vegetables from Venables and began to think, by God, that I was turning into one or the other myself."

He groaned with relief, stretched his mighty arms, shook himself like a great shaggy lion. In all this welter of red clay and Indians and shirt sleeves and tobacco juice and drought he seemed to find a beauty and an exhilaration that eluded Sabra quite. But then Sabra, after those first two days, had ceased to search for a reason for anything. She met and accepted the most grotesque, the most fantastic happenings. When she looked back on the things she had done and the things she had said in the first few hours of her Oklahoma experience it was as though she were tolerantly regarding the naïvetés of a child. Ten barrels of water a day! She knew now that water, in this burning land, was a precious thing to be measured out like wine. Life here was an anachronism, a great crude joke. It was hard to realize that while the rest of the United States, in this year of 1889, was living a conventionally civilized and primly Victorian existence, in which plumbing, gaslight, trees, gardens, books, laws, millinery, Sunday churchgoing, were taken for granted, here in this Oklahoma country life had been set back according to the frontier standards of half a century earlier. Literally she was pioneering in a wilderness surrounded but untouched by civilization.

Yancey had reverted. Always—even in his staidest Wichita incarnation —a somewhat incredibly romantic figure, he now was remarkable even in this town of fantastic humans gathered from every corner of the brilliantly picturesque Southwest. His towering form, his curling locks, his massive head, his vibrant voice, his dashing dress, his florid speech, his magnetic personality drew attention wherever he went. On the day following their arrival Yancey had taken from his trunk a pair of silver-mounted ivory-handled six-shooters and a belt and holster studded with silver. She had never before seen them. She had not known that he possessed these grim and gaudy trappings. His white sombrero he had banded with a rattlesnake skin of gold and silver, with glass eyes, a treasure also produced from the secret trunk, as well as a pair of gold-mounted spurs which further enhanced the Texas star boots. Thus bedecked for his legal and editorial pursuits he was by far the best dressed and most spectacular male in all the cycloramic Oklahoma country. He had always patronized a good tailor, and because the local talent was still so limited in this new community he later sent as far as San Antonio, Texas, when his wardrobe needed replenishing.

Sabra learned many astounding things in these first few days, and among the most terrifying were the things she learned about the husband to whom she had been happily married for more than five years. She learned, for example, that this Yancey Cravat was famed as the deadliest shot in all the deadly shooting Southwest. He had the gift of being able to point his six-shooters without sighting, as one would point with a finger. It was a direction-born gift in him and an enviable one in this community. He was one of the few who could draw and fire two six-shooters at once with equal speed and accuracy. His hands would go to his hips with a lightning gesture that yet was so smooth, so economical that the onlooker's eye scarcely followed it. He could hit his mark as he walked, as he ran, as he rode his horse. He practised a great deal. From the back door of their cabin Sabra and Cim and rolling-eyed Isaiah used to stand watching him. He sometimes talked of wind and trajectory. You had to make allowance mathematically, he said, for this ever-blowing Oklahoma wind. Sabra was vaguely uneasy. Wichita had not been exactly effete, and Dodge City, Kansas, was notoriously a gun-play town. But here no man walked without his six-shooters strapped to his body. On the very day of her harrowing encounter with Doc Nisbett and the cowboy, Sabra, her composure regained, had gone with Yancey to see still another house owner about the possible renting of his treasure. The man was found in his crude one-room shack which he used as a combination dwelling and land office. He and Yancey seemed to know each other. Sabra was no longer astonished to find that Yancey, twenty-four hours after his arrival, appeared to be acquainted with everyone in the town. The man glanced up at them from the rough pine table at which he was writing.

"Howdy, Yancey!"

"Howdy, Cass!"

Yancey, all grace, performed an introduction. The lean, leather-skinned house owner wiped his palm on his pants' seat in courtly fashion and, thus purified, extended a hospitable hand to Sabra. Yancey revealed to him their plight.

"Well, now, say, that's plumb terr'ble, that is. Might be I can help you out—you and your good lady here. But say, Yancey, just let me step out, will you, to the corner, and mail this here letter. The bag's goin' any minute now."

He licked and stamped the envelope, rose, and took from the table beside him his broad leather belt with its pair of holstered six-shooters, evidently temporarily laid aside for comfort while writing. This he now strapped quickly about his waist with the same unconcern that another man would use in slipping into his coat. He merely was donning conventional street attire for the well-dressed man of the locality. He picked up his sheaf of envelopes and stepped out. In three minutes he was back, and affably ready to talk terms with them.

It was, perhaps, this simple and sinister act, more than anything she had hitherto witnessed, that impressed Sabra with the utter lawlessness of this new land to which her husband had brought her.

This house, so dearly held by the man called Cass, turned out to be a four-room dwelling inadequate to their needs, and they were in despair at the thought of being obliged to wait until a house could be built. Then Yancey had a brilliant idea. He found a two-room cabin made of rough boards. This was hauled to the site of the main house, plastered, and—added to it—provided them with a six-room combination dwelling, newspaper plant, and law office. There was all the splendor of sitting room, dining room, bedroom, and kitchen to live in. One room of the small attached cabin was a combination law and newspaper office. The other served as composing room and print shop. The Hefner Furniture and Undertaking Parlors provided them with furniture—a large wooden bedstead to fit Sabra's mattress and spring; a small bed for Cim; tables, chairs—the plainest of everything. The few bits of furnishing and ornament that Sabra had brought with her from Wichita were fortunately—or unfortunately—possessed of the enduring beauty of objects which have been carefully made by hands exquisitely aware of line, texture, color, and further enhanced by the rich mellow patina that comes with the years. Her pieces of silver, of china, of fine linen were as out of place in this roughly furnished cabin of unpainted lumber as a court lady in a peasant's hovel. In two days Sabra was a housewife established in her routine as though she had been at it for years. A pan of biscuits in the oven of the wood-burning kitchen stove; a dress pattern of calico, cut out and ready for basting, on the table in the sitting room.

Setting up the newspaper plant and law office was not so simple. Yancey, for example, was inclined to write his first editorial entitled Whither Oklahoma? before the hand press had been put together. He was more absorbed in the effect of the sign tacked up over the front of the shop than he was in the proper mechanical arrangement of the necessary appliances inside. THE OKLAHOMA WIGWAM, read the sign in block letters two feet high, so that the little cabin itself was almost obscured. Then, beneath, in letters scarcely less impressive: YANCEY

CRAVAT, PROP. AND EDITOR. ATTORNEY AT LAW. NO-
TARY.

The placing of this sign took the better part of a day, during which
time all other work was suspended. While the operation was in progress
Yancey crossed the road fifty times, ostensibly to direct matters from a
proper vantage point of criticism, but really to bask in the dazzling effect
of the bold fat black letters. As always in the course of such proceedings
on the part of the laboring male there was much hoarse shouting, gesticu-
lation, and general rumpus. To Sabra, coming to the door from time to
time, dish towel or ladle in hand, the clamor seemed out of all proportion to the results achieved. She thought (privately) that two women
could have finished the job in half the time with one tenth the fuss.
She still was far too feminine, tactful, and in love with her husband to
say so. Cim enjoyed the whole thing enormously, as did his black satel-
lite, bodyguard, and playmate, Isaiah. They capered, shouted, whooped,
and added much to the din.

Yancey, from across the road—"Lift her up a little higher that end!"

"What say?" from the perspiring Jesse Rickey, his assistant.

"That end—up! NO! UP! I said, UP!"

"Well, which end, f'r Chris' sakes, right or left?"

"Right! RIGHT! God Almighty, man, don't you know your right
from your left?"

"Easy now. E-e-e-esy! Over now. Over! There! That's—no—yeh—now
head her a little this way. . . ."

"How's that?"

"Oh, my land's sakes alive!" thought Sabra, going back to her orderly
kitchen. "Men make such a lot of work of nothing."

It was her first admission that the male of the species might be fallible.
A product of Southern training, even though a daily witness, during her
girlhood, to the dominance of her matriarchal mother over her weak
and war-shattered father, she had been bred to the tradition that the
male was always right, always to be deferred to. Yancey, still her passionate lover, had always treated her, tenderly, as a charming little fool,
and this rôle she had meekly—even gratefully—accepted. But now suspicion began to rear its ugly head. These last three weeks had shown
her that the male was often mistaken, as a sex, and that Yancey was
almost always wrong as an individual. But these frightening discoveries
she would not yet admit even to herself. Also that he was enthralled
by the dramatics of any plan he might conceive, but that he often was
too impatient of its mechanics to carry it through to completion.

"Yancey, this case of type's badly pied." Jesse Rickey, journeyman
printer and periodic drunkard, was responsible for this misfortune, hav-

ing dropped a case, face down, in the dust of the road while assisting Yancey in the moving. "It'll have to be sorted before you can get out a paper."

"Oh, Rickey'll tend to that. I've got a lot of important work to do. Editorials to write, news to get, lot of real estate transfers—and I'm going to find out who killed Pegler and print it in the first issue if it takes the last drop of blood in me."

"Oh, please don't. What does it matter! He's dead. Maybe he did shoot himself. And besides, you've got Cim and me to think of. You can't let anything happen to you."

"Let that Yountis gang get away with a thing like that and anything *is* likely to happen to me; the same thing that happened to him. No, sir! I'll show them, first crack, that the *Oklahoma Wigwam* prints all the news, all the time, knowing no law but the Law of God and the government of these United States! Say, that's a pretty good slogan. Top of the page, just above the editorial column."

In the end it was she who sorted the case of pied type. The five years of Yancey's newspaper ownership in Wichita had familiarized her, almost unconsciously, with many of the mechanical aspects of a newspaper printing shop. She even liked the smell of printer's ink, of the metal type, of the paper wet from the hand press. She found that the brass and copper thin spaces, used for setting up ads, had no proper container, and at a loss to find one she hit upon the idea of using a muffin tin until a proper receptacle could be found. It never was found, and the muffin tin still served after a quarter of a century had gone by. She was, by that time, sentimental about it, and superstitious.

The hand press was finally set up, and the little job press, and the case rack containing the type. The rollers were in place, and their little stock of paper. Curiously enough, though neither Yancey nor Sabra was conscious of it, it was she who had directed most of this manual work and who had indeed actually performed much of it, with Isaiah and Jesse Rickey to help her. Yancey was off and up the street every ten minutes. Returning, he would lose himself in the placing of his law library, his books of reference, and his favorite volumes, for which he contended there was not enough shelf room in the house proper. He had brought along boxes of books stowed away in the covered wagons. If the combined book wealth contained in all the houses, offices, and shops of the entire Oklahoma country so newly settled could have been gathered in one spot it probably would have been found to number less than this preposterous library of the paradoxical Yancey Cravat. Glib and showy though he was with his book knowledge Yancey still had in these volumes of his the absorption of the true book lover. He gave more attention to the carpenter who put up these crude bookshelves than he had bestowed upon the actual coupling of the two cabins when first they had moved in. The books he insisted on placing himself, picking them up, one by one, and losing himself now in this page, now in that, so that at the end of the long hot afternoon he had accomplished nothing. Blackstone and Kent (ineffectual enough in this lawless land) were shocked to find themselves hobnobbing side by side with Childe Harold and the Decameron. Culpepper's Torts nestled cosily between the shameless tale of the sprightly Wife of Bath and Yancey's new and joyously discovered copy of Fitzgerald's Omar Khayyám.

Lost to all else he would call happily in to Sabra as she bent over the case rack, her cheek streaked with ink, her fingers stained, her head close to Jesse Rickey's bleary-eyed one as she sorted type or filled the muffin tin with the metal thin spaces: "Sabe! Oh, Sabe—listen to this." He would clear his throat. " 'Son of Nestor, delight of my heart, mark the flashing of bronze through the echoing halls, and the flashing of gold and of amber and of silver and of ivory. Such like, methinks, is the court of Olympian Zeus within, for the world of things that are here; wonder comes over me as I look thereon.' . . . God, Sabra, it's as fine as the Old Testament. Finer!"

" 'The world of things that are here,' " echoed Sabra, not bitterly, but with grave common sense. "Perhaps if you'd pay more attention to those, and less to your nonsense in books about gold and silver and ivory, we might get settled."

But he was ready with a honeyed reply culled from the same book so dear to his heart and his grandiloquent tongue. " 'Be not wroth with me hereat, goddess and queen.' "

The goddess and queen pushed her hair back from her forehead with a sooty hand, leaving still another smudge of printer's ink upon that worried surface.

Jesse Rickey, the printer (known, naturally, to his familiars as "Gin" Rickey, owing to his periods of intemperance) and black Isaiah were, next to Sabra, most responsible for the astounding fact that the Cravat family finally was settled in house and office. The front door, which was the office entrance, faced the wide wallow of the main street. The back and the side doors of the dwelling looked out on a stretch of Oklahoma red clay, littered with the empty tin cans that mark any new American settlement, and especially one whose drought is relieved by the thirst-quenching coolness of tinned tomatoes and peaches. Perhaps the canned tomato, as much as anything, made possible the settling of the vast West and Southwest. In the midst of this clay and refuse, in a sort of shed-kennel, lived little Isaiah; rather, he slept there, like a faithful dog, for all day long he was about the house and the printing office, tireless, willing, invaluable. He belonged to Sabra, body and soul, as completely as though the Civil War had never been. A little servant of twelve, born to labor, he became as dear to Sabra, as accustomed, as one of her own children, despite her Southern training and his black skin. He dried the dishes, a towel tied round his neck; he laid the table; he was playmate and nursemaid for Cim; he ran errands, a swift and splay-footed Mercury; he was a born reporter, and in the course of his day's scurrying about the town on this errand or that brought into Sabra's kitchen more items of news and gossip (which were later transferred to the newspaper office) than a whole staff of trained newspaper men could have done. He was so little, so black, so lithe, so harmless looking, that his presence was, more often than not, completely overlooked. The saloon loungers, cowboys, rangers, and homesteaders in and about the town alternately spoiled and plagued him. One minute they were throwing him dimes in the dust for his rendition of his favorite song:

> King Jesus come a-ridin' on a milk-white steed,
> Wid a rainbow on his shoulder.

The next moment they were making his splay-feet dance frenziedly as the bullets from their six-shooters plopped playfully all about him and his kinky hair seemed to grow straight and dank with terror.

Sabra, in time, taught him to read, write, and figure. He was quick to learn, industrious, lovable. He thought he actually belonged to her. Cim was beginning to learn the alphabet, and as Sabra bent over the child, Isaiah, too, would bring his little stool out of its corner. Perched on it like an intelligent monkey he mastered the curlycues in their proper sequence. He cleared the unsightly back yard of its litter of tin cans and refuse. Together he and Sabra even tried to plant a little garden in this barren sanguine clay. More than anything else, Sabra missed the trees and flowers. In the whole town of almost ten thousand inhabitants there were two trees: stunted jack oaks. Sometimes she dreamed of lilies of the valley—the translucent, almost liquid green of their stems and leaves, the perfumed purity of their white bells.

All this, however, came later. These first few days were filled to overflowing with the labor of making the house habitable and the office and plant fit for Yancey's professional pursuits. Already his talents as a silver-tongue were being sought in defense of murderers, horse thieves, land grabbers, and more civil offenders in all the surrounding towns and counties. It was known that the average jury was wax in his hands. Once started on his plea it was as though he were painting the emotions that succeeded each other across the faces of the twelve (or less, depending on the number available in the community) good men (or good enough) and true. A tremolo tone—their eyes began to moisten, their mouth muscles to sag with sympathy; a wave of the hand, a lilt of the golden voice—they guffawed with mirth. Even a horse thief, that blackest of criminals in this country, was said to have a bare chance for his life if Yancey Cravat could be induced to plead for him—and provided always, of course, that the posse had not dealt with the offender first.

Yancey, from the time he rose in the morning until he went to bed late at night, was always a little overstimulated by the whisky he drank. This, together with a natural fearlessness, an enormous vitality, and a devouring interest in everybody and everything in this fantastic Oklahoma country, gained him friends and enemies in almost equal proportion.

In the ten days following their arrival in Osage, his one interest seemed to be the tracing of the Pegler murder—for he scoffed at the idea that his predecessor's death was due to any other cause.

He asked his question everywhere, even in the most foolhardy circumstances, and watched the effect of his question. Pegler had been a Denver newspaper man; known, respected, decent. Yancey had sworn to bring his murderers to justice.

Sabra argued with him, almost hysterically, but in vain. "You didn't do anything about helping them catch the Kid, out there on the prairie, when they were looking for him, and you knew where he was—or just about—and he had killed a man, too, and robbed a bank, and I don't know what all."

"That was different. The Kid's different," Yancey answered, unreasonably and infuriatingly.

"Different! How different? What's this Pegler to you! They'll kill you, too—they'll shoot you down—and then what shall I do?—Cim—Cim—and I here, alone—Yancey, darling—I love you so—if anything should happen to you——" She waxed incoherent.

"Listen, honey. Hush your crying and listen. Try to understand. The Kid's a terror. He's a bad one. But it isn't his fault. The government at Washington made him an outlaw."

"Why, Yancey Cravat, what are you talking about? Don't you ever say a thing like that before Cim."

"The Kid's father rode the range before there were fences or railroads in Kansas, and when this part of the country was running wild with longhorn cattle that had descended straight from the animals that the Spaniards had brought over four centuries ago. The railroads began coming in. The settlers came with it, from the Gulf Coast, up across Texas, through the Indian Territory to the end of steel at Abilene, Kansas. The Kid was brought up to all that. Freighters, bull whackers, mule skinners, hunters, and cowboys—that's all he knew. Into Dodge City, with perhaps nine months' pay jingling in his pocket. I'll bet neither the Kid nor his father before him ever saw a nickel or a dime. They wouldn't have bothered with such chicken feed. Silver dollars were the smallest coin they knew. They worked for it, too. I've seen seventy-five thousand cattle at a time waiting shipment to the East, with lads like the Kid in charge. The Kid's grandfather was a buffalo hunter. The range was the only life they wanted. Along comes the government. What happens?"

"What?" breathed Sabra, as always enthralled by one of Yancey's arguments, forgetting quite that she must oppose this very plea.

"They take the range away from the cattle men and cowboys—the free range that never belonged to them really, but that they had come to think of as theirs through right of use. Squatters come in, Sooners, too, and Nesters, and then the whole rush of the Opening. The range is cut up into town sites, and the town into lots, before their very eyes. Why, it must have sickened them—killed them almost—to see it."

"But that's progress, Yancey. The country's got to be settled."

"This was different. There's never been anything like this. Settling a great section of a country always has been a matter of years—decades—centuries, even. But here they swept over it in a day. You know that as well as I do. Wilderness one day; town sites the next. And the cowboys and rangers having no more chance than chips in a flood. Can't you see it? Shanties where the horizon used to be; grocery stores on the old buffalo trails. They went plumb locoed, I tell you. They couldn't fight progress, but they could get revenge on the people who had taken their world away from them and cut it into little strips and dirtied it."

"You're taking the part of criminals, of murderers, of bad men! I'm ashamed of you! I'm afraid of you! You're as bad as they are."

"Now, now, Sabra. No dramatics. Leave that for me. I'm better at it. The Kid's bad, yes. They don't come worse than he. And they'll get him, eventually. But he never kills unless he has to. When he robs a bank or holds up a train it's in broad daylight, by God, with a hundred guns against him. He runs a risk. He doesn't shoot in the dark. The other fellow always has a chance. It's three or four, usually, against fifty. He was brought up a reckless, lawless, unschooled youngster. He's a killer now, and he'll die by the gun, with his boots on. But the man who fathered him needn't be ashamed of him. There's no yellow in the Kid."

For one dreadful sickening second something closed with iron fingers around Sabra Cravat's heart and squeezed it, and it ceased to beat. White faced, her dark eyes searched her husband's face. Wichita whispers. Kansas slander. But that face was all exaltation, like the face of an evangelist, and as pure. His eyes were glowing. The iron fingers relaxed.

"But Pegler. The men who killed Pegler. Why are they so much worse——"

"Skunks. Dirty jackals hired by white-livered politicians."

"But why? Why?"

"Because Pegler had the same idea I have—that here's a chance to start clean, right from scratch. Live and let live. Clean politics instead of the skulduggery all around; a new way of living and of thinking, because we've had a chance to see how rotten and narrow and bigoted the other way has been. Here everything's fresh. It's all to do, and we can do it. There's never been a chance like it in the world. We can make a model empire out of this Oklahoma country, with all the mistakes of the other pioneers to profit by. New England, and California, and the settlers of the Middle West—it got away from them, and they fell into the rut. Ugly politics, ugly towns, ugly buildings, ugly minds." He was off again. Sabra, all impatience, stopped him.

"But Pegler. What's that got to do with Pegler?" She hated the name. She hated the dead man who was stalking their new life and threatening to destroy it.

"I saw that one copy of his paper. He called it the *New Day*—poor devil. And in it he named names, and he outlined a policy and a belief something like—well—along the lines I've tried to explain to you. He accused the government of robbing the Indians. He accused the settlers of cheating them. He told just how they got their whisky, in spite of its being forbidden, and how their monthly allotment was pinched out of their foolish fingers——"

"Oh, my heavens, Yancey! Indians! You and your miserable dirty Indians! You're always going on about them as if they mattered! The sooner they're all dead the better. What good are they? Filthy, thieving, lazy things. They won't work. You've said so yourself. They just squat there, rotting."

"I've tried to explain to you," Yancey began, gently. "White men can't do those things to a helpless——"

"And so they killed him!" Sabra cried, irrelevantly. "And they'll kill you, too. Oh, Yancey—please—please—I don't want to be a pioneer woman. I thought I did, but I don't. I can't make things different. I liked them as they were. Comfortable and safe. Let them alone. I don't want to live in a model empire. Darling! Darling! Let's just make it a town like Wichita . . . with trees . . . and people being sociable . . . not killing each other all the time . . . church on Sunday . . . a school for Cim. . . ."

The face she adored was a mask. The ocean-gray eyes were slate-gray now, with the look she had seen and dreaded—cold, determined, relentless.

"All right. Go back there. Go back to your trees and your churches and your sidewalks and your Sunday roast beef and your whole god-damned, smug, dead-alive family. But not me! Me, I'm staying here. And when I find the man who killed Pegler I'll face him with it, and I'll publish his name, and if he's alive by then I'll bring him to justice and I'll see him strung up on a tree. If I don't it'll be because I'm not alive myself."

"Oh, God!" whimpered Sabra, and sank, a limp bundle of misery, into his arms. But those arms were, suddenly, no haven, no shelter. He put her from him, gently, but with iron firmness, and walked out of the house, through the newspaper office, down the broad and sinister red road.

VIII

YANCEY put his question wherever he came upon a little group of three or four lounging on saloon or store porch or street corner. "How did Pegler come to die?" The effect of the question always was the same. One minute they were standing sociably, gossiping, rolling cigarettes; citizenry at ease in their shirt sleeves. Yancey would stroll up with his light, graceful step, his white sombrero with the two bullet holes in its crown, his Prince Albert, his fine high-heeled boots. He would ask his question. As though by magic the group dispersed, faded, vanished.

He visited Coroner Hefner, of Hefner's Furniture Store and Under-taking Parlor. That gentleman was seated, idle for the moment, in his combination office and laboratory. "Listen, Louie. How did Pegler come to die?"

Hefner's sun-kissed and whisky-rouged countenance became noticeably less roseate. His pale blue pop-eyes stared at Yancey in dismay. "Are you going around town askin' that there question, or just me?"

"Oh—around."

Hefner leaned forward. He looked about him furtively. He lowered his voice. "Yancey, you and your missus, you bought your furniture and so on here in my place, and what's more, you paid cash for it. I want you as a customer, see, but not in the other branch of my business. Don't go round askin' that there question."

"Think I'd better not, h'm?"

"I know you better not."

"Why not?"

The versatile Hefner made a little gesture of despair, rose, vanished by way of his own back door, and did not return.

Yancey strolled out into the glaring sunshine of Pawhuska Avenue. Indians, Mexicans, cowboys, solid citizens lounged in whatever of shade could be found in the hot, dry, dusty street. On the corner stood Pete Pitchlyn talking to the Spaniard, Estevan Miro. They were the gossips of the town, these two. This Yancey knew. News not only of the town, but of the Territory—not alone of the Territory but of the whole brilliant burning Southwest, from Texas through New Mexico into Arizona, sieved through this pair. Miro not only knew; he sold his knowledge. The Spaniard made a gay splash of color in the drab prairie street. He wore a sash of purple wound round his middle in place of a belt and his neckerchief was of scarlet. His face was tiny, like the face of a child, and pointed; his hair was thick, blue-black, and lay in definite strands, coarse and glossy, like fine wire. His two upper incisor teeth were separated by, perhaps, the width of an eighth of an inch. He was very quiet, and his movements appeared slow because of their feline grace. Eternally he rolled cigarettes in the cowboy fashion, with exquisite deftness, manipulating the tobacco and brown paper magically between the thumb and two fingers of his right hand. The smoke of these he inhaled, consuming a cigarette in three voracious pulls. The street corner on which he lounged was ringed with limp butts.

Pete Pitchlyn, famous Indian scout of a bygone day, had grown potbellied and flabby, now that the Indians were rotting on their reservations and there was no more work for him to do. He was a vast fellow, his height of six feet three now balanced by his bulk. His wife, a full-blood Cherokee squaw, squatted on the ground in the shade of a near-by frame shack about ten feet away, as befits a wife whose husband is conversing with another male. On the ground all around her, like a litter of puppies tumbling about a bitch, were their half-breed children. Late in his hazardous career as a scout on the plains Pitchlyn had been shot in the left heel by a poisoned Indian arrow. It was thought he would surely die. This failing, it was then thought he would lose that leg. But a combination of unlimited whisky, a constitution made up of chilled steel, and a determination that those varmints should never kill him, somehow caused him not only to live but to keep the poison-ravaged

leg clinging to his carcase. Stubbornly he had refused to have it ampu-
tated, and by a miracle it had failed to send its poison through the rest
of that iron frame. But the leg had withered and shrunk until now it
was fully twelve inches shorter than the sound limb. He refused to use
crutches or the clumsy mechanical devices of the day, and got about
with astonishing speed and agility. When he stood on the sound leg he
was, with his magnificent breadth of shoulders, a giant of six feet three.
But occasionally the sound leg tired, and he would rest it by slumping
for a moment on the other. He then became a runt five feet high.

The story was told of him that when he first came to Osage in the
rush of the Run he, with hundreds of others, sought the refreshment
of the Montezuma Saloon, which hospice—a mere tent—had opened its
bar and stood ready for business as the earliest homesteader drew his
red-eyed sweating horse up before the first town site to which claim was
laid in the settlement of Osage (at that time—fully a month before—a
piece of prairie as bare and flat as the palm of your hand). The crowd
around the rough pine slab of the hastily improvised bar was parched,
wild eyed, clamorous. The bartenders, hardened importations though
they were, were soon ready to drop with fatigue. Even in this milling
mob the towering figure of Pete Pitchlyn was one to command attention.
Above the clamor he ordered his drink—three fingers of whisky. It was
a long time coming. He had had a hard day. He leaned one elbow on
the bar, while shouts emerged as croaks from parched throats, and
glasses and bottles whirled all about him. Dead tired, he shifted his
weight from the sound right leg to the withered left, and conversed
half-heartedly with the thirsty ones on this side and that. The harried
bartender poured Pitchlyn's whisky, shoved it toward him, saw in his
place only a wearily pensive little man whose head barely showed above
the bar, and, outraged, his patience tried beyond endurance, yelled:

"Hey, you runt! Get out of there! Where's the son of a bitch who ordered this whisky?"

Like a python Pete Pitchlyn uncoiled to his full height and glared
down on the bewildered bartender.

Crowded though it was, the drinks were on the house.

These two specimens of the Southwest it was that Yancey now approached, his step a saunter, his manner carefree, even bland. Almost
imperceptibly the two seemed to stiffen, as though bracing themselves
for action. In the old scout it evidenced itself in his sudden emergence
from lounging cripple to statuesque giant. In the Spaniard you sensed,
rather than saw, only a curiously rippling motion of the muscles beneath
the smooth tawny skin, like a snake that glides before it really moves
to go.

"Howdy, Pete!"

"Howdy, Yancey!"

He looked at the Spaniard. Miro eyed him innocently. "*Que tal?*"

"*Bien. Y tu?*"

They stood, the three, wary, silent. Yancey balanced gayly from shining boot toe to high heel and back again. The Cherokee woman kept her sloe eyes on her man, as though, having received one signal, she were holding herself in readiness for another.

Yancey put the eternal question of the inquiring reporter. "Well, boys, what do you know?"

The two were braced for a query less airy. Their faces relaxed in an expression resembling disappointment. It was as when gunfire fails to explode. The Spaniard shrugged his shoulders, a protean gesture intended on this occasion to convey to the beholder the utter innocence and uneventfulness of the daily existence led by Estevan Miro. Pete Pitchlyn's eyes, in that ravaged face, were coals in an ash heap. It was not for him to be seen talking on the street corner with the man who was asking a fatal question—fatal not only to the asker but to the one who should be foolhardy enough to answer it. He knew Yancey, admired him, wished him well. Yet there was little he dared say now before the reptilian Miro. Yancey continued, conversationally:

"I understand there's an element rarin' around town bragging that they're going to make Osage the terror of the Southwest, like Abilene and Dodge City in the old days; and the Cimarron." The jaws of Pete Pitchlyn worked rhythmically on the form of nicotine to which he was addicted. Estevan Miro inhaled a deep draught of his brand of poison and sent forth its wraith, a pale gray jet, through his nostrils. Thus each maintained an air of nonchalance to hide his nervousness. "I'm interviewing citizens of note," continued Yancey, blandly, "on whether they think this town ought to be run on that principle or on a Socratic one that the more modern element has in mind." He lifted his great head and turned his rare gaze full on the little Spaniard. His gray eyes, quizzical, mocking, met the black eyes, and the darker ones shifted. "Are you at all familiar with the works of Socrates—'Socrates . . . whom well inspir'd the oracle pronounced wisest of men'?"

Again Estevan Miro shrugged. This time the gesture was exquisitely complicated in its meaning, even for a low-class Spaniard. Slight embarrassment was in it, some bewilderment, and a grain—the merest fleck—of something as nearly approaching contempt as was possible in him for a man whom he feared.

"Yancey," said Pete Pitchlyn, deliberately, "stick to your lawy'in'."

"Why?"

"Anybody's got the gift of gab like you have is wastin' their time doin' anything else."

"Oh, I wouldn't say that," Yancey replied, all modesty. "Running a newspaper keeps me in touch with folks. I like it. Besides, the law isn't very remunerative in these parts. Running a newspaper's my way of earning a living. Of course," he continued brightly, as an afterthought, "there have been times when running a newspaper has saved the editor the trouble of ever again having to earn a living." The faces of the two were blank as a sponged slate. Suddenly—"Come on, boys. Who killed Pegler?"

Pete Pitchlyn, his Cherokee squaw, and the litter of babies dispersed. It was magic. They faded, vanished. It was as though the woman had tossed her young into a pouch, like a kangaroo. As for the cripple, he might have been a centipede. Yancey and the Spaniard were left alone on the sunny street corner. The face of Miro now became strangely pinched. The eyes were inky slits. He was summoning all his little bravado, pulling it out of his inmost depths.

"I know something. I have that to tell you," he said in Spanish, his lips barely moving.

Yancey replied in the same tongue, "Out with it."

The Spaniard did not speak. The slits looked at Yancey. Yancey knew that already he must have been well paid by someone to show such temerity when his very vitals were gripped with fear. "You know something, h'm? Well, Miro, *mas vale saber que haber*." With which bit of philosophy he showed Miro what a Westerner can do in the way of a shrug; and sauntered off.

Miro leaped after him in one noiseless bound, like a cat. He seemed now to be more afraid of not revealing that which he had been paid to say than of saying it. He spoke rapidly, in Spanish. His hard *r* sounds drummed like hail on a tin roof. "I say only that which was told to me. The words are not mine. They say, 'Are you a friend of Yancey Cravat?' I say, 'Yes.' They say then, 'Tell your friend Yancey Cravat that wisdom is better than wealth. If he does not keep his damn mouth shut he will die.' The words are not mine."

"Thanks," replied Yancey, thoughtfully, speaking in English now. Then with one fine white hand he reached out swiftly and gave Miro's scarlet neckerchief a quick strong jerk and twist. The gesture was at once an insult and a threat. "Tell them——" Suddenly Yancey stopped. He opened his mouth, and there issued from it a sound so dreadful, so unearthly as to freeze the blood of any within hearing. It was a sound between the gobble of an angry turkey cock and the howl of a coyote. Throughout the Southwest it was known that this terrible sound, famed as the gobble, was Cherokee in origin and a death cry among the Territory Indians. It was known, too, that when an Indian gobbled it meant sudden destruction to any or all in his path.

The Spaniard's face went a curious dough gray. With a whimper he ran, a streak of purple and scarlet and brown, round the corner of the nearest shack, and vanished.

Unfortunately, Yancey could not resist the temptation of dilating to Sabra on this dramatic triumph. The story was, furthermore, told in the presence of Cim and Isaiah, and illustrated—before Sabra could prevent it—with a magnificent rendering of the blood-curdling gobble. They were seated at noonday dinner, with Isaiah slapping briskly back and forth between stove and table. Sabra's fork, halfway to her mouth, fell clattering on her plate. Her face blanched. Her appetite was gone. Cim, tutored by that natural Thespian and mimic, black Isaiah, spent the afternoon attempting faithfully to reproduce the hideous sound, to the disastrous end that Sabra, nerves torn to shreds, spanked him soundly and administered a smart cuff to Isaiah for good measure. Luckily, the full import of the sinister Indian gobble was lost on her, else she might have taken even stronger measures.

It was all like a nightmarish game, she thought. The shooting, the carousing, the brawls and high altercations; the sounds of laughter and ribaldry and drinking and song that issued from the flimsy cardboard false-front shacks that lined the preposterous street. Steadfastly she refused to believe that this was to be the accepted order of their existence. Yancey was always talking of a new code, a new day; live and let live. He was full of wisdom culled from the Old Testament, with which he pointed his remarks. " 'The fathers have eaten sour grapes, and the children's teeth are set on edge,' " when Sabra reminded him of this or that pleasant Wichita custom. But Sabra prepared herself with a retort, and was able, after some quiet research, to refute this with:

" 'Stand ye in the ways, and see, and ask for the old paths, where is the good way, and walk therein.' There! Now perhaps you'll stop quoting the Bible at me every time you want an excuse for something you do."

"The devil," retorted Yancey, "can cite Scripture for his purpose." But later she wondered whether by this he had intended a rather ungallant fling at her own quotation or a sheepish excuse for his own.

She refused to believe, too, that this business of the Pegler shooting was as serious as Yancey made it out to be. It was just one of his whims. He would, she told herself, publish something or other about it in the first edition of the *Oklahoma Wigwam*. Yancey stoutly maintained it was due off the press on Thursday. Privately, Sabra thought that this would have to be accomplished by a miracle. This was Friday. A fort-night had gone by. Nothing had been done. Perhaps he was exaggerating the danger as well as the importance of all this Pegler business. Some-thing else would come up to attract his interest, arouse his indignation, or outrage his sense of justice.

She was overjoyed when, that same day, a solemn deputation of citi-zens, three in number, *de rigueur* in sombreros and six-shooters, called on Yancey in his office (where, by some chance, he happened momen-tarily to be) with the amazing request that he conduct divine service the following Sunday morning. Osage was over a month old. The women folks, they said, in effect, thought it high time that some contact be es-tablished between the little town sprawled on the prairie and the Power supposedly gazing down upon it from beyond the brilliant steel-blue dome suspended over it. Beneath the calico and sunbonnets despised of Sabra on that first day of her coming to Osage there apparently glowed the same urge for convention, discipline, and the old order that so fired her to revolt. She warmed toward them. She made up her mind that, once the paper had gone to press, she would don the black silk and the hat with the plumes and go calling on such of the wooden shacks as she knew had fostered this meeting. Then she recollected her mother's training and the stern commands of fashion. The sunbonnets had been residents of Osage before she had arrived. They would have to call first. She pictured, mentally, a group of Mother Hubbards balanced stylishly on the edge of her parlor chairs, making small talk in this welter of Southwestern barbarism.

She got out a plaid silk tie for Cim. "Church meeting!" she exclaimed, joyously. Here, at last, was something familiar; something on which she could get a firm foothold in this quagmire. Yancey temporarily aban-doned his journalistic mission in order to make proper arrangements for Sunday's meeting. There was, certainly, no building large enough to hold the thousands who, surprisingly enough, made up this settlement spawned overnight on the prairie. Yancey, born entrepreneur, took hold with the enthusiasm that he always displayed in the first spurt of a new enterprise. Already news of the prospective meeting had spread by the mysterious means common to isolated settlements. Nesters, homestead-ers, rangers, cowboys for miles around somehow got wind of it. Saddles were polished, harnesses shined, calicoes washed and ironed, faces scrubbed. Church meeting.

Yancey turned quite naturally to the one shelter in the town ade-quate to the size of the crowd expected. It was the gambling tent that stood at the far north end of Pawhuska Avenue, flags waving gayly from its top in the brisk Oklahoma wind. For the men it was the social center of Osage. Faro, stud poker, chuckaluck diverted their minds from the stern business of citizenship and saved them the trouble of counting their ready cash on Saturday night. Sunday was, of course, the great day in the gambling tent. Rangers, cowboys, a generous sprinkling of professional bad men from the near-by hills and plains, and all the town women who were not respectable flocked to the tent on Sunday for recreation, society, and excitement. Shouts, the tinkle of glass, the sound of a tubercular piano playing Champagne Charley assailed the ears of the passers-by. The great canvas dome, measuring ninety by one hundred and fifty feet, was decorated with flags and bunting; cheerful, bright, gay.

It was a question whether the owner and dealer would be willing to sacrifice any portion of Sunday's brisk trade for the furtherance of the Lord's business, even though the goodwill of the townspeople were to be gained thereby. After all, he might argue, it was not this element that kept a faro game going.

Yancey, because of his professional position and his well-known power to charm, was delegated to confer with that citizen *du monde*, Mr. Grat Gotch, better known as Arkansas Grat, proprietor and dealer of the gambling tent. Mr. Gotch was in. Not only that, it being mid-afternoon and a slack hour for business, he was superintending the placing of a work of art recently purchased by him and just arrived via the Missouri, Kansas & Texas Railroad, familiarly known throughout the Territory, by a natural process of elision, as the Katy. The newly acquired treasure was a picture, done in oils of a robust and very pink lady of full habit who, apparently having expended all her energy upon the arrangement of her elaborate and highly modern coiffure, was temporarily unable to proceed further with her toilette until fortified by refreshment and repose. To this end she had flung herself in a complete state of nature (barring the hairpins) down on a convenient couch where she lolled at ease, her lips parted to receive a pair of ripe red cherries which she held dangling between thumb and forefinger of a hand whose little finger was elegantly crooked. Her eyes were not on the cherries but on the beholder, of whom she was, plainly, all unaware.

As a tent naturally boasts no walls, it was impossible properly to hang this *objet d'art*, and it was being suspended by guy ropes from the tent top so that it dangled just in front of the bar, as it properly should, flanked by mirrors. Arkansas Grat had pursued his profession in the bonanza days of Denver, San Francisco, White Oaks, and Dodge City. In these precocious cities his artistic tastes had been developed. He knew that the eye, as well as the gullet, must have refreshment in hours of ease. A little plump man, Grat, with a round and smiling countenance, strangely unlined. He looked like an old baby.

He now, at Yancey's entrance, called his attention to the newly acquired treasure, expressing at the same time his admiration for it.

"Ain't she," he demanded, "a lalapaloosa!"

Yancey surveyed the bright pink lady. He had come to ask a favor of Grat, but he would not sell his artistic soul for this mess of pottage.

"It's a calumny," he announced, with some vehemence, "on nature's fairest achievement."

The word was not contained in Mr. Gotch's vocabulary. He mistook Yancey's warmth of tone for enthusiasm. "That's right," he agreed, in triumphant satisfaction. "I was sayin' to the boys only this morning when she come."

Yancey ordered his drink and invited Gotch to have one with him. Arkansas Grat was not one of those abstemious characters frequently found in fiction who, being dispensers of alcoholic refreshment, never sample their own wares. Over the whisky Yancey put his case.

"Listen, Grat. The women folks have got it into their heads that there ought to be a church service Sunday, now that Osage is over a month old, with ten thousand inhabitants, and probably the metropolis of the great Southwest in another ten years. They want the thing done right. I'm chosen to conduct the meeting. There's no building in town big enough to hold the crowd. What I want to know is, can we have the loan of your tent here for about an hour Sunday morning for the purpose of divine worship?"

Arkansas Grat set down his glass, made a sweeping gesture with his right hand that included faro tables, lolling cherry eater, bar, piano, and all else that the tent contained.

"Divine worship! Why, hell, yes, Yancey," he replied, graciously.

They went to work early Sunday. So as not to mar the numbers they covered the faro and roulette tables with twenty-two-foot boards. Such of the prospective congregation as came early would use these for seats. There were, too, a few rude benches on which the players usually sat. The remainder must stand. The meeting was to be from eleven to twelve. As early as nine o'clock they began to arrive. They seemed to spring out of the earth. The horizon spewed up little hurrying figures, black against the brilliant Oklahoma sky. They came from lonely cabins, dugouts, tents. Ox carts, wagons, buggies, horsemen, mule teams. They were starving for company. It wasn't religion they sought; it was the stimulation that comes of meeting their kind in the mass. They brought picnic baskets and boxes, prepared for a holiday. The cowboys were gorgeous. They wore their pink and purple shirts, their five-gallon hats, their gayest neckerchiefs, their most ornate high-heeled boots. They rode up and down before the big tent, their horses curveting and stepping high. "Whoa there! Don't crowd the cattle! . . . You figgerin' on gettin' saved, Quince? . . . Yessir, I'm here for the circus and I'm stayin' for the concert and grand olio besides. . . . Say, you're too late, son. Good whisky and bad women has ruined you."

The town seemed alive with blanketed Indians.

They squatted in the shade of the wooden shacks. They walked in from their near-by reservations, or rode their mangy horses, or brought in their entire families—squaw, papoose, two or three children of assorted sizes, dogs. The family rarely was a large one. Sabra had once remarked this.

"They don't have big families, do they? Two or three children. You'd think savages like that—I mean——"

Yancey explained. "The Indian is a cold race—passionless, or almost. I don't know whether it's the food they eat—their diet—or the vigorous outdoor life they've lived for centuries, or whether they're a naturally sterile race. Funny. No hair on their faces—no beards. Did you ever see an Indian festival dance?"

"Oh, no! I've heard they——"

"They work themselves up, you know, at those dances. Insidious music, mutilations, hysteria—all kinds of orgies to get themselves up to pitch."

Sabra had shuddered with disgust.

This Sunday morning they flocked in by the dozens, with their sorry nags and their scabrous dogs. The men were decked in all their beads and chains with metal plaques. They camped outside the town, at the end of the street.

Sabra, seeing them, told herself sternly that she must remember to have a Christian spirit, and they were all God's children; that these red men had been converted. She didn't believe a word of it. "They're just where they were before Joshua," Mother Bridget had said.

Rangers, storekeepers, settlers. Lean squatters with their bony wives and their bare-legged, rickety children, as untamed as little wolves.

Sabra superintended the toilettes of her men folk from Yancey to Isaiah. She herself had stayed up the night before to iron his finest shirt. Isaiah had polished his boots until they glittered. Sabra sprinkled a drop of her own cherished cologne on his handkerchief. It was as though they were making ready a bridegroom.

He chided her, laughing, "My good woman, do you realize that this is no way to titivate for the work of delivering the Word of God? Sack-

cloth and ashes is, I believe, the prescribed costume." He poured and
drank down three fingers of whisky, the third since breakfast.

Cim cavorted excitedly in his best suit, with the bright plaid silk tie
and the buttoned shoes, tasseled at the top. The boy, Sabra thought as
she dressed him, grew more and more like Yancey, except that he
seemed to lack his father's driving force, his ebullience. But he was high
spirited enough now, so that she had difficulty in dressing him.

"I'm going to church!" he shouted, his voice shrill. "Hi, Isaiah! Blessed
be the name of the Lawd Amen hall'ujah glory be oh my fren's come
and be save hell fire and brimstone——"

"Cimarron Cravat, stop that this minute or you'll have to stay home."
Evidently he and Isaiah, full of the Sunday meeting, had been playing
church on Saturday afternoon. This was the result of their rehearsal.

Yancey's sure dramatic instinct bade him delay until he could make
an effective entrance. A dozen times Sabra called to him, as he sat in
the front office busy with paper and pencil. This was, she decided, his
sole preparation for the sermon he would be bound to deliver within
the next hour. Later she found in the pocket of his sweeping Prince Albert the piece of paper on which he had made these notes. The paper
was filled with those cabalistic whorls, crisscrosses, parallel lines and
skulls with which the hand unconsciously gives relief to the troubled or
restless mind. One word he had written on it, and then disguised it
with meaningless marks—but not quite. Sabra, studying the paper after
the events of the morning, made out the word "Yountis."

At last he was ready. As they stepped into the road they saw that
stragglers were still hurrying toward the tent. Sabra had put on, not her
second-best black grosgrain, but her best, and the hat with the plumes,
none of which splendor she had worn since that eventful first day. She
and Yancey stepped sedately down the street, with Cim's warm wriggling fingers in her own clasp. Sabra was a slimly elegant little figure in
her modish black; Yancey, as always, a dashing one; Cim's clothes were
identical with those being worn, perhaps, by a million little boys all
over the United States, now on their unwilling way to church. Isaiah,
on being summoned from his little kennel in the back yard, had announced that his churchgoing toilette was not quite completed, urged
them to proceed without him, and promised to catch up with them before they should have gone a hundred feet.

They went on their way. It occurred neither to Sabra nor to Yancey
that there was anything bizarre or even unusual in their thus proceeding,
three well-dressed and reasonably conventional figures, toward a gambling tent and saloon which, packed to suffocation with the worst and

the best that a frontier town has to offer, was for one short hour to become a House of God.

"Are you nervous, Yancey dear?"

"No, sugar. Though I will say I'd fifty times rather plead with a jury of Texas Panhandle cattlemen for the life of a professional horse thief than stand up to preach before this gang of——" He broke off abruptly. "What's everybody laughing at and pointing to?" Certainly passers-by were acting strangely. Instinctively Sabra and Yancey turned to look behind them. Down the street, perhaps fifty paces behind them, came Isaiah. He was strutting in an absurd and yet unmistakably recognizable imitation of Yancey's stride and swing. Around his waist was wound a red calico sash, and over that hung a holstered leather belt so large for his small waist that it hung to his knees and bumped against them at every step. Protruding from the holsters one saw the ugly heads of what seemed at first glance to be two six-shooters, but which turned out, on investigation by the infuriated Mrs. Cravat, to be the household monkey wrench and a bar of ink-soaked iron which went to make up one of the printing shop metal forms. On his head was a battered—an unspeakable —sombrero which he must have salvaged from the back-yard débris. But this was not, after all, the high point of his sartorial triumph. He had found somewhere a pair of Yancey's discarded boots. They were high heeled, slim, star trimmed. Even in their final degradation they still had something of the elegance of cut and material that Yancey's footgear always bore. Into these wrecks of splendor Isaiah had thrust, as far as possible, his own great bare splay feet. The high heels toppled. The arched insteps split under the pressure. Isaiah teetered, wobbled, walked now on his ankles as the treacherous heel betrayed him; now on his toes. Yet he managed, by the very power of his dramatic gift, to give to the appreciative onlooker a complete picture of Yancey Cravat in ludicrous—in grotesque miniature.

He advanced toward them, in spite of his pedestrian handicaps, with an appalling imitation of Yancey's stride. Sabra's face went curiously sallow, so that she was, suddenly, Felice Venable, enraged. Yancey gave a great roar of laughter, and at that Sabra's blazing eyes turned from the ludicrous figure of the black boy to her husband. She was literally panting with fury. Her idol, her god, was being mocked.

"You—laugh! . . . Stop. . . ."

She went in a kind of swoop of rage toward the now halting figure of Isaiah. Though Cim's hand was still tightly clutched by her own she had quite forgotten that he was there so that, as she flew toward the small mimic, Cim was yanked along as a cyclone carries small objects in its trail by the very force of its own velocity. She reached him. The black face, all eyes now (and those all whites), looked up at her, startled, terrorized. She raised her hand in its neat black kid glove to cuff him smartly. But Yancey was too quick for her. Swiftly as she had swooped upon Isaiah, Yancey's leap had been quicker. He caught her hand halfway in its descent. His fingers closed round her wrist in an iron grip.

"Let me go!" For that instant she hated him.

"If you touch him I swear before God I'll not set foot inside the tent. Look at him!"

The black face gazed up at him. In it was worship, utter devotion. Yancey, himself a born actor, knew that in Isaiah's grotesque costume, in his struttings and swaggerings, there had been only that sincerest of flattery, imitation of that which was adored. The eyes were those of a dog, faithful, hurt, bewildered.

Yancey released Sabra's wrist. He turned his brilliant winning smile on Isaiah. He put out his hand, removed the mangy sombrero from the child's head, and let his fine white hand rest a moment on the woolly poll.

Isaiah began to blubber, his fright giving way to injury. "Ah didn't go fo' to fret nobody. You-all was dress up fine fo' ch'ch meetin' so I crave to dress myself up Sunday style——"

"That's right, Isaiah. You look finer than any of us. Now listen to me. Do you want a real suit of Sunday clothes?"

The white teeth now vied with the rolling eyes. "Sunday suit fo' me to wear! Fo' true!"

"Listen close, Isaiah. I want you to do something for me. Something big. I don't want you to go to the church meeting." Then, as the black boy's expressive face, all smiles the instant before, became suddenly doleful: "Isaiah, listen hard. This is something important. Everybody in town's at the church meeting. Jesse Rickey's drunk. The house and the newspaper office are left alone. There are people in town who'd sooner set fire to the newspaper plant and the house than see the paper come out on Thursday. I want you to go back to the house and into the kitchen, where you can see the back yard and the side entrance, too. Patrol duty, that's what I'm putting you on."

"Yes, *suh*, Mr. Yancey!" agreed Isaiah. "Patrol." His dejected frame now underwent a transformation as it stiffened to fit the new martial rôle.

"Now listen close. If anybody comes up to the house—they won't come the front way, but at the back, probably, or the side—you take this—and shoot." He took from beneath the Prince Albert a gun which, well on the left, under the coat, was not visible as were the two sixshooters that he always carried at his belt. It was a six-shooter of the kind known as the single action. The trigger was dead. It had been put out of commission. The dog—that part of the mechanism by which the hammer was held cocked and which was released at the pulling of the trigger—had been filed off. It was the deadliest of Southwestern weapons, a six-shooter whose hammer, when pulled back by the thumb, would fall again as soon as released. No need for Isaiah's small forefinger to wrestle with the trigger.

"Oh, Yancey!" breathed Sabra, in horror. She made as though to put Cim behind her—to shield him with her best black grosgrain silk from sight of this latest horror of pioneer existence. "Yancey! He's a child!" Now it was she who was protecting the black boy from Yancey. Yancey ignored her.

"You remember what I told you last week," he went on, equably. "When we were shooting at the tin can on the fence post in the yard. Do it just as you did it then—draw, aim, and shoot with the one motion."

"Yes, *suh*, Mr. Yancey! I kill 'em daid."

"You'll have a brand-new suit of Sunday clothes next week, remember, and boots to go with it. Now, scoot!"

Isaiah turned on the crazy high-heeled boots. "Take them off!" screamed Sabra. "You'll kill yourself. The gun. You'll stumble!"

But he flashed a brilliant, a glorified smile at her over his shoulder and was off, a ludicrous black Don Quixote miraculously keeping his balance; the boots slapping the deep dust of the road now this way, now that.

All Sabra's pleasurable anticipation in the church meeting had fled. "How could you give a gun to a child like that! You'll be giving one to Cim, here, next. Alone in the house, with a gun."

"It isn't loaded. Come on, honey. We're late."

For the first time in their married life she doubted his word absolutely. He strode along toward the tent. She hurried at his side. Cim trotted to keep up with her, his hand in hers.

"What did you mean when you said there were people who would set fire to the house? I never heard of such . . . Did you really mean that someone . . . or was it an excuse to send Isaiah back because of the way he looked?"

"That was it."

For the second time she doubted him. "I don't believe you. There's something going on—something you haven't told me. Yancey, tell me."

"I haven't time now. Don't be foolish. I just don't like the complexion of—I just thought that maybe this meeting was the idea of somebody who isn't altogether inspired by a desire for a closer communion with

God. Just occurred to me. I don't know why. Good joke on me, if it's true."

"I'm not going to the meeting. I'm going back to the house." She was desperate. Her house was burning up, Isaiah was being murdered. Her linen, the silver in the DeGrasse pattern, the cake dish, the green nun's veiling.

"You're coming with me." He rarely used this tone toward her.

"Yancey! Yancey, I'm afraid to have you stand up there, before all those people. I'm afraid. Let's go back. Tell them you're sick. Tell them I'm sick. Tell them——"

They had reached the tent. The flap was open. A roar of talk came to them from within. The entrance was packed with lean figures smoking and spitting. "Hi, Yancey! How's the preacher? Where's your Bible, Yancey?"

"Right here, boys." And Yancey reached into the capacious skirt of his Prince Albert to produce in triumph the Word of God. "Come in or stay out, boys. No loafing in the doorway." With Sabra on his arm he marched through the close-packed tent. "They've saved two seats for you and Cim down front—or should have. Yes, there they are."

Sabra felt faint. She had seen the foxlike face of Lon Yountis in the doorway. "That man," she whispered to Yancey. "He was there. He looked at you as you passed by—he looked at you so——"

"That's fine, honey. Better than I hoped for. Nothing I like better than to have members of my flock right under my eye."

IX

RANGED along the rear of the tent were the Indians. Osages, Poncas, Cherokees, Creeks. They had come from miles around. The Osages wore their blankets, striped orange, purple, green, scarlet, blue. The bucks wore hats—battered and dirty sombreros set high up on their heads. The thin snaky braids of their long black hair hung like wire ropes over their shoulders and down their breasts. Though they wore, for the most part, the checked gingham shirt of the white man there was always about them the gleam of metal, the flash of some brightly dyed fabric, the pattern of colored beads. The older women were shapeless bundles, with the exception of those of the Osage tribe. The Osage alone had never intermarried with the negro. Except for intermingled white blood, the tribe was pure. The Indian children tumbled all about. The savages viewed the proceedings impassively, their faces bronze masks in which only the eyes moved. Later, on their reservations, with no white man to see and hear, they would gossip like fishwives; they would shake with laughter; they would retail this or that absurdity which, with their own eyes, they had seen the white man perform. They would slap their knees and rock with mirth.

"Great jokers, the Indians," Yancey had once said, offhand, to Sabra. She had felt sure that he was mistaken. They were sullen, taciturn, grave. They did not speak; they grunted. They never laughed.

Holding Cim's hand tightly in her own, Sabra, escorted by Yancey, found that two chairs had been placed for them. Other fortunate ones sat perched on the saloon bar, on the gambling tables, on the benches, on upturned barrels. The rest of the congregation stood. Sabra glanced shyly about her. Men—hundreds of men. They were strangely alike, all those faces; young-old, weather-beaten, deeply seamed, and, for the most part, beardless. The Plains had taken them early, had scorched them with her sun, parched them with her drought, buffeted them with her wind, stung them with her dust. Sabra had grown accustomed to these faces during the past two weeks. But the women—she was not prepared for the women. Calico and sunbonnets there were in plenty; but the wives of Osage's citizenry had taken this first opportunity to show what they had in the way of finery; dresses that they had brought with them from Kansas, from Texas, from Arkansas, from Colorado, carefully laid away in layers of papers which in turn were smoothed into pasteboard boxes or into trunks. Headgear trembled with wired roses. Cheviot and lady's-cloth and henrietta graced shoulders that had known only cotton this month past. Near her, and occupying one of the seats evidently reserved for persons of distinction, was a woman who must be, Sabra thought, about her own age; perhaps twenty or twenty-one, fair, blue eyed, almost childlike in her girlish slimness and purity of contour. She was very well dressed in a wine-color silk-warp henrietta, bustled, very tightly basqued, and elaborate with fluting on sleeves and collar. Dress and bonnet were city made and very modish. From Denver, Sabra thought, or Kansas City, or even Chicago. Sabra further decided, with feminine unreason, that her nose was the most exquisite feature of the kind she had ever seen; that her fair skin could not long endure this burning, wind-deviled climate and that the man beside her, who looked old enough to be her father, must be, after all, her husband. It was in the way he spoke to her, gazed at her, touched her. Yancey had pointed

him out one day. She remembered his name because it had amused her
at the time: Waltz, Evergreen Waltz. He was a notorious Southwest
gambler, earned his living by the cards, and was supposed to be the
errant son of the former governor of some state or other—she thought it
was Texas. The girl looked unhappy; and beneath that, rebellious.

Still, the sight of this lovely face, and of the other feminine faces
looking out from at least fairly modish and decent straw bonnets and
toques, gave Sabra a glow of reassurance. Immediately this was
quenched at the late, showy, and dramatic entrance, just before Yancey
took his place, of a group of women of whom Sabra had actually been
unaware. As a matter of fact, the leader of this spectacular group, whose
appearance caused a buzz and stir throughout the tent, had arrived in
Osage only the day before, accompanied by a bevy of six young ladies.
The group had stepped off the passenger coach of the Katy at the town
of Wahoo arrayed in such cinder-strewn splendor as to cause the depot
loafers to reel. The Katy had not yet been brought as far as Osage. It
terminated at Wahoo, twenty-two miles away. The vision, in her purple
grosgrain silk, with a parasol to match, and two purple plumes in her
hat, with her six gayly bedecked companions had mounted a buckboard
amid much shrill clamor and many giggles and a striking display of
ankle. In this crude vehicle, their silks outspread, their astounding parasols unfurled, they had bumped their way over the prairie to the town.
Osage, since that first mad day of its beginning, had had its quota of
shady ladies, but these had been raddled creatures, driftwood from this
or that deserted mining camp or abandoned town site, middle aged,
unsavory, and doubtless slightly subnormal mentally.

These were different. The leader, a handsome black-haired woman
of not more than twenty-two or -three, had taken for herself and her
companions such rooms as they could get in the town. Osage gazed on
the parasols, bedazzled. Within an hour it was known that the woman
claimed the name of Dixie Lee. That she was a descendant of decayed
Southern aristocracy. That her blooming companions boasted such fancy
nomenclature as Cherry de St. Maurice, Carmen Brown, Belle Mansero,
and the like. That the woman, shrewd as a man and sharp as a knife,
had driven a bargain whereby she was to come into possession, at a stiff
price, of the building known as the Elite Rooming House and Café,
situated at the far end of Pawhuska Avenue, near the gambling tent;
and that she contemplated building a house of her own, planned for her
own peculiar needs, if business warranted. Finally, she brought the
news, gained God knows how or where, that the Katy was to be extended
to Osage and perhaps beyond it. Thus harlotry, heretofore a sordid
enough slut in a wrapper and curling pins, came to Osage in silks and

plumes, with a brain behind it and a promise of prosperity in its gaudy train.

Dixie Lee, shrewd saleswoman, had been quick to learn of Sunday's meeting, and quicker still to see the advantage of this opportunity for a public advertisement of her business. So now, at Osage's first church meeting, in marched the six, with Dixie Lee at their head making a seventh. They rustled in silks. The air of the close-packed tent became as suffocating with scent as a Persian garden at sunset. Necks were craned; whispers became a buzz; seats were miraculously found for these representatives of a recognized social order, as for visiting royalty. The dazzling tent top, seeming to focus rather than disseminate the glare of the Oklahoma sun, cast its revealing spotlight upon painted cheeks and beaded lashes. The nude and lolling lady of the cherries in Grat Gotch's newly acquired art treasure stared down at them, open-mouthed, with the look of one who is surprised and vanquished by an enemy from her own camp. The hard-working worthy wives of Osage, in their cheviots and their faded bonnets and cotton gloves, suddenly seemed sallow, scrawny, and almost spectacularly unalluring.

All this Sabra beheld in a single glance, as did the entire congregation. Only the Indians, standing or squatting in a row at the back, like an Egyptian frieze against the white of the tent, remained unagitated, remote. Yancey, having lifted Cim into the chair next his mother, looked up at the entrance of this splendid procession.

"God Almighty!" he said. His tone was as irreverent as the words were sacred. A dull flush suffused his face, a thing so rare in him as to startle Sabra more than the words he had uttered or the tone in which he had said them.

"What is it? Yancey! What's wrong?"

"That's the girl."

"What girl?"

"That one—Dixie Lee—she's the girl in the black tights and the skull-cap . . . in the Run . . . on the thoroughbred . . ." he was whispering.

"Oh, no!" cried Sabra, aloud. It was wrung from her. Those near by stared.

So this was the church meeting toward which she had looked with such hope, such happy assurance. Harlots, pictures of nude women, Indians, heat, glare, her house probably blazing at this moment, Isaiah weltering in his own gore, Lon Yountis's sinister face sneering in the tent entrance. And now this woman, unscrupulous, evil, who had stolen Yancey's quarter section from him by a trick.

Yancey made his way through the close-packed crowd, leaped to the top of the roulette table which was to be his platform, flung his broad-

brimmed white sombrero dexterously to the outjutting base of a suspended oil lamp, where it spun and then clung, cocked rakishly; and,
lifting the great lolling head, swept the expectant congregation with
his mysterious, his magnetic eyes.

Probably never in the history of the Christian religion had the Word
of God been preached by so romantic and dashing a figure. His long
black locks curled on his shoulders; the fine eyes glowed; the Prince Albert swayed with his graceful movements; his six-shooters, one on each
side, bulged reassuringly in their holsters.

His thrilling voice sounded through the tent, stilling its buzz and
movement.

"Friends and fellow citizens, I have been called on to conduct this
opening meeting of the Osage First Methodist, Episcopal, Lutheran,
Presbyterian, Congregational, Baptist, Catholic, Unitarian Church. In
the course of my career as a lawyer and an editor I have been required
to speak on varied occasions and on many subjects. I have spoken in
defense of my country and in criticism of it; I have been called on to
defend and to convict horse thieves, harlots, murderers, samples of
which professions could doubtless be found in any large gathering in the
Indian Territory to-day. I name no names. I point no finger. Whether
for good or for evil, the fact remains that any man or woman, for whatever purpose, found in this great Oklahoma country to-day is here because in his or her veins, actuated by motives lofty or base, there is the
spirit of adventure. I ask with Shakespeare, 'Why should a man, whose
blood is warm within, sit like his grandsire cut in alabaster?' Though
I know the Bible from cover to cover, and while many of its passages
and precepts are graven on my heart and in my memory, this, fellow
citizens of Osage, is the first time that I have been required to speak
the Word of God in His Temple." He glanced around the gaudy, glaring tent. "For any shelter, however sordid, however humble—no offense, Grat—becomes, while His Word is spoken within it, His Temple.
Suppose, then, that we unite in spirit by uniting in song. We have, you
will notice, no hymn books. We will therefore open this auspicious occasion in the brief but inevitably glorious history of the city of Osage by
singing—uh—what do you all know, boys, anyway?"

There was a moment's slightly embarrassing pause. The hard-bitten
faces of the motley congregation stared blankly up at Yancey. Yancey,
self-possessed, vibrant, looked warmly down on them. He raised an arm
in encouragement. "Come on, boys! Name it! Any suggestions, ladies
and gentlemen?"

"How about Who Were You At Home? just for a starter," called out a
voice belonging to a man with a shining dome-shaped bald head and a

flowing silky beard, reddish in color. He was standing near the rear of the tent. It was Shanghai Wiley, up from Texas; owner of more than one hundred thousand long-horn cattle and of the Rancho Palacios, on Tres Palacios Creek. He was the most famous cattle singer in the whole Southwest, besides being one of its richest cattle and land owners. Possessed of a remarkably high sweet tenor voice that just escaped being a clear soprano, he had been known to quiet a whole herd of restless cattle on the verge of a mad stampede. It was an art he had learned when a cowboy on the range. Many cowboys had it, but none possessed the magic soothing quality of Shanghai's voice. It was reputed to have in it the sorcery of the superhuman. It was told of him that in a milling herd, their nostrils distended, their flanks heaving, he had been seen to leap from the back of one maddened steer to another, traveling the moving mass that was like a shifting sea, singing to them in his magic tenor, stopping them just as they were about to plunge into the Rio Grande.

Yancey acknowledged this suggestion with a grateful wave of the hand. "That's right, Shanghai. Thanks for speaking up. A good song, though a little secular for the occasion, perhaps. But anyway, you all know it, and that's the main thing. Kindly favor us with the pitch, will you, Shanghai? Will the ladies kindly join in with their sweet soprano voices? Now, then, all together!"

It was a well-known song in the Territory where, on coming to this new and wild country, so many settlers with a checkered—not to say plaid—past had found it convenient to change their names.

The congregation took it up feelingly, almost solemnly:

> *Who were you at home?*
> *Who were you at home?*
> *God alone remembers*
> *Ere you first began to roam.*
> *Jack or Jo or Bill or Pete,*
> *Anyone you chance to meet,*
> *Sure to hit it just as neat,*
> *Oh, who were you at home?*

"Now, all together! Again!"

Somebody in the rear suddenly produced an accordion, and from the crowd perched on the saloon bar came the sound of a jew's harp. The chorus now swelled with all the fervor of song's ecstasy. They might have been singing Onward, Christian Soldiers. Through it all, high and clear, sounded Shanghai Wiley's piercing tenor, like brasses in a band,

and sustaining it from the roulette table platform the 'cello of Yancey Cravat's powerful, rich barytone.

> Oh, WHO were you at home?
> WHO were you at HOME?

They had not risen to sing for the reason that most of the congregation was already standing, and the few who were seated were afraid to rise for fear that their seats would be snatched from under them.

Sabra had joined in the singing, not at first, but later, timidly. It had seemed, somehow, to relieve her. This, she thought, was better. Perhaps, after all, this new community was about to make a proper beginning. Yancey, she thought, looked terribly handsome, towering there on the roulette table, his eyes alight, his slim foot, in its shining boot, keeping time to the music. She began to feel prim and good and settled at last.

"Now, then," said Yancey, all aglow, "the next thing in order is to take up the collection before the sermon."

"What for?" yelled Pete De Vargas.

Yancey fixed him with a pitying gray eye. "Because, you Spanish infidel, part of a church service is taking up a collection. Southwest Davis, I appoint you to work this side of the house. Ike Bixler, you take that side. The collection, fellow citizens, ladies and gentlemen—and you, too, Pete—is for the new church organ."

"Why, hell, Yancey, we ain't even got a church!" bawled Pete again, aggrieved.

"That's all right, Pete. Once we buy an organ we'll have to build a church to put it in. Stands to reason. Members of the congregation, anybody putting in less than two bits will be thrown out of the tent by me. Indians not included."

The collection was taken up, in two five-gallon sombreros, the contents of which, as they passed from one hairy sunburned paw to the next, were watched with eagle eyes by Southwest Davis and Ike Bixler, and, in fact, by the entire gathering. The sombreros were then solemnly and with some hesitation brought to the roulette table pulpit for Yancey's inspection.

"Mr. Grat Gotch, being used to lightning calculations in the matter of coins, will kindly count the proceeds of the collection."

Arkansas Grat, red-faced and perspiring, elbowed his way to the pulpit and made his swift and accurate count. He muttered the result to Yancey. Yancey annnounced it publicly. "Fellow citizens, the sum of the first collection for the new church organ for the Osage church, whose denomination shall be nameless, is the gratifying total of one hundred and thirty-three dollars and fifty-five cents.—Heh, wait a minute, Grat! Fifty-five—did you say fifty-five cents?"

"That's right, Yancey."

Yancey's eye swept his flock. "Some miserable tight-fisted skinflint of a—— But maybe it was a Ponca or an Osage, by mistake."

"How about a Cherokee, Yancey!" came a taunting voice from somewhere in the rear.

"No, not a Cherokee, Sid. Recognized your voice by the squeak. A Cherokee—as you'd know if you knew anything at all—you and Yountis and the rest of your outfit—is too smart to put anything in the contribution box of a race that has robbed him of his birthright." He did not pause for the titter that went round. He now took from the rear pocket of the flowing Prince Albert the small and worn little Bible. "Friends! We've come to the sermon. What I have to say is going to take fifteen minutes. The first five minutes are going to be devoted to a confession by me to you, and I didn't expect to make it when I accepted the job of conducting this church meeting. Walt Whitman—say, boys, there's a poet with red blood in him, and the feel of the land, and a love of his fellow beings!—Walt Whitman has a line that has stuck in my memory. It is: 'I say the real and permanent grandeur of these states must be their religion.' That's what Walt says. And that's the text I intended to use for the subject of my sermon, though I know that the Bible should furnish it. And now, at the eleventh hour, I've changed my mind. It's from the Good Book, after all. I'll announce my text, and then I'll make my confession, and following that, any time left will be devoted to the sermon. Any lady or gent wishing to leave the tent will kindly do so now, before the confession, and with my full consent, or remain in his or her seat until the conclusion of the service, on pain of being publicly held up to scorn by me in the first issue of my newspaper, the *Oklahoma Wigwam*, due off the press next Thursday. Anyone wishing to leave the tent kindly rise now and pass as quietly as may be to the rear. Please make way for all departing—uh—worshipers."

An earthquake might have moved a worshiper from his place in that hushed and expectant gathering: certainly no lesser cataclysm of nature. Yancey waited, Bible in hand, a sweet and brilliant smile on his face. He waited quietly, holding the eyes of the throng in that stifling tent. A kind of power seemed to flow from him to them, drawing them, fixing them, enthralling them. Yet in his eyes, and in the great head raised now as it so rarely was, there was that which sent a warning pang of fear through Sabra. She, too, felt his magnetic draw, but mingled with it was a dreadful terror—a stab of premonition. The little pitted places in the skin of forehead and cheeks were somehow more noticeable. Twice she had seen his eyes look like that.

Yancey waited yet another moment. Then he drew a long breath. "My text is from Proverbs. 'There is a lion in the way; a lion is in the streets.' Friends, there is a lion in the streets of Osage, our fair city, soon to be Queen of the Great Southwest. A lion is in the streets. And I have been a liar and a coward and an avaricious knave. For I pretended not to have knowledge which I have; and I went about asking for information of this lion—though I would change the word lion to jackal or dirty skunk if I did not feel it to be sacrilege to take liberties with Holy Writ—when already I had proof positive of his guilt—proof in writing, for which I paid, and about which I said nothing. And the reason for this deceit of mine I am ashamed to confess to you, but I shall confess it. I intended to announce to you all today that I had this knowledge, and I meant to announce to you from this pulpit—" he glanced down at the roulette table—"from this platform—that I would publish this knowledge in the columns of the *Oklahoma Wigwam* on Thursday, hoping thereby to gain profit and fame because of the circulation which this would gain for my paper, starting it off with a bang!" At the word "bang," uttered with much vehemence, the congregation of Osage's First Methodist, Episcopal, Lutheran, etc., church jumped noticeably and nervously. "Friends and fellow citizens, I repent of my greed and of my desire for self-advancement at the expense of this community. I no longer intend to withhold, for my own profit, the name of the jackal in a lion's skin who, by threats of sudden death, has held this town abjectly terrorized. I stand here to announce to you that the name of that skunk, that skulking fiend and soulless murderer who shot down Jack Pegler when his back was turned—that coward and poltroon—" he was gesturing with his Bible in his hand, brandishing it aloft—"was none other than——"

He dropped the Bible to the floor as if by accident, in his rage. As he stooped for it, on that instant, there was the crack of a revolver, a bullet from a six-shooter in the rear of the tent sang past the spot where his head had been, and there appeared in the white surface of the tent a tiny circlet of blue that was the Oklahoma sky. But before that dot of blue appeared Yancey Cravat had raised himself halfway from the hips, had fired from the waist without, seemingly, pausing to take aim. His thumb flicked the hammer. That was all. The crack of his six-shooter was, in fact, so close on the heels of that first report that the two seemed almost simultaneous. The congregation was now on its feet, en masse, its back to the roulette table pulpit. Its eyes were on one figure; its breath was suspended. That figure—a man—was seen to perform some curious antics. He looked, first of all, surprised. With his left hand he had gripped one of the taut tent ropes, and now, with his hand still grasping the hempen line, his fingers slipping gently along it, as though loath to let go, he sank to the floor, sat there a moment, as if in meditation, loosed his hand's hold of the rope, turned slightly, rolled over on one side and lay there, quite still.

"—Lon Yountis," finished Yancey, neatly concluding his sentence and now holding an ivory-mounted six-shooter in right and left hand.

Screams. Shouts. A stampede for the door. Then the voice of Yancey Cravat, powerful, compelling, above the roar. He sent one shot through the dome of the tent to command attention. "Stop! Stand where you are! The first person who stampedes this crowd gets a bullet. Shut that tent flap, Jesse, like I told you to this morning. Louie Hefner, remove the body and do your duty."

"Okeh, Yancey. It's self-defense and justifiable homicide."

"I know it. Louie, . . . Fellow citizens! We will forego the sermon this morning, but next Sabbath, if requested, I shall be glad to take the pulpit again, unless a suitable and ordained minister of God can be procured. The subject of my sermon for next Sabbath will be from Proverbs xxvi, 27: 'Whoso diggeth a pit shall fall therein' . . . This church meeting, brethren and sisters, will now be concluded with prayer." There was a little thudding, scuffling sound as a heavy, inert burden was carried out through the tent flap into the noonday sunshine. His six-shooters still in his hands, Yancey Cravat bowed his magnificent buffalo head—but not too far—and sent the thrilling tones of his beautiful voice out into the agitated crowd before him.

". . . bless this community, O Lord. . . ."

X

MOURNFULLY, and in accordance with the custom of the community, Yancey carved a notch in the handsome ivory and silver-mounted butt of his six-shooter. It was then for the first time that Sabra, her eyes widening with horror, noticed that there were five earlier notches cut in the butts of Yancey's two guns—two on one, three on the other. This latest addition brought the number up to six.

Aghast, she gingerly investigated further. She saw that the two ter-

rifying weapons were not worn completely encased in the holster but
each was held within it by an ingenious steel clip, elastic and sensitive
as a watch spring. This spring gripped the barrel securely and yet so
lightly that the least effort would set it free. Yancey could pull his gun
and thumb the hammer with but one motion, instead of two. The infinitesimal saving of time had saved his life that day.

"Oh, Yancey, you haven't killed six men!"

"I've never killed a man unless I knew he'd kill me if I didn't."

"But that's murder!"

"Would you have liked to see Yountis get me?"

"Oh, darling, no! I died a thousand deaths while you were standing
there. That terrible prayer, when I thought surely someone else would
shoot you. But wasn't there some other way? Did you have to kill him?
Like that?"

"Why, no, honey. I could have let him kill me."

"Cim has seen his own father shoot a man and kill him."

"Better than seeing a man shoot and kill his own father."

There was nothing more that she could say on this subject. But still
another question was consuming her.

"That woman. That woman. I saw you talking to her, right on the
street, in broad daylight to-day, after the meeting. All that horrible
shooting—all those people around you—Cim screaming—and then to
find that woman smirking and talking. Bad enough if you'd never seen
her before. But she stole your land from you in the Run. You stood
there, actually talking to her. Chatting."

"I know. She said she had made up her mind that day of the Run to
get a piece of land, and farm it, and raise cattle. She wanted to give up
her way of living. She's been at it since she was eighteen. Now she's
twenty-six. Older than she looks. She comes of good stock. She was
desperate."

"What she doing here, then!"

"Before the month was up she saw she couldn't make it go. One
hundred and sixty acres. Then the other women homesteaders found out
about her. It was no use. She sold out for five hundred dollars, added to
it whatever money she had saved, and went to Denver."

"Why didn't she stay there?"

"Her business was overcrowded there. She got a tip that the railroad
was coming through here. She's a smart girl. She got together her outfit, and down she came."

"You talk as though you admired her! That—that—" Felice Venable's
word came to her lips—"that hussy!"

"She's a smart girl. She's a—" he hesitated, as though embarrassed—"in a way she's a—well, in a way, she's a good girl."

Sabra's voice rose to the pitch of hysteria.

"Don't you quote your Bible at me, Yancey Cravat! You with your Lukes and your Johns and your Magdalenes! I'm sick of them."

The first issue of the *Oklahoma Wigwam* actually appeared on Thursday, as scheduled. It was a masterly mixture of reticence and indiscretion. A half column, first page, was devoted to the church meeting. The incident of the shooting was not referred to in this account. An outsider, reading it, would have gathered that all had been sweetness and light. On an inside column of the four-page sheet was a brief notice:

> It is to be regretted that an unimportant but annoying shooting affray somewhat marred the otherwise splendid and truly impressive religious services held in the recreation tent last Sunday, kindness of the genial and popular proprietor, Mr. Grat Gotch. A ruffian, who too long had been infesting the streets of our fair city of Osage, terrorizing innocent citizens, and who was of the contemptible ilk that has done so much toward besmirching the dazzling fame of the magnificent Southwest, took this occasion to create a disturbance, during which he shot, with intent to kill, at the person presiding. It was necessary to reply in kind. The body, unclaimed, was interred in Boot Hill, with only the prowling jackals to mourn him, their own kin. It is hoped that his nameless grave will serve as a warning to others of his class.

Having thus modestly contained himself in the matter of the actual shooting, Yancey let himself go a little on the editorial page. His editorials, in fact, for a time threatened the paper's news items. Sabra and Jesse Rickey had to convince him that the coming of the Katy was of more interest to prospective subscribers than was the editorial entitled, Lower than the Rattlesnake. He was prevailed upon to cut it slightly, though under protest.

> The rattlesnake has a bad reputation. People accuse him of a great many mean things, and it cannot be denied that the world would be better off if his species were exterminated. Nine times out of ten his bite is fatal, and many homes have been saddened because of his venomous attacks. But the rattlesnake is a gentleman and a scholar beside some snakes. He always gives warning. It is the snake that takes you unawares that hurts the worst. . . .

Thus for a good half column.

Sabra, reading the damp galley proof, was murmurous with admiration. "It's just wonderful! But, Yancey, don't you think we ought to have more news items? Gossip, sort of. I don't mean gossip, really, but about

people, and what they're doing, and so on. Those are the things I like to
read in a newspaper. Of course men like editorials and important things
like that. But women——"

"That's right, too," agreed Jesse Rickey, looking up, ink smeared,
from his case. "Get the women folks to reading the paper."

Sabra was emerging slowly from her rôle of charming little fool. By
degrees she was to take more and more of a hand in the assembling of
the paper's intimate weekly items, while Yancey was concerned with
cosmic affairs. Indeed, had it not been for Sabra and Jesse Rickey that
first issue of the *Oklahoma Wigwam* might never have appeared, for the
front office of the little wooden shack that served as newspaper plant was
crowded, following that eventful Sunday, with congratulatory committees, so that it seemed stuffed to suffocation with sombreros, six-
shooters, boots, tobacco, and repetitious talk.

"Yessir, Yancey, that was one of the quickest draws I ever see. . . .
And you was on to him all the time, huh? Sa-a-ay, you're a slick one,
all right. They don't come no slicker. . . . The rest of the gang has took
to the Hills, I understand. That shows they're scairt, because they got a
feud with the Kid and his outfit, and the Kid sees 'em he'll drop 'em like
a row of gobblers at a turkey shootin'. Yessir, Yancey, you're the kind
of stuff this country needs out here. First thing you know you'll be
Governor of the Territory. How's that, boys! Come on out and have a
drink to the future new Governor, the Honorable Yancey Cravat!"

The group moved in a body across the dusty street into the Sunny
Southwest Saloon, from whence came further and more emphatic
sounds of approbation.

Sabra, in her checked gingham kitchen apron, was selecting fascinating
facts from the stock of ready-print brought with them from Wichita,
fresh supplies of which they would receive spasmodically by mail or
express via the Katy or the Santa Fé.

SWIMMING BRIDES

Girls inhabiting the Island of Himla, near Rhodes, are not allowed
to marry until they have brought up a specified number of sponges,
each taken from a certain depth. The people of the Island earn their
living by the sponge fishery.

STRENGTH OF THE THUMB

The thumb is stronger than all the other fingers together.

COMPRESSED AIR FOR MINE HAULAGE

During the last ten years a great many mines have replaced animal
haulage with compressed air motors.

As the printing plant boasted only a little hand press, the two six-column forms had to be inked with a hand roller. Over this was placed the damp piece of white print paper. Each sheet was done by hand. The first issue of the *Oklahoma Wigwam* numbered four hundred and fifty copies, and before it was run off, Yancey, Jesse Rickey, Sabra, Isaiah—every member of the household except little Cim—had taken a turn at the roller. Sabra's back and arm muscles ached for a week.

Yancey made vigorous protest. "What! Ink on the white wonder of dear Juliet's hand! Out, damned spot! See here, honey. This will never do. My sweet Southern jasmine working over a miserable roller! I'd rather never get out a paper, I tell you."

"It looks as if you never would, anyway." The sweet Southern jasmine did not mean to be acid; but the events of the past two or three weeks were beginning to tell on her nerves. The ready-print contained the opening chapters of a novel by Bertha M. Clay in which beauty and virtue triumphed over evil. An instalment of this would appear weekly. The second half of it was missing. But Sabra sagely decided that this fragment, for a time at least, would compensate the feminine readers of the *Oklahoma Wigwam* for the preponderance of civic and political matter and the scarcity of social and personal items. She made up her mind that she would conquer her shyness and become better acquainted with some of those cheviots and straw bonnets seen at the Sunday church meeting.

Yancey and Jesse Rickey seemed to have some joke between them. Sabra, in her kitchen, could hear them snickering like a couple of school-girls. They were up to some mischief. Yancey was possessed of the rough and childlike notion of humor that was of the day and place.

"What are you boys up to?" she asked him at dinner.

He was all innocence. "Nothing. Not a thing! What a suspicious little puss you're getting to be."

The paper came out on Thursday afternoon, as scheduled. Sabra was astonished and a little terrified to see the occasion treated as an event, with a crowd of cowboys and local citizens in front of the house, pistols fired, whoops and yells; and Yancey himself, aided by Jesse Rickey, handing out copies as if they had cost nothing to print. Perhaps twenty-five of these were distributed, opened eagerly, perused by citizens leaning against the porch posts, and by cowboys on horseback, before Sabra, peeking out of the office window, saw an unmistakable look of surprise—even of shock—on their faces and heard Cass Bixby drawl, "Say, Yancey, that's a hell of a name for a newspaper."

She sent Isaiah out to get hold of a copy. He came back with it, grinning. It was a single sheet. The *Oklahoma Galoot*. Motto: Take It or Leave It. Beneath this a hastily assembled and somewhat pied collection of very personal items, calculated to reveal the weaknesses and foibles of certain prominent citizens now engaged in perusing the false sheet.

The practical joke being revealed and the *bona fide* paper issued, this was considered a superb triumph for Yancey, and he was again borne away to receive the congratulatory toasts of his somewhat sheepish associates.

It was a man's town. The men enjoyed it. They rode, gambled, swore, fought, fished, hunted, drank. The antics of many of them seemed like those of little boys playing robber's cave under the porch. The saloon was their club, the brothel their social rendezvous, the town women their sweethearts. Literally there were no other young girls of marriageable age; for the men and women who had come out here were, like Sabra and Yancey, married couples whose ages ranged between twenty and forty. It was no place for the very young, the very old, or even the middle-aged. Through it all wove the Indians, making a sad yet colorful pattern. The Osage reservation was that nearest the town of Osage. There now was some talk of changing the name of the town because of this, but it never was done. It had been named in the rush of the Run. The Osages, unlike many of the other Territory Plains tribes, were a handsome people—tall, broad shouldered, proud. The women carried themselves well, head up, shoulders firm, their step leisurely and light. Their garments were mean enough, but over them they wore the striped blanket of the tribe, orange and purple and scarlet and blue, dyed with the same brilliant lasting dyes that Mother Bridget had used in Sabra's coverlet. They came in from the Reservation on foot; sometimes a family rattled along the red clay road that led into town, huddled in a wagon, rickety, mud spattered. Sometimes a buck rode a scrofulous horse, his lean legs hugging its sorry flanks. The town treated them with less consideration than the mongrel curs that sunned themselves in the road. They bought their meager supplies with the stipend that the government allowed them; the men bought, stole, or begged whisky when they could, though fire water was strictly forbidden them, and to sell or give it to an Indian was a criminal offense. They lolled or squatted in the sun. They would not work. They raised a little corn which, mixed with lye, they called soffica. This mess, hot or cold, was eaten with a spoon made from the horn of a cow. Sabra hated them, even feared them, though Yancey laughed at her for this. Cim was forbidden by her to talk to them. This after she discovered that Yancey had taken him out to visit the Reservation one afternoon. Here, then, was the monstrous society in which Sabra Cravat now found herself. For her, and the other respectable women of the town, there was nothing but their housework, their children, their memories of the homes they had left.

And so the woman who was, after all, the most intelligent among them, set about creating some sort of social order for the good wives of the community. All her life Sabra had been accustomed to the open-handed hospitality of the South. The Venable household in Wichita had been as nearly as possible a duplicate of the Mississippi mansion which had housed generations of Sabra's luxury-loving and open-handed ancestors. Hordes of relatives came and went. Food and drink were constantly being passed in abundance. White muslin dresses and blue sashes whirled at the least provocative tinkle of the handsome old square piano with its great blobs of grapevine carving. Friends drove up for midday dinner and stayed a week. Felice Venable's musical drawl was always tempting the sated guest to further excesses. "I declare, Cousin Flora May, you haven't eaten enough to keep a bird alive. Angie'll think you don't fancy her cooking. . . . Lacy, just another quail. They're only a mouthful. . . . Mittie, pass the currant jell."

Grimly Sabra (and, in time, the other virtuous women of the community) set about making this new frontier town like the old as speedily as possible. Yancey, almost single handed, tried to make the new as unlike the old as possible. He fought a losing fight from the first. He was muddled; frequently insincere; a brilliant swaggerer. He himself was not very clear as to what he wanted, or how to go about getting it. He only knew that he was impatient of things as they were; that greed, injustice, and dishonesty in office were everywhere; that here, in this wild and virgin land, was a chance for a Utopian plan. But he had no plan. He was sentimental about the under dog; overgallant to women; emotional, quick-tempered, impulsive, dramatic, idealistic. And idealism does not flourish in a frontier settlement. Yancey Cravat, with his unformed dreams—much less the roistering play boys of saloon and plain and gambling house—never had a chance against the indomitable materialism of the women.

Like Sabra, most of the women had brought with them from their homes in Nebraska, in Arkansas, in Missouri, in Kansas, some household treasure that in their eyes represented elegance or which was meant to mark them as possessed of taste and background. A chair, a bed, a piece of silver, a vase, a set of linen. It was the period of the horrible gimcrack. Women all over the country were covering wire bread toasters with red plush, embroidering sulphurous yellow chenille roses on this, tying the whole with satin ribbons and hanging it on the wall to represent a paper rack (to be used on pain of death). They painted the backsides of frying pans with gold leaf and daisies, enhanced the handles of these, too, with bows of gay ribbon and, the utilitarian duckling thus turned into a swan, hung it on the wall opposite the toaster. Rolling pins were gilded or sheathed in velvet. Coal scuttles and tin shovels were surprised to find themselves elevated from the kitchen to the parlor, having first been subjected to the new beautifying process. Sabra's house became a sort of social center following the discovery that she received copies of *Harper's Bazaar* with fair regularity. Felice Venable sometimes sent it to her, prompted, no doubt, by Sabra's rather guarded account of the lack of style hints for the person or for the home in this new community. Sabra's social triumph was complete when she displayed her new draped jars, done by her after minute instructions found in the latest copy of *Harper's*. She then graciously printed these instructions in the *Oklahoma Wigwam*, causing a flurry of excitement in a hundred homes and mystifying the local storekeepers by the sudden demand for jars.

As everything [the fashion note announced, haughtily] is now draped, we give an illustration [Sabra did not—at least in the limited columns of the *Wigwam*] of a china or glass jar draped with India silk and trimmed with lace and ribbon, the decoration entirely concealing any native hideousness in the shape or ornamentation of the jar. Perfectly plain jars can also be draped with a pretty piece of silk and tied with ribbon bows or ornamented with an odd fragment of lace and thereby makes a pretty ornament at little or no cost.

Certainly the last four words of the hint were true.

With elegancies such as these the womenfolk of Osage tried to disguise the crudeness and bareness of their glaring wooden shacks. Usually, there was as well a plush chair which had survived the wagon journey; a tortured whatnot on which reposed painted seashells and the *objets d'art* above described; or, on the wall, a crayon portrait or even an oil painting of some stern and bewhiskered or black-silk and fichued parent looking down in surprised disapproval upon the ructions that comprised the daily activities of this town. From stark ugliness the house interiors were thus transformed into grotesque ugliness, but the Victorian sense of beauty was satisfied. The fact was that these women were hungry for the feel of soft silken things; their eyes, smarting with the glare, the wind, the dust, ached to rest on that which was rich and soothing; their hands, roughened by alkali water, and red dust, and burning sun and wind, dwelt lovingly on these absurd scraps of silk and velvet, snipped from an old wedding dress, from a bonnet, from finery that had found its way to the scrap bag.

Aside from the wedding silver and linen that she had brought with her, the loveliest thing that Sabra possessed was the hand-woven blue coverlet that Mother Bridget had given her. It made a true and brilliant spot of color in the sitting room, where it lay neatly folded at the foot of the sofa, partly masking the ugliness of that utilitarian piece of furniture. This Sabra did not know. As silk patchwork quilts, made in wheel and fan patterns, and embroidered in spider webs of bright-colored threads were quite the fashion, the blue coverlet was looked on with considerable disrespect. Thirty years later, its color undimmed, Sabra contributed it temporarily to an exhibition of early American handiwork held in the Venetian room of the Savoy-Bixby Hotel, and it was cooed and ah'd over by all the members of Osage's smart set. They said it was quaint and authentic and very native and a fine example of pioneer handicraft and Sabra said yes indeed, and told them of Mother Bridget. They said she must have been quaint, too. Sabra said she was.

Slowly, in Sabra's eyes, the other women of the town began to emerge from a mist of drabness into distinct personalities. There was one who had been a school teacher in Cairo, Illinois. Her husband, Tracy Wyatt, ran the spasmodic bus and dray line between Wahoo and Osage. They had no children. She was a sparse and simpering woman of thirty-nine, who talked a good deal of former trips to Chicago during which she had reveled in the culture of that effete city. Yancey was heard learnedly discoursing to her on the subject of Etruscan pottery, of which he knew nothing. The ex-school teacher rolled her eyes and tossed her head a good deal.

"You don't know what a privilege it is, Mr. Cravat, to find myself talking to someone whose mind can soar above the sordid life of this horrible town."

Yancey's ardent eyes took on their most melting look. "Madam, it is you who have carried me with you to your heights. 'In youth and beauty wisdom is but rare!'" It was simply his way. He could not help it.

"Ah, Shakespeare!" breathed Mrs. Wyatt, bridling.

"Shakespeare—hell!" said Yancey to Sabra, later. "She doesn't know Pope when she hears him. No woman ought to pretend to be intelligent. And if she is she ought to have the intelligence to pretend she isn't. And this one looks like Cornelia Blimber, to boot."

"Cornelia? . . ."

"A schoolmarm in Dickens's *Dombey and Son*. A magnificent book, honey. I want you to read it. I want Cim to read it by the time he's twelve. I've got it somewhere here on the shelves." He was searching among the jumble of books. Five minutes later he was deep in a copy of Plutarch which he had bewailed as lost.

Sabra persisted. "But why did you make her think she was so smart and attractive when you were talking to her?"

"Because she is so plain, darling."

"It's just that you can't bear not to have everybody think you're fascinating."

She never read *Dombey and Son*, after all. She decided that she preferred exchanging recipes and discussing the rearing of children with the other women to the more intellectual conversation of Mrs. Wyatt.

It was Sabra who started the Philomathean Club. The other women clutched at the idea. It was part of their defense against these wilds. After all, a town that boasted a culture club could not be altogether lost. Sabra had had no experience with this phase of social activity. The languorous yet acid Felice Venable had always scorned to take part in any civic social life that Wichita knew. Kansas, even then, had had its women's clubs, though they were not known by this title. The Ladies' Sewing Circle, one was called; the Twentieth Century Culture Society; the Hypatias.

Felice Venable, approached as a prospective member, had refused languidly.

"I just naturally hate sewing," she had drawled, looking up from the novel she was reading. "And as for culture! Why, the Venables and the Marcys have had it in this country for three hundred years, not to speak of England and France, where they practically started it going. Besides, I don't believe in women running around to club meetings. They'll be going into politics next."

Sabra timidly approached Mrs. Wyatt with her plan to form a woman's club, and Mrs. Wyatt snatched at it with such ferocity as almost to make it appear her own idea. Each was to invite four women of the town's élite. Ten, they decided, would be enough as charter members.

"I," began Mrs. Wyatt promptly, "am going to ask Mrs. Louie Hefner, Mrs. Doc Nisbett——"

"Her husband's horrid! I hate him. I don't want her in my club." The ten barrels of water still rankled.

"We're not asking husbands, my dear Mrs. Cravat. This is a ladies' club."

"Well, I don't think the wife of any such man could be a lady."

"Mrs. Nisbett," retorted Mrs. Wyatt, introducing snobbery into that welter of mud, Indians, pine shacks, drought, and semi-barbarism known as Osage, Indian Territory, "was a Krumpf, of Ouachita, Arkansas."

Sabra, descendant of the Marcys and the Venables, lifted her handsome black eyebrows. Privately, she decided to select her four from among the less vertebrate and more ebullient of Osage's matrons.

Culture was all very well, but the thought of mingling once every fort-
night with nine versions of the bony Mrs. Wyatt or the pedigreed Mrs.
Nisbett (née Krumpf) was depressing. She made up her mind that next
day, after the housework was done, she would call on her candidates,
beginning with that pretty and stylish Mrs. Evergreen Waltz. Sabra had
inherited a strain of frivolity from Felice Venable. At supper that evening
she told Yancey of her plans.

"We're going to take up literature, you know. And maybe early American history."

"Why, honey, don't you know you're making it?"

This she did not take seriously. "And then current events, too."

"Well, the events in this town are current enough. I'll say that for
them. The trick is to catch them as they go by. You girls'll have to be
quick." She told him of her four prospective members.

"Waltz's wife!" Surprise and amusement, too, were in his voice, but
she was too full of her plans to notice. Besides, Yancey often was mysti-
fyingly amused at things that seemed to Sabra quite serious. "Why, that's
fine, Sabra. That's fine! That's the spirit!"

"I noticed her at church meeting last Sunday. She's so pretty, it rests
me to look at her, after all these—not that they're—I don't mean they're
not very nice ladies. But after all, even if it's a culture club, someone
nearer my own age would be much more fun."

"Oh, much," Yancey agreed, still smiling. "That's what a town like
this should be. No class distinctions, no snobbery, no highfalutin no-
tions."

"I saw her washing hanging on the line. Just by accident. You can
tell she's a lady. Such pretty underthings, all trimmed with embroidery,
and there were two embroidery petticoats all flounced and every bit as
nice as the ones Cousin Belle French Vian made for me by hand, for
my trousseau."

"I'm not surprised." Yancey was less loquacious than usual. But then,
men were not interested in women's clothes.

"She looks kind of babyish and lonely, sitting there by the window
sewing all day. And her husband's so much older, and a cripple, too, or
almost. I noticed he limps quite badly. What's his trouble?"

"Shot in the leg."

"Oh." She had already learned to accept this form of injury as a matter of course. "I thought I'd ask her to prepare a paper for the third
meeting on Mrs. Browning's 'Aurora Leigh.' I could lend her yours to
read up on, if you don't mind, just in case she hasn't got it."

Yancey thought it unlikely.

Mrs. Wyatt's house was one of the few in Osage which were used for dwelling purposes alone. No store or office occupied the front of it. Tracy Wyatt's bus and dray line certainly could not be contained in a pine shack intended for family use. Mrs. Wyatt had five rooms. She was annoyingly proud of this, and referred to it on all possible occasions.

"The first meeting," she said, "will be held at my house, of course. It will be so much nicer."

She did not say nicer than what, but Sabra's face set itself in a sort of mask of icy stubbornness. "The first meeting of the Philomathean Society will be held at the home of the Founder." After all, Mrs. Wyatt's house could not boast a screen door, as Sabra's could. It was the only house in Osage that had one. Yancey had had Hefner order it from Kansas City. The wind and the flies seemed to torture Sabra. It was so unusual a luxury that frequently strangers came to the door by mistake, thinking that here was the butcher shop, which boasted the only other screen door in the town.

"I'll serve coffee and doughnuts," Sabra added, graciously. "And I'll move to elect you president. I"—this not without a flick of malice—"am too busy with my household and my child and the newspaper—I often assist my husband editorially—to take up with any more work."

The paper on Mrs. Browning's "Aurora Leigh" never was written by the pretty Mrs. Evergreen Waltz. Three days later Sabra, chancing to glance out of her sitting-room window, saw the crippled and middle-aged gambler passing her house, and in spite of his infirmity he was walking with great speed—running, almost. In his hand was a piece of white paper—a letter, Sabra thought. She hoped it was not bad news. He had looked, she thought, sort of odd and wild.

Evergreen Waltz, after weeks of tireless waiting and watching, had at last intercepted a letter from his young wife's lover. As he now came panting up the street the girl sat at the window, sewing. The single shot went just through the center of the wide white space between her great babyish blue eyes. They found her with the gold initialed thimble on her finger, and the bit of work on which she had been sewing, now brightly spotted with crimson, in her lap.

"Why didn't you tell me that when she married him she was a girl out of a—out of a—house!" Sabra demanded, between horror and wrath.

"I thought you knew. Women are supposed to have intuition, or whatever they call it, aren't they? All those embroidered underthings on the line in a town where water's scarce as champagne—scarcer. And then 'Aurora Leigh.'"

She was thoroughly enraged by now. "What, for pity's sake, has 'Aurora Leigh' got to do with her!"

He got down the volume. "I thought you'd been reading it yourself, perhaps." He opened it. " 'Dreams of doing good for good-for-nothing people.' "

XI

SABRA's second child, a girl, was born in June, a little more than a year after their coming to Osage. It was not as dreadful an ordeal there in those crude surroundings as one might have thought. She refused to send for her mother; indeed, Sabra insisted that Felice Venable be told nothing of the event until after her granddaughter had wailed her way into the Red Man's country. Yancey had been relieved at Sabra's decision. The thought of his luxury-loving and formidable mother-in-law with her flounced dimities and her high-heeled slippers in the midst of this Western wallow to which he had brought her daughter was a thing from which even the redoubtable Yancey shrank. Curiously enough, it was not the pain, the heat, nor the inexpert attention she received that most distressed Sabra. It was the wind. The Oklahoma wind tortured her. It rattled the doors and windows; it whirled the red dust through the house; its hot breath was on her agonized face as she lay there; if allowed its own way it leaped through the rooms, snatching the cloth off the table, the sheets off the bed, the dishes off the shelves.

"The wind!" Sabra moaned. "The wind! The wind! Make it stop." She was a little delirious. "Yancey! With your gun. Shoot it. Seven notches. I don't care. Only stop it."

She was tended, during her accouchement, by the best doctor in the county and certainly the most picturesque man of medicine in the whole Southwest, Dr. Don Valliant. Like thousands of others living in this new country, his past was his own secret. He rode to his calls on horseback, in a black velveteen coat and velveteen trousers tucked into fancy leather boots. His soft black hat, rivaling Yancey's white one, intensified the black of his eyes and hair. It was known that he often vanished for days, leaving the sick to get on as best they could. He would reappear as inexplicably as he had vanished; and it was noticed then that he was worn looking and his horse was jaded. It was no secret that he was often called to attend the bandits when one of their number, wounded in some out-

law raid, had taken to their hiding place in the Hills. He was tender
and deft with Sabra, though between them he and Yancey consumed
an incredible quantity of whisky during the racking hours of her confinement. At the end he held up a caterwauling morsel of flesh torn
from Sabra's flesh—a thing perfect of its kind, with an astonishing mop
of black hair.

"This is a Spanish beauty you have for a daughter, Yancey. I present
to you Señorita Doña Cravat."

And Donna Cravat she remained. The town, somewhat scandalized,
thought she had been named after Dr. Don himself. Besides, they did
not consider Donna a name at all. The other women of the community
fed their hunger for romance by endowing their girl children with such
florid names as they could conjure up out of their imagination or from
the novels they read between dish washings. The result was likely to
range from the pathetic to the ridiculous. Czarina McKee; Emmeretta
Folsom; Gazelle Slaughter; Maurine Turket; Cassandra Sipes; Jewel
Riggs.

The neighborhood wives showered the Cravat household with the
customary cakes, pies, meat loaves, and bowls of broth. Black Isaiah was
touching, was wonderful. He washed dishes, he mopped floors, he actually cooked as though he had inherited the art from Angie, his vast
black mother, left behind in Wichita. One of Sabra's gingham kitchen
aprons, checked blue and white, was always hitched up under his arms,
and beneath this utilitarian yet coquettish garment his great bare feet
slapped in and out as he did the work of the household. He was utterly
fascinated by the new baby. "Looka dat! She know me! Hi, who yo'
rollin' yo' eyes at, makin' faces!" He danced for her, he sang negro songs
to her, he rocked her to sleep. He was, as Donna grew older, her nursemaid, pushing her baby buggy up and down the dusty street, and later
still her playmate as well as Cim's.

When Sabra Cravat arose from that bed something in her had crystal-
lized. Perhaps it was that, for the first time in a year, she had had hours
in which to rest her tired limbs; perhaps the ordeal itself worked a
psychic as well as a physical change in her; it might have been that she
realized she must cut a new pattern in this Oklahoma life of theirs.
The boy Cim might surmount it; the girl Donna never. During the
hours through which she had lain in her bed in the stifling wooden
shack, mists seemed to have rolled away from before her eyes. She saw
clearly. She felt light and terribly capable—so much so that she made the
mistake of getting up, dizzily donning slippers and wrapper, and tottering
into the newspaper office where Yancey was writing an editorial and

shouting choice passages of it into the inattentive ear of Jesse Rickey, who was setting type in the printing shop.

". . . the most stupendous farce ever conceived by the mind of man in a civilized country. . . ."

He looked up to see in the doorway a wraith, all eyes and long black braids. "Why, sugar! What's this? You can't get up!"

She smiled rather feebly. "I'm up. I felt so light, so——"

"I should think you would. All that physic."

"I feel so strong. I'm going to do so many things. You'll see. I'm going to paper the whole house. Rosebuds in the bedroom. I'm going to plant two trees in the front. I'm going to start another club—not like the Philomathean—I think that's silly now—but one to make this town . . . no saloons . . . women like that Dixie Lee . . . going to have a real hired girl as soon as the newspaper begins to . . . feel so queer . . . Yancey . . ."

As she began to topple, Yancey caught the Osage Joan of Arc in his arms.

Incredibly enough, she actually did paper the entire house, aided by Isaiah and Jesse Rickey. Isaiah's ebony countenance splashed with the white paste mixture made a bizarre effect, a trifle startling to anyone coming upon the scene unawares. Also Jesse Rickey's inebriate eye, which so often resulted in many grotesque pied print lines appearing in unexpected and inconvenient places in the *Oklahoma Wigwam* columns, was none too dependable in the matching of rosebud patterns. The result, in spots, was Burbankian, with roses grafted on leaves and tendrils emerging from petals. Still, the effect was gay, even luxurious. The Philomathean Club, as one woman, fell upon wall paper and paste pot, as they had upon the covered jars in Sabra's earlier effort at decoration. Within a month Louie Hefner was compelled to install a full line of wall paper to satisfy the local demand.

Slowly, slowly, the life of the community, in the beginning so wild, so unrelated in its parts, began to weave in and out, warp and woof, to make a pattern. It was at first faint, almost undiscernible. But presently the eye could trace here a motif, there a figure, here a motif, there a figure. The shuttle swept back, forward, back, forward.

"It's almost time for the Jew," Sabra would say, looking up from her sewing. "I need some number forty sewing-machine needles."

And then perhaps next day, or the day after, Cim, playing in the yard, would see a familiar figure, bent almost double, gnomelike and grotesque, against the western sky. It was Sol Levy, the peddler, the Alsatian Jew. Cim would come running into the house, Donna, perhaps, trotting at his heels. "Mom, here comes the Jew!"

Sabra would fold up her work, brush the threads from her apron; or if her hands were in the dough she would hastily mold and crimp her pie crust so as to be ready for his visit.

Sol Levy had come over an immigrant in the noisome bowels of some dreadful ship. His hair was blue-black and very thick, and his face was white in spite of the burning Southwest sun. A black stubble of beard intensified this pallor. He had delicate blue-veined hands and narrow arched feet. His face was delicate, too, and narrow, and his eyes slanted ever so little at the outer corners, so that he had the faintly Oriental look sometimes seen in the student type of his race. He belonged in crowded places, in populous places, in the color and glow and swift drama of the bazaars. God knows how he had found his way to this vast wilderness. Perhaps in Chicago, or in Kansas City, or Omaha he had heard of this new country and the rush of thousands for its land. And he had bummed his way on foot. He had started to peddle with an oil-cloth-covered pack on his back. Through the little hot Western towns in summer. Through the bitter cold Western towns in winter. They turned the dogs on him. The children cried, "Jew! Jew!" He was only a boy, disguised with that stubble of beard. He would enter the yard of a farm-house or a dwelling in a town such as Osage. A wary eye on the dog. Nice Fido. Nice doggie. Down, down! Pins, sewing-machine needles, rolls of gingham and calico, and last, craftily, his Hamburg lace. Hamburg lace for the little girls' petticoats, for the aprons of the lady of the house; the white muslin apron edged with Hamburg lace, to be donned after the midday dinner dishes were done, the house set to rights, her hair tidied with a wet comb, the basket of mending got out, or the roll of strips for the rag rug, to be plaited in the precious hours between three and five. He brought news, too.

"The bridge is out below Gray Horse. . . . The Osages are having a powwow at Hominy. All night they kept me awake with their drums, those savages. . . . The Kid and his gang held up the Santa Fé near Wetoka and got thirty-five thousand dollars; but one of them will never hold up a train again. A shot in the head. Verdigris Bob, they call him. A name! They say the posse almost caught the Kid himself because this Verdigris Bob when he finds he is dying he begs the others to leave him and go on, but first they must stop to take his boots off. His boots he wants to have off, that murderer, to die a respectable man! The Kid stops to oblige him, and the posse in ten more minutes would have caught him, too. A feather in that sheriff's cap, to catch the Kid! . . . A country! My forefathers should have lived to see me here!"

His beautiful, civilized face, mobile as an actor's, was at once expressive of despair and bitter amusement. His long slender hands were spread in a gesture of wondering resignation.

Later he bought a horse—a quadruped possessed unbelievably of the power of locomotion—a thing rheumy-eyed, cadaverous, high rumped, like a cloth horse in a pantomime. Sol Levy was always a little afraid of it; timorous of those great square white teeth, like gravestones. He came of a race of scholars and traders. Horses had been no part of their experience. He had to nerve himself to wait on it, to give it the feed bag, an occasional apple or lump of sugar. With the horse and rickety wagon he now added kitchenware to his stock, coarse china, too; bolts of woollen cloth; and, slyly, bright colored silks and muslin flowers and ribbons. Dixie Lee and her girls fell upon these with feverish fingers and shrill cries, like children. He spread his wares for them silently. Sometimes they teased him, these pretty morons; they hung on his meager shoulders, stroked his beard. He regarded them remotely, almost sadly.

"Come on, Solly!" they said. "Why don't you smile? Don't you never have no fun? I bet you're rich. Jews is all rich. Ain't that the truth, Maude?"

His deep-sunk eyes looked at them. *Schicksas*. They grew uncomfortable under his gaze, then sullen, then angry. "Go on, get the hell out of here! You got your money, ain't you? Get, sheeny!"

He sometimes talked to Dixie Lee. There existed between these two a strange relation of understanding and something resembling respect. Outcasts, both of them, he because of his race, she because of her calling. "A smart girl like you, what do you want in such a business?"

"I've got to live, Solly. God knows why!"

"You come from a good family. You are young yet, you are smart. There are other ways."

"Ye-e-e-s? I guess I'll take up school teaching. Tell a lot of snotty-nosed brats that two and two make four and get handed eleven dollars at the end of the month for it. I tried a couple of things. Nix, nix!"

In a year or two he opened a little store in Osage. It was, at first, only a wooden shack containing two or three rough pine tables on which his wares were spread. He was the town Jew. He was a person apart. Sometimes the cowboys deviled him; or the saloon loungers and professional bad men. They looked upon him as fair game. He thought of them as savages. Yancey came to his rescue one day in the spectacular fashion he enjoyed. Seated at his desk in the *Wigwam* office Yancey heard hoots, howls, catcalls, and then the crack and rat-a-tat-tat of a fusillade. The porch of the Sunny Southwest Saloon was filled with grinning faces beneath sombreros. In the middle of the dusty road, his back against a Howe scale, stood Sol Levy. They had tried to force him to drink a great glass of whisky straight. He had struggled, coughed, sputtered; had succeeded in spitting out the burning stuff. They had got another. They were holding it up from their vantage point on the porch. Their six-shooters were in their hands. And they were shooting at him—at his feet, at his head, at his hands, expertly, devilishly, miraculously, never hitting him, but always careful to come within a fraction of an inch. He had no weapon. He would not have known how to use it if he had possessed one. He was not of a race of fighters.

"Drink it!" The yells were high and less than human. "You're a dead Jew if you don't. Dance, gol darn you! Dance for your drink!"

The bullets spat all about him, sang past his ears, whipped up the dust about his feet. He did not run. He stood there, facing them, frozen with fear. His arms hung at his sides. His face was deathly white. They had shot off his hat. He was bareheaded. His eyes were sunken, suffering, stricken. His head lolled a little on one side. His thick black locks hung dank on his forehead. At that first instant of seeing him as he rushed out of his office, Yancey thought, subconsciously, "He looks like—like ——" But the resemblance eluded him then. It was only later, after the sickening incident had ended, that he realized of Whom it was that the Jew had reminded him as he stood there, crucified against the scale.

Yancey ran into the road. It is impossible to say how he escaped being killed by one of the bullets. He seemed to leap into the thick of them like a charmed thing. As he ran he whipped out his own ivory-handled guns, and at that half the crowd on the saloon porch made a dash for the door and were caught in it and fell sprawling, and picked themselves up, and crawled or ran again until they were inside. Yancey stood beside Sol Levy, the terrible look in his eyes, the great head thrust forward and down, like a buffalo charging. Here was a scene to his liking.

"I'll drill the first son of a bitch that fires another shot. I will, so help me God! Go on, fire now, you dirty dogs. You filthy loafers. You stinking spawn of a rattlesnake!"

He was, by now, a person in the community—he was, in fact, the person in the town. The porch loafers looked sheepish. They sheathed their weapons, or twirled them, sulkily.

"Aw, Yancey, we was foolin'!"

"We was only kiddin' the Jew. . . . Lookit him, the white-livered son of a gun. Lookit—Holy Doggie, look at him! He's floppin'."

With a little sigh Sol Levy slid to the dust of the road and lay in a crumpled heap at the foot of the Howe scale. It was at that moment, so curiously does the human mind work, that Yancey caught that elusive resemblance. Now he picked the man up and flung him over his great shoulder as he would a sack of meal.

"Yah!" hooted the jokesters, perhaps a little shamefaced now.

Yancey, on his way to his own house so near by, made first a small detour that brought him to the foot of the tobacco-stained saloon porch steps. His eyes were like two sword blades flashing in the sun.

"Greasers! Scum of the Run! Monkey skulls!"

His limp burden dangling over his shoulder, he now strode through the *Wigwam* office, into the house, and laid him gently down on the sitting-room couch. Revived, Sol Levy stopped to midday dinner with the Cravats. He sat, very white, very still, in his chair and made delicate pretense of eating. Sabra, because Yancey asked her to, though she was mystified, had got out her DeGrasse silver and a set of her linen. His long meager fingers dwelt lingeringly on the fine hand-wrought stuff. His deep-sunk haunting eyes went from Sabra's clear-cut features, with the bold determined brows, to Yancey's massive head, then to the dazzling freshness of the children's artless countenances.

"This is the first time that I have sat at such a table in two years. My mother's table was like this, in the old country. My father—peace to his soul!—lighted the candles. My mother—sainted—spread the table with her linen and her precious thin silver. Here in this country I eat as we would not have allowed a beggar to eat that came to the door for charity."

"This Oklahoma country's no place for you, Sol. It's too rough, too hard. You come of a race of dreamers."

The melancholy eyes took on a remote—a prophetic look. There was, suddenly, a slight cast in them, as though he were turning his vision toward something the others could not see. "It will not always be like this. Wait. Those savages to-day will be myths, like the pictures of monsters you see in books of prehistoric days."

"Don't worry about those dirty skunks, Sol. I'll see that they leave you alone from now on."

Sol Levy smiled a little bitter smile. His thin shoulders lifted in a weary shrug. "Those barbarians! My ancestors were studying the Talmud and writing the laws the civilized world now lives by when theirs were swinging from tree to tree."

XII

In the three and a half years of her residence in Osage Sabra had yielded hardly an inch. It was amazing. It was heroic. She had set herself certain standards, and those she had maintained in spite of almost overwhelming opposition. She had been bred on tradition. If she had yielded at all it was in minor matters and because to do so was expedient. True, she could be seen of a morning on her way to the butcher's or the grocer's shielded from the sun by one of the gingham sunbonnets which in the beginning she had despised. Certainly one could not don a straw bonnet, velvet or flower trimmed, to dart out in a calico house dress for the purchase of a pound and a half of round steak, ten cents worth of onions, and a yeast cake.

Once only in those three years had she gone back to Wichita. At the prospect of the journey she had been in a fever of anticipation for days. She had taken with her Cim and Donna. She was so proud of them, so intent on outfitting them with a wardrobe sufficiently splendid to set off their charms, that she neglected the matter of her own costuming and found herself arriving in Wichita with a trunk containing the very clothes with which she had departed from it almost four years earlier. Prominent among these was the green nun's veiling with the pink ruchings. She had had little enough use for it in these past years or for the wine-colored silk-warp henrietta.

"Your skin!" Felice Venable had exclaimed at sight of her daughter. "Your hands! Your hair! As dry as a bone! You look a million. What have you done to yourself?"

Sabra remembered something that Yancey once had said about Texas. Mischievously she paraphrased it in order to shock her tactless mother. "Oklahoma is fine for men and horses, but it's hell on women and oxen."

The visit was not a success. The very things she had expected to enjoy fell, somehow, flat. She missed the pace, the exhilarating uncertainty of the Oklahoma life. The teacup conversation of her girlhood friends seemed to lack tang and meaning. Their existence was orderly, calm, accepted. For herself and the other women of Osage there was everything still to do. There lay a city, a county, a whole vast Territory to be swept and garnished by an army of sunbonnets. Paradoxically enough, she was trying to implant in the red clay of Osage the very forms and institutions that now bored her in Wichita. Yet it was, perhaps, a very human trait. It was illustrated literally by the fact that she was, on her return, more thrilled to find that the scrawny elm, no larger than a baby's arm, which she had planted outside the doorway in Osage, actually had found some moisture for its thirsty roots, and was now feebly vernal, than she had been at sight of the cool glossy canopy of cedar, arbor vitae, sweet locust, and crêpe myrtle that shaded the Kansas garden. She took a perverse delight in bringing the shocked look to the faces of her Wichita friends, and to all the horde of Venables and Marcys and Vians that swarmed up from the South to greet the pioneer. Curiously enough, it was not the shooting affrays and Indian yarns that ruffled them so much as her stories of the town's social life.

". . . rubber boots to parties, often, because when it rains we wade up to our ankles in mud. We carry lanterns when we go to the church sociables. . . . Mrs. Buckner's sister came to visit her from St. Joseph, Missouri, and she remarked that she had noticed that the one pattern of table silver seemed to be such a favorite. She had seen it at all the little tea parties that had been given for her during her visit. Of course it was my set that had been the rounds. Everybody borrowed it. We borrow each other's lamps, too, and china, and even linen."

At this the Venables and Marcys and Vians and Goforths looked not only shocked but stricken. Chests of lavender-scented linen, sideboards flashing with stately silver, had always been part of the Venable and Marcy tradition.

Then the children. The visiting Venables insisted on calling Cim by his full name—Cimarron. Sabra had heard it so rarely since the day of his birth that she now realized, for the first time, how foolish she had been to yield to Yancey's whim in the naming of the boy. Cimarron. Spanish: wild, or unruly. The boy had made such an obstreperous entrance into the world, and Yancey had shouted, in delight, "Look at him! See him kick with his feet and strike out with his fists! He's a wild one. Heh, Cimarron! *Peceno Gitano.*"

Cousin Jouett Goforth or Cousin Dabney Venable said, pompously, "And now, Cimarron, my little man, tell us about the big red Indians. Did you ever fight Indians, eh, Cimarron?" The boy surveyed them from beneath his long lashes, his head lowered, looking for all the world like his father.

Cimarron was almost eight now. If it is possible for a boy of eight to be romantic in aspect, Cimarron Cravat was that. His head was not large, like Yancey's, but long and fine, like Sabra's—a Venable head. His eyes were Sabra's, too, dark and large, but they had the ardent look of

Yancey's gray ones, and he had Yancey's absurdly long and curling
lashes, like a beautiful girl's. His mannerisms—the head held down, the
rare upward glance that cut you like a sword thrust when he turned it
full on you—the swing of his walk, the way he gestured with his delicate
hands—all these were Yancey in startling miniature.

His speech was strangely adult. This, perhaps, because of his close
association with his elders in those first formative years in Osage. Yancey
had delighted in talking to the boy; in taking him on rides and drives
about the broad burning countryside. His skin was bronzed the color
of his father's. He looked like a little patrician Spaniard or perhaps (the
Venables thought privately) part Indian. Then, too, there had been few
children of his age in the town's beginning. Sabra had been, at first, too
suspicious of such as there were. He would, probably, have seemed a
rather unpleasant and priggish little boy if his voice and manner had not
been endowed miraculously with all the charm and magnetism that his
father possessed in such disarming degree.

He now surveyed his middle-aged cousins with the concentrated and
disconcerting gaze of the precocious child.

"Indians," he answered, with great distinctness, "don't fight white men
any more. They can't. Their—uh—spirit is broken." Cousin Dabney
Venable, who still affected black stocks (modified), now looked slightly
apoplectic. "They only fought in the first place because the white men
took their buff'loes away from them, that they lived on and ate and
traded the skins and that was all they had; and their land away from
them."

"Well," exclaimed Cousin Jouett Goforth, of the Louisiana Goforths,
"this is quite a little Redskin you have here, Cousin Sabra."

"And," continued Cimarron, warming to his subject, "look at the
Osage Indians where my father took me to visit the reservation near
where we live. The white people made them move out of Missouri to
Kansas because they wanted their land, and from there to another place
—I forget—and then they wanted that, too, and they said, 'Look, you
go and live in the Indian Territory where we tell you,' and it's all bare
there, and nothing grows in that place—it's called the Bad Lands—unless
you work and slave and the Osages they were used to hunting and fishing not farming, so they are just starving to death and my father says
some day they will get their revenge on the white——"

Felice Venable turned her flashing dark gaze on her daughter.

"Aha!" said Cousin Jouett Goforth.

Cousin Dabney Venable, still the disgruntled suitor, brought malicious
eyes to bear on Sabra. "Well, well, Cousin Sabra! Look out that you don't
have a Pocahontas for a daughter-in-law some fine day."

Sabra was furious, though she tried in her pride to conceal it. "Oh, Cim has just heard the talk of the men around the newspaper office—the Indian agent, Mr. Heeney, sometimes drops in on his trips to Osage—they're talking now of having the Indian Agent's office transferred to Osage, though Oklahoma City is fighting for it—Yancey has always been very much stirred by the wretched Indians—Cim has heard him talking."

Cim sensed that he had not made the desired effect on his listeners. "My father says," he announced, suddenly, striding up and down the room in absurd and unconscious imitation of his idol—one could almost see the Prince Albert coat tails switching—"my father says that some day an Indian will be President of the United States, and then you bet you'll all be sorry you were such dirty skunks to 'em."

The eyes of the visiting Venables swung, as one orb, from the truculent figure of the boy to the agitated face of the mother.

"My poor child!" came from Felice Venable in accents of rage rather than pity. She was addressing Sabra.

Sabra took refuge in hauteur. "You wouldn't understand. Our life there is so different from yours here. Yancey's Indian editorials in the *Wigwam* have made a sensation. They were spoken of in the Senate at Washington." Felice dismissed all Yancey's written works with a wave of her hand. "In fact," Sabra went on—she who hated Indians and all their ways—"in fact, his editorials on the subject have been so fearless and free that he has been in danger of his life from the people who have been cheating the Indians. It has been even more dangerous than when he tracked down the murderer of Pegler."

"Pegler," repeated the Venables, disdainfully, and without the slightest curiosity in their voices.

Sabra gave it up. "You don't understand. The only thing you care about is whether the duck runs red or not."

Even little Donna was not much of a success. The baby was an eerie little elf, as plain as the boy was handsome. She resembled her grandmother, Felice Venable, without a trace of that redoubtable matron's former beauty. But she had that almost indefinable thing known as style. At the age of two she wore with undeniable chic the rather clumsy little garments that Sabra had so painstakingly made for her; and when she was dressed, for the first time, in one of the exquisitely hemstitched, tucked and embroidered white frocks that her grandmother had wrought for her, that gifted though reluctant needlewoman said, tartly, "Thank God, she's got style, at least. She'll have to make out with that."

All in all, Sabra found herself joyously returning to the barren burning country to which, four years earlier, she had gone in such dread and terror. She resented her mother's do-this, do-that. She saw Felice Venable now, no longer as a power, an authority in all matters of importance, but as a sallow old lady who tottered on heels that were too high and who, as she sat talking, pleated and unpleated with tremulous fingers the many ruffles of her white dimity wrapper. The matriarch had lost her crown. Sabra was matriarch now of her own little kingdom; and already she was planning to extend that realm beyond and beyond its present confines into who knows what vastness of demesne.

She decided that she must take the children more than ever in hand. No more of this talk of Indians, of freedom, or equality of man. She did not realize (it being long before the day of psychology as applied so glibly to the training of children) that she was, so far as Cim was concerned, years too late. At eight his character was formed. She had taught him the things that Felice Venable had taught her—stand up straight; eat your bread and butter; wash your hands; say how do you do to the lady; one and one are two; somebody has been eating *my* porridge, said the little wee bear. But Yancey had taught him poetry far beyond his years, and accustomed his ears to the superb cadences of the Bible; Yancey had told him, bit by bit, and all unconsciously, the saga of the settling of the great Southwest.

"Cowboys wear big sombreros to shield their faces from the rain and the sun when they're riding the range, and the snow from dripping down their backs. He wears a handkerchief knotted at the back of the neck and hanging down in front so that he can wipe the sweat and dust from his face with it, and then there it is, open, drying in the wind; and in a dust storm he pulls it over his mouth and nose, and in a blizzard it keeps his nose and chin from freezing. He wears chaps, with the hairy side out, to keep his legs warm in winter and to protect them from being torn by chaparral and cactus thorns in summer. His boots are high heeled to keep his feet from slipping in the stirrups when he has to work standing in the saddle, and because he can sink them in the sod when he's off his horse and roping a plunging bronc. He totes a six-shooter to keep the other fellow from shooting."

The child's eyes were enormous, glowing, enthralled. Yancey told him the story of the buffalo; he talked endlessly of the Indians. He even taught him some words of Comanche, which is the court language of the Indian. He put him on a horse at the age of six. A sentimentalist and a romantic, he talked to the boy of the sunset; of Spanish gold; of the wild days of the Cimarron and the empire so nearly founded there. The boy loved his mother dutifully, and as a matter of course, as a child loves the fount of food, of tender care, of shelter. But his father he worshiped, he adored.

Sabra's leave-taking held one regret, one pain. Mother Bridget had died two weeks before Sabra arrived in Wichita. It was not until she learned this sad news that Sabra realized how tremendously she had counted on telling her tale of Osage to the nun. She would have understood. She would have laughed at the story of the ten barrels of water; of the wild cowboy's kiss in the road; she would have sympathized with Sabra's terror during that Sunday church meeting. She had known that very life a half century ago, there in Kansas. Sabra, during her visit, did not go to the Mission School. She could not.

She had meant, at the last, to find occasion to inform her mother and the minor Venables that it was she who ironed Yancey's fine white linen shirts. But she was not a spiteful woman. And she reflected that this might be construed as a criticism of her husband.

So, gladly, eagerly, Sabra went back to the wilds she once had despised.

XIII

Before the Katy pulled in at the Osage station (the railroad actually had been extended, true to Dixie Lee's prediction, from Wahoo to Osage and beyond) Sabra's eyes were searching the glaring wooden platform. Len Orsen, the chatty and accommodating conductor, took Donna in his arms and stood with her at the foot of the car steps. His heavy gold plated watch chain, as broad as a cable, with its concomitant Masonic charm, elk's tooth, gold pencil and peach pit carved in the likeness of an ape, still held Donna enthralled, though she had snatched at it whenever he passed their seat or stood to relate the gossip of the Territory to Sabra. She was hungry for news, and Len was a notorious fishwife. Now, as she stepped off the train, Sabra's face wore that look of radiant expectancy characteristic of the returned traveler, confident of a welcome.

"Well, I guess I know somebody'll be pretty sorry to see you," Len said, archly. He looked about for powerful waiting arms in which to deposit Donna. The engine bell clanged, the whistle tooted. His kindly and inquisitive blue eyes swept the station platform. He plumped Donna, perforce, into Sabra's strangely slack arms, and planted one foot, in its square-toed easy black shoe, onto the car step in the nick of time, the other leg swinging out behind him as the train moved on.

Yancey was not there. The stark red-painted wooden station sat blistering in the sun. Yancey simply was not there. Not only that, the station platform, usually graced by a score of vacuous faces and limp figures gathered to witness the exciting event of the Katy's daily arrival and departure, was bare. Even the familiar figure of Pat Leary, the station agent, who always ran out in his shirt sleeves to wrestle such freight or express as was left on the Osage platform, could not be seen. From within the ticket office came the sound of his telegraph instrument. Its click was busy; was frantic. It chattered unceasingly in the hot afternoon stillness.

Sabra felt sick and weak. Something was wrong. She left her boxes and bags and parcels on the platform where Len Orsen had obligingly dumped them. Half an hour before their arrival in Osage she had entrusted the children to the care of a fellow passenger while she had gone to the washroom to put on one of the new dresses made in Wichita and bearing the style cachet of Kansas City: green, with cream colored ruchings at the throat and wrists, and a leghorn hat with pink roses. She had anticipated the look in Yancey's gray eyes at sight of it. She had made the children spotless and threatened them with dire things if they sullied their splendor before their father should see them.

And now he was not there.

With Donna in her arms and Cim at her heels she hurried toward the sound of the clicking. And as she went her eyes still scanned the dusty red road that led to the station, for sight of a great figure in a white sombrero, its coat tails swooping as it came.

She peered in at the station window. Pat Leary was bent over his telegraph key. A smart tight little Irishman who had come to the Territory with the railroad section crew when the Katy was being built. Station agent now, and studying law at night.

"Mr. Leary! Mr. Leary! Have you seen Yancey?" He looked up at her absently, his hand still on the key. Click . . . click . . . clickclick-clickety—clicketyclickclick.

"Wha' say?"

"I'm Mrs. Cravat. I just got off the Katy. Where's my husband? Where's Yancey?"

He clicked on a moment longer; then wiped his wet forehead with his forearm protected by the black sateen sleevelet. "Ain't you heard?"

"No," whispered Sabra, with stiff lips that seemed no part of her. Then, in a voice rising to a scream, "No! No! No! What? Is he dead?"

The Irishman came over to her then, as she crouched at the window.

"Oh, no, ma'am. Yancey's all right. He ain't hurt to speak of. Just a nick in the arm—and left arm at that."

"Oh, my God!"

"Don't take on. You goin' to faint or——?"

"No. Tell me."

"I been so busy. . . . Yancey got the Kid, you know. Killed him. The whole town's gone crazy. Pitched battle right there on Pawhuska Avenue in front of the bank, and bodies layin' around like a battlefield. I'm sending it out. I ain't got much time, but I'll give you an idea. Biggest thing that's happened in the history of the Territory—or the whole Southwest, for that matter. Shouldn't wonder if they'd make Yancey President. Governor, anyway. Seems Yancey was out hunting up in the Hills last Thursday——"

"Thursday! But that's the day the paper comes out."

"Well, the *Wigwam* ain't been so regular since you been away." She allowed that to pass without comment. "Up in the Hills he stumbles on Doc Valliant, drunk, but not so drunk he don't recognize Yancey. Funny thing about Doc Valliant. He can be drunker'n a fool, but one part of his brain stays clear as a diamond. I seen him take a bullet out of Luke Slaughter once and sew him up when he was so drunk he didn't know his right hand from his left, or where he was at, but he done it. What? Oh, yeh—well, he tells Yancey, drunk as he is, that he's right in the camp where the Kid and his gang is hiding out. One of them was hurt bad in that last Santa Fé hold-up at Cimarron. Like to died, only they sent for Doc, and he come and saved him. They got close to thirty thousand that trick, and it kind of went to their head. Valliant overheard them planning to ride in here to Osage, like to-day, and hold up the Citizens' National in broad daylight like the Kid always does. They was already started. Well, Yancey off on his horse to warn the town, and knows he's got to detour or he'll come on the gang and they'll smell a rat. Well, say, he actually did meet 'em. Came on 'em, accidental. The Kid sees him and grins that wolf grin of his and sings out, 'Yancey, you still runnin' that paper of yourn down at Osage?' Yancey says, 'Yes.' 'Well, say,' he says, 'how much is it?' Yancey says a dollar a year. The Kid reaches down and throws Yancey a shot sack with ten silver dollars in it. 'Send me the paper for ten years,' he says. 'Where to?' Yancey asks him. Well, say, the Kid laughs that wolf laugh of his again and he says, 'I never thought of that. I'll have to leave you know later.' Well, Yancey, looking as meek and mealy-mouthed as a baby, he rides his way, he's got a little book of poems in his hand and he's reading as he rides, or pretending to, but first chance he sees he cuts across the Hills, puts his horse through the gullies and into the draws and across the scrub oaks like he was a circus horse or a centipede or something. He gets into Osage, dead tired and his horse in a lather, ten minutes before the Kid and his gang sweeps down Pawhuska Avenue, their six-shooters barking like a regiment was coming, and makes a rush for the bank. But the town is expecting them. Say! Blood!"

Sabra waited for no more. She turned. And as she turned she saw coming down the road in a cloud of dust a grotesque scarecrow, all shanks and teeth and rolling eyes. Black Isaiah.

"No'm, Miss Sabra, he ain't hurt—not what yo' rightly call hurt. No, ma'am. Jes' a nip in de arm, and he got it slung in a black silk hank'chief and looks right sma't handsome. They wouldn't let him alone noways. Ev'ybody in town they shakin' his hand caze he shoot the shot dat kill de Kid. An' you know what he do then, Miss Sabra? He kneel down an' he cry like a baby. . . . Le' me tote dis yere valise. Ah kin tote Miss Donna, too. My, she sho' growed!"

The newspaper office, the print shop, her parlor, her kitchen, her bedroom, were packed with men in boots, spurs, sombreros; men in overalls; with women; with children. Mrs. Wyatt was there—the Philomatheans as one woman were there; Dixie Lee, actually; everyone but—sinisterly——Louie Hefner.

"Well, Mis' Cravat, I guess you must be pretty proud of him! . . . This is a big day for Osage. I guess Oklahoma City knows this town's on the map now, all right. . . . You missed the shootin', Mis' Cravat, but you're in time to help Yancey celebrate. . . . Say, the Santa Fé alone offered five thousand dollars for the capture of the Kid, dead or alive. Yancey gets it, all right. And the Katy done the same. And they's a government price on his head, and the Citizens' National is making up a purse. You'll be ridin' in your own carriage, settin' in silks, from now."

Yancey was standing at his desk in the *Wigwam* office. His back was against the desk, as though he were holding this crowd at bay instead of welcoming them as congratulatory guests. His long locks hung limp on his shoulders. His face was white beneath the tan, like silver under lacquer. His great head lolled on his chest. His left arm lay in a black and scarlet silk sling made of one of his more piratical handkerchiefs.

He looked up as she came in, and at the look in his face she forgave him his neglect of her; forgave him the house full of what Felice Venable would term riffraff and worse; his faithlessness to the *Wigwam*. Donna, tired and frightened, had set up a wail. Cim, bewildered, had gone on a rampage. But as Yancey took a stumbling step toward her she had only one child, and that one needed her. She thrust Donna again into Isaiah's arms; left Cim whirling among the throng; ran toward him. She was in his great arms, but it was her arms that seemed to sustain him.

"Sabra. Sugar. Send them away. I'm so tired. Oh, God, I'm so tired."

Next day they exhibited the body of the Kid in the new plate glass show window of Hefner's Furniture Store and Undertaking Parlors. All Osage came to view him, all the county came to view him; they rode in on trains, on horses, in wagons, in ox carts for miles and miles around. The Kid. The boy who, in his early twenties, had sent no one knew how many men to their death—whose name was the symbol for terror and daring and merciless marauding throughout the Southwest. Even in the East—in New York—the name of the Kid was known. Stories had been written about him. He was, long before his death, a mythical figure. And now he, together with Clay McNulty, his lieutenant, lay side by side, quite still, quite passive. The crowd was so dense that it threatened Louie Hefner's window. He had to put up rope barriers to protect it, and when the mob surged through these he stationed guards with six-shooters, and there was talk of calling out the militia from Fort Tipton. Sabra said it was disgusting, uncivilized. She forbade Cim to go within five hundred yards of the place—kept him, in fact, virtually a prisoner in the yard. Isaiah she could not hold. His lean black body could be seen squirming in and out of the crowds; his ebony face, its eyes popping, was always in the front row of the throng gloating before Hefner's window. He became, in fact, a sort of guide and unofficial lecturer, holding forth upon the Kid, his life, his desperate record, the battle in which he met his death in front of the bank he had meant to despoil.

"Well, you got to hand it to him," the men said, gazing their fill. "He wasn't no piker. When he held up a train or robbed a bank or shot up a posse it was always in broad daylight, by God. Middle of the day he'd come riding into town. No nitroglycerin for him, or shootin' behind fence posts and trees in the dark. Nosiree! Out in the open, and takin' a bigger chance than them that was robbed. Ride! Say, you couldn't tell which was him and which was horse. They was one piece. And shoot! It wa'n't shootin'. It was magic. They say he's got half a million in gold cached away up in the Hills."

For weeks, for months, the hills were honeycombed with prowlers in search of this buried treasure.

Sabra did a strange, a terrible thing. Yancey would not go near the grisly window. Sabra upheld him; denounced the gaping crowd as scavengers and ghouls. Then, suddenly, at the last minute, as the sun was setting blood red across the prairie, she walked out of the house, down the road, as if impelled, as if in a trance, like a sleep walker, and stood before Hefner's window. The crowd made way for her respectfully. They knew her. This was the wife of Yancey Cravat, the man whose name appeared in headlines in every newspaper throughout the United States, and even beyond the ocean.

They had dressed the two bandits in new cheap black suits of store clothes, square in cut, clumsy, so that they stood woodenly away from the lean hard bodies. Clay McNulty's face had a faintly surprised look. His long sandy mustaches drooped over a mouth singularly sweet and resigned. But the face of the boy was fixed in a smile that brought the lips in a sardonic snarl away from the wolf-like teeth. He looked older in death than he had in life, for his years had been too few for lines such as death's fingers usually erase; and the eyes, whose lightning glance had pierced you through and through like one of the bullets from his own dreaded six-shooters, now were extinguished forever behind the waxen shades of his eyelids.

It was at the boy that Sabra looked; and having looked she turned and walked back to the house.

They gave them a decent funeral and a burial with everything in proper order, and when the minister refused to read the service over these two sinners Yancey consented to do it and did, standing there with the fresh-turned mounds of red Oklahoma clay sullying his fine high-heeled boots, and the sun blazing down upon the curling locks of his uncovered head.

" 'Whoso sheddeth man's blood, by man shall his blood be shed. . . . His hand will be against every man, and every man's hand against him. . . . The words of his mouth were smoother than butter, but war was in his heart. . . . Fools make mock at sin. . . .' "

They put up two rough wooden slabs, marking the graves. But souvenir hunters with little bright knives soon made short work of those. The two mounds sank lower, lower. Soon nothing marked this spot on the prairie to differentiate it from the red clay that stretched for miles all about it.

They sent to Yancey, by mail, in checks, and through solemn committees in store clothes and white collars, the substantial money rewards that, for almost five years, had been offered by the Santa Fé road, the M.K. & T., the government itself, and various banks, for the capture of the Kid, dead or alive.

Yancey refused every penny of it. The committees, the townspeople, the county, were shocked and even offended. Sabra, tight lipped, at last broke out in protest.

"We could have a decent house—a new printing press—Cim's education—Donna——"

"I don't take money for killing a man," Yancey repeated, to each offer of money. The committees and the checks went back as they had come.

XIV

SABRA noticed that Yancey's hand shook with a perceptible palsy before breakfast, and that this was more than ever noticeable as that hand approached the first drink of whisky which he always swallowed before he ate a morsel. He tossed it down as one who, seeking relief from pain, takes medicine. When he returned the glass to the table he drew a deep breath. His hand was, miraculously, quite steady.

More and more he neglected the news and business details of the *Wigwam.* He was restless, moody, distrait. Sabra remembered with a pang of dismay something that he had said on first coming to Osage. "God, when I think of those years in Wichita! Almost five years in one place—that's the longest stretch I've ever done."

The newspaper was prospering, for Sabra gave more and more time to it. But Yancey seemed to have lost interest, as he did in any venture once it got under way. It was now a matter of getting advertisements, taking personal and local items, recording the events in legal, real estate, commercial, and social circles. Mr. and Mrs. Abel Dagley spent Sunday in Chuckmubbee. The Rev. McAlestar Couch is riding the Doakville circuit.

Even in the courtroom or while addressing a meeting of townspeople Yancey sometimes would behave strangely. He would stop in the midst of a florid period. At once a creature savage and overcivilized, the flaring lamps, the hot, breathless atmosphere, the vacuous white faces looming up at him like balloons would repel him. He had been known to stalk out, leaving them staring. In the courtroom he was an alarming figure. When he was defending a local county or Territorial case they flocked from miles around to hear him, and the crude pine shack that was the courtroom would be packed to suffocation. He towered over any jury of frontiersmen—a behemoth in a Prince Albert coat and fine linen, his great shaggy buffalo's head charging menacingly at his opponent. His was the florid highfalutin oratory of the day, full of sentiment, hyperbole, and wind. But he could be trenchant enough when needs be; and his charm, his magnetic power, were undeniable, and almost invariably he emerged from the courtroom victorious. He was not above employing tricks to win his case. On one occasion, when his client was being tried for an affair of gunplay which had ended disastrously, the jury, in spite of all that Yancey could do, turned out to be one which would be, he was certain, heavily for conviction. He deliberately worked himself up into an appearance of Brobdingnagian rage. He thundered, he roared, he stamped, he wept, he acted out the events leading up to the killing and then, while the jury's eyes rolled and the weaker among them wiped the sweat from their brows, he suddenly whipped his two well known and deadly ivory-handled and silver six-shooters from their holsters in his belt. "And this, gentlemen, is what my client did." He pointed them. But at that, with a concerted yelp of pure terror the jury rose as one man and leaped for the windows, the doors, and fled.

Yancey looked around, all surprise and injured innocence. The jury had disbanded. According to the law, a new jury had to be impaneled. The case was retried. Yancey won it.

Sabra saw more and more to the editing and to the actual printing of the *Oklahoma Wigwam*. She got in as general houseworker and helper an Osage Indian girl of fifteen who had been to the Indian school and who had learned some of the rudiments of household duties: cleaning, dishwashing, laundering, even some of the simpler forms of cookery. She tended Donna, as well. Her name was Arita Red Feather, a quiet gentle girl who went about the house in her calico dress and moccasins and had to be told everything over again, daily. Isaiah was beginning to be too big for these duties. He was something of a problem in the household. At the suggestion that he be sent back to Wichita he set up a howling and wailing and would not be consoled until both Sabra and Yancey assured him that he might remain with them forever. So he now helped Arita Red Feather with the heavier housework; did odd jobs about the printing shop; ran errands; saw that Donna kept from under horses' hoofs; he could even beat up a pan of good light biscuits in a pinch. When Jesse Rickey was too drunk to stand at the type case and Yancey was off on some legal matter, he slowly and painstakingly helped Sabra to make possible the weekly issue of the *Oklahoma Wigwam*. Arita Red Feather's dialect became a bewildering thing in which her native Osage, Sabra's refined diction, and Isaiah's Southern negro accent were rolled into an almost unintelligible jargon. "I'm gwine wash um clothes big rain water extremely nice um make um clothes white fo' true."

"That's fine!" Sabra would say. Then, an hour later, "Oh, Arita, don't you remember I've told you a hundred times you put the bluing in *after* they're rubbed, not before?"

Arita's dead black Indian eyes, utterly devoid of expression, would stare back at her.

Names of families of mixed Indian and white blood appeared from time to time in the columns of the *Wigwam*, for Sabra knew by now that there were in the Territory French-Indian families who looked upon themselves as aristocrats. This was the old French St. Louis, Missouri, background cropping up in the newly opened land. The early French who had come to St. Louis, there to trade furs and hides with the Osages, had taken Indian girls as squaws. You saw, sprinkled among the commonplace nomenclature of the frontier, such proud old names as Bellieu, Revard, Revelette, Tayrien, Perrier, Chouteau; and their owners had the unmistakable coloring and the bearing of the Indian. These dark-skinned people bore, often enough, and ridiculously enough, Irish names as well, for the Irish laborers who had come out with pickax and shovel and crowbar to build the Territory railroads had wooed and married the girls of the Indian tribes. You saw little Indian Kellys and Flahertys and Riordans and Caseys.

All this was bewildering to Sabra. But she did a man's job with the paper, often against frightening odds, for Yancey was frequently absent now, and she had no one but the wavering Jesse Rickey to consult. There were times when he, too, failed her. Still the weekly appeared regularly, somehow.

> Grandma Rosey, living eleven miles northwest of town, is very ill with the la grippe. Mrs. Rosey is quite aged and fears are entertained for her recovery.
>
> Preaching next Sunday morning and evening at the Presbyterian church by Rev. J. H. Canby. Come and hear the new bell.
>
> Mrs. Wicksley is visiting with the Judge this week.
>
> A movement is on foot to fill up the sink holes on Pawhuska Avenue. The street in its present state is a disgrace to the community.
>
> C. H. Snack and family expect to leave next week for an extended visit with Mrs. Snack's relatives in southeastern Kansas. Mr. Snack disposed of his personal property at public sale last Monday. Our loss is Kansas's gain.

(A sinister paragraph this. You saw C. H. Snack, the failure, the defeated, led back to Kansas there to live the life of the nagged and unsuccessful husband tolerated by his wife's kin.)

Sabra, in a pinch, even tried her unaccustomed hand at an occasional editorial, though Yancey seldom failed her utterly in this department. A rival newspaper set up quarters across the street and, for two or three months, kept up a feeble pretense of existence. Yancey's editorials, during this period, were extremely personal.

> The so-called publishers of the organ across the street have again been looking through glasses that reflect their own images. A tree is known by its fruit. The course pursued by the *Dispatch* does not substantiate its claim that it is a Republican paper.

The men readers liked this sort of thing. It was Yancey who brought in such items as:

> Charles Flasher, wanted for murder, forgery, selling liquor without a license and breaking jail at Skiatook, was captured in Oklahoma City as he was trying to board a train in the Choctaw yards.

But it was Sabra who held the women readers with her accounts of the veal loaf, cole slaw, baked beans, and angel-food cake served at the church supper, and the somewhat touching decorations and costumes worn at the wedding of a local or county belle.

If, in the quarter of a century that followed, every trace of the settling of the Oklahoma country had been lost, excepting only the numbers of the *Oklahoma Wigwam*, there still would have been left a clear and inclusive record of the lives, morals, political and social and economic workings of this bizarre community. Week by week, month by month, the reader could have noticed in its columns whatever of progress was being made in this fantastic slice of the Republic of the United States.

It was the day of the practical joke, and Yancey was always neglecting his newspaper and his law practice to concoct, with a choice group of conspirators, some elaborate and gaudy scheme for the comic downfall of a fellow citizen or a newcomer to the region. These jokes often took weeks for their successful consummation. Frequently they were founded on the newcomer's misapprehension concerning the Indians. If this was the Indian Territory, he argued, not unreasonably, it was full of Indians. He had statistics. There were 200,000 Indians in the Territory. Indians meant tomahawks, scalpings, burnings, raidings, and worse. When the local citizens assured him that all this was part of the dead past the tenderfoot quoted, sagely, that there was no good Indian but a dead Indian. Many of the jokes, then, hinged on the mythical bad Indian. The newcomer was told that there was a threatened uprising; the Cheyennes had been sold calico—bolts and bolts of it—with the stripes running the wrong way. This, it was explained, was a mistake most calculated to madden them. The jokesters armed themselves to the teeth. Six-shooters were put in the clammy, trembling hand of the tenderfoot. He was told that the nights were freezing cold. He was led to a near-by field that was man-high with sunflowers and cautioned not to fire unless he heard the yells of the maddened savages. There, shaking and sweating in overcoat, overshoes, mufflers, ear muffs, and leggings, he cowered for hours while all about him (at a safe distance) he heard the horrid, blood-curdling yells of the supposed Indians. His scalp, when finally he was rescued, usually was found to be almost lifted of its own accord.

Next day, Yancey would spend hours writing a humorous account of this Indian uprising for the Thursday issue of the *Wigwam*. The drinks were on the newcomer. That ceremony also took hours.

> *O jest unseen, inscrutable, invisible,*
> *As a nose on a man's face, or a weathercock on a steeple.*

Thus Yancey's article would begin with a quotation from his favorite poet.

"Oh, Yancey darling, sometimes I think you're younger than Cim."

"What would you like me to be, honey? A venerable Venable? 'A man whose blood is very snow-broth; one who never feels the wanton stings and motions of the sense'?"

Sabra, except for Yancey's growing restlessness, was content enough. The children were well; the paper was prospering; she had her friends; the house had taken on an aspect of comfort; they had added another bedroom; Arita Red Feather and Isaiah together relieved her of the rougher work of the household. She was, in a way, a leader in the crude social life of the community. Church suppers; sewing societies; family picnics.

One thing rankled deep. Yancey had been urged to accept the office of Territorial delegate to Congress (without vote) and had refused. All sorts of Territorial political positions were held out to him. The city of Guthrie, Capital of the Territory, wooed him in vain. He laughed at political position, rejected all offers of public nature. Now he was being offered the position of Governor of the Territory. His oratory, his dramatic quality, his record in many affairs, including the Pegler murder and the shooting of the Kid, had spread his fame even beyond the Southwest.

"Oh, Yancey!" Sabra thought of the Venables, the Marcys, the Vians, the Goforths. At last her choice of a mate was to be vindicated. Governor!

But Yancey shook his great head. There was no moving him. He would go on the stump to make others Congressmen and Governors, but he himself would not take office. "Palavering to a lot of greasy office seekers and panhandlers! Dancing to the tune of that gang in Washington! I know the whole dirty lot of them."

Restless. Moody. Irritable. Riding out into the prairies to be gone for days. Coming back to regale Cim with stories of evenings spent on this or that far-off Reservation, smoking and talking with Chief Big Horse of the Cherokees, with Chief Buffalo Hide of the Chickasaws, with old Black Kettle of the Osages.

But he was not always like this. There were times when his old fiery spirit took possession. He entered the fight for the statehood of Oklahoma Territory, and here he encountered opposition enough even for him. He was for the consolidation of the Oklahoma Territory and the Indian Territory under single statehood. The thousands who were opposed to the Indians—who looked upon them as savages totally unfit for citizenship—fought him. A year after their coming to Oklahoma the land had been divided into two territories—one owned and occupied by the Indian Tribes, the other owned by the whites. Here the Cravats lived, on the border line. And here was Yancey, fighting week after week, in the editorial and news columns of the *Oklahoma Wigwam*, for the rights of the Indians; for the consolidation of the two halves as one state. Yet, unreasonably enough, he sympathized with the Five Civilized Tribes in their efforts to retain their tribal laws in place of the United States Court laws which were being forced upon them. He made a thousand bitter enemies. Many of the Indians themselves were opposed to him. These were for separate statehood for the Indian Territory, the state to be known as Sequoyah, after the great Cherokee leader of that name.

Sabra, who at first had paid little enough heed to these political problems, discovered that she must know something of them as protection against those times (increasingly frequent) when Yancey was absent and she must get out the paper with only the uncertain aid of Jesse Rickey.

She dared not, during these absences of Yancey, oppose outright his political and Territorial stand. But she edged as near the line as she could, for her hatred of the Indians was still deep and (she insisted) unconquerable. She even published—slyly—the speeches and arguments of the Double Statehood party leaders, stating simply that these were the beliefs of the opposition. They sounded very reasonable and convincing as the *Wigwam* readers perused them.

Sabra came home one afternoon from a successful and stirring meeting of the Twentieth Century Philomathean Culture Club (the two had now formed a pleasing whole) at which she had read a paper entitled, Whither Oklahoma? It had been received with much applause on the part of Osage's twenty most exclusive ladies, who had heard scarcely a word of it, their minds being intent on Sabra's new dress. She had worn it for the first time at the club meeting, and it was a bombshell far exceeding any tumult that her paper might create.

Her wealthy Cousin Bella French Vian, visiting the World's Fair in Chicago, had sent it from Marshall Field's store. It consisted of a blue serge skirt, cut wide and flaring at the hem but snug at the hips; a waist-length blue serge Eton jacket trimmed with black soutache braid; and a garment called a shirtwaist to be worn beneath the jacket. But astounding—revolutionary—as all this was, it was not the thing that caused the eyes of feminine Osage to bulge with envy and despair. The sleeves! The sleeves riveted the attention of those present, to the utter neglect of Whither Oklahoma? The balloon sleeve now appeared for the first time in the Oklahoma Territory, sponsored by Mrs. Yancey Cravat. They were bouffant, enormous; a yard of material at least had gone into each of them. Every woman present was, in her mind, tearing to rag strips, bit by bit, every gown in her own scanty wardrobe.

Sabra returned home, flushed, elated. She entered by way of the newspaper office, seeking Yancey's approval. Curtseying and dimpling she stood before him. She wanted him to see the new costume before she must thriftily take it off for the preparation of supper. Yancey's comment, as she pirouetted for his approval, infuriated her.

"Good God! Sleeves! Let the squaws see those and they'll be throwing away their papoose boards and using the new fashion for carrying their babies, one in each sleeve."

"They're the very latest thing in Chicago. Cousin Bella French Vian wrote that they'll be even fuller than this, by autumn."

"By autumn," echoed Yancey. He held in his hand a slip of paper. Later she knew that it was a telegram—one of the few telegraphic messages which the *Wigwam's* somewhat sketchy service received. He was again completely oblivious of the new costume, the balloon sleeves. "Listen, sugar. President Cleveland's just issued a proclamation setting September sixteenth for the opening of the Cherokee Strip."

"Cherokee Strip?"

"Six million, three hundred thousand acres of Oklahoma land to be opened for white settlement. The government has bought it from the Cherokees. It was all to be theirs—all Oklahoma. Now they're pushing them farther and farther out."

"Good thing," snapped Sabra, still cross about the matter of Yancey's indifference to her costume. Indians. Who cared! She raised her arms to unpin her hat.

Yancey rose from his desk. He turned his rare full gaze on her, his handsome eyes aglow. "Honey, let's get out of this. Clubs, sleeves, church suppers—God! Let's get our hundred and sixty acre allotment of Cherokee Strip land and start a ranch—raise cattle—live in the open—ride—this town life is no good—it's hideous."

Her arms fell, leaden, to her side. "Ranch? Where?"

"You're not listening. There's to be a new Run. The Cherokee Strip Opening. You know. You wrote news stories about it only last week, before the opening date had been announced. Let's go, Sabra. It's the biggest thing yet. The 1889 Run was nothing compared to it. Sell the *Wigwam*, take the children, make the Run, get our hundred and sixty, start a ranch, stock up with cattle and horses, build a ranch house and patio; in the saddle all day——"

"Never!" screamed Sabra. Her face was distorted. Her hands were clutching the air, as though she would tear to bits this plan of his for the future. "I won't. I won't go. I'd rather die first. You can't make me."

He came to her, tried to take her in his arms, to pacify her. "Sugar, you won't understand. It's the chance of a lifetime. It's the biggest thing in the history of Oklahoma. When the Territory's a state we'll own forever one hundred and sixty acres of the finest land anywhere. I know the section I want."

"Yes. You know. You know. You knew the last time, too. You let that slut—that hussy—take it away from you—or you gave it to her. Go and take her with you. You'll never make me go. I'll stay here with my children and run the paper. Mother! Cim! Donna!"

She had a rare and violent fit of hysterics, after which Yancey, aided clumsily by Arita Red Feather, divested her of the new finery, quieted the now screaming children, and finally restored to a semblance of suppertime order the household into which he had hurled such a bomb. Felice Venable herself, in her heyday, could not have given a finer exhibition of Marcy temperament. It was intended, as are all hysterics (no one ever has hysterics in private), to intimidate the beholder and fill him with remorse. Yancey was properly solicitous, tender, charming as only he could be. From the shelter of her husband's arms Sabra looked about the cosy room, smiled wanly upon her children, bade Arita Red Feather bring on the belated supper. "That," thought Sabra to herself, bathing her eyes, smoothing her hair, and coming pale and wistful to the table, her lip quivering with a final effective sigh, "settles that."

But it did not. September actually saw Yancey making ready to go. Nothing that Sabra could say, nothing that she could do, served to stop him. She even negotiated for a little strip of farm land outside the town of Osage and managed to get Yancey to make a payment on it, in the

hope that this would keep him from the Run. "If it's land you want you
can stay here and farm the piece at Tuskamingo. You can raise cattle
on it. You can breed horses on it."

Yancey shook his head. He took no interest in the farm. It was Sabra
who saw to the erection of a crude little farmhouse, arranged for the
planting of such crops as it was thought that land would yield. It was
very near the Osage Reservation land and turned out, surprisingly
enough, doubtless owing to some mineral or geological reason (they
knew why, later), to be fertile, though the Osage land so near by was
barren and flinty.

"Farm! That's no farm. It's a garden patch. D'you think I'm settling
down to be a potato digger and chicken feeder, in a hayseed hat and
manure on my boots!"

September, the month of the opening of the vast Cherokee Strip, saw
him well on his way. Cim howled to be taken along, and would not be
consoled for days.

Sabra's farewell was intended to be cold. Her heart, she told herself,
was breaking. The change that these last four years had made in her
never was more apparent than now.

"You felt the same way when I went off to the first Run," Yancey
reminded her. "Remember? You carried on just one degree less than
your mother. And if I hadn't gone you'd still be living in the house in
Wichita, with your family smothering you in Southern fried chicken
and advice." There was much truth in this, she had to admit. She
melted; clung to him.

"Yancey! Yancey!"

"Smile, sugar. Wait till you see Cim and Donna, five years from now,
riding the Cravat acres."

After all, a hundred other men in Osage were going to make the
Cherokee Strip Run. The town—the whole Territory—had talked of
nothing else for months.

She dried her eyes. She even managed a watery smile. He was making
the Run on a brilliant, wild-eyed mare named Cimarron, with a strain
of Spanish in her for speed and grace, and a strain of American mustang
for endurance. He had decided to make the trip from Osage to the
Cherokee Outlet on horseback by easy stages so as to keep the animal
in condition, though the Santa Fé and the Rock Island roads were to
run trains into the Strip. He made a dashing, a magnificent figure as he
sat the strong, graceful animal that now was pawing and pirouetting
to be off. Though a score of others were starting with him, it was
Yancey that the town turned out to see. He rode in his white sombrero,
his fine white shirt, his suit with the Prince Albert coat, his glittering

high-heeled Texas star boots with the gold-plated spurs. The start was made shortly after sunrise so as to make progress before the heat of the day. But a cavalcade awoke them before dawn with a rat-a-tat-tat of six-shooters and a blood-curdling series of cowboy yips. The escort rode with Yancey and the others for a distance out on the Plains. Sabra, at the last minute, had the family horse hitched to the buggy, bundled Cim and Donna in with her, and—Isaiah hanging on behind, somehow —the prim little vehicle bumped and reeled its way over the prairie road in the wake of the departing adventurers.

At the last Sabra threw the reins to Isaiah, sprang from the buggy, ran to Yancey as he pulled up his horse. He bent far over in his saddle, picked her up in one great arm, held her close while he kissed her long and hard.

"Sabra, come with me. Let's get clear away from this."

"You've gone crazy! The children!"

"The children, too. All of us. Come on. Now." His eyes were blazing. She saw that he actually meant it. A sudden premonition shook her.

"Where are you going? Where are you going?"

He set her down gently and was off, turned halfway in his saddle to face her, his white sombrero held aloft in his hand, his curling black locks tossing in the Oklahoma breeze.

Five years passed before she saw him again.

XV

DIXIE LEE's girls were riding by on their daily afternoon parade. Sabra recognized their laughter and the easy measured clatter of their horses' hoofs before they came into view. She knew it was Dixie Lee's girls. Somehow, the virtuous women of Osage did not laugh much, though Sabra did not put this thought into words, ever in her mind. She glanced up now as they drove by. She was seated at her desk by the window in the front office of the *Oklahoma Wigwam*. Their plumes, their parasols, their brilliant-hued dresses made a gay garden of color in the monotony of Pawhuska Avenue. They rode in open phaëtons, but without the usual top, so that they had only their parasols to shade their brightly painted faces from the ardent Southwest sun. The color of the parasols and plumes and dresses was changed from day to day, but they always were done in ensemble effect. One day the eyes of Osage's male population were dazzled (and its female population's eyes affronted) by a burst of rosy splendor shading from pale pink to scarlet. The next day they would shade from palest lavender to deepest purple. The next, from delicate lemon to orange; the day following they ran the gamut of green. They came four by four, and usually one in each carriage handled the reins, though occasionally a negro driver occupied the front seat alone. They were not boisterous. Indeed, they conducted themselves in seemly enough fashion except perhaps for the little bursts of laughter and for the fact that they were generous with the ankles beneath the ruffled skirts. Often they carried dolls in their arms. Sometimes—rarely—they called to each other. Their voices were high and curiously unformed, like the voices of little children, and yet with a metallic note in them.

"Madge, looka! When we get to the end of Pawhuska we'll race you to Coley's Gulch and back." These afternoon races became almost daily sporting events, and the young bloods of Osage got into the habit of stationing themselves along the road to bet on the pale pink plumes or the deep rose plumes.

"Heh, go it, Clemmie! Whip him up, Carmen. Give him the whip! Come on! Whoop-ee! Yi!" Plumes whirling, parasols bobbing, skirts flying, shrill shouts and screams of laughter from the edge of town. But on the return drive their behavior was again seemly enough, their cheeks flushed with a natural color beneath the obvious red.

Sabra's face darkened now as she saw them driving slowly by. Dixie Lee never drove with them. Sabra knew where she was this afternoon. She was down in the back room of the Osage First National Bank talking business to the President, Murch Rankin. The business men of the town were negotiating for the bringing of the packing house and a plough works and a watch factory to Osage. Any one of these industries required a substantial bonus. The spirit of the day was the boom spirit. Boom the town of Osage. Dixie Lee was essentially a commercial woman—shrewd, clear headed. She had made a great success of her business. It was one of the crude town's industries, and now she, as well as the banker, the hardware man, the proprietor of the furniture store, the meat market, the clothing store, contributed her share toward coaxing new industries to favor Osage. That way lay prosperity.

Dixie Lee was a personage in the town. Visitors came to her house now from the cities and counties round about. She had built for herself and her thriving business the first brick structure in the wooden town; a square, solid, and imposing two-story house, its bricks formed from the native Oklahoma red clay. Cal Bixby had followed close on it with the

Bixby Block on Pawhuska Avenue, but Dixie Lee had led the way. She had commissioned Louie Hefner to buy her red velvet and gold furniture and her long gilt-framed mirrors, her scarlet deep-pile carpet—that famous velvet-pile carpet in which Shanghai Wiley, that bearded, cultured, and magnetic barbarian, said he sank so deep that for a terrified moment he fell into a panic, being unable to tell which was red carpet and which his own flowing red beard. Dixie herself had gone East for her statues and pictures. The new house had been opened with a celebration the like of which had never been seen in the Southwest. Sabra Cravat, mentioning no names, had had an editorial about it in which the phrases "insult to the fair womanhood of America" and "orgy rivaling the Bacchanalian revels of history" (Yancey's library stood her in good stead these days) figured prominently. Both the Philomathean Society and the Twentieth Century Culture Club had, for the duration of one meeting at least, deserted literature and culture for the discussion of the more vital topic of Dixie Lee's new mansion.

It was—this red brick brothel—less sinister than these good and innocent women suspected. Dixie Lee, now a woman of thirty or more, ruled it with an iron hand. Within it obtained certain laws and rules of conduct so rigid as to be almost prim. In a crude, wild, and nearly lawless country the brick mansion occupied a strange place, filled a want foreign to its original purpose. It was, in a way, a club, a rendezvous, a salon. For hundreds of men who came there it was all they had ever known of richness, of color, of luxury. The red and gold, the plush and silk, the perfume, the draperies, the white arms, the gleaming shoulders sank deep into their hard-bitten senses, long starved from years on windswept ranches, plains dust bedeviled, prairies baked barren by the fierce Southwest sun. Here they lolled, sunk deep in rosy comfort, while they talked Territory politics, swapped yarns of the old cattle days, played cards, drank wines which tasted like sweet prickling water to their whisky-scarred palates. They kissed these women, embraced them fiercely, thought tenderly of many of them, and frequently married them; and these women, once married, settled down contentedly to an almost slavish domesticity.

A hard woman, Dixie Lee; a bad woman. Sabra was morally right in her attitude toward her. Yet this woman, as well as Sabra, filled her place in the early life of the Territory.

Now, as the laughter sounded nearer and the equipages came within her view, Sabra, seated at her desk in the newspaper office, put down the soft pencil with which she had been filling sheet after sheet of copy paper. She wrote easily now, with no pretense to style, but concisely and with an excellent sense of news values. The *Oklahoma Wigwam* had flourished in these last five years of her proprietorship. She was thinking seriously of making it a daily instead of a weekly; of using the entire building on Pawhuska Avenue for the newspaper plant and building a proper house for herself and the two children on one of the residence streets newly sprung up—streets that boasted neatly painted houses and elm and cottonwood trees in the front yards.

Someone came up the steps of the little porch and into the office. It was Mrs. Wyatt. She often brought club notices and social items to the *Wigwam:* rather fancied herself as a writer; a born woman's club corresponding secretary.

"Well!" she exclaimed now, simply, but managing to put enormous bite and significance into the monosyllable. Her glance followed Sabra's. Together the two women, tight lipped, condemnatory, watched the gay parade of Dixie Lee's girls go by.

The flashing company disappeared. A whiff of patchouli floated back to the two women standing by the open window. Their nostrils lifted in disdain. The sound of the horses' hoofs grew fainter.

"It's a disgrace to the community"—Mrs. Wyatt's voice took on its platform note—"and an insult to every wife and mother in the Territory. There ought to be a law."

Sabra turned away from the window. Her eyes sought the orderly rows of books, bound neatly in tan and red—Yancey's law books, so long unused now, except, perhaps, for occasional newspaper reference. Her face set itself in lines of resolve. "Perhaps there is."

It had taken almost three of those five years to bring those lines into Sabra Cravat's face. They were not, after all, lines. Her face was smooth, her skin still fresh in spite of dust and alkali water and sun and wind. It was, rather, that a certain hardening process had taken place—a crystallization. Yancey had told her, tenderly, that she was a charming little fool, and she had believed it—though perhaps with subconscious reservations. It was not until he left her, and the years rolled round without him, that she developed her powers. The sombrero had ridden gayly away. The head under the sunbonnet had held itself high in spite of hints, innuendoes, gossip.

A man like Yancey Cravat—spectacular, dramatic, impulsive—has a thousand critics, scores of bitter enemies. As the weeks had gone by and Yancey failed to return—had failed to write—rumor, clouded by scandal, leaped like prairie fire from house to house in Osage, from town to town in the Oklahoma Country, over the Southwest, indeed. All the old stories were revived, and their ugly red tongues licked a sordid path through the newly opened land.

They say he is living with the Cherokee squaw who is really his wife.

They say he was seen making the Run in the Kickapoo Land Opening in 1895.

They say he killed a man in the Cherokee Strip Run and was caught by a posse and hung.

They say he got a section of land, sold it at a high figure, and was seen lording it around the bar of the Brown Palace Hotel in Denver, in his white sombrero and his Prince Albert coat.

They say Dixie Lee is his real wife, and he left her when she was seventeen, came to Wichita, and married Sabra Venable; and he is the one who has set Dixie up in the brick house.

They say he drank five quarts of whisky one night and died and is buried in an unmarked grave in Horseshoe Ranch, where the Doolin gang held forth.

They say he is really the leader of the Doolin gang.

They say. They say. They say.

It is impossible to know how Sabra survived those first terrible weeks that lengthened into months that lengthened into years. There was in her the wiry endurance of the French Marcys; the pride of the Southern Venables. Curiously enough, in spite of all that had happened to her she still had that virginal look—that chastity of lip, that clearness of the eye, that purity of brow. Men come back to the women who look as Sabra Cravat looked, but the tempests of men's love pass them by.

She told herself that he was dead. She told the world that he was dead. She knew, by some deep and unerring instinct, that he was alive. Donna had been so young when he left that he now was all but wiped from her memory. But Cim, strangely enough, spoke of Yancey Cravat as though he were in the next room. "My father says . . ." Sometimes, when Sabra saw the boy coming toward her with that familiar swinging stride, his head held down and a little thrust forward, she was wrenched by a physical pang of agony that was almost nausea.

She ran the paper competently; wrung from it a decent livelihood for herself and the two children. When it had no longer been possible to keep secret from her parents the fact of Yancey's prolonged absence, Felice Venable had descended upon her prepared to gather to the family bosom her deserted child and to bring her, together with her offspring, back to the parental home. Lewis Venable had been too frail and ill to accompany his wife, so Felice had brought with her the more imposing among the Venables, Goforths, and Vians who chanced to be visiting the Wichita house at the time of her departure. Osage had looked upon these stately figures with much awe, but Sabra's reception of them had been as coolly cordial as her rejection of their plans for her future was firm.

"I intend to stay right here in Osage," she announced, quietly, but in a tone that even Felice Venable recognized as inflexible, "and run the paper, and bring up my children as their father would have expected them to be brought up."

"Their father!" Felice Venable repeated, in withering accents.

The boy Cimarron, curiously sensitive to sounds and moods, stood before his grandmother, his head thrust forward, his handsome eyes glowing. "My father is the most famous man in Oklahoma. The Indians call him Buffalo Head."

Felice Venable pounced on this. "If that's what you mean by bringing them up as their father . . ."

The meeting degenerated into one of those family bickerings. "I do wish, Mamma, that you wouldn't repeat everything I say and twist it by your tone into something poisonous."

"I say! I can't help it if the things you say sound ridiculous when they are repeated. I simply mean——"

"I don't care what you mean. I mean to stay here in Osage until Yancey—until——" She never finished that sentence.

The Osage society notes became less simple. From bare accounts of quiltings, sewing bees, and church sociables they blossomed into flowery imitations of the metropolitan dailies' descriptions of social events. Refreshments were termed elegant. Osage matrons turned from the sturdy baked beans, cole slaw, and veal loaf of an earlier day to express themselves in food terms culled from the pictures in the household magazines. They heard about fruit salads. They built angel-food cakes whose basis was the whites of thirteen eggs, and their husbands, at breakfast, said, "What makes these scrambled eggs so yellow?" Countrified costumes were described in terms of fashion. The wilted prairie flowers that graced weddings and parties were transformed into rare hothouse blooms by the magic touch of the *Oklahoma Wigwam* hand press. Sabra cannily published all the brilliant social news items that somewhat belatedly came her way via the ready-print and the paper's scant outside news service.

Newport. Oct. 4—One of the most brilliant weddings which Newport has seen for many years was solemnized in old Trinity Church to-day. The principals were Miss Georgina Harwood and Mr. Harold Blake, both members of families within the charmed circle of the 400. The bride wore a gown of ivory satin with draperies and rufflings of rarest point lace, the lace veil being caught with a tiara of pearls and diamonds. After the ceremony a magnificent collation . . .

The feminine population of Osage—of the county—felt that it had seen the ivory satin, the point lace, the tiara of pearls and diamonds, as these splendors moved down the aisle of old Trinity on the person of Miss Georgina Harwood of Newport. They derived from it the vicarious satisfaction that a dieting dyspeptic gets from reading the cook book.

Sabra was, without being fully aware of it, a power that shaped the social aspect of this crude Southwestern town. The Ladies of the new Happy Hour Club, on her declining to become a member, pleading lack of time and press of work (as well she might) made her an honorary member, resolved to have her influential name on their club roster, somehow. They were paying unconscious tribute to Oklahoma's first feminist. She still ran the paper single handed, with the aid of Jesse Rickey, the most expert printer in the Southwest (when sober), and as good as the average when drunk.

Sabra, serene in the knowledge that the attacked could do little to wreak vengeance on a woman, printed stories and statements which for boldness and downright effrontery would have earned a male editor a horse-whipping. She publicly scolded the street loafers who, in useless sombreros and six-shooters and boots and spurs, relics of a bygone day, lolled limply on Pawhuska Avenue corners, spitting tobacco juice into the gutter. Sometimes she borrowed Yancey's vigorous and picturesque phraseology. She denounced a local politician as being too crooked to sleep in a roundhouse, and the phrase stuck, and in the end defeated him. Law, order, the sanctity of the home, prunes, prisms. Though the Gyp Hills and the Osage Hills still were as venomous with outlaws as the Plains were with rattlesnakes; though the six-shooter still was as ordinary a part of the Oklahoma male costume as boots or trousers; though outlawry still meant stealing a horse rather than killing a man; though the Territory itself had been settled and peopled, in thousands of cases, by men who had come to it, not in a spirit of adventure, but from cowardice, rapacity, or worse, Sabra Cravat and the other basically conventional women of the community were working unconsciously, yet with a quiet ferocity, toward that day when one of them would be able to say, standing in a doorway with a stiff little smile:

"Awfully nice of you to come."

"Awfully nice of you to ask me," the other would reply.

When that day came, Osage would no longer need to feel itself looked down upon by Kansas City, Denver, Chicago, St. Louis, and San Francisco.

Slowly, slowly, certain figures began to take on the proportions of personalities. No one had arisen in the Territory to fill Yancey Cravat's romantic boots. Pat Leary was coming on as a Territory lawyer, with an office in the Bixby Block and the railroads on which he had worked as section hand now consulting him on points of Territorial law. In his early railroad days he had married an Osage girl named Crook Nose. People shook their heads over this and said that he regretted it now, and that a lawyer could never hope to get on with this marital millstone round his neck.

There still was very little actual money in the Territory. People traded this for that. Sabra often translated subscriptions to the *Oklahoma Wigwam*—and even advertising space—into terms of fresh vegetables, berries, wild turkey, quail, prairie chickens, dress lengths and shoes and stockings for the children.

Sol Levy's store, grown to respectable proportions now, provided Sabra with countless necessities in return for the advertisement which, sent through the country via the *Oklahoma Wigwam*, urged its readers to Trade at Sol Levy's. Visit the Only Zoo in the Territory. This invitation, a trifle bewildering to the uninitiated, was meant to be taken literally. In the back of his store Sol Levy kept a sizable menagerie. It had started through one of those chance encounters. A gaunt and bearded plainsman had come into the store one day with the suggestion that the proprietor trade a pair of pants for a bear cub. The idea had amused Sol Levy; then he had glanced out into the glare of Pawhuska Avenue and had seen the man's ocherous wife, his litter of spindling children, huddled together in a crazy wagon attached by what appeared to be ropes, strings, and bits of nail and wire, to horses so cadaverous that his amusement was changed to pity. He gave the man the pants, stockings for the children, and—the sentimentalist in him—a piece of bright-colored cotton stuff for the woman.

The bear cub, little larger than a puppy, had been led gingerly into the welter of packing cases, straw, excelsior, and broken china which was the Levy Mercantile Company's back yard, and there tied with a piece of rope which he immediately bit in two. Five minutes later a local housewife, deep in the purchase of a dress length of gingham, and feeling something rubbing against her stout calves, looked down to see the bear cub sociably gnawing his way through her basket of provisions, carelessly placed on the floor by her side.

One week later the grateful ranger brought in a pair of catamounts. A crude wire cage was built. There were added coyotes, prairie dogs, an eagle. The zoo became famous, and all the town came to see it. It brought trade to the Mercantile Company, and free advertising. It was the nucleus for the zoo which, fifteen years later, Sol Levy shyly presented to the Osage City Park, and which contained every wild thing that the Southwest had known, from the buffalo to the rattlesnake.

In a quiet, dreamy way Sol Levy had managed to buy a surprising amount of Osage real estate by now. He owned the lot on which his

store stood, the one just south of it, and, among other pieces, the building and lot which comprised the site of the *Wigwam* and the Cravat
house. In the year following Yancey's departure Sabra's economic sur-
vival was made possible only through the almost shamefaced generosity
of this quiet, sad-eyed man.

"I've got it all down in my books," Sabra would say, proudly. "You
know that it will all be paid back some day."

He began in the *Oklahoma Wigwam* a campaign of advertising out of
all proportions to his needs, and Sabra's debt to him began to shrink to
the vanishing point. She got into the habit of talking to him about her
business problems, and he advised her shrewdly. When she was utterly
discouraged he would say, not triumphantly, but as one who states an
irrefutable and not particularly happy fact:

"Some day, Mrs. Cravat, you and I will look back on this and we will
laugh—but not very loud."

"How do you mean—laugh?"

The little curious cast came into his eyes. "Oh—I will be very rich,
and you will be very famous. And Yancey——"

"Yancey!" The word was wrenched from her like a cry.

"They will tell stories about Yancey until he will grow into a legend.
He will be part of the history of the Southwest. They will remember
him and write about him when all these mealy-faced governors are dead
and gone and forgotten. They will tell the little children about him, and
they will dispute about him—he did this, he did that; he was like this,
he was like that. You will see."

Sabra thought of her own children, who knew so little of their father.
Donna, a thin secretive child of almost seven now, with dark, straight
black hair and a sallow skin like Yancey's; Cim, almost thirteen, moody,
charming, imaginative. Donna was more like her grandmother Felice
Venable than her own mother; Cim resembled Yancey so strongly in
mood, manner, and emotions as to have almost no trace of Sabra. She
wondered, with a pang, if she had failed to impress herself on them
because of her absorption in the town, in the newspaper, in the resolve
to succeed. She got out a photograph of Yancey that she had hidden
away because to see it was to feel a stab of pain, and had it framed,
and hung it on the wall where the children could see it daily. He was
shown in the familiar costume—the Prince Albert, the white sombrero,
the six-shooters, the boots, the spurs, the long black locks curling beneath the hat brim, the hypnotic eyes startling you with their arresting
gaze, so that it was as if he were examining you rather than that you
were seeing his likeness in a photograph. One slim foot, in its high-

heeled boot, was slightly advanced, the coat tails flared, the whole picture was somehow endowed with a sense of life and motion.

"Your father——" Sabra would begin, courageously, resolved to make him live again in the minds of the children. Donna was not especially interested. Cim said, "I know it," and capped her story with a tale of his own in which Yancey's feat of derring-do outrivaled any swashbuckling escapade of D'Artagnan.

"Oh, but Cim, that's not true! You mustn't believe stories like that about your father."

"It is true. Isaiah told me. I guess he ought to know." And then the question she dreaded. "When are Isaiah and Father coming back?"

She could answer, somehow, evasively, about Yancey, for her instinct concerning him was sure and strong. But at the fate that had overtaken the negro boy she cowered, afraid even to face the thought of it. For the thing that had happened to the black boy was so dreadful, so remorseless that when the truth of it came to Sabra she felt all this little world of propriety, of middle-class Middle West convention that she had built up about her turning to ashes under the sudden flaring fire of hidden savagery. She tried never to think of it, but sometimes, at night, the hideous thing took possession of her, and she was swept by such horror that she crouched there under the bedclothes, clammy and shivering with the sweat of utter fear. Her hatred of the Indians now amounted to an obsession.

It was in the fourth year of Yancey's absence that, coming suddenly and silently into the kitchen from the newspaper office, where she had been busy as usual, she saw Arita Red Feather twisted in a contortion in front of the table where she had been at work. Her face was grotesque, was wet, with agony. It was the agony which only one kind of pain can bring to a woman's face. The Indian girl was in the pangs of childbirth. Even as she saw her Sabra realized that something about her had vaguely disturbed her in the past few weeks. Yet she had not known, had not dreamed of this. The loose garment which the girl always wore—her strong natural slenderness—the erect dignity of her Indian carriage—the stoicism of her race—had served to keep secret her condition. She had had, too, Sabra now realized in a flash, a way of being out of the room when her mistress was in it; busy in the pantry when Sabra was in the kitchen; busy in the kitchen when Sabra was in the dining room; in and out like a dark, swift shadow.

"Arita! Here. Come. Lie down. I'll send for your father—your mother." Her father was Big Knee, well known and something of a power in the Osage tribe. Of the tribal officers he was one of the eight members of the Council and as such was part of the tribe's governing body.

Dreadful as the look on Arita Red Feather's face had been, it was now contorted almost beyond recognition. "No! No!" She broke into a storm of pleading in her own tongue. Her eyes were black pools of agony. Sabra had never thought that one of pure Indian blood would thus give way to any emotion before a white person.

She put the girl to bed. She sent Isaiah for Dr. Valliant, who luckily was in town and sober. He went to work quietly, efficiently, aided by Sabra, making the best of such crude and hasty necessities as came to hand. The girl made no outcry. Her eyes were a dull, dead black; her face was rigid. Sabra, passing from the kitchen to the girl's bedroom with hot water, cloths, blankets, saw Isaiah crouched in a corner by the wood box. He looked up at her mutely. His face was a curious ash gray. As Sabra looked at him she knew.

The child was a boy. His hair was coarse and kinky. His nose was wide. His lips were thick. He was a negro child. Doc Valliant looked at him as Sabra held the writhing red-purple bundle in her arms.

"This is a bad business."

"I'll send for her parents. I'll speak to Isaiah. They can marry."

"Marry! Don't you know?"

Something in his voice startled her. "What?"

"The Osages don't marry negroes. It's forbidden."

"Why, lots of them have. You see negroes who are Indians every day. On the street."

"Not Osages. Seminoles, yes. And Creeks, and Choctaws, and even Chickasaws. But the Osages, except for intermarriage with whites, have kept the tribe pure."

This information seemed to Sabra to be unimportant and slightly silly. Purity of the tribe, indeed! Osages! She resolved to be matter of fact and sensible now that the shocking event was at hand, waiting to be dealt with. She herself felt guilty, for this thing had happened in her own house. She should have foreseen danger and avoided it. Isaiah had been a faithful black child in her mind, whereas he was, in reality, a man grown.

Dr. Valliant had finished his work. The girl lay on the bed, her dull black eyes fixed on them; silent, watchful, hopeless. Isaiah crouched in the kitchen. The child lay now in Sabra's arms. Donna and Cim were, fortunately, asleep, for it was now long past midnight. The tense excitement past, the whole affair seemed to Sabra sordid, dreadful. What would the town say? What would the members of the Philomathean Club and the Twentieth Century Culture Club think?

Doc Valliant came over to her and looked down at the queer shriveled morsel in her arms. "We must let his father see him."

Sabra shrank. "Oh, no!"

He took the baby from her and turned toward the kitchen. "I'll do it. Let me have a drink of whisky, will you, Sabra? I'm dead tired."

She went past him into the dining room, without a glance at the negro boy cowering in the kitchen. Doc Valliant followed her. As she poured a drink of Yancey's store of whisky, almost untouched since he had left, she heard Valliant's voice, very gentle, and then the sound of Isaiah's blubbering. All the primness in her was outraged. Her firm mouth took on a still straighter line. Valliant took the child back to the Indian girl's bed and placed it by her side. He stumbled with weariness as he entered the dining room where Sabra stood at the table. As he reached for the drink Sabra saw that his hand shook a little as Yancey's used to do in that same gesture. She must not think of that. She must not think of that.

"There's no use talking now, Doctor, about what the Osages do or don't do that you say is so pure. The baby's born. I shall send for the old man—what's his name?—Big Knee. As soon as Arita can be moved he must take her home. As for Isaiah, I've a notion to send him back to Kansas, as I wanted to do years ago, only he begged so to stay, and Yancey let him. And now this."

Doc Valliant had swallowed the whisky at a gulp—had thrown it down his throat as one takes medicine to relieve pain. He poured another glass. His face was tired and drawn. It was late. His nerves were not what they had been, what with drink, overwork, and countless nights without sleep as he rode the country on his black horse, his handsome figure grown a little soft and sagging now. But he still was a dashing sight when he sat the saddle in his black corduroys and his soft-brimmed black hat.

He swallowed his second drink. His face seemed less drawn, his hand steadier, his whole bearing more alert. "Now listen, Sabra. You don't understand. You don't understand the Osages. This is serious."

Sabra interrupted quickly. "Don't think I'm hard. I'm not condemning her altogether, or Isaiah, either. I'm partly to blame. I should have seen. But I am so busy. Anyway, I can't have her here now, can I? With Isaiah. Even you . . ."

He filled his glass. She wished he would stop drinking; go home. She would sit up the night with the Indian girl. And in the morning—well, she must get someone in to help. They would know, sooner or later.

He was repeating rather listlessly what he had said. "The Osages have kept the tribe absolutely free of negro blood. This is a bad business."

Her patience was at an end. "What of it? And how do you know? How do you know?"

"Because they remove any member of the tribe that has had to do with a negro."

"Remove!"

"Kill. By torture."

She stared at him. He was drunk, of course. "You're talking nonsense," she said crisply. She was very angry.

"Don't let this get around. They might blame you. The Osages. They might—— I'll just go and take another look at her."

The girl was sleeping. Sabra felt a pang of pity as she gazed down at her. "Go to bed—off with you," said Doc Valliant to Isaiah. The boy's face was wet, pulpy with tears and sweat and fright. He walked slackly, as though exhausted.

"Wait." Sabra cut him some bread from the loaf, sliced a piece of meat left from supper. "Here. Eat this. Everything will be all right in the morning."

The news got round. Perhaps Doc Valliant talked in drink. Doubtless the girl who came in to help her. Perhaps Isaiah, who after a night's exhausted sleep had suddenly become proudly paternal and boasted loudly about the house (and no doubt out of it) of the size, beauty, and intelligence of the little lump of dusky flesh that lay beside Arita Red Feather's bed in the very cradle that had held Donna when an infant. Arita Red Feather was frantic to get up. They had to keep her in bed by main force. She had not spoken a dozen words since the birth of the child.

On the fourth day following the child's birth Sabra came into Arita Red Feather's room early in the morning and she was not there. The infant was not there. Their beds had been slept in and now were empty. She ran straight into the yard where Isaiah's little hut stood. He was not there. She questioned the girl who now helped with the housework and who slept on a couch in the dining room. She had heard nothing, seen nothing. The three had vanished in the night.

Well, Sabra thought, philosophically, they have gone off. Isaiah can make out, somehow. Perhaps he can even get a job as a printer somewhere. He was handy, quick, bright. He had some money, for she had given him, in these later years, a little weekly wage, and he had earned a quarter here, a half dollar there. Enough, perhaps, to take them by train back to Kansas. Certainly they had not gone to Arita's people, for Big Knee, questioned, denied all knowledge of his daughter, of her child, of the black boy. He behaved like an Indian in a Cooper novel. He grunted, looked blank, folded his arms, stared with dead black, expressionless eyes. They could make nothing of him. His squaw, stout, silent, only shook her head; pretended that she neither spoke nor understood English.

Then the rumor rose, spread, received credence. It was started by Pete Pitchlyn, the old Indian guide and plainsman who sometimes lived with the Indians for months at a time on their reservations, who went with them on their visiting jaunts, hunted, fished, ate with them, who was married to a Cherokee, and who had even been adopted into the Cherokee tribe. He had got the story from a Cherokee who in turn had had it from an Osage. The Osage, having managed to lay hands on some whisky, and becoming very drunk, now told the grisly tale for the first time.

There had been an Osage meeting of the Principal Chief, old Howling Wolf; the Assistant Chief; the eight members of the Council, which included Big Knee, Arita's father. There the news of the girl's dereliction had been discussed, her punishment gravely decided upon, and that of Isaiah.

They had come in the night and got them—the black boy, the Indian girl, the infant—by what means no one knew. Arita Red Feather and her child had been bound together, placed in an untanned and uncured steer hide, the hide was securely fastened, they were carried then to the open, sun-baked, and deserted prairie and left there, with a guard. The hide shrank and shrank and shrank in the burning sun, closer and closer, day by day, until soon there was no movement within it.

Isaiah, already half dead with fright, was at noonday securely bound and fastened to a stake. Near by, but not near enough quite to touch him, was a rattlesnake so caught by a leather thong that, strike and coil and strike as it might, it could not quite reach, with its venomous head, the writhing, gibbering thing that lay staring with eyes that protruded out of all semblance to human features. But as dusk came on the dew fell, and the leather thong stretched a little with the wet. And as twilight deepened and the dew grew heavier the leather thong holding the horrible reptile stretched more and more. Presently it was long enough.

XVI

REMEMBER the *Maine!* To hell with Spain!" You read this inflaming sentiment on posters and banners and on little white buttons pinned to coat lapels or dress fronts. There were other buttons and pennants bearing the likeness of an elderly gentleman with a mild face disguised behind a martial white mustache; and thousands of male children born within the United States in 1898 grew up under the slight handicap of the christened name of Dewey. The *Oklahoma Wigwam* bristled with new words: Manila Bay—Hobson—Philippines. Throughout the Southwest sombreros suddenly became dust-colored army hats with broad, flat brims and peaked crowns. People who, if they had thought of Spain at all, saw it in the romantic terms of the early Southwest explorers— Coronado, De Soto, Moscoso—and, with admiration for these intrepid and mistaken seekers after gold, now were told that they must hate Spain and the Spanish and kill as many little brown men living in the place called the Philippines as possible. This was done as dutifully as could be, but with less than complete enthusiasm.

Rough Riders! That was another matter. Here was something that the Oklahoma country knew and understood—tall, lean, hard young men who had practically been born with a horse under them and a gun in hand; riders, hunters, dead shots; sunburned, keen eyed, daredevil. Their uniforms, worn with a swagger, had about them a dashing something that the other regiments lacked. Their hat crowns were dented, not peaked, and the brims were turned romantically up at one side and caught with the insignia of the Regiment—the crossed sabers. And their lieutenant-colonel and leader was that energetic, toothy young fellow who was making something of a stir in New York State—Roosevelt, his name was. Theodore Roosevelt.

Osage was shaken by chills and fever; the hot spasms of patriotism, the cold rigors of virtue. One day the good wives of the community would have a meeting at which they arranged for a home-cooked supper, with coffee, to be served to this or that regiment. Their features would soften with sentiment, their bosoms heave with patriotic pride. Next day, eyes narrowed, lips forming a straight line, they met to condemn Dixie Lee and her ilk, and to discuss ways and means for ridding the town of their contaminating presence.

The existence of this woman in the town had always been a festering sore to Sabra. Dixie Lee, the saloons that still lined Pawhuska Avenue, the gambling houses, all the paraphernalia of vice, were anathema lumped together in the minds of the redoubtable sunbonnets. A new political group had sprung up, ostensibly on the platform of civic virtue. In reality they were tired of seeing all the plums dropping into the laps of the early-day crew, made up of such strong-arm politicians as had been the first to shake the Territorial tree. In the righteous ladies of the Wyatt type they saw their chance for a strong ally. The saloons and the gamblers were too firmly intrenched to be moved by the reform element: they had tried it. Sabra had been urged to help. In the columns of the *Oklahoma Wigwam* she had unwisely essayed to conduct a campaign against Wick Mongold's saloon, in whose particularly lawless back room it was known that the young boys of the community were in the habit of meeting. With Cim's future in mind (and as an excuse) she wrote a stirring editorial in which she said bold things about shielding criminals and protecting the Flower of our Southwest's Manhood. Two days later a passer-by at seven in the morning saw brisk flames licking the foundations of the *Oklahoma Wigwam* office and the Cravat dwelling behind it. The whole had been nicely soaked in coal oil. But for the chance passer-by, Sabra, Cim, Donna, newspaper plant, and house would have been charred beyond recognition. As the town fire protection was still of the scantiest, the alarmed neighbors beat out the fire with blankets wet in the near-by horse trough. It was learned that a Mexican had been hired to do the job for twenty dollars. Mongold skipped out.

After an interval reform turned its attention to that always vulnerable objective known then as the Scarlet Woman. Here it met with less opposition. Almost five years after Yancey's departure it looked very much as though Dixie Lee and her fine brick house and her plumed and parasoled girls would soon be routed by the spiritual broomsticks and sunbonnets of the purity squad.

It was characteristic that at this moment in Osage's history, when the town was torn, now by martial music, now by the call of civic virtue, Yancey Cravat should have chosen to come riding home; and not that alone, but to come riding home in full panoply of war, more dashing, more romantic, more mysterious than on the day he had ridden away.

It was eight o'clock in the morning. The case of Dixie Lee (on the charge of disorderly conduct) was due to come up at ten in the local court. Sabra had been at her desk in the *Wigwam* office since seven. One ear was cocked for the sounds that came from the house; the other was intent on Jesse Rickey's erratic comings and goings in the printing shop just next the office.

"Cim! Cim Cravat! Will you stop teasing Donna and eat your breakfast. Miss Swisher's report said you were late three times last month, and all because you dawdle while you dress, you dawdle over breakfast, you dawdle—— Jesse! Oh, Jesse! The Dixie Lee case will be our news lead. Hold two columns open. . . ."

Horse's hoofs at a gallop, stopping spectacularly in front of the *Wigwam* office in a whirl of dust. A quick, light step. That step! But it couldn't be. Sabra sprang to her feet, one hand at her breast, one hand on the desk, to steady herself. He strode into the office. For five years she had pictured him returning to her in dramatic fashion; in his white sombrero, his Prince Albert, his high-heeled boots. For five years she had known what she would say, how she would look at him, in what manner she would conduct herself toward him—toward this man who had deserted her without a word, cruelly. In an instant, at sight of him, all this left her mind, her consciousness. She was in his arms with an inarticulate cry, she was weeping, her arms were about him, the buttons of his uniform crushed her breasts. His uniform. She realized then, without surprise, that he was in the uniform of the Oklahoma Rough Riders.

It is no use saying to a man who has been gone for five years, "Where have you been?" Besides, there was not time. Next morning he was on his way to the Philippines. It was not until he had gone that she realized her failure actually to put this question that had been haunting her for half a decade.

Cim and Donna took him for granted, as children do. So did Jesse Rickey, with his mind of a child. For that matter, Yancey took his own return for granted. His manner was nonchalant, his spirits high, his exuberance infectious. He set the pitch. There was about him nothing of the delinquent husband.

He now strode magnificently into the room where the children were at breakfast, snatched them up, kissed them. You would have thought he had been gone a week.

Donna was shy of him. "Your daughter's a Venable, Mrs. Cravat," he said, and turned to the boy. Cim, slender, graceful, taller than he seemed because of that trick of lowering his fine head and gazing at you from beneath his too-long lashes, reached almost to Yancey's broad shoulders. But he had not Yancey's heroic bulk, his vitality. The Cravat skull structure was contradicted by the narrow Venable face. The mouth was oversensitive, the hands and feet too exquisite, the smile almost girlish in its wistful sweetness. " 'Gods! How the son degenerates from the sire!' "

"Yancey!" cried Sabra in shocked protest. It was as though the five years had never been.

"Do you want to see my dog?" Cim asked.

"Have you got a pony?"

"Oh, no."

"I'll buy you one this afternoon. A pinto. Here. Look."

He took from his pocket a little soft leathern pouch soiled and worn from much handling. It was laced through at the top with a bit of stout string. He loosed this, poured the bag's contents onto the breakfast table; a little heap of shining yellow. The three stood looking at it. Cim touched it with one finger.

"What is it?"

Yancey scooped up a handful of it and let it trickle through his fingers. "That's gold." He turned to Sabra. "It's all I've got to show, honey, for two years and more in Alaska."

"Alaska!" she could only repeat, feebly. So that was it.

"I'm famished. What's this? Bacon and eggs?" He reached for a slice of bread from the plate on the table, buttered it lavishly, clapped a strip of coldish bacon on top of that, and devoured it in eager bites. Sabra saw then, for the first time, that he was thinner; there were hollow shadows in the pock-marked cheeks; there was a scarcely perceptible sag to the massive shoulders. There was something about his hand. The forefinger of the right hand was gone. She felt suddenly faint, ill. She reeled a little and stumbled. As always, he sprang toward her. His lips were against her hair.

"Oh, God! How I've missed you, Sabra, sugar!"

"Yancey! The children!" It was the prim exclamation of a woman who had forgotten the pleasant ways of dalliance. Those five years had served to accentuate her spinsterish qualities; had made her more and more powerful; less human; had slowed the machinery of her emotional equipment. A man in the house. A possessive male, enfolding her in his arms; touching her hair, her throat with urgent fingers. She was embarrassed almost. Besides, this man had neglected her, deserted her, had left his children to get on as best they could. She shrugged herself free. Anger leaped within her. He was a stranger.

"Don't touch me. You can't come home like this—after years—after years——"

"Ah, Penelope!"

She stared. "Who?"

" 'Strange lady, surely to thee above all womankind the Olympians have given a heart that cannot be softened. No other woman in the world would harden her heart to stand thus aloof from her husband, who after travail and sore had come to her . . . to his own country.'"

"You and your miserable Milton!"

He looked only slightly surprised and did not correct her.

One by one, and then in groups and then in crowds, the neighbors and townspeople began to come in—the Wyatts, Louie Hefner, Cass Peery, Mott Bixler, Ike Hawes, Grat Gotch, Doc Nisbett—the local politicians, the storekeepers, their wives. They came out of curiosity, though they felt proper resentment toward this strange—this baffling creature who had ridden carelessly away, leaving his wife and children to fend for themselves, and now had ridden as casually back again. They would have stayed away if they could, but his enchantment was too strong. Perhaps he represented, for them, the thing they fain would be or have. When Yancey, flouting responsibility and convention, rode away to be gone for mysterious years, a hundred men, bound by ties of work and wife and child, escaped in spirit with him; a hundred women, faithful wives and dutiful mothers, thought of Yancey as the elusive, the romantic, the desirable male.

Well, they would see how she had met it, and take their cue from her. A smart woman, Sabra Cravat. Throw him out, likely as not, and serve him right. But at sight of Yancey Cravat in his Rough Rider uniform of khaki, U.S.V. on the collar, the hat brim dashingly caught up on the left side with the insignia of crossed sabers, they were snared again in the mesh of his enchantment. The Rough Riders. Remember the *Maine*, to hell with Spain! There'll Be a Hot Time in the Old Town To-night. He became a figure symbolic of the war, of the Oklahoma country, of the Territory, of the Southwest—impetuous, romantic, adventuring.

"Hi, Yancey! Well, say, where you been, you old son of a stampedin' steer!"

"Howdy, Cimarron! Where at's your white hat?"

"You and this Roosevelt get goin' in this war, I guess the Spaniards'll wish Columbus never been born."

And Yancey, in return, "Hello, Clint! Howdy, Sam! Well, damn' if it isn't you, Grat! H'are you, Ike, you old hoss thief!"

The great figure towered even above these tall plainsmen; the fine eyes glowed; the mellifluous voice worked its magic. The renegade was a hero; the outcast had returned a conqueror.

Alaska. Oklahoma had not been so busy with its own growing pains that it had failed to hear of Alaska and the Gold Rush. "Alaska! Go on, you wasn't never in Alaska! Heard you'd turned Injun. Heard you was buried up in Boot Hill along of the Doolins."

He got out the little leather sack. While they gathered round him he poured out before their glistening eyes the shining yellow heap of that treasure with which the whole history of the Southwest was intertwined. Gold. The hills and the plains had been honeycombed for it; men had hungered and fought and parched for it; had died for it; had been killed for it; had sacrificed honor, home, happiness in the hope of finding it. And here was the precious yellow stuff from far-off Alaska trickling through Yancey Cravat's slim white fingers.

"Damn it all, Yancey, some folks has all the luck."

And so he stood, this Odysseus, and wove for them this new chapter in his saga. And they listened, and wondered, and believed and were stirred with envy and admiration and the longing for like adventure. He talked, he laughed, he gesticulated, he strode up and down, and they never missed the flirt of the Prince Albert coat tails, for there were brass buttons and patch pockets and gold embroidery and the glitter of crossed sabers to take their place.

"Luck! Call it luck, do you, Mott, to be frozen, starved, lost, snow-blinded! One whole winter shut up alone in a one-room cabin with the snow piled to the roof-top and no living soul to talk to for months. Luck to have your pardner that you trusted cheat you out of your claim and rob you of your gold in the bargain! All but this handful. I was going to see Sabra covered in gold like an Aztec princess."

The eyes of listening Osage swung to the prim blue serge figure of the cheated Aztec princess, encountered the level gaze, the unsmiling lips; swung back again hastily to the dashing, the martial figure of the lately despised wanderer.

A tale of another world; a story of a land so remote from the brilliant scarlet and orange of the burning Southwest country that the very sound of the words he used in describing it fell with a strange cadence on the ears of the eager listeners. And as always when Yancey was telling the tale, he filled his hearers with a longing for the place he described; a longing that was like a nostalgia for something they had never known. Well, folks, winters at fifty below zero. Two hours of bitter winter sunshine, and then blackness. Long splendid summer days in May and June, with twenty hours of sunshine and four hours of twilight. Sabra, listening with the others, found this new vocabulary as strange, as terrifying, as the jargon of the Oklahoma country had been to her when first she had encountered it years ago.

Yukon. Chilkoot Pass. Skagway. Kuskokwim. Klondike. Moose. Caribou. Huskies. Sledges. Nome. Sitka. Blizzards. Snow blindness. Frozen fingers. Pemmican. Cold. Cold. Cold. Gold. Gold. Gold. To the fascinated figures crowded into the stuffy rooms of this little frame house squatting on the sun-baked Oklahoma prairie he brought, by the magic of his voice and his eloquence, the relentless movement of the glaciers, the black menace of icy rivers, the waste plains of blinding, treacherous snow. Two years of this, he said; and looked ruefully down at the stump that had been his famous trigger finger.

They, too, looked. Two years. Two years, and he had been gone five. That left three unaccounted for, right enough. The old stories seeped up in their minds. Their eyes, grown accustomed to the uniform, were less dazzled now. They saw the indefinable break that had come to the magnificent figure—not a break, really, but a loosening, a lowering of the resistance such as comes to steel that has been too often in the flaming furnace. You looked at the massive shoulders—they did not droop. The rare glance still pierced you like a sword thrust. The buffalo head, lowered, menaced you; lifted, thrilled you. Yet something had vanished.

"Where'd you join up, Yancey?"

"San Antonio. Leonard Wood's down there—Colonel Wood now— and young Roosevelt, Lieutenant Colonel. He's been drilling the boys. Most of them born on a horse and weaned on a Winchester. We're better equipped than the regulars that have been at it for years. Young Roosevelt's to thank for that. They were all for issuing us winter clothing, by God, to wear through a summer campaign in the tropics—those nincompoops in Washington—and they'd have done it if it hadn't been for him."

Southwest Davis spoke up from the crowd. "That case, you'll be leaving right soon, won't you? Week or so."

"Week!" echoed Yancey, and looked at Sabra. "I go back to San Antonio to-morrow. The regiment leaves for Tampa next day."

He had not told her before. Yet she said nothing, gave no sign. She had outfaced them with her pride and her spirit for five years; she would give them no satisfaction now. Five years. One day. San Antonio— Tampa—Cuba—the Philippines—War. She gave no sign. Curiously, the picture that was passing in her mind was this: she saw herself, as though it were someone she had known in the dim, far past, standing in the cool, shady corridor of the Mission School in Wichita. She saw, through the open door, the oblong of Kansas sunshine and sky and garden; there swept over her again that wave of nostalgia she had felt for the scene she was leaving; she was shaken by terror of this strange Indian country to which she was going with her husband.

". . . but here in this land, Sabra, my girl, the women, they've been the real hewers of wood and drawers of water. You'll want to remember that."

Sabra remembered it now, well enough.

Slowly the crowd began to disperse. The men had their business; the women their housework. Wives linked their arms through those of husbands, and the gesture was one of perhaps not entirely unconscious cruelty, accompanied as it was by a darting glance at Sabra.

"Rough Rider uniform, sack of gold, golden voice, and melting eye," that glance seemed to say. "You're welcome to all the happiness you can get from those. Security, permanence, home, husband—I wouldn't change places with you."

"Come on, Yancey!" shouted Strap Buckner. "Over to the Sunny Southwest and have a drink. We got a terrible lot of drinking to do, ain't we, boys? Come on, you old longhorn. We got to drink to you because you're back and because you're going away."

"And to the war!" yelled Bixler.

"And the Rough Riders!"

"And Alaska!"

Their boots clattered across the board floor of the newspaper office. They swept the towering figure in its khaki uniform with them. He turned, waved his hat at her. "Back in a minute, honey." They were gone.

Sabra turned to the children, Cim and Donna, flushed, both, with the unwonted excitement; out of hand. Her face set itself with that look of quiet resolve. "Half the morning's gone. But I want you to go along to school, anyway. Now, none of that! It's no use your staying around here. The paper must be got out. Jesse'll be no good to me the rest of the day. It's easy to see that. I'll write a note to your teachers. . . . Run along now. I must go to court."

She actually had made up her mind that she would see the day through as she had started it. The Dixie Lee case, seething for weeks, was coming to a crisis this morning—this very minute. She would be late if she did not hasten. She would not let the work of months go for nothing because this man—this stranger had seen fit to stride into her life for a day.

She pinned on her hat, saw that her handbag contained pencil and paper, hurried into the back room that was printing shop, composing room, press room combined. She had been right about Jesse Rickey. That consistently irresponsible one was even now leaning a familiar elbow on the polished surface of the Sunny Southwest bar as he helped toast the returned wanderer or the departing hero or the war in the semi-tropics, or the snows of Alaska "—or God knows what!" concluded Sabra, in her mind.

Cliff Means, the ink-smeared printer's devil who, at fifteen, served as

Jesse Rickey's sole assistant in the mechanical end of the *Wigwam* office, looked up from his case rack as Sabra entered.

"It's all right, Mis' Cravat. I got the head all set up like you said. 'Vice Gets Death Blow. Reign of Scarlet Woman Ends. Judge Issues Ban.' Even if Jesse don't—even if he ain't—why, you and me can set up the story this afternoon so we can start the press goin' for Thursday. We ain't been late with the paper yet, have we?"

"Out on time every Thursday for five years," Sabra said, almost defiantly.

Suddenly, sharp and clear, Yancey's voice calling her from the office porch, from the front office, from the print-shop doorway; urgent, perturbed. "Sabra! Sabra! Sabra!"

He strode into the back shop. She faced him. Instinctively she knew. "What's this about Dixie Lee?" His news-trained eye leaped to the form. He read the set-up head, upside down, expertly. "When's this case come up?"

"Now."

"Who's defending her?"

"Nobody in town would touch the case. They say she got a lawyer from Denver. He didn't show up. He knew better than to take her money."

"Prosecuting?"

"Pat Leary."

Without a word he turned. She caught him at the door, gripped his arm. "Where are you going?"

"Court."

"What for? What for?" But she knew. She actually interposed her body between him and the street door then, as though physically to prevent him from going. Her face was white. Her eyes stared enormous.

"You can't take the case of that woman."

"Why not?"

"Because you can't. Because I've been fighting her. Because the *Wigwam* has come out against all that she stands for."

"Why, Sabra, honey, where are you thinking of sending her?"

"Away. Away from Osage."

"But where?"

"I don't know. I don't care. Things have changed since you went away. Went away and left me."

"Nothing's changed. It's all the same. Dixie's been stoned in the market place for two thousand years and more. Driving her out is not going to do it. You've got to drive the devil out of——"

"Yancey Cravat, are you preaching to me? You who left your wife and children to starve, for all you cared! And now you come back and you take this creature's part against every respectable woman in Osage —against me!"

"I know it. I can't help it, Sabra."

"I'll tell you what I think," cried Sabra—the Sabra Cravat who had been evolved in the past five years. "I think you're crazy! They've all said so. And now I know they are right."

"Maybe so."

"If you dare to think of disgracing me by defending her. And your children. I've fought her for months in the paper. A miserable creature like that! Your own wife—a laughing stock—for a—a——"

"The Territory's rotten. But, by God, every citizen's still got the legal right to fight for existence!" He put her gently aside.

She went mad. She became a wildcat. She tried to hold him. She beat herself against him. It was like an infuriated sparrow hurling itself upon a mastodon. "If you dare! Why did you come back? I hate you. What's she to you? I say you won't. I'd rather see you dead. I'd kill you first. That scum! That filth! That harlot!"

Her dignity was gone. He lifted her, scratching, kicking, clawing, set her gently down in the chair in front of her desk. The screen slammed. His quick, light step across the porch, down the stair. Crumpled, tear-stained, wild as she was, and with her hat on one side she reached automatically for her pencil, a pad of copy paper, and wrote a new head. Vice Again Triumphs Over Justice. Then, with what composure she could summon, she sped down the dusty road to where the combination jail and courthouse—a crude wooden building—sat broiling in the sun.

Because of the notoriety of the defendant the inadequate little courtroom would have been crowded enough in any case. But the news of Yancey's abrupt departure from the Sunny Southwest Saloon—and the reason for it—had spread from house to house through the little town with the rapidity of a forest fire leaping from tree to tree. Mad Yancey Cravat's latest freak. Men left their offices, their stores; women their cooking, their cleaning. The courtroom, stifling, fly infested, baked by the morning sun, was packed beyond endurance. The crowd perched on the window sills, stood on boxes outside the windows, suffocated in the doorway, squatted on the floor. The jury so hastily assembled, Pat Leary in a solemn suit of black, Dixie Lee with her girls, even Judge Sipes himself seemed in momentary danger of being trampled by the milling mob. It was a travesty of a courtroom. The Judge nervously champing his cud of tobacco, the corners of his mouth stained brown; Pat Leary neat, tight, representing law and order in his glittering celluloid collar; Dixie Lee, with a sense of the dramatic, all in black, her white cheeks unrouged, her dark abundant hair in neat smooth bands under the prim brim of her toque. But her girls were in full panoply of plumes. It was rather exhilarating to see them in that assemblage of drab respectability.

The jury was a hard-faced lot for the most part. Plucked from the plains or the hills; halting of speech, slow of mind, quick on the trigger. Two or three in overalls; one or two in the unaccustomed discomfort of store clothes. The rest in the conventional boots, corduroys or jeans, and rough shirt. A slow, rhythmic motion of the jaw was evidence that a generous preliminary bite of plug served as a precaution to soothe the nerves and steady the judgment.

This legal farce had already begun before Yancey made his spectacular entrance.

XVII

"CASE of the Territory of Oklahoma versus Dixie Lee!" (So they had made it a Territorial case. . . .) "Counsel for the Territory of Oklahoma!" Pat Leary stood up. ". . . for the defense." No one. The close-packed courtroom was a nightmare of staring eyes and fishlike mouths greedily devouring Dixie Lee's white, ravaged face. Oddly enough, compared to these, she seemed pure, aloof, exquisite. "The defendant having failed to provide herself with counsel, it is my duty, according to the laws of the gover'ment of the United States and the Territory of Oklahoma to appoint counsel for the defendant." He shifted his quid, the while his cunning, red-rimmed eyes roved solemnly through the crowd seeking the shyster, Gwin Larkin. A stir in the close-packed crowd; a murmur. "I hereby appoint——" The murmur swelled. "Order in the court!"

"Your Honor!"

Towering above the crowd, forging his way through it like some relentless force of nature, came the great buffalo head, the romantic Rough Rider hat with its turned-up brim caught by the crossed sabers; the massive khaki-clad figure. It was dramatic, it was melodramatic, it was ridiculous. It was superb. The fish faces turned their staring eyes and their gasping mouths away from the white-faced woman and upon him. Here was the kind of situation that the Southwest loved and craved; here was action, here was blood-and-thunder, here was adventure. Here, in a word, was Cimarron.

He stood before the shoddy judge. He swept off his hat with a gesture that invested it with plumes. "If it please Your Honor, I represent the defendant, Dixie Lee."

No Territorial judge, denying Yancey Cravat, would have dared to face that crowd. He cast another glance round—a helpless, baffled one, this time—waved the approaching Gwin Larkin back with a feeble gesture, and prepared to proceed with the case according to the laws of the Territory. Certainly the look that he turned on Sabra Cravat as she entered a scant ten minutes later, white faced, resolute, and took her place as representative of the press, was one of such mingled bewilderment and reproach as would have embarrassed anyone less utterly preoccupied than the editor and publisher of the *Oklahoma Wigwam*.

Objection on the part of the slick Pat Leary. Overruled, perforce, by the Judge. A shout from the crowd. Order! Bang! Another shout. Law in a lawless community not yet ten years old; a community made up, for the most part, of people whose very presence there meant impatience of the old order, defiance of the conventions. Ten minutes earlier they had been all for the cocky little Leary, erstwhile station agent; eager to cast the first stone at the woman in the temple. Now, with the inexplicable fickleness of the mob, the electric current of sympathy flowed out from them to the woman to be tried, to the man who would defend her. Hot and swift and plenty of action—that was the way the Southwest liked its justice.

Pat Leary. Irish, ambitious, fiery. His temper, none too even at best, had been lost before he ever rose. The thought of Yancey ahead of him, the purity brigade behind him, spurred him to his frantic, his disorderly charge.

His years as section hand on the railroad had equipped him with a vocabulary well suited to scourge this woman in black who sat so quietly, so white faced, before him, for all the crowd to see. Adjective on adjective; vituperation; words which are considered obscenity outside the Bible and the courtroom.

". . . all the vicious influences, Your Honor, with which our glorious Territory is infested, can be laid at this woman's leprous door. . . . A refuge for the evil, for the diseased, for the criminal . . . waxed fat and sleek in her foul trade, on the money that should have been spent to help build up, to ennoble this fair Southwest land of ours . . . scavenger . . . vilest of humans . . . disgrace to the fair name of woman. . . ." Names, then, that writhed from his tongue like snakes.

A curious embarrassment seized the crowd. There were many in the packed room who had known the easy hospitality of Dixie's ménage; who had eaten at her board, who had been broken in Grat Gotch's gambling place and had borrowed money from Dixie to save themselves from rough frontier revenge. She had plied her trade and taken the town's money and given it out again with the other merchants of the town. The banker could testify to that; the mayor; this committee; that committee. Put Dixie Lee's name down for a thousand. Part of the order of that disorderly, haphazard town.

Names. Names. Names. The dull red of resentment deepened the natural red of their sunburned faces. The jurors shifted in their places. A low mutter, ominous, like a growl, sounded its distant thunder. Blunt. Sharp. Ruthless. Younger than Yancey, less experienced, he still should have known better. These men of the inadequate jury, these men in the courtroom crowd, had come of a frontier background, had lived in the frontier atmosphere. In their rough youth, and now, women were scarce, with the scarcity that the hard life predicated. And because they were scarce they were precious. No woman so plain, so hard, so undesirable that she did not take on, by the very fact of her sex, a value far beyond her deserts. The attitude of a whole nation had been touched by this sentimental fact which was, after all, largely geographic. For a full century the countries of Europe, bewildered by it, unable to account for it, had laughed at this adolescent reverence of the American man for the American woman.

Here was Pat Leary, jumping excitedly about, mouthing execrations, when he himself, working on the railroads ten years before, had married an Indian girl out of the scarcity of girls in the Oklahoma country. Out of the corner of his eye, as he harangued, he saw the great lolling figure of Yancey Cravat. The huge head was sunk on the breast; the eyelids were lowered. Beaten, Pat Leary thought. Defeated, and he knows it. Cravat, the wind bag, the wife deserter. He finished in a burst of oratory so ruthless, so brutal that he had the satisfaction of seeing the painful, unaccustomed red surge thickly over Dixie Lee's pale face from her brow down to where the ladylike white turnover of her high collar met the line of her throat.

The pompous little Irishman seated himself, chest out, head high, eye roving the crowd and the bench, lips open with self-satisfaction. A few more cases like this and maybe they'd see there was material for a Territory governor right here in Osage.

The crowd shifted, murmured, gabbled. Yancey still sat sunk in his chair as though lost in thought. The gabble rose, soared. "He's given it up," thought Sabra, exulting. "He sees how it is."

The eyes of the crowd so close packed in that suffocating little court-room were concentrated on the inert figure lolling so limply in its chair. Perhaps they were going to be cheated of their show after all.

Slowly the big head lifted, the powerful shoulders straightened, he rose, he seemed to rise endlessly, he walked to Judge Sipes's crude desk with his light, graceful stride. The lids were still cast down over the lightning eyes. He stood a moment, that singularly sweet and winning smile wreathing his lips. He began to speak. The vibrant voice, after Leary's shouts, was so low pitched that the crowd held its breath in order to hear.

"Your Honor. Gentlemen of the Jury. I am the first to bow to achievement. Recognition where recognition is due—this, gentlemen, has ever been my way. May I, then, before I begin my poor plea in defense of this lady, my client, most respectfully call your attention to that which, in my humble opinion, has never before been achieved, much less duplicated, in the whole of the Southwest. Turn your eye to the figure which has so recently and so deservedly held your attention. Gaze once more upon him. Regard him well. You will not look upon his like again. For, gentlemen, in my opinion this gifted person, Mr. Patrick Leary, is the only man in the Oklahoma Territory—in the Indian Territory—in the whole of the brilliant and glorious Southwest—nay, I may even go so far as to say the only man in this magnificent country, the United States of America!—of whom it actually can be said that he is able to strut sitting down."

The puffed little figure in the chair collapsed, then bounded to its feet, red faced, gesticulating. "Your Honor! I object!"

But the rest was lost in the gigantic roar of the delighted crowd.

"Go it, Yancey!"

"That's the stuff, Cimarron!"

Here was what they had come for. Doggone, there was nobody like him, damn if they was!

Even to-day, though more than a quarter of a century has gone by, there still are people in Oklahoma who have kept a copy, typed neatly now from records made by hand, of the speech made that day by Yancey Cravat in defense of the town woman, Dixie Lee. Yancey Cravat's Plea for a Fallen Woman, it is called; and never was speech more sentimental, windy, false, and utterly moving. The slang words hokum and bunk were not then in use, but even had they been they never would have been applied, by that appreciative crowd, at least, to the flowery and impassioned oratory of the Southwest Silver Tongue, Yancey Cravat.

Cheap, melodramatic, gorgeous, impassioned. A quart of whisky in

him; an enthralled audience behind him; a white-faced woman with
hopeless eyes to spur him on; the cry of his wronged and righteous
wife still sounding in his ears—Booth himself, in his heyday, never gave
a more brilliant, a more false performance.

"Your Honor! Gentlemen of the Jury! You have heard with what
cruelty the prosecution has referred to the sins of this woman, as if her
condition was of her own preference. A dreadful—a vicious—a revolting
picture has been painted for you of her life and surroundings. Tell me—
tell me—do you really think that she willingly embraced a life so repel-
lent, so horrible? No, gentlemen! A thousand times, no! This girl was
bred in such luxury, such refinement, as few of us have known. And
just as the young girl was budding into womanhood, cruel fate snatched
all this from her, bereft her of her dear ones, took from her, one by one,
with a terrible and fierce rapidity, those upon whom she had come to
look for love and support. And then, in that moment of darkest terror
and loneliness, came one of our sex, gentlemen. A wolf in sheep's clothing. A fiend in the guise of a human. False promises. Lies. Deceit so
palpable that it would have deceived no one but a young girl as innocent, as pure, as starry eyed as was this woman you now see white and
trembling before you. One of our sex was the author of her ruin, more
to blame than she. What could be more pathetic than the spectacle she
presents? An immortal soul in ruin. The star of purity, once glittering
on her girlish brow, has set its seal, and forever. A moment ago you
heard her reviled, in the lowest terms a man can employ toward a
woman, for the depths to which she has sunk, for the company she
keeps, for the life she leads. Yet where can she go that her sin does not
pursue her? You would drive her out. But where? Gentlemen, the very
promises of God are denied her. Who was it said, 'Come unto me all
ye that are heavy laden, and I will give you rest'? She is indeed heavy
laden, this trampled flower of the South, but if at this instant she were
to kneel down before us all and confess her Redeemer, where is the
Church that would receive her, where the community that would take
her in? Scorn and mockery would greet her; those she met of her own
sex would gather their skirts the more closely to avoid the pollution of
her touch. Our sex wrecked her once pure life. Her own sex shrinks
from her as from a pestilence. Society has reared its relentless walls
against her. Only in the friendly shelter of the grave can her betrayed
and broken heart ever find the Redeemer's promised rest. The gentleman who so eloquently spoke before me told you of her assumed
names, of her sins, of her habits. He never, for all his eloquence, told
you of her sorrows, her agonies, her hopes, her despairs. But I could
tell you. I could tell you of the desperate day—the red-letter day in the

banner of the great Oklahoma country—when she tried to win a home for herself where she could live in decency and quiet. . . . When the remembered voices of father and mother and sisters and brothers fall like music on her erring ears . . . who shall tell what this heavy heart, sinful though it may seem to you and to me . . . understanding, pity, help, like music on her erring soul . . . oh, gentlemen . . . gentlemen . . ."

But by this time the gentlemen, between emotion and tobacco juice, were having such difficulty with their Adam's apples as to make a wholesale strangling seem inevitable. The beautiful flexible voice went on, the hands wove their enchantment, the eyes held you in their spell. The pompous figure of little Pat Leary shrank, dwindled, disappeared before their mind's eye. The harlot Dixie Lee, in her black, became a woman romantic, piteous, appealing. Sabra Cravat, her pencil flying over her paper, thought grimly:

"It isn't true. Don't believe him. He is wrong. He has always been wrong. For fifteen years he has always been wrong. Don't believe him. I shall have to print this. How lovely his voice is. It's like a knife in my heart. I mustn't look at his eyes. His hands—what was that he said?—I must keep my mind on . . . music on her erring soul . . . oh, my love . . . I ought to hate him . . . I do hate him. . . ."

Dixie Lee's head drooped on her ravaged breast. Even her plumed satellites had the wit to languish like crushed lilies and to wipe their eyes with filmy handkerchiefs the while they sniffled audibly.

It was finished. Yancey walked to his seat, sat as before, the great buffalo head lowered, the lids closed over the compelling eyes, the beautiful hands folded, relaxed.

The good men and true of the jury filed solemnly out through the crowd that made way for them. As solemnly they crossed the dusty road and repaired to a draw at the roadside, where they squatted on such bits of rock or board as came to hand. Solemnly, briefly, and with utter disregard of its legal aspect, they discussed the case—if their inarticulate monosyllables could be termed discussion. The courtroom throng, scattering for refreshment, had barely time to down its drink before the jury stamped heavily across the road and into the noisome courtroom.

". . . find the defendant, Dixie Lee, not guilty."

XVIII

IT WAS as though Osage and the whole Oklahoma country now stopped and took a deep breath. Well it might. Just ahead of it, all unknown, waited years of such clangor and strife as would make the past years seem uneventful in comparison. Ever since the day of the Run, more than fifteen years ago, it had been racing helter-skelter, devil take the hindmost; shooting into the air, prancing and yelping out of sheer vitality and cussedness. A rough roof over its head; coarse food on its table; a horse to ride; a burning drink to toss down its throat; border justice; gyp water; a girl to hug; mud roads to the edge of the sun-baked prairie, and thereafter no road; grab what you need; fight for what you want— the men who had come to the wilderness of the Oklahoma country had expected no more than this; and this they had got. A man's country it seemed to be, ruled by men for men. The women allowed them to think so. The word feminism was unknown to the Sabra Cravats, the Mrs. Wyatts, the Mrs. Hefners, the Mesdames Turket and Folsom and Sipes. Prim, good women and courageous, banded together by their goodness and by their common resolve to tame the wilderness. Their power was the more tremendous because they did not know they had it. They never once said, during those fifteen years, "We women will do this. We women will change that." Quietly, indomitably, relentlessly, without even a furtive glance of understanding exchanged between them, but secure in their common knowledge of the sentimental American male, they went ahead with their plans.

The Philomathean Club. The Twentieth Century Culture Club. The Eastern Star. The Daughters of Rebekah. The Venus Lodge.

"Ha-ha!" and "Ho-ho!" roared their menfolk. "What do you girls do at these meetings of yours? Swap cooking receipts and dress patterns?"

"Oh, yes. And we talk."

"I bet you do. Say, you don't have to tell any man that. Talk! Time about ten of you women folks start gabblin' together I bet you get the whole Territory settled—politics, Injuns, land fights, and all."

"Just about."

Yancey had come home from the Spanish-American War a hero. Other men from Osage had been in the Philippines. One had even died there (dysentery and ptomaine from bad tinned beef). But Yancey was the town's Rough Rider. He had charged up San Juan Hill with Roosevelt. Osage, knowing Yancey and never having seen Roosevelt, assumed that Yancey Cravat—the Southwest Cimarron—had led the way, an ivory- and silver-mounted six-shooter in either hand, the great buffalo head lowered with such menace that the little brown men had fled to their jungles in terror.

His return had been the occasion for such a celebration as the town had never known and never would know again, they assured each other, between drinks, until the day when statehood should come to the Territory. He returned a captain, unwounded, but thin and yellow, with the livery look that confirmed the stories one had heard of putrid food, typhoid, dysentery, and mosquitoes more deadly, in this semi-tropical country, than bullets or cannon.

Poisoned and enfeebled though he was, his return seemed to energize the crude little town. Wherever he might be he lived in a swirl of events that drew into its eddy all that came within its radius. Hi, Yancey! Hi, Clint! He shed the khaki and the cocked hat and actually appeared again in the familiar white sombrero, Prince Albert, and high-heeled boots. Osage breathed a sigh of satisfaction. His dereliction was forgiven, the rumors about him forgotten—or allowed to subside, at least. Again the editorial columns of the *Oklahoma Wigwam* blazed with hyperbole.

It was hard for Sabra to take second place (or to appear to take second place) in the office of the *Wigwam*. She had so long ruled there alone. Her word had been law to the wavering Jesse Rickey and to the worshiping Cliff Means. And now to say, "You'd better ask Mr. Cravat."

"He says leave it to you. He's went out."

Yancey did a good deal of going out. Sabra, after all, still did most of the work of the paper without having the satisfaction of dictating its policy. A linotype machine, that talented iron monster, now chattered and chittered and clanked in the composing room of the *Wigwam*. It was the first of its kind in the Oklahoma country. Very costly and uncannily human, Sabra never quite got over her fear of it. The long arm reached down with such leisurely assurance, snatched its handful of metal, carried it over, descended, dropped it. It opened its capacious maw to be fed bars of silvery lead which it spat forth again in the shape of neat cakes of type. Its keys were like grinning teeth. It grunted, shivered, clumped, spoke—or nearly.

"I never come near it," Sabra once admitted, "that I don't expect the thing to reach down with its iron arm and clap me on the shoulder and clatter, 'Hello, Sabra!'"

She was proud of the linotype machine, for it had been her five years at the head of the *Wigwam* that had made it possible. It was she who had gone out after job printing contracts; who had educated the local merchants to the value of advertising. Certainly Yancey, prancing and prating, had never given a thought to these substantial foundations on which the entire business success of the paper rested. They now got out with ease the daily *Wigwam* for the Osage townspeople and the weekly for county subscribers. Passing the windows of the *Wigwam* office on Pawhuska Avenue you could hear the thump and rattle of the iron monster. Between them Jesse Rickey and Cliff Means ran the linotype. Often they labored far into the night on job work, and the late passer-by would see the little light burning in the printing shop and hear the rattle and thump of the machine. In a pinch Sabra herself could run it. Yancey never went near it, and, strangely enough, young Cim had a horror of it, as he had of most things mechanical. After one attempt at the keyboard, during which he had hopelessly jammed the machine's delicate insides, he was forbidden ever to go near it again. For that matter, Cim had little enough taste for the newspaper business. He pied type at the case rack. He had no news sense. He had neither his father's gift for mingling with people and winning their confidence nor his mother's more orderly materialistic mind. He had much of Yancey Cravat's charm, and something of the vagueness of his grandfather, old Lewis Venable (dead these two years), but combining the worst features of both.

"Stop dreaming!" Sabra said to him, often and often. "What are you dreaming about?"

She had grown to love the atmosphere of the newspaper office and resented the boy's indifference to it. She loved the very smell of it—the mixed odor of hot metal, printer's ink, dust, white paper, acid, corncob pipe, and cats.

"Stop dreaming!" Yancey, hearing her thus admonishing Cim, whirled on her in one of his rare moments of utter rage. "God A'mighty, Sabra! That's what Ann Hathaway said to Shakespeare. Don't you women know that 'Dreams grow holy put in action; work grows fair through starry dreaming'? Leave the boy alone! Let him dream! Let him dream!"

"One starry dreamer in a family is enough," Sabra retorted, tartly.

Five years had gone by—six years since Yancey's return. Yet, strangely enough, Sabra never had a feeling of security. She never forgot what he had said about Wichita. "Almost five years in one place. That's the longest stretch I've ever done, honey." Five years. And this was well into the sixth. He had plunged head first into the statehood fight, into the Indian Territory situation. The anti-Indian faction was bitterly opposed to the plan for combining the Oklahoma Territory and the Indian Territory under the single state of Oklahoma. Their slogan was The White Man's State for the White Man.

"Who brought the Indian here to the Oklahoma country in the first place?" shouted Yancey in the editorial columns of the *Wigwam.* "White men. They hounded them from Missouri to Arkansas, from Arkansas to southern Kansas, then to northern Kansas, to northern Oklahoma, to southern Oklahoma. You white men sold them the piece of arid and barren land on which they now live in squalor and misery. It isn't fit for a white man to live on, or the Indians wouldn't be living on it now. Deprived of their tribal laws, deprived of their tribal rites, herded together in stockades like wild animals, robbed, cheated, kicked, hounded from place to place, give them the protection of the country that has taken their country away from them. Give them at least the right to become citizens of the state of Oklahoma."

He was obsessed by it. He traveled to Washington in the hope of lobbying for it, and made quite a stir in that formal capital with his white sombrero, his Prince Albert, his Texas star boots, his great buffalo head, his charm, his grace, his manner. Roosevelt was characteristically cordial to his old campaign comrade. Washington ladies were captivated by the flowery speeches of this romantic, this story-book swaggerer out of the Southwest.

It was rumored on good authority that he was to be appointed the next Governor of the Oklahoma Territory.

"Oh, Yancey," Sabra said, "do be careful. Governor of the Territory! It would mean so much. It would help Cim in the future. Donna, too. Their father a governor." She thought, "Perhaps everything will be all right now. Perhaps all that I've gone through in the last ten years will be worth it, now. Perhaps it was for this. He'll settle down. . . . Mamma can't say now . . . and all the Venables and the Vians and the Goforths and the Greenwoods. . . ." She had had to endure their pity, even from a distance, all these years.

The rumor took on substance. My husband, Yancey Cravat, Governor of the Territory of Oklahoma. And then, when statehood came, as it must in the next few years, perhaps Governor of the state of Oklahoma. Why not!

At which point Yancey blasted any possibility of his appointment to the governorship by hurling a red-hot editorial into the columns of the *Wigwam.* The gist of it was that the hundreds of thousands of Indians now living on reservations throughout the United States should be al-

lowed to live where they pleased, at liberty. The whites of the Oklahoma
Territory and the Indian Territory, with an Indian population of about
one hundred and twenty thousand of various tribes—Poncas, Cherokees,
Chickasaws, Creeks, Osages, Kiowas, Comanches, Kaws, Choctaws,
Seminoles, and a score of others—read, emitted a roar of rage, and
brandishing the paper ran screaming into the streets, cursing the name
of Yancey Cravat.

Sabra had caught the editorial in the wet proof sheet. Her eye leaped
down its lines.

> Herded like sheep in a corral—no, like wild animals in a cage—they
> are left to rot on their reservations by a government that has taken
> first their land, then their self-respect, then their liberty from them.
> The land of the free! When the very people who first dwelt on it are
> prisoners! Slaves, but slaves deprived of the solace of work. What hope
> have they, what ambition, what object in living! Their spirit is broken.
> Their pride is gone. Slothful, yes. Why not? Each month he receives
> his dole, his pittance. Look at the Osage Nation, now dwindled to a
> wretched two thousand souls. The men are still handsome, strong, vital;
> the women beautiful, dignified, often intelligent. Yet there they huddle
> in their miserable shanties like beaten animals eating the food that is
> thrown them by a great—a munificent—government. The government
> of these United States! Let them be free. Let the Red Man live a free
> man as the White Man lives. . . .

Much that he wrote was true, perhaps. Yet the plight of the Indian
was not as pitiable as Yancey painted it. He cast over them the glamour
of his own romantic nature. The truth was that they themselves cared
little—except a few of their tribal leaders, more intelligent than the rest.
They hunted a little, fished, slept, visited from tribe to tribe, the Poncas
visiting the Osages, the Osages the Poncas, gossiping, eating, holding
powwows. The men were great poker players, having learned the game
from the white man, and spent hours at it.

They passed through the town of Osage in their brilliant striped
blankets, sometimes walking, sometimes on sorry nags, sometimes in
rickety wagons laden with pots, poles, rags, papooses, hounds. The
townspeople hastily removed such articles as might please the pilfering
fancy.

Sabra picked up the proof sheet, still damp from the press, and
walked into Yancey's office. Her face was white, set.

"You're going to run this, Yancey?"

"Yes."

"You'll never be Governor of the Territory."

"Never."

She stood a moment, her face working. She crushed the galley proof in her hand so that her knuckles stood out, white.

"I've forgiven you many, many things, God knows, in the last ten years. I'll never forgive you for this. Never."

"Yes, you will, honey. Never is a long time. Not while I'm alive, maybe. But some day, a long time from now—though not so very long, maybe—you'll be able to turn back to the old files of the *Oklahoma Wigwam* and lift this editorial of mine right out of it, word for word, and run it as your own."

"Never. . . . Donna . . . Cim . . ."

"I can't live my children's lives for them, Sabra, honey. They've got to live their own. I believe what I believe. This town is rotten—the Territory—the whole country. Rotten."

"You're a fine one to say what is or isn't rotten. You with your whisky and your Indians and your women. I despise you. So does everyone in the town—in the Territory."

" 'A prophet is not without honor, save in his own country and in his own home.' " A trifle sonorously.

She never really knew whether he had done this thing with the very purpose of making his governorship impossible. It was like him.

Curiously enough, the editorial, while it maddened the white population of the Territory, gained the paper many readers. The *Wigwam* prospered. Osage blossomed. The town was still rough, crude, wide open, even dangerous. But it began to take on an aspect of permanence. It was no longer a camp; it was a town. It began to build schools, churches, halls. Arkansas Grat's gambling tent had long ago been replaced by a solid wooden structure, just as gambling terms of the West and the Southwest had slowly been incorporated into the language of daily use. I'm keeping cases on him . . . standing pat . . . bluffing . . . bucking the tiger. Terms filched from the gaming table; poker and faro and keno.

Sol Levy's store—the Levy Mercantile Company—had two waxen ladies in the window, their features only slightly affected by the burning Southwest sun. Yancey boomed Sol Levy for mayor of Osage, but he never had a chance. It was remarkable how the *Oklahoma Wigwam* persisted, though its position in most public questions was violently unpopular. Perhaps it, like Yancey, had a vitality and a charm that no one could withstand.

Although Sol Levy was still the town Jew, respected, prosperous, the town had never quite absorbed this Oriental. A citizen of years' standing, he still was a stranger. He mingled little with his fellow townsmen outside business hours. He lived lonesomely at the Bixby House and ate the notoriously bad meals served by Mrs. Bixby. He was shy of the town women though the Women of the Town found him kindly, passionate, and generous. The business men liked him. They put him on committees. Occasionally Sabra or some other woman who knew him well enough would say, half playfully, half seriously, "Why don't you get married, Sol? A nice fellow like you. You'd make some girl happy."

Sometimes he thought vaguely of going to Wichita or Kansas City or even Chicago to meet some nice Jewish girl there, but he never did. It never entered his head to marry a Gentile. The social life of the town was almost unknown to him. Sometimes if a big local organization—the Elks, the Odd Fellows, the Sons of the Southwest—gave a benefit dance, you would glimpse him briefly, in the early part of the evening, standing shyly against the wall or leaning half hidden in the doorway, a darkling, remote, curiously Oriental figure in the midst of these robust red-faced plainsmen and ex-cowmen.

"Come on, Sol, mix in! Grab off one of the girls and get to dancin', why don't you? What you scairt of?" But Sol remained aloof. He regarded the hot, sweaty, shouting dancers with a kind of interested bewilderment and wonder, much as the dancers themselves sometimes watched the Indians during one of the Festival Dances on the outlying reservations. On occasion he made himself politely agreeable to a stout matron well past middle age. They looked up at his tragic dark eyes; they noticed his slim ivory hand as it passed them a plate of cake or a cup of coffee. "He's real nice when you get to know him," they said. "For a Jew, that is."

Between him and Yancey there existed a deep sympathy and understanding. Yancey campaigned for Sol Levy in the mayoralty race—if a thing so one-sided could be called a race. The *Wigwam* extolled him.

Sol Levy, the genial proprietor of the Levy Mercantile Company, is the *Wigwam's* candidate for mayor. It behooves the people of Osage to do honor to one of its pioneer citizens whose career, since its early days, has been marked by industry, prosperity, generosity. He comes of a race of dreamers and doers. . . .

"Why, the very idea!" snorted the redoubtable virago, Mrs. Tracy Wyatt, whose husband was the opposing candidate. "A Jew for mayor of Osage! They'll be having an Indian mayor next. Mr. Wyatt's folks are real Americans. They helped settle Arkansas. And as for me, why, I can trace my ancestry right back to William Whipple, who was one of the signers of the Declaration of Independence."

Sol Levy never had a chance for public honor. He, in fact, did practically nothing to further his own possible election. He seemed to regard the whole matter with a remoteness slightly tinged with ironic humor. Yancey dropped into Sol's store to bring him this latest pronouncement of the bristling Mrs. Wyatt. Sol was busy in the back of the store, where he was helping the boy unpack a new invoice of china and lamps just received, for the Levy Mercantile Company had blossomed into a general store of parts. His head was in a barrel, and when he straightened and looked up at the towering Yancey there were bits of straw and excelsior clinging to his shirt sleeves and necktie and his black hair.

"Declaration of Independence!" he exclaimed, thoughtfully. "Tell her one of my ancestors wrote the Ten Commandments. Fella name of Moses."

Yancey, roaring with laughter, used this in the *Wigwam*, and it naturally helped as much as anything to defeat the already defeated candidate.

Sometimes the slim, white-faced proprietor, with his friend Yancey Cravat, stood in the doorway of the store, watching the town go by. They said little. It was as though they were outsiders, looking on at a strange pageant.

"What the hell are you doing here in this town, anyway, Sol?" Yancey would say, as though musing aloud.

"And you?" Sol would retort. "A civilized barbarian."

The town went by—Indians, cowboys up from Texas, plainsmen, ranchers. They still squatted at the curb, as in the early days. They chewed tobacco and spat. The big sombrero persisted, and even the boots and spurs.

"Howdy, Yancey! Howdy, Sol! H'are you, Cim!"

There was talk of paving Pawhuska Avenue, but this did not come for years. The town actually boasted a waterworks. The *Wigwam* office still stood on Pawhuska, but it now occupied the entire house. Two years after Yancey's return they had decided to build a home on Kihekah Street, where there actually were trees now almost ten years old.

Sabra had built the house as she wanted it, though at first there had been a spirited argument about this. Yancey's idea had been, of course, ridiculous, fantastic. He said he wanted the house built in native style.

"Native! What in the world! A wickiup?"

"Well, a house in the old Southwest Indian style—almost pueblo, I mean. Or Spanish, sort of, made of Oklahoma red clay—plaster, maybe. Not brick. And low, with a patio where you can be out of doors and yet away from the sun. And where you can have privacy."

Sabra made short work of that idea. Or perhaps Yancey did not persist. He withdrew his plan as suddenly as he had presented it; shrugged his great shoulders as though the house no longer interested him.

Osage built its new houses with an attached front porch gaping so-cially out into the street. It sat on the front porch in its shirt sleeves and kitchen apron. It called from porch to porch, "How's your tomato plants doing? I see the Packses got out-of-town company visiting." It didn't in the least want privacy.

Sabra built a white frame house in the style of the day, with turrets, towers, minarets, cupolas, and scroll work. There was a stained glass window in the hall, in purple and red and green and yellow, which, con-fronting the entering caller, gave him the look of being suddenly stricken with bubonic plague. There were parlor, sitting room, dining room, kitchen on the first floor; four bedrooms on the second floor, and a bathroom, actually, with a full-size bathtub, a toilet, and a marble wash-stand with varicose veins. In the cellar there was a hot air furnace. In the parlor were brown brocade-and-velvet settee and stuffed chairs. In the sitting room was a lamp with a leaded glass shade in the shape of a strange and bloated flower—a Burbankian monstrosity, half water lily, half petunia.

"As long as we're building and furnishing," Sabra said, "it might as well be the best." She had gone about planning the house, and furnish-ing it, with her customary energy and capability. With it all she found time to do her work on the *Wigwam*—for without her the paper would have been run to the ground in six months. Osage had long since ceased to consider it queer that she, a woman, and the wife of one of its most prominent citizens, should go to work every morning like a man.

By ten every morning she had attended to her household, seen it started for the day, had planned the meals, ordered them on her way downtown, and was at her desk in the *Wigwam* office, sorting mail, reading exchanges, taking ads, covering news, writing heads, pasting up. Yancey's contributions were brilliant but spasmodic. The necessary de-partmental items—real estate transfers, routine court news, out-of-town district and county gleanings—bored him, though he knew well that they were necessary to the success of the paper. He left these to Sabra, among many other things.

Sabra, in common with the other well-to-do housewives of the com-munity, employed an Indian girl as a house servant. There was no other kind of help available. After her hideous experience with Arita Red Feather she had been careful to get Indian girls older, more settled, though this was difficult. She preferred Osage girls. These married young, often before they had finished their studies at the Indian school.

Ruby Big Elk had been with Sabra now for three years. A curious, big, silent girl of about twenty-two—almost handsome—one of six children —a large family for an Osage. Sabra was somewhat taken aback, after the girl had been with her for some months, to learn that she already had been twice married.

"What became of your husbands, Ruby?"

"Died."

She had a manner that bordered on the insolent. Sabra put it down to Indian dignity. When she walked she scuffed her feet ever so little, and this, for some inexplicable reason, seemed to add insolence to her bearing. "Oh, do lift your feet, Ruby! Don't scuffle when you walk." The girl made no reply. Went on scuffling. Sabra discovered that she was lame; the left leg was slightly shorter than the right. She did not limp— or, rather, hid the tendency to limp by the irritating sliding sound. Her walk was straight, leisurely, measured. Sabra was terribly embarrassed; apologized to the Indian girl. The girl only looked at her and said nothing. Sabra repressed a little shiver. She had never got accustomed to the Indians.

Sabra was a bustler and a driver. As she went about the house in the morning, performing a dozen household duties before leaving for the *Wigwam* office, her quick tapping step drummed like hail on a tin roof. It annoyed her intensely, always, to see Ruby Big Elk making up the beds with that regal manner, or moving about the kitchen with the pace and air of a Lady Macbeth. The girl's broad, immobile face, her unspeaking eyes, her secret manner all worked a slow constant poison in Sabra. She spoke seldom; never smiled. When Sabra spoke to her about some household task she would regard her mistress with an unblinking gaze that was highly disconcerting.

"Did you understand about the grape jell, Ruby? To let it get thoroughly cool before you pour on the wax?"

Ruby would majestically incline her fine head, large, like a man's head. The word sinister came into Sabra's mind. Still, Sabra argued, she was good to the children, fed them well, never complained about the work. Sometimes—on rare occasions—she would dig a little pit in the back yard and build a slow hot smothered fire by some secret Indian process, and there, to the intense delight of young Cim, she would roast meats deliciously in the Indian fashion, crisp and sweet, skewered with little shafts of wood that she herself whittled down. Donna refused to touch the meat, as did Sabra. Donna shared her mother's dislike of the Indians—or perhaps she had early been impressed with her mother's feeling about them. Sometimes Donna, the spoiled, the pampered, the imperious (every inch her grandmother Felice Venable) would feel Ruby Big Elk's eye on her—that expressionless, dead black Indian eye. Yet back of its deadness, its utter lack of expression, there still seemed to lurk a cold contempt.

"What are you staring at, Ruby?" Donna would cry, pettishly. Ruby would walk out of the room with her slow scuffling step, her body erect, her head regal, her eyes looking straight ahead. She said nothing. "Miserable squaw!" Donna would hiss under her breath. "Gives herself the airs of a princess because her greasy old father runs the tribe or something."

Ruby's father, Big Elk, had in fact been Chief of the Osage tribe by election for ten years, and though he no longer held this highest office, was a man much looked up to in the Osage Nation. He had sent his six children and actually his fat wife to the Indian school, but he himself steadfastly refused to speak a word of English, though he knew enough of the language. He conversed in Osage, and when necessary used an interpreter. It was a kind of stubborn Indian pride in him. It was his enduring challenge to the white man. "You have not defeated me."

His pride did not, however, extend to more material things, and Sabra was frequently annoyed by the sight of the entire Big Elk family, the old ex-Chief, his squaw, and the five brothers and sisters, squatting in her kitchen doorway enjoying such juicy bits as Ruby saw fit to bestow upon them from the Cravat larder. When Sabra would have put a stop to this, Yancey intervened.

"He's a wise old man. If he had a little white blood in him he'd be as great as Quanah Parker was, or Sequoyah. Everything he says is wisdom. I like to talk with him. Leave him alone."

This did not serve to lessen Sabra's irritation. Often she returned home to find Yancey squatting on the ground with old Big Elk, smoking and conversing in a mixture of Osage and English, for Big Elk did not refuse to understand the English language, even though he would not speak it. Yancey had some knowledge of Osage. Sabra, coming upon the two grunting and muttering and smoking and staring ahead into nothingness or (worse still) cracking some Indian joke and shaking with silent laughter, Indian fashion, was filled with fury. Nothing so maddened her.

It slowly dawned on Sabra that young Cim was always to be found lolling in the kitchen, talking to Ruby. Ruby, she discovered to her horror, was teaching Cim to speak Osage. A difficult language to the white, he seemed to have a natural aptitude for it. She came upon them, their heads close together over the kitchen table, laughing and talking and singing. Rather, Ruby Big Elk was singing a song with a curious rhythm, and (to Sabra's ear, at least) no melody. There was a pulsation of the girl's voice on sustained notes such as is sometimes produced on a violin when the same note is sounded several times during a single bow stroke. Cim was trying to follow the strange gutturals, slurs, and accents, his eyes fixed on Ruby's face, his own expression utterly absorbed, rapt.

"What are you doing? What is this?"

The Indian girl's face took on its customary expression of proud disdain. She rose. "Teach um song," she said; which was queer, for she spoke English perfectly.

"Well, I must say, Cimarron Cravat! When you know your father is expecting you down at the office——" She stopped. Her quick eye had leaped to the table where lay the little round peyote disk or mescal button which is the hashish of the Indian.

She had heard about it; knew how prevalent among the Indian tribes from Nebraska down to Mexico had become the habit of eating this little buttonlike top of a Mexican cactus plant. In shape a disk about an inch and a half in diameter and a quarter of an inch thick, the mescal or peyote gave the eater a strange feeling of lightness, dispelled pain and fatigue, caused visions of marvelous beauty and grandeur. The use of it had become an Indian religious rite.

Like a fury Sabra advanced to the table, snatched up the little round button of soft green.

"Peyote!" She whirled on Cim. "What are you doing with this thing?"

Cim's eyes were cast down sullenly. His hands in his pockets, he leaned against the wall, very limp, very bored, very infuriating and insolent.

"Ruby was just teaching me one of the Mescal Ceremony songs. Darned interesting. It's the last song. They sing it at sunrise when they're just about all in. Goes like this."

To Sabra's horror he began an eerie song as he stood there leaning against the kitchen wall, his eyes half closed.

> Ya na hi yo hi ya na
> Ya na hi . . . . ya na hi . . . . yo

"Stop it!" screamed Sabra. With the gesture of a tragedy queen she motioned him out of the kitchen. He obeyed with very bad grace, his going more annoying, in its manner, than his staying. Sabra followed him, silently. Suddenly she realized she hated his walk, and knew why. He walked with a queer little springing gait, on the very soles of his feet. It came over her that it always had annoyed her. She remembered that someone had laughingly told her what Pete Pitchlyn, the old Indian scout, lounging on his street corner, had said about young Cim:

"Every time I see that young Cimarron Cravat a-comin' down the street I expect to hear a twig snap. Walks like a story-book Injun."

In the privacy of the sitting room Sabra confronted her son, the bit of peyote still crushed in her hand.

"So you've come to this! I'm ashamed of you!"

"Come to what?"

She opened her hand to show the button of pulpy green crushed in her palm. "Peyote. A son of mine. I'd rather see you dead——"

"Oh, for heaven's sake, Mom, don't get Biblical, like Dad. To hear you a person would think you'd found me drugged in a Chinese opium den."

"I think I'd almost rather."

"It's nothing but a miserable little piece of cactus. And what was I doing but sitting in the kitchen listening to Ruby tell how her father——"

"I should think a man of almost eighteen could find something better to do than sit in a kitchen in the middle of the day talking to an Indian hired girl. Where's your pride!"

Cim's eyes were still cast down. He still lounged insolently, his hands in his pockets. "How about these stories you've told me all your life about the love you Southerners had for your servants and how old Angie was like a second mother to you?"

"Niggers are different. They know their place."

He raised the heavy eyelids then and lifted his fine head with the menacing look that she knew so well in his father. "You're right. They are different. In the first place, Ruby isn't an Indian hired girl. She is the daughter of an Osage chief."

"Osage fiddlesticks! What of it!"

"Ruby Big Elk is just as important a person in the Osage Nation as Alice Roosevelt is in Washington."

"Now, listen here, Cimarron Cravat! I've heard about enough. A lot of dirty Indians! Just you march yourself down to the *Wigwam* office, young man, and don't you ever again let me catch you talking in that disrespectful manner about the daughter of the President of the United States. And if I ever hear that you've eaten a bite of this miserable stuff" —she held out her hand, shaking a little, the mescal button crushed in her palm—"I'll have your father thrash you within an inch of your life, big as you are. As it is, he shall hear of this."

But Yancey, on being told, only looked thoughtful and a little sad. "It's your own fault, Sabra. You're bound that the boy shall live the life you've planned for him instead of the one he wants. So he's trying to escape into a dream life. Like the Indians. It's all the same thing."

"I don't know what you're talking about. I don't think you know, either."

"The Indians started to eat peyote after the whites had taken their religious and spiritual and decent physical life away from them. They had owned the plains and the prairies for centuries. The whites took those. The whites killed off the buffalo, whose flesh had been the Indians' food, and whose skins had been their shelter, and gave them bacon and tumbledown wooden houses in their place. The whites told them that the gods they had worshiped were commonplace things. The Sun was a dying planet—the Stars lumps of hot metal—the Rain a thing that could be regulated by tree planting—the Wind just a current of air that a man in Washington knew all about and whose travels he could prophesy by looking at a piece of machinery."

"And they ought to be grateful for it. The government's given them food and clothes and homes and land. They're a shiftless good-for-nothing lot and won't work. They won't even plant crops."

"'Man cannot live by bread alone.' He has got to have dreams, or life is unendurable. So the Indian turned to the peyote. He finds peace and comfort and beauty in his dreams."

A horrible suspicion darted through Sabra. "Yancey Cravat, have you ever——"

He nodded his magnificent head slowly, sadly. "Many times. Many times."

XIX

CIM was twenty-one, Donna fifteen. And now Sabra lived quite alone in the new house on Kihekah Street, except for a colored woman servant sent from Kansas. She ran the paper alone, as she wished it run. She ordered the house as she wished it. She very nearly ran the town of Osage. She was a power in the Territory. And Yancey was gone, Cim was gone, Donna was gone. Sabra had refused to compromise with life, and life had taken matters out of her hands.

Donna was away at an Eastern finishing school—Miss Dignum's on the Hudson. Yancey had opposed that, of course. It had been Sabra's idea to send Donna east to school.

"East?" Yancey had said. "Kansas City?"

"Certainly not."

"Oh—Chicago."

"I mean New York."

"You're crazy."

"I didn't expect you to approve. I suppose you'd like her to go to an Indian school. Donna's an unusual girl. She's not a beauty and never will be, but she's brilliant, that's what she is. Brilliant. I don't mean intellectual. You needn't smile. I mean that she's got the ambition and the insight and the foresight, too, of a woman of twice her age."

"I'm sorry to hear that."

"I'm not. She's like Mamma in many ways, only she's got intelligence and drive. She doesn't get along with the girls here—Maurine Turket and Gazelle Slaughter and Jewel Riggs and Czarina McKee, and those. She's different. They go switching up and down Pawhuska Avenue. They'll marry one of these tobacco-chewing loafers and settle down like vegetables. Well, she won't. I'll see to that."

"Going to marry her off to an Eastern potentate—at fifteen?"

"You wait. You'll see. She knows what she wants. She'll get it, too."

"Sure it isn't you who know what you want her to want?"

But Sabra had sent her off to Miss Dignum's on a diet of prunes and prisms that even her high-and-mighty old grandmother Felice Venable approved.

Cim, walking the prairies beyond Osage with that peculiar light step of his, his eyes cast down; prowling the draws and sprawling upon the clay banks of the rivers that ran so red through the Red Man's Territory, said that he wanted to be a geologist. He spoke of the Colorado School of Mines. He worked in the *Wigwam* office and hated it. He could pi a case of type more quickly and completely than a drunken tramp printer. The familiar "shrdlu etaoin" was likely to appear in any column in which he had a hand. Even Jesse Rickey, his mournful mustaches more drooping than ever, protested to Yancey.

"She can't make a newspaper man out of that kid," he said. "Not in a million years. Newspaper men are born, not made. Cim, he just naturally hates news, let alone a newspaper office. He was born without a nose for news, like a fellow that's born without an arm, or something. You can't grow it if you haven't got it."

"I know it," said Yancey, wearily. "He'll find a way out."

For the first time a rival newspaper flourished in the town of Osage. The town was scarcely large enough to support two daily papers, but Yancey's political attitude so often was at variance with the feeling of the Territory politicians that the new daily, slipshod and dishonest though it was, and owned body and soul by Territorial interests, achieved a degree of popularity.

Sabra, unable to dictate the policy of the *Wigwam* with Yancey at its head, had to content herself with the management of its mechanical workings and with its increasingly important social and club columns. Osage swarmed with meetings, committees, lodges, Knights of This and Sisters of That. The Philomathean and the Twentieth Century clubs began to go in for Civic Betterment, and no Osage merchant or professional man was safe from cajoling and unattractive females in shirtwaists and skirts and eyeglasses demanding his name signed to this or that petition (with a contribution. Whatever you feel that you can give, Mr. Hefner. Of course, as a leading business man . . .).

They planted shrubs about the cinder-strewn environs of the Santa Fé and the Katy depots. They agitated for the immediate paving of Pawhuska Avenue (it wasn't done). The Ladies of the Eastern Star. The Venus Lodge. Sisters of Rebekah. Daughters of the Southwest. They came into the *Wigwam* office with notices to be printed about lodge suppers and church sociables. Strangely enough, they were likely to stay longer and to chat more freely if Yancey and not Sabra were there to receive them. Sabra was polite but businesslike to her own sex encountered in office hours. But Yancey made himself utterly charming. He could no more help it than he could help breathing. It was almost functional with him. He made the stout, commonplace, middle-aged women feel that they were royal—and seductive. He flattered them with his fine eyes; he bowed them to the door; their eyeglasses quivered. He was likely, on their departure, to crumple their carefully worded notice and throw it on the floor. Sabra, though she made short work of the visiting Venuses and Rebekahs, ran their notice and, if necessary, carefully rewrote it.

"God A'mighty!" he would groan at noonday dinner. "The office was full of Wenuses this morning. Like a swarm of overstuffed locusts."

Sabra was at the head of many of these Betterment movements. Also if there could be said to be anything so formal as society in Osage, Sabra Cravat was the leader of it. She was the first to electrify the ladies of the Twentieth Century Culture Club by serving them Waldorf salad —that abominable mixture of apple cubes, chopped nuts, whipped cream, and mayonnaise. The club fell upon it with little cries and murmurs. Thereafter it was served at club meetings until Osage husbands, returning home to supper after a day's work, and being offered this salvage from the feast, would push it aside with masculine contempt for its contents and roar, "I can't eat this stuff. Fix me some bacon and eggs."

From this culinary and social triumph Sabra proceeded to pineapple and marshmallow salad, the recipe for which had been sent her by Donna in the East. Its indirect effects were fatal.

When it again became her turn to act as hostess to the members of
the club she made her preparations for the afternoon meeting, held at
the grisly hour of half-past two. Refreshments were invariably served at
four. With all arrangements made, she was confronted by Ruby Big Elk
with the astounding statement that this was a great Indian Festival day
(September, and the corn dances were on) and that she must go to the
Reservation in time for the Mescal Ceremony.

"You can't go," said Sabra, flatly. Midday dinner was over. Yancey had
returned to the office. Cim was lounging in the hammock on the porch.
For answer Ruby turned and walked with her stately, irritating step into
her own room just off the kitchen and closed the door.

"Well," shouted Sabra in the tones of Felice Venable herself, "if you
do go you needn't come back." She marched out to the front porch,
where the sight of the lounging Cim only aggravated her annoyance.

"This ends it. That girl has got to leave."

"What girl?"

"Ruby. Twenty women this afternoon, and she says she's going to the
Reservation. They'll be here at half-past two." It was rather incoherent,
but Cim, surprisingly enough, seemed to understand.

"But she told you a month ago."

"Told me what? How do you know?"

"Because she told me she told you, ever so long ago."

"Maybe she did. She never mentioned it again. I can't be expected to
remember every time the Indians have one of their powwows. I told her
she couldn't go. She's in there getting ready. Well, this ends it. She
needn't come back."

She flounced into the kitchen. There stood a mild-mannered young
Indian girl unknown to her.

"What do you want?"

"I am here," the girl answered, composedly, "to take Ruby Big Elk's
place this afternoon. I am Cherokee. She told me to come." She plucked
Ruby's blue and white checked gingham kitchen apron off the hook behind the door and tied it around her waist.

"Well!" gasped Sabra, relieved, but still angry. Through the kitchen
window she saw Cim hitching up the two pintos to the racy little yellow
phaëton that Yancey had bought. She must run out and tell him before
he left. He had seemed disturbed. She was glad he was clearing out. She
liked having the men folks out of the way when afternoon company was
due.

Ruby's door opened. The girl came out. Her appearance was amazing.
She wore a dress of white doeskin hanging straight from shoulders to
ankles, and as soft and pliable as velvet. The hem was fringed. Front,

sleeves, collar were finely beaded in an intricate pattern that was more like embroidery than beading. On her feet were moccasins in ivory white and as exquisitely beaded as the dress. It was the robe of a princess. Her dark Indian eyes were alive. Her skin seemed to glow in contrast with the garment. The girl was, for the moment, almost beautiful.

"Hello, Theresa Jump. . . . This is Theresa Jump. She will do my work this day. I have told her. She knows about the pineapple and marshmallow salad." For a moment it seemed to Sabra that just the faintest shadow of amusement flitted over Ruby's face as she said this. But then, Sabra never had pretended to understand these Indians. "I will be back to-morrow morning."

She walked slowly out of the house by way of the kitchen door, across the yard with her slow insolent dragging step. A stab of suspicion cut Sabra. She flew to the back porch, stood there a moment. Ruby Big Elk walked slowly toward the barn. Cim drove out with the phaëton and pintos. He saw the Indian woman in her white doeskin dress. His eyes shone enormous. He lifted his head as though to breathe deeply. At that look in his face Sabra ran across the yard. One hand was at her breast, as though an Indian arrow had pierced her. Ruby had set one foot in its cream white moccasin on the buggy step. Cim held out his free hand.

Sabra reached them, panting. "Where are you going?"

"I'm driving Ruby out to the Reservation."

"No, you're not. No, you're not." She put one hand in a futile gesture on the buggy wheel, as though to stop them by main force. She knew she must not lose her dignity before this Indian woman—before her son. Yet this thing was, to her way of thinking, monstrous.

Cim gathered up the reins, his eyes on the restive ponies. "I may stay to see some of the dancing and the Mescal Ceremony. Father says it's very interesting. Big Elk has invited me."

"Your father knows you're going? Like this?"

"Oh, yes." He cast a slight, an oblique glance at her hand on the wheel. Her hand dropped heavily to her side. He spoke to the horses. They were off. Ruby Big Elk looked straight ahead. She had uttered no word. Sabra turned and walked back to the house. The hot tears blinded her. She was choking. But her pride spoke, even then. You must not go the kitchen way. That Indian girl will see you. They are all alike. You must go around by the front way. Pretend it is nothing. Oh, God, what shall I do! All those women this afternoon. Perhaps I am making a fuss over nothing. Why shouldn't he take the Indian girl out to the Reservation and stop an hour or two to see the dances and the rites? . . . His face! His face when he saw her in that dress.

She bathed her eyes, powdered her nose, changed her dress, came into the kitchen, smiling. ". . . the pineapple cut into chunks about like this. Then you snip the marshmallow into it with the scissors. Mix whipped cream into your mayonnaise . . . a cherry on top . . . little thin sandwiches . . . damp napkin . . ." She went into the sitting room, adjusted a shade, plumped a pillow. The door bell rang. "Howdy-do, Mrs. Nisbett. . . . No, you're not. You're just on time. It's everybody else who's late." She thought, "Women are wonderful. No man could do what I am doing. Smiling and chatting when I am almost crazy." Her fine dark eyes were luminous. Her clear ivory skin was tinged now with a spot of red on either cheek. She looked very handsome.

Theresa Jump proved clumsy and unteachable. Sabra herself mixed and served the pineapple and marshmallow salad, and though this novelty proved a great success, the triumph of serving it was spoiled for Sabra. She bundled the girl off at six, after the dishes were done. Wearily she began to set the house to rights, but Yancey came home to a confusion of chairs and squashed pillows, a mingled odor of perfumery and coffee; a litter of cake crumbs, bits of embroidery silk, and crumpled tea napkins. His huge frame moving about the cluttered sitting room made these feminine remnants seem ridiculous. The disorder of the household irked him. Worst of all, Sabra, relieved now of her guests, was free to pour out upon him all the pent-up wrath, anxiety, and shock of the past few hours. Ruby. Cim. Theresa Jump. Peyote. Osages. If his own father allows such things—what will people say—no use trying to make something of yourself.

Yancey, usually so glib with quotations from this or that sonorous passage of poetry, said little. He did not even try to cajole her into a better humor with his flattery, his charm, his tenderness. His eyes were bloodshot, his hand more unsteady than usual. He had been drinking even more than was his wont, she knew that at once. By no means drunk (she had never seen him really drunk—no one had—he was seemingly incapable of reaching a visible state of drunkenness), he was in one of his fits of moody depression. The great shoulders sagged. The splendid head lolled on his breast. He seemed sunk in gloomy thought. She felt that he hardly heard what she was saying. She herself could eat nothing. She set a place for him at the dining-room table and plumped down before him a dish of the absurd salad, a cup of coffee, some cake, a plate of the left-over sandwiches, their edges curled dismally.

"What's this?" he said.

"Pineapple and marshmallow salad. With Ruby gone and all, I didn't get anything for your supper—I was so upset—all those women . . ."

He sat looking down at the slippery mass on his plate. His great arms were spread out on the table before him. The beautiful hands were opening and closing convulsively. So a mastodon might have looked at a worm. "Pineapple and marshmallow salad," he repeated, thoughtfully, almost wonderingly. Suddenly he threw back the magnificent head and began to laugh. Peal after peal of Herculean laughter. "Pineapple and marsh——" choking, the tears running down his cheeks. Sabra was angry, then frightened. For as suddenly as he had begun to laugh he became serious. He stood up, one hand on the table. Then he seemed to pull his whole body together like a tiger who is about to spring. He stood thus a moment, swaying a little. "*'Actum est de republica.'*"

"What?" said Sabra, sharply.

"Latin, Latin, my love. Pineapple and marshmallow salad! 'It is all over with the Republic.'" She shrugged her shoulders impatiently. Yancey turned, stiffly, like a soldier, walked out of the room, flicked his white sombrero off the hall rack and put it on at the usual jaunty angle, went down the porch stair with his light, graceful step, to the sidewalk and up the street, the great head lowered, the arms swinging despondently at his sides.

Sabra went on with her work of tidying up the house. Her eyes burned, her throat was constricted. Men! Men! Cim off with that squaw. Yancey angry because she had given him this very feminine dish of left-overs. What was the use of working, what was the use of pride, what was the use of ambition for your children, your home, your town if this was all it amounted to? Her work done, she allowed herself the luxury of a deliberate and cleansing storm of tears.

Eight o'clock. She heated some of the afternoon coffee and drank it sitting at the kitchen table. She went out on the front porch. Darkness had come on. A hot September evening. The crickets squeaked and ground away in the weeds. She was conscious of an aching weariness in all her body, but she could not sleep. Her eyes felt as though they were being pulled apart by invisible fingers. She put her palms over them, to shut them, to cool them. Nine. Ten. Eleven. Twelve. She undressed, unpinned the braids of her thick hair, brushed it, plaited it for the night. All the time she was listening. Listening. One.

Suddenly she began to dress again with icy fumbling fingers. She did up her hair, put on her hat and a jacket. She closed the door behind her, locked it, slipped the key into the mail box. The *Wigwam* office. Yancey was not there. The office was dark. She shook the door, rattled the knob, peered in, unlocked it with the key in her handbag. Her heart was pounding, but she was not afraid of the darkness. A cat's eyes gleamed at her from the printing shop. She struck a light. No one. No one. The linotype machine grinned at her with its white teeth. Its iron arm and hand shook tauntingly at her in the wavering light. With a sudden premonition she ran to Yancey's desk, opened the drawer in which he kept his holster and six-shooters, now that Osage had become so effete as to make them an unessential article of dress. They were not there. She knew then that Yancey had gone.

Doc Valliant. She closed and locked the door after her, stepped out into the quiet blackness of Pawhuska Avenue. Doc Valliant. He would go with her. He would drive her out there. But his office and the room at the rear, which was his dwelling, gave forth no response. Gone out somewhere—a case. Down the rickety wooden steps of the two-story brick building. She stood a moment in the street, looking this way and that. She struck her palms together in a kind of agony of futility. She would go alone if she had a horse and buggy. She could rent one at the livery stable. But what would they think—those men at the livery stable? They were the gossips of the town. It would be all over Osage, all over the county. Sabra Cravat driving out into the prairie alone in the middle of the night. Something up. Well, she couldn't help that. She had to go. She had to get him.

Toward the livery stable, past the Bixby House. A quiet little figure rose from the blackness of the porch where all through the day the traveling men and loafers sat with their chairs tilted back against the wall. The red coal of his cigar was an eye in the darkness.

"Sabra! What is this! What are you doing running around at this hour of the night?"

Sol Levy, sitting there in the Oklahoma night, a lonely little figure, sleepless, brooding. He had never before called her Sabra.

"Sol! Sol! Cim's out at the Reservation. Something's happened. I know. I feel it."

He did not scoff at this, as most men would. He seemed to understand her fear, her premonition, and to accept it with Oriental fatalism.

"What do you want to do?"

"Take me out there. Hitch up and drive me out there. Cim's got the buggy. He went out with her."

He did not ask where Yancey was. He asked nothing. "Go home," he said. "Wait on your porch. I will get my rig and come for you. They shouldn't see you. Do you want me to go home with you first?"

"No, no. I'm not afraid. I'm not afraid of anything."

Sol Levy had two very fine horses; really good animals. They won the races regularly at the local fairs. The little light rig with its smart rubber tires whirled behind them over the red dusty Oklahoma prairie roads. His slim hands were not expert with horses. He was a nervous, jerky driver. They left the town behind them, were swallowed up by the prairie. The Reservation was a full two hours distant. Sabra took off her hat. The night air rushed against her face, cooling it. A half hour.

"Let me drive, will you, Sol?"

Without a word he entrusted the reins to her strong, accustomed hands; the hands of one who had come of generations of horse lovers. The animals sensed the change. They leaped ahead in the darkness. The light buggy rocked and bounced over the rutted roads. Sol asked her nothing. They drove in silence. Presently she began to talk, disjointedly. Yet, surprisingly enough, he seemed intuitively to understand, to fill in the gaps with his own instinct and imagination. What she said sounded absurd; he knew it for tragedy.

". . . pineapple and marshmallow salad . . . hates that kind of thing . . . queer for a long time . . . moody . . . drinking . . . Ruby Big Elk . . . Cim . . . his face . . . peyote . . . Mescal Ceremony . . . Osage . . . white doeskin dress . . . Theresa Jump . . ."

"I see," said Sol Levy, soothingly. "Sure. Well, sure. The boy will be all right. The boy will be all right. Well, Yancey—you know how he is— Yancey. Do you think he has gone away again? I mean—gone?"

"I don't know." Then, "Yes."

Three o'clock and after. They came in sight of the Osage Reservation, a scattered settlement of sterile farms and wooden shanties sprawled on the bare unlovely prairie.

Darkness. The utter darkness that precedes the dawn. Stillness, except for the thud of their horses' flying hoofs and the whir and bump of the buggy wheels. Then, as Sabra slowed them down, uncertainly, undecided as to what they might best do, they heard it—the weird wavering cadences of the Mescal song, the hail-like clatter of the gourd rattle shaken vigorously and monotonously; and beneath and above and around it all, reverberating, haunting, ominous, the beat of the buckskin drum. Through the still, cool night air of the prairie it came to them —to the overwrought woman, and to the little peaceful Jew. Barbaric sounds, wild, sinister. She pulled up the horses. They sat a moment, listening. Listening. The drum. The savage sound of the drum.

Fear was gnawing at her vitals, wringing her very heart with clammy fingers, yet Sabra spoke matter-of-factly, her voice holding a hard little note because she was trying to keep it from quavering.

"He'll be in the Mescal tepee next to Big Elk's House. They built it there when he was Chief, and they still use it regularly for the ceremony. Yancey showed it to me once, when he drove me out here." She stopped and cleared her throat, for her voice was suddenly husky. She wondered, confusedly, if that sound was the drum or her own heart beating. She gave a little cracked laugh that bordered on hysteria. "A drum in the night. It sounds so terrible. So savage."

Sol Levy took the reins from her shaking fingers. "Nothing to be frightened about. A lot of poor ignorant Indians trying to forget their misery. Come." Perhaps no man ever made a more courageous gesture, for the little sensitive Jew was terribly frightened.

Uncertainly, in the blackness, they made their way toward the drum beat. Nearer and nearer, louder and louder. And yet all about, darkness, silence. Only that pulsing cry and rattle and beat pounding through the night like the tide. What if he is not there? thought Sabra.

Sol Levy pulled up in the roadway before the trampled yard that held the Mescal tepee, round, to typify the sun, built of wood, larger than any other building on the Reservation. The horses were frightened, restive. All about in the blackness you heard the stamp of other horses' hoofs, heard them crunching the dried herbage of the autumn prairie. With difficulty he groped his way to a stump that served as hitching post, tied the horses. As he helped Sabra down her knees suddenly bent, and he caught her as she sank. "Oh! It's all right. Stiff, I guess—from the ride." She leaned against him a moment, then straightened determinedly. He took her arm firmly. Together they made their way toward the tent-shaped wooden tepee.

Two great, silent blanketed figures at the door through which the fitful flame of the sacred fire flared. The figures did not speak. They stood there, barring the way. The little Jew felt Sabra's arm trembling in his hand. He peered up into the faces of the silent, immobile figures.

Suddenly, "Hello, Joe!" He turned to Sabra. "It's Joe Yellow Eyes. He was in the store only yesterday. Say, Joe, the lady here—Mrs. Cravat—she wants her son should come out and go home."

The blanketed figures stood silent.

Suddenly Sabra thought, "This is ridiculous."

She loosed her arm. She took a step forward, her profile sharp and clear in the firelight. "I am the woman of Yancey Cravat, the one you call Buffalo Head. If my son is in there I want to take him home now. It is time."

"Sure take um home," replied the blanket that Sol had addressed as Joe Yellow Eyes. He stood aside. Blinking, stumbling a little, Sol and Sabra entered the crowded Mescal tepee.

The ceremony was almost at an end. With daybreak it would be finished. Blinded by the light, Sabra at first could discern nothing except the central fire and the figure crouched before it. Yet her eyes went this way and that, searching for him. Gradually her vision cleared. The figures within the tepee paid no attention to those two white intruders. They stood there in the doorway, bewildered, terrified, brave.

In the center a crescent of earth about six inches high curved around a fire built of sticks so arranged that as the ashes fell they formed a second crescent within the other. A man squatted, tending this fire, watchfully, absorbedly. In the center of the crescent, upon a little star of sage twigs, lay the mescal, symbol of the rite. Facing them was the Chief, old Stump Horn, in the place of honor, the emblems of office in his hands—the rattle, the wand, the fan of eagle plumes. All about the tepee crouched or lay blanketed motionless figures. Some sat with heads bowed, others gazed fixedly upon the central mescal button. All had been eating the mescal or drinking a brew in which it had steeped. Now and then a figure would slowly draw the blanket over his head and sink back to receive the vision. And the song went on, the shaking of the gourd rattle, the beat-beat of the buckskin drum. The air of the room was stifling, the room itself scrupulously clean.

At intervals around the wall, and almost level with the dirt floor, were apertures perhaps sixteen inches square. A little wooden door was shut upon most of these. Near each lay figures limper, more spent even than the other inert bodies. As Sabra and Sol stood, blinking, they learned the use of these openings. For suddenly nausea overcame one of the Indians crouched in the semicircle near the flame. The man crawled swiftly to one of the little doors, opened it, thrust head and shoulders out into the night air, relieved his body of the drug's overdose.

Sabra only turned her eyes away, searching, searching. Then she saw where the boy lay under his gay striped blanket. His face was covered, but she knew. She knew well how the slim body curled in its blankets, how it lay at night, asleep. This was a different sleep, but she knew. They went to him, picking their way over the crouching figures with the fixed trancelike gaze; the recumbent forms that lay so still. She turned back the blanket. His face was smiling, peaceful, lovely.

She thought, "This is the way I should look at him if he were dead." Then, "He is dead." The boy lay breathing quietly. All about the room was an atmosphere of reverie, of swooning bliss. If the Indians looked at all at Sabra, at the Jew, at their efforts to rouse the boy, it was with the eyes of sleep-walkers. Their lips were gently smiling. Sometimes they swayed a little. The sacred fire leaped orange and scarlet and gold. Old Stump Horn wielded his eagle feather fan, back and forth, back and forth. The quavering cadences of the Mescal song rose and fell to the accompaniment of the gourd rattle and the unceasing drum. The white man and woman, frail both, tugged and strained at the inert figure of the boy.

"Oh, God!" whimpered Sabra. "He's so heavy. What shall we do?" They bent again, tugged with all their strength, lifted but could not carry him.

"We must drag him," Sol said, at last.

They took an arm each. So, dragging, tugging, past those rapt still forms, past those mazed smiling faces, they struggled with him to the door. The little beads of sweat stood out on her forehead, on her lip. She breathed in choking gasps. Her eyes were wide and staring and dreadful in their determination. The rattle. The drum beat. The high eerie song notes, wordless.

The blackness of the outer air; past the two towering motionless blanketed figures at the door. Dragging him along the earth, through the trampled weeds.

"We can't lift him into the buggy. We can't——" She ran back to the two at the door. She clasped her hands before the one called Joe Yellow Eyes. She lifted her white, agonized face to him. "Help me. Help me." She made a futile gesture of lifting.

The Indian looked at her a moment with a dead, unseeing gaze. Flecks of gold and red and yellow danced, reflected in the black pools of his eyes, and died there. Leisurely, wordless, he walked over to where the boy lay, picked him up lightly in his great arms as though he were a sack of meal, swung him into the buggy seat. He turned, then, and went back to his place at the door.

They drove back to the town of Osage. Cim's body leaned heavily, slackly against hers; his head lay in her lap, like a little boy's. One aching arm she held firmly about him to keep him from slipping to the floor of the buggy, so that finally it ceased to ache and became numb. The dawn came, and then the sunrise over the prairie, its red meeting the red of the Oklahoma earth, so that they drove through a fiery furnace.

She had been quiet enough until now, with a kind of stony quiet. She began to sob; a curious dry racking sound, like a hiccough.

"Now, now," said Sol Levy, and made a little comforting noise between tongue and teeth. "So bad it isn't. What did the boy do, he went out to see the sights on the Reservation and try what it was like to eat this dope stuff—this peyote. Say, when I was a boy I did lots worse."

She did not seem to pay much heed to this, but it must have penetrated her numbed brain at last, for presently she stopped the painful sobbing and looked down at his lovely smiling face in her lap, the long lashes, like a girl's, resting so fragilely on the olive cheek.

"He wanted to go. I wouldn't let him. Is it too late, Sol?"

"Go? Go where?"

"The Colorado School of Mines. Geology."

"Too late! That kid there! Don't talk foolish. September. This is the time to go. It just starts. Sure he'll go."

They drove through the yard, over Sabra's carefully tended grass, of which she was so proud, right to the edge of the porch steps, and so, dragging again and pulling, they got him in, undressed him; she washed his dust-smeared face.

"Well," said Sol Levy. "I guess I go and open the store and then have a good cup of coffee."

She put out her hand. Her lower lip was caught between her teeth, sharp and tight. Her face was distorted absurdly with her effort not to cry. But when he would have patted her grimed and trembling hand with his own, in a gesture of comforting, she caught his hand to her lips and kissed it.

The sound of the horses' hoofs died away on the still morning air. She looked down at Cim. She thought, I will take a bath, and then I will have some coffee, too. Yancey has gone again. Has left me. I know that. How do I know it? Well, nothing more can happen to me now. I have had it all, and I have borne it. Nothing more can happen to me now.

XX

For years Oklahoma had longed for statehood as a bride awaits the dawn of her wedding day. At last, "Behold the bridegroom!" said a paternal government, handing her over to the Union. "Here is a star for your forehead. Meet the family."

Then, at the very altar, the final words spoken, the pact sealed, the bride had turned to encounter a stranger—an unexpected guest, dazzling, breath-taking, embodying all her wildest girlish dreams.

"Bridegroom—hell!" yelled Oklahoma, hurling herself into the stranger's arms. "What's family to me! Go away! Don't bother me. I'm busy."

The name of the gorgeous stranger was Oil.

Oil. Nothing else mattered. Oklahoma, the dry, the wind-swept, the burning, was a sea of hidden oil. The red prairies, pricked, ran black and slimy with it. The work of years was undone in a day. The sunbonnets shrank back, aghast. Compared to that which now took place the early days following the Run in '89 were idyllic. They swarmed on Oklahoma from every state in the Union. The plains became black with little eager delving figures. The sanguine roads were choked with every sort of vehicle. Once more tent and shanty towns sprang up where the day before had been only open prairie staring up at a blazing sky. Again the gambling tent, the six-shooter, the roaring saloon, the dance hall, the harlot. Men fought, stole, killed, died for a piece of ground beneath whose arid surface lay who knew what wealth of fluid richness. Every barren sun-baked farm was a potential fortune; every ditch and draw and dried-up creek bed might conceal liquid treasure. The Wildcat Field—Panhandle—Cimarron—Crook Nose—Cartwright—Wahoo—Bear Creek—these became magic names; these were the Seven Cities of Cibola, rich beyond Coronado's wildest dream. Millions of barrels of oil burst through the sand and shale and clay and drenched the parched earth. Drill, pump, blast. Nitroglycerin. Here she comes. A roar. Oklahoma went stark raving mad.

Sabra Cravat went oil mad with the rest of them. Just outside the town of Osage, for miles around, they were drilling. There was that piece of farm land she had bought years ago, when Yancey first showed signs of restlessness. She had thought herself shrewd to have picked up this fertile little oasis in the midst of the bare unlovely plain. She was proud of her bit of farm land with its plump yield of alfalfa, corn, potatoes, and garden truck. She knew now why it had been so prolific. By a whim of nature rich black oil lay under all that surrounding land, rendering it barren through its hidden riches. No taint of corroding oil ran beneath that tract of Cravat farm land, and because of this it lay there now, so green, so lush, with its beans, its squash, its ridiculous onions, taunting her, deriding her, like a mirage in the desert. Queerly enough, she had no better luck with her share in an oil lease for which she had paid a substantial sum—much more than she could afford to lose. Machinery, crew, days of drilling, weeks of drilling, sand, shale, salt. The well had come up dry—a duster.

That which happened to Sabra happened to thousands. The stuff was elusive, tantalizing. Here might be a gusher vomiting millions. Fifty feet away not so much as a spot of grease could be forced to the surface. Fortune seemed to take a delight in choosing strange victims for her pranks. Erv Wissler, the gawk who delivered the milk to Sabra's door each morning, found himself owner of a gusher whose outpourings yielded him seven thousand dollars a day. He could not grasp it. Seven dollars a day his mind might have encompassed. Seven thousand had no meaning.

"Why, Erv!" Sabra exclaimed, when he arrived at her kitchen door as usual, smelling of the barnyard. "Seven thousand dollars a day! What in the world are you going to do with it!"

Erv's putty features and all his loose-hung frame seemed to stiffen with the effort of his new and momentous resolve. "Well, I tell you, Mis' Cravat, I made up my mind I ain't going to make no more Sunday delivery myself. I'm a-going to hire Pete Lynch's boy to take the milk route Sundays."

Everyone in Osage knew the story of Ferd Sloat's wife when the news was brought to her that weeks of drilling on the sterile little Sloat farm had brought up a gusher. They had come running to her across the trampled fields with the news. She had stood there on the back porch of the shabby farmhouse, a bony drudge, as weather-beaten and unlovely as the house itself.

"Millions!" they shouted at her. "Millions and millions! What are you going to do?"

Ferd Sloat's wife had looked down at her hands, shriveled and gnarled from alkali water and rough work. She wiped them now on a corner of her gingham apron with a gesture of utter finality. Her meager shoulders straightened. The querulous voice took on a note of defiance.

"From now on I'm goin' to have the washin' done out."

In those first few frenzied weeks there was no time for scientific methods. That came later. Now, in the rush of it, they all but burrowed in the red clay with their finger nails. Men prowled the plains with divining rods, with absurd things called witch sticks, hoping thus to detect the precious stuff beneath the earth's surface.

For years the meandering red clay roads that were little more than trails had seen only occasional buggies, farm wagons, horsemen, an Indian family creeping along in a miserable cart or—rarely—an automobile making perilous progress through the thick dust in the dry season or the slippery dough in the wet. Now those same roads were choked, impassable. The frail wooden one-way bridges over creeks and draws sagged and splintered with the stream of traffic, but no one took the time to repair them. A torrent of vehicles of every description flowed without ceasing, night and day. Frequently the torrent choked itself with its own volume, and then the thousands were piled there, locked, cursing, writhing, battling, on their way to the oil fields. From the Crook Nose field to Wahoo was a scant four miles; it sometimes took half a day to cover it in a motor car. Trucks, drays, wagons, rigs, Fords, buckboards. Every day was like the day of the Opening back in '89. Millionaire promoters from the East, engineers, prospectors, drillers, tool dressers, shooters, pumpers, roustabouts, Indians. Men in oil-soaked overalls that hadn't been changed for days. Men in London tailored suits and shirts from Charvet's. Only the ruthless and desperate survived. In the days of the covered wagon scarcely twenty years earlier those roads had been trails over the hot, dry plains marked by the bleaching skull of a steer or the carcass of a horse, picked clean by the desert scavengers and turned white and desolate to the blazing sky. A wagon wheel, a rusted rim, a split wagon tongue lay at the side of the trail, mute evidence of a traveler laboriously crawling his way across the prairie. Now the ditches by the side of these same roads were strewn with the bodies of wrecked and abandoned automobiles, their skeletons stripped and rotting, their lamps staring up at the sky like sightless eyes, testimony to the passing of the modern ravisher of that tortured region. Up and down the dust-choked roads, fenders ripped off like flies' wings, wheels interlocking, trucks overturned, loads sunk in the mud, plank bridges splitting beneath the strain. Devil take the hindmost. It was like an army push, but without an army's morale or discipline. Bear Creek boasted a killing a day and not a jail nor a courthouse for miles around. Men and women, manacled to a common chain, were marched like slave convicts down the road to the nearest temple of justice, a rough pine shack in a town that had sprung overnight on the prairie. There were no railroads where there had been no towns.

Boilers loaded on two wagons were hauled by twenty-mule-team outfits. Stuck in the mud as they inevitably were, only mules could have pulled the load out. Long lines of them choked the already impassable road. Wagons were heaped with the pipes through which the oil must be led; with lumber, hardware, rigs, tools, portable houses—all the vast paraphernalia of sudden wealth and growth in a frontier community.

Tough careless young boys drove the nitroglycerin cars, a deadly job on those rough and crowded roads. It was this precious and dreadful stuff that shot the oil up out of the earth. Hard lads in corduroys took their chances and pocketed their high pay, driving the death-dealing wagons, singing as they drove, a red shirt tail tied to a pole flaunting its warning at the back of the load. Often an expected wagon would fail to appear. The workers on the field never took the trouble to trace it or the time to wait for it. They knew that somewhere along the road was a great gaping hole, with never a sizable fragment of wood or steel or bone or flesh anywhere for yards around to tell the tale they already knew.

Acres that had been carefully tended so that they might yield their scanty crop of cabbages, onions, potatoes were abandoned to oil, the garden truck rotting in the ground. Rawboned farmers and their scrawny wives and pindling brats, grown spectacularly rich overnight, walked out of their houses without taking the trouble to move the furniture or lock the door. It was not worth while. They left the sleazy curtains on the windows, the pots on the stove. The oil crew, clanking in, did not bother to wreck the house unless they found it necessary. In the midst of an inferno of oil rigs, drills, smoke, steam, and seeping oil itself the passer-by would often see a weather-beaten farmhouse, its windows broken, its front askew, like a beldame gone mad, gray hair streaming about her crazed face as she stared out at the pandemonium of oil hell about her.

The farmers moved into Osage, or Oklahoma City, or Wahoo. They bought automobiles and silk shirts and gew-gaws, like children. The men sat on the front porch in shirt sleeves and stocking feet and spat tobacco juice into the fresh young grass.

Mile on mile, as far as the eye could see, were the skeleton frames of oil rigs outlined against the sky like giant Martian figures stalking across the landscape. Horrible new towns—Bret Harte wooden-front towns— sprang up overnight on the heels of an oil strike; towns inhabited by people who never meant to stay in them; stark and hideous houses thrown up by dwellers who never intended to remain in them; rude frontier crossroad stores stuffed with the necessities of frontier life and the luxuries of sudden wealth all jumbled together in a sort of mercantile miscegenation. The thump and clank of the pump and drill; curses, shouts; the clatter of thick dishes, the clink of glasses, the shrill laughter of women; fly-infested shanties. Oil, smearing itself over the prairies like a plague, killing the grass, blighting the trees, spreading over the surface of the creeks and rivers. Signs tacked to tree stumps or posts; For Ambulance Call 487. Sim Neeley Undertaker. Call 549. Call Dr. Keogh 735.

Oklahoma—the Red People's Country—lay heaving under the hot summer sun, a scarred and dreadful thing with the oil drooling down its face a viscid stream.

Tracy Wyatt, who used to drive the bus and dray line between Wahoo and Osage, standing up to the reins like a good-natured red-faced charioteer as the wagon bumped over the rough roads, was one of the richest men in Oklahoma—in the whole of the United States, for that matter. Wyatt. The Wyatt Oil Company. In another five years the Wyatt Oil Companies. You were to see their signs all over the world. The Big Boys from the East were to come to him, hat in hand, to ask his advice about this; to seek his favor for that. The sum of his daily income was fantastic. The mind simply did not grasp it. Tracy himself was, by now, a portly and not undignified looking man of a little more than fifty. His good-natured, rubicund face wore the grave slightly astonished look of a commonplace man who suddenly finds himself a personage.

Mrs. Wyatt, plainer, more horse-faced than ever in her expensive

New York clothes, tried to patronize Sabra Cravat, but the Whipple blood was no match for the Marcy. The new money affected her queerly. She became nervous, full of spleen, and the Eastern doctors spoke to her of high blood pressure.

Sabra frankly envied these lucky ones. A letter from the adder-tongued Felice Venable to her daughter was characteristic of that awesome old matriarch. Sabra still dreaded to open her mother's letters. They always contained a sting.

All this talk of oil and millions and everyone in Oklahoma rolling in it. I'll be bound that you and that husband of yours haven't so much as enough to fill a lamp. Trust Yancey Cravat to get hold of the wrong piece of land. Well, at least you can't be disappointed. It has been like that from the day you married him, though you can't say your mother didn't warn you. I hope Donna will show more sense.

Donna, home after two years at Miss Dignum's on the Hudson, seemed indeed to be a granddaughter after Felice Venable's own heart. She was, in coloring, contour, manner, and outlook, so unlike the other Oklahoma girls—Czarina McKee, Gazelle Slaughter, Jewel Riggs, Maurine Turket—as to make that tortured, wind-deviled day of her birth on the Oklahoma prairie almost nineteen years ago seem impossible. Even during her homecomings in the summer vacations she had about her an air of cool disdain together with a kind of disillusioned calculation very disconcerting to her former intimates, not to speak of her own family.

The other girls living in Osage and Oklahoma City and Guthrie and Wahoo were true products of the new raw Southwest country. They liked to dress in crude high colors—glaring pinks, cerise, yellow, red, vivid orange, magenta. They made up naïvely with white powder and big daubs of carmine paint on either cheek. The daughters of more wealthy parents drove their own cars in a day when this was considered rather daring for a woman. Donna came home tall, thin to the point of scrawniness in their opinion; sallow, unrouged, drawling, mysterious. She talked with an Eastern accent, ignored the letter *r*, said eyether and nyether and rih'ally and altogether made herself poisonously unpopular with the girls and undeniably stirring to the boys. She paid very little heed to the clumsy attentions of the Oklahoma home-town lads, adopting toward them a serpent-of-the-Nile attitude very baffling to these frank and open-faced prairie products.

Her school days finished, and she a finished product of those days, she now looked about her coolly, calculatingly. Her mother she regarded with a kind of affectionate amusement.

"What a rotten deal you've had, Sabra dear," she would drawl. "Really, I don't see how you've stood it all these years."

Sabra would come to her own defense, goaded by something strangely hostile in herself toward this remote, disdainful offspring. "Stood what?"

"Oh—you know. This being a pioneer woman and a professional Marcy and head-held-high in spite of a bum of a husband."

"Donna Cravat, if you ever again dare to speak like that of your father I shall punish you, big as you are."

"Sabra darling, how can you punish a grown woman? You might slap me, and I wouldn't slap you back, of course. But I'd be terribly embarrassed for you. As for Father—he is a museum piece. You know it."

"Your father is one of the greatest figures the Southwest has ever produced."

"Mm. Well, he's picturesque enough, I suppose. But I wish he hadn't worked so hard at it. And Cim! There's a brother! A great help to me in my career, the men folks of this quaint family."

"I wasn't aware that you were planning a career," Sabra retorted, very much in the manner of Felice Venable. "Unless getting up at noon, slopping around in a kimono most of the day, and lying in the hammock reading is called a career by Dignum graduates. If it is, you're the outstanding success of your class."

"Darling, I adore you when you get viperish and Venable like that. Perhaps you influenced me in my early youth. That's the new psychology, you know. You used to tell me about Grandma trailing around in her white ruffled dimity wrappers and her high heels, never lifting a lily hand."

"At least your grandmother didn't consider it a career."

"Neither do I. This lovely flower-like head isn't so empty as you think, lolling in the front porch hammock. I know it's no use counting on Father, even when he's not off on one of his mysterious jaunts. What is he doing, anyway? Living with some squaw? . . . Forgive me, Mother darling. I didn't mean to hurt you. . . . Cim's just as bad, and worse, because he's weak and hasn't even Dad's phony ideals. You're busy with the paper. That's all right. I'm not blaming you. If it weren't for you we'd all be on the town—or back in Wichita living on Grandma in genteel poverty. I think you're wonderful, and I ought to try to be like you. But I don't want to be a girl reporter. Describing the sumptuous decorations of dandelions and sunflowers at one of Cassandra Sipes' parties."

Goaded by curiosity and a kind of wonder at this unnatural creature, Sabra must put her question: "What do you want to do, then?"

"I want to marry the richest man in Oklahoma, and build a palace that I'll hardly ever live in, and travel like royalty, and clank with emeralds. With my skin and hair they're my stone."

"Oh, emeralds, by all means," Sabra agreed, cuttingly. "Diamonds are so ordinary. And the gentleman that you consider honoring—let me see. From your requirements that would have to be Tracy Wyatt, wouldn't it?"

"Yes," replied Donna, calmly.

"You've probably overlooked Mrs. Wyatt. Of course, Tracy's only fifty-one, and you being nineteen, there's plenty of time if you'll just be patient." She was too amused to be really disturbed.

"I don't intend to be patient, Mamma darling."

Something in her hard, ruthless tone startled Sabra. "Donna Cravat, don't you start any of your monkey business. I saw you cooing and ah-ing at him the other day when we went over the Wyatts' new house. And I heard you saying some drivel about his being a man that craved beauty in his life, and that he should have it; and sneering politely at the new house until I could see him beginning to doubt everything in it, poor fellow. He had been so proud to show it. But I thought you were just talking that New York talk of yours."

"I wasn't. I was talking business."

Sabra was revolted, alarmed, and distressed, all at once. She gained reassurance by telling herself that this was just one of Donna's queer jokes—part of the streak in her that Sabra had never understood and that corresponded to the practical joker in Yancey. That, too, had always bewildered her. Absorbed in the workings of the growing, thriving newspaper the conversation faded to a dim and almost unimportant memory.

Sabra was sufficiently shrewd and level headed to take Sol Levy's sound advice. "You settle down to running your paper, Sabra, and you won't need any oil wells. You can have the best-paying paper and the most powerful in the Southwest. Bigger than Houston or Dallas or San Antonio. Because Osage is going to be bigger and richer than any of them. You mark what I say. Hardly any oil in the town of Osage, but billions of barrels of oil all around it. This town won't be torn to pieces, then. It'll grow and grow. Five years from now it'll look like Chicago."

"Oh, Sol, how can that be?"

"You'll see. There where the gambling tent stood with a mud hole in front of it a few years ago you'll see in another five years a skyscraper like those in New York."

She laughed at that.

Just as she had known that Yancey had again left her on that night of the Mescal ceremony, so now she sensed that he would come back in the midst of this new insanity that had seized all Oklahoma. And come back he did, from God knows where, on the very crest of the oil wave, and bringing with him news that overshadowed his return. He entered as he had left, with no word of explanation, and, as always, his entrance was so dramatic, so bizarre as to cause everything else to fade into the background.

He came riding, as always, but it was a sorry enough nag that he bestrode this time; and his white sombrero was grimed and battered, the Prince Albert coat was spotted, the linen frayed, the whole figure covered with the heavy red dust of the trampled road. He must have ridden like an avenging angel, for his long black locks were damp, his eyes red rimmed. And when she saw this Don Quixote, so sullied, so shabby, her blood turned to water within her veins for pity.

She thought, it will always be like this as long as he lives, and each time he will be a little more broken, older, less and less the figure of splendor I married, until at last . . .

She only said, "Yancey," quietly.

He was roaring, he was reeling with Jovian laughter as he strode into the *Wigwam* office where she sat at her neat orderly desk just as she had sat on that day years before. For a dreadful moment she thought that he was drunk or mad. He flung his soiled white sombrero to the desk top, he swept her into his arms, he set her down.

"Sabra! Here's news for you. Jesse! Heh, Jesse! Where's that rum-soaked son of a printer's devil? Jesse! Come in here! God, I've been laughing so that I almost rolled off my horse." He was striding up and down as of old, his shabby coat tails spreading with the vigor of his movements, the beautiful hands gesticulating, the fine eyes—bloodshot now—still flashing with the fire that would burn until it consumed him.

"Oil, my children! More oil than anybody ever thought there was in any one spot in the world. And where! Where! On the Osage Indian Reservation. It came in an hour ago, like the ocean. It makes every other field look like the Sahara. There never was such a joke! It's cosmic— it's terrible. How the gods must be roaring. 'Laughter unquenchable among the blessed gods!' "

"Yancey dear, we're used to oil out here. It's an old story. Come now. Come home and have a hot bath and clean clothes." In her mind's eye she saw those fine white linen shirts of his all neatly stacked in the drawer as he had left them.

For answer he reached out with one great arm and swept a pile of exchanges, copy paper, galley proofs, and clippings off the desk, while with the other hand he seized the typewriter by its steel bar and plumped it to the floor with a force that wrung a protesting whine and zing from its startled insides. He had always scorned to use a typewriter. The black swathes of his herculean pencil bit deeper into the paper's surface than any typewriter's metal teeth.

"Hot bath! Hot hell, honey! Do you realize what this means? Do you understand that two thousand Osage Indians, squatting in their rags in front of their miserable shanties, are now the richest nation in the world? In the world, I tell you. They were given that land—the barest, meanest desert land in the whole of the Oklahoma country. And the government of these United States said, 'There, you red dogs, take that and live on it. And if you can't live on it, then die on it.' God A'mighty, I could die myself with laughing. Millions and millions of dollars. They're spattering, I tell you, all over the Osage Reservation. There's no stopping that flow. Every buck and squaw on the Osage Reservation is a millionaire. They own that land, and, by God, I'm going to see that no one takes it away from them!"

"Oh, Yancey, be careful."

He was driving his pencil across the paper. "Send this out A.P. They tried to keep it dark when the flow came, but I'll show them. Sabra, kill your editorial lead, whatever it was. I'll write it. Make this your news lead, too. Listen. 'The gaudiest star-spangled cosmic joke that ever was played on a double-dealing government burst into fireworks to-day when, with a roar that could be heard for miles around, thousands of barrels of oil shot into the air on the miserable desert land known as the Osage Indian Reservation and occupied by those duped and wretched——!'"

"We can't use that, I tell you."

"Why not?"

"This isn't the Cimarron. It's the state of Oklahoma. That's treason —that's anarchy——"

"It's the truth. It's history. I can prove it. They'll be down on those Osages like a pack of wolves. At least I'll let them know they're expected. I'll run the story, by God, as I want it run, and they can shoot me for it."

"And I say you won't. You can't come in here like that. I'm editor of this paper."

He turned quietly and looked at her, the great head jutting out, the eyes like cold steel. "Who is?"

"I am."

Without a word he grasped her wrist and led her out, across the old porch, down the steps and into the street. There, on Pawhuska Avenue, in the full glare of noonday, he pointed to the weather-worn sign that he himself, aided by Jesse Rickey, had hung there almost twenty years before. She had had it painted and repainted. She had had it repaired. She had never replaced it with another.

THE OKLAHOMA WIGWAM

YANCEY CRAVAT PROP. AND EDITOR.

"When you take that down, Sabra honey, and paint your own name up in my place, you'll be the editor of this newspaper. Until you do that, I am."

As they stood there, she in her neat blue serge, he in his crumpled and shabby attire, she knew that she never would do it.

XXI

Young Cim came home from Colorado for the summer vacation, was caught up in the oil flood, and never went back. With his geological knowledge, slight as it was, and his familiarity with the region, he was shuttled back and forth from one end of the state to the other. Curiously enough Cim, like his father, was more an onlooker than a participant in this fantastic spectacle. The quality of business acumen seemed to be lacking in both these men; or perhaps a certain mad fastidiousness in them kept them from taking part in the feverish fight. A hint of oil in this corner, a trace of oil in that, and the thousands were upon it, pushing, scrambling, nose to the ground, down on all-fours like pigs in a trough. A hundred times Yancey could have bought an oil lease share for a song. Head lolling on his breast, lids lowered over the lightning eyes, he shrugged indifferent shoulders.

"I don't want the filthy muck," he said. "It stinks. Let the Indians have it. It's theirs. And the Big Boys from the East—let them sweat and scheme for it. They know where Oklahoma is now, all right."

His comings and goings had ceased to cause Sabra the keen agony of earlier days. She knew now that their existence, so long as Yancey lived, would always be made up of just such unexplained absences and melodramatic homecomings. She had made up her mind to accept the inevitable.

She did not mind that Yancey spent much time on the oil fields. He knew the men he called the Big Boys from the East, and they often sought him out for his company, which they found amusing, and for a certain regional wisdom that they considered valuable. He despised them and spent most of his time with the pumpers and roustabouts, drillers and tool dressers and shooters—a hard-drinking, hard-talking, hard-fighting crew. In his white sombrero and his outdated Prince Albert and his high-heeled boots he was known as a picturesque character. Years of heavy drinking were taking their toll of the magnificent body and mind. The long locks showed streaks of gray.

Local townsmen who once had feared and admired him began to patronize him or to laugh at him, tolerantly. Many of them were rich now, counting their riches not in thousands but in millions. They had owned a piece of Oklahoma dirt, or a piece of a piece of dirt—and suddenly, through no act of theirs, it was worth its weight in diamonds. Pat Leary, the pugnacious little Irish lawyer who had once been a section hand in the early days of the building of the Santa Fé road, was now so rich through his vast oil holdings that his Indian wife, Crook Nose, was considered a quaint and picturesque note by the wives of Eastern operators who came down on oil business.

After the first shrill excitement of it Sabra Cravat relinquished the hope of making sudden millions as other luckier ones had done. Her land had yielded no oil; she owned no oil leases. It was a curious fact that Sabra still queened it in Osage and had actually become a power in the state. The paper was read, respected, and feared throughout the Southwest. It was said with pride by Osage's civic minded that no oil was rich enough to stain the pages of the *Oklahoma Wigwam*. Though few realized it, and though Sabra herself never admitted it, it was Yancey who had made this true. He neglected it for years together, but he always turned up in a crisis, whether political, economic, or social, to hurl his barbed editorials at the heads of the offenders, to sting with the poison of his ridicule. He championed the Indians, he denounced the oil kings, he laughed at the money grabbers, he exposed the land thieves. He was afraid of nothing. He would absent himself for six months. The *Wigwam* would run along smoothly, placidly. He would return, torch in hand, and again set fire to the paper until the town, the county, the state were ablaze. The Osages came to him with their legal problems, and he advised them soundly and took a minimum fee. He seemed always to sense an important happening from afar and to emerge, growling like an old lion, from his hidden jungle lair, broken, mangy, but fighting, the fine eyes still alight, the magnificent head still as menacing as that of a buffalo charging. He had, on one occasion, come back just in time to learn of Dixie Lee's death.

Dixie had struck oil and had retired, a rich woman. She had closed her house and gone to Oklahoma City, and there she bought a house in a decent neighborhood and adopted a baby girl. She had gone to Kansas City for it, and though she had engaged a capable and somewhat bewildered nurse on that trip, Dixie herself carried the child home in her arms, its head close against the expensive satin bosom.

No one knew what means she had used to pull the wool over the eyes of the Kansas City authorities. She never could have done it in Oklahoma. She had had the child almost a year when the women of Osage got wind of it. They say she took it out herself in its perambulator daily, and perhaps someone recognized her on the street, though she looked like any plump and respectable matron now, in her rich, quiet dress and her pince nez, a little gray showing in the black, abundant hair.

Sabra Cravat heard of it. Mrs. Wyatt. Mrs. Doc Nisbett. Mrs. Pack.

They took the child away from her by law. Six months later Dixie Lee died; the sentimental said of a broken heart. It was Yancey Cravat who wrote her obituary:

> Dixie Lee, for years one of the most prominent citizens of Osage and a pioneer in the early days of Oklahoma, having made the Run in '89, one of the few women who had the courage to enter that historic and terrible race, is dead.
>
> She was murdered by the good women of Osage. . . .

The story was a nine-days' wonder, even in that melodramatic state. Sabra read it, white faced. The circulation of the *Wigwam* took another bound upward.

"Some day," said Osage, over its afternoon paper, "somebody is going to come along and shoot old Cimarron."

"I should think his wife would save them the trouble," someone suggested.

If Yancey's sporadic contributions increased the paper's circulation it was Sabra's steady drive that maintained it. It was a gigantic task to keep up with the changes that were sweeping over Osage and all of Oklahoma. Yet the columns of the *Wigwam* recorded these changes in its news columns, in its editorial pages, in its personal and local items and its advertisements, as faithfully as on that day of its first issue when Yancey had told them who killed Pegler. Perhaps it was because Sabra, even during Yancey's many absences, felt that the paper must be prepared any day to meet his scathing eye.

Strange items began to appear daily in the paper's columns—strange to the eye not interested in oil; but there was no such eye in Oklahoma, nor, for that matter, in the whole Southwest. Cryptic though these items might be to dwellers in other parts of the United States, they were of more absorbing interest to Oklahomans than front-page stories of war, romance, intrigue, royalty, crime.

Indian Territory Illuminating Oil Company swabbed 42 barrels in its No. 3 Lizzie in the northwest corner of the southwest of the northwest of 11–8–6 after having plugged back to 4,268 feet, and shooting with 52 quarts.

The wildcat test of McComb two miles north of Kewoka which is No. 1 Sutton in the southwest corner of the southeast of the northeast of 35–2–9 was given a shot of 105 quarts in the sand from 1,867 feet and hole bridged. As it stands it is estimated good for 450 barrels daily.

The paper's ads reflected the change. The old livery stable, with its buggies and phaëtons, its plugs to be hired, its tobacco-chewing loungers, its odor of straw, manure, and axle grease, was swept away, and in its place was Fink's Garage and Auto Livery. Repairs of All Kinds. Buy a Stimson Salient Six. The smell of gasoline, the hiss of the hose, lean young lads with grease-grimed fingers, engine wise.

Come to the Chamber of Commerce Dinner. The Oklahoma City College Glee Club will sing.

Osage began to travel, to see the world. Their wanderings were no longer local. Where, two years ago, you read that Dr. and Mrs. Horace McGill are up from Concho to do their Christmas buying, you now saw that Mr. and Mrs. W. Fletcher Busby have left for a trip to Europe, Egypt, and the Holy Land. You knew that old Wick Busby had made his pile in oil and that Nettie Busby was out to see the world.

Most astounding of all were the Indian items, for now the *Oklahoma Wigwam* and every other paper in the county regularly ran news about those incredible people who in one short year had leaped from the Neolithic Age to Broadway.

The Osage Indians, a little more than two thousand in number, who but yesterday were a ragged, half-fed, and listless band, squatting wretchedly on the Reservation allotted them, waiting until time, sickness, and misery should blot them forever from the land, were now, by a miracle of nature, the richest nation in the world. The barren ground on which they had lived now yielded the most lavish oil flow in the state. Yancey Cravat's news story and editorial had been copied and read all over the country. A stunned government tried to bring order out of a chaos of riches. The two thousand Osages were swept off the Reservation to make way for the flood of oil that was transmuted into a flood of gold. They were transported to a new section called Wazhazhe, which is the ancient Indian word for Osage.

Agents appointed. Offices established. Millions of barrels of oil. Millions of dollars. Millions of dollars yearly to be divided somehow among two thousand Osage Indians, to whom a blanket, a bowl of soffica, a mangy pony, a bit of tobacco, a disk of peyote had meant riches. And now every full blood, half blood, or quarter blood Osage was put on the Indian Roll, and every name on the Indian Roll was entitled to a Head Right. Every head right meant a definite share in the millions. Five in a family—five head rights. Ten in a family—ten head rights. The Indian Agent's office was full of typewriters, files, pads, ledgers, neat young clerks all occupied with papers and documents that read like some fantastic nightmare. The white man's eye, traveling down the tidy list, with its story-book Indian names and its hard, cold, matter-of-fact figures, rejected what it read as being too absurd for the mind to grasp.

Clint Tall Meat	$523,000
Benny Warrior	$192,000
Ho ki ah se	$265,887
Long Foot Magpie	$387,942

The government bought them farms with their own oil money, and built big red brick houses near the roadside and furnished them in plush and pianos and linoleum and gas ranges and phonographs. You saw their powerful motor cars, dust covered, whirling up and down the red clay Oklahoma roads—those roads still rutted, unpaved, hazardous, for Oklahoma had had no time to attend to such matters. Fifty years before, whole bands of Osages on their wiry little ponies had traveled south in the winter and north in the summer to visit their Indian cousins. Later, huddled miserably on their Reservation, they had issued forth on foot or in wretched wagons to pay their seasonal visits and to try to recapture, by talk and song and dance and ritual, some pale ghost of their departed happiness. A shabby enough procession, guarded, furtive, smoldering.

But now you saw each Osage buck in his high-powered car, his inexpert hands grasping the wheel, his enormous sombrero—larger even than the white man's hat—flapping in the breeze that he made by his speed. In the back you saw the brilliance of feathers and blankets worn by the beady-eyed children and the great placid squaw crouched in the bottom of the car. The white man driving the same road gave these Indian cars a wide berth, for he knew they stopped for no one, kept the middle of the road, flew over bridges, draws, and ditches like mad things.

Grudgingly, for she still despised them, Sabra Cravat devoted a page of the *Wigwam* to news of the Osages, those moneyed, petted wards of a bewildered government. The page appeared under the title of Indian News, and its contents were more than tinged with the grotesque.

Long Foot Magpie and wife were week-end visitors of Plenty Horses at Watonga recently.

Grandma Standing Woman of near Hominy was a visitor at the home of Red Paint Woman.

Mr. and Mrs. Sampson Lame Bull have returned from Osage after accompanying Mrs. Twin Woman, who is now a patient in the Osage Hospital.

Albert Short Tooth and Robert White Eyes are batching it at the home of Mrs. Ghost Woman during her absence.

Laura Bird Woman and Thelma Eagle Nest of near here motored to Grey Horse to visit Sore Head but he was not at home.

Woodson Short Man and wife were shopping in Osage one day last week.

Red Bird Scabby has left the Reservation for a visit to Colorado Springs and Manitou.

Squaw Iki has returned recently after being a patient at the Concho Hospital for some time.

Joe Stump Horn and his wife Mrs. Long Dead are visiting Red Nose Scabby for a few days.

Sun Maker has given up the effort to find a first-class cook in Waz-hazhe and is looking around in Osage.

The Osages were *Wigwam* subscribers. They read the paper, or had it read to them if they were of the older and less literate generation. Sabra was accustomed to seeing the doorway suddenly darkened by a huge blanketed form or to look up, startled, to behold the brilliant striped figure standing beside her desk in the business office. If Yancey chanced to be in the occasion became very social.

"How!"

"How!"

"Want um paper."

"All right, Short Tooth. Five dollars."

The blanketed figure would produce a wallet whose cheeks were plump to bursting with round silver dollars, for the Osage loved the sound and feel of the bright metal disks. Down on the desk they clinked.

The huge Osage stood then, waiting. Yancey knew what was wanted, as did Sabra.

"Me want see iron man. Make um name."

Whereupon Yancey or Sabra would conduct the visitor into the composing room. There were three linotype machines now, clanking and chattering away. Once Yancey had taken old Big Elk, Ruby's father, back there to see how the linotype turned liquid lead into printed words. He had had Jesse Rickey, at the linotype's keyboard, turn out old Big

Elk's name in the form of a neat metal bar, together with the paper slip of its imprint.

There was no stopping it. The story of the iron monster that could talk and write and move spread like a prairie fire through Wazhazhe. Whole families subscribed separately for the *Oklahoma Wigwam*— bucks, squaws, girls, boys, papooses in arms. The iron monster had for them a fascination that was a mingling of admiration, awe, and fear. It was useless to explain that they need not take out a subscription in order to own one of these coveted metal bars. It had been done once. They always would do it that way. Sabra, if she happened to be in charge, always gave the five dollars to her pet charity, after trying in vain to refuse it when proffered. Yancey took it cheerfully and treated the boys at the new Sunny South Saloon, now a thing of splendor with its mahogany bar, its brass rail, its mirror, chandeliers, and flesh-tinted oil paintings.

Up and down the dusty Oklahoma roads at terrific speed, up and down Pawhuska Avenue, went the blanketed figures in their Packard and Pierce Arrow cars. The merchants of Osage liked to see them in town. It meant money freely spent on luxuries. The Osage Indian men were broad shouldered, magnificent, the women tall, stately. Now they grew huge with sloth and overfeeding. They ate enormously and richly. They paced Pawhuska Avenue with slow measured tread; calm, complete, grandly content. The women walked bareheaded, their brilliant blankets, striped purple and orange and green and red, wrapped about their shoulders and enveloping them from neck to heels. But beneath this you saw dresses of silk, American in make and style. On their feet were slippers of pale fine kid, high-heeled, or of patent-leather, ornamented with buckles of cut steel, shining and costly. The men wore the blanket, too, but beneath it they liked a shirt of silk brocade in gorgeous colors— bright green or purple or cerise—its tail worn outside the trousers, and the trousers often as not trimmed with a pattern of beadwork at the side. On their heads they wore huge sombreros trimmed with bands of snake-skin ornamented with silver. They hired white chauffeurs to drive their big sedan cars and sat back grandly after ordering them to drive round and round and round the main business block. Jewelry shops began to display their glistening wares in Osage, not so much in the hope of winning the favor of the white oil millionaire as the red. Bracelets, watches, gaudy rings and pins and bangles and beads and combs and buckles. Diamonds. These the Indians seemed instinctively to know about, and they bought them clear and blue-white and costly.

The Levy Mercantile Company had added a fancy grocery and market department to its three-story brick store. It was situated on the street floor and enhanced with a great plate-glass window. In this window Sol displayed a mouth-watering assortment of foods. Juicy white stalks of asparagus in glass, as large around as a man's two thumbs; great ripe olives, their purple-black cheeks glistening with oil; lobster, mushrooms, French peas, sardines, mountainous golden cheeses, tender broilers, peaches in syrup, pork roasts dressed in frills. Dozens of chickens, pounds of pork, baskets of delicacies were piled in the cars of home-ward bound Osages. Often, when the food bills mounted too high, the Indian Agent at Wazhazhe threatened to let the bill go unpaid. He alone had the power to check the outpouring of Indian gold, and even he frequently was unable to cope with their mad extravagances.

"It's disgusting," Sabra Cravat said, again and again. "What are they good for? What earthly good are they? Ignorant savages who do nothing but eat and sleep and drive around in their ridiculous huge automobiles."

"Keep money in circulation," Sol Levy replied, for she often took him to task after seeing a line of Indian cars parked outside the Osage Mercantile Company's store.

"You ought to be ashamed of yourself."

"Now, now, Sabra. Not so grand, please. I don't do like dozens of other merchants here in town. Make out bills for goods they haven't bought and give them the money. Or charge them double on the bill that the Indian Agent sees, and return them the overcharge. They come in my store, they buy, they pay what the article is marked, and they get what they pay for. Inez Bull comes in and gets a silk step-in, or Sun Maker he buys twelve pounds of chicken and ten pounds of pork. I should tell them they can't have it! Let the President of the United States do it. The Big White Father."

Not only did Yancey agree with Sol, he seemed to find enormous satisfaction in the lavishness with which they spent their oil money; in the very absurdity of the things they bought.

"The joke gets better and better. We took their land away from them and exterminated the buffalo, then expected them to squat on the Reservations weaving baskets and molding pottery that nobody wanted to buy. Well, at least the Osages never did that. They're spending their money just as the white people do when they get a handful of it—chicken and plush and automobiles and phonographs and silk shirts and jewelry."

"Why don't they do some good with it?" Sabra demanded.

"What good's Wyatt doing? Or Nisbett, or old Buckner, or Ike Hawes, or their wives! Blowing it on houses and travel and diamonds and high-priced cars."

"The Osages could help the other tribes—poor Indian tribes that haven't struck oil."

"Maybe they will—when Bixby gives away his millions to down-and-out hotel keepers who are as poor as he was when he ran the Bixby House, back in the old days."

"Filthy savages!"

"No, honey. Just blanket Indians—horse Indians—Plains Indians, with about twenty-five millions of dollars a year gushing up out of the earth and splattering all around them. The wonder to me is that they don't die laughing and spoil their own good time."

Sometimes Sabra encountered old Big Elk and his vast squaw and Ruby Big Elk, together with others of the family—a large one for an Osage—driving through Pawhuska Avenue. With their assembled head rights the family was enormously rich—one of the wealthiest on the Wazhazhe Reservation. When the Big Elks drove through the town it was a parade. No one car could have contained the family, though they would have scorned such economy even if it had been possible.

They made a brilliant Indian frieze in the modern manner. Old Big Elk and his wife, somewhat conservatively, lolled in a glittering Lincoln driven by a white chauffeur. Through the generous glass windows you saw the two fat bronze faces, the massive bodies, the brilliant colors of their blankets and chains and beads. One of the Big Elk boys drove a snow-white Pierce Arrow roadster that tore and shrieked like an avenging demon up and down the dusty road between Osage and Wazhazhe. Ruby herself, and a sister-in-law or so, and a brother, might follow in one of the Packards, while still another brother or sister preferred a Cadillac. If they walked at all it was to ascend with stately step the entrance to the Indian Agent's Office. The boys wore American dress, with perhaps an occasional Indian incongruity—beaded pants, a five-gallon hat with an eagle feather in it, sometimes moccasins. Ruby and her sisters and her sister-in-law wore the fine and gaudy blanket over their American dresses, they were hatless, and their long bountiful hair was done Indian fashion. The dress of old Big Elk and his wife was a gorgeous mixture of Indian and American, with the Indian triumphantly predominating. About the whole party, as in the case of any of the Osage oil families, there was an air of quiet insolence, of deep rich triumph.

Sabra always greeted them politely enough. "How do you do, Ruby," she would say. "What a beautiful dress." Ruby would say nothing. She would look at Sabra's neat business dress of dark blue or gray, at Sabra's plain little hat and sensible oxford ties. "Give my regards to your father and mother," Sabra would continue, blandly, but inwardly furious to find herself feeling uncomfortable and awkward beneath this expressionless Indian gaze. She fancied that in it there was something menacing, something triumphant. She wondered if Ruby, the oft-married, had married yet again. Once she asked young Cim about her, making her tone casual. "Do you ever see that girl who used to work here—Ruby, wasn't that it? Ruby Big Elk?"

Cim's tone was even more casual than hers. "Oh, yes. We were working out Wazhazhe way, you know, on the Choteau field. That's near by."

"They're terribly rich, aren't they?"

"Oh, rotten. A fleet of cars and a regular flock of houses."

"It's a wonder that some miserable white squaw man hasn't married that big greasy Ruby for her head right. Mrs. Conn Sanders told me that one of the Big Elk boys was actually playing golf out at the Westchester Apawamis Club last Saturday. It's disgusting. He must know there's a rule against Indians. Mrs. Sanders reported him to the house committee."

"There's a rule, all right. But you ought to see the gallery when Standing Bear whams it out so straight and so far that he makes the pro look like a ping-pong player."

"How is he in a tomahawk contest?"

"Oh, Mother, you talk like Grandma when she used to visit here."

"The Marcys and the Venables didn't hobnob with dirty savages in blankets."

"Standing Bear doesn't wear his blanket when he plays golf," retorted Cim, coolly. "And he took a shower after he'd made the course in seven below par."

Donna came home from a bridge party one afternoon a week later, the creamy Venable pallor showing the Marcy tinge of ocherous rage. She burst in upon Sabra, home from the office.

"Do you know that Cim spends his time at the Big Elks' when we think he's out in the oil fields?"

Sabra met this as calmly as might be. "He's working near there. He told me he had seen them."

"Seen them! That miserable Gazelle Slaughter said that he's out there all the time. All the time, I tell you, and that he and Ruby drive around in her car, and he eats with them, he stays there, he——"

"I'll speak to your father. Cim's coming home Saturday. Gazelle is angry at Cim, you know that, because he won't notice her and she likes him."

She turned her clear appraising gaze upon this strange daughter of hers. She thought, suddenly, that Donna was like a cobra, with that sleek black head, that cold and slanting eye, that long creamy throat in which a pulse sometimes could be seen to beat and swell a little—the only sign of emotion in this baffling creature.

"I'll tell you what, Donna. If you'd pay a little less attention to your brother's social lapses and a little more to your own vulgar conduct, perhaps it would be better."

Donna bestowed her rare and brilliant smile upon her forthright mother. "Now, now, darling! I suppose I say, 'What do you mean?' And you say, 'You know very well what I mean.'"

"You certainly do know what I mean. If you weren't my own daughter I'd say your conduct with Tracy Wyatt was that of a—a——"

"Harlot," put in Donna, sweetly.

"Donna! How can you talk like that? You are breaking my heart. Haven't I had enough? I've never complained, have I? But now—you——"

Donna came over to her and put her arms about her, as though she were the older woman protecting the younger. "It's all right, Mamma darling. You just don't understand. Life isn't as simple as it was when you were a frontier gal. I know what I want and I'm going to get it."

Sabra shrugged away from her; faced her with scorn. "I've seen you. I'm ashamed for you. You press against him like a—like a——" Again she could not say it. Another generation. "And that horse you ride. You say he loans it to you. He gave it to you. It's yours. What for?"

She was weeping.

"I tell you it's all right, Mamma. He did give it to me. He wants to give me lots of things, but I won't take them, yet. Tracy's in love with me. He thinks I'm young and beautiful and stimulating and wonderful. He's married to a dried-up, vinegary, bitter old hag who was just that when he married her, years ago. He's never known what love is. She has never given him children. He's insanely rich, and not too old, and rather sweet. We're going to be married. Tracy will get his divorce. Money does anything. It has taken me a year and a half to do it. I've never worked so hard in all my life. But it's going to be worth it. Don't worry, darling. Tracy's making an honest woman of your wayward daughter."

Sabra drew herself up, every inch the daughter of her mother, Felice Venable, née Marcy. "You are disgusting."

"Not really, if you just look at it without a lot of sentiment. I shall be happy, and Tracy, too. His wife will be unhappy, I suppose, for a while. But she isn't happy anyway, as it is. Better one than three. It'll work out. You'll see. Don't bother about me. It's Cim that needs looking

after. He's got a streak of—of——" She looked at her mother. Did not
finish the sentence. "When he comes home Saturday I wish you'd speak
to him."

XXII

BUT Cim did not come home on Saturday. On Saturday, at noon, when
Sabra and Yancey drove from the office in their little utility car to the
house on Kihekah Street for their noonday dinner they saw a great
limousine drawn up at the curb. A chauffeur, vaguely familiar, lounged
in front. The car was thick with the red dust of the country road.

A vague pang of premonition stabbed at Sabra's vitals. She clutched
Yancey's arm. "Whose car is that?"

Yancey glanced at it indifferently. "Somebody drove Cim home, I
suppose. Got enough dinner for company?"

Donna had gone to Oklahoma City to spend the week-end. It must
be Cim.

"Cim!" Sabra called, as she entered the front door. "Cim!" But there
was no answer. She went straight to the sitting room. Empty. But in the
stiff little parlor, so seldom used, sat two massive, silent figures. With
the Indian sense of ceremony and formality old Big Elk and his squaw
had known the proper room to use for an occasion such as this.

"Why—Big Elk!"

"How!" replied Big Elk, and held up his palm in the gesture of
greeting.

"Yancey!" cried Sabra suddenly, in a terrible voice. The two pairs of
black Indian eyes stared at her. Sabra saw that their dress was elaborate;
the formal dress reserved for great occasions. The woman wore a dark
skirt and a bright cerise satin blouse, ample and shaped like a dressing
sacque. Over her shoulders was the fine bright-hued blanket. Her hair
was neatly braided and wound about her hatless head. She wore no
ornaments. That was the prerogative of the male. Old Big Elk was a
structure of splendor. His enormous bulk filled the chair. His great
knees were wide apart. His blue trousers were slashed and beaded elaborately at the sides and on his feet were moccasins heavy with intricate
beadwork. His huge upper body was covered with a shirt of brilliant

green brocade worn outside the trousers, and his striped blanket hung regally from his shoulders. About his neck and on his broad breast hung chains, beads, necklaces. In the bright silk neckerchief knotted about his throat you saw the silver emblem of his former glory as chief of the tribe. There were other insignia of distinction made of beaten silver—the star, the crescent, the sun. On his head was a round high cap of brown beaver like a Cossack's. Up the back of this was stuck an eagle feather. His long locks, hanging about his shoulders, straight and stiff, were dyed a brilliant orange, like an old burlesque queen's, a startling, a fantastic background for the parchment face, lined and creased and crisscrossed with a thousand wrinkles. One hand rested on his knee. The other wielded languidly, back and forth, back and forth, an enormous semicircular fan made of eagle feathers. Side by side the two massive figures sat like things of bronze. Only their eyes moved, and that nightmarish eagle feather fan, back and forth, back and forth, regally.

Those dull black unsmiling eyes, that weaving fan, moved Sabra to nameless terror. "Yancey!" she cried again, through stiff lips. "Yancey!"

At the note of terror in her voice he was down the stairs and in the room with his quick light step. But at sight of old Big Elk and his wife his look of concern changed to one of relief. He smiled his utterly charming smile.

"How!"

"How!" croaked Big Elk.

Mrs. Big Elk nodded her greeting. She was a woman younger, perhaps, by thirty years than her aged husband; his third wife. She spoke English; had even attended an Indian Mission school in her girlhood. But through carelessness or indifference she used the broken, slovenly English of the unlettered Indian.

Now the two relapsed into impassive silence.

"What do they want? Ask them what they want."

Yancey spoke a few words in Osage. Big Elk replied with a monosyllable.

"What did he say? What is it?"

"I asked them to eat dinner with us. He says he cannot."

"I should hope not. Tell her to speak English. She speaks English."

Big Elk turned his great head, slowly, as though it moved on a mechanical pivot. He stared at his fat, round-faced wife. He uttered a brief command in his own tongue. The squaw smiled a little strange, embarrassed smile, like a schoolgirl—it was less a smile than a contortion of the face, so rare in her race as to be more frightening than a scowl.

"Big Elk and me come take you back to Wazhazhe."

"What for?" cried Sabra, sharply.

"Four o'clock big dinner, big dance. Your son want um come tell you. Want um know he marry Ruby this morning."

She was silent again, smiling her foolish fixed smile. Big Elk's fan went back and forth, back and forth.

"God A'mighty!" said Yancey Cravat. He looked at Sabra, came over to her quickly, but she waved him away.

"Don't. I'm not going to—it's all right." It was as though she shrank from his touch. She stood there, staring at the two barbaric figures staring so stonily back at her with their dead black Indian eyes. It was at times like this that the Marcy in her stood her in good stead. She came of iron stock, fit to stand the fire. Only beneath her fine dark eyes you now suddenly saw a smudge of purplish brown, as though a dirty thumb had rubbed there; and a sagging of all the muscles of her face, so that she looked wattled, lined, old.

"Don't look like that, honey. Come. Sit down."

Again the groping wave of her hand. "I'm all right, I tell you. Come. We must go there."

Yancey came forward. He shook hands formally with Big Elk, with the Indian woman. Sabra, seeing him, suddenly realized that he was not displeased. She knew that no formal politeness would have prevented him from voicing his anger if this monstrous announcement had shattered him as it had her, so that her very vitals seemed to be withering within her.

"Sugar, shake hands with them, won't you?"

"No. No." She wet her dry lips a little with her tongue, like one in a fever. She turned, woodenly, and walked to the door, ignoring the Indians. Across the hall, slowly, like an old woman, down the porch steps, toward the shabby little car next to the big rich one. As she went she heard Yancey's voice (was there an exultant note in it?) at the telephone.

"Jesse! Take this. Get it in. Ready! . . . Ex-Chief Big Elk, of the Osage Nation, and Mrs. Big Elk, living at Wazhazhe, announce the marriage of their daughter Ruby Big Elk to Cimarron Cravat, son of—don't interrupt me—I'm in a hurry—son of Mr. and Mrs. Yancey Cravat, of this city. The wedding was solemnized at the home of the bride's parents and was followed by an elaborate dinner made up of many Indian and American dishes, partaken of by the parents of the bride and the groom, many relatives and numerous friends of the young . . ."

Sabra climbed heavily into the car and sat staring at the broad back of the car ahead of her. Chief Big Elk and his wife came out presently, unreal, bizarre in the brilliant noonday Oklahoma sunshine, ushered by

Yancey. He was being charming. They heaved their ponderous bulk into the big car. Yancey got in beside Sabra. She spoke to him once only.

"I think you are glad."

"This is Oklahoma. In a way it's what I wanted it to be when I came here twenty years ago. Cim's like your father, Lewis Venable. Weak stuff, but good stock. Ruby's pure Indian blood and a magnificent animal. It's hard on you now, my darling. But their children and their grandchildren are going to be such stuff as Americans are made of. You'll see."

"I hope I shall die before that day."

The shabby little middle-class car followed the one whirling ahead of them over the red clay Oklahoma roads. Eating the dust of the big car just ahead.

She went through it and stood it, miraculously, until one grotesquerie proved too much for her strained nerves and broke them. But she went into the Indian house, and saw Cim sitting beside the Indian woman, and as she looked at his beautiful weak face she thought, I wish that I had never found him that day when he was lost on the prairie long ago. He came toward her, his head lowered with that familiar look, his fine eyes hidden by the lids.

"Look at me!" Sabra commanded, in the voice of Felice Venable. The boy raised his eyes. She looked at him, her face stony. Ruby Big Elk came toward her with that leisurely, insolent, scuffling step. The two women gazed at each other; rather, their looks clashed, like swords held high. They did not shake hands.

There were races, there were prizes, there was dancing. In the old Indian days the bucks had raced on foot for a prize that was a pony tethered at a distance and won by the fleetest to reach him, mount, and ride him back to the starting point. To-day the prize was a magnificent motor car that stood glittering in the open field half a mile distant. Sabra thought, I am dying, I am dying. And Donna. This squaw is her sister-in-law. Miss Dignum's on the Hudson.

Ruby's handsome head right had bought the young couple the house just across the road from Big Elk's—a one-story red brick bungalow, substantial, ugly. They showed Sabra and Yancey through it. It was furnished complete. Mongrel Spanish furniture in the living room—red plush, fringe, brass nail heads as big as twenty-dollar gold pieces. An upright piano. An oak dining-room set. A fine bathroom with heavy rich bath towels neatly hung on the racks. A shining stained oak bedroom set with a rose-colored taffeta spread. Sabra felt a wave of nausea. Cim's face was smiling, radiant. Yancey was joking and laughing with the Indians. In the kitchen sat a white girl in a gingham dress and a kitchen apron. The girl's hair was so light a yellow as to appear almost white.

Her unintelligent eyes were palest blue. Her skin was so fair as to be quite colorless. In the midst of the roomful of dark Indian faces the white face of the new Cravat hired girl seemed to swim in a hazy blob before Sabra's eyes. But she held on. She felt Ruby's scornful dark eyes on her. Sabra had a feeling as though she had been disemboweled and now was a hollow thing, an empty shell that moved and walked and talked.

Dinner. White servants and negro servants to wait on them. A long table seating a score or more, and many such tables. Bowls and plates piled with food all down the length of it. Piles of crisp pork, roasted in the Indian fashion over hot embers sunk in a pit in the yard, and skewered with a sharp pointed stick. Bowls of dried corn. Great fat, black ripe olives. Tinned lobster. Chicken. Piles of dead ripe strawberries. Vast plateaus of angel-food cake covered with snow fields of icing.

Sabra went through the motions of eating. Sometimes she put a morsel into her mouth and actually swallowed it. There was a great clatter of knives and forks and dishes. Everything was eaten out of one plate. Platters and bowls were replenished. Sabra found herself seated beside Mrs. Big Elk. On her other side was Yancey. He was eating and laughing and talking. Mrs. Big Elk was being almost comically polite, solicitous. She pressed this tidbit, that dainty, on her stony guest.

Down the center of the table, at intervals, were huge bowls piled with a sort of pastry stuffed with forcemeat. It was like a great ravioli, and piles of it vanished beneath the onslaught of appreciative guests.

"For God's sake, pretend to eat something, Sabra," Yancey murmured, under his breath. "It's done now. They consider it an insult. Try to eat something."

She stirred the pastry and chopped meat that had been put on her plate.

"Good," said Mrs. Big Elk, beside her, and pointed at the mass with one dusky maculate finger.

Sabra lifted her fork to her lips and swallowed a bit of it. It was delicious—spicy, rich, appetizing. "Yes," she said, and thought, I am being wonderful. This is killing me. "Yes, it is very good. This meat—this stuffing—is it chopped or ground through a grinder?"

The huge Indian woman beside her turned her expressionless gaze on Sabra. Ponderously she shook her head from side to side in negation.

"Naw," she answered, politely. "Chawed."

The clatter of a fork dropped to the plate, a clash among the cups and saucers. Sabra Cravat had fainted.

XXIII

Osage was so sophisticated that it had again become simple. The society editor of the *Oklahoma Wigwam* used almost no adjectives. In the old days, you had read that "the house was beautifully decorated with an artistic arrangement of smilax, sent from Kansas City, pink and purple asters in profusion making a bower before which the young couple stood, while in the dining room the brilliance of golden glow, scarlet salvia, and autumn leaves gave a seasonal touch." But now the society column said, austerely, "The decorations were orchids and Pernet roses."

Osage, Oklahoma, was a city.

Where, scarcely two decades ago, prairie and sky had met the eye with here a buffalo wallow, there an Indian encampment, you now saw a twenty-story hotel: the Savoy-Bixby. The Italian head waiter bent from the waist and murmured in your ear his secret about the veal sauté with mushrooms or the spaghetti Caruso du jour. Sabra Cravat, Congresswoman from Oklahoma, lunching in the Louis XIV room with the members of the Women's State Republican Committee, would say, looking up at him with those intelligent dark eyes, "I'll leave it to you, Nick. Only quickly. We haven't much time." Niccolo Mazzarini would say yes, he understood. No one had much time in Osage, Oklahoma. A black jackanapes in a tight scarlet jacket with brass buttons and even tighter bright blue pants, an impudent round red cap cocked over one ear, strolled through the dining room bawling, "Mistah Thisandthat! Mistah Whoandwhat!" He carried messages on a silver salver. There were separate ice-water taps in every bedroom. Servidors. Ring once for the waiter. Twice for the chambermaid. A valet is at your service.

Twenty-five years earlier anybody who was anybody in Oklahoma had dilated on his or her Eastern connections. Iowa, if necessary, was East.

They had been a little ashamed of the Run. Bragged about the splendors of the homes from which they had come.

Now it was considered the height of chic to be able to say that your parents had come through in a covered wagon. Grandparents were still rather rare in Oklahoma. As for the Run of '89—it was Osage's *Mayflower*. At the huge dinner given in Sabra Cravat's honor when she was elected Congresswoman, and from which they tried to exclude Sol Levy over Sabra's vigorous (and triumphant) protest, the chairman of the Committee on Arrangements explained it all to Sol, patronizingly.

"You see, we're inviting only people who came to Oklahoma in the Run."

"Well, sure," said the former peddler, genially. "That's all right. I walked."

The Levy Mercantile Company's building now occupied an entire square block and was fifteen stories high. In the huge plate-glass windows on Pawhuska postured ladies waxen and coquettish, as on Fifth Avenue. You went to the Salon Moderne to buy Little French Dresses, and the saleswomen of this department wore black satin and a very nice little strand of imitation pearls, and their eyes were hard and shrewd and their phrases the latest. The Osage Indian women had learned about these Little French Dresses, and they often came in with their stately measured stride: soft and flaccid from easy living, rolls of fat about their hips and thighs. They tried on sequined dresses, satin dresses, chiffon. Sometimes even the younger Osage Indian girls still wore the brilliant striped blanket, in a kind of contemptuous defiance of the whites. And to these, as well as to the other women customers, the saleswomen said, "That's awfully good this year. . . . That's dreadfully smart on you, Mrs. Buffalo Hide. . . . I think that line isn't the thing for your figure, Mrs. Plenty Vest. . . . My dear, I want you to have that. It's perfect with your coloring."

The daughter of Mrs. Pat Leary (née Crook Nose) always caused quite a flutter when she came in, for accustomed though Osage was to money and the spending of it, the Learys' lavishness was something spectacular. Hand-made silk underwear, the sheerest of cobweb French stockings, model hats, dresses—well, in the matter of gowns it was no good trying to influence Maude Leary or her mother. They frankly wanted beads, spangles, and paillettes on a foundation of crude color. The saleswomen were polite and acquiescent, but they cocked an eyebrow at one another. Squaw stuff. Now that little Cravat girl—Felice Cravat, Cimarron Cravat's daughter—was different. She insisted on plain, smart tailored things. Young though she was, she was Oklahoma State Woman Tennis Champion. She always said she looked a freak in fluffy things—like a boy dressed up in girl's clothes. She had long, lean, muscular arms and a surprising breadth of shoulder, was slim flanked and practically stomachless. She had a curious trick of holding her head down and looking up at you under her lashes and when she did that you forgot her boyishness, for her lashes were like fern fronds, and her eyes, in her dark face, an astounding ocean gray. She was a good sport, too. She didn't seem to mind the fact that her mother, when she accompanied her, wore the blanket and was hatless, just like any poor Kaw, instead of being one of the richest of the Osages. She was rather handsome for a squaw, in a big, insolent, slow-moving way. Felice Cravat, everyone agreed, was a chip of the old block, and by that they did not mean her father. They were thinking of Yancey Cravat—old Cimarron, her grandfather, who was now something of a legend in Osage and throughout Oklahoma. Young Cim and his Osage wife had had a second child—a boy—and they had called him Yancey, after the old boy. Young Yancey was a bewilderingly handsome mixture of a dozen types and forbears—Indian, Spanish, French, Southern, Southwest. With that long narrow face, the dolicho-cephalic head, people said he looked like the King of Spain—without that dreadful Hapsburg jaw. Others said he was the image of his grand-mother, Sabra Cravat. Still others contended that he was his Indian mother over again—insolence and all. A third would come along and say, "You're crazy. He's old Yancey, born again. I guess you don't re-member him. There, look, that's what I mean! The way he closes his eyes as if he were sleepy, and then when he does look at you straight you feel as if you'd been struck by lightning. They say he's so smart that the Osages believe he's one of their old gods come back to earth."

Mrs. Tracy Wyatt (she who had been Donna Cravat) had tried to adopt one of her brother's children, being herself childless, but Cim and his wife Ruby Big Elk had never consented to this. She was a case, that Donna Cravat, Oklahoma was agreed about that. She could get away with things that any other woman would be shot for. When old Tracy Wyatt had divorced his wife to marry this girl local feeling had been very much against her. Everyone had turned to the abandoned middle-aged wife with attentions and sympathy, but she had met their warmth and friendliness with such vitriol that they fell back in terror and finally came to believe the stories of how she had deviled and nagged old Tracy all through their marriage. They actually came to feel that he had been justified in deserting her and taking to wife this young and fascinating girl. Certainly he seemed to take a new lease on life, lost five inches around the waist line, played polo, regained something of the high color and good spirits of his old dray-driving days, and made a great hit in London during the season when Donna was presented at court. Besides, there was no withstanding the Wyatt money. Even in a country blasé of millionaires Tracy Wyatt's fortune was something to marvel about. The name of Wyatt seemed to be everywhere. As you rode in trains you saw the shining round black flanks of oil cars, thou-sands of them, and painted on them in letters of white, "Wyatt Oils." Motoring through Oklahoma and the whole of the Southwest you passed miles of Wyatt oil tanks, whole silent cities of monoliths, like something grimly Egyptian, squatting eunuch-like on the prairies.

As for the Wyatt house—it wasn't a house at all, but a combination of the palace of Versailles and the Grand Central Station in New York. It occupied grounds about the size of the duchy of Luxembourg, and on the grounds, once barren plain, had been set great trees brought from England.

A mile of avenue, planted in elms, led up to the mansion, and each elm, bought, transported, and stuck in the ground, had cost fifteen hundred dollars. There were rare plants, farms, forests, lakes, tennis courts, golf links, polo fields, race tracks, airdromes, swimming pools. Whole paneled rooms had been brought from France. In the bathrooms were electric cabinets, and sunken tubs of rare marble, and shower baths glass enclosed. These bathrooms were the size of bedrooms, and the bedrooms the size of ballrooms, and the ballroom as big as an auditorium. There was an ice plant and cooling system that could chill the air of every room in the house, even on the hottest Oklahoma windy day. The kitchen range looked like a house in itself, and the kitchen looked like that of the Biltmore, only larger. When you entered the dining room you felt that here should be seated solemn diplomats in gold braid signing world treaties and having their portraits painted doing it. Sixty gardeners manned the grounds. The house servants would have peopled a village.

Sabra Cravat rarely came to visit her daughter's house, and when she did the very simplicity of her slim straight little figure in its dark blue georgette or black crêpe was startling in the midst of these marble columns and vast corridors and royal hangings. She did come occasionally, and on those occasions you found her in the great central apartment that was like a throne room, standing there before the portraits of her son's two children, Felice and Yancey Cravat. Failing to possess either of the children for her own, Donna had had them painted and hung there, one either side of the enormous fireplace. She had meant them to be a gift to her mother, but Sabra Cravat had refused to take them.

"Don't you like them, Sabra darling? They're the best things Segovia has ever done. Is it because they're modern? I think they look like the kids—don't you?"

"They're just wonderful."

"Well, then?"

"I'd have to build a house for them. How would they look in the sitting room of the house on Kihekah! No, let me come here and look at them now and then. That way they're always a fresh surprise to me."

Certainly they were rather surprising, those portraits. Rather, one of them was. Segovia had got little Felice well enough, but he had made the mistake of painting her in Spanish costume, and somehow her angular contours and boyish frame had not lent themselves to these gorgeous lace and satin trappings. The boy, Yancey, had refused to dress up for the occasion—had, indeed, been impatient of posing at all. Segovia had caught him quickly and brilliantly, with startling results. He wore a pair of loose, rather grimy white tennis pants, a white woolly sweater with a hole in the elbow, and was hatless. In his right hand—that slim, beautiful, speaking hand—he held a limp, half-smoked cigarette, its blue-gray smoke spiraling faintly, its dull red eye the only note of color in the picture. Yet the whole portrait was colorful, moving, alive. The boy's pose was so insolent, so lithe, so careless. The eyes followed you. He was a person.

"Looks like Ruby, don't you think?" Donna had said, when first she had shown it to her mother.

"No!" Sabra had replied, with enormous vigor. "Not at all. Your father."

"Well—maybe—a little."

"A little! You're crazy! Look at his eyes. His hands. Of course they're not as beautiful as your father's hands were—are . . ."

It had been five years since Sabra had heard news of her husband, Yancey Cravat. And now, for the first time, she felt that he was dead, though she had never admitted this. In spite of his years she had heard that Yancey had gone to France during the war. The American and the English armies had rejected him, so he had dyed his graying hair, lied about his age, thrown back his still magnificent shoulders, and somehow, by his eyes, his voice, his hands, or a combination of all these, had hypnotized them into taking him. An unofficial report had listed him among the missing after the carnage had ceased in the shambles that had been a wooded plateau called the Argonne.

"He isn't dead," Sabra had said, almost calmly. "When Yancey Cravat dies he'll be on the front page, and the world will know it."

Donna, in talking it over with her brother Cim, had been inclined to agree with this, though she did not put it thus to her mother. "Dad wouldn't let himself die in a list. He's too good an actor to be lost in a mob scene."

But a year had gone by.

The *Oklahoma Wigwam* now issued a morning as well as an afternoon edition and was known as the most powerful newspaper in the Southwest. Its presses thundered out tens of thousands of copies an hour, and hour on hour—five editions. Its linotype room was now a regiment of iron men, its staff boasted executive editor, editor in chief, managing editor, city editor, editor, and on down into the dozens of minor minions. When Sabra was in town she made a practice of driving down to the office at eleven every night, remaining there for an hour looking over the layout, reading the wet galley proof of the night's news lead, scanning the A.P. wires. Her entrance was in the nature of the passage of royalty, and when she came into the city room the staff all but saluted. True, she wasn't there very much, except in the summer, when Congress was not in session.

The sight of a woman on the floor of the Congressional House was still something of a novelty. Sentimental America had shrunk from the thought of women in active politics. Woman's place was in the Home, and American Womanhood was too exquisite a flower to be subjected to the harsh atmosphere of the Assembly floor and the committee room.

Sabra stumped the state and developed a surprising gift of oratory.

"If American politics are too dirty for women to take part in, there's something wrong with American politics. . . . We weren't too delicate and flowerlike to cross the plains and prairies and deserts in a covered wagon and to stand the hardships and heartbreaks of frontier life . . . history of France peeking through a bedroom keyhole . . . history of England a joust . . . but here in this land the women have been the hewers of wood and drawers of water . . . thousands of unnamed heroines with weather-beaten faces and mud-caked boots . . . alkali water . . . sun . . . dust . . . wind. . . . I am not belittling the brave pioneer men but the sunbonnet as well as the sombrero has helped to settle this glorious land of ours. . . ."

It had been so many years since she had heard this—it had sunk so deep into her consciousness—that perhaps she actually thought she had originated this speech. Certainly it was received with tremendous emotional response, copied throughout the Southwest, the Far West, the Mid-West states, and it won her the election and gained her fame that was nation wide.

Perhaps it was not altogether what Sabra Cravat said that counted in her favor. Her appearance must have had something to do with it. A slim, straight, dignified woman, yet touchingly feminine. Her voice not loud, but clear. Her white hair was shingled and beautifully waved and beneath this her soft dark eyes took on an added depth and brilliance. Her eyebrows had remained black and thick, still further enhancing her finest feature. Her dress was always dark, becoming, smart, and her silken ankles above the slim slippers with their cut-steel buckles were those of a young girl. The aristocratic Marcy feet and ankles.

Her speeches were not altogether romantic, by any means. She knew her state. Its politics were notoriously rotten. Governor after governor was impeached with musical comedy swiftness and regularity, and the impeachment proceedings stank to Washington. This governor was practically an outlaw and desperado; that governor, who resembled a traveling evangelist with his long locks and his sanctimonious face, flaunted his mistress, and all the office plums fell to her rapscallion kin. Sabra had statistics at her tongue's end. Millions of barrels of oil. Millions of tons of zinc. Third in mineral products. First in oil. Coal. Gypsum. Granite. Live stock.

In Washington she was quite a belle among the old boys in Congress and even the Senate. The opposition party tried to blackmail her with publicity about certain unproved items in the life of her dead (or missing) husband Yancey Cravat: a two-gun man, a desperado, a killer, a drunkard, a squaw man. Then they started on young Cim and his Osage Indian wife, but Sabra and Donna were too quick for them.

Donna Wyatt leased a handsome Washington house in Dupont Circle, staffed it, brought Tracy Wyatt's vast wealth and influence to bear, and planned a coup so brilliant that it routed the enemy forever. She brought her handsome, sleepy-eyed brother Cim and his wife Ruby Big Elk, and the youngsters Felice and Yancey to the house in Dupont Circle, and together she and Sabra gave a reception for them to which they invited a group so precious that it actually came.

Sabra and Donna, exquisitely dressed, stood in line at the head of the magnificent room, and between them stood Ruby Big Elk in her Indian dress of creamy white doeskin all embroidered in beads from shoulder to hem. She was an imposing figure, massive but not offensively fat as were many of the older Osage women, and her black abundant hair had taken on a mist of gray.

"My daughter-in-law, Mrs. Cimarron Cravat, of the Osage Indian tribe."

"My son's wife, Ruby Big Elk—Mrs. Cimarron Cravat."

"My sister-in-law, Mrs. Cimarron Cravat. A full-blood Osage Indian. . . . Yes, indeed. We think so, too."

And, "How do you do?" said Ruby, in her calm, insolent way.

For the benefit of those who had not quite been able to encompass the Indian woman in her native dress Ruby's next public appearance was made in a Paris gown of white. She became the rage, was considered picturesque, and left Washington in disgust, her work done. No one but her husband, whom she loved with a doglike devotion, could have induced her to go through this ceremony.

The opposition retired, vanquished.

Donna and Tracy Wyatt then hired a special train in which they took fifty Eastern potentates on a tour of Oklahoma. One vague and not very bright Washington matron, of great social prestige, impressed with what she saw, voiced her opinion to young Yancey Cravat, quite confused as to his identity and seeing only an attractive and very handsome young male seated beside her at a country club luncheon.

"I had no idea Oklahoma was like this. I thought it was all oil and dirty Indians."

"There is quite a lot of oil, but we're not all dirty."

"We?"

"I'm an Indian."

Osage, Oklahoma, was now just as much like New York as Osage could manage to make it. They built twenty-story office buildings in a city that had hundreds of miles of prairie to spread in. Tracy Wyatt built the first skyscraper—the Wyatt building. It was pointed out and advertised all over the flat prairie state. Then Pat Leary, dancing an Irish jig of jealousy, built the Leary building, twenty-three stories high. But the sweet fruits of triumph soon turned to ashes in his mouth. The Wyatt building's foundations were not built to stand the added strain of five full stories. So he had built a five-story tower, slim and tapering, a taunting finger pointing to the sky. Again Tracy Wyatt owned the tallest building in Oklahoma.

On the roof of the Levy Mercantile Company's Building Sol had had built a penthouse after his own plans. It was the only one of its kind in all Oklahoma. That small part of Osage which did not make an annual pilgrimage to New York was slightly bewildered by Sol Levy's roof life. They fed one another with scraps of gossip got from servants, clerks, stenographers who claimed to have seen the place at one time or another. It was, these said, filled with the rarest of carpets, rugs, books, hangings. Super radio, super phonograph, super player piano. Music hungry. There he lived, alone, in luxury, of the town, yet no part of it. At sunset, in the early morning, late of a star-spangled night he might have been seen leaning over the parapet of his sky house, a lonely little figure, lean, ivory, aloof, like a gargoyle brooding over the ridiculous city sprawled below; over the oil rigs that encircled it like giant Martian guards holding it in their power; beyond, to where the sky, in a veil of gray chiffon that commerce had wrought, stooped to meet the debauched red prairie.

Money was now the only standard. If Pat Leary had sixty-two million dollars on Tuesday he was Oklahoma's leading citizen. If Tracy Wyatt had seventy-eight million dollars on Wednesday then Tracy Wyatt was Oklahoma's leading citizen.

Osage had those fascinating little specialty shops and interior decorating shops on Pawhuska just like those you see on Madison Avenue, whose owners are the daughters of decayed Eastern aristocracy on the make. The head of the shop appeared only to special clients and then with a hat on. She wore the hat from morning until night, her badge of revolt against this position of service. "I am a lady," the hat said. "Make no mistake about that. Just because I am a shopkeeper don't think you can patronize me. I am not working. I am playing at work. This is my fad. At any moment I can walk out of here, just like any of you."

Feminine Osage's hat, by the way, was cut and fitted right on its head, just like Paris.

Sabra probably was the only woman of her own generation and social position in Osage who still wore on the third finger of her left hand the plain broad gold band of a long-past day. Synchronous with the permanent wave and the reducing diet the oil-rich Osage matrons of Sabra's age cast sentiment aside for fashion, quietly placed the clumsy gold band in a bureau drawer and appeared with a slim platinum circlet bearing, perhaps, the engraved anachronism, "M. G.–K. L. 1884." Certainly it was much more at ease among its square-cut emerald and oblong-diamond neighbors. These ladies explained (if at all) that the gold band had grown too tight for the finger, or too loose. Sabra looked down at the broad old-fashioned wedding ring on her own gemless finger. She had not once taken it off in over forty years. It was as much a part of her as the finger itself.

Osage began to rechristen streets, changing the fine native Indian names to commonplace American ones. Hetoappe Street became the Boston Road; very fashionable it was, too. Still, the very nicest people were building out a ways in the new section (formerly Okemah Hill) now River View. The river was the ruddy Canadian, the view the forest of oil rigs bristling on the opposite shore. The grounds sloped down to the river except on those occasions when the river rose in red anger and sloped down to the houses. The houses themselves were Italian palazzi or French châteaux or English manors; none, perhaps, quite so vast or inclusive as Tracy Wyatt's, but all provided with such necessities as pipe organs, sunken baths, Greek temples, ancient tapestries, Venetian glass, billiard rooms, and butlers. Pat Leary, the smart little erstwhile section hand, had a melodramatic idea. Not content with peacocks, golf links, and swimming pools on his estate he now had placed an old and weathered covered wagon, a rusted and splintered wagon tongue, the bleached skull of a buffalo, an Indian tepee, and a battered lantern on a little island at the foot of the artificial lake below the heights on which his house stood. At night a searchlight, red, green, or orange, played from the tower of the house upon the mute relics of frontier days.

"The covered wagon my folks crossed the prairies in," Pat Leary explained, with shy pride. Eastern visitors were much impressed. It was considered a great joke in Osage, intimately familiar with Pat's Oklahoma beginnings.

"Forgot something, ain't you Pat, in that outfit you got rigged up in the yard?" old Bixby asked.

"What's that?"

"Pickax and shovel," Bixby replied, laconically. "Keg of spikes and a hand car."

Old Sam Pack, who had made the Run on a mule, said that if Pat Leary's folks had come to Oklahoma in a covered wagon then his had made the trip in an airplane.

All the Oklahoma millionaire houses had libraries. Yards and yards of fine leather libraries, with gold tooling. Ike Hawkes's library had five sets of Dickens alone, handsomely bound in red, green, blue, brown, and black, and Ike all unaware of any of them.

Moving picture palaces, with white-gloved ushers, had all the big Broadway super-films. Gas filling stations on every corner. Hot dog, chili con carne, and hamburger stands on the most remote country road. The Arverne Grand Opera Company at the McKee Theater for a whole week every year, and the best of everything—*Traviata, Bohême, Carmen, Louise, The Barber of Seville.* The display of jewels during that week made the Diamond Horseshoe at the Metropolitan look like the Black Hole of Calcutta.

SMART DANCING PARTY

Social events of the week just closed were worthily concluded with the smart dancing party at which Mr. and Mrs. Clint Hopper entertained a small company at the Osage Club. The roof garden of the club . . .

SMALL DINNER

Mr. and Mrs. James Click honored two distinguished Eastern visitors on Wednesday at the small dinner at which they entertained in courtesy to Mr. and Mrs. C. Swearingen Church, of St. Paul, Minnesota. There were covers for eighty. . . .

Mr. and Mrs. Buchanan Ketcham and Miss Patricia Ketcham left for New York last night, from which city they will sail for Europe, there to meet the J. C. McConnells on their yacht at Monaco. . . .

Le Cercle Français will meet Tuesday evening at the home of Mr. and Mrs. Everard Pack. . . .

The sunbonnets had triumphed.

XXIV

STILL, oil was oil, and Indians were Indians. There was no way in which either of those native forces could quite be molded to fit the New York pattern.

The Osages still whirled up and down the Oklahoma roads, and those roads, for hundreds of miles, were still unpaved red prairie dust. They crashed into ditches and draws and culverts as of old, walked back to town and, entering the automobile salesroom in which they had bought the original car, pointed with one dusky finger at a new and glittering model.

" 'Nother," they said, succinctly. And drove out with it.

It was common news that Charley Vest had smashed eight Cadillac cars in a year, but then Charley had a mysterious source through which he procured fire water. They bought airplanes now, but they were forbidden the use of local and neighboring flying fields after a series of fatal smashes. They seemed, for the most part (the full bloods, at least), to be totally lacking in engine sense.

They had electric refrigerators—sometimes in the parlor, very proud. They ate enormously and waxed fatter and fatter. The young Osages now wore made-to-order shirts with monograms embroidered on them the size of a saucer. The Osages had taken to spending their summers in Colorado Springs or Manitou. At first the white residents of those cities had refused to rent their fine houses, furnished, to the Indians for the season. But the vast sums offered them soon overcame their reluctance. The Indian problem was still a problem, for he was considered legitimate prey, and thousands of prairie buzzards fed on his richness.

Sabra Cravat had introduced a bill for the further protection of the Osages, and rather took away the breath of the House assembled by advocating abolition of the Indian Reservation system. Her speech, radical though it was, and sensational, was greeted with favor by some of the more liberal of the Congressmen. They even conceded that this idea of hers, to the effect that the Indian would never develop or express himself until he was as free as the negro, might some day become a reality. These were the reformers—the long-hairs—fanatics.

Oklahoma was very proud of Sabra Cravat, editor, Congresswoman, pioneer. Osage said she embodied the finest spirit of the state and of the Southwest. When ten of Osage's most unctuous millionaires contributed fifty thousand dollars each for a five-hundred-thousand-dollar statue that should embody the Oklahoma Pioneer no one was surprised to hear that the sculptor, Masja Krbecek, wanted to interview Sabra Cravat.

Osage was not familiar with the sculpture of Krbecek, but it was impressed with the price of it. Half a million dollars for a statue!

"Certainly," said the committee, calmly. "He's the best there is. Half a million is nothing for his stuff. He wouldn't kick a pebble for less than a quarter of a million."

"Do you suppose he'll do her as a pioneer woman in a sunbonnet? Holding little Cim by the hand, huh? Or maybe in a covered wagon."

Sabra received Krbecek in a simple (draped) dress. He turned out to be a quiet, rather snuffy little Pole in eyeglasses, who looked more like a tailor—a "little" tailor—than a sculptor. His eye roamed about the living room of the house on Kihekah. The old wooden house had been covered with plaster in a deep warm shade much the color of the native clay; the gimcrack porch and the cupolas had been torn away and a great square veranda and a terrace built at the side, away from the street and screened by a thick hedge and an iron grille. It was now, in fact, much the house that Yancey had planned when Sabra first built it years ago. The old pieces of mahogany and glass and silver were back, triumphant again over the plush and brocade with which Sabra had furnished the house when new. The old, despised since pioneer days, was again the fashion in Osage. There was the DeGrasse silver; the cake dish with the carefree cupids, the mantelpiece figures of china, even the hand-woven coverlet that Mother Bridget had given her that day in Wichita so long ago. Its rich deep blue was unfaded.

"You are very comfortable here in Oklahoma," said Masja Krbecek. He pronounced it syllable by syllable, painfully. O-kla-ho-ma.

"It is a very simple home," Sabra replied, "compared to the other places you have seen hereabouts."

"It is the home of a good woman," said Krbecek, dryly.

Sabra was a trifle startled, but she said thank you, primly.

"You are a Congress member, you are editor of a great newspaper, you are well known through the country. You American women, you are really amazing."

Again Sabra thanked him.

"Tell me, will you, my dear lady," he went on, "some of the many interesting things about your life and that of your husband, this Yancey Cravat who so far preceded his time."

So Sabra told him. Somehow, as she talked, the years rolled back, curtain after curtain, into the past. The Run. Then they were crossing the prairie, there was the first glimpse of the mud wallow that was Osage, the church meeting in the tent, the Pegler murder, the outlaws, the early years of the paper, the Indians, oil. She talked very well in her clear, decisive voice. At his request she showed him the time-yellowed photographs of Yancey, of herself. Krbecek listened. At the end, "It is touching," he said. "It makes me weep." Then he kissed her hand and went away, taking one or two of the old photographs with him.

The statue of the Spirit of the Oklahoma Pioneer was unveiled a year later, with terrific ceremonies. It was an heroic figure of Yancey Cravat stepping forward with that light graceful stride in the high-heeled Texas star boots, the skirts of the Prince Albert billowing behind with the vigor of his movements, the sombrero atop the great menacing buffalo head, one beautiful hand resting lightly on the weapon in his two-gun holster. Behind him, one hand just touching his shoulder for support, stumbled the weary, blanketed figure of an Indian.

XXV

Sabra Cravat, Congresswoman from Oklahoma, had started a campaign against the disgraceful condition of the new oil towns. With an imposing party of twenty made up of front-page oil men, Senators, Congressmen, and editors, she led the way to Bowlegs, newest and crudest of the new oil strikes.

Cities like Osage were suave enough in a surface way. But what could a state do when oil was forever surging up in unexpected places, bringing the days of the Run back again? At each newly discovered pool there followed the rush and scramble. Another Bret Harte town sprang up on the prairie; fields oozed slimy black; oil rigs clanked; false-front wooden shacks lined a one-street village. Dance halls. Brothels. Gunmen. Brawls. Heat. Flies. Dirt. Crime. The clank of machinery. The roar of traffic boiling over a road never meant for more than a plodding wagon. Nitroglycerin cars bearing their deadly freight. Overalls, corduroys, blue prints, engines. The human scum of each new oil town was like the scum of the Run, but harder, crueler, more wolfish and degraded.

The imposing party, in high-powered motor cars, bumped over the terrible roads, creating a red dust barrage.

"It is all due to our rotten Oklahoma state politics," Sabra explained to the great Senator from Pennsylvania who sat at her right and the great editor from New York who sat at her left in the big luxurious car. "Our laws are laughed at. The Capitol is rotten with graft. Anything goes. Oklahoma is still a Territory in everything but title. This town of Bowlegs. It's a throw-back to the frontier days of forty years ago—and worse. It's like the old Cimarron. People who have lived in Osage all their lives don't know what goes on out here. They don't care. It's more oil, more millions. That's all. Any one of you men, well known as you are, could come out here, put on overalls, and be as lost as though you had vanished in the wilderness."

The Pennsylvania Senator laughed a plump laugh and with the elbow nearest Sabra made a little movement that would have amounted to a nudge—in anyone but a Senator from Pennsylvania. "What they need out here is a woman Governor—eh, Lippmann!" to the great editor.

Sabra said nothing.

On the drive out from Osage they stopped for lunch in an older oil town hotel dining room—a surprisingly good lunch, the Senators and editors were glad to find, with a tender steak, and little green onions, and near beer, and cheese, and coffee served in great thick cups, hot and strong and refreshing. The waitress was deft and friendly: a tall angular woman with something frank and engaging about the two circles of vermilion on the parchment of her withered cheeks.

"How are you, Nettie?" Sabra said to her.

"I'm grand, Mis' Cravat. How's all your folks?"

The Senator from Ohio winked at Sabra. "You're a politician, all right."

Arrived at Bowlegs, Sabra showed them everything, pitilessly. The dreadful town lay in the hot June sun, a scarred thing, flies buzzing over it, the oil drooling down its face, a slimy stream. A one-street wooden shanty town, like the towns of the old Territory days, but more sordid. A red-cheeked young Harvard engineer was their official guide: an engaging boy in bone-rimmed glasses and a very blue shirt that made his pink cheeks pinker. That is what I wanted my Cim to be, Sabra thought with a great wrench at her heart. I mustn't think of that now.

The drilling of the oil. The workmen's shanties. The trial of a dance-hall girl in the one-room pine shack that served as courtroom. The charge, nonpayment of rent. The little room, stifling, stinking, was already crowded. Men and women filled the doorway, lounged in the windows. The judge was a yellow-faced fellow with a cud of tobacco in his cheek, and a Sears-Roebuck catalogue and a single law book on a shelf as his library. It was a trial by jury. The jurors were nine in number, their faces a rogues' gallery. There had happened to be nine men loafing near by. It might have been less or more. Bowlegs did not consider these fine legal points. They wore overalls and shirts. The defendant was a tiny rat-faced girl in a soiled green dress that parodied the fashions, a pathetic green poke bonnet, down-at-heel shoes, and a great run in her stocking. Her friends were there—a dozen or more dance-hall girls in striped overalls and jockey caps or knee-length gingham dresses with sashes. Their ages ranged from sixteen to nineteen, perhaps. It was incredible that life, in those few years, could have etched that look on their faces.

The girls were charming, hospitable. They made way for the imposing visitors. "Come on in," they said. "How-do!"—like friendly children. The mid-afternoon sun was pitiless on their sick eyes, their bad skin, their unhealthy hair. Clustered behind the rude bench on which the jury sat, the girls, from time to time, leaned a sociable elbow on a juryman's shoulder, occasionally enlivening the judicial proceedings by a spirited comment uttered in defense of their sister, and spoken in the near-by ear or aloud, for the benefit of the close-packed crowd.

"She never done no such thing!"

"He's a damn liar, an' I can prove it."

No one, least of all the tobacco-chewing judge, appeared to find these girlish informalities at all unusual in the legal conduct of the case.

In the corner of the little room was a kind of pen made of wooden slats, like a sizable chicken coop, and in it, on the floor, lay a man.

"What's he there for?" Sabra asked one of the girls. "What is that?"

"That's Bill. He's in jail. He shot a man last night, and he's up for carrying concealed weapons. It ain't allowed."

"I'm going to talk to him," said Sabra. And crossed the room, through the crowd. The jurors had just filed out. They repaired to a draw at the side of the road to make their finding. Two or three of the dance-hall girls, squatted on the floor, were talking to Bill through the bars. They asked Sabra her name, and she told them, and they gave her their own. Toots. Peewee. Bee.

The face of the boy on the floor was battered and blood-caked. There was a festering sore on his left hand, and the hand and arm were swollen and angry looking.

"You were carrying a concealed weapon?" Sabra asked, squatting there with the girls. A Senator or two and an editor were just behind her.

An injured look softened Bill's battered features. He pouted like a child. "No, ma'am. I run the dance hall, see? And I was standing in the middle of the floor, working, and I had the gun right in my hand. Anybody could see. I wasn't carrying no concealed weapon."

The jury filed back. Not guilty. The rat-faced girl's shyster lawyer said something in her ear. She spoke in a dreadful raucous voice, simpering.

"I sure thank you, gents."

The dance-hall girls cheered feebly.

Out of that fetid air into the late afternoon blaze. "The dance halls open about nine," Sabra said. "We'll wait for that. In the meantime I'll show you their rooms. Their rooms——" she looked about for the fresh-cheeked Harvard boy. "Why, where——"

"There's some kind of excitement," said the New York editor. "People have been running and shouting. Over there in that field we visited awhile ago. Here comes our young friend now. Perhaps he'll tell us."

The Harvard boy's color was higher still. He was breathing fast. He had been running. His eyes shone behind the bone-rimmed spectacles.

"Well, folks, we'll never have a narrower squeak than that."

"What?"

"They put fifty quarts in the Gypsy pool but before she got down the oil came up——"

"Quarts of what?" interrupted an editorial voice.

"Oh—excuse me—quarts of nitroglycerin."

"My God!"

"It's in a can, you know. A thing like a can. It never had a chance to explode down there. It just shot up with the gas and oil. If it had hit the ground everything for miles around would have been shot to hell and all of us killed. But he caught it. They say he just ran back like an outfielder and gauged it with his eye while it was up in the air, and ran to where it would fall, and caught it in his two arms, like a baby, right on his chest. It didn't explode. But he's dying. Chest all caved in. They've sent for the ambulance."

"Who? Who's he?"

"I don't know his real name. He's an old bum that's been around the field, doing odd jobs and drinking. They say he used to be quite a fellow in Oklahoma in his day. Picturesque pioneer or something. Some call him old Yance and I've heard others call him Sim or Simeon or——"

Sabra began to run across the road.

"Mrs. Cravat! You mustn't—where are you going?"

She ran on, across the oil-soaked field and the dirt, in her little buckled high-heeled slippers. She did not even know that she was running. The crowd was dense around some central object. They formed a wall—roustabouts, drillers, tool dressers, shooters, pumpers. They were gazing down at something on the ground.

"Let me by! Let me by!" They fell back before this white-faced woman with the white hair.

He lay on the ground, a queer, crumpled, broken figure. She flung herself on the oil-soaked earth beside him and lifted the magnificent head gently, so that it lay cushioned by her arm. A little purplish bubble rose to his lips, and she wiped it away with her fine white handkerchief, and another rose to take its place.

"Yancey! Yancey!"

He opened his eyes—those ocean-gray eyes with the long curling lashes like a beautiful girl's. She had thought of them often and often, in an agony of pain. Glazed now, unseeing.

Then, dying, they cleared. His lips moved. He knew her. Even then, dying, he must speak in measured verse.

" 'Wife and mother—you stainless woman—hide me—hide me in your love!' "

She had never heard a line of it. She did not know that this was Peer Gynt, humbled before Solveig. The once magnetic eyes glazed, stared; were eyes no longer.

She closed them, gently. She forgave him everything. Quite simply, all unknowing, she murmured through her tears the very words of Solveig.

"Sleep, my boy, my dearest boy."